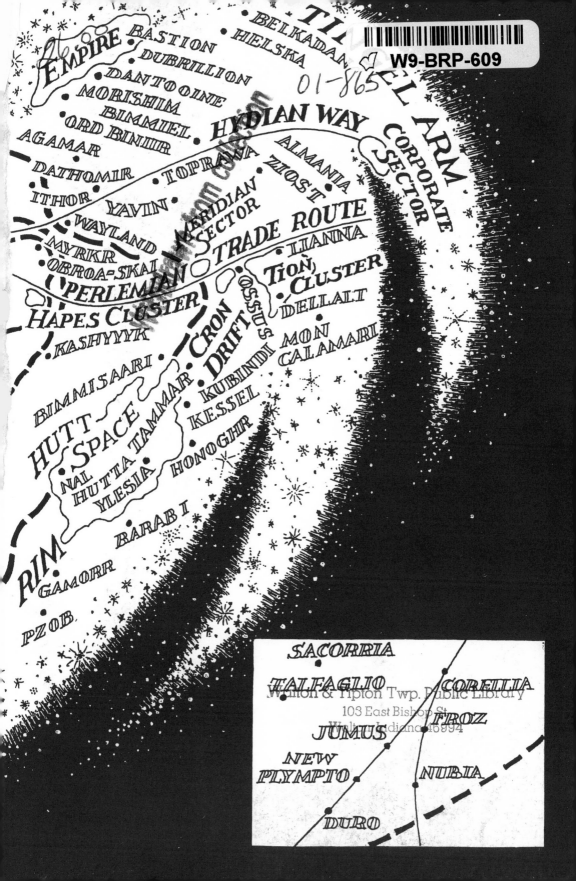

W9-BRP-609

01-865

Walton & Tipton Twp. Public Library
103 East Bishop St
Walton, Indiana 46994

THE NEW JEDI ORDER

STAR BY STAR

THE STAR WARS NOVELS TIMELINE

44 YEARS BEFORE
STAR WARS: A New Hope

Jedi Apprentice series

33 | YEARS BEFORE STAR WARS: A New Hope

Cloak of Deception
Darth Maul: Shadow Hunter

32 | YEARS BEFORE STAR WARS: A New Hope

STAR WARS: EPISODE I
THE PHANTOM MENACE

29 | YEARS BEFORE STAR WARS: A New Hope

Rogue Planet
The Approching Storm

22 | YEARSBEFORE STAR WARS: A New Hope

STAR WARS: EPISODE II

20 | YEARS BEFORE STAR WARS: A New Hope

STAR WARS: EPISODE III

10-8 | YEARS BEFORE STAR WARS: A New Hope

The Han Solo Trilogy:
The Paradise Snare
The Hutt Gambit
Rebel Dawn

5-2 | YEARS BEFORE STAR WARS: A New Hope

The Adventures of Lando Calrissian:
Lando Calrissian and the
  Mindharp of Sharu
Lando Calrissian and the
  Flamewind of Oseon
Lando Calrissian and the
  Starcave of ThonBoka

The Han Solo Adventures:
Han Solo at Stars' End
Han Solo's Revenge
Han Solo and the Lost Legacy

STAR WARS: A New Hope
YEAR 0

STAR WARS: EPISODE IV

0-3 | YEARS AFTER STAR WARS: A New Hope

Tales from the Mos Eisley
  Cantina
Splinter of the Mind's Eye

3 | YEARS AFTER STAR WARS: A New Hope

STAR WARS: EPISODE I
THE EMPIRE STRIKES BACK

Tales of the Bounty Hunters

3.5 | YEARS AFTER STAR WARS: A New Hope

Shadows of the Empire

4 | YEARS AFTER STAR WARS: A New Hope

STAR WARS: EPISODE I
THE PHANTOM MENACE

The Truce at Bakura
Tales from Jabba's Palace

The Bounty Hunter Wars:
The Mandalorian Armor
Slave Ship
Hard Merchandise

6.5-7.5 YEARS AFTER
STAR WARS: A New Hope

X-Wing:
Rogue Squadron
Wedge's Gamble
The Krytos Trap
The Bacta War
Wraith Squadron
Iron Fist
Solo Command

8 *YEARS AFTER STAR WARS: A New Hope*

The Courtship of Princess Leia

9 *YEARS AFTER STAR WARS: A New Hope*

X-Wing: Isard's Revenge

The Thrawn Trilogy:
Heir to the Empire
Dark Force Rising
The Last Command

11 *YEARS AFTER STAR WARS: A New Hope*

I, Jedi

The Jedi Academy Trilogy:
Jedi Search
Dark Apprentice
Champions of the Force

12-13 *YEARS AFTER STAR WARS: A New Hope*

Children of the Jedi
Darksaber
Planet of Twilight
X-Wing: Starfighters of Adumar

14 *YEARS AFTER STAR WARS: A New Hope*

The Crystal Star

16-17 *YEARS AFTER STAR WARS: A New Hope*

The Black Fleet Crisis Trilogy:
Before the Storm
Shield of Lies
Tyrant's Test

17 *YEARS AFTER STAR WARS: A New Hope*

The New Rebellion

18 *YEARS AFTER STAR WARS: A New Hope*

The Corellian Trilogy:
Ambush at Corellia
Assault at Selonia
Showdown at Centerpoint

19 *YEARS AFTER STAR WARS: A New Hope*

The Hand of Thrawn Duology:
Specter of the Past
Vision of the Future

22 *YEARS AFTER STAR WARS: A New Hope*

Junior Jedi Knights series

23-24 *YEARS AFTER STAR WARS: A New Hope*

Young Jedi Knights series

25-30 YEARS AFTER
STAR WARS: A New Hope

The New Jedi Order:
Vector Prime
Dark Tide I: Onslaught
Dark Tide II: Ruin
Agents of Chaos I: Hero's Trial
Agents of Chaos II: Jedi Eclipse
Balance Point
Edge of Victory I: Conquest
Edge of Victory II: Rebirth
Star by Star
Dark Journey

Books by Troy Denning

STAR WARS®

THE NEW JEDI ORDER

STAR BY STAR

TROY DENNING

 THE BALLANTINE PUBLISHING GROUP
NEW YORK

To Andria
For advice, encouragement, and more

A Del Rey® Book
Published by The Ballantine Publishing Group

Copyright © 2001 by Lucasfilm Ltd. & ™.
All Rights Reserved. Used Under Authorization.

All rights reserved under International and Pan-American Copyright Conventions.
Published in the United States by The Ballantine Publishing Group, a division of
Random House, Inc., New York, and simultaneously in Canada by Random House of
Canada Limited, Toronto.

Del Rey is a registered trademark and the Del Rey colophon is a trademark
of Random House, Inc.

www.starwars.com
www.starwarskids.com
www.delreydigital.com

Library of Congress Catalog Card Number: 2001094037

ISBN 0-345-42828-X

Manufactured in the United States of America

First Edition: November 2001

10 9 8 7 6 5 4 3 2 1

ACKNOWLEDGMENTS

Many people helped make this book possible. I would like to thank them all, especially Curtis Smith for introducing me to *Star Wars* writing all those years ago; Mary Kirchoff, who drew my attention to the possibility; and Matthew Caviness, Kevin McConnell, and Ross Martin, three special *Star Wars* fans who were never far from my thoughts during the writing. Thanks are also due to: Mike Friedman and Jenni Smith; fellow NJO writers R. A. Salvatore— what a setup!—Mike Stackpole, Jim Luceno, Kathy Tyers, Greg Keyes, Elaine Cunningham, Aaron Allston, and Matt Stover, who all contributed to this story through endless compromising and brainstorming; Shelly Shapiro and all the people at Del Rey, especially Chris Schluep, Kathleen David, and Lisa Collins; to Sue Rostoni and Lucy Autrey Wilson at Lucasfilm, as well as Chris Cerasi, Leland Chee, Dan Wallace, and everyone else there who made this project such a pleasure. And, of course, thanks to George Lucas for letting me play in his galaxy.

Dramatis Personae

Alema Rar; Jedi Knight (female Twi'lek)

Anakin Solo; Jedi Knight (male human)

Bela Hara; Jedi Knight (female Barabel)

Borsk Fey'lya; chief of state (male Bothan)

C-3PO; protocol droid

Cilghal; Jedi Master (female Mon Calamari)

Eryl Besa; Jedi Knight (female human)

Ganner Rhysode; Jedi Knight (male human)

Han Solo; captain, *Millennium Falcon* (male human)

Jacen Solo; Jedi Knight (male human)

Jaina Solo; Jedi Knight (female human)

Jovan Drark; Jedi Knight (male Rodian)

Krasov Hara; Jedi Knight (female Barabel)

Kyp Durron; Jedi Master (male human)

Lando Calrissian; resistance fighter (male human)

Leia Organa Solo; former New Republic diplomat (female human)

Lowbacca; Jedi Knight (male Wookiee)

Luke Skywalker; Jedi Master (male human)

Mara Jade Skywalker; Jedi Master (female human)

Nom Anor; executor (male Yuuzhan Vong)

R2-D2; astromech droid
Raynar Thul; Jedi Knight (male human)
Saba Sebatyne; Jedi Knight (female Barabel)
Tahiri Veila; Jedi Knight (female human)
Tekli; Jedi Knight (female Chadra-Fan)
Tenel Ka; Jedi Knight (female human)
Tesar Sebatyne; Jedi Knight (male Barabel)
Tsavong Lah; warmaster (male Yuuzhan Vong)
Ulaha Kore; Jedi Knight (female Bith)
Vergere; adviser to Tsavong Lah (female Fosh)
Viqi Shesh; senator (female human)
Zekk; Jedi Knight (male human)

They appeared without warning from beyond the edge of galactic space: a warrior race called the Yuuzhan Vong, armed with surprise, treachery, and a bizarre organic technology that proved a match—too often more than a match—for the New Republic and its allies. Even the Jedi, under the leadership of Luke Skywalker, found themselves thrown on the defensive, deprived of their greatest strength. For somehow, inexplicably, the Yuuzhan Vong seemed to be utterly devoid of the Force.

The alien assault caught the New Republic unawares. Before they could rally and strike back, several worlds were destroyed and countless beings killed—among them the Wookiee Chewbacca, loyal friend and partner of Han Solo.

The New Republic won the day—the first of a series of costly victories. Behind that alien advance fleet came a seemingly endless stream of ships and warriors. The planet Ithor fell to Yuuzhan Vong treachery—a devastating loss for the New Republic and a personal one for Jedi Corran Horn, who took the blame.

The New Republic government unraveled a little more with each setback. Even the Jedi Knights began to splinter under the strain. And while Luke Skywalker struggled with the dilemma of how to handle the Jedi, he struggled with a private crisis, as well: His beloved wife, Mara, was ill and possibly dying from a debilitating and utterly mystifying disease, and it was taking much of her energy simply to stay alive. Lacking strong leadership, some of the Jedi fell under the sway of Kyp Durron, who advocated using every available resource to defeat the Yuuzhan Vong—including unbridled aggression, which could lead only to the dark side. Even the Solo children—Jedi Knights all—found themselves on different sides of the argument.

Consumed with grief and guilt for Chewbacca's death, Han Solo turned away from his family, seeking expiation in action—and foiled a Yuuzhan Vong plot to eliminate the Jedi. He returned with what seemed to be an antidote to Mara Jade Skywalker's illness, but not even that victory could erase the loss of his dearest friend—or mend his marriage to Leia.

Leia, too, was beset by guilt. She had disregarded a vision of the future, and now she blamed herself for the devastation of the Hapan fleet at Fondor—a mass destruction caused by the uncontrollable power of Centerpoint Station, a weapon armed by her younger son, Anakin.

The elder Solo son, Jacen, also had a vision, one in which he saw the galaxy moving toward darkness. Afraid of tipping the balance farther, the young Jedi temporarily abandoned the use of the Force altogether. Only the near-loss of his mother, Leia, compelled him to return to the Force.

But in saving Leia's life Jacen had bested none other than the great Yuuzhan Vong warmaster Tsavong Lah. In retaliation, the warmaster declared a temporary truce on the condition that all Jedi—and Jacen in particular—be handed over to the Yuuzhan Vong.

Now the Jedi were being hunted. When the youngsters at the Jedi academy were threatened, Anakin Solo raced off to help, going undercover among the Yuuzhan Vong lower castes to rescue his friend Tahiri Veila. He ended up a hero—but the Jedi Temple on Yavin 4 was destroyed.

Luke and Mara found themselves declared traitors by the New Republic. As a pregnant Mara struggled with the recurrence of her disease, Luke began to assert his leadership over the Jedi. With Jaina Solo's help, Kyp Durron convinced Luke and the military to let him lead a mission to destroy a Yuuzhan Vong superweapon. The mission was successful . . . but Jaina learned, too late, that what they had destroyed was not a weapon but a worldship in the making—one filled with civilians and intended for Yuuzhan Vong young. Once again the balance seemed to be tipping toward darkness. The only ray of light was the birth of Luke and Mara's son, Ben Skywalker.

Their new worldship destroyed and their attempts to capture the Jedi frustrated, the Yuuzhan Vong have declared the truce broken. Once again worlds will fall, as the alien forces push inexorably Coreward. And the Jedi may be the last hope in a galaxy that no longer wants them . . .

Chapter 1

The dark sliver of a distant starliner crept into view, a blue needle of ion efflux pushing it across the immense sweep of a brilliant orange sun. Like a million such suns in the Core region alone, this one lacked any world with a civilization or even a sapient species, and it was too inconsequential for any name except an obsolete Imperial survey number. With so much emptiness, so many planets untouched, it seemed to Jaina Solo that there should have been no need for fighting, that there should have been room for all. But comfort was always easier to steal than to earn, peace easier to break than to keep—as her mother so often said—and so the Yuuzhan Vong had invaded a galaxy that might have welcomed them with open arms. It was a mistake the aliens had yet to understand, but one day, Jaina knew . . . one day the Jedi would teach them.

R2-D2 chirped an inquiry from the droid station at the rear of the *Jade Shadow*'s flight deck.

"Stay connected, Artoo." Jaina did not turn around. "They still haven't sent the signal, and Mara needs her rest."

The droid whistled a lengthy objection.

Jaina glanced at the interface readout, then threw her hands into the air. "Fine. If that's what she said, go wake her up."

R2-D2 unplugged and whirred off toward the passenger cabin, leaving Jaina alone on the flight deck of the *Jade Shadow*. Even in a standby orbit, with all systems powered down and the ion drives resting cold and quiet, the vessel felt more like a suit of formfitted battle armor than a seventy-ton starship. The flow-form seat, drop-deck helm, and full-view canopy gave her the sense of floating in open space, while a new retinal tracker kept the heads-up status holos centered just below her plane of vision. Communications and countermeasures could be controlled from an array of glide switches on the throttle; a similar set on the stick managed sensors, weapons, and shields. Even the life-support system could be regulated by voice with an astromech unit plugged into the flight deck droid station. It was the perfect cockpit, and when the time came to have her own ship, Jaina intended to duplicate every detail—especially the seating arrangement, with the pilot alone down low in the front and the navigator and copilot seated side by side behind her. She liked that part the best.

Jaina's reverie was interrupted by a sudden sense of deep disquiet, an unexpected stirring in the Force that soon built to a strange feeling of frenzy. She opened herself to it further and experienced an instant of terrible longings and ravenous hunger, not quite evil, but dark and feral—and brutal enough to make her gasp and withdraw from its touch.

A cold sweat running down her brow, Jaina slid the throttle comm switch to intercom and called Mara to the flight deck. While she waited, she studied the sensors. There was nothing unexpected, but Jaina knew better than to place too much faith in the instruments. They had put the *Shadow* into orbit around the orange sun's closest planet, a rubble-ringed magma ball little more than twenty million kilometers from its star. Without R2-D2 at his station making constant resolution adjustments, all she could see was electromagnetic blast.

Catching a glimmer of movement in the canopy reflections, Jaina glanced at an activation reticle in the front of the cockpit. A small section of plexalloy opaqued into a mirror, and she saw the willowy form of Mara Jade Skywalker slipping onto the flight deck. Mara's cascade of red-gold hair was a tangle of sleep snarls, but her complexion was no longer quite so ashen nor her green eyes quite so sunken. Jaina stood and, feeling a little like a child caught with her hand under the candy dropper, turned to vacate the pilot's station.

Mara waved her down. "Sit. You're entitled." She dropped into the navigator's chair, sweetening the filter-scrubbed air with a hint of talc and stericlean that seemed to cling to her even with her new baby thousands of light-years away. She lifted her chin toward the distant starliner. "That our two troublemakers?"

"The transponder identifies it as the *Nebula Chaser*," Jaina said. R2-D2 plugged back into the droid station and confirmed the identity with a chirp. "But there's been no rendezvous signal, and a moment ago I felt something, uh, strange in the Force."

Mara nodded. "It's still there. But I don't think it's our passengers. It doesn't feel right."

"Nothing feels right about this," Jaina said. A thousand-meter Corellian cruiser with a customized Hoersch-Kessel sublight drive, the *Nebula Chaser* had already traversed half the face of the orange sun. It was now the size of Jaina's finger, with a blue efflux tail three times that long. "They still haven't signaled. Maybe we should give them one more orbit, then duck behind the planet and blow ions."

Mara shook her head. "Luke's right about these two; they're getting people killed with their saber-flashing. We'd better snag them while they need the ride." She pulled her crash webbing over her shoulders and clipped the buckle. "But let's be ready. Power up."

"Me?" Though Jaina had piloted the *Shadow* before, her aunt had done all the flying on the way out—perhaps because it had been Mara's first real chance to fly her beloved vessel since giving birth to Ben, or perhaps because she had simply needed to keep her mind occupied on her first trip away from her new son. "It's your ship."

"I want to sleep some more anyway. You won't believe what a luxury that is until you have a baby." Mara was silent for a moment, then added sternly, "And that's not a suggestion."

"Check!" Jaina's laugh was a little wistful. At nineteen, she had certainly been on dates, but the war had kept her too busy to pursue any serious relationships. Even now, she was only on temporary leave from Rogue Squadron—until the anti-Jedi sentiment in the senate faded. "Like I'd have time."

Jaina reached over to toggle the ion drives active, but stopped when R2-D2 whistled an alarm. The heads-up display holo contorted through a maddening array of colors and shapes, then settled on the image of a tiny, tube-shaped craft swinging toward them well beneath the luminous haze of the sun's orange corona.

"That explains their silence," Mara said. Though the navigator's station lacked a heads-up holo, the seat was surrounded by a complete set of conventional displays. "Can we can take it, Artoo?"

A message appeared on both displays, sternly informing Jaina and Mara that the representation was not to scale. A series of sensor readouts began to relate the craft's true size, velocity, and probable hull composition. Jaina whistled softly and glanced through the tinted canopy, where the new arrival's speckish silhouette was streaking up behind the *Nebula Chaser*.

"Looks like a frigate analog," Jaina said. "What do you want to do?"

"The only thing we can." There was a note of caution in Mara's voice that would have seemed foreign to her before Ben's arrival. "Damp down all systems and wait."

In Captain Pollux's private quarters aboard the *Nebula Chaser*, the Rar sisters stood shoulder to shoulder in front of the offbridge vidconsole, their long head-tails—lekku—writhing nervously as they watched a large piece of yorik coral detach from the frigate and start toward the *Nebula Chaser*. Pocked and lumpy, the smaller craft looked more like a mined-out asteroid than a boarding skiff, but the sensor displays showed the heat signatures of at least a hundred warriors inside. There was also some other creature, larger and colder, but the sisters needed no sensor readings to know this. When they reached out with the Force, they could feel the same hungry presence that had touched them as the frigate appeared from behind the sun. Whatever the Yuuzhan Vong were bringing across, it was attuned to their galaxy in a way its masters would never be.

Alema isolated the creature's heat signature and asked the computer to find a match, then turned to see Numa already at the captain's bunk laying out their disguises: a pair of diaphanous dancing shifts, some face paint, and not much else. Having spent the last year leading a fierce resistance movement on the occupied world of New Plympto, the sisters were certainly the object of the boarding party's search. Fortunately, their enemy would be searching for a single human woman instead of two Twi'lek dancing girls; in their role as the resistance leader, they had taken the precaution of never appearing together and always in disguise, with their lekku hidden beneath the cowl of a Jedi robe.

By the time the sisters changed out of their jumpsuits and returned to the vidconsole, the Yuuzhan Vong were disembarking in the docking bay. With bald sloping brows and saggy eyes rimmed underneath by drooping blue membranes, they were half a head taller than a typical human and much heavier. Their brutal faces had been reshaped into leathery masks of disjoined cartilage and torn flesh, and their powerful bodies were adorned with religious tattoos and ritual disfigurements. Most wore shells of living vonduun crab armor, and all carried the ubiquitous Yuuzhan Vong amphistaff, a serpent that could change on command into a cudgel, razor-sharp polearm, or poison-fanged whip. The most hideous of the warriors, a stoop-shouldered brute with only dark cavities where there should have been a nose, pushed arrogantly past the guards surrounding Captain Pollux.

"You have *Jeedai* aboard?"

"No," Pollux lied smoothly. "Is that why you stopped us?"

The warrior ignored the captain's question. "You come from Talfaglio . . . or Sacorria?"

"You can't believe I would tell you that," Pollux said. "The last I heard, our whole galaxy was at war with you."

The retort drew a grudging sneer of respect. "We are only a picket ship, Captain, and you are carrying refugees. You have nothing to fear from us . . . provided you tell me now if you have *Jeedai* among your passengers."

"We have none." Pollux did not look away when he answered, and his voice did not crack. Even civilian starship captains knew the Yuuzhan Vong were blind to the Force. "Feel free to search."

The warrior cracked a smile. "But I do, Captain. I do." He glanced toward his boarding skiff and, in his own language, ordered, *"Duwin tur voxyn."*

A seam appeared near the back of the craft and began to open, the yorik coral puckering outward like a set of pursed lips. A pair of yellow oval eyes appeared in the darkness, and Alema felt the hunger in the Force grow more distinct. Then, when the aperture had opened a half meter, an ebony streak shot from the portal and clattered to the deck in a ripple of darkness.

"Clouds of fire!" Numa gasped.

The creature—the *voxyn,* Alema guessed from what she had learned of the Yuuzhan Vong language—began to pad around the deck on eight bandy legs. Though it stood no higher than a human waist, it was more than four meters long, with a flattish head and an undulating body covered in black scales. A line of coarse sensory bristles ran down its spine, and a white barb protruded from its flickering whip of a tail. The beast circled the captain and his wary guards only once, then went off toward the rear of the docking bay.

In the vidscreen, Pollux fixed his gaze on the Yuuzhan Vong warrior. "Why have you brought that . . . that thing on my ship?"

The warrior knocked Pollux to the deck with a backhand slap. "You can't believe I would tell you that," he laughed.

Though Pollux's guards did not appear in danger of attacking, the captain signaled them to stand down and returned to his feet with as much dignity as possible.

Alema rotated an idle narrow-beam antenna toward the dark planet where their rendezvous craft would be waiting, then keyed in a secret Jedi comm channel and began to broadcast what they were seeing. The proximity of the orange sun would interfere with the signal, but signals could be enhanced—and it would be better than nothing if she and Numa failed to escape.

The voxyn circled away from the shuttles and wandered the docking bay for a few minutes more, then exited into an adjoining passage. The sisters lost sight of it until Alema found the right scanner, and by then it was padding down the main boulevard as though it had been riding slidewalks all its life. Along one side of the passage raced a company of Yuuzhan Vong, their distrust of lifeless technology keeping them on the stationary band at the edge of the broad corridor. Eventually, they gave up trying to keep pace and spread through the ship in small groups.

Alema activated a surveillance lock on the voxyn, and for the next hour she and Numa watched it roam the *Nebula Chaser*'s primary activities deck, occasionally circling a petrified refugee or cocking its head at some eruption of machine noise. Finally, it leapt into a decorative water fountain and began to circle the statue of a Calamarian star-urchin, its sensory bristles on end and its yellow eyes fixed on the ceiling. With a drooping feeling, Alema turned to the holopad and called up a three-dimensional schematic of the

Nebula Chaser. After a few adjustments, it grew clear that Captain Pollux's cabin was directly over the creature, ten levels above.

"Unpleasant," Numa said. The tips of her lekku flicked sharply. "It seems to have an idea of our location."

"That makes no sense." Alema reached out with the Force and felt the same hungry stirring as before, but now much stronger and distinctly below. "Unless it's using the Force to track us."

A shudder ran down Numa's lekku, and she glared at Alema out of the corner of a slanted eye. "You do have a way of springing to the most alarming explanation, sister."

"Alarming, but no less likely." Alema pointed to the vidscreen, where the voxyn was bounding down the corridor toward the nearest lift tube.

Numa studied the image for a moment, then said, "You seem to have a point. Perhaps we should shut down."

They took a moment to meditate, then began to pull in on themselves, shutting down their presence in the Force. When they could not even feel each other, Alema looked back to the vidscreen. The voxyn had just reached the lift tube. It slapped the activation pad with a front claw, then pushed its foresection into the cylinder and allowed the repulsor current to pull its long body up into the shaft. She traced the lift to an officers' deck outlet less than a hundred meters away, perhaps twice that distance by the time the creature found its way through the corridor grid.

"No good, sister. It still senses us." She turned toward the satchel holding their jumpsuits and lightsabers. "We can catch it as it steps out of the tube."

"Then what?" Numa asked. "The scarheads will know Captain Pollux was lying to them."

"They'll know anyway when it comes scratching at his door." Sorry there was no time to change back into her jumpsuit, Alema pulled her lightsaber from the travel satchel and activated its silver blade. "And I'd just as soon take a few Yuuzhan Vong with us."

"No." Numa reached over and shut down Alema's lightsaber. "I won't have that, not after New Plympto."

Frustrated by the planet's stubborn resistance, the Yuuzhan Vong had released a life-destroying plague that wiped the whole world clean. The sisters and a few thousand others had waited out the destruction inside a small fleet of intrasystem ore freighters, then sneaked into space after the enemy abandoned the dead world.

"They're *Yuuzhan Vong,* sister," Alema said. "Do you think they'll just forgive the captain's lie?"

"Hardly." Numa returned to the console. "We must make them think their creature is wrong."

She called up a hologram that showed the Yuuzhan Vong frigate floating half a kilometer beyond the *Nebula Chaser*'s docking bay. At only two hundred meters, the enemy craft was a mere fraction of the starliner's size, but the weapon nodules bristling along its flank left no doubt about its destructive capabilities.

Alema saw at once what her sister was thinking. "We'll pick our escape pod on the way."

She returned her lightsaber to their travel satchel and tossed the bag to Numa, then grabbed a datapad from the captain's bunkside table and comlinked it to the offbridge vidconsole. The sisters left the captain's suite and scurried toward the opposite end of the officers' deck. At the lift tube, Alema consulted the datapad and found the voxyn splashing through a Damp Deck basin two levels below. Its yellow eyes were fixed on the ceiling, tracing their path.

"It knows we're moving," Alema said.

"But its sense of distance is poor." Numa was ever the optimist. "Where are we going?"

Alema called up a display of midship escape stations, then chose the one most directly opposite the Yuuzhan Vong frigate. "Engineering deck, Bulkhead Forty-two." She performed a sectional security scan and found a team of Yuuzhan Vong smashing a droid in gravitational control. "We'll have to trick a squad of scarheads."

"Alternate?"

Alema checked the other escape stations, then shook her head. "Nothing, unless we leave the *Chaser*'s sensor shadow."

"Out of the question." Numa's lekku curled inward at the tips. "We'll have to go bare."

"Bare?" It was the term they had used on New Plympto for caching their weapons and disguising themselves as slaves. "You must be brightsick. I'm not leaving my lightsaber behind!"

"You would risk the lives of everyone aboard?" Numa pulled her lightsaber from their travel satchel and twisted the handle open, then plucked the Adegan focusing crystal from its mount and secured it over her navel with a few drops of fleshglue. Through her filmy shift, the golden jewel looked like a dancer's decoration. "Do you think such selfishness worthy of the memory of Daeshara'cor?"

Alema coiled her lekku, then let them slap against her back. Though not exactly their Master, Daeshara'cor had certainly been the sisters' deliverer. During one of the Jedi's rare visits to Ryloth, she had recognized the Rar sisters' innate Force talents and rescued them from one of the darkest ryll dens in Kala'uun, then arranged their transport to the Jedi training academy. Alema sighed and held out her hand.

"If we must."

Numa placed Alema's lightsaber in her palm. Alema removed the Adegan crystal and secured the silver jewel over her own navel. They tossed their Jedi robes and the remains of their weapons into a disintegration chute, then stepped into the lift, descended twenty levels to the engineering deck, and left their satchel on the floor halfway across the tube threshold. Though a far less obvious act of sabotage than smashing the actuation panel, it was just as effective. A collision override circuit would hold the tube static until the safety hazard was removed.

"Time to look flighty," Alema said.

She called up a banal emotidrama on the datapad, and the sisters started toward Bulkhead 42. As they advanced down the corridor, they peered into each room they passed and called loudly for someone named Travot. When they reached inducer control, a Yuuzhan Vong warrior stepped out to confront them. With only three long scars on each cheek and a single disfigured ear, he was clearly a warrior of low rank. The sisters pressed themselves against the corridor's far wall and, doing their best to look shocked and repulsed, started to ease past.

He blocked their way with a lowered amphistaff. "Where do you go?"

"To s-see Travot?" Numa made her voice sound frightened and tentative. "He works in the coil room."

"The coil room?" the Yuuzhan Vong echoed.

Alema shrugged and glanced back to her datapad, as though unable to resist the emotidrama. "His workstation."

A second Yuuzhan Vong with the crooked nose and scar-laced face of a minor officer stepped into the corridor. He scrutinized the sisters briefly and, seeing there was no place beneath their dancing shifts to hide a lightsaber or anything else, pointed back the way they had come.

"This ship is under seizure. Return to your berthings."

Numa and Alema put on looks of fear and confusion and remained where they were.

"Obey!" the subordinate said.

"We c-can't," Alema said.

"They sealed off the staff deck," Numa said. "And they closed our lounge."

"See?" Alema called up a schematic of the ship and shoved the datapad at the officer. "We don't have anyplace to go."

"Do not pollute me with your profane devices!" The officer knocked the instrument from Alema's hand and smashed it beneath his heel, then motioned to someone inside the room. "Bring the infidel machine shaper."

A third Yuuzhan Vong appeared in the doorway with a bruise-mottled human female. One eyelid had split open and covered the side of her face in coppery-smelling blood.

"You have one called Travot in your squad?"

Numa saw her sister catch the engineer's eye and give a barely perceptible nod, using the Force to plant the suggestion that the woman knew Travot. Taking full advantage of the Yuuzhan Vong's insensitivity to the Force, Alema reached out and felt the presence of more than a hundred beings in the immediate area, most of them frightened, a few angry or in pain. She did not feel the invaders, of course; the Yuuzhan Vong were as invisible to the Force as it was to them—but she did feel the voxyn's hungry presence descending toward them. It had found another lift tube.

After a moment of confusion, the engineer finally said, "There's a Travot in engineering, but he's not on my crew."

The officer considered the two sisters, no doubt trying to puzzle out the proper procedure for dealing with them. Alema decided to help him along by simply assuming the answer she wanted—a subtle means of enticement both she and her sister had put to good use in the ryll dens of Kala'uun.

"Engineering is just down there, isn't it? At Bulkhead Forty-two?"

"That's right," the engineer said. "Bulkhead Forty-two."

Alema stepped to her sister's side and eyed the amphistaff blocking their way. The subordinate looked to his officer, who scowled and waved him down the corridor.

"See to it and return."

Not waiting for the warrior to lead the way, the sisters slipped past his amphistaff and started down the corridor. The bulkheads appeared to be simple structural arches that spanned the passage every ten meters, but each one contained a thin durasteel door that would descend automatically at the first sign of a pressure drop. The doors could also be triggered by voice, but the crew had wisely refrained from using the code to seal off the Yuuzhan Vong search parties.

As they scurried down the corridor, Alema reached out with the Force again and felt the voxyn behind them, on the same level and coming fast. They were at Bulkhead 33, still ninety meters from the escape pod.

"I'm cold, sister." Alema rubbed her bare arms. "Do you feel that chill?"

"Quiet," their guard ordered. "Your complaints are an insult to the gods."

Alema's palm ached for her lightsaber.

The faint clatter of claws on metal echoed down the corridor behind them. She looked over her shoulder and saw a distant ripple of darkness bounding down the sterile tunnel.

"What's that?" she gasped, finding it difficult to pretend she did not know. "What's it doing?"

Numa glanced back, then let out a convincing shriek and raced down the corridor flailing her arms. Alema screamed and started after her, leaving their astonished guard to stomp after them yelling for them to stop. As they passed Bulkhead 38, he cried out in astonishment, then yelled something angry in his own language as the voxyn bowled him off his feet.

Alema did not even glance back. "Close Bulkhead Thirty-eight!" she yelled. "Authorization code: nebula rubantine!"

The bulkhead door clanged down behind her and sealed itself with a hiss—then tolled deeply as the voxyn slammed into it. Alema knew that closing the door would draw attention from the Yuuzhan Vong commander—but so would allowing the voxyn to catch them. She hoped that the thing had broken its neck, but there was no such luck. It was up and slamming itself into the durasteel almost instantly.

They passed Bulkhead 42. Numa turned toward the outer wall and slapped her palm against the escape bay door-pad.

"Attention: You have requested entrance to an escape pod launching bay." The computer spoke in the same cheery female voice it used to announce dinner seatings. "Are you sure you wish to proceed?"

"Yes!" Numa said.

"If you proceed, an alarm will sound in the security—"

"Override alarm, code: Pollux eight one six!" Alema called. "Confidential departure."

"Override accepted."

As the launching bay's iris hatch swirled open, a soft pop sounded from Bulkhead 38, and Alema knew the hermetic seal had been broken. Her first thought was that someone on the bridge was raising the door, but then she heard the muffled voice of the female engineer.

The door rose, and the voxyn came scurrying down the corridor, sensory bristles on end, white tail whipping back and forth. The creature's yellow eyes were fixed on the floor and it was licking the air with a long forked tongue, and Alema's hand ached more than ever for her lightsaber.

"Ready the escape pod," Numa ordered, pushing Alema into the launching bay's bluish light. "*Now*, sister."

Alema found herself looking into the nozzle of the escape pod's primitive rocket engine. It was barely a meter across, just large enough to start the hundred-person capsule toward the nearest habitable planet.

In the corridor, Numa called, "Close Bulkhead Forty-two! Authorization code: nebula rubantine!"

"The bulkhead emergency code is temporarily suspended," the computer returned in its sweet voice. "Please report valid emergencies to any engineering supervisor."

"Override!" Numa ordered. "And disarm safety sensors! Code: Pollux . . ."

As Numa finished the authorization code, Alema slipped past

the rocket nozzle to the side of the pod. A sickening crunch sounded out in the corridor, but she could no longer see what was happening outside the bay. She pressed her palm to the escape pod's activation pad. The hatch slid open, revealing a starkly lit interior crammed with ten cramped rows of acceleration chairs. There was no cockpit or viewport, only a droid pilot stationed at the craft's single control panel.

The droid pointed to the chair farthest from the door. "Welcome to Escape Pod Four-twenty-one. Please take your seat and wait for the other passengers. There is no need—"

"Prepare for a cold launch." Alema would have preferred the speed of a hot launch, but the flare of rockets would be noticed on the bridge—and however faint their fast-dwindling hopes of escaping unnoticed, she still had to try. "On my command. Authorization code: Pollux—"

"The override authorization code has already been given," the droid said, turning to its duties. "There is no need to repeat the override authorization code once the launching bay is entered."

A wet burping noise sounded from out in the corridor, then Numa screamed. Alema stepped out of the escape pod and saw her sister staggering into the launching bay, arms raised to cover her face. She missed the center of the hatch and stumbled over the rim, then fell with her feet across the threshold. Her face and chest were covered in sizzling brown mucus, and her lekku were thrashing against the durasteel floor.

Alema did not experience Numa's pain, as she had heard sometimes happened between Force-sensitive siblings, but she did receive a heightened impression of her sister's thoughts. Numa was afraid of being blind, but more than that, she was frightened they would be unveiled as Jedi and cause the deaths of yet more innocents. And she was angry—angry at her own carelessness in letting the creature surprise her.

"Sister!"

Alema sprang toward Numa and saw the voxyn pinned beneath Bulkhead 42, struggling to pull itself forward. Though its torso was pressed almost flat, she was astounded to see it moving at all. Bulkhead doors had safety sensors precisely because they closed with so much force; they had sensor overrides because it was sometimes necessary to crush anything beneath them to save the ship.

As Alema neared her sister, the creature swung its broad snout in her direction and sprayed a jet of brown saliva through the hatchway. Prepared by the attack on her sister, she opened herself to the Force and, with an almost unconscious wave of her fingertips, sent the stream washing back toward her attacker. The voxyn, fast as a blaster bolt, closed its eyes and turned away before the mucus struck.

Alema hardly cared. Numa's thoughts were growing disorganized and distant, her cries fading to groans. Alema grabbed her sister beneath the arms, smearing her own fingers in the burning mucus, and tried not to think about what the stuff was doing to Numa's face and eyes.

"Find your center, sister." She pulled Numa into the launching bay. "Let the Force flow into you."

Numa fell completely quiet, her mind alarmingly calm—and then the calmness vanished, leaving in its place only a lingering peace and a vague sense of emptiness. Alema cried out and started to look down, then felt the mucus burning into the bones of her fingers and knew she did not have the courage.

Alema carried her sister's body around to the escape pod hatch and glanced back toward the door, where the voxyn, still trapped beneath the bulkhead, continued to watch. One side of its head was covered in the residue of its acid mucus, the scales beneath pocked and smoking as they continued to dissolve. The heads of several amphistaffs appeared in the narrow gap next to the creature's head and began—hopelessly—to pry.

A part of Alema—the part not mourning her sister, the part that was still a Jedi Knight—realized her last faint hope of slipping away unnoticed had vanished. The Yuuzhan Vong would hear the whir of the closing hatch and feel the thump of the pod's separation. Still, she could do nothing but go on. Pollux's life was forfeit—even if she surrendered, she knew the Yuuzhan Vong better than to think the commander would forgive his lies—but it would take time to destroy a ship as large as the *Nebula Chaser*. Perhaps, if she launched quickly, the frigate would be forced to pursue the escape pod instead of attacking the starliner. It was her best hope—her only hope.

She looked back toward the hatchway. "Close launching bay—"

The voxyn's snout—all of the creature Alema could still see—turned toward her and opened half a meter. A deafening shriek filled her ears, then the fist of a powerful compression wave slammed her in the stomach. She suddenly felt dizzy and sick, and in the next second she was slumped against the escape pod, cradling her sister's dead body in her arms. She felt something warm trickling out of her ear and touched it with a fleshless finger; when she lowered her hand, the tip of the bone was red with blood.

Alema tried to rise, nearly retched, then dropped back to her haunches, head spinning and stomach churning. Still holding Numa in her lap, she kicked her way through the escape pod door.

"Launch!" Alema gasped. "Launch right now!"

The pod hatch closed, the lights dimmed—and that was all. The capsule remained eerily silent and still. Puzzled, Alema dragged herself past a row of acceleration chairs and looked forward. The droid pilot was facing her, vocabulator flashing rapidly as he endeavored to explain proper launching procedure. Alema could not hear a word.

"Override!" she yelled. "Authorization code—"

The escape pod shot forward, hurling Alema into a durasteel chair-mounting. She had already given the authorization code.

Walton & Tipton Twp. Public Library,
103 East Bishop St.
Walton, Indiana 46994

*   *   *

Jaina missed the launch. She was staring at the heads-up display, trying to bring the *Shadow*'s comm array into perfect alignment with the *Nebula Chaser*'s tight-beam antenna. With the starliner drifting dead only twenty million kilometers in front of an orange sun, the task would have been difficult under the best circumstances. With the presence of a Yuuzhan Vong frigate limiting them to air thrusters, it was nearly impossible.

After several minutes of trying, Jaina finally aligned the comm pip inside the targeting reticle and matched the *Shadow*'s rotation to the *Nebula Chaser*'s progress across the face of the orange sun.

"How's that?"

R2-D2 scrolled a message down the heads-up.

"No, I don't think I can," Jaina snapped. "If you're getting anything at all, put it on!"

Half a dozen fuzzy two-dimensional vids appeared inside the canopy, neatly arrayed in a row across the plexalloy. Half the displays showed Yuuzhan Vong warriors being Yuuzhan Vong warriors, smashing droids, throwing electronics down disintegration tubes, beating helpless refugees. One screen showed some sort of eight-legged reptile—maybe it was a reptile—pinned beneath a bulkhead door, its head badly acid-burned and one eye burst from sudden decompression. Another display showed an empty escape pod bay, but it was the last screen that caught Jaina's interest.

It showed the *Nebula Chaser*'s bridge, where Captain Pollux and his entire flight crew stood surrounded by Yuuzhan Vong warriors. Even had Jaina known Pollux personally and the vid display been better than it was, she would not have recognized him. His face had been reduced to a misshapen lump.

A Yuuzhan Vong with no nose cut the captain's ear off his head. "I ask the last time: Where did you pick up the *Jeedai*?"

Somehow, Pollux found the strength to laugh. "What Jedi?"

The Yuuzhan Vong chuckled. "You are a funny man, Captain."

He folded the dismembered ear into the captain's palm, then turned to his subordinates. "Kill the crew."

Heart sinking, Jaina turned to Mara. "Can we do anything?"

Mara kept her attention fixed on her navicomputer. "Not for the crew. But look at this."

She keyed a command, and a golden trajectory line appeared inside the canopy. It ran from the *Nebula Chaser* more or less across the *Shadow*'s bow, then curved sharply toward the planet.

"An escape pod?" Jaina glanced back to the starliner and found the Yuuzhan Vong frigate still sitting idle off the *Chaser*'s docking bay deck. "They endangered thousands of refugees, then snuck away in an escape pod? *Jedi* did that?"

"That's how it looks, doesn't it?" Mara began to plot an interception course. "Let's pick 'em up before they do any more damage."

Chapter 2

A mere kilometer beyond the transparisteel wall, the antenna-strewn horizon plunged away into a bottomless abyss of tumbling asteroids and drifting stars. Tiny blue halos winked into existence and slowly swelled into the backlit rectangles of enormous cargo barges returning with loads of durasteel from outlying fabrication plants. Crew transports laced the darkness with long tails of ions, racing from task to task on more than a hundred orbiting dry docks, and enormous welding droids traced ship skeletons in brilliant spark storms.

On the way in, Han Solo had counted nearly five hundred warships under construction in the old Bilbringi Shipyards. They were mostly escorts, corvettes, and other small stuff that could be finished in a hurry, but there were also two *Imperial*-class Star Destroyers. While these huge ships probably would not be ready before the Yuuzhan Vong captured the facility, the hulls were nearly closed and the drive units already mounted. Clearly, young General Muun was a Sullustan with a plan, just the sort of careful deskpilot who always impressed Coruscant Command—and seldom failed to exhaust Han's limited supply of patience.

Wishing he could use one of those Jedi calming techniques his son Jacen was always talking about, Han forced an insincere smile and turned toward the center of the room. Leia sat on a small couch with the general, her face glowing with the same stunning brown-eyed intensity that had caught Han's eye so long ago. Though he would never understand how she had kept that fervor burning so brightly through thirty years of service to the galaxy, it had become a mooring for him, the one constant that never seemed to change through so many decades of struggle, loss, and death. Now, when occasionally her legs—healed from her near-fatal ordeal on Duro but still sometimes weak—tired and stumbled, the pain of almost losing her made his heart stop, and he swore he would never, *ever* shut her out again.

". . . hundred thousand lives are at stake, General," she was saying. "The Vray are a gentle species. Without an escort, the evacuation convoy will be defenseless against the Yuuzhan Vong."

"And how many lives will the New Republic lose if Bilbringi falls before the fleet is completed?" Muun asked. His heavy Sullustan jowls rippled gently as he spoke, but his feelings remained otherwise hidden behind his flat mask of a face. "Whole worlds will perish, and that will mean millions."

"She's only asking for twenty ships," Han said.

The general turned his black eyes on Han. "She is asking for five cruisers and fifteen corvettes—a quarter of Bilbringi's defense, and the Yuuzhan Vong are already probing our outer security posts."

"We're letting you keep the *Dauntless.*" Han spoke in his most reasonable tone. "And the other ships will be back in a week standard . . . two, tops."

"I am sorry, no." Muun shook his head and started to rise.

A buzz sounded from the secure comm station on the general's desk. C-3PO, who had been standing behind the couch, raised his head and inquired, "Would you like me to take that for you, General?"

Muun nodded. "Unless it's urgent priority, I'll reply in a few minutes."

"Thanks, Threepio," Han said. Any interruption would only reduce their chances of getting the escort. He dropped into a seat opposite Muun. "You seem to be forgetting who you're talking to, General."

Leia's brown eyes flashed in alarm. "Han—"

"It wasn't so long ago she could have demanded the ships," Han continued. "If anyone deserves—"

"I know what the Princess deserves." Muun reluctantly returned to his seat. "I studied the history vids at the academy."

"*History* vids?" Han growled. "So they activated you when? About last year?" He glanced through the transparisteel dome at the bustling dry docks. "You must have had some test scores to get a command like this."

An indignant shudder ran through the Sullustan's jowls, but before he could reply, C-3PO spoke again.

"Excuse me for interrupting, but there is a Yuuzhan Vong emissary asking to see Princess Leia."

"What?" Han and Leia asked together.

"Tell him no," Han said.

And Leia asked, "How did he find me?"

C-3PO spouted a millisecond of digital squeal into the comm station. The reply came a moment later.

"The Yuuzhan Vong emissary refuses to reveal that information to the picket officer, but he does swear in the name of Yun-Yammka to do you no harm. He wishes to discuss the fate of some refugees."

"No," Han said.

Leia flashed him a scowl, then said to C-3PO, "Tell him I'll send instructions shortly."

"Have you gone spacesick?" Han knew he would never win this argument, but he had to try. Having already lost his best friend to the Yuuzhan Vong, he was determined not to lose his wife. "Or maybe you've forgotten Elan and the bo'tous attempt—or how close you came to losing your legs last year on Duro?"

"I haven't forgotten," Leia said evenly. She turned to their host. "But I'm sure General Muun wants to hear how the Yuuzhan Vong knew I was here—almost as much as I do."

The Sullustan nodded. "Indeed."

"You can't let a Yuuzhan Vong into Bilbringi!" Han said, realizing that Muun was his best hope of preventing Leia from taking such a risk. "The ship counts alone—"

"Will be of use to our enemies only if they are accurate." The Sullustan did not even look in Han's direction. His jowls lifted into a sort of stiff grin, and he said to Leia, "We have been waiting for just such an opportunity."

"Then it is my pleasure to give it to you." Leia turned to C-3PO. "You may relay to the Yuuzhan Vong that we will grant him safe passage."

"As long as he presents himself unarmed and unmasked," Han added glumly. Leia's Noghri bodyguards, waiting in the corridor outside Muun's office, would like this even less than he did, but they stood no chance at all of changing her mind. "And if there's any funny business—"

"He has already promised honorable conduct," C-3PO replied. "Though, if you ask me, a Yuuzhan Vong's promise is worth precisely as much as a Jawa's."

General Muun stepped over to his desk and opened a comm channel to his security chief. "Commence Operation Restbreak. This is not a drill."

Han and the two bodyguards spent the next two hours converting one of the base's old Imperial interrogation chambers into an interview room he considered safe enough for his wife. The main safety feature was the transparisteel panel through which the discussion would be held, but there were also the biosensor arrays to monitor the Yuuzhan Vong's body state, the negative air pressure to confine any poisons he might release to the original room, and a "void button" that would open the chamber to the near-vacuum outside.

General Muun's preparations were just as thorough and twice as fast. He had barely given the order before the orbiting dry docks began to fall dark and still, making the shipyard look more and more abandoned. By the time the picket ship appeared above the planetoid, only three dilapidated dry docks remained in operation, skeleton crews scurrying about their work as though rushing to put the final touches on half a dozen inconsequential corvettes. The vast majority of the dry docks were not even visible, and the few that could be seen contained only half-built craft that appeared to have been abandoned in the haste of an over-early evacuation. Whether or not the general deserved his command at such a young age, Han had to admire his cleverness; based on what could be seen from the surface, the Yuuzhan Vong would be in no hurry to attack the Bilbringi Shipyards.

C-3PO announced the emissary's arrival, then a dozen guards entered the interrogation chamber with their charge. The Yuuzhan Vong had been afforded few diplomatic courtesies; something that looked like an artificial eye had been confiscated and now rested in a security officer's hand, and in place of his own clothes, he wore a thin fleet watchcloak with the hood up. In his hands he carried a spongelike creature that resembled the villips Yuuzhan Vong used to communicate over long distances, though this one was larger and more gelatinous. The shipyard science officers had screened the creature for every known form of Yuuzhan Vong attack and confirmed it to be an organic communication device, but Leia's Noghri bodyguards, Adarakh and Meewalh, insisted on performing their own inspection, sniffing, prodding, and squeezing the thing until Han thought it would burst. He put his hand over the void button anyway; until someone could tell him how an overgrown protozoan could send messages across the galaxy as efficiently as the HoloNet, he wasn't taking anyone's word for anything.

Once everyone was satisfied, the escorts pushed the emissary into the room's single chair, then left and locked the door.

Leia stepped to the transparisteel. "I am Leia Organa Solo."

"Yes, we have met before, on the planet Rhommamool." The emissary's voice was throaty and arrogant, and it instantly caused Leia's face to go white. He set his creature on the table and peeled back his hood, revealing a smashed Yuuzhan Vong face with one empty eye socket. "And at Duro, we even worked together for a time."

"Cree'Ar?" Leia's hand dropped instinctively to her lightsaber—the one Luke had made for her years ago. Tsavong Lah had destroyed her other lightsaber on Duro. "Nom Anor!"

"You have an excellent memory." The Yuuzhan Vong glared at Leia coldly. "How is your son Jacen? And Mara, is she still in remission? As you know, I have a special interest in your sister-in-law's condition."

Han felt the void button tickle his palm and realized he was dangerously close to pressing it. "Keep talking, fella." During the fall of Duro, Nom Anor had attempted to kill Mara and Jaina, tried to orchestrate the deaths of Leia and Jacen, and before that he had infected Mara with a deadly disease that had required more than two years to overcome. "There's nothing I'd enjoy more than vaccing you."

Nom Anor's smile remained snide. "Before you hear what I came to say? Besides, I do not think Leia Organa Solo the type to break a promise of safe passage."

"My promise, not Han's," Leia said. "And his self-control isn't what it used to be. How did you know I was here?"

"With the Vray evacuating, where else would you look for a convoy escort?" Nom Anor gestured at the creature on the desk. "If I may?"

"The Vray have been evacuating for weeks," Leia said, continuing to press for an answer. Han doubted Nom Anor would tell them if there was a spy inside Bilbringi, but what was left unsaid would prove just as useful to General Muun. "We've only been here a few hours."

"We are, of course, watching Bilbringi—and that is really all I am going to say on the matter." Without asking permission this time, Nom Anor coaxed his creature awake with a brief stroke. "Tsavong Lah wishes you to see this."

The creature melted into a flat disk, then began to glow with yellow bioluminescence. The light coalesced into a long starship with a blocky stern and the distinctive hammerhead bridge of one of the Corellian Engineering Corporation's large civilian cruisers. Judging by the lack of efflux from the ion drives and the open doors of its docking bay deck, the ship was standing dead in space.

"The starliner *Nebula Chaser*," Nom Anor said. "The image is current."

Han's heart leapt into his throat. The *Nebula Chaser* was the ship Mara and Jaina had gone to meet. The mission was supposed to be simple, a quick rendezvous in a safe sector and then home— but something had clearly gone wrong. He put on his best sabacc face and forced himself not to look in his wife's direction.

"Very impressive," Leia said. Though she had to be just as worried as Han, her voice remained dry and mocking. "You've learned to transmit holograms. I'll look forward to your holodramas on the 'Net."

"The Yuuzhan Vong have made living light for centuries," Nom Anor snapped. "I am showing you this ship because the warmaster thought you might wish to trade."

Here it comes, Han thought. He moved his hand away from the void button, not trusting himself to resist if Nom Anor announced the Yuuzhan Vong had his daughter.

"Tsavong Lah thought wrong," Leia said. Her voice was a little too cold, the only hint of the ice ball that had to be filling in her stomach. "I'd rather trade with a Hutt."

"The Hutts do not have what you want." Nom Anor stabbed a clawlike finger into the hologram. "There are ten thousand refugees aboard, and their peril is your doing."

"I doubt that. If this is what Tsavong Lah wished me to see, our business is done."

Leia turned her back on Nom Anor and stepped away from the transparisteel. It was all Han could do not to remind her that their daughter's life might be at stake, but he held his tongue, knowing she was only trying to undermine their opponent's confidence.

She made it as far as the door before Nom Anor called, "You can save them." He rose to peer over the living light. "Just tell me where to find the Jedi base."

Leia glanced at Han, clearly wondering whether Nom Anor meant they could save the refugees or Jaina and Mara, then said, "There is no Jedi base."

Nom Anor sighed theatrically. "Princess Leia, you discredit me again in the eyes of Tsavong Lah." He let his chin slump. "I advised him you would never sacrifice so many to save so few, but he believes you are willing to sacrifice more—much more—to protect the Jedi."

As Nom Anor spoke, a salvo of plasma balls streaked into the hologram and erupted against the shieldless starliner, opening flash-melted holes in the durasteel hull. Dark clouds of speck-sized flotsam and atmospheric vapor began to jet into space, and another salvo of plasma boiled into view. Many of the balls entered through the same holes as the previous fusillade and tore through the ship's interior bulkheads. The clouds darkened as more flotsam poured into the cold vacuum, then the image shifted, magnifying the breach area and revealing the specks to be the tumbling, pressure-ruptured bodies of the ship's passengers.

"Truly, the wisdom of Tsavong Lah is as boundless as the

galaxy itself." Nom Anor rolled his one good eye as though sharing a joke, then gestured at the starliner. "They are dying because there were Jedi aboard. If the Jedi do not want more to die, they will surrender within one of your standard weeks."

"More?" Han knew it was exactly the question Nom Anor wanted him to ask, but he could not restrain himself. He had to know what had become of Jaina. "How many more?"

"Your scouts will confirm that our fleets have surrounded the world of Talfaglio; for the next week, all refugee ships are being held in orbit. If the Jedi surrender, the convoy will be allowed to leave. If the Jedi do not, it will be destroyed." Nom Anor glanced down at Han's hand, which was hovering over the void button, then added, "As they will if I fail to return."

"You expect the Jedi to surrender?" Han asked. He was too relieved by Nom Anor's failure to mention Jaina or Mara to feel any real outrage at the deaths of ten thousand strangers. Maybe he should have felt guilty about that, he didn't know, but all that mattered at the moment was that Jaina and Mara were safe. "Won't happen, fella. I might as well get things started."

Han locked gazes with Nom Anor and lowered his hand toward the void button, grinning crookedly and taking his time to give Leia a chance to stop him. The Yuuzhan Vong met his gaze with a sneer and did not look away, even when Han's palm touched the button. He paused there, waiting for Leia to stop him, but she said nothing. Han glanced over and saw her glaring at the emissary, her brown eyes burning with raw rage.

"What are you waiting for?" she demanded.

"Really?"

Leia nodded. "Do it."

The edge in her voice unsettled Han, and it occurred to him that Nom Anor might have failed to mention Jaina or Mara for another reason—a reason Leia had already thought of. It was entirely possible the pair had been aboard when the *Nebula Chaser* was destroyed, and the Yuuzhan Vong simply did not realize who they had killed.

Han pushed the void button, and a seal hissed open along the edge of the ceiling panel. Nom Anor's one eye grew wide.

"Are you mad?" He jumped to his feet. "You'll kill millions!"

Leia reached over and depressed the void button again, stopping the ceiling panel where it was. "Not us, you."

The air continued to hiss out of the chamber, causing the image of the *Nebula Chaser* to flicker out of existence as the villip creature curled in on itself. Nom Anor glanced at the ceiling, then back to Leia, his gruesome face slack with surprise. She waited until he pressed his fingers to his ears, then hit the void button again and closed the panel.

When Nom Anor took his hands away from his ears, Leia said, "Go back to your warmaster and tell him how you were treated. Tell him the Jedi accept no responsibility for the lives he threatens, and that any emissary issuing a similar threat will not be returned."

Nom Anor nodded, if not meekly, then at least not haughtily. "I will tell him, but that will change nothing." He went to the door and waited until it opened, then added, "The warmaster believes this will work, and he has not been wrong yet."

Luke Skywalker knew that a few days in the bacta tank would heal the physical damage, but there was an anguish in Alema that would never fade. He could feel it even now, while she floated in a restless healing trance, and the torment would only grow worse when she awakened to the news of the *Nebula Chaser*'s fate. There would be more feelings of guilt, more anger, more fear of the . . . *thing* that had killed her sister. Already perilously close to the dark side in her leadership of the New Plympto resistance, now she would find it an irresistible alternative to accepting whatever responsibility she bore for her sister's death, for New Plympto's destruction, and for the starliner's fate. It was not a question of whether Alema Rar would turn to the dark side, but how soon and for how long.

The infirmary door whispered open behind Luke, and he turned to find Cilghal's liquid eyes studying him from the threshold.

"I am sorry to interrupt, Luke, but your brother-in-law is demanding to speak with you. He seems to think we're keeping something from him."

Luke smiled. "Good old Han. It's nice to have him back to normal."

Cilghal's huge mouth parted in a Calamarian grin. "Yes, isn't it?"

Luke followed her into a round corridor and started toward the conference vault. Like much of the new base, the tunnel had been laser-cut from solid rock, but it had been sealed against vacuum leaks with a white plastifoam that made it appear much softer and brighter than the typical cave warren. The foam was also an excellent insulator, trapping equipment-generated heat so efficiently that most species elected to wear their vacuum emergency suits—still necessary far too often—with all closures open. Engineering was trying to correct the problem, but most inhabitants already referred to their sleeping quarters as sweat lodges.

Luke entered the conference vault and found his nephews, Jacen and Anakin, waiting with Danni Quee, Tahiri Veila, and a group of other Jedi. A small hologram of Han and Leia hovered above the holoprojector in the center of the conference table. Han was grilling his sons about exactly *why* their sister was not in the room; Leia was looking a little embarrassed.

Luke joined the others at the table and, much to the gratitude of his two nephews, took their place in the holo's sensor arc. "Han, Jaina is in the signals center with Artoo, trying to enhance a transmission they received from the *Nebula Chaser*. She'll be here as soon as she can, but she can't drop what she's doing."

Han frowned, but appeared to accept this. "You heard about the threat?"

Luke nodded. "A few minutes ago."

"Then what took you so long?"

"I was with Alema Rar," he said. "She wasn't strapped in when the pod ejected and got beat up. She couldn't say much on the way back except 'voxyn,' so I was hoping to get a subconscious impression of what happened to her sister."

Han narrowed his eyes. "Subconscious impression?"

"Through the Force, Han," Luke said, beginning to lose patience with his brother-in-law. Though Han was largely back to himself, his grief over Chewbacca's death continued to manifest itself in peculiar ways. The latest was a nervous streak that had both Leia and his children ready to walk asteroids. "Jaina is fine—so is Mara."

The attempt at subtlety was lost on Han. "So how come Mara isn't there?"

"Mara can't exactly drop what she's doing either," Luke answered. "She's feeding Ben."

"You'll have to excuse us for being a little nervous." Leia flashed an annoyed look at her husband, then continued, "That was quite a demonstration Nom Anor put on. Ten thousand people dead, and I doubt he would have stopped if I *had* told him where to find Eclipse. What are we going to do about Talfaglio?"

"First, remember that by allowing the Yuuzhan Vong to make the responsibility ours, we would only be playing into their hands," Luke said. "We must always remember that they're the murderers here, not us."

"That is true as far as it goes, Master Skywalker," Cilghal said, addressing Luke more formally now that they were in a larger group. "But I am not comfortable closing my eyes to the death of so many. Whether the responsibility is ours or not, we must do something if we can prevent it."

"And we're not entirely innocent in this, either." Jaina entered the vault leading R2-D2 and several Jedi. News of Tsavong Lah's threat was spreading fast, and base personnel were pouring into the conference vault. "There were Jedi on the *Nebula Chaser,* and those Jedi were leading the resistance on New Plympto. The Rar sisters put the whole starliner at risk by boarding it—as we did by rendezvousing with it."

"And you know the Yuuzhan Vong wouldn't have taken them for sacrifices *how?*" Danni Quee asked, always quick to pinpoint the flaw in any argument. A small-framed woman with green eyes and curly blond hair, Danni had been one of the first Yuuzhan Vong prisoners—and the first to witness their breaking tortures. "We can't presume to know how these killers think," she went on. "It will cause mistakes. Bad ones."

As Danni spoke, she stepped aside to let Jaina join Luke in the holocomm's sensor arc.

"Hi, Dad, Mom," Jaina said. "Sorry to keep you waiting."

"We weren't waiting that long," Leia said.

The tension drained from Han's face, and he added, "Yeah, no problem."

The calm lasted about a second before Anakin Solo, his brown hair as unruly as ever, stepped forward to kick the discussion into hyperdrive. "Look, it doesn't really matter whether we're responsible or not. There are hundreds of thousands—maybe millions—of lives at risk. We've got to do something, that's all."

"What would you have us do, Anakin?" Luke asked.

Tahiri answered for him. "Break their blockade, of course." Blond and willowy, Tahiri resembled in many respects a fifteen-year-old version of Danni Quee—even down to having been a Yuuzhan Vong prisoner, until Anakin rescued her from a shaper laboratory. "We make them pay, so they don't try it again. It's the only way we turn this back on them."

"And that may be exactly what the Yuuzhan Vong expect us to

do," Danni said. "If they see the Jedi as warriors like themselves, they will expect an honorable response."

Han nodded in the hologram. "They're calling the Jedi out. You'd be fools to go—especially when they're waiting for you."

"So we let a world die?" Jacen's quiet voice was a stark contrast to the rising tension in the room. He turned toward Tahiri and Anakin. "But waving our lightsabers around will only get more people killed, too."

Anakin scowled, as he so often did when talking with his older brother these days. "Maybe you can just stand aside and watch—"

Jacen raised a hand. "Let me finish, Anakin. I'm saying that neither choice is good." He glanced at the others in the room. "If we fight, the Yuuzhan Vong kill more people; if we don't fight, they kill them anyway. We can't permit either. The Jedi are supposed to be the defenders of life in this galaxy."

"What are you saying, Jacen?" Han demanded. "That the Jedi have to surrender?" He closed his eyes and winced. "Tell me that's not what you're saying."

"Nobody is going to surrender, Han," Luke said.

He was sympathetic to Han's concern. Of all the young Jedi Knights who had come to Eclipse, Jacen was the most philosophical, often struggling with the paradoxical idea that it was sometimes necessary to destroy in order to preserve. Luke knew his nephew's concerns to be the result of a disturbing vision on the planet Duro, in which Jacen had seen the galaxy tipping toward darkness and been unable to stop it. Fearful of tipping the balance even farther, the young Jedi had temporarily abandoned the Force altogether. Though he had resumed its use when events necessitated it in order to save his mother's life, Jacen remained uncertain enough about his vision that at times his uneasiness still moved him close to inaction—a situation as perilous, in its own way, as the one that would soon be leading Alema into danger.

"We're not surrendering," Luke repeated. "And we won't let

the Yuuzhan Vong lure us into battle unprepared." He turned to Danni and Cilghal. "Does the Eclipse Program have anything to offer yet?"

Danni shook her head. "Nothing. We can tell from the holos when there's a yammosk coordinating the battle, but it's been impossible to identify posting patterns or determine how it communicates. We just have to get closer."

Luke looked to Cilghal. "And the villips?"

"I fear my group has made even less progress," she said. "The Yuuzhan Vong obviously stop using the villips we have captured, which leaves us only with dissection. So far, we haven't the faintest idea how they work."

Luke nodded to both scientists. "It's too early to expect progress, but it will come." He turned to the others—now numbering nearly fifty, including Mara, their infant son, Ben, and more than a dozen non-Jedi support volunteers. "Our path is not yet clear, but I am confident in this much: It would be folly to let the Yuuzhan Vong draw us out before we are ready. I hope you can be patient and trust in the Force to steer blame for the *Nebula Chaser*'s destruction onto the proper shoulders."

As the group murmured its consent and began to break up, Mara came to his side. "Well said, Luke." Cradling Ben in one arm, she rose to her toes and kissed him on the cheek. "But I'd feel better if the Force weren't blind to Yuuzhan Vong shoulders."

Chapter 3

One of a thousand pagan blasphemies excluded from the redemption of Obroa-skai, the Museum of Applied Photonics rose above the surrounding bugyards in a glittering massif of transparisteel towers and crystalplas galleries. Though Nom Anor had spent too much time among the infidels to find the sight offensive, he knew better than to let his comfort with the place show. He paused at the threshold to cast a yearning glance out over the droning black plain, then put on a sneer of disgust and followed his escorts into the lobby, where a hundred Verpine captives stood watching their Yuuzhan Vong guards with unfathomable insectoid eyes. After a brief conversation with the subaltern of the detachment, Nom Anor's escorts led him through a maze of corridors profanely lit by wandering balls of pure light.

They found Tsavong Lah in a chamber surrounded by what looked like a hundred kilometers of snarled translucent threads. A fully tattooed warrior with fringed lips and bone-implanted armor, the warmaster was holding a small holopad in his hand, gazing at its projector disk with a look most others would reserve for cowards and slaves.

"Now," he said into the instrument.

Tsavong Lah had barely spoken before an instantaneous flash lit the whole thread tangle, then leapt through the empty air into the holopad. A millisecond later, the full-sized image of an infidel X-wing appeared over his hand, obscuring the warmaster's upper body and much of the room. The starfighter turned slowly toward the door and opened fire; only Nom Anor did not duck for cover.

"Do you know what I would do with this, were I the infidels?" Tsavong Lah asked, speaking from inside the hologram.

"Destroy it, I am certain," Nom Anor answered. "Such lifeless things are an abomination to the gods. I cannot tell you how it disgusted me to abide them while I prepared the way for our invasion."

"We all do what is necessary, Executor, and you have already been commended for enduring the enemy's filth." Tsavong Lah's tone was irritated, and perhaps a little distracted. "We cannot defeat what we do not understand. For instance, our coralskipper pilots could easily be misled by an image such as this. Were I the enemy, the galaxy would be littered with these devices."

"The galaxy *is* littered with them," Nom Anor answered, bristling. "They are not really much to admire, Great One. They are as limited in their capacities as are our enemies."

The X-wing vanished, then Tsavong Lah dropped the holopad to the floor and crushed it beneath the armored vua'sa claw that he now stood upon in place of the foot taken by Jacen Solo.

"The enemy has proven challenging enough to thwart *you* several times." The warmaster's voice was full of loathing; a true believer in the supremacy of the Yuuzhan Vong gods, he disavowed the influence of chance and viewed any failure as a sign of the instrument's spiritual decadence. "I trust that was not the case this time?"

"The chilab worked beautifully." Nom Anor tipped his head to one side, then covered his nostrils and blew air into his sinuses. Though he lacked the faith to truly enjoy the pain of the neural grub's detachment, he feigned a smile of satisfaction as the thing tore its dendrites from his optic chiasma and exited through his nasal cavity. He let it drop into his palm, then presented it to Tsavong Lah. "I had a good view on the way in. I am certain the chilab's memories will prove useful in planning your attack."

"No doubt." Tsavong Lah slipped the grub into the pocket of the sharp-clawed cape clinging to his shoulders. "I will view them later. Your meeting with Leia Solo went well?"

"Very well." It would have been unthinkable to answer anything else. "I have no doubt that the Jedi will respond to our challenge."

"You are more confident than I would be in your place," a wispy voice said, low and behind him. "The Jedi will smell our trap and be wary."

Nom Anor turned and saw a motley featherball hopping past the guards on thin, reverse-jointed legs. Her willowy ears and corkscrew antennae bestowed on her a vaguely mothlike aspect, though Nom Anor considered her a pest more on the magnitude of a radank.

"Vergere," he fumed. "I was not aware you knew the ways of the Jedi."

"Vergere knows them better than I," Tsavong Lah said. "She was the one who said the *Jeedai* would let you live. I believed they would kill you outright."

"You were perhaps closer to the truth than your pet." Nom Anor refused to call Vergere an aide, for the peculiar little creature was no more than the familiar of an agent who had perished during an ill-fated attempt to disease the Jedi. She had become an adviser to Tsavong Lah after a brief captivity in the hands of New Republic Intelligence, where she managed to learn as much about the enemy in a few weeks as had Nom Anor in all his years as an agent provocateur. Questions had been raised about her loyalties, but once the reliability of her information had been established, she had quickly become Nom Anor's greatest rival.

"Leia Solo and her consort did attempt to kill me as you

expected," Nom Anor continued, "but I was able to play on her human emotions to save my life."

"So now you can control the emotions of the Jedi?" Vergere mocked. "Then perhaps you should make them surrender."

"One can lure a tana into the spatter pit with a smile and soft words." Nom Anor spread his hands and turned to Tsavong Lah. "Even I cannot persuade it to lay its neck in the cleaving yoke."

The warmaster rewarded him with a curt nod. "I am more interested in what Leia Solo said than why you are still alive. How did she respond when the *Gift of Anguish* destroyed the infidels?"

"She wanted to kill me."

"But she did not," the warmaster observed. "What did she do instead?"

"I convinced her she would also be killing millions of refugees." Even Nom Anor realized he was clinging to the claim a little too closely—perhaps because of the shame he had already suffered at Leia's hands on Duro. "She yielded."

"Not yielded—she refused to accept blame." Vergere stated her rebuttal as fact, not supposition. She hopped over to Tsavong Lah. "She's been a diplomat all her life. For her to fall into such a trap would be akin to you flying into an ambush."

Tsavong Lah considered her argument for only an instant. "It may appear so, but something else is happening." He looked over Vergere's feathery back at Nom Anor. "She let you live for a reason. What is it?"

The answer, of course, was because she had given her word, but Nom Anor knew better than to say so. Such an answer would contradict the opinion the warmaster had expressed earlier, and while a Yuuzhan Vong subordinate could insinuate, thwart, even subvert and still hope to live, he could never contradict. Sometimes Nom Anor wondered if the infidels' way was not better, and he supposed the fact that he did not immediately cower in fear of the gods' retribution was in itself a sign that he had spent too long away from his people. Leaving aside for the moment the question of why he had been forced to endure the painful introduction of the chilab if the warmaster had not expected him to return, Nom Anor shrugged.

"Before she released me, she gave me a warning. She said to tell you that the Jedi accept no responsibility for the hostages, and that any emissary you send with a similar threat will not be returned."

If Tsavong Lah noticed the slight contradiction of Nom Anor's contention that he had been the one controlling Leia, he showed no sign. He simply looked to Vergere.

"Right again, my servant."

She smiled up at him. "Have I not said the Jedi will prove worthy foes?"

"You have indeed," the warmaster said. "But the refugees will be their undoing yet. They will become the wedge that drives the New Republic away from the *Jeedai*."

Chapter 4

*T*he one good thing to come of Tsavong Lah's threat was that General Muun decided now would be a bad time to appear indifferent to the fate of refugees—and a particularly good time to boost his career by "rescuing" a group of evacuees. Not only did he send ten vessels to escort the Vray to safety, he insisted on leading the operation himself—freeing Leia and Han to return directly to Eclipse.

One of the many bad things to come of the threat was that when they arrived, Luke was waiting with a mission and a request to borrow C-3PO. The Solos barely had a chance to say hello to Anakin and the twins before they were on their way again, this time to Nova Station in what had once been the Carida system.

Surrounded as it was by the still-cooling ejecta of the explosion that had turned its sun into a supernova, space outside Nova Station was the reddest space Leia had ever seen. Wispy curtains of crimson gas swept slowly past the turning station, obscuring the distant stars and calling to mind the flash-boiled blood of billions of perished Caridans. Sitting there with Han in the wryly named Big Boom cantina, sipping an eyeblaster and trying to ignore Bobolo Baker's All-

Bith Band, Leia could not help feeling a little sickened by the knowledge that this had been an artificial cataclysm, one wrought by her own species' boundless thirst for vengeance and destruction.

An electronic attention bell chimed three times, temporarily drowning out Bobolo's flighty melody, then a male voice said something garbled over the public-address system. Along with every other being in the cantina, Leia and Han turned their heads toward a hologram projector hanging over the All-Bith Band. The name *Asteroid Dancer* appeared, with a line beneath designating the vessel a YT-1500 freighter. A few moments later, the word *Confirmed* was added, and a hologram depicting the craft's distinctive cockpit arrangement appeared.

Han grunted in frustration and reached for the pitcher of eye-blasters sitting in front of him. "They should've been here by now." He filled his glass, took a sip, then tried not to make a sour face and returned the drink to the table. "Booster's not coming."

"He has to," Leia said, glad to see the distaste in Han's expression. For a long time after Chewbacca's death he would drink anything, the fouler the better. The healing of his taste buds was yet one more sign of the healing inside. "Even the *Errant Venture* needs to resupply. Could we have missed them?"

Han gave her one of his patented dumb-question looks, then waved at the holo display. "How do we miss a Star Destroyer?"

"We don't," Leia agreed. "Not here."

Built to replace Carida as a way stop on the Perlemian Trade Route, Nova Station floated just inside the supernova's expanding gas shell, moving along behind the edge at the same three kilometers per second. As a result, any starship wishing to dock with the station had to leave hyperspace and enter the cloud at sublight speed, then use its sensors to obtain a final location. This gave station security and anyone else with a decent sensor package a chance to identify the ship long before it arrived, making the station an ideal haunt for smugglers, criminals, and anyone else with reason to appreciate a head start.

Han looked across the table. "What do you think, Red?" He was referring to Leia's neon-colored hair—now almost down to her collar after being shaved off during a decon alert on Duro last year. Along with a blastback pilot's jacket and stretchtight flight suit she could still pull off, the temporary dye job was part of her smuggler's-moll disguise. "Time to go?"

Leia smiled and shook her head. "How about something to eat?"

She reached over to thumb the service pad, but stopped when she noticed Han being eyed from the next table. The watcher was a small mountain of a Weequay, with a broad nose and a deeply creased face almost as gruesome as a Yuuzhan Vong's. "I think you're about to be recognized."

"Me?" Han turned to gaze out the viewport and see if he could spy the watcher in its reflection. "It's not *my* face that's been flashing over the 'Net for the last twenty years."

Long resentful of the loss of anonymity that came with being a hero of the Rebellion, Han had limited his disguise to a brush-bottle mustache and a pair of cheek pads. Along with a two-day growth of beard, the costume had worked so far, probably because people did not expect to see the husband of a former chief of state in a place like the Big Boom.

Clearly, their luck was changing. The big Weequay picked up his drink and stood, flight duster flapping open to reveal the hilt of a big vibroblade on his hip. Knowing that her Noghri bodyguard would be growing nervous, Leia glanced quickly in Meewalh's direction. Gaunt, wiry, and no more than a meter and a half tall, Meewalh was nevertheless such an intimidating sight with her leathery skin and wild eyes that even the Big Boom's clientele gave her wide berth. Leia signaled the Noghri to wait with a double eyeflick, then pretended not to notice as the stranger started toward Han.

"Wait a minute," Han said, more to himself than Leia. "I know this guy."

Leia casually lowered a hand beneath the table and loosened the blaster on her hip. The mere fact that her husband knew someone was no guarantee that the party in question did not have murder in mind. The big Weequay stopped beside their table and, after casting an appraising glance at Leia, turned to Han.

"Thought it was you," he said. "I'd recognize that smell anywhere."

"Yeah?" Han narrowed his eyes at the Weequay, clearly trying to recall where he had seen him before. "I get that a lot."

"Didn't see your ship come in on the board, Miek." The Weequay's smile was almost a sneer; clearly, he enjoyed watching Han struggle to remember him. "You still with the *Sunlight?*"

"You might say that." Han flashed a conspiratorial smile, then took a long drink of his eyeblaster to buy himself some time. *Sunlight Franchise* was one of a dozen false transponder codes the *Falcon* used regularly. They had docked with Nova Station under the name *Longshot,* and Han had more aliases than even he could track. Finally, he returned the glass to the table and refilled it from the pitcher. "Only you'd have to try a different name."

The Weequay laughed. "I thought as much. That captain of yours was a tricky one." He pulled up a chair and sat down, then glanced around the room. "Haven't seen any Ryn around, though."

That hardness only a wife can see came to Han's eyes, and Leia knew he had finally placed their uninvited guest.

"Droma doesn't run things anymore," Han said. Droma and Han had fallen in together for a time after the capture of Ord Mantell, then spent half a year tracking down Droma's lost Ryn clanmates and bringing them together in a Duros refugee camp. Though Droma and his people had since vanished into space, they had given Han a focus when Leia could not and would therefore always have a warm place in her heart. "He and I parted ways nearly a year ago."

"Really?" The Weequay turned to Leia again, half leering and half appraising. "This your new captain?"

Han looked hurt. "I'm captain. She's the mate."

"You might say that." Leia glared across the table at her husband. "On a good day."

The Weequay laughed heartily, then surprised Leia by reaching under the table to lay a meaty hand on her knee. "The next time you have a bad day, come over and see me on the *Sweet Surprise*. I'm the mate there, but you can have any post you want."

"That's enough, Plaan. She's not looking." Han's voice was serious now. "What are you doing off Tholatin, anyway? I thought you were the security chief."

The small amount of humor Leia saw in the situation vanished. Tholatin was the home of a group of traitorous smugglers who were not above aiding the Yuuzhan Vong when the price was high enough.

"Change of jobs. Like I said, I'm first mate on the *Sweet Surprise* now." He removed his hand from Leia's thigh. "Reason I came over, we're short of help this run. Pay's good."

Han waited just long enough for Leia to shake her head, then raised his hand to silence her. "How good?"

"*Captain,*" Leia interrupted. Whether it was through the Force or because of all their years together, the role he wanted her to play came to her almost instinctively. "What about that load we're waiting for?"

Han did not look at her. "It's late."

"But we've already been paid for the job." Leia was playing the role, but she was also truly irritated at being dismissed. "And you know how he is about runners who don't keep their contracts. I'd hate to see you frozen in carbonite or something."

Han winced, then took another long drink of his eyeblaster.

"There's a clause," he said. "If the load's more than a day late, we pick it up later. Let's hear him out."

"Can't say much until you're in," Plaan said.

"We don't need much," Han said. "As long as it's not that refugee scam. The last thing I want is a New Republic fleet breathing down my neck."

Plaan shook his head. "No more of that. This time they get where they're going, a sweet deal for them and us. You won't believe it."

Leia slumped back and folded her arms across her ribs, doing her best imitation of an angry moll. It wasn't hard.

"How long would it take?" Han asked.

"We have to hop out and pick up the rest of our cargo," Plaan said. "Then it's a two-day run, no more."

Han looked across the table. "What do you think, Red?"

Realizing he was still probing for information, Leia said, "What about the *Longshot*, Miek? Are we hitchhiking back?"

"We'll drop you," Plaan said. "We'll be coming back by."

"How much?" Han asked.

"Five thousand," Plaan answered.

"Each?" Leia asked.

Plaan frowned. "For both—and that covers the docking fees for leaving the *Longshot* here."

Han looked to Leia. "Well?"

Leia rolled her eyes and reached for her eyeblaster.

"We'll think about it," Han said.

Plaan started to make a higher offer, then looked at Leia and changed his mind. "Don't think too long. We're pulling out in an hour."

He took his drink and left, weaving his way through the crowd toward another pair of likely looking prospects. Leia watched as he sat down and began his pitch, then she glanced up with everyone else when the electronic attention bell chimed. This time, the name *Light Racer* appeared above the Bith's heads.

"So, where's he going?" she asked.

"With that schedule, three possibilities," Han replied. "Kuat, Borleias, or Coruscant."

"Coruscant," Leia surmised. "Kuat and Borleias are turning away refugees. If he expects to get where he's going, it's Coruscant."

Plaan found his two crew members and stood, waving to Han and Leia as he shouldered his way toward the exit with a pair of flop-eared Ossan. Han raised his glass to the big Weequay and took a long drink, then waited until they were gone and thumbed the service pad on the table.

"Where are you going?" Leia put the emphasis on *you*.

"To gargle—I can't stand eyeblasters," Han replied. "And then *we're* going to Coruscant."

Leia remained seated. "I can't. You know how worried my brother is about his students."

The young students of Luke's Jedi academy were currently aboard the *Errant Venture* with Booster Terrik, jumping around the galaxy at random to prevent the Yuuzhan Vong from tracking them down. Unfortunately, in the two days since Alema Rar had awakened on Eclipse and described the attack on her sister, two more Jedi had fallen to voxyn—one on the supposedly secure world of Kuat. Concerned the *Venture* might stumble across one of the Jedi-killers during a supply stop, Luke had asked Han and Leia to pass Booster the coordinates of the new Jedi base at Eclipse and suggest that he resupply only from there. Booster being Booster, he was now three days overdue for his regularly scheduled rendezvous, and even Leia had to admit it seemed unlikely he meant to keep it.

"Let's wait one more day," she suggested. "The *Longshot* is fast. If Booster doesn't show, we can still reach Coruscant ahead of Plaan."

"Well, I'm not leaving here without you," Han sighed. "But

Rogue Squadron is rotating through Coruscant right now, and Wedge owes me a favor. At least let me talk to him and make sure the *Sweet Surprise* receives a warm welcome."

"Wedge Antilles owes you a favor?"

"Everybody owes me a favor," Han said.

Booster failed to show, of course, and Wedge—General Antilles—was reluctant to order the boarding of a properly registered starship without "evidence of suspicion," in this case the presence of the complaining witness. Knowing this to be no more than an essential concession to the anti-Jedi sentiments on the Advisory Council, Leia reluctantly kept her promise to Han and informed Luke it was impossible to wait for the *Errant Venture* any longer. They left Nova Station and jumped into hyperspace at the Perlemian Trade Route. Han guessed they would be fast enough to beat the *Sweet Surprise* to Coruscant.

Han's calculations were a little off. They emerged from hyperspace to the news that Rogue Squadron was already on its way to intercept the *Surprise*. Wedge asked Han to meet him at Orbital Control to file a report, and Han surprised no one by promising to be there *after* he saw what happened with the *Surprise*.

Coruscant's usual aura of flickering starship light was now squeezed into a stack of luminous halos. To guard against the possibility of a Yuuzhan Vong surprise attack, the military had surrounded the planet with a shell of orbiting space mines, leaving open only a few dozen narrow travel bands—and slowing the normal traffic-storm to a crawl.

Han took the *Falcon* over the top of a travel band and came down within a few hundred meters of the *Sweet Surprise*'s blocky stern, drawing an ear-popping comm squeal from the thousand-meter cargo hauler he had cut off. He reached for the comm unit to return the affront and Leia practically had to throw herself out of the Wookiee-sized copilot's seat to stop him.

"Easy, flyboy. This is no place to start a screech fight."

When Han removed his hand, she opened a private frequency to the freighter. "Sorry to cut in, Freight. There's about to be a military delay ahead. Suggest you veer port."

"Delay?" an icy Duros voice responded. "What do you call *this?*"

The huge freighter began to slide across the traffic band, prompting such a squall of random comm squeals that Leia had to turn down the volume.

"Who needs the military?" Han asked. "Let the Yuuzhan Vong into this traffic-storm and see how long they last."

The storm grew worse as four tiny X-wings streaked into view, then pivoted on their noses and fell in behind the *Sweet Surprise*. Leia scanned comm channels until she heard Gavin Darklighter's familiar voice.

". . . and stand for inspection, *Sweet Surprise*."

"What for?" Plaan's voice replied. "We aren't violating any trade laws. We haven't even entered customs control."

"Be advised this is a New Republic military inspection." In a more reassuring voice, Gavin added, "No need to worry. It's just random."

"Random?" Plaan sounded doubtful. "I'll talk to my captain."

"Remind him we're not interested in customs regulations," Gavin said. "But we are armed."

The discussion between Plaan and his captain must have been a lively one, because the *Sweet Surprise* continued forward until the traffic band narrowed to a mere three hundred meters. The space mines became a tangible presence, more because of the vast swaths of darkness they occupied than because of the tiny shapes Leia occasionally saw silhouetted against Coruscant's scintillating surface. Gavin again warned the ship that his X-wings were armed and authorized to fire, and Plaan replied that the *Surprise* was carrying a thousand innocent refugees.

"They're not going to stop," Leia said.

Monitoring the exchange from its network of orbital weapon platforms, the Planetary Defense Force was slowly coming to the same conclusion. Over the *Falcon*'s military comm unit, Leia listened to a series of increasingly senior officers query first Gavin Darklighter, then Wedge Antilles about what was happening. Finally, the groggy voice of General Rieekan, who had been called out of retirement to command the PDF, demanded an explanation from Han.

Han told him who Plaan was, the Weequay's refugee-selling history, and what had transpired aboard Nova Station.

"So, basically, you're telling me you've got a bad feeling about these guys?"

Han winced. "That's about it, General."

There was a crackle as the general switched comm channels, then his voice came over the unsecured channel being used between Rogue Squadron and the *Surprise*. "Colonel Darklighter, you know who this is?"

"General Rieekan, yes, sir."

"Good. As commander of Coruscant's Planetary Defense Force, I am ordering you not to allow the *Sweet Surprise* inside the mine shell. Do you understand?"

Leia looked at Han. No more than three kilometers ahead of the *Falcon,* traffic was already passing under the minefield. By the time Gavin responded, both Rogue Squadron and the *Surprise* would be between the mines.

"Uh, sir, we're already entering the safe lane."

"You have your orders, Colonel Darklighter. Rieekan out."

That was all it took. Save for the *Falcon* and the X-wings, every ship within ten kilometers of the *Sweet Surprise* began to veer away.

"What about it, *Sweet Surprise?*" Gavin asked. "Come to a halt and prepare for boarding."

The proper response would have been to fire a burst of braking rockets from the bow thrusters. Instead, the *Surprise* nosed sharply up.

"We don't want any trouble," Plaan said.

"Negative, *Surprise*." The voice belonged to Colonel Tycho Celchu, Gavin Darklighter's immediate superior and a veteran Rogue Squadron pilot himself. "You can't pull a flipover here. You're too long for the safe lane."

"You let us worry about that," Plaan's reply came. As he spoke, all three hundred meters of the *Sweet Surprise* shot straight up in front of the *Falcon*, then began to arc back overhead.

"Colonel?" Gavin called. "Orders?"

"Shields!" Tycho's reply came.

"Good idea," Han muttered, reaching for the controls.

Leia's hand was already bringing the glide switches up. "Full power?"

"You Jedi—always reading minds."

Leia locked the glides at maximum, then opened an intercom channel to the main hold and crew quarters. "Strap in, back there. We're about to have some fun."

The Noghri, of course, said nothing. A pair of mine rockets flared to life. The *Sweet Surprise*'s belly laser flashed in response, and both mines erupted before they had traveled a hundred meters.

"Wormheads!" Han nosed the *Falcon* down.

On the military channel, Gavin called frantically, "Mine control, deactivate—"

The ten closest mines fired their rockets and streaked toward the *Sweet Surprise* in a funnel-shaped web of orange. The freighter's belly laser lashed out again, destroying three more mines. Another ten ignited.

"You'd think they'd learn," Leia said, struggling to cinch her crash webbing. It was still Wookiee-sized, and she almost said something about replacing it, then realized how that would sound to

Han and grabbed hold in a cross-chest grip. "We should have filed the report first."

The first wave of mines blossomed into white fire against the *Sweet Surprise*'s shields. So did most of the second. But three devices passed through the shields, their vibropoint heads penetrating the ship's durasteel walls. One erupted on the bridge, shattering the transparisteel viewing panels, spraying X-wing-sized shards down through the safe lane. A second warhead vaporized the ion drives and sent the crippled freighter tumbling down behind the *Falcon*. Leia did not see where the third detonated. She was distracted by several orange halos expanding above their own cockpit.

"Han—"

"I know," he said. With the *Sweet Surprise* falling away, the *Falcon* had become the largest target mass. "Just hold on. I think . . ."

The halos went dark, and a half-dozen black silhouettes bounced harmlessly off the *Falcon*'s shields.

Han finished, ". . . they'll deactivate."

He rolled the *Falcon* down after the *Surprise*. Leia sank into her oversized chair, then grunted as she snapped back up into her loose shoulder restraints.

Han glanced over. "This could get tricky. Dial up the inertial compensator. Tighten your crash webbing."

"It's as tight as it goes," Leia said. "I'll just hold on."

If Han heard, he was too busy to answer. They were diving through the next band of traffic.

Rogue's X-wings were spiraling after the tumbling *Sweet Surprise*.

Startled starships were looping in all directions, their deflector shields rubbing, forks of blue lightning dancing between their hulls. Han swerved away from a space yacht, bounced the *Falcon* off a particle shield, slipped between two Gallofree transports, then shot out the bottom of the traffic band.

Pilots below began to respond to Rogue Squadron's emergency warnings, and a series of gaps opened ahead of the *Sweet Surprise*. Leia reached out with the Force to see how many survivors there were. She felt a wave of fear that convinced her Plaan had not been lying about his hostages—and also a feral stirring, a strange sense of hungry agitation unlike anything she had ever experienced.

"Han . . ."

"In a minute."

Below, a trio of X-wings were struggling to align themselves with the *Sweet Surprise*'s center of gravity. Leia glimpsed the freighter's belly and saw where the third mine had struck. A plume of cargo and vapor streamed from the hole. The three X-wings finally arranged themselves and advanced at berthing speed, their laser cannons blasting a docking breach in the ship's hull.

The maneuver was desperate but effective, standard military protocol for entering out-of-control craft. Inside, the last pilot would seal the breach with his shields. The other two would close their vac suits and do what could be done.

The feral stirring faded, just like the stirring aboard the *Nebula Chaser* that Jaina and Mara had described. Leia opened a scrambled channel to Rogue Squadron.

"Colonels Celchu and Darklighter, this is Leia Solo. Your men will find more than smugglers on board. There may be a voxyn."

Han looked over wide-eyed, but she ignored him and waited.

"Copy," Gavin said. "Voxyn?"

"Yuuzhan Vong monsters, Jedi-killers," Leia explained. "Stay away from anything that looks like an eight-legged reptile. Far away. These things spit acid and screech blastwaves. Maybe they do worse."

"I'll keep that in mind. Darklighter out."

Leia looked to Han. "He went in himself?"

"First one," Han confirmed.

Han and Leia spent a nervous quarter hour following the *Surprise* into an unstable orbit around Coruscant. Gavin was not only Jaina's commanding officer in Rogue Squadron, he was also a good friend of Han and Leia and the cousin of Biggs Darklighter, who had died helping Luke destroy the first Death Star at the Battle of Yavin. Both Solos were afraid of losing him to an accident or one of the voxyn, but trying to grab the freighter with the *Falcon*'s tractor beam would only drag them out of control. They could do nothing but sit by while someone else performed the heroics; Leia could tell by Han's white knuckles that he found their helplessness even more frustrating than she did.

As they waited, the freighter tumbled through the last traffic band and swung into an erratic polar orbit. The PDF agreed to deactivate the appropriate sectors of the mine shell as the *Sweet Surprise* passed through, but the ship's trajectory would decay in forty-two minutes. With Orbital Control's rescue tractors busy cleaning up collisions the freighter had caused trying to escape, there would be no choice except to destroy the *Surprise* before it crashed into Coruscant. The refugees would have to be evacuated via civilian rescue or perish with the ship.

Gavin reached the backup controls in engineering and began to fire the *Surprise*'s attitude thrusters. Orbital Control called for evacuation help and received a reply from a bulk cruiser with room for a thousand passengers.

The cruiser, a sleek fast-hauler named *Steady Lady*, appeared behind the *Falcon* and began to maneuver its five-hundred-meter body into position over the topside rescue hatch. Han dropped behind the *Sweet Surprise*'s stern, clearly galled at having to sit back and wait for others. Leia reached out with the Force again. The passengers were near the top of the freighter, moving toward the center in a large mass. She did not sense the voxyn, but that meant nothing. Jaina and Mara had not felt Numa Rar's killer after the initial stirring.

By the time the *Steady Lady* began to descend toward the escape hatch, the *Sweet Surprise* was above Coruscant's south pole. The navicomputer showed thirty-three minutes to orbital decay—barely time, Leia hoped, to transfer a thousand frightened passengers.

Gavin Darklighter's voice came over the comm. "Leia, how'd you say to kill these things?"

"Things?" Leia echoed.

"Four," Gavin confirmed.

Han groaned.

"About a meter high, four long," Gavin continued. "Not attacking, but between us and the air lock."

Han opened a separate channel to the *Steady Lady.* "Hold still a minute, *Lady.*" Not waiting for a reply, he eased the *Falcon* up under the larger ship's belly and started forward. "We've got to take care of a small problem."

Leia did not hear what the *Lady*'s pilot shrieked back. She was busy on the other channel.

"Gavin, sit tight. We'll clear them for you."

"Clear them?" the reply came. "How?"

Leia looked to Han.

Han shrugged. *We'll think of something,* he mouthed.

Leia shot her husband a scowl, but said, "We have a plan."

The *Falcon* slid over the *Sweet Surprise*'s mangled stern and shot down the narrowing cleft between the big freighters, orange tongues of rocket fire licking all around as the *Steady Lady* fired her braking thrusters. A loud clunk sounded from the roof, and the long-range displays went to static. Han barely looked up. He had lost the sensor dish so many times he now carried a spare; it could be plugged into the new breakaway sockets in minutes.

Leia released her crash webbing, grabbed her lightsaber, and turned to go.

"Hold on!" Han said. He was struggling to keep the *Falcon* from becoming a durasteel sandwich. "Where are you—"

"The docking hatch."

"Too dangerous!" Han actually looked away from the viewport. "You're staying here."

"If you like." Leia had to remind herself that Han's protectiveness was a *good* thing, a stage in the healing process. "You can lure the voxyn out with the Force, and *I* can scrape off the cannon mounts."

She gestured ahead. The gap between the *Lady* and *Sweet Surprise* could not have been much wider than the *Falcon* itself.

Han cringed. "Use the emergency hatch in the aft freight lift," he said. "When you draw them out, stay on *this* side of the air lock."

"Whatever you say, dear." Leia was already halfway down the access tunnel.

She collected the Noghri from the crew deck and went aft. Adarakh removed the floor of the freight lift, Meewalh prepared the emergency docking hatch, and Leia used the intercom to guide Han into place. The space was narrow, and they had to tip the *Falcon* up against the *Steady Lady* to slip the cofferdam over the *Sweet Surprise*'s escape hatch. Leia could feel the voxyn below, four killers thirsty for her blood. Adarakh equalized the pressures.

A clunk echoed up through the hull. No need to draw them out. They were coming.

Leia spun toward the inner hatch, thumbed her lightsaber active. "Let's go!"

A wave of excitement rippled through the Force. A heavy body slammed into the still-sealed hatch on the *Falcon*'s end of the cofferdam. Adarakh and Meewalh stopped and reached for their blasters.

"Come on!" Leia ordered.

She reached the hatch, hit the slap pad, heard the seal break, and exhaled in relief. Had the voxyn triggered the emergency hatch first, a decompression safety would have prevented hers from opening. Leia led Adarakh and Meewalh into the access corridor, then sealed the hold and waited.

The emergency hatch did not open.

"Leia?" Han called over the intercom. "How's it going?"

"It's not. They haven't opened the emergency hatch."

"Not a problem."

The hatch slid open to reveal a passage full of scaly black legs and wary yellow eyes. One creature extended its neck to peer into the empty hold, then withdrew and remained inside the air lock.

"Well?" Han called.

"They smell a trap."

Han was silent for a moment, then said, "Our side is airtight. I could pull away now."

Leia stood on her toes and tried to see how many voxyn were in the cofferdam, but her angle was hopeless. "No good. I need to draw them out."

"Draw them out *how?*" The disapproval in Han's voice could not be missed. "I'm coming back there."

"Stay put." Leia palmed the hatch open and stepped through. "Someone has to fly—"

Han yelled something over the intercom, but the voxyn were suddenly boiling out of the cofferdam, scales rattling and claws squealing. Leia brought her lightsaber around and stood fast— stood fast for about two seconds, until the third set of yellow eyes came over the rim and looked in her direction. She decided the fourth voxyn could not be far behind and used the Force to spring back through the hatchway.

Adarakh and Meewalh poured blasterfire through the door, and the lead voxyn, only three meters away, exploded into a cloud of acid vapor. Its blood reeked, like smoke and ammonia. Leia's eyes flooded with tears. She started to call the Noghri back. Bad mistake. Her lungs erupted in acid agony.

The second voxyn leapt over the first, screeching. An invisible wall slammed into Leia, and her ears rang with pain. Adarakh and Meewalh collapsed in front of her. Leia pressed herself to the wall and reached out with the Force, depressed the slap pad. The voxyn opened its mouth again, this time burping out a brown stream.

The mucus splatted against the closing hatch, but a few drops shot past and splashed the unconscious Noghri. Counting them lucky, Leia hit the lock—then cursed as the crush safety prevented the door from sealing. A round reptilian foot protruded from under the hatch, gouging at the floor. She brought her light-saber down. The blade droned, cutting through something hard as durasteel.

A yowl came from the hold, and the voxyn stuck its muzzle under the door.

Leia hit the crush-safety override. Then, hoping one of the ship's three droid brains would not—for a change—challenge the veracity of the command, she hit it again.

The door hesitated an instant, then crunched shut on the voxyn's muzzle. Another yowl, more muffled. A caustic odor— worse than before. Six inches of scaly snout in a pool of purplish blood. Leia grew queasy, lightheaded; her lungs burned down to her knees.

She glanced up. The other two voxyn were a meter away, staring at her through the hatch viewport. They opened their mouths, and a sound like a meteor strike rang through the duras-teel. She stumbled back, fell.

"Leia, what's happening back there?" Han shouted. "Answer me!"

"We've got . . ." The rest was lost to coughing.

"Leia? You don't sound so—"

"No time!" Leia staggered up, vision darkening, head spinning. "Han, just . . ."

It was hard to tell. She might have made it as far as *go*.

Chapter 5

ara looked away as the hologram shifted, zooming in on the flash-frozen bodies tumbling out of the *Nebula Chaser*'s breached hull. At the time, she and Jaina had been too busy recovering the escape pod to notice the Yuuzhan Vong attack, but she had seen the hologram too many times to want to view it again. In the privacy of her apartment on Eclipse, she had made R2-D2 play it repeatedly, trying to see some way she could have saved the refugees. After a hundred times, she had given up, convinced she could have done nothing differently—and little comforted by the knowledge.

Nom Anor's smug voice—captured by the surveillance equipment in the Bilbringi interrogation chamber—sounded from R2-D2's speakers. Mara focused on the others in the dank chamber—a hangar storeroom on the free-drifting supply base *Solistation*, one of a thousand anonymous rendezvous points where Jedi could meet and be gone before the Peace Brigade learned of their presence. A flash of hatred showed in Kyp Durron's cold eyes, then he clenched his still-boyish jaw and pushed his anger down into the dark pit where he stowed such emotions. The reaction of Saba Sebatyne was more difficult to read, perhaps because Mara did not know what signaled anger in the scaly face of a Barabel. With huge dark eyes, heavy brow folds, and a thin-lipped muzzle, Saba's reptilian features betrayed nothing.

Luke allowed the hologram to play itself out. By the time R2-D2's projector shut down, Kyp's outrage was a tangible thing in the Force, filling the room with a crackling energy that seemed in danger of blasting the doors off their quiet meeting place. Saba's feelings, if she had any, remained secret. Mara might have been able to probe them by reaching out with the Force, but knew how a Barabel would react to such an intrusion.

Kyp Durron surprised no one by speaking before Luke. "That wasn't my fault." He pointed at R2-D2 as though the droid had been the one threatening the refugee fleet. "I'm not responsible for what the Yuuzhan Vong do."

"Who said you were?" Luke responded mildly. "But you were running supplies to the New Plympto resistance."

Kyp nodded reluctantly. "I won't apologize. If there were Jedi doing the same thing on every—"

"Kyp, no one's asking you to apologize." Luke passed a data card to the younger Jedi. "We only came to give you our data on the voxyn and discuss how the Jedi should react to the Yuuzhan Vong threat."

"Ignore it." Kyp pocketed the data card and turned to go. "Thanks for the warning."

"Kyp, we're talking about a million people," Mara said. "The Jedi can't just ignore them."

Kyp paused at the door, but did not turn around. "What else can we do? We'd be fools to attack—they'd be waiting to wipe us out. If we surrender. . . . Forget it. I won't surrender."

"Neither will I," Luke said. "But now is not the time to keep harassing them. Our enemies in the senate will use this—"

"I don't care about the senate," Kyp replied. "And the Dozen are not harassing the enemy, *Master* Skywalker, we're killing them. More Jedi should be doing the same."

Mara was not sure whether the flash of irritation she felt was her own or her husband's. Luke was not all that fond of being called Master in the first place, and he particularly loathed it when it was used in a spirit of scorn.

Kyp palmed a touchpad on the wall. The storeroom door slid open, much to the surprise of the eleven flight-suited pilots trying to eavesdrop on the other side.

"Well?" Kyp stood in the door glaring. "Are we leaving or not?"

The pilots scattered across the hangar, running for the brand-new XJ3 X-wings—the latest and most lethal version of the venerable starfighter—scattered at the landing bay entrance. Before Kyp could follow, Mara stepped to the door and caught him by the arm.

"Kyp, no one's saying you're wrong, but it's time for the Jedi to act in concert," she said. "The Yuuzhan Vong are smart. If we keep going our own ways, they'll kill us one by one."

Kyp nodded. "I know that better than anyone." He had already lost an apprentice, Miko Reglia, to the enemy. He looked past Mara to Luke. "When the rest of you are ready to fight, I'll be there."

"And when you are ready to join the rest of us," Luke replied, "you know how to reach me."

Once Kyp passed out of earshot, Saba Sebatyne came to stand in the door and spoke in a raspy voice, "That one is trouble."

Mara turned. "So you do speak Basic." She glanced at C-3PO. "I was beginning to think we would have to ask Threepio to translate."

"Forgive this one." Saba broke into a fit of amused sissing, then struggled to add, "Jedi Eelysa taught her the wisdom of waiting."

Eelysa was a native of Coruscant, born soon after Palpatine's death and untainted by the poisons that had corrupted so many who came before her. Now a grown woman, she was one of Luke's most resourceful and trusted Jedi Knights, often living for years at a time in the wildest parts of galaxy in service to the Jedi cause. She had discovered Saba while on a long-term spying mission to Barab I, but the circumstances of her cover had prevented her from sending the Barabel to Yavin 4 to train with other Jedi students. Instead, she had taken Saba as her own apprentice, teaching her what she could of the Force before being chased off the planet by a hunting pack trying to import the human-hating doctrine of Nolaa Tarkona's Ryloth-based Diversity Alliance.

When her sissing fit finally passed, Saba rasped something in her own language that C-3PO dutifully translated as, "She also taught this one the wisdom of listening quietly."

"Yes, Eelysa has proven herself an expert in that regard many times over." Luke laughed, joining the pair at the door. "I should have known that any Jedi of hers would be full of surprises."

"This one is glad her silence did not offend you," Saba said. "The taste of Kyp Durron was not pleasing to her. How does one like him earn a new squadron of X-wingz?"

"There are some in the military who admire his courage— misplaced as it is," Luke said.

He caught Mara's eye and directed it to the motley assortment of Y-wings, Headhunters, and Howlrunners resting in a neat line beside Saba's plasma-scored blastboat. Having fought her way in from the Outer Rim only recently, Saba was not as well known as Kyp Durron or as well equipped, but her habit of keeping a low profile had attracted an entire squadron of like-minded Jedi pilots.

"The reputation of your squadron is also admired by those in a position to know," Mara said. "I'm sure the same officers who supply Kyp would happily lose a shipment in your direction."

Saba's slit pupils widened almost into diamonds. "The Wild Knightz would never dishonor the Jedi by taking such a shipment."

Mara was taken aback by the disapproval in Saba's voice, but Luke only smiled and laid a hand—his real one—on her scaly shoulder. C-3PO had warned them that such intimacies with the

Barabel had been known to result in the loss of the hand, but somehow Luke's familiarity drew only an accepting curl of Saba's thick tail.

"In your hands, such a gift would do the Jedi no dishonor," Luke said. "But I'm glad to know you're concerned. Have you given any thought to Tsavong Lah's threat against the refugees, and how we will be hurt if the senate believes us insensitive to so many deaths?"

Saba looked away. "The path is not clear."

She opened her mouth as though to continue, but rippled her scales and simply stopped. Luke and Mara waited for her to continue, then shared a moment of bewilderment and reached out around them with the Force. Mara felt nothing unusual, and she could tell by Luke's puzzled reaction that he did not either.

"Saba?" Luke asked.

The Barabel turned back to Luke. "You did not feel that?"

"No," Mara said. She could sense that Saba was uneasy with her—especially after she had suggested something the Barabel considered less than honorable—but she also knew that standing quietly by would do nothing to allay that uneasiness. "And neither did Luke."

"Strange." Saba looked around for a moment, then flipped her tail in the reptilian equivalent of a shrug. "Master Skywalker, this one knowz the senate disapproves of us and otherz like us—but when are cowardz not threatened by the brave?" She glanced across the hangar to her pilots, who all stood patiently beside their battle-scarred craft. "The Jedi are few and the Yuuzhan Vong many, yet look at the forcez they direct against us: voxyn, blockades, whole hunting fleetz. We are doing something they fear, and the Force tellz this one she must continue."

Mara started to suggest that they would be more effective if they all worked together, but sensed a sudden acceptance in Luke and remained quiet.

"The Barabel are hunters," Luke said to Saba. "And hunters work best in small packs."

Saba rewarded him with a crooked grin. "Truly, Master Skywalker is as wise as Jedi Eelysa claimz. Perhaps he would honor this one with a great favor?"

Luke did not hesitate. "Of course."

She turned to Mara. "And you? This will be a burden on you, as well, and you have the new hatchling in your nest."

Mara thought of Ben and instantly felt him aboard the *Shadow* with Jaina and Danni, sleeping contentedly in the arms of one of the two young women. Mara would *never* do anything to jeopardize her baby's well-being, but she sensed the inherent trust Luke felt for this Jedi they had never met, and Mara's trust in him was such that there could be no doubt of her answer.

"Please, we Jedi must do what we can for each other," Mara said. "And we have plenty of help on Eclipse."

"Good. You may have need of it," Saba said, not smiling. She turned to C-3PO and rasped something in her own language.

"Oh my." The droid's photoreceptors lit in alarm. "Truly?"

Saba snarled something back.

"It's only an expression," C-3PO said, scurrying toward Saba's blastboat. "I wasn't calling you a liar!"

Luke and Mara exchanged curious glances, and Mara realized they also had a favor to ask of Saba. She was about to suggest this, but Luke, as usual, knew what she was thinking almost before she did.

"Saba, perhaps the Wild Knights would also do us a great service?" Luke asked. "It would mean carrying a fair amount of equipment into battle."

"And a scientist," Mara added. "It could mean the war, especially if you know where to find a yammosk war coordinator."

Mara was not sure Saba heard them. The Barabel was looking somewhere beyond their shoulders, brow folds creased deeper than ever.

"Master Skywalker, do you know where Eelysa is?"

Mara felt the growing apprehension that accompanied Luke's answer. "She's still monitoring the situation on Corellia for us."

Saba's gaze returned to Luke. "Do you think she could be in danger?"

And now Mara had a sinking feeling. As much as Luke cared for all of the academy's former students, it had been impossible to spend enough time with each one to develop the kind of bond that would connect them closely through the Force. But Eelysa had spent years training Saba one on one in a very stressful environment. It was not surprising that their bond would be an especially close one—and strong enough to inform Saba of her Master's danger.

"It's always impossible to say what Thrackan Sal-Solo and his ilk will do next," Mara said. "But we didn't expect Eelysa's mission to be dangerous. The Corellians don't even know she's there."

"Perhaps they have found out," Saba said. "Or perhaps it is something else, but Eelysa is frightened."

"Frightened?" Luke asked. He looked at Mara. "That doesn't sound like Eelysa."

Saba shook her head. "No, it does not. We will investigate once we have loaded your scientist and the equipment. There will be no trouble finding a yammosk—they come to us."

"Thank you," Luke said. "I'll have Danni start the transfer."

Luke activated his comlink and informed Danni, who sounded happy—perhaps *ecstatic* was a better word—to be flying with Saba Sebatyne instead of Kyp Durron. The *Shadow*'s cargo ramp descended, then Danni and the pilots from Saba's squadron began to transfer equipment.

In the meantime, C-3PO returned with three burly Barabels.

Though a little larger than Saba, all three had the purple-green scales of young adults. There were also lightsabers hanging from their belts.

"If you please, Master Skywalker, we were on our way to Yavin Four when the war blocked us," Saba said. "Please take these young Jedi Knightz and show them the true path to becoming a Jedi. There remainz too much of the hunter in this one to teach them well."

Luke and Mara exchanged startled looks, then Mara asked, "Are these your children, Saba?"

"They are hatchmates, but only the male is of me," Saba said. "The females share a mother. One also shares a father with my own son, but of course it is impossible to say which."

The affiliations were horribly lost on the two humans, but Mara suspected they would figure it out in time. "We'll care for them as though they were our own."

Saba's eyes widened. "They are old enough to find their own food; just give them a territory. Any subbasement or scrub lot will do."

Now it was Mara's turn to be shocked. *This is going to be interesting.*

The slight smile that came to Luke's lips suggested he had perceived the sense of her thoughts, then Saba let out a chain of long hisses. Mara mistook the sound for the Barabel's sissing laughter—until Saba cried out in grief and dropped into a fighting crouch. Her needlelike teeth folded down into view, and she let out a long mournful growl.

Mara and Luke stepped away in unison, their hands instinctively dropping toward their lightsabers. C-3PO rasped at her in Barabel. She snarled something in reply, then dropped to all fours and crouched low. The other Barabels reacted to their Master's distress, also dropping to all fours and adding their own raspy voices to the rumble, and they all began to scratch at the durasteel floor.

Mara and Luke exchanged startled glances, then the Force grew heavy with anger and disbelief. Mara knelt beside Saba and, ignoring C-3PO's admonition not to touch a strange Barabel, laid a hand on the Jedi's back.

"Saba? What's wrong?"

The Barabel's head turned slowly toward Mara, her reptilian pupils narrowed to slits, her fangs wet with saliva.

"Eelysa," she rasped. "Something caught her."

"Something?" Luke asked.

Saba beat her tail against the ground, prompting C-3PO to explain unnecessarily that tail-banging was a typical reptilian expression of rage.

"This one doesn't know," the Barabel said. "But she is gone. Eelysa is no more."

Mara and Luke glanced across her back, each knowing without speaking what the other was thinking.

Voxyn.

Chapter 6

With a hologram of the strategic situation lighting the overhead darkness and dozens of tactical displays hovering in the pit below, the New Republic Defense Force Fleet Command room looked more like a galaxarium than a council chamber. The overhead display depicted the barest outlines of the galaxy, a broad ribbon of crimson marking the Yuuzhan Vong invasion route. In just two years, the aliens had cut a swath from the Tingel Arm almost to Bothan space, with three distinct salients punching through the Inner Rim at Fondor and Duro. A third offshoot, the one threatening Bilbringi, had not quite reached the Inner Rim, but Leia knew it soon would. The invaders were destroying ships faster than the New Republic could build them, and even Bilbringi did not warrant a major defense. She wondered how much importance NRMOC—the New Republic Military Oversight Committee— would place on the lives of the Talfaglion refugees. She wondered how much they could afford to.

Less than happy to find herself once again negotiating Coruscant's twisted corridors of power, Leia leaned on her son's arm and advanced along the mezzanine. Though it had been more than a day since she was knocked unconscious by the voxyn's noxious blood, she still felt the need of support when she moved—and considered herself lucky. The Noghri, who had taken the brunt of the attacks, remained in bacta tanks with severe ear and lung damage.

"This is encouraging," Jacen said. He had come to stay with her while Han returned to Eclipse with the voxyn bodies. "If they'll let us in here, our reputation in the senate can't be all that bad."

"Don't read too much into this," Leia said. "There is a reason behind the reason Borsk Fey'lya does anything. Listen with your eyes, Jacen; see with your ears."

As they advanced, Leia barely glanced at the tactical displays below the mezzanine. There was a less elaborate situation room on Eclipse—kept up to date by a secret feed from a friendly command officer—so she knew the holograms would show several dozen fleets orbiting on-station, as well as an alarming number of pitched space battles. The situation had been much the same for nearly a year, with the Yuuzhan Vong steadily widening their swath of occupied territory while their main advance remained stalled in the Corellian sector.

Leia and Jacen passed a hologram depicting the frantic work at the Bilbringi Shipyards, then a large lift rose into view from behind a minor engagement near Vortex. Borsk Fey'lya himself was on the lift, his feral Bothan features twisted into a snarl of greeting, creamy fur rippling with what Leia had long ago learned to recognize as his species' way of cringing.

"Princess Leia, you honor us."

"You could not find room on the agenda for a former chief of state to address the senate in body?" Leia demanded. With the war going badly, Fey'lya's support was slipping, and she stood to win more allies than she lost by treating him sharply. "Surely, the war isn't going that poorly?"

Fey'lya's insincere smile remained frozen on his face. "It's nice to see you recovered so soon from your fray with the Jedi-killers."

He opened the gate himself—a sure sign of how tenuous his power had become. "We can certainly put you on the agenda if you wish, but NRMOC will consider your request more carefully in closed session. Please come aboard."

Leia released Jacen's arm and led the way onto the lift. They descended directly onto the committee's conferencing balcony, and Leia went straight to the speaker's rostrum. Several tiers of senators were seated in a semicircle at the opposite end.

"Thank you for coming," Fey'lya said, joining her. "And welcome to your Jedi companion, as well."

"Jacen is here as my bodyguard," Leia said, both explaining her son's presence and sidestepping any question of why the Jedi had not sent a higher-ranking member. "This has nothing to do with the Jedi. It's entirely a SELCORE matter."

"Of course," Fey'lya said agreeably. "We have studied your report. This is certainly worthy of NRMOC's attention."

Wary of the Bothan's unexpected support, Leia asked, "And?"

"And, unfortunately, this *does* concern the Jedi," a honeyed female voice said. "Are they not the reason the Yuuzhan Vong are holding Talfaglion hostages at all?"

Leia turned to see a slender woman with long jet-black hair rising from her seat. A sultry young senator from the shipbuilding world of Kuat, Viqi Shesh had parlayed her world's importance to the war effort into a position on the Advisory Council and several coveted bottom-tier seats on the senate's most powerful oversight committees. She had also proven an adept deal maker who traded loyalties with a facility that awed Bothans, and who did not hesitate to use her position for personal gain. Less than a year ago, as the administrating senator of the Senate Select Committee for Refugees—SELCORE—Shesh had not hesitated to strike a deal for her personal gain by diverting vital supplies from the refugee camps on Duro. Leia had been unable to marshal sufficient proof to have the woman removed from the senate, but she had created enough of a stink to have her rotated off the committee. How the unscrupulous senator had managed to win an influential—and highly secret—posting on NRMOC was a mystery, but the Kuati's opening salvo made clear that Leia had made a powerful enemy for both herself and the Jedi.

Drawing on the Force for strength—and patience—Leia met the senator's gaze evenly. "The Yuuzhan Vong have threatened to destroy the convoy unless the Jedi surrender, yes. Were the Jedi to do so, I have no doubt the Yuuzhan Vong's next demand would be the surrender of Kuat Drive Yards."

"It has never been the New Republic's policy to yield to coercion," Fey'lya said, deftly cutting off the argument before it started. "The question is, what can we do *without* surrendering?"

"I submit there is nothing we can do." Shesh looked to Fey'lya. "If we can see the Corellian sector?"

The Bothan used a remote to send the command, and the holo rotated to display the appropriate sector. The Corellian system was surrounded by a shell of New Republic frigates, the ones on the Duro side glowing slightly brighter to show they were lightly engaged against a wall of enemy probe ships facing them. Talfaglio was encircled by a swarm of Yuuzhan Vong corvette-analog patrol craft, with a single cruiser centrally positioned to provide support. But it was the Jumus system that was most alarming. Just a short hyperspace jump from either Corellia or Talfaglio, it was now home to much of the fleet that had captured Duro.

"As you can see, the Yuuzhan Vong are hoping we'll try to break their blockade." Shesh pointed to the all-too-small cluster of capital ships orbiting Corellia. "The moment we move, they'll sweep in and grab the prize."

"Not if we come the back way," Jacen said. He pointed above their heads, tracing a route along the edge of the Deep Core into the back of the sector. "If we sneak three Star Destroyers along here, we can wipe out their blockade and be gone with the convoy before they can react."

"Now *that* would teach them to take hostages," Kvarm Jia, a gray-bearded senator from Tapani sector, said. "Where can we find the Star Destroyers?"

"Yes, where *do* we find three expendable Star Destroyers?" Shesh echoed, quick to turn Jia's support on its head. "Or do you suggest sacrificing yet another world to Jedi ineptitude?"

A pair of senators began to speak at the same time, realized they were on opposite sides of the issues, and immediately tried to talk over each other. Fey'lya called for order, only to be shouted down by senators from the anti-Jedi coalition, who were in turn shouted down by Jia's supporters. Soon, all the senators on the balcony were bellowing at once.

Jacen looked over at Leia and shook his head in dismay. More accustomed to the rancorous nature of republican politics, Leia occupied herself with counting heads and quickly realized the committee was split almost down the center. She borrowed Jacen's lightsaber—she had left her own behind, hoping to emphasize that she was appearing on SELCORE's behalf and not as a Jedi—then turned to Fey'lya.

"If I may?" She nearly had to shout to make herself heard.

The Bothan nodded—and stepped back. "By all means."

Leia ignited the blade, its brilliance and distinctive *snap-hiss* bringing the tumult to an instant silence. Suppressing a smile at this reminder of the continuing power of the Jedi, she thumbed the blade off.

"Please forgive the theatrics." Leia returned the weapon to her son. "In appearing before you, it was not my intention to cause such discord in NRMOC. That's the last thing the Republic needs. Perhaps the committee should simply vote on Jacen's suggestion and be done with it."

"Vote *now?*" Shesh's eyes narrowed. "So you and your son can use your Jedi mind tricks?"

Leia forced a tolerant smile. "Those tricks work only on the weak of will—which I can assure you no one on this committee is."

The joke drew a tension-draining laugh from both camps, and Jia mocked, "Unless you're afraid of losing, Senator Shesh?"

"It would not be I who lose, Senator Jia, it would be the New Republic," Shesh said. "But let us vote, by all means."

Fey'lya went to his dais and authorized the vote, and the balcony's droid brain announced the results almost before the last senator had keyed his voting pad. As Leia had expected, the resolution passed with a bare two-vote majority—not enough to authorize the action without the full senate's approval, but enough for Fey'lya to use his authority under the military secrets act to bypass the security risk of a full senate vote and "declare" the necessary majority. Given the deference he had shown Leia earlier, she expected him to do just that.

Uneasy at finding herself in debt to a Bothan, she turned to Fey'lya. "Will you declare the majority, Chief Fey'lya? This is your chance to save a million lives."

Fey'lya's fur rippled again, betraying just how weak his position as chief of state had become. "A chance to save a million—or lose billions."

"What?" Leia was astonished at the ire in her own voice. Perhaps it was because of her fatigue, or perhaps because of her surprise at having miscalculated so badly, but she found herself struggling to hold back a string of invectives on the tip of her tongue. "Chief Fey'lya, the plan is a sound one—"

Fey'lya raised a placating hand. "And I haven't said no. But you must know what the loss of three Star Destroyers would mean to us. We could lose another dozen planets." He stroked the creamy tufts on his cheek, then spoke in a deliberately thoughtful voice. "I will ask the military for a study."

"A study?" Jacen burst out. "The convoy will be drifting slag by the time they finish!"

"I'm sure General Bel Iblis will expedite matters," Fey'lya said evenly. "In the meantime, we'll stall."

"Stall?" In her weakened state, Leia did not trust herself to keep a civil tone. She knew Garm Bel Iblis, who like Wedge Antilles had been reactivated at the outbreak of the war, would move as quickly as possible. But even he could push the plodding command bureaucracy along only so fast, and there was no guarantee that he would reach the conclusion she hoped for. "How can you stall the Yuuzhan Vong?"

Fey'lya flashed a snarl she was sure he meant as reassuring. "We'll ask Tsavong Lah for an envoy to discuss the matter."

"An envoy?" Jia shouted the question. "It will look like we're asking for terms!"

Fey'lya's ears pricked mischievously forward. "Precisely, Senator—and it will buy time." The Bothan was quick to look back to Leia. "But rest assured, Princess. Whatever General Bel Iblis's conclusion, we shall tell the envoy only this: that Yuuzhan Vong threats merely strengthen the ties between the New Republic and her Jedi."

Jia actually grinned. "A point that will be underscored when we rescue the hostages."

"Or even if we must let them die," Shesh added. She nodded her approval. "I believe we have a consensus, Chief Fey'lya."

The consensus only angered Leia more, for she had worked with Borsk Fey'lya long enough to know that his plans served only himself; whatever he intended to say to the Yuuzhan Vong, she felt sure that he would not allow the Jedi to stand in the way of making an accommodation that would save his own position.

"What you have, Senators," she said icily, "is a consensus of fools."

"Mother?"

Leia felt Jacen reach out to her through the Force, laving her with soothing emotions, and she realized how *young* he really was. The New Republic Senate was far from the unblemished body he imagined, and the good-faith compromises described in C-3PO's civics lessons were all too rare. The senate was a power-grubbing club of people who too often saw their duty in terms of their own interests, who measured their success by how long they held office, and it made Leia ashamed to think she had played such a prominent role in its founding. She spun on her heel and would have stepped into the lift's gate—perhaps even flipped over it—if not for a gentle telekinetic tug from her son.

To cover for herself, she reached for the gate and said, "I have wasted all the time I care to with NRMOC."

Borsk Fey'lya stepped in front of her. "You really have no reason to be upset, Princess. General Bel Iblis's integrity is beyond question."

"It is not Garm's integrity I question, Chief."

Leia used the Force to open the gate behind Fey'lya, then brushed him aside and stepped onto the lift. Jacen came to her side, one hand ready to catch her at the first sign of weakness.

When they reached the mezzanine and started for the exit, he asked, "Was that wise? We have enough enemies in the senate."

"Jacen, I'm done with the senate. Again."

As Leia spoke, an unexpected calmness came to her. She began to feel stronger and less weary, more at harmony with herself, and she knew her words had been more than the usual frustration with politicians. She had lost control with Fey'lya not because she was weak and tired—though she was—but because she no longer belonged in the halls of power, no longer believed in the process that placed selfish bureaucrats in positions of power over those they were sworn to serve. The Force was guiding her, telling her the

New Republic had changed, the galaxy had changed, most of all *she* had changed. She had stepped onto a new path, and it was time that she realized it and stopped trying to follow the old one.

Leia took Jacen's arm and, in a more peaceful voice, said, "I'll never appear before them or their committees again."

Jacen remained silent, but his distress and concern were as thick in the Force as the air over a Dagobah swamp. Leia wrapped an arm around his waist and, surprised as always at how far her nineteen-year-old son now towered above her, pulled him close.

"Jacen, sometimes it can be dangerous to assume the best about people," she said quietly. "Borsk is our worst enemy in the senate, and he just proved it."

"He did?"

They left the committee room and started down the familiar corridor. "Think," Leia said. "The reason behind the reason. Why would Borsk want to talk to a Yuuzhan Vong envoy? What can he bargain with?"

Jacen walked a few silent steps, then stopped when the answer finally struck him. "Us."

Chapter 7

lood still streaming from a network of hastily inflicted slashes, Nom Anor presented himself to the sentry outside Tsavong Lah's private warren aboard the *Sunulok*.

"I have been summoned." Nom Anor struggled to mask his excitement, for the warmaster rarely called subordinates to his private refuge—and never during the sleep cycle. "I was told not to concern myself with appearance."

The sentry nodded curtly and pressed a palm to the receptor pores in the door valve. The portal took a moment to recognize the warrior's scent, then puckered open to reveal a small contemplation chamber lit softly by bioluminescent wall lichen. Tsavong Lah sat on the far side of the room, absorbed in conversation with a master villip. Nom Anor stomped a foot politely, then waited for permission to enter.

Vergere came out from behind a table and waved him over. "He wants you to see this."

Irritated to find his rival there, Nom Anor rounded the table to look over the warmaster's shoulder. The villip had assumed the visage of a human female with high cheeks and sharp features. Nom Anor's annoyance immediately vanished, for he knew the woman well. He had been the one who turned her to the Yuuzhan Vong cause.

". . . see you have put the vornskrs I sent to good use," Viqi Shesh was saying. "Four Jedi have died already. Your voxyn are proving most effective."

"Voxyn? How do you know their names?"

Shesh's eyes widened slightly, though subtly enough that the warmaster might not have noticed her surprise. "That's what the Jedi call them. I don't know how they came by the name—they're becoming very tight-lipped about the matter."

"Are they?" Tsavong Lah turned thoughtful. "Interesting."

Vergere astonished Nom Anor by touching the warmaster's arm. "Your agent is here."

Tsavong Lah did not strike her or chastise her in any manner. He merely told Shesh to wait and turned to "his agent," as Vergere had so dismissively called Nom Anor, and studied the bloodstains seeping through his websilk tunic.

"My summons interrupted your devotions." His tone was apologetic and sincere. "Perhaps something can be done about that."

Tsavong Lah surprised Nom Anor yet again by rising and fetching—himself—a thorn seat from the far corner. He put it in front of Shesh's villip and motioned his guest to sit. The lack of a blood crust suggested the chair's last feeding had been less than sating, but it would have been an insult to hesitate. Nom Anor sat down and, as the hungry thorns sank into his back and buttocks, consoled himself with the thought that the warmaster believed he enjoyed such indulgences.

"I am honored."

Tsavong Lah was already returning to the villip. "Viqi, I have an old friend of yours here."

"Really?" Shesh replied. She would not have seen Nom Anor

enter the room. Her villip would be of the type linked directly to the warmaster and able to relay only his image and words. "Who's there?"

"I am certain you recall Pedric Cuf," Tsavong Lah said, using the alias by which Shesh knew Nom Anor.

The smile that came to the villip's lips was less than sincere, for Viqi had seized the first opportunity to bypass Nom Anor and offer her services directly to the warmaster. "What a delight."

"Viqi, repeat what happened today." Tsavong Lah gave Nom Anor no chance to reply to her greeting. "Pedric Cuf needs to hear all."

Viqi obediently recounted what had happened in the committee room earlier, emphasizing Jacen's plan to ambush the Talfaglio blockade. She lingered a little too long on how cleverly she had manipulated Borsk Fey'lya into asking for a military study, buying the Yuuzhan Vong time to prepare a counterambush.

"You may have as much as two weeks," Shesh finished. "I will keep you informed."

"You did well," Tsavong Lah said, though Nom Anor knew they already had a fleet lying in wait for just such a purpose. "But tell Pedric Cuf about the envoy, Viqi."

If she understood that Tsavong Lah was slighting her by consistently speaking only half her name, Viqi Shesh showed no sign. "There was some concern about the time required for a study, but I persuaded Borsk to ask for an envoy." Her villip smiled. "He has no real interest in talking to you, but I convinced him the request might save the refugees long enough for the military to complete its study."

"Very clever," Tsavong Lah said. "You buy us time, but make them think they are the ones who stall. You are truly gifted, Viqi. On the day of our victory, your reward will be beyond imagining. Is there anything you need now?"

"Only the usual funds," she replied.

"You will have them and more," the warmaster promised. "Through the customary channels."

Tsavong Lah broke the connection by stroking the villip, then turned to Nom Anor as the creature reverted into an inert blob.

"That one angers me," he growled. "She takes me for a fool."

"Humans often cast themselves in the best light," Nom Anor said, unsure whether the warmaster's displeasure extended to him as Shesh's recruiter. "They seem unable to see the shadows they also cast."

"A pity for you then, Nom Anor," Tsavong Lah said.

Nom Anor sat forward, stifling a cry as the chair's thorns tore free of his back. "Me, Warmaster?"

Tsavong Lah nodded. "Tell me, do you believe what she says about the Bothan? That he has no interest in talking to us?"

"No more than I believe *she* persuaded him to ask for an envoy," Nom Anor said. "Borsk Fey'lya wants to talk, and Viqi Shesh fears he has something to make us listen. She hopes to protect her own position."

"Our thinking is the same on this, Nom Anor," the warmaster said. "All the more reason I must command you to return to the infidels."

"Him?" Vergere asked.

Nom Anor glared fire at the feathery pet. "Who else? Perhaps you were thinking of yourself?"

Vergere lowered her arms. "My objection praises you, Nom Anor. You have caused the New Republic too much damage. Borsk Fey'lya could not talk to you if he wanted to. The senate would vote him out of office."

"Truly?" Tsavong Lah smiled slyly, then turned to Nom Anor and gestured at the thorn chair. "Take that with you, my servant. Consider it a gift."

Chapter 8

The door opened to an unfamiliar soughing sound, and Cilghal's skin went dry. The voxyn were dead.

The *Millennium Falcon* had pulled away from the *Sweet Surprise* with its emergency hatch still open and the aft hold exposed to cold space. It was true the creatures had sealed themselves into scale cocoons and survived the resulting decompression. They had even endured the vacuum—for a time—by dropping into deep hibernation. But the cold had killed them, eventually. Han had kept the hold in a sealed vacuum and near absolute zero the entire trip, and by the time they arrived on Eclipse, the voxyn were frozen solid. She had probed their molecular structures with the Force and found every cell in their bodies burst. She had confirmed her findings via ultrasonic probe *and* thermal scan, then performed a dozen different bioscans on their space-frozen carcasses to search out any lingering sign of life. Just to be certain, she had done it all again, and only after confirming her results had she cut their claws out of the *Falcon*'s durasteel deck. They had to be dead.

Still, Cilghal was not taking chances—not with creatures that spat flesh-eating acid and stunned their prey with sonic blasts, creatures whose blood became a neurotoxin in most kinds of air, whose toe pads harbored a hundred deadly retroviruses. She was too fatigued to analyze the situation, too prone to mistakes lately to gamble with the lives of everyone on Eclipse. Cilghal backed quietly out the door, then slipped the comlink from her pocket and raised it to her lips.

A plaintive Wookiee groan rolled out of the room, and she grew aware of a strange heaviness in the Force. With a start, she realized the sound she had heard was crying.

Human crying.

Cilghal peered through the door and saw a line of young Jedi standing on the other side of the room, looking through a transparisteel observation panel into the frozen tissue locker. At one end of the group stood Anakin, tall, lanky, and broad-shouldered in the way of human males as they crossed from adolescence into adulthood, recognizable even from behind by his sandy-brown tousled mane. Beside him, as always, stood Tahiri, small and svelte with short-cropped blond hair, feet customarily bare, her EV footwear in one hand and Anakin's arm in the other. The Wookiee groan had come from the opposite end of the line, where russet-furred Lowbacca stood with Jaina Solo's slender form wrapped into his hairy arm. Next to them stood Zekk and Tenel Ka, Zekk a wiry young man with shaggy black hair hanging over his collar, Tenel Ka a tall and willowy beauty with rust-colored hair and an arm amputated just above the elbow. And more or less in the center was the one Cilghal had heard crying, blond-haired Raynar Thul, standing alone with his fists pressed against the transparisteel, his shoulders rising and falling as he sobbed.

Cilghal remained outside, trying to decide whether collecting yet another tissue sample justified the intrusion. The young Jedi Knights were a close-knit group, having spent many of their formative years studying at Luke's Jedi academy on Yavin 4. Together, they had fought off Imperial kidnappers, Dark Jedi, ruthless crime organizations, and more hazards than the Mon Calamari healer could name. Whatever was grieving them, it did not seem right to trespass on their gathering now.

She started to back away, but her presence had not gone unnoticed. Tenel Ka turned and fixed a pair of red-rimmed eyes on her.

"Do not mind us," she said. "We are not here to disturb your work."

Feeling the companions' anguish through the Force but unsure of what to do about it, Cilghal entered the room and went to the closet where she kept the cryosuit she would need to collect her samples.

"Someone else has died?" she asked, fearing the truth even as she surmised it.

"Lusa," Anakin said, voice cracking. Lusa was one of their close friends from the academy on Yavin 4, a nature-loving Chironian female. Anakin gestured vaguely toward the frozen carcasses in the tissue locker. "A pack of voxyn ran her down."

"We just heard over the subspace," Tahiri added. "She was at home, just running through a meadow."

"She was supposed to be safe," Jaina added, finally pulling her face out of Lowbacca's fur. "Chiron is long way from the Yuuzhan Vong."

Cilghal felt a stab of guilt. "I am sorry to be so slow. I have learned much about these creatures, but nothing of use."

Raynar mumbled a suggestion that she work harder. Out of respect for his grief, Cilghal pretended not to hear and began to fumble into her cryosuit.

Lowbacca was not so generous, groaning softly and admonishing the young Jedi for his rudeness. Raynar started to say something in reply, but his throat failed him and he turned back toward the tissue locker.

Jaina stepped away from Lowbacca and patted Raynar's arm, then turned to Cilghal. "Forgive Raynar, Cilghal. He and Lusa were very close." Though Jaina's eyes were puffy from crying, Cilghal could feel that the red came from anger. "No one is angry at you. Jedi are dying, and the senate blames us for losing the war. Sometimes, I think we should just go off into the Unknown Regions and leave the New Republic to the Yuuzhan Vong."

"I understand," Cilghal said. Grief—especially young grief—had to have an outlet, or it would eat away the vessel. "But what will we do when the Yuuzhan Vong come for us there?"

Jaina's eyes hardened, but she nodded. "I know—and I suppose there's no guarantee the Chiss would welcome us."

"Then I suppose we must find a way to defend this part of the galaxy." Cilghal nearly fell as she thrust her leg into the cryosuit. "If we can."

"Don't these creatures have a weakness?" Tahiri asked. "The Sand People say everyone has a weakness—everyone except them."

"The voxyn have no weakness I have found," Cilghal answered. "As we suspected, they are part of this galaxy and part of the Yuuzhan Vong's, but I have not gone far beyond that. There is so much that makes no sense."

"You are tired." Tenel Ka came over and held one of the suit's bulky arms. "I will help you."

"Maybe she should rest." Anakin turned around, revealing eyes as red as Tenel Ka's. "It's hard to think straight when you can't even stand."

Cilghal smiled at his concern. "You're right, of course, but I cannot bring myself to sleep while others are dying." She pushed her arm through the second sleeve. "I may as well work."

"Is there anything we can do?" Tenel Ka asked. "We have sentry duty in an hour, but—"

"You can watch," Cilghal said. "You can tell me how I keep contaminating these samples."

"Contaminating them?" Tahiri asked. "What do you mean?"

"Their genetic codes always map the same," Cilghal said. "It's not the equipment—I have checked—so I must be contaminating the samples when I collect them."

Tenel Ka exchanged glances with her friends, then laid a hand on Cilghal's arm to stop her from closing the suit. "How many times have you tried?"

"Four," Cilghal said.

"And they always map the same?" Jaina asked. "Exactly the same?"

Cilghal nodded, struggling to see what the young Jedi were driving at. "Even when Tekli gathers the samples." Tekli was her apprentice, a young Chadra-Fan no older than Jaina. "We are making a systematic error somewhere."

"And what if you are not?" Tenel Ka asked.

A wave of weariness came over Cilghal, and she shook her head. "We are. No two genetic sequences are identical. There are always differences."

"Not always," Jaina said.

Cilghal frowned, then felt her skin brighten to a pale green. "Clones?" she gasped. "They're cloning the voxyn!"

"Why would they do that?" Tenel Ka asked. "Would it not make more sense to breed them?"

"Perhaps." Cilghal was suddenly wide awake, her thoughts flying at lightspeed. "Unless they have only one."

Anakin's eyes lit with excitement—or perhaps it was determination. "That would be a weakness, definitely."

"But these voxyn all came from the same shipment," Tenel Ka observed. "Can we be sure that a pack from another shipment would not come from a different master?"

Cilghal thought for a moment, going over all the different kinds of tests—both scientific and through the Force—she could run. She kept coming to the same conclusion.

"There is no way to be sure," she said. "Not from one set of samples."

"Then we need more samples." Anakin was already half out the door before he seemed to realize that Tahiri was the only one following. He scowled back at the others. "We need them *now*."

Chapter 9

The signal was scratchy, but clear enough to recognize a familiar name as the Corellian newscaster's sober voice filled Anakin's cockpit.

"Kuati senator Viqi Shesh said the New Republic will receive the envoy with cautious optimism."

Anakin opened a channel to the rest of his small task force. "Are you guys getting this?" They were sitting on an asteroid on the outskirts of the Froz system, powered down and quietly keeping tabs on inbound traffic. With Kyp Durron supplying from here, it seemed a good place to look for the voxyn Cilghal needed. "The Yuuzhan Vong are sending an envoy after all."

"Neg that commclutter, Little Brother," Jaina ordered. Anakin was in command of the mission, but, being a veteran Rogue Squadron pilot, Jaina was in charge of tactical aspects. As Luke had put it before allowing them to leave Eclipse, Anakin decided what to do, Jaina decided how. "Stay passive. Let's not spray rays on idle chatter. Never know who might be listening."

Anakin clicked an acknowledgment, then Viqi Shesh's cloying voice replaced that of the newscaster.

"I'm the last to condone bargaining with murderers, but I

do think we have something to talk about," she said. "If we can make our foes understand that the New Republic has no control over the Jedi, perhaps the Yuuzhan Vong will apply pressure where it belongs."

"Would making the Yuuzhan Vong understand include helping them find the Jedi's secret base?" the newscaster asked. "Isn't that why they took hostages in the first place?"

"I've been a friend of the Jedi since I joined the senate, but in this case, Luke Skywalker is thinking only of his followers. The rash acts of the Jedi have endangered the citizens of an entire world, and now he refuses to take responsibility."

"How do you like that?" Zekk said, ignoring Jaina's request for comm silence. While he and Jaina had been close when they were younger, they had drifted apart since she volunteered for Rogue Squadron, and now he sometimes seemed to place a premium on annoying her. "The Yuuzhan Vong threaten a billion lives, we get blamed."

"Bounty Hunter, what did I say?"

"Excuse me," Tenel Ka said. Along with Lowbacca, Raynar, and Ulaha Kore—who in addition to being a talented musician was also a Force-gifted tactical analyst—Tenel Ka was manning their sensor platform, a converted blastboat named the *Big Eye*. "We have a contact entering the system. Their transponder identifies them as the freighter *Speed Queen*."

Tenel Ka fed the coordinates directly to the X-wing astromech droids, then added, "A second craft has exited hyperspace. It is on a convergence course to the first."

"Enemy interdictor?" Jaina asked.

A favorite tactic of the Yuuzhan Vong interdiction forces was to lurk outside their assigned system, then catch inbound traffic with a quick hyperspace hop.

Tenel Ka took only a moment to confirm Jaina's deduction. "It does not register on the sensors, and there is no ion efflux. It masses out at corvette size."

"Little Brother?" Jaina said.

"Give me a sec."

Being the group's most powerful in the Force, Anakin reached out, stretching his awareness to just shy of the population concentration around Froz. He felt no voxyn aboard the corvette, nor even the Yuuzhan Vong flying it. This latter was no surprise. Though the living crystal he had stolen from the enemy base on Yavin 4 enabled him to sense Yuuzhan Vong—in a different, much hazier way than Jedi sensed most other beings—his perceptions at such distances were too weak to discern anything less than a massive concentration. He *was* somewhat surprised to detect a more ordinary presence on a frozen moon near the edge of the system, something that was startled to feel his touch.

"Negative voxyn," he reported. "Something on that moon in Orbit Twelve, but I can't tell what. Not Yuuzhan Vong, though."

"Nor did we three feel anything hungry," the rasping voice of one of Saba Sebatyne's Barabel apprentices agreed. Anakin had been reluctant to bring the newcomers along until Luke pointedly reminded him that they had survived more than fifty space battles flying ancient Y-wings for the Wild Knights. On the way out, they had also proven adept pilots in the new XJ3—with variable-stutter lasers, decoy-enhanced proton torpedoes, and grab-proof shields, the newest and most sophisticated X-wing yet. "But the presence in Orbit Twelve was human."

Unsure of whether the Barabel was trying to show him up or be helpful, Anakin assumed the latter. "Thanks for the backup, uh, One?"

There was a rhythmic hissing that suggested chuckling. "Tail Two, Little Brother."

Anakin felt the heat rise to his cheeks. "Sorry."

Tail One was the male, Tesar Sebatyne. Two and Three were Bela and Krasov Hara—not sisters, they insisted, but *hatchmates.* Whatever that meant, their sense of humor gave Anakin the shudders. They had been the ones to suggest the Tail code names, which they seemed to find hilarious for some reason no one understood.

Raynar saved Anakin the embarrassment of a more protracted silence. "Why are we sitting here? Let's do something."

"We can't interfere, Merchantman," Anakin said. He was as eager as Raynar to avenge Lusa's death, but Luke had ordered them to focus solely on the mission. With Viqi Shesh and her allies already suggesting the Jedi should surrender for the greater good, the slightest incident could turn the rest of the senate against them. "And the *Speed Queen* is better off without us. If the Yuuzhan Vong see us coming, they'll blast and run. This way, they might let it off with a search."

"Fact," Tenel Ka confirmed. "They have used their dovin basals to bring the *Speed Queen* to a halt, and a small launch is separating from their hull."

A trio of blips, one marked in New Republic red and two in Yuuzhan Vong blue, appeared on Anakin's tactical display. He had his astromech droid, Fiver, call up the technical data and saw no reason to disagree with Tenel Ka. Even the Yuuzhan Vong did not destroy every vessel they found; if the ship was not carrying war matériel or Jedi, they often released it in the hope of picking it up outbound filled with refugees.

A raspy Barabel voice—Anakin thought it was Krasov—said, "Little Brother, we feel . . . someone does not obey the orderz of Uncle Master."

An instant later, a swarm of blips appeared on Anakin's sensor display. He called, *"Big Eye?"*

"A flight of X-wings," Tenel Ka reported. "Twelve XJ3s."

"Likelihood ninety-nine point . . ." Ulaha paused, then said, "Well, that *is* Kyp's Dozen. Undoubtedly."

"*Big Eye,* open a secure subspace channel," Anakin said. "And download the coordinates for a microjump."

"Little Brother," Jaina warned, "remember what—"

"Just in case." Anakin's subspace comm light came on, and he activated his microphone. "X-wing flight, you know who this is."

He reached out with the Force to identify himself, and felt a presence almost as strong as his own in return.

"Request you break off," he said. "You'll cause some real trouble for us—for all of us."

"Trouble, yes," the familiar voice of Kyp Durron replied, "but not for us."

On Anakin's tactical display, the Yuuzhan Vong boarding shuttle dissolved into static and vanished. Simply vanished, no sign of attack from the X-wings—no propellant trails, no energy flashes, nothing.

"*Big Eye?*" Anakin asked. "Is something wrong with—"

The corvette lashed out with plasma cannons and magma missiles, and Anakin's display filled with streaks of red energy. Nothing wrong with *Big Eye*'s sensor package. Kyp had destroyed the shuttle . . . how? The Force? It didn't seem possible. Only the most powerful Jedi could use it that way; only Dark Jedi would. Killing with the Force directly opened a Jedi to corruption, made him hungry for power. At least that was what Luke said. Anakin knew his uncle and Mara had been disappointed by their latest meeting with Kyp; perhaps this was the reason.

The Dozen began to juke and jink, lacing the tactical display with flashes of laserfire. Enemy plasma balls flared against their shields or streaked off and vanished, then the corvette's blip was engulfed in static. Anakin thought maybe a proton torpedo, but his display had not shown any propellant trails.

When the static faded, the corvette remained, its fire faded to a mere dribble. The XJ3 X-wings swarmed, blasting it with laser bolts and finishing it with proton torpedoes. This time, propellant trails glowed brilliant blue on Anakin's display.

Kyp's voice came over the subspace. "See? No trouble."

The *Speed Queen* fired its sublight drives and lumbered off. Though Anakin knew rogue attacks would ultimately prove harmful to both the Jedi and the New Republic, Lusa's death was still too fresh for him to feel anything but glad.

"Nice shooting," he said.

He was about to ask after the two strange detonations when Tenel Ka's voice came over their squadron comm channel.

"New contacts," she reported. "Two—no, three vessels. They appear somewhat larger."

Fiver whistled in alarm as he displayed the blips on Anakin's sensor screen. The three were arrayed in a perfect "stacked triangle": a ship above, on, and below the Dozen's tactical plane, each vessel situated so that its firing lane passed safely between the other two. Anakin was about to ask for a tactical readout when a data line appeared beneath each ship, identifying all three as assault frigates— slow and clumsy, but heavily armed and well protected.

"Ambush!" Anakin cried.

"Fact," Tenel Ka said. "Launching coralskippers now."

Clouds of faint blips swarmed from the frigates' off-battle side. Most moved to take up positions around the killing zone, but a half dozen turned to pursue the fleeing *Speed Queen*.

The Dozen broke formation, but the bigger ships had already loosed a salvo of corkscrewing lava missiles. A pair of Kyp's X-wings flared briefly and vanished.

Anakin was already lifting off the asteroid.

"Hold on, Little Brother," Jaina said. Despite her words, her X-wing was rising along with everyone else's. "We're not exactly following orders here."

"Are we exactly disobeying them?" Anakin demanded. He truly did not know what his uncle would want; whether Kyp had turned to the dark side or not, Luke would not want him killed—or, worse, captured. "We can't let them have another of us—not after Lusa."

"This is different," Tenel Ka said. "The argument could be made that Kyp has brought this on himself."

"Maybe," Anakin said.

He took a moment to collect himself. People had been accusing him of being reckless since Yavin 4, and the last thing he needed was to give them more ammunition. On the other hand, he had made up his mind.

"Is that an argument you want to make?" he asked.

Tenel Ka was quiet for a moment, then the blastboat rose. "No."

"Fine. We're going in. Jaina, tell us how."

As the squadron formed around the *Big Eye,* Jaina said, "Our hop brings us out behind the low frigate. No fancy stuff, and don't get carried away. Just blast an escape hole and head for home. Tails, you fly cover. No offense, but we haven't worked together."

"No offense taken, Stickz," a Barabel said. Worried that she might not respond as automatically to a different call sign, Jaina had asked the squadron to use her Rogue Squadron nickname. "We are honored to cover your backz. If Tail One may offer a suggestion?"

Tenel Ka began the countdown, and Jaina said, "Seven seconds, One."

"Their missile crewz will be facing away when you arrive. If you send the blastboat on the first pasz—"

"Risky, but it could work in a hurry," Jaina said. "Odds, Minstrel?"

"The probability of success is . . . eighty-two percent, with a margin of error—"

Lowbacca rumbled his commitment to the Barabel plan, then Tenel Ka said, "Two, one, mark!"

Anakin pushed the throttle and toggled the hyperdrive. The stars stretched into lines. Two seconds later, Fiver chirped to announce their arrival half a system away. To prevent the return to realspace from disorienting him, Anakin kept his eyes squeezed shut.

He reached out with the Force and felt his squadron in formation behind him. Kyp and the Dozen were a short distance to the left, swirling about in the killing zone trying to avoid plasma balls and magma missiles. Now that he was close enough, he could also feel the Yuuzhan Vong over at the battle, an indistinct quaver just powerful enough to divert his attention at a crucial moment. He was tempted to remove his lightsaber's lambent focusing crystal. A starfighter battle was no place to get distracted.

The X-wing banked sharply right as Fiver, acting in tandem with the other astromech droids, lined up on target. Now past any danger of becoming disoriented, Anakin opened his eyes and saw the battle ahead, a tiny web of flashing color.

"Everybody ready to play?" Jaina asked.

Anakin keyed his microphone to answer affirmative and counted the right number of clicks as others did likewise. Through the Force, he sensed a strange resignation in his sister, not at all similar to his own adrenaline-charged excitement. She seemed more weary than tense, almost detached. Maybe that was how an ace pilot survived so many blinding-fast starfighter battles—or maybe it was the price of coming back alive, the all-too-organic result of stress overload. Perhaps senate politics weren't the only reason Jaina's leave from Rogue Squadron was indefinite. Perhaps the flight surgeons had suggested to Gavin that she needed a long rest.

"Fiver, open a private channel to Jaina."

Before the droid could obey, Jaina said, "We're whole and hot. Green to go, Jedi, and good shooting."

Her X-wing leapt ahead, racing into a light-laced panorama

now so large it spilled across the entire front panel of Anakin's canopy. Putting aside any thought of suggesting she stay behind, he toggled his weapons live and selected laser cannons. The target swelled into view, first a blocky silhouette hiding the stars, then a megalithic darkness spewing plasma and magma into the maelstrom beyond.

Jaina nosed down to meet the only coralskipper in position to intercept the Jedi and soon had it juking and jinking to avoid her laserfire. The enemy pilot poured the power of his dovin basal into shielding his craft instead of maneuvering it. Not smart. Jaina dodged past the few plasma balls he lobbed in her direction and raked the skip with low-power stutter blasts. When the first hit scored, she immediately quadded her weapons and unloaded.

"Now that's shooting!" Zekk said.

"Neg that commclutter, Bounty Hunter," Jaina ordered.

Zekk keyed his microphone.

With nothing between him and the frigate, Anakin switched to proton torpedoes and laid his targeting reticle on the ship's bow. Tesar had guessed right about the missile crews; the plasma nodules and rock spitters on their side of the vessel remained quiet.

"Fiver, what's happening with those skips chasing the *Speed Queen?*"

Fiver shifted the tactical display's scale. The missing coralskippers were swarming the *Queen.*

"Not good," Anakin groaned. "Really not good. Uncle Luke will like that about as much as rancor fighting."

Fiver displayed a readout noting how long it would take the skips to return. They were out of the fight, but they might try to cut off the Jedi retreat.

"Keep an eye on them."

Fiver whistled an acknowledgment, then Anakin's targeting

reticle lit as he entered torpedo range. The frigate filled the front of the canopy now, an asteroidlike rock that was all Anakin could see.

"Little Brother green," he reported.

"Bounty Hunter green," Zekk said. "Back and forth?"

"You first."

A dozen white circles—three proton torpedoes and their decoy flares—streaked past and spread along the frigate's flank. The Yuuzhan Vong shielding crews activated their gravity-focusing dovin basals, projecting a string of miniature black holes that swallowed everything coming at them. Zekk switched to laser cannons and sprayed the frigate with stutter blasts. Over the last two years, space combat between the New Republic and the Yuuzhan Vong had evolved into a game of bait and switch, each side trying to bluff the other into squandering its limited reserve of power on unneeded defenses and ineffectual attacks. The XJ3 updates had been designed to win that game.

Anakin fired his first torpedo salvo, then switched weapons and sprayed laserfire. The shield crews were slower to grab his attacks, and the proximity fuses detonated within meters of the ship. Melt circles pocked the hull. Out of one small crack shot a geyser of atmosphere. Anakin hit the fissure with a pair of laser bursts, and a plume of bodies and equipment tumbled out. Zekk added a quadded burst and triggered a flurry of internal explosions, and then they were too close and had to pull up.

Anakin felt a pair of Yuuzhan Vong eyes on him—the lambent wasn't always a distraction—and jinked right. A magma missile spiraled past from somewhere beyond the frigate, and he felt his alarm mirrored back to him through the Force. He checked the heads-up display and saw Zekk sliding in behind him as another rock missile corkscrewed past.

"Thanks for the warning!" Zekk commed.

A pair of skips shot up from behind the frigate and hurled past, volcano cannons spitting plasma balls in the blastboat's direction.

Anakin started to loop around. "Get 'em!"

"Neg that, boys." Jaina's X-wing came swinging up behind the skips, her nose already leveling off to fire. "Take the pair going under."

She flashed past, a single proton torpedo streaking after the rear skip. No need to check the tactical display; with Jaina on their tail, the two Yuuzhan Vong were already dead. Anakin and Zekk nosed down over the frigate, weaving through a storm of magma missiles and circling under the vessel's belly before the surprised gunnery crews could target them. Three hundred meters ahead, two skips were angling up under the *Big Eye,* trading fire with the blastboat's big laser cannons.

Anakin felt Zekk find him through the Force. He quadded his cannons and positioned his targeting reticle. Lead flier ready. They depressed their triggers together. Their weapons flashed together. The skips disintegrated . . . together.

"Very nice shooting," Tenel Ka said. "Now please get clear."

Anakin pushed his throttle forward. There should have been another coralskipper, but it was nowhere on his display.

"Where's that last skip?" he said.

"Got it," Jaina replied. "On the way under."

Fiver let out a whistle.

"Yeah, four of 'em," Anakin said. "And she's not even excited."

The blastboat lit the darkness with flashing color. Anakin used his rearview vidscreen to watch the enemy shielding crews catch the entire first salvo. They missed four missiles from the next salvo, though, and one entered the breach Anakin and Zekk had opened earlier. The blast blew a hole through the far hull. The third salvo broke the vessel in two, and the ship tumbled away in separate pieces, its truncated halves bleeding bodies and vapor.

Anakin looped his X-wing back toward the battle and found another frigate angling to cut off the Dozen. The *Big Eye* launched all torpedoes and, no match for the larger ship's firepower, fled.

Jaina led Anakin and Zekk after the volleys, but Kyp's voice came over their comm channel.

"You've done enough, Sticks. We've got it from here."

"Sure." Jaina's reply was sarcastic, perhaps because the blast-boat's torpedoes were arcing into a gravitic singularity. "They'll just let you past."

"Well, not *let*."

A brilliant flash lit the frigate's bow, incinerating the bridge and leaving the vessel dead in space. The Dozen's eight survivors launched a torpedo volley at the crippled ship, then streaked out of the killing zone with a comfortable lead on the pursuing coralskippers.

"Kyp?" Anakin gasped. "How did you—"

"The Force."

The answer was curt, and even without the Force, Anakin would have sensed Kyp's anger at losing so many pilots. The two groups joined formations in cold silence and remained silent. Kyp had yielded to his anger before, and all Jedi knew the danger of that.

But Anakin was beginning to wonder. On Yavin 4, a bitter Yuuzhan Vong outcast had betrayed his people to help Anakin rescue Tahiri—and from him, Anakin had learned that there was a dark side even without the Force, that strength of will counted for as much as purity of heart. Now, more than ever, it seemed to him that the Force was one tool among many, to be used for a greater good. And if Kyp Durron had discovered some way to use the Force to destroy enemy ships, it seemed to Anakin that Eclipse should investigate it—that a strong Jedi with a focused will and pure heart might be able to use it without turning to the dark side.

Kyp allowed the silence to hang on the comm channels until they were clear of the enemy, then asked, "Anakin, did those explosions remind you of anything?"

"Their spectrographic signature was that of a proton torpedo," Tenel Ka said helpfully. "But there was no propellant trail."

"And what does that tell you?" Kyp asked smugly. "Think about it. 'Size matters not,' and all that."

"Telekinesis?" Anakin gasped. "You're using the Force to throw torpedoes?"

"I'm not as fast as a propellant charge—yet—but the Yuuzhan Vong have a hard time seeing proton torpedoes without a big, bright propellant glow to give them away."

Anakin was almost disappointed. He had been hoping for a secret weapon, something the Force-blind Yuuzhan Vong could never counter. Instead, it was just one more move in the game, one more trick the enemy would soon learn to defeat.

If Kyp expected someone to congratulate him on his cleverness, he was disappointed. Tenel Ka remarked that it would save the New Republic a few propellant cylinders if nothing else, then an urgent warble drew Anakin's attention to his tactical display. Fiver shifted scales, showing the *Speed Queen*'s derelict hulk dead in space. The six coralskippers that had destroyed it were rushing to cut off his group's escape path.

"We are not done yet, I fear," Tenel Ka said.

The six skip pilots were hopelessly outnumbered and would no doubt die, but they would also buy the rest of the task force time to catch the X-wings from behind. Anakin hissed a curse— then cursed again as three X-wings appeared ahead of the skips, rushing to meet them.

"Please continue on course, Little Brother," a Barabel rasped. "This will not take long. There are only six."

The three X-wings merged into one blip and continued toward the enemy, forcing the Yuuzhan Vong to choose between being torn apart piecemeal and abandoning their screen. Not surprisingly, they closed ranks, spraying a flurry of stripes and corkscrew lines at the Barabels.

Outside the canopy, Anakin could barely see the battle ahead, mere pinpoints of light flashing in the distant darkness. He looked back to the tactical display and saw the corkscrew lines winking out as they approached the X-wings.

"They can't do that!" Zekk gasped.

"If you think they are shooting missiles out of space, then they *can*," Tenel Ka said. "Optical magnification shows a seventy-two percent correlation between their laser flashes and the disappearance of the missiles."

Anakin was not as impressed by their shooting as by their flying. To merge into one blip, they had to be on top of each other, no more than a meter apart, at a velocity that might well be 10 percent of light. Aside from demoralizing the enemy, he could think of no battle use for such a display of precision, but he *was* impressed.

At last, one magma missile got through to the X-wings. Anakin's eyes remained glued to the tactical display, awaiting the horrible flash that would mean the end of one or—as close as they were—all three Barabels.

It never came. The missile reappeared on the other side of the blip in a different trajectory. Someone had used the Force to redirect its flight.

"I need some Jedi in my squadron," Kyp said. "I need some *Barabel* Jedi."

Anakin looked up again. The battle was brighter now, more like a flickering phosflea, but there was no question of reaching it in time to help the Barabels.

The Yuuzhan Vong gave up on the magma missiles and concentrated on plasma balls. To Anakin's amazement, the Barabels wasted no effort trying to dodge. They took the attacks head-on, one after the other, and continued straight on long after their shields should have fallen.

"How can they do that?" Zekk asked. "Are they reinforcing each other's shields?"

"Not enough overlap." Jaina's voice was full of admiration—the first sign of emotion she had displayed during the battle. "They must be leapfrogging, taking turns out front while the others reenergize."

"Fact," Tenel Ka confirmed. "There are fluctuating ion pulses consistent with variations in drive output."

"Now I'm really impressed," Anakin said.

A Yuuzhan Vong blip vanished. The X-wings swung toward another skip. It disappeared, too. Anakin was not surprised by this tactic, but he was awed by its precision. The hatchmates were concentrating their fire, simply overwhelming their targets with the sheer volume of laser blasts. A third skip blinked out. The survivors closed on the X-wings' flanks, trying to swing around behind them.

The Barabels' blip quivered and slowed. Anakin knew the Yuuzhan Vong were using dovin basals to pull at the X-wings' shields. He wanted to open a channel and yell at them to toggle their grab-safety, which would release the shields and bring them back up a millisecond later. He did not dare interfere with their concentration.

The Barabels surprised him again, this time shutting down their sublight drives completely. With the skips pulling on their shields, the distance closed in a heartbeat. Then there were three X-wings again, each nose to nose with a coralskipper. The tactical display burst into an indecipherable tangle of propellant trails, then dissolved into static as the rapid-fire proton bursts overloaded the blastboat's sensors. Anakin glanced through his canopy and saw a novalike burst of light.

When he looked back to his display, there was nothing but static.

"Fiver?"

The droid tweedled and set to work filtering the overload.

"Tails?" Jaina called. "Are you there?"

They did not reply, but Tenel Ka said, "Our sensors are coming back on-line. There appear to be three X-wings."

"Tails, are you there?" Jaina repeated. "One? Two? Three?"

She was answered by a long outburst of sissing, what passed for laughter among the Barabel.

"We are here, Stickz," one of the hatchmates rasped. "One, Two, Three."

Chapter 10

*N*early a hundred senatorial balconies sat empty in support of the Ithorian boycott. The Wookiees were hurling pieces of their conferencing console at the speaker's dais, where a hologram of the Thyferran senator offered a nine-point plan to open peace negotiations with the Yuuzhan Vong. The entire consular staff of Talfaglio wandered the walkways shouting—actually shouting—their demand that the Jedi surrender to save the hostages. Balmorra was channel-blasting an offer of free orbital turbolaser platforms to any world that sent a fleet to its defense, and security droids were whirring back and forth through the air, searching in vain for a Dathomiri assassin rumored to be hiding in the chamber.

It was not how Borsk Fey'lya would have liked to meet Tsavong Lah's envoy. He would have preferred to receive him in the State Reception Hall and, over a decanter of fine Endorian port, quietly work out an acceptable script for their public confrontation. But the emissary had balked at the invitation, suggesting instead that the chief of state greet him as he debarked his ship—a deferential gesture that would have further split the senate and undermined Borsk's already sagging support. So, unable to reach a compromise, here they were, meeting for the first time in the Grand Convocation Chamber of the New Republic Senate, the whole galaxy watching, and neither one with a clue as to what the other would do or say. It was, as the phrase went, a Great Moment in History, when empires rose or fell on the words of politicians and posterity's favor was won or lost in a second. Chief of State Fey'lya felt like he was going to throw up.

The Yuuzhan Vong, looking faintly Jedi-like in a hooded cape over scarlet vonduun crab armor, made Borsk wait while he descended three hundred meters of stairs at the pace of a Dagobah swamp sloth. The envoy brought no bodyguards, giving the impression that he needed no protection but his living armor and the long amphistaff in his hands. He paid no attention to the hisses and jeers many senators cast his way, and even less to the fools who stepped forward to suggest private meetings. The only time he looked away was when the Togorians hurled a volley of caf mugs at him, and even then it was only to cast a shadowed glare upon the security droids who intercepted the fusillade.

Borsk suddenly wished he had instructed the sergeant at arms to disarm the Yuuzhan Vong. He had thought facing an armed warrior would make him look brave on the HoloNet, but now he was not so sure. Though the security droids would blast the envoy senseless at the first sign of an attack, Borsk knew himself well enough to realize even holocams would not ease his anxiety.

When the Yuuzhan Vong finally reached the chamber floor, he stopped on one side of the speaker's rostrum and waited. As their negotiators had agreed, Borsk left the chief of state's console and came down to stand across from him. He was followed by two members of the Advisory Council, Viqi Shesh of Kuat and Fyor Rodan of Commenor. No one exchanged pleasantries or greetings.

"I am Borsk Fey'lya. I have invited you here to discuss the Talfaglion hostages."

"What is there to discuss?" The envoy reached up and pulled

his hood back, revealing the usual wreck of a Yuuzhan Vong face. "My words to Leia Solo were clear enough."

The uproar in the chamber faded to an electric drone as consular aides scoured data banks for facemap fits and voiceprint matches. Borsk needed no such help. Though he had not stood toe to toe with many invaders—none, actually—he had watched the hologram of Leia's Bilbringi meeting a hundred times. Nom Anor's gnarled visage was almost as familiar to him as his own—even with a new false eye fitted in what had been an empty socket on the holo.

"Leia Solo is no longer a representative of this government," Borsk said. Though his fur was standing on end, his tone was dismissive. "If you have something to say to the New Republic, you must say it to me."

The envoy glared out of his one good eye, clearly surprised by Borsk's impudence. "You do not know of our terms?"

An indignant murmur built in the chamber as the consular aides began to inform their masters of the envoy's identity, and Borsk knew he had to work quickly. Nom Anor's role in both the Rhommamool-Osarian conflict and the fall of Duro were well documented, and selecting him as an envoy was an open insult.

"I know you have threatened to kill millions of New Republic citizens," Borsk said. "I *summoned* you here to provide an explanation."

The murmur in the chamber rose to a near-din, and the Wookiees whooped in approval. Borsk did nothing to quell the noise, which the Talfaglions correctly interpreted as encouragement and attempted to rebut by urging their allies to shout down the Wookiees. This drew a deafening counterroar from the Jedi-supporters, and it occurred to Borsk that he might have found the way to shore up his support. He locked gazes with Nom Anor and allowed the uproar to continue, until Viqi Shesh finally returned to the Advisory Council's dais and used the gallery address to plead for quiet.

Borsk was not as troubled by the betrayal of his patronage as by how quickly her efforts were rewarded.

When the uproar had died, Nom Anor turned from Borsk and looked directly into the galleries. "What a pity the courage of your Jedi does not match that of your bureaucrats."

The chorus of jeers was not nearly so loud as Borsk would have liked, and for a moment he worried he was making a mistake. While many of the systems supporting the Jedi were almost fanatical in their loyalties, they tended to be already conquered or separated from the rest of the New Republic by the invasion route. On the other hand, the worlds that favored appeasing the Yuuzhan Vong were mostly rich Core systems, with resources vital to the war effort and political power bases critical to Borsk's continued tenure as chief of state. The Yuuzhan Vong knew all that, which was why they had sent a notorious spy to represent them in the first place. They were trying to divide the senate between those they could intimidate and those they could not—and Borsk had been in politics long enough to know what happened to those who were easily intimidated.

He waited while Nom Anor's gaze circled the gallery, passing over those who taunted him with a confident sneer, lingering on the ones who remained quiet until they grew uncomfortable and looked away. Borsk had to admire the envoy's technique. It was classic intimidation politics, rendered all the more effective by the fact that the Yuuzhan Vong had proven time and again they would not hesitate to carry through even the most unthinkable threat. Fortunately for the New Republic—in the humble opinion of its chief of state, at least—they were playing this game against a master.

When Nom Anor's gaze finally returned to the speaker's rostrum, Borsk stepped to within a hand's breadth of the Yuuzhan Vong's chest. Purposely contrasting his stubby figure against his counterpart's more massive build, he craned his neck back and stared at the underside of the other's crooked chin.

"The Yuuzhan Vong must be worried about our Jedi indeed, to think a handful worth so many lives."

Borsk spoke so softly that the sound droid had to float nearly between them to pick up his words, and, as he had planned, Nom Anor was forced to step back to glare down at him.

"Your lives mean nothing to us."

"Indeed?" Borsk glanced into the high galleries, searching out the peace-loving senator from Thyferra. "I thought as much."

A silence fell over the chamber, and the Bothan knew he was succeeding when he heard the rustle of a thousand senatorial backsides shifting in their seats. He was holding his audience rapt; this was not what they had expected, and they barely dared breathe for fear of missing what would happen next.

Then Viqi Shesh stepped over beside them, and Borsk could almost hear the excitement drain from the room.

"What the chief of state means to say, Ambassador, is that the Yuuzhan Vong may not understand the New Republic's relationship with the Jedi. We lack control—"

"No." Borsk shot Shesh a look that would have melted durasteel. "That is not what the chief of state means to say."

Shesh paled, but refused to retreat. "I beg your pardon."

"The senator from Kuat is welcome to express her opinion in the proper forums, but she may not presume to speak for the chief of state." Borsk glared at her until she retreated, then he turned back to Nom Anor. "What the chief of state means to say is that the Yuuzhan Vong are cowards and murderers. If they had the courage of the least of their slaves, they would stop hiding behind helpless refugees and go do battle with the Jedi!"

"We are not hiding!" Nom Anor shot back. "It is the Jedi."

"Really?" Borsk answered in a sarcastic tone. "Then I suggest you look in the Corellian sector. There were recently quite a few at Froz, from what I understand."

Much of the chamber erupted into laughter, for the "irresponsible Jedi ambush" at Froz had dominated the HoloNet over the last few days. It was too early to tell whether Borsk's comment would change the slant of the coverage, but it was sure to keep the incident—and the chief of state—in the newsvids for days to come.

Nom Anor's meandering eye swiveled down toward Borsk, and the Bothan's stomach went sour. He had read the reports on the false eye confiscated at Bilbringi and knew the unpleasant death that awaited anyone unfortunate enough to have its poison emptied in his face. But he refused to back down. He could feel the support of the Jedi-lovers swelling behind him, and he knew that to show fear now was to throw away all he had just won.

Then, in a flash of inspiration, Borsk knew what to say, exactly how to crystallize his support. "And you might try looking in Bothan space. I have it on good authority that the Jedi are well loved there."

This drew an even bigger laugh than the Froz suggestion, for Borsk and the Jedi had not been on good terms since—well, ever. It was a weak point in his rapidly developing plan, and one he hoped to fix by openly pledging his home system's support to the Jedi. He glanced up at the Bothan gallery and saw Mak Sezala, the Bothan senator, staring daggers at him. Borsk flattened his ears in warning, and Sezala obediently rose and began to suggest planets where the Yuuzhan Vong might start searching. None of the worlds were inhabited, but it was enough to bring the senators of a hundred other systems to their feet with similar suggestions.

Nom Anor's eyes narrowed. Borsk thought he had finally pushed too far, but the Yuuzhan Vong stepped back.

"I will relay your suggestions." He turned toward the stairs and glanced into the galleries. "All of them."

"Fine, but you will do so by villip," Borsk said.

Nom Anor looked over his shoulder. "What?"

"You may relay your suggestions by villip." Borsk did not want to miss this chance to mock the infamous spy. "I summoned you here to explain the taking of a million hostages. You aren't leaving until you do."

Nom Anor's reply was lost to a tumult of Wookiee roaring. The cheers felt good to Borsk. He would never again be able to set foot inside Bothan space, but the cheers felt good.

Chapter 11

The villip everted at last, assuming the likeness of the warmaster's disfigured visage. Rugged and bold-featured, with pensive eyes and a fringed mouth, it had once been a face Viqi Shesh might have found alluring. Now, laced with devotional scars and rearranged by ritual breakings, the best she could call it was interesting. So how come her stomach fluttered whenever she saw it? Why should she be annoyed that he had taken so long to respond to her villip? It had to be his power. She was drawn to powerful men—well, males. She was not proud of this weakness—it was considered something of a perversion back on Kuat, where women of her station normally purchased telbun servants to serve as their mates—but there it was, her secret shame. For a while—a very brief while—she had even been rather taken with furry little Borsk.

"Viqi, you have something to report?" Tsavong Lah asked.

"Yes." She liked how he always called her by her first name. It bespoke a certain intimacy he did not share with most others. "It was a surprising session."

"Nom Anor says successful."

"Then he saw something I did not," she replied. "Nom Anor

110

misread the situation from the start. His arrogance forced Borsk to throw his support to the Jedi."

"Truly?" The warmaster did not seem all that surprised. "And he assured me he would do so well."

"I have been all day salvaging the situation."

"You have?" Tsavong Lah sounded surprised, no doubt because he was not accustomed to underlings showing such initiative. "What have you done?"

"The senate split roughly along Core boundaries," she explained. "Those inside the Core—and coincidentally in your invasion path—favored turning against the Jedi. The others support them."

"That was expected," Tsavong Lah said impatiently.

Seeing that the significance was lost on the warmaster, Viqi tried a confident tone. "The Core Worlds have most of the resources still available to the New Republic, and those who control the purse strings control the government."

"Yes?"

"I've spent all morning talking to Core senators. We don't have the votes to win a no-confidence call, but I'm convinced that were Borsk to meet an untimely end, the next chief of state would be less favorably disposed toward the Jedi."

Tsavong Lah's brow rose. "You are thinking of murder?"

Viqi was surprised to feel a shudder run down her spine. Murder was such an ugly way to put it, but how like the Yuuzhan Vong to say it in the ghastliest way possible. "Nom Anor was close enough today. He could do it."

"Nom Anor?" Tsavong Lah echoed. "Are you not the one who will be elected chief of state when Borsk dies?"

Not *if*, Viqi noted, *when*. She smiled confidently. "That's my plan, yes."

The warmaster scowled. "Then you do it, Viqi."

Her smile vanished. "Me?" Thoughts swirled through her

mind, trying to sort through the possible purposes behind his words. Was he testing her courage? Joking? Perhaps he simply did not understand the ramifications of his suggestion. Yes, that had to be it. "I don't think politics work the same way in the New Republic as among the Yuuzhan Vong. Were I to murder Borsk, I'd be disgraced and sent to a rehabilitation facility—not elected chief of state."

"Only if you were caught."

Viqi paused. Tsavong Lah could certainly smuggle her some means of killing Borsk secretly, but knowing the Yuuzhan Vong— and the warmaster in particular—she felt sure the method would involve some horrible mutilation to her own body, and still require her to look in the Bothan's eye as she murdered him. Though she had never killed anyone face to face before, she believed she could do it, considering the prize. But what of the investigation that followed? As fierce as the Yuuzhan Vong were as warriors, they knew nothing of the New Republic's investigative technology— technology that would be brought fully to bear to identify Borsk's assassin.

Viqi shook her head. "It wouldn't work."

"You're refusing me?"

"I am." Her insides went cold. She already regretted proposing the assassination in the first place, but she knew better than to show fear now. The warmaster would see hesitation as a sign of weakness and pounce on it like the predator he was, and she had worked too hard—done too many things that repulsed even her—to throw it all away recklessly. "I won't do either of us any good on a prison planet."

Tsavong Lah's tone grew dangerously even. "I have ways to force your cooperation. I'm sure Belindi Kalenda would be very interested to learn of our association."

"I'm sure she would. But then you would lose that steady little flow of memories from the NRMOC situation room." To illustrate her point, she tipped her head to one side and ground her teeth together, then winced as the chilab detached itself and slithered down her nasal passage. "And I'm sure New Republic Intelligence would also be very interested in these."

The neural grub dropped out of her nostril exactly on cue, and a small smile of respect crept across Tsavong Lah's face.

"As you wish, Viqi Shesh," he said. "But Nom Anor cannot be trusted with a task this important. A vermin hunter named Bjork Umi will contact you soon."

"Yes?"

"Give him a time and a place," Tsavong Lah said. "And you will become chief of state—*our* chief of state."

Chapter 12

The YVH-One is a top-notch war droid with flaw-less search-and-identify engineering, the heavy-weapons punch of a four-seater blastcar, and, with the optional laminanium layered armor, the durability to survive even the most hazardous postings. Ladies and gentlemen, I give you the ultimate answer to the invasion of the New Republic, Tendrando Arms' Yuuzhan Vong Hunter One!"

The hulking war droid sprang into view, a skull-headed blur of black-and-gray camouflage bouncing across the floor in a dizzying array of evasive flips and midair twists. It crashed through a ferrocrete wall that had apparently been erected for just that purpose, dived over a hovering landspeeder, and finished by positioning itself precisely at the entrance of the proving facility. It pivoted exactly ninety degrees left and clanged to attention in front of the spectator hoversled, then snapped its blaster-cannon arm against its chest in salute.

With a death's-head face and red photoreceptors gleaming in socket mountings as deep as a blaster burn, the droid bore a faint but nightmarish resemblance to the enemy it had been built to destroy. Its wedge-shaped torso, the massive proportions of its system-packed limbs, even the way its armor overlapped at the joints reminded Leia of a Yuuzhan Vong warrior trapped in a droid's shell. She wondered if Lando's designers had intended the similarity—perhaps to cause judgment lapses by goading their foes into a rage—or if the insult had just been lucky coincidence.

In an ultradeep, ultramale version of Lando Calrissian's voice, the droid said, "YVH One-One-A reporting all systems functional. Ready to proceed in demonstration mode."

Leia rolled her eyes at Lando's characteristic vanity, then looked at Han, who had returned to Coruscant immediately after dropping the voxyn at Eclipse. "I don't see why I have to be here."

"Think of it as a favor." Han nodded toward the front of the hoversled, where Borsk Fey'lya stood flanked by two generals, Garm Bel Iblis and Wedge Antilles. "Borsk wouldn't meet with Lando unless you came."

"And why is the chief of state meeting with an arms supplier in the first place?" Leia demanded. "You know what this is."

Han shrugged. "They're good droids."

"As if anyone here were qualified to judge that." Leia was silent for a moment, then said, "He's trying to draw me back in."

"Look, all Lando's trying to do is sell a few droids and help win the war," Han said.

"I was talking about Borsk."

"I know," Han answered. "But what's wrong with using *him* for a change?"

"It's politics. I'm done with that."

She fell silent as Lando explained he would be demonstrating the YVH's capabilities in the most challenging combat environment of all, the urban battleground. YVH 1-1A turned and began to stalk down the simulation maze of a fairly modern glasteel city. The hoversled followed a dozen meters above, where the occupants would have a clear view of the action. Adarakh and Meewalh were still in bacta tanks recovering from their acid burns, or Leia knew they would have insisted on being even farther from the action. Demonstrations of war droids were notorious for going tragically astray.

The first test came when a pair of what looked like Yuuzhan Vong quietly stepped into an alley around the corner from 1-1A. They were armed with amphistaffs and bandoliers of thud bugs.

"There's nothing to be concerned about," Lando said. "They're actually training droids, built off the same frame as the YVH, but programmed with Yuuzhan Vong battle tactics and equipped with emitter packages that mimic enemy heart rates, heat signatures, and odor characteristics."

"Yuuzhandroids—the ultimate abomination," Bel Iblis said, grinning. "I admire a man who has confidence in his own product."

"I have confidence in everything I manufacture," Lando said, returning the general's smile. "But why do you find that so admirable . . . in this case?"

"No particular reason." Bel Iblis shrugged. "I was just thinking of what the enemy will do when they hear you've begun manufacturing them."

Lando's smile grew queasy.

The Yuuzhandroids made it only three steps down the alley before 1-1A sprang around the corner to meet them, the servo motors of his repulsor-enhanced legs hissing slightly as they propelled his enormous mass. One Yuuzhandroid made the mistake of raising his amphistaff and was immediately struck down by a green blaster bolt. The other was smarter, making a headlong dive and reaching for his bandolier of thud bugs. He actually had a hand on it before 1-1A's blaster bolt knocked him senseless.

"For the purposes of this demonstration, One-One-A's blaster cannon is powered down to a nonlethal setting modulated specifically to paralyze the Yuuzhandroid circuitry," Lando explained. "In true combat, One-One-A would automatically select the energy level needed to annihilate any target up to the size of a coralskipper. We'll see his destructive capabilities in the second part of the demonstration."

YVH 1-1A paused while a remote sensor scan confirmed that he "downed" his targets, then he continued along the main avenue. For the next hour, Leia and the others watched the war droid work his way through a broad assortment of combat problems, locating concealed Yuuzhandroids through solid durasteel, tracking multiple escapees, and, most impressive to Leia, capturing a trio of ooglith-masqued infiltrators without harming anyone in a crowd of bystanders. The finale came when 1-1A was ordered into a simulated ambush—simulated because 1-1A's sensors alerted him to it well in advance and Lando ordered him in anyway. Of the half a dozen Yuuzhandroids trapped in the cul-de-sac with him, four hit him with thud bugs. Only one managed a second strike before being blasted unconscious. By the time 1-1A's sensors confirmed that he had downed all six targets, the bug pits in his laminanium armor were already filling themselves.

"Self-healing metals," General Bel Iblis observed. "Nice."

"Just one of the YVH's many design innovations." Lando's smile was one of genuine pride, more sincere than Leia had seen in decades. "Of course, it's impossible to simulate a full-scale battle here. The Yuuzhan Vong would have heavier weapons that we just can't use in a demonstration, but this should provide some idea of the YVH's capabilities. It's totally immune to biological agents, hermetically seals itself in the presence of corrosive chemicals, and the laminanium armor can take a coralskipper plasma ball in the chest without breaching."

"How long to repair that?" Wedge asked.

"Less than a day standard, but it will need to recharge its power pack and replace its laminanium ingot." Lando signaled to 1-1A, who drew an appreciative murmur from the generals by riding the repulsorlifts concealed in his feet onto the deck of the hoversled. "If we can proceed to the firing range, One-One-A will demonstrate his destructive capability."

Fey'lya nodded to the pilot droid, and they started across the mock city toward a distant blast tunnel.

"The YVH's primary weapon is the variable-output blaster cannon in his right arm," Lando said. "But his left arm can be fitted with a wide variety of weapons, including a fifty-missile seeker battery, sonic rifles, heavy lasers . . ."

As Lando ticked off the options, Fey'lya motioned for him to continue for the generals, then joined Leia and Han in the back.

"Impressive." He addressed himself to both Leia and Han, as though he were only making casual conversation. "I can see an army of these droids defending the New Republic. What would it take? A million?"

"Three million would be better," Han answered, immediately slipping into bargaining mode on his friend's behalf. "There are a lot of Yuuzhan Vong, and these things are bound to make them mad. That's worth something."

"*Three* million?" Fey'lya considered the number, then looked to Leia. "That's a lot of laminanium. It would require a great deal of support to push through."

Leia had a hollow feeling in her stomach. She had known this moment was coming since watching the hologram of Fey'lya dressing Nom Anor down in front of the full senate, and—for a change—she was almost eager to give the Bothan what he wanted. After the destruction of the *Speed Queen* in the battle at Froz, the Jedi were taking more of a battering in the senate than ever. The chief of state's support would do much to alleviate that, but her feeling as she left the NRMOC situation room that day had been unmistakable. The Force was guiding her away from politics, and she had no doubt that the Bothan hoped to bring her back into the senate as his ally—a move that would both add to his support and give the Jedi an audible voice.

It was a sacrifice she could no longer make. The feeling had been too clear. "I'm sure you'll find all the support you need, if you truly believe it's the right thing."

The fur around Fey'lya's collar ruffled uncertainly. "What do my beliefs matter? We're talking about the senate."

"The senate *you* made," Leia said. "You and those like you. I'm no part of that."

Fey'lya's ears flattened, and Leia heard her husband mutter something under his breath. They had talked this over before coming. Han was sympathetic to her determination to have no more to do with the senate, but, in typical Han Solo fashion, he thought she simply ought to fake it. To his way of thinking, all she had to do was smile a few times and make a couple of public appearances with Fey'lya. Then the Jedi would be off the hook, Lando would have enough credits to buy an entire sector, and the New Republic would have the finest droid army in a dozen galaxies. Han just could not understand that to play Fey'lya's game would be to countenance the Bothan's way of doing things, to become a part of the rot that had made the New Republic such a soft target for the Yuuzhan Vong in the first place.

After a long pause, Fey'lya cast a meaningful glance at the lightsaber hanging from Leia's belt. "Come now, Princess. You know how this works. I cannot support the Jedi unless the Jedi support me."

"Do the right thing, and you will have their support," Leia said. Lando and the generals had given up all pretense of discussing the YVH's merits and were now openly eavesdropping. "I am no longer in the business of making behind-the-scenes deals."

"What a pity, when there is such a need for them to hold the New Republic together."

Lando's eyes widened at Fey'lya's acid tone, and he shot Han a look of appeal.

Han could only shrug. "Sorry, pal. I promised she'd come, not what she'd say."

The hoversled slowed and began to descend toward the blast tunnel, where several Tendrando technicians were unloading two huge crates of YVH munitions.

Lando rallied with one of his slickest smiles. "No problem, Han. This baby sells itself." He jerked a thumb toward a squad of big human bodyguards rushing to secure the hoversled's landing pad. "When the chief of state sees what One-One-A's depleted baradium pellets do to yorik coral, he'll want a dozen to replace those jokers."

From behind them came 1-1A's ultramasculine voice. "Remain calm. Seek shelter immediately." The hoversled shuddered beneath the war droid's heavy steps. "This is a military emergency. Seek shelter immediately."

It was the same warning the droid had given in the search-and-identify demonstration, just before disabling three Yuuzhandroid "infiltrators" as they tried to slip through a crowd of Tendrando "pedestrians." Leia cocked a querying brow at Lando. He shook his head, then moved to intercept the war droid.

"One-One-A, the demonstration is over," he said.

"Affirmative, demonstration completed," the droid replied. "Please seek shelter. There are Yuuzhan Vong ahead."

YVH 1-1A brushed Lando aside and jerked the pilot droid away from the control column, then jacked into the socket himself. The sled was so close to the landing area that Leia had to step to the safety rail to look down on the bodyguards. They were arraying themselves on all sides of the pad, facing outward as was proper. Once the sled descended, it would take only an instant to spin around and catch the group in a deadly cross fire.

The war droid turned the hoversled away from the landing area.

"Calrissian!" General Bel Iblis barked. "Enough is enough."

Leia reached out with the Force, felt nothing from the guards. "No, Garm," she said. "They're impostors."

YVH 1-1A laid his arm on the rail and loosed a flurry of blaster bolts. A pair of Yuuzhan Vong detached the sleeves of their blast armor and turned their shoulders toward the hoversled, and something black and winged shot out of the first warrior's sleeve. YVH 1-1A continued to bank away.

The thing—whatever it was—smashed into the hoversled and nearly flipped it. Four black pincers came through the durasteel floor, ripping a hole, and a beetlelike insect about the size of Leia's arm started to come through. Han, Bel Iblis, and Wedge vaporized it with blasterfire.

Another jolt. The hoversled turned on edge and angled down into the simulated city.

"Impact imminent," 1-1A warned. "Brace—"

Even cushioned by repulsorlift engines, the crash was a mad and confusing thing. Leia ricocheted off durasteel and dropped face-first onto ferrocrete, bodies thudding all around. The hoversled fell against a wall above her, remained there leaning. Han called out. She reached for him through the Force and felt more worry than pain.

"I'm fine," she said. "Everyone?"

Fey'lya answered first. "Thankfully, I am unhurt."

"Sound and strong," Bel Iblis reported.

"Same here," Wedge said.

Only Lando did not answer. Leia picked herself up and found him crouched behind the overturned sled, watching 1-1A spray blaster bolts down a one-block street. The *whumpf-whumpf* of the droid's blaster cannon sounded somehow all too gentle.

"Lando?" Leia pulled the lightsaber from her belt. The handle felt familiar enough, but the weapon still seemed a thing in her hand, not at all the extension of herself she knew it should have been. "Tell One-One-A to let loose with the heavy stuff."

"Can't. There's a power governor on his weapons systems." Lando sounded almost sick. "With two generals and the chief of state here, we didn't want to chance a programming glitch."

"Power governor?" This from both Han and Fey'lya.

"You think I'm not disappointed?" Lando retorted. "An opportunity like this?"

Thud bugs began to ping the bottom of the hoversled.

"What was he supposed to do in the blast tunnel?" Han asked. "Put on a lightshow?"

"It only takes a second to change a programming card," Lando said. "It's with the munitions."

Leia peered around the platform edge. YVH 1-1A stood in a storm of thud bugs pouring blasterfire at the assassins and accomplishing nothing against their stolen blast armor. Finally, he gave an electronic bellow and stomped down the street.

A pair of Yuuzhan Vong pressed themselves into a doorway and opened their breastplates, each drawing a long eel-like creature from beneath his armor and throwing it at 1-1A. The things turned rigid and streaked at the droid, their heads pulsing with white energy, their tails shooting threads of flame.

YVH 1-1A fired twice on the run. The eels exploded. He fired twice more, and both attackers dropped.

Then the droid was crashing into the others. Two more fell to his flailing arms, but the rest slipped past, and Han, Lando, and the generals took out another pair with blaster pistols. Wedge stopped firing long enough to shove Han and Leia toward Fey'lya.

"Take him. We'll hold here."

Han started to object, but Fey'lya was already fleeing, shouting into his comlink for someone to answer. Judging by the panic in his voice, no one was.

Leia grabbed Han and started after the Bothan. Like it or not, Fey'lya was chief of state. Behind them, another assassin fell, then

Wedge took a thud bug in the shoulder and tumbled into the others, and the last trio of Yuuzhan Vong charged under the hover-sled and raced past, 1-1A stomping into view behind them, still scorching their armor with ineffective blasterfire. The droid's lami-nanium armor was pitted to the underskeleton and his circuits were showing, but he kept coming, kept firing even with his allies in front of him. Precision targeting.

Seeing the advantage of the situation, Leia ignited her light-saber. "Time to make a stand."

"Too dangerous!" The near-panic in Han's voice surprised Leia. "You go."

He shoved her after Fey'lya, nearly losing a hand as he reached past her lightsaber, then dropped the nearest Yuuzhan Vong with an impressive under-the-arm shot. Bad timing. A blaster bolt—one of 1-1A's nonlethal green bolts—caught him in the chest and hurled him into Leia. He dropped, not dead she could tell, but out, really, really out. She caught her balance and stumbled around to meet the last two Yuuzhan Vong, one slashing at her head, the other slipping past after Fey'lya.

Leia dropped to a crouch and tumbled backward, using the Force to carry her along. A flying somersault would have been better, but she was no dueling master. She rolled to her feet and spun, catching Borsk's would-be assassin across the back. Her ruby blade cleaved him nearly in two, and the smell was sickening.

Leia continued her spin and found the last Yuuzhan Vong where she expected, whipping his amphistaff at her legs, also as expected. She blocked low. He dropped his weapon and reached for his utility pouch.

Something struck at Leia's knee. She caught it on her blade, saw the amphistaff had reverted to snake form, and flung the thing away. The Yuuzhan Vong's hand was in his utility pouch. Leia sum-moned the Force and kicked with everything she had. The blow caught the assassin square and sent him stumbling back all of two steps.

The warrior sneered and withdrew his hand from the utility pouch. Vowing for the thousandth time to spend more time practicing her Jedi skills, Leia hurled her lightsaber at his arm. Still sneering, he pivoted to let it pass . . . and suddenly found himself folded into 1-1A's laminanium arms.

The droid crushed the stolen blast armor like an eggshell, squeezing black gore out onto the ground. "Blasters ineffectual," he said, stunned and confused. "Alternate tactics required."

Chapter 13

With the milky splendor of the galactic core pouring down through its transparisteel ceiling, the crater room on Eclipse was one of the few that still had light. An attempt to feed more power to the central cooling system had blown a primary switching bank, shutting down all nonvital systems and compelling the Jedi to hold their assembly in one of the Eclipse Program's labs. Several empty villip tanks—even Cilghal could not make the things grow—had been moved aside to create a gathering area. Han and Lando stood a little off to the side with Leia's Noghri bodyguards. After the close call on Coruscant, the Noghri had emerged from their bacta tanks a day early and now refused to let Leia out of their sight.

Leia was near the front with Mara, Cilghal, and the older Jedi, while Jacen and Jaina stood with Tenel Ka, Lowie, Raynar, Zekk, and the more thoughtful of the younger Jedi Knights. Anakin, with his pretty friend Tahiri at his side, was surrounded by his growing gaggle of companions, now including the three Barabel hatchmates, Ulaha Kore, a red-haired human woman named Eryl Besa, and the Twi'lek dancer, Alema Rar.

Han was only slightly less pleased than Tahiri to see how closely Alema pressed into his son's space. Though the Twi'lek was about the same age as Anakin, he could tell by how she used her eyes and touch that she was much older in at least one sense—and now was not a particularly good time for Anakin to learn those lessons. Though Luke had called the gathering to report a breakthrough in Cilghal's research, they had just received word that Anakin's friend Lyric had fallen to the voxyn. Almost as alarming, Corran Horn had been seen with his wife, Mirax, fleeing a pack of the creatures while resupplying on Corellia. No one had been able to contact them since.

Cilghal was the first to break the silence. "I asked Master Sky-walker to call this meeting because I wanted to give you some hopeful news. Instead, I must again apologize for my tardiness in solving the problem." The Mon Calamari turned her bulbous eyes toward the floor. "Forgive me."

"Don't think like that." Though Anakin's eyes were wet with barely restrained tears, his tone was warm. "No one could do better. Without you, we wouldn't even know these things were part vornskr."

Anakin's words made Han proud. He knew from his own experience how difficult it was not to lash out after the loss of someone close, and his son's reassurances would help ease Cilghal's over-active conscience.

"That's right," Ganner Rhysode agreed. The big man's scarred cheek lent a dangerous air to an otherwise rakishly handsome face. "Everyone knows how hard you've been working—just by how hard we've been working."

This drew a chorus of agreement, for Cilghal was keeping many of the Jedi busy trying to identify the location of the original voxyn—the queen, as they now called her. Ganner had retraced the *Sweet Surprise*'s route to and from Nova Station, Streen had searched the log for suspicious gaps, and Cheklev was still keeping a dozen scientists busy analyzing pieces of the destroyed ship. Meanwhile, Anakin and his group rushed from planet to planet retrieving voxyn corpses for Cilghal, who plotted dispersal patterns and correlated data. The result of all that effort had been to confirm that all voxyn were indeed clones of a single creature, but also—and more importantly—to establish that their cells deteriorated at an accelerated rate. Cilghal estimated that the creatures could survive no more than a few months after release, and Han knew she had been searching for a way to use the Force to make them age even more rapidly. With any luck, she had called today's meeting to announce her success.

Luke allowed everyone a chance to express their support, then raised a hand to quiet the gathering. "We have no complaints about Cilghal's progress, but there is reason for concern. If Corran and Mirax are missing, Booster Terrik may take it on himself to go into the war zone after them."

"Not with Tionne and Kam aboard," Han said. He and Leia had finally caught up to Booster between trips to Coruscant. "They know where to find us. They won't let him try anything stupid without swinging by here to drop the students off."

"You're sure?" Luke asked. "That ship is carrying the next generation of Jedi Knights."

"Two of whom are his own grandchildren," Leia said. "Booster won't risk Valin and Jysella, even for Mirax."

Luke considered this, then nodded. "Good. I've been friends with Corran long enough to know he can take care of himself, but we'll all breathe easier if we don't have to worry about the academy students." He fell silent for a moment, then said, "Let's turn our attention to preventing the voxyn from taking any more of us. Cilghal has some interesting news."

Luke stepped over to Mara and smiled at the infant sleeping in her arms. The sight filled Han with a sense of calm, and he wondered if that was what it felt like to touch the Force. For a moment, the galaxy did not seem to be coming apart after all; the glue that held it together remained, and Yuuzhan Vong or not, it would still be there tomorrow.

Cilghal blinked twice and choked on her emotion, then found her voice. "My friends, I discovered something very interesting in that last voxyn retrieved by Ulaha and Eryl." She tipped her head toward the pair, both standing with the flock of young females that always seemed to gather around Anakin these days. "In its stomach was a full-grown ysalamiri, and in the ysalamiri's stomach were several olbio leaves."

"So these things eat ysalamiri?" Raynar asked. During Han's visits to Yavin 4, he had noticed that questions seemed to boil out of the boy the way words bubbled out of young Tahiri—two more things that had survived the invasion of the Yuuzhan Vong. "Is that what you're telling us?"

"No, Cilghal is telling us where to find the queen," Jacen said. "You ran a metals study on the leaves?"

Cilghal smiled. "A perfect match. The leaves came from Myrkr."

Lando let out a low whistle, and Han drew a disapproving glance from Leia by expressing his emotions in a less eloquent fashion. Myrkr was famous among smugglers for the high metal content of its trees, a trait that rendered orbital sensor readings unreliable and made the place perfect for secret bases. It was also the world of origination for both vornskrs and ysalamiri—the former being nasty four-legged predators that hunted the Force in their prey, the latter being docile reptiles that pushed the Force away from them in small areas. Under the best of conditions, it was hardly an ideal place to go voxyn hunting, and the task was bound to be complicated by the fact that it lay about four hundred light-years behind Yuuzhan Vong lines.

"Okay," Raynar said. "So what's the good news?"

"It's a start." Mara passed Ben to Luke, then looked to Cilghal. "You're sure the queen is there? The ysalamiri couldn't have come from another place?"

It was Jacen who answered. "Not with those leaves in its stomach. If the leaves had come from somewhere else, the metal content would be far less."

"The ysalamiri ate on Myrkr shortly before its death," Cilghal agreed. "And was eaten itself a short time later. I saw no sign of freezing or other preservation in the leaves."

The room fell eerily silent. The question before the group was as obvious as it was pressing, and the Jedi were well-enough attuned to each other to realize their next task was making a plan.

"Let us dismiss any thought of a massive attack out of hand," Ulaha Kore said. "Even if we could assemble a large-enough fleet—and we cannot—our probability of success is below single digits."

"And the mere attempt would telegraph our intentions," Luke said. "We must think of a better way."

"A commando force," Zekk said. "We sneak a small strike team in the back way—"

"Not unless you're better at it than Wraith Squadron," Han interrupted. Before leaving Coruscant, he had stopped by the New Republic Defense Force medcenter to check on Wedge and found the general in a garrulous mood. "They've been trying to penetrate the frontier between Corellia and Vortex for six months. The Yuuzhan Vong have dovin basal interdictors everywhere; the Wraiths were pulled out of every hyperspace lane they tried. And the stretch between the Perlemian Trade Route and the Hydian Way was especially bad; they were jumped this side of the frontier."

"Now we know why," Luke surmised. "The Yuuzhan Vong

suspect we will discover this secret, and they're prepared for us to take action."

"I think they're counting on it," Tahiri said. Despite her age—at just over fifteen, she was the youngest Jedi present—her comment commanded attention. Having survived a Yuuzhan Vong shaper's attempt to turn her into a Jedi-hunting slave, she understood the Yuuzhan Vong better than anyone present. "They have a saying, 'Let the enemy fight.' I don't think they're trying to be fair."

"You are very right, Tahiri," Alema said. The praise drew only an icy glare in response, but the Twi'lek pretended not to notice. She addressed herself to Luke and the senior Jedi. "On New Plympto, the Yuuzhan Vong always tried to anticipate our response and build a trap around it. You can be sure they're looking for us now."

"Then we have to fool them," Anakin said, speaking in his typical tone of teenage certainty. He turned to the younger Jedi gathered around him. "The Yuuzhan Vong want us to surrender, right? So we do—and let *them* ferry us across the frontier."

"Go on," Luke said, deftly drawing attention back to the assembly's more mature side. "We're listening."

Anakin disengaged himself from Tahiri and stepped toward his uncle. "It'll buy time for Talfaglio, too."

"That would be a plus," Luke said. "How do we do this?"

"*You* don't," Anakin said. "*We* do."

Han felt Lando's hand on his arm even before he realized he was starting forward. Lando had been there when Leia finally laid into Han for nearly getting her killed at the droid demonstration. In no uncertain terms, she had told him that while she was glad to have him back, she would not tolerate overprotectiveness in a husband any more than she would in a Noghri bodyguard—who was certainly much better at it. The next time Han smothered her or one of their children with his deranged need to control, she had warned, he would find himself flying the *Falcon* alone. Han vowed to hear his younger son out, then stepped back and quietly thanked Lando for the reminder.

Anakin looked back to his group. "We'll have a traitor turn us over to the Yuuzhan Vong on the pretext of buying time for the Talfaglion hostages. We'll set up a transfer for somewhere near Obroa-skai, let them cross the frontier, then take over the ship and fly to Myrkr." He turned to his older sister. "I know Wedge—General Antilles—has let you fly a couple of captured Yuuzhan Vong vessels. Can you teach Zekk?"

Jaina studied him suspiciously. "Why would I need to? You're not doing something that crazy without me."

A look of distress came to Anakin's face. "But you're only on temporary leave. The Rogues could call you back anytime."

"Sure they could." Jaina rolled her eyes; then her face grew hard in the same way Leia's did when she would abide no argument. "If you go, I go."

"Me, too," Tahiri said.

Anakin frowned. "You? You're too—"

"If you say *young*, I'll kick you where you really don't want to be kicked," Tahiri interrupted. "Nobody here knows the Yuuzhan Vong from the inside like I do. Can anyone else—except you, maybe—be sure they'd know a shaper laboratory? Can anyone else understand the language?"

"Good point," Jaina said. "We'll need her help to run the ship."

Anakin frowned at his sister. "Can you fly a Yuuzhan Vong ship or not? If Wedge just had you put on the cognition hood or something—"

"I've flown—and so has Tahiri, unless you've forgotten," Jaina said. She was referring to Anakin's narrow escape in the Yag'Dhul system a few months before, when, along with Corran Horn and Tahiri, he escaped an almost certain death by capturing a Yuuzhan Vong scouting ship. "Most of the piloting stuff is symbolic, but who knows about the rest? There's more to this than flying."

"And what happens when they start hailing us?" Tahiri asked. "You'll need to know what they're saying—and how to answer."

She glanced around the room expectantly. When no one responded, Han bit his tongue and waited for his brother-in-law to shoot down the plan.

Luke was very patient. Han counted the seconds, determined to heed his wife's warning, yet just as determined to keep his family safe. *All* of it.

Han made it to five seconds before his brother-in-law's silence grew unbearable. "What are you waiting for, Luke?" Han shook off Lando's hand and stepped into the Jedi circle. "Tell him why this isn't going to work."

Anakin's blue eyes darkened to angry amethyst. "Why don't *you* tell me, Dad?"

"All right, I will." He spun toward his son. "It won't work because . . ." Han was so angry he found it difficult to think of a reason. "Because you can't be certain you'll escape."

"Actually, I think I can—at least reasonably certain." Despite the indignation in his eyes, Anakin's voice remained calm. "I went behind Yuuzhan Vong lines to rescue Tahiri, and I have this." He touched his lambent-modulated lightsaber. "But most of all, I know how they think."

"*We* know how they think," Tahiri corrected.

"You know how they *think*?" Han stormed. "They aren't going to be *thinking* thud bugs at you."

Leia took his arm. "Han—"

He shook her off. "And I'll give you another reason. You can't do it because it's crazy." He shook a finger in his son's face and was vaguely surprised to realize he was shaking it at the height of his own nose. "Because you're not going, that's why."

"Han!" Leia pulled him away. "This isn't your decision."

Han turned to scowl. "It sure isn't Anakin's!"

When he turned back to Anakin, he was surprised to find his son glaring at him, more hurt than angry, yet unyielding and completely sure of himself. It was so teenage, so classically rebellious. But there was also a stoniness that even Han could not miss, a hardness born of battles already lost and won, tempered by the anguish of fallen comrades and missing friends. At seventeen, Anakin was as much a man as Han had been at thirty, had probably seen as much combat and spilled more blood than Han had in the Rebellion. And he was still so young.

"Han, the decision is Luke's," Leia said. "Not Anakin's, not yours."

She interposed herself between father and son, then gently turned Han away, leaving him to wonder where he had been when his son, when *all* his children, had grown into adults. The answer, of course, was lost—lost and wallowing in his grief as the object of that grief would never have wanted.

But the old Han Solo was back now, and the old Han Solo was not about to let the Yuuzhan Vong—or anyone else—take his family from him. He turned to Luke.

"This isn't a mission, it's a sacrifice. You can't send him in there—not Anakin, not any of them."

Luke studied the floor for a moment, then turned to Anakin. "It feels right, Anakin, but I'll lead the strike team. You stay here."

Anakin's face fell—and with it Han's heart, but that did not stop him from feeling relieved. Luke had done this sort of thing before. Han had been there helping, and, despite the queasy look on Mara's face, he knew Luke would come back—especially if Han went along to keep him out of trouble. He looked over to Mara to reassure her and saw that no reassurance was needed. Mara's jaw was set and her eyes were hard, but there was a calmness in her expression that Han found difficult to understand—a knowledge of the danger and all it might cost her, and yet a stoic acceptance of fact. *Somebody* had to kill the voxyn, and if it had to be Luke, then it had to be.

Anakin studied his uncle for moment, then managed a curt nod and stepped back into his group. He refused to meet his father's eye. For a time Han thought Anakin would leave the chamber, but his son had grown into a man in so many more ways than he realized. Seeming to sense how his reaction would dictate that of his large circle of friends, Anakin remained with the group, ready to offer Luke his full support.

After a tense moment of silence, Tenel Ka stepped forward, her usual Dathomir warrior's dress now covered by the ubiquitous vacuum emergency suit still necessary everywhere on Eclipse. "Master Skywalker, forgive me for speaking so candidly, but have you lost your mind?"

The young woman's customary bluntness filled the room with uneasy chuckles.

Even Luke smiled. "I don't think so, why?"

"Because you must know that Anakin's plan would never work for you," she said. "It depends on the Yuuzhan Vong taking us for granted, and that would never happen with *any* Jedi Master. Even if they did not kill you on the spot, they would take every precaution to render you helpless."

"She has a point," Ganner said. "The leader has to be someone they won't be too worried about—and someone they'll believe could be duped by a traitor." He flashed a white smile beneath his mustache. "Someone like me."

Even Han could sense the reluctance of the other Jedi.

When no one volunteered to join the handsome Jedi Knight, Jacen said, "Maybe *none* of us should be going."

This drew a frown from both of his siblings, and Anakin said, "Jacen, this is no time to stand around debating good and evil. Either we kill those things, or those things kill the Jedi."

"And if we destroy the queen, the Yuuzhan Vong will retaliate against New Republic citizens even more severely," Jacen replied. "Do we want that on our heads?"

"Jacen, the blood is not on *our* hands," Alema said, lekku trembling angrily. "It is on theirs."

"A convenient position, but will it save more lives than it costs?" Ulaha asked. "As Jedi, that must be our only concern."

And they were off, voices rising and gestures growing sharp as they argued the same point they had been contesting since the destruction of the *Nebula Chaser*. Alema spoke most forcefully against Jacen, no doubt because she could not bear the burden of New Plympto's destruction and her sister's death. Ulaha and Jacen led the argument for Jedi responsibility; they were supported by a surprisingly large number, including Streen, Cilghal, and, most astonishingly, the Barabel hatchmates.

In the end, the debate grew so heated that C-3PO had to be summoned to take a crying Ben to his nursery, and Luke was forced to call repeatedly for quiet. Finally, he used the Force to project his voice directly into the mind of everyone present, and a silence as tense as it was embarrassed fell over the room.

Luke glanced over the Jedi calmly, then spoke in barely a whisper. "It comes down to a simple question: How do we fight a brutal, evil enemy without growing brutal and evil ourselves?"

"This is so," Tenel Ka confirmed.

Luke looked at her for a moment, then shook his head wearily. "I wish I had the answer, but the Force has refused to guide me in this—as it has all of you, I think." He waited a moment, and when no one denied this, continued, "What has grown clear to me is that the time has come for us to choose one path. I assume there is no one among us who believes we should actually surrender to the Yuuzhan Vong?"

Though Jacen alarmed Han by briefly looking as though he might disagree, he remained as silent as the rest of the Jedi.

Luke nodded. "As I thought. So, do we destroy the voxyn and risk more retaliation? Or do we accept our losses in the hope that doing so will save the New Republic many more lives than it costs us?"

"What are you asking for?" Ganner demanded. "A vote?"

"Your opinion," Luke clarified. "Whatever I decide, I want to know that everyone has been heard."

Ganner considered this for a moment, then nodded. "All right, I say we go after the queen."

"Accept our losses," the first Barabel, Tesar Sebatyne, rasped.

His female hatchmates echoed his sentiment, and Luke started around the circle. Though Han felt in his heart that they should go after the queen, he could not help giving a silent cheer every time someone supported accepting their losses. Tenel Ka had been right about a Jedi Master not being able to lead the strike team, which meant that Anakin—and no doubt Jaina, too—would be trusting their lives to a plan almost as foolhardy as trying to break Leia out of the Death Star's detention center. If the Jedi opted for accepting their losses, at least he and Leia would be close by in the *Falcon* to keep an eye on their children—until a pack of voxyn caught them. Sooner or later, somebody was going to have to destroy that queen. Han just did not see why it had to be *his* children.

By the time the question came around to Leia's end of the circle, opinion was divided almost evenly, with a slight edge toward destroying the voxyn.

Lando leaned close to Han. "You can breathe easy, old buddy. Leia and Mara will want to go after the queen, but Cilghal and Streen are against it."

Though Han knew no gambler in the galaxy could read faces as well as Lando Calrissian, he did not feel as relieved as he might have. The way Leia looked at him made clear enough how she felt about Anakin's injured pride, but there was more to it than her anger. Han was being selfish and she knew it—and she knew what his selfishness might cost the Jedi in the end.

"Han?"

Caught by surprise, Han looked from Leia to her brother. "Yeah?"

"Your opinion?"

"Mine?"

"You're part of this," Luke said. "You have a say."

Han glanced back to Leia and, seeing the silent plea in her eyes, wondered how she could be so strong.

"Okay, give me a minute."

He closed his eyes and, wishing someone could teach him one of those Jedi relaxation techniques, tried to calm himself with a few deep breaths. It didn't help, not really. He knew why his son wanted to lead this mission, why Anakin had fought in every major Jedi battle since the invasion began, why he had charged off alone to rescue Tahiri.

Chewbacca.

No matter how much Anakin claimed otherwise, it all came down to Chewbacca.

"Dad," Anakin said. "Just do what you think's right."

"I didn't need to hear that—I really didn't." Han opened his eyes and found his son standing in front of him. He started to take the boy by his shoulders, but realized how ridiculous he would look spreading his arms so wide and clasped a forearm instead. "You don't have to do this, you know."

"I know." The hurt in Anakin's face was instantly replaced by an alarming brashness. "But I'm going to."

With the uneasy feeling that he had seen the same cocky look in the mirror thirty years before, Han turned and found Leia staring at him openmouthed.

He shrugged and gave her a lopsided grin. "Kids. What can you do?"

"I take it you favor destroying the queen," Luke said.

He finished the polling, which came out exactly as Lando had predicted—except that, with Han behind the mission, Luke decided to go after the voxyn queen.

"I expect everyone present to support this decision," he said. "We'll do what we can to protect the innocent, but we *will* be sending a strike team to Myrkr."

Jacen turned to his brother. "Then let me be the first to volunteer."

"You?" No one looked more surprised than Anakin. "But you're against it."

"That doesn't matter," Jacen said. "Nobody is as good with animals as I am. If you have to track down the queen or something, you're going to need me."

"When he's right, he's right, Little Brother," Jaina said, stepping to her twin's side. "And I believe we've already agreed that I'm coming."

"Like I had a choice." Anakin smiled, then turned to the other young Jedi around him. "Anyone who wants to volunteer, see me later—after we've put together some kind of plan."

Han felt like his knees would buckle. All three of them were going, all of his children on the same crazy mission—and he wouldn't be there to protect them, couldn't even consider going along because he wasn't a Jedi.

Leia looked no happier than he. Her face was pale, her lip trembling, and still she somehow found the strength to hold her head up and look proud. "There is one condition," she said, turning to Lando. "I want you to deliver them."

For the first time in a very long while, Lando looked surprised. "Me?"

"You're the only one who can make this work," Leia said. "I know I wasn't much help with Borsk, but if you'll do this—"

Lando raised his hands. "We're way past favors here," he said. "I'll help any way I can."

Chapter 14

The hulking war droid rotated two hundred degrees on his waist coupling and pointed the business end of his blaster arm at Raynar Thul. "Plan point fourteen, Private."

"I'm not a private." Raynar was dressed as usual in the colors of his family's merchant house, in this case scarlet breeches, purple waist sash, and a golden tunic that matched the color of his bristly blond hair. "We're not in the military."

"Point fourteen," 1-1A insisted.

Raynar rolled his eyes. "The crew bursts into the dining area and gets the drop on the Jedi," he said. "Point fifteen. The Jedi yield their weapons."

"Lightsabers," 1-1A corrected. "And I did not ask for point fifteen, soldier."

"I'm not a soldier," Raynar said wearily.

Anakin and the sixteen members of his strike team were sitting on the lush conform couches on the observation deck of Lando Calrissian's private space yacht, rehearsing the plan Anakin had worked out with Luke, Lando, his father, mother, and about half the Jedi on Eclipse. There were a thousand little details, but basically the scheme called for the *Lady Luck*'s crew to "surprise" the Jedi when the Yuuzhan Vong boarded. As the invaders took their prisoners away, a pair of YVH war droids would slip out of the disposal lock with an equipment pod and attach to the bottom of the enemy boarding shuttle. When the shuttle returned to its mothership, the droids would ride along, concealed from view by the shuttle itself. To make certain the droids went undetected, the strike team would stage a diversion.

"Point thirty-two, sir."

Recalling that the droid considered him the group officer, Anakin looked up to find 1-1A's blaster arm leveled at his face. As usual, staring down the black tunnel of death brought his thoughts into sharp focus.

"I use the Force to tear open the weapons locker and pass out blasters," Anakin said. "The blasters will be stored with power packs disengaged."

"This part troubles me," Tenel Ka said. "Surely, the Yuuzhan Vong will find it too convenient."

"Consider the alternative," Lando said, stepping onto the observation deck with them. "My crew is all volunteer, but they won't die just to make things look good."

"Which only proves her point," Ganner said. As the oldest Jedi Knight aboard, he would serve as a decoy commander so that Anakin would remain free—or as free as possible—to quietly lead the group. "The Yuuzhan Vong aren't stupid."

"No, they're not, which is why I can sell this," Lando said. "Disengaging power packs is a common safety procedure—one that anyone about to betray a shipload of Jedi would certainly take."

"This came up in the planning meeting," Anakin said. "Dad thought it was a good idea."

Ganner shrugged, then—much to Anakin's relief—nodded.

Serving as a decoy leader had been Ganner's own suggestion, and Anakin's biggest worry so far was that the older man would have trouble separating the two roles.

"I have a question," Raynar said.

"Why am I not surprised," Jaina muttered.

Lando smiled. "Ask away. You need to be confident in this plan."

"Yuuzhan Vong ships are alive, right?" he asked. "So how come this one isn't going to feel the droids attaching?"

"That would be like a shenbit feeling something on itz shell," Bela Hara rasped. "Armor serves no purpose if one feelz pain when it is struck."

"These are hulls, not armor," Raynar objected. "And if the ships are alive—"

"They're not alive like that," Jaina said. "They have brains, but the brains only control certain functions, like computers do aboard our ships. And they *don't* have feeling in their hulls—at least none of the ships I've been on did."

"They couldn't," Jacen said. "Feeling requires nerve endings, and nerve endings close enough to feel the exterior of the hull would freeze solid. Imagine standing on Hoth barefoot."

This seemed to convince Raynar. He winced and nodded to Lando. "Thanks—*now* I'm confident."

YVH 1-1A swiveled toward Lowbacca. "Point thirty-three, Private."

Lowbacca groaned something long and low that Anakin recognized as a crude offer involving a memory wipe. The Wookiee's translation droid, Em Teedee, flitted down in front of him.

"Are you sure you want to say that to a war droid, Master Lowbacca?"

When Lowbacca answered with a growl, Em Teedee zipped around behind Tekli and emitted a burst of static that caused 1-1A's photoreceptors to light.

Lando interposed himself between Lowbacca and the war droid. "That's all for now, One-One-A. Stand down." He shot Lowbacca a weary look, then turned to the others. "We've transferred the extra two YVHs and your equipment pod, and Tendra is down on the bridge plotting our route with the crew."

"We're ready," Tahiri said confidently. "One-One-A has seen to that."

Lando's expression grew even more stern. "One-One-A is a droid. He can make you drill and practice, but he can't prepare you—not for something like this."

"I'm not sure I understand," Ulaha Kore ventured. "Our rehearsals have been flawless. Certainly, we must be ready to improvise—every good ensemble is—but current projections give us a . . . seventy-two percent chance of success."

Anakin did not want to ask about the margin of error. There were still so many unknowns that he suspected the swing could place their chances either above 100 percent or below 50.

Lando sat across from the Bith and stared into her glassy eyes, his own gaze harder and colder than Anakin had ever seen. "What I'm talking about can't be measured." He glanced at the others. "Things are going to go wrong. No matter how many times we rehearse, no matter how well we plan, this isn't going to happen the way we expect. You'll need to react fast."

"No different from any battle," Ganner said.

"This isn't a battle, Rhysode. Get that into your head." Lando glared at Ganner until Ganner looked away, then continued to glare some more. "You're not going as warriors, you're going as spies. You'll have to do things that don't sit well inside. You can't balk. You can't even hesitate."

"We won't." It was Alema Rar who said this, and Anakin knew by the look in her eyes that she, at least, understood exactly what Lando was telling them. "*I* won't."

Lando studied the Twi'lek only a moment before nodding.

"You've been there, I know." He turned to the others and said, "Watch Alema. She'll do what's necessary, and so should you."

"What are you saying?" Jacen asked. "That any means justify the ends?"

"He means we have only two concerns," Alema said, the silkiness of her voice belying the steel of her words. "The first is to complete our mission. The second is to return alive."

"That way lies the dark side," Jacen insisted. "If we have no concern for the methods we use to win our goals, we are no better than the Emperor . . . or the Yuuzhan Vong."

"Perhaps so," Alema agreed. "But if the path before us is dark, we dare not shy away—not for our own sakes, but for the sake of those who will fall if we fail."

"And for Numa and Lusa and Eelysa and everyone else the voxyn have taken already," Raynar added.

Alema rewarded his support with a vaguely promising smile. "Of course. For their sakes most of all."

"No. Vengeance leads to the dark side," Zekk said. "I won't be a part of something like that."

Everyone started to talk at once, Alema and Raynar arguing that destroying the voxyn and defeating the Yuuzhan Vong would justify any action, Zekk telling them they didn't know what they were talking about, Jacen insisting it was wrong to put the ends before the means. Though the others seemed to fall somewhere between the two poles, they spoke just as loudly, drawing even Eryl Besa and Jovan Drark, an imperturbable Rodian, into the argument on opposite sides. Only the Barabels, squatting in the corner with their reptilian pupils narrowed to vertical slits, seemed in possession of themselves.

Anakin sighed deep inside, then noticed Lando watching him and realized just how wise his mother had been in choosing the arms merchant to ferry them to the enemy. As sincere as Lando's warning about not hesitating might be, there was a hidden agenda behind his words. Knowing the strike team was going to have this argument eventually, he had intentionally provoked it while they could take time to work things through—and now he was waiting for Anakin to solve the problem.

"Quiet." Anakin waited a moment, then tried again, and when that failed, shouted, "Shut up! That's an order!"

His rudeness, and the Force he used to augment his voice, finally got through to the others. Before the argument could resume, he continued, "Nobody is turning to the dark side on this mission." He glared at Raynar and Alema. "Is that clear?"

"I didn't mean to suggest we should," Alema began quietly. "Only that we can't shy—"

"Is *that* clear?" Anakin demanded again.

Alema's lekku curled at the tips, but she pushed her lip out and said, "Of course, Anakin."

Anakin felt more than glimpsed the strange smirk that came to Tahiri's face. While she was not fond of any of the strike team's female Jedi, she seemed to truly dislike Alema. Deciding to puzzle over the matter later, he turned to Raynar and cocked his brow.

Raynar nodded. "Fine. Who'd want to anyway?"

Anakin accepted this and turned to Zekk and Jacen. "But Lando's right. We may have to do some things we don't feel good about, and do them quickly. If you can't live with that, maybe you should catch a ride home on the freighter."

"What kind of things?" Jacen asked. "If we talk about our limits now—"

"*Jacen!*" Anakin hissed. "Can you do this?"

Instead of answering, Jacen looked around for support. He found it, of course, especially from Zekk and Tenel Ka, but Anakin began to think even his brother's special talent for handling animals might not be worth the discord he would bring to the team. He looked to Lando for guidance, but found only the expressionless face of a seasoned gambler. Anakin would have to solve this problem on his own; where they were going, there would be no advice from old heroes of the Rebellion.

Anakin took a deep breath, using a Jedi relaxation technique to clear his mind so he could concentrate. Throughout the Yuuzhan Vong invasion, he and Jacen had been drifting apart, until they had reached a point where they had barely been able to speak to each other without an undercurrent of resentment and blame. Those wounds were only now beginning to heal. The last thing Anakin wanted to do was remove his brother from the team and open them again, but he had to think of the mission—and of the others who would be on it.

Anakin turned to his brother. "Jacen, maybe—"

"Anakin, I've had a brainstorm!" Though Jaina's tone was enthusiastic, Anakin could feel his sister's agitation through the Force. Nearly as troubled by the schism as the brothers themselves, she had spoken to them both about trying to bridge it. "You know how we've been worried about the breaking?"

"Yeah?" Anakin answered cautiously. Everyone on Eclipse knew how much value the Yuuzhan Vong placed on trying to break the will of Jedi prisoners. His biggest concern was that their "captors" would start it aboard the transfer vessel, and that someone in the group would not be able to endure it long enough to cross the frontier. "What's that have to do with what we're talking about?"

"You remember how we used that telepathic Force union during that first Yuuzhan Vong attack at Dubrillion?" Jaina asked. The three siblings had reached out to each other through the Force to share perceptions. "What if Jacen could help us *all* do that? We could use the link to bolster each other mentally and emotionally."

"This is a good plan," Tenel Ka said. "Every interrogator knows that mental isolation is key to breaking a victim's resistance."

Anakin saw the potential—just as he saw how desperately his sister was trying to prevent the gulf between him and Jacen from widening any farther. Cautiously, he asked, "How can we do that?"

Jaina's expression grew confident. "I've been talking to Tesar and his hatchmates about the Wild Knights' combat tactics." She glanced in the Barabels' direction. "I think we could adapt a couple to our situation."

"Yes, this one thinkz we could," Tesar said. "Perhapz we could even use the bond to create a big meld-fight."

Anakin raised his brow. Meld-fight was what the Barabels had called their incredible display of cohesion during the confused battle at Froz. "An interesting possibility."

"But we'd need Jacen," Jaina pressed. "He's the only one with enough empathic power to bind us all together."

Or to drive us apart, Anakin thought. But, as he studied the expectant faces watching him, he realized much of the damage had been done already. Sending Jacen back now would not only disappoint his sister, it would alienate Zekk, Tenel Ka, and many of the others who shared his concerns about the dark side. It would also widen the gulf between the two brothers—and Anakin wanted that about as much as he wanted another Yuuzhan Vong slave seed implanted in his head.

"Jacen, you have to do what I say when I say it." Anakin caught his brother's gaze and held it. "If something feels wrong, it's on my head, not yours. If you can't live with that, I'm sorry, but you can't come."

Having sensed how close Anakin had been to sending him home before, Jacen knew better than to hesitate. He nodded and said, "I trust your judgment, Anakin. I really do."

Chapter 15

The data readouts went wild, then Danni was slammed back into her g-seat as Wonetun put them into a tight turn. A stocky Brubb reptoid from gravity-heavy Baros, Wonetun kept the inertial compensators dialed down to 92 percent because he liked to know when the blastboat shuddered; if someone in the crew got sick or blacked out for a few seconds, that was better than stressing the ancient hull welds. Danni fought to keep the purple out of her vision and strained to watch her display. The readouts continued to dance. It didn't mean she had solved her riddle—Saba Sebatyne had not even said there was a yammosk present—but it meant something.

The gunners vaporized the skips with a volley of stutter-fire from the blastboat's big laser cannons, then Danni's skin prickled with sudden apprehension. Still, she resisted the temptation to look away from her instruments. The readouts were rising and falling in intermittent surges that looked suspiciously contrived, and Danni would not let herself be distracted. Her fingers began to fly over her control panels, defining sensor sweeps and activating recorders.

"Saba, could there be a yammosk out there?" She still did not look away from her instruments. "Please tell me there's a yammosk out there."

"Oh yes, there is a yammosk. No doubt." Saba's tone was distracted, and she did not seem to catch the significance of Danni's question. Speaking into the blastboat's comm unit, she ordered, "Wild Knightz, prepare for return to the *Jolly Man*. Break left on this one's mark . . ."

Danni braced herself. The *Jolly Man* was not the cramped blastboat in which she was riding, but a fast-freighter standing some distance off in a pocket of space dust. It served the squadron as a mobile base, and to carry the Vigilances and Howlrunners—which had no hyperdrives—into and out of battle.

"Three, two, mark!"

Danni strained to keep her head turned toward her data screens as Wonetun whipped the blastboat around. Several more readouts jumped to life, hovered there an instant, then dropped back to close-zero. When the data bars she had been watching answered with a flurry of oscillations, Danni ruled out coincidence. She was seeing a comm code, not some random graviton eddy.

Saba must have felt her excitement through the Force, for the Barabel rasped, "You have found something, Danni Quee?"

"I think so." The blastboat's hull thrummed as the gunners opened up. "Gravitic modulation. That's how the yammosk communicates."

"Ah." For the Barabel, it was almost a cry of excitement. Crimson flashes filled the ship interior as plasma balls started to burst against the shields. "If this one may make a suggestion, you should open a comm feed so your data will not be lost."

Danni tore her eyes away from her data screens. "Sith sabers!"

Curving through space to intercept them was what at first looked like an entire ring of asteroids, but which the plasma-burping nodules on the closest monoliths quickly identified as an enemy fleet. She could not believe even the Wild Knights warranted such an effort—then she realized they did not.

For the past few days, the squadron had been working a choke point not far from the gem-mining world of Arkania, ambushing Yuuzhan Vong corvettes as they felt their way out of the war zone. Everyone had assumed these patrols were merely scouting New Republic positions, but now it seemed obvious they had been clearing an invasion route. Danni did not need a galactic holograph to know that capturing Arkania would put the Yuuzhan Vong close to both the Perlemian Trade Route and the Hydian Way, and in position to threaten much of the Colonies region. She opened the data feed to the *Jolly Man,* then added an urgent alert for the subspace emergency band.

The leading elements of the fleet fired a volley of magma missiles, forcing Wonetun to put the blastboat into a stomach-churning series of loops and rolls. Saba ordered him to turn up the inertial compensator so she could stay conscious. The enemy fleet was now so close it looked like one huge spray of yorik coral.

One of the large lumps opened its nose and vomited grutchins, half-meter insects resembling turfhoppers. The blastboat's gunners switched targets, laying a barrage of laserfire in the creatures' path. Those things could eat through a titanium hull in seconds.

Saba spoke into the comm unit. "There is our target—the cruiser at the bottom of the formation. Do you see it?"

"The one on the end?" Drif Lij, pilot of one of the squadron's old T-65 X-wings, commed.

"No, that they will expect," Saba said. "Three shipz in. He is ahead of himself."

"Got it," Drif replied.

A flurry of comm clicks confirmed everyone else did, too, and Danni sensed the squadron's fear changing to resolve.

Saba said, "Glowball in five, four . . ."

Izal Waz, an Arcona gunner with a nasty salt habit, stopped firing and drew inward. Though his compound eyes were incapable of distinguishing shapes, their sensitivity to movement made him the best gunner in the squadron. As Saba continued her count-down, those golden eyes grew glassy and distant, like they did during a salt binge, and the veins on his anvil-shaped head popped in concentration.

"Mark," Saba said.

A white sphere of illumination engulfed the blastboat. Danni thought *shield overload,* but Wonetun straightened out and they accelerated. When no plasma balls came boiling through the hull, she looked outside and found the squadron camouflaged in a sun-bright orb.

"What's this?" Danni gasped.

"You have seen ghost sunz?" Saba asked.

"Parhelions? Of course," Danni said. "Sometimes from two suns at once."

"It is like that," Saba explained. "Izal Waz callz it his glowball. He is using the Force to collect light."

Danni eyed Izal with newfound respect. "What's it do?"

"What does it do?" Saba sissed at this. "It hides us. Is that not enough?"

Though the sphere had to be a kilometer across, the Wild Knights were clustered close to the blastboat, a dozen ghostly shapes pooling defenses. Drif's X-wing hung just meters away. Its ion engines were pouring blue efflux into the glowball, feeding the intensity of the general radiance. Plasma balls and magma missiles continued to pour blindly into the glowball, but most missed by a wide margin, and those that came close were defeated by the Wild Knights' combined defenses.

"Does the *Jolly Man* have enough data yet?" Saba asked.

Danni checked her instruments. The readouts were dancing like crazy. "This is good stuff," she said. "The longer we stay, the better."

Saba's diamond-shaped pupils narrowed. "But do they have *enough?*"

Danni did a quick statistical calculation in her head, then nodded. "We could use a higher significance level, but—"

"We must train you to fly an A-wing, Danni Quee. The Wild Knightz could use someone as crazy as you." Saba turned and commed, "Shorthopperz, break for the *Jolly Man*. We'll see you at home."

Shielded by the still-expanding glowball, the squadron's two Howlrunners and three Vigilances broke for the fast-freighter.

"Passive sensors, no lasers," Saba ordered. She turned to Danni and pointed at Izal, who was slumped in a trance in the upper cannon turret. "Change places. The glowball requires his concentration."

Danni eyed the big Arcona, trying to imagine how she was going to move someone more than twice her size without breaking his concentration. "Uh, I don't think I can lift him," she said. "Maybe you could—"

"This one *could*, but she told *you* to." Saba glared out of one dark eye. "You are Jedi, Danni Quee. Size matterz not."

Danni swallowed. She had been studying the Force for almost two years now, but no one seemed able to explain the theory behind it—even Luke always spoke of *feeling* and *doing*, never how or why—and it was still the last solution that came to mind. An impatient tongue began to flicker between Saba's pebbly lips. Danni let out a long relaxing breath, then pictured the tall Arcona slipping out of his seat and coming to a rest in the one opposite her, then reached out with the Force and made it so.

To her relief, Izal settled into the chair as though he had moved himself, and the glowball remained intact. Danni started to climb into the turret as ordered, but Saba caught her by the shoulder and pulled her back down.

"Do you never train, Danni Quee?" She climbed into the turret. "This one will save us herself. Watch. Learn."

Danni did not understand until a moment later, when a volley of magma missiles came streaking in and her heart leapt into her throat. She felt the Y-wing weapon operators reach out and start nudging, and then there was no time for questions. A crimson spiral loomed large. Saba pushed, and it shot past meters above her turret. Someone else redirected a grutchin, and Danni spent the next eternity watching the Barabel use the Force to push, lift, and turn Yuuzhan Vong missiles.

Finally, Saba asked, "What does your machine say now, Danni Quee? Has the yammosk seen through our ruse?"

Danni stepped over to look at her display. The gravity arrow readouts were dancing.

"Same as before," she reported. "The yammosk seems to be giving orders, everyone else is quiet. What that means, I have no idea."

Saba bared her needle-teeth and sissed in satisfaction. "It meanz it thinkz it has us." She dropped out of the turret and motioned Danni back into the gunner's seat. "Ready all weapons. Back out and drop the block on this one's mark. Three, two . . ."

Danni barely climbed into the turret before "mark." The cargo door thumped open, expelling a two-ton square of durasteel, and the blastboat decelerated and slammed her into the transparisteel dome, and she grabbed for the cannon triggers and pushed herself into the firing seat. Outside, the sunlike sphere of the glowball was shrinking away, with a comet's tail of magma missiles, plasma balls, and grutchins trailing behind.

An uproarious rasp erupted from the blastboat's main deck, where Saba stood over the instrument panel, scaly shoulders shaking as the data readouts danced.

"Oh, that got them," she sissed. "That got them good."

A plasma ball erupted against the shields, and Drif's voice came over the comm speaker.

"Danni, the hostiles are *behind* us."

"Sorry."

She spun the turret around to see the Wild Knights' fighters looping up to meet a dozen coralskippers. Pointing more than aiming, she squeezed the triggers and felt the twin laser cannons come to life. Long streaks of crimson stained the starlit darkness, forcing the skips to roll and twist as they descended on the squadron.

The blastboat jerked forward, then Wonetun announced, "The cruiser wants to pull our shields."

"Squadron, form on the blastboat on this one's mark," Saba said. "Five—"

The blastboat slipped backward, and Wonetun reported, "Shields gone."

"Twoonemark!" Saba finished.

The blastboat accelerated. Danni's laser cannons went wild, catching a coralskipper by sheer chance and reducing it to pebbles. The X-wings and Y-wings looped back to encircle the blastboat, masking the larger ship behind their own shields.

"Keep firing, Danni," Drif urged. "You've got our backs."

Danni swung the cannons toward the largest lump in the sky—a corvette analog angling down to cut them off—and squeezed the triggers. Her crimson bolts shot straight into its nose—and vanished into a black hole. She strafed the hull at full power, back and forth, back and forth. The shielding crews continued to catch her attacks, but the corvette fell behind as its dovin basals diverted to protecting the ship.

Danni fired a few more seconds, until the battle drew too close to the enemy cruiser, and the corvette and coralskippers broke off. She swung her cannons forward. A mere two hundred meters distant, the glowball was as large as a class-three comet, and space beyond was filled by the Yuuzhan Vong cruiser—a lumpy silhouette as big as some moons, spewing plasma and magma into the glowball. The golden sphere flattened and began to shrink as the enemy shielding crews drew it toward one of their singularities.

"Ready missiles and torpedoes. Spread pattern," Saba ordered. "Hold . . . hold . . ."

The glowball distorted into an undulating flower pattern and shrank to the size of Danni's thumbnail.

"Fire all!" Saba commanded. "Cancel glowball."

The glowball blinked out of existence, then Izal thumped to the deck, exhausted. The Yuuzhan Vong cruiser fell ominously dark as the weapons crews struggled to retrain their weapons. The Wild Knights launched a second, then third volley of concussion missiles and proton torpedoes, and suddenly the darkness ahead was all spiraling ion trails and looping plasma trails.

"Darken blast tinting." Saba used the Force to lift Izal back into a seat, then swung around and strapped him in. "Prepare for concussion impact."

"Concussion impact?" Danni cried, grabbing her seat restraints. "You're ramming it?"

"Ramming it?" Saba erupted into a fit of sissing, and even Wonetun rumbled with laughter. "Danni Quee, you are so crazy!"

Then Danni remembered the block—the block the Yuuzhan Vong could not have seen when they grabbed the glowball—the two tons of durasteel accelerated to no small percentage of light-speed. The energy on impact would be equal to mass multiplied by velocity squared, divided by . . .

Danni was still doing the calculations when space turned white.

Chapter 16

*T*he coufee fell, and the sanctum filled with the strange odor of alien blood and an endless, undulating wail. Tsavong Lah waited until the priests began their real work, then stepped away from the spatter pit so he could focus his thoughts on the bungled sneak attack.

"You do not wish to know Yun-Yammka's will?" Vergere asked, one eye still fixed on the howling slave.

"The Slayer's will is no mystery. How to accomplish it . . . that is another matter." He waved his hand toward the priests and their sacrifice. "They serve in their way, I in mine."

Vergere's beaklike mouth cracked open in what Tsavong Lah had come to recognize as a mocking smile. "You doubt the accuracy of Vaecta's seers?"

"Only the gods are infallible." Tsavong Lah glanced into the pit and smiled at what was happening there. "The priests are faithful servants, but until they can tell me how the *Jeedai* work their magic, I must do my own work."

"You make too much of these Jedi."

Vergere looked back to the spatter pit and fixed her eye on the shrieking sacrifice. The Ithorian's T-shaped head curled in her direction, his gaze lingering on hers as his eyes grew glassy and distant. His screams subsided much sooner than they should have, and he slipped into that strange tranquility that sometimes came over slaves even in their most anguished moments. A priest stepped in front of the Ithorian and tried unsuccessfully to draw him back into his pain.

"A pity for the invasion." Vergere's tone was that of a thwarted child. "The priests are sure to take a dim view of that."

Tsavong Lah glanced down to find her feathers hanging flat in disappointment. Sometimes she seemed more a Yuuzhan Vong to him than his own warriors.

"It was a *Jeedai* squadron that intercepted the invasion of Arkania," he said, returning to her earlier remark. "And it was only two *Jeedai* who forced us to sacrifice New Plympto."

"Then destroy the Talfaglion convoys," Vergere said. "That will draw them out."

Tsavong Lah raised his brow. "And sacrifice Nom Anor?"

"It would not be such a sacrifice."

Tsavong Lah smiled faintly. "You have high ambitions for such an unassuming creature."

Vaecta stepped over to their side of the spatter pit and looked up. A stoop-shouldered female with an aged and wrinkled face, she did not bow to Tsavong Lah or cross her blood-streaked arms in salute. During a ritual, the priestess was beholden to Lord Shimrra himself and would die—gladly—before offering deference to any other.

"The slave's silence will not please the Slayer. You should not go through with the attack."

Tsavong Lah looked away from her. "The decision is mine."

"Lord Shimrra has made that clear," she agreed. "I was given to believe Lord Shimrra also made clear you should consider the will of the gods in all things."

Tsavong Lah continued to look away. "But the decision is mine."

Vaecta did not disagree.

"Good." Tsavong Lah looked back to the priestess. "You will ask Yun-Yammka to punish the commanders who allowed the *Jeedai* squadron to escape. I will order their replacements to make a halfhearted assault on the planet and withdraw."

"If you tease Yun-Yammka, he will want lives," Vaecta warned. "Many lives."

"Of course." Though Tsavong Lah felt certain the god of war would understand the value of a good feint, it was better to be safe about these things. "He shall have eight thousand."

"Twenty thousand would be better," Vaecta retorted.

"Twenty, then."

Tsavong Lah turned and left the sanctum, already adjusting his plans to accommodate the ritual. The extra sacrifices would require a full escort instead of a single ship, putting an unnecessary strain on his already overextended logistics train.

Vergere waddled up to his side. "Why take that from Vaecta? Even with reinforcements, the New Republic can't hold Arkania. Capture it and make a fool of her."

Tsavong Lah whirled on Vergere. "You question my judgment?" He raised his foot as though to kick her. "You think you know better than I how to win battles?"

Vergere gave his leg a contemptuous glance, then bristled her feathers and moved a step closer. "If you have a better idea, all you need do is say so."

It was all Tsavong Lah could do not to burst out laughing. "Around you? I think not." Supreme commanders and high prefects trembled at his slightest frown, yet Vergere, this ugly little bird, dismissed his fury as though it were nothing. "You, I must watch. It will amuse me, if nothing else."

Chapter 17

Lando let his sweaty palm brush against his pant leg, then transferred the datapad to the somewhat drier hand and displayed the screen to the subaltern of the Yuuzhan Vong boarding party. The picture showed seventeen young Jedi Knights crowded around the *Lady Luck*'s dining table. Though their bowls were filled with green thakitillo—Lando had ordered his chef to serve only the finest fare on this journey—none of the Jedi were eating. Most were not even holding their spoons.

"They seem agitated," the subaltern said. A brutish warrior with a fringe of spindly black hair, he stared at the datapad from arm's length, as though keeping his distance would prevent the instrument from defiling him. "You are sure they do not know we are here?"

"They're Jedi," Lando answered, feigning irritation at a foolish question. "They can certainly sense my crew's apprehension, but I won't claim to know what's in their minds. All I can say is the viewports have been closed the entire trip."

After a moment, the subaltern nodded to himself and turned to an unarmed—but heavily armored—superior waiting outside the *Lady Luck*'s air lock.

"Eia dag lightsabers, *Duman Yaght. Yenagh doa Jeedai."*

The superior stepped out of the red-ribbed transfer tunnel. A little smaller than his subordinates, this one had sculpted his face into a gridwork of raised scars. Like the subaltern of the boarding party, he wore two small villips on his shoulders instead of the usual one. He stopped across from Lando and looked expectant.

"This is Fitzgibbon Lane, holder of the *Stardream,*" the subaltern said, supplying the false names Lando was traveling under. "He is the one who sent the message."

Lando stared at the subaltern and waited for him to introduce his leader. When the warrior grew uncomfortable and looked down, Lando shifted his gaze to the superior and continued to wait. As nervous as he was about this particular swindle, he knew better than to open negotiations on anything less than equal footing.

After a moment, the superior said, "I am Duman Yaght, commander of the *Exquisite Death.* You have some *Jeedai* for me?"

"For your warmaster," Lando corrected. Taking the commander's presence as a sign of eagerness, he turned the datapad toward the Yuuzhan Vong and dangled the bait. "I have seventeen, in fact."

The subaltern scowled and reached out to knock the profane instrument aside, but the commander raised a hand.

"No. This I must see for myself."

Duman Yaght peered into the vidscreen, where Anakin and a few others were halfheartedly spooning thakitillo into their mouths. The strike team had not been warned about the boarding, in part because Lando wanted their reactions to appear genuine, in part because the Yuuzhan Vong had come so quickly. The *Lady Luck* had been drifting along beside an outbound comet, waiting for the nav computer to plot the final leg of their journey, when the boarding shuttle came swinging out of the tail. It had headed straight for the docking portal, a wormlike transfer tunnel already extending to make contact.

There was barely time to alert Tendra before the bridge alarm announced contact at the air lock. Lando authorized equalization and rushed back to find the subaltern already opening the exterior hatch. A check on his datapad revealed a corvette-sized coral ship swinging over the comet to cover the shuttle's approach, and Lando realized the vessel was lying in wait when he entered the system. He had almost felt foolish—until he realized what the clever maneuver told him about the eagerness of the Yuuzhan Vong commander.

"Satisfied?" Lando asked. "I'd ask them to levitate, but that might give us away."

"That won't be necessary. We have already confirmed their nature."

"Really?" Lando did not like the sound of that, but knew better than to ask for details. "If you want them, let the Talfaglion hostages go."

"If I want them, I will take them," Duman Yaght said.

Lando raised his datapad and depressed a function key. "We both know what seventeen Jedi can do with warning. Don't make me release this button."

The commander stepped closer. "You think that would matter to me?"

"Of course not." Lando sneered with more confidence than he felt. "Even a space boulder like the *Exquisite Death* would destroy this barge in about three seconds. And what a pity that would be— no sacrifices for Yun-Yammka, and no more Jedi deliveries for your warmaster."

"More *Jeedai* deliveries?" The blue beneath Duman Yaght's eyes grew brighter. "You can bring more?"

"Only if Talfaglio is spared—I'm not doing this because I like you," Lando said. "If you knew to intercept me here, then you know who I am. You know I can deliver."

Duman Yaght lowered his chin in a vague nod. "I heard your message, yes."

In the message, sent to what the Wraiths had identified as a Yuuzhan Vong listening post, Lando had claimed to be a Talfaglion native active in the Great River Jedi rescue organization. He had given just enough details of past operations to sound like a low-level pilot, then rambled on for a few minutes about how the Jedi were betraying him by allowing Talfaglio's destruction. He had finished by naming a time and place and promising that anyone meeting him would be well rewarded.

Duman's eyes remained fixed on the datapad, where the Jedi were beginning to discuss something in low tones. "You must know I cannot make promises on the warmaster's behalf."

"Then go ask for authority and meet me at the rendezvous," Lando said. The next step had to be the Yuuzhan Vong's; the mark had to think he was the one pushing things. "I'm not turning them over until I have his promise."

The Yuuzhan Vong considered this a moment, then said, "You won't make it that far." He tapped the vid display with a blackened fingernail. "Your *Jeedai* are nervous. Let me take them now, and we will see what happens. The warmaster is certain to be interested—I *can* promise you that."

"I don't know," Lando said, setting the hook. "I don't see how you can handle so many Jedi aboard that little rock."

"How we handle the slaves will not be your concern," Duman Yaght said.

"It will be when they escape and hunt me down," Lando said.

"They will not escape. You may be assured of that."

"Sure I can," Lando scoffed. Now that he had his mark pushing him, he could afford to take a few risks, and he wanted to know why Duman Yaght had been so quick to confirm he was carrying Jedi. "Maybe I should just go to the rendezvous point—"

"That is not one of your choices." Duman Yaght's voice remained mild. "You may turn them over to me and know that they will reach the warmaster, who may or may not be sufficiently impressed by your token of faith to spare Talfaglio's refugees. Or you may release that button and be assured that when we die, a million of your people will die with us."

Lando looked down and stroked his lip, not feigning his thoughtfulness at all. Duman Yaght's confidence in his ability to control the Jedi concerned him, but he had pushed his quest for information as far as he dared. He could release the function key on his datapad and sound the abort alarm; he would almost certainly die, but they had planned for just such an emergency. The transfer deck's inner hatch would seal automatically, then the detonite charges concealed in the exterior hatch of the air lock would explode into the boarding shuttle. Duman Yaght and the boarding party would be sucked out into space, and the *Lady Luck* would shoot around the comet and be in hyperspace before the *Exquisite Death* realized what was happening.

But the mission would be lost, more Jedi doomed—and why? Because Lando had an uneasy feeling about something Duman Yaght said? He shook his head in resignation.

"If you put it like that," Lando said. It was not his place to abort the mission—not with so much riding on it, not even with the children of his best friend at risk. "But I'm no fool. I know how this works."

"Good," Duman Yaght said. "Then you also know that the lives of your fellows will rest on your shoulders. I'll give you a villip so you can contact me when the next delivery is ready."

Lando's only response was a sigh of disgust.

"No need for rude noises." Duman Yaght grabbed the back of

Lando's neck in what may have been a gesture of domination or friendship—or both. "This will work out well for both of us."

The Yuuzhan Vong waved his subaltern and the boarding party forward, but Lando quickly blocked their way.

"No, I've got this all planned out," he said. "My ship, my way—or you might as well call the volcano cannons down."

The subaltern glowered, but looked to his commander for orders.

"As he wishes," Duman Yaght smirked. "His ship, his way."

Jacen had sensed only the single stirring in the Force, but everyone else had felt it, too, and now it was gone. He lifted another spoonful of green thakitillo to his mouth, but hardly tasted the zest of the dissolving curds. Even without Alema's abrupt paleness and fluttering lekku, he would have recognized the burst of hungry agitation. Cilghal theorized that the initial disturbance came from the voxyn reaching out to find its prey, but Jacen wondered if it might be something simpler. To him, it felt more like raw animal excitement.

It was a feeling surprisingly close to that held by a number of Jacen's fellow Jedi. The members of the strike team had opened their emotions to each other the instant they sensed the voxyn, and he could feel the eagerness of Ganner, Zekk, the Barabels, Eryl Besa, even Raynar to destroy the creature. Others—Tahiri, Lowbacca, Tekli, Ulaha—were surprised at how fast things were happening. Alema Rar was terrified—more of herself than the creature. Tenel Ka was grimly determined, Anakin absorbed in concerns about everyone else, Jovan Drark eager to begin the game. To Rodians, everything was a game.

Only Jaina, whose feelings Jacen could always sense through their bond as twins, seemed calm. Whatever came, warning or no warning, voxyn or not, they would handle it—or not. They had cast their fate to the Force, and now they had no choice but to trust where it carried them. It was a strange sort of composure born of battle and death and suffering, the grim serenity of the soldier, who was both maker and victim of the all-devouring cataclysm.

Jacen put another spoonful of thakitillo in his mouth. Beyond the dining area, he could feel the crew's fear, Lando's apprehension about something unknown to him, Tendra's guilt as she approached the cabin door. He pressed his tongue to the roof of his mouth and crushed the curds, then savored the tangy explosion of their melting.

The galley door hissed open. Yarsroot, the ship's Ho'Din chef, stepped into the dining cabin with his human assistant, both holding blasters behind their backs. It was the signal to follow the primary plan. Jacen extended himself to the other Jedi, going beyond the simple emotional connection the Barabels had taught them to a much deeper level, melding with the others until it seemed to him that he was them and they were all him. As the meld coordinator, he was to a certain extent trusting the others with his body; they had discovered that, at times, he might become so consumed by the sensations and feelings of others that he forgot to keep track of himself.

Lando's tall wife entered the dining room from the main cabin, a nasty G-9 power blaster cradled in her arms. Zekk and Jovan instantly pushed away from the table and reached for their lightsabers. Tendra loosed a flurry of blue stun bolts, blasting both Jedi and red-haired Eryl into the wall—all as planned. Lowbacca and Krasov tried to rise and were dropped by stun shots from Yarsroot and his assistant, also as planned.

Feeling the impact of each bolt through the team's battle meld, Jacen groaned and would have tumbled from his chair, had Tenel Ka not steadied him.

That was not part of the plan.

Tendra flipped her power blaster to full automatic/lethal. "Anyone else moves—or even looks my way—you all die." She glanced at Ganner, supporting the role he was to play as the decoy leader. "That clear?"

"As transparisteel." Ganner kept his eyes fixed on the center of the table. "Do as she says."

"Good." Tendra motioned two crew members behind her into the room. "Now sit very still and no one gets hurt."

The two crew members started around the table, unclipping the strike team's lightsabers and tossing them down the food disposal chute—along with Lowbacca's protesting translation droid, Em Teedee. Jacen experienced a moment of panic from Anakin and realized they had just run into their first problem. The disposal chutes still led to the flushlock instead of their weapons pod; they had intended to make the changeover after the evening meal. Jacen reached out to Jaina and moved some of her serenity toward Anakin. Nothing to be done about it. Follow the Force.

"Tendra, what's all this about?" Ganner asked. This wasn't in the script, but Ganner knew what was needed—Jacen could feel it. Ganner *always* knew. "Haven't we been good guests?"

"The best," Tendra replied. "Fitzgibbon just doesn't like cowards."

Jacen did not even feel Yarsroot's assistant remove his lightsaber; he only saw it go down the chute with the others.

"Cowards?" Ganner asked. "What are you—"

"Talfaglio," Tendra said simply. A native of nearby Sacorria, she did not need to work to make herself sound angry. "Now shut that fly hangar of yours and stand up. There's someone who wants to see you—all of you."

Back to the script. Jacen felt himself stand and turn toward the door, Tenel Ka close behind. She would be his watcher, her one arm strong enough to carry them both. Tendra stepped aside and motioned the strike team through the door. Down the corridor past the guest cabins and up three stairs onto the transfer deck. Things would be crowded—air lock, escape pods, who knows how many Yuuzhan Vong. Would the voxyn be there? Probably not— nobody could feel it yet.

Alema began to tremble, frightened not of the Yuuzhan Vong—she had killed dozens with her own hands, eluded hundreds more—but of herself. She had not expected to encounter a voxyn on the transit ship. Could she face one again, knowing what the first had done to her sister?

Jacen fed her the feelings of Raynar, who was comforting himself with the knowledge that the Twi'lek had done this stuff many times before. She had denied the Yuuzhan Vong New Plympto. She would get them through this. Alema's lekku stopped shaking, and Jacen followed the unconscious Jedi—who were being levitated by five of their fellows—past Lando's suite toward the guest cabins.

A door slid open behind Tenel Ka, and something blunt caught her between the shoulder blades. Jacen dropped to his knees and started to black out, then realized it was Tenel Ka's body he was feeling and reached out to the others, calling upon their strength to keep them both conscious. When his vision cleared, Yuuzhan Vong filled the corridor.

At the head of the line, Ganner lunged for Lando. "You double-crossing—"

The blunt edge of an amphistaff caught the big Jedi across the back of the head, dropping him into a dark pit before Jacen could call on the others to keep him conscious. Not in the script—but probably for the best.

Point thirty: The crew departs. Tendra and Yarsroot retreated into the ship, leaving the strike team in the hands of the Yuuzhan Vong. There were only six guards on the transfer deck with Lando. The rest were down in the access corridor behind Anakin, flanking the long line of Jedi. Tesar Sebatyne, who was second in line, hesitated at the transfer deck and stared down at Ganner's unconscious form.

A Yuuzhan Vong warrior, a large one with a spindly fringe of black hair, grabbed the Barabel and shoved him into the boarding suite. "Forward—all of you!"

Anakin suppressed a smirk and stepped over Ganner's unconscious form. Tesar had played his role perfectly, forcing the Yuuzhan Vong to order the strike team to do exactly what the strike team wanted to. Anakin followed the Barabel to the far end of the deck and took his place across from the weapons locker. Tahiri and the other Jedi crowded after him, packing themselves just tightly enough to make room for the whole team—and not much else.

So far, events were proceeding more or less as planned. True, their lightsabers had been dropped into the flushlock. But Tendra and Yarsroot had taken extra "precautions" during the turnover to give the war droids time to retrieve the weapons. Anakin could feel the strike team's confidence growing with every success. The empathic sharing strengthened everyone's resolve and bound them to a common purpose, just as the Barabels had said it would, and Jacen was keeping him in touch with the group. Anakin sensed Alema Rar's resolve harden and shared Tenel Ka's surprise when she was struck from behind, and now he perceived Lowie's mind stirring. No sooner had Anakin begun to worry about how a groggy Wookiee would impact their plans than he sensed Jacen reaching out to calm their waking friend. This was going to work great.

Once the crew was safely out of sight, Lando turned to a scarfaced Yuuzhan Vong and gestured at a fiberplast crate in front of the *Lady Luck*'s escape pod. "Perhaps the commander of the *Exquisite Death* would allow me to present him with a small gift?"

It was a subtle variation on point thirty-one, but a useful one. No one had expected the commander of the transit ship to supervise the transfer personally. This officer was an eager one.

When the enemy commander did not object, Lando removed several pairs of stun cuffs from the crate. Anakin expelled a long calming breath, using a Jedi relaxation technique to let a spike of anxiety flow out with it.

Lando held the cuffs in front of the commander. "A little something to keep the prisoners in line, Duman Yaght."

Duman Yaght regarded the cuffs with a sneer. "What are those profanities?"

"Wrist restraints." Lando opened a metal sleeve and displayed it proudly. "You see, I've thought of everything."

Duman knocked the stun cuffs aside. "We have our own bindings." He glared at Ganner's unconscious form, which one of the strike team had levitated and placed in the center of the transfer deck with the other unconscious Jedi Knights. "Bindings that teach as well as restrain."

Point thirty-two: The enemy acknowledges the offer. Anakin turned his palm toward the weapons locker and reached out with the Force, buckling the door panel inward. Lando and the Yuuzhan Vong spun toward the *screal* of crumpling durasteel. Ulaha closed the pressure hatch at her end of the transfer deck, sealing the rest of the enemy boarding party out in the access corridor.

Anakin twisted the door free and slammed it into Duman Yaght's head. One Yuuzhan Vong warrior stepped over to defend his stunned commander, and the others—finding the space too cramped for amphistaffs—reached for their coufees. The strike team counterattacked in a flurry of kicks and blows, taking full advantage of the battle meld to keep the enemy too busy dodging and blocking to actually draw a weapon.

With the Force, Anakin jerked the blaster pistols from their locker mounts and hurled them across the transfer deck into the grasps of ten waiting Jedi. From the other side of the sealed hatch came muffled shouts and metallic thuds as the rest of the boarding party tried to break into the transfer deck, then Tesar half turned, whipping his thick reptilian tail into the ankles of Duman Yaght and his defender and sweeping both Yuuzhan Vong off their feet. He leveled his blaster at the commander's head.

"Call off your scarheads," the Barabel rasped.

Duman Yaght's eyes flared with anger, and his guard, now lying behind Tesar, reached for his coufee. Anakin started to shout a warning, but Jacen had already felt his alarm and relayed it through the battle meld. The Barabel pivoted and brought his heel down, a long spike folding out to pin the warrior's hand to the durasteel floor.

The tumult on the other side of the hatch suddenly fell silent, and Anakin guessed the situation on the transfer deck had been relayed to the officers of the *Exquisite Death*. He leveled his blaster pistol at Duman Yaght's wounded protector and began to count. The war droids would need at least a thirty-second distraction to slip out of the *Lady Luck*'s disposal lock with the equipment pod and attach to the enemy shuttle. Anakin would have liked to give them a safety margin of twice that, but sixty seconds seemed like an eternity.

Tesar took his time pulling his heel spike out of the guard's hand, then pressed his blaster to Duman Yaght's face.

"Tell your warriorz to drop their weaponz," the Barabel rasped.

Duman Yaght surprised Anakin and everyone else by responding with an admiring smirk. "Impressive. The reputation of the *Jeedai* is well deserved."

Tesar's only response was a hiss. If not for the battle meld, Anakin would have thought the Barabel confused, but he sensed through Jacen that Tesar was only stalling for time.

Two seconds later, Tesar snarled, "This one wantz surrender, not complimentz."

"Then you are to be disappointed," Duman replied. "You must know that before allowing seventeen *Jeedai* to escape, I'll destroy this ship and everyone aboard it—myself included."

"Wait a second," Lando objected. He stepped forward, and Anakin's count reached eight. "There's no call for—"

"Silence! If you know anything about the Yuuzhan Vong, then you know we have no fear of death." Duman looked back to Tesar. "You have five breaths."

Finally, something they had not planned for. Desperate to thwart the deadline, Anakin stepped over and kicked the villips off the commander's shoulder, crushed them beneath his foot.

"That will not save you," the commander said. "I have a personal villip on the bridge of my ship, relaying every word I say." He looked back to Tesar. "Three breaths."

Though Anakin's count had barely passed ten seconds, he knew better than to challenge the commander's word. Having proclaimed his willingness to die, it was now a matter of honor to follow through. He watched Duman Yaght's chest rise and fall two more times.

Lando must have been watching, as well; after the second breath, he snorted loudly. "Nobody's going to slag my ship." He started across the transfer deck to the inner hatch. "Not when there's no reason for it."

Alema Rar blocked his way and pointed her blaster at his face, then pulled the trigger as he moved to step past. There was a loud pop of a tripping safety breaker, then she cried out and dropped the smoking pistol.

Lando kicked the weapon aside. "You see? I've thought of everything." He snatched Raynar's blaster out of his hand, popped a retaining clip, reversed the power pack, adjusted the discharge setting, and dropped Tesar with a stun bolt. "Reversed power packs—standard safety precaution, at least when you're turning traitor on a company of Jedi."

Anakin and several others popped their retaining clips, but even Jedi were not that quick. Duman Yaght's protector caught Anakin in a leg scissors and whipped him to the floor, and Anakin found himself struggling to continue his count beneath a rain of blows.

The rest of the Yuuzhan Vong were also attacking, forgoing their coufees to lash out at the blasters in the hands of their foes. Even Duman Yaght joined the fray, leaping up to hurl Tahiri into an escape pod hatch. Blaster and power pack flew in two directions, and she wisely let herself slump to the deck.

The commander turned to Lando, pointed to the inner hatch. "Open it!"

Lando stepped forward, his hand reaching for the override. By Anakin's count, they were at twenty-five seconds. The two war droids would be searching the bottom of the shuttle for a place to anchor. Jacen sensed Anakin's worry, and Ulaha stepped forward to block the path, a long-fingered Bith hand flicking forward as she opened herself to the Force.

Jacen screamed first. Anakin experienced an instant of hot pain and thought his brother had been wounded, but then he heard Ulaha's whistle and saw the Bith stumbling forward, the handle of a coufee protruding from her back. Shock shot through the strike team like a stun bolt. No one had seen the attack coming, and the sudden pain dazed them badly. Anakin took two hard blows and felt the others reeling, too, and then bodies began to fall.

Across the deck, Ulaha lay facedown, too pained to scream, her fingernails raking the durasteel floor. Lando stood above her, dark eyes dazed with horror, but too much the gambler to show anything more. His knee flexed as though he might kneel down to pull out the coufee. Then he caught himself and stepped over the anguished Jedi and opened the inner hatch.

Another fist crashed down on Anakin, this time summoning misty shadows of unconsciousness. He forgot his count, but it had to be thirty—or as close as they were going to get. The floor began to reverberate with heavy footfalls, the rest of the boarding party rushing onto the transfer deck. Anakin reached out with the Force and hurled a discarded blaster pistol into his attacker's head and was rewarded with another blow, then the tip of a coufee touched his throat.

"Done, *Jeedai!*" the warrior hissed. "Understand?"

Anakin did not even dare to nod.

Duman Yaght barked an order. A pair of Yuuzhan Vong lifted Ulaha off the floor and passed her into the air lock, the coufee still protruding from her back. A familiar hollowness came to Anakin then—the same hollowness he had felt on Sernpidal, when he had been forced to raise the *Falcon's* nose and leave Chewie behind— and a cold fear rose inside him. They had barely made contact, and he had already gotten someone injured. Maybe this mission was too much for them. Maybe everyone was going to get killed just like Chewbacca—Lowie, Tahiri, even Jacen and Jaina. Maybe it would be his fault.

Jacen reached out to him, gently laving him with the emotions of the others. There was fear, anger, guilt. Anakin could not tell who was feeling what, except for Alema Rar.

Alema seemed to be relieved. No one had actually died yet, and she had made it this far without breaking down in terror. Things were going pretty well, it seemed to her.

Duman Yaght's voice sounded from somewhere beyond Anakin's feet. "I must admit, Fitzgibbon Lane, that I now understand why you destroyed their lightsabers. Had they gotten to those . . . well, let us say I am happy they were disintegrated."

A pair of Yuuzhan Vong jerked Anakin to his feet, and he saw the commander standing with Lando as the boarding party lined the Jedi up for transfer. Anakin fixed his stare on Lando, wondering if there was not some way for the silky-tongued gambler to keep Ulaha aboard the *Lady Luck*.

Lando caught Anakin staring at him and allowed his gaze to linger a moment, then turned back to Duman Yaght. "It's all in the planning, but next time, I want some warning. If we catch them during a sleep cycle—"

"You will have your villip," the Yuuzhan Vong interrupted. "That is all I can promise."

Anakin's guards pushed him into the air lock. He stumbled on the threshold, but kept his gaze turned over his shoulder. He knew there was no safe way for Lando to retrieve Ulaha, but Lando Calrissian had a way of doing the impossible. Lando had spent his youth outwitting Imperial agents and swindling the deadliest criminals in the galaxy, and he had been rescuing the Solo children and their parents for longer than Anakin had been alive. Surely, Lando Calrissian could outwit one ambitious Yuuzhan Vong.

Lando met Anakin's gaze again. A haunted and fearful look came to his eyes, then Duman Yaght said something that required a laugh, and Lando had to turn his back.

Chapter 18

Instead of taking the sanibuffed corridor to the *Errant Venture*'s parade deck, where two dozen eager academy students stood waiting to display their Force skills, Luke and his companions followed a freshly preened Booster Terrik into a lift tube and ascended directly to the bridge. The Star Destroyer could orbit Eclipse only so long before it risked exposing the base's location, so the last thing anyone in the group wanted was to spend time watching the HoloNet. Unfortunately, they had just received word that Nom Anor was about to address the senate regarding the Talfaglion hostages, and that Borsk Fey'lya himself had asked both Wedge Antilles and Garm Bel Iblis to attend. There could be no doubt that something major was about to happen, and that it would be of great importance to the Jedi.

Booster led them along the back of the bridge into the ship's comm center, where an old Imperial holoprojector sat at the far end of a conference table littered with datapads, science projects, and flimsiplast dye-paintings. In addition to Luke and Booster, there were Corran and Mirax Horn, Han and Leia, R2-D2 and C-3PO, and, fussing discontentedly in Mara's arms, Ben. Tionne and Kam Solusar were on the parade deck with their students, explaining that

Master Skywalker was looking forward to seeing them very much and would be along soon.

Luke had not yet heard how Corran and Mirax had escaped from the voxyn on Corellia. Their story had been interrupted by news of Nom Anor's address, but they claimed it was nothing too exciting, save that they would need to find some way of quietly reimbursing Corellian Transport Services for a badly corroded hovertaxi.

Ben grew more disgruntled as the group gathered around the transceiver pad. He was normally the most imperturbable of babies—but there were times when he simply could not be consoled. Now, as R2-D2 tuned the ancient transceiver to the senate holoband, Ben broke into a fit of wailing. Luke felt Mara reaching out through the Force to calm him. When that did not help, he did so himself. Ben only cried harder. Mara sighed heavily and turned to take the baby into the next room.

Leia intercepted her. "Let me. I really don't need to see this."

Mara nodded and passed Ben over.

The infant calmed almost instantly.

Luke and Mara exchanged surprised glances, both feeling a little distressed that they had not been able to comfort their son themselves, but knowing there was more to it than that.

"I was thinking about Anakin," Leia said, her eyes fixed on Ben's face. "I was watching Mara and wishing there had been more time for me to hold him when he was this age."

Luke smiled and turned back to the holopad, where the cam was zooming in on a figure in the Grand Convocation Chamber.

To Viqi Shesh's eye, Nom Anor looked too certain of himself. Though Fey'lya had denied him the privilege of appearing in warrior's garb, the executor carried himself tall and haughtily, all but deaf to the taunts of the jeering senators, his one eye fixed on the high councilors' dais. He wore a shimmering robe of living glistaweb, nearly as proof against blaster bolts as vonduun crab armor, but far more innocuous—at least to those who did not know the secret of its charge-neutralizing fibers.

Nom Anor stepped to the center of the speaker's platform and waited for silence. It would be a long wait, Viqi knew. After Fey'lya's public declarations of support for the Jedi, the Jedi-lovers were content to wait for the Bothan's signal before they stopped heckling. Never one to miss a chance to bully an enemy, Fey'lya did not give Nom Anor a chance to correct his mistake. He leaned forward, peering down from behind his chief of state's console, and spoke into the microphone.

"You asked for this audience." Fey'lya's amplified voice reverberated through the chamber, quieting the hecklers. "Have you come to explain the Talfaglion hostages?"

Nom Anor's now-empty eye socket twitched. "Hardly. You understand the situation. I have come to inform you the warmaster has extended the deadline for the Jedi surrender."

The chamber burst into an astonished rustle. Viqi was as shocked as everyone else, for the warmaster was not the type to yield to Fey'lya's empty threats. Perhaps Nom Anor was playing some game of his own. Now that Fey'lya had thrown his support behind the Jedi, perhaps the executor believed he could strike a deal with the appeasers. Such a plan would have to be stopped and quickly, or it might be Nom Anor instead of her who replaced Fey'lya when Tsavong Lah's killers finally attacked. She did not understand what was taking the assassins so long. Most of the opportunities she had listed for them were already past, and so far she had not heard of even a suspicious loiterer near the chief of state.

Not waiting for the commotion to fade, Viqi activated her own microphone. "How do you explain this sudden attack of conscience, Mr. Ambassador?"

Nom Anor's expression remained far too smug. "The warmaster has come to realize it may be difficult for the New Republic to comply with his orders on short notice." He paused and turned away from the high councilors' dais to look directly into the galleries. "Last night, a concerned citizen turned over seventeen young Jedi—"

The convocation chamber burst into such an uproar that it was impossible to hear the rest of Nom Anor's statement. Viqi fell back in her chair, as stunned as the others in the room, and began to wonder how such a thing could happen. No bounty hunter in the galaxy could just fly out and collect seventeen Jedi—she doubted that even a company of bounty hunters could do it.

To restore order, Fey'lya was forced to darken the chamber, and even then he had to wait several minutes before he could make himself heard enough to order the sergeant at arms to have the security droids remove any senator who continued to yell. When light was finally restored, the Bothan's ears were flattened, and a long ridge of hair was standing along the back of his neck.

"I don't believe you," he said.

Viqi was inclined to agree, as was most of the senate. A rising murmur threatened to crest into another uproar, until the security droids brought the noise under control by issuing stern warnings about decibel levels.

Nom Anor sneered. "I have a list." He made a show of consulting a sheet of what looked like the shed skin of a snake, then said, "The leader is Ganner Rhysode. His assistants seem to be Tesar Sebatyne and a Wookiee named Lowbacca."

A plaintive howl echoed down from the Wookiee gallery, and a security droid was slapped out of the air by a hairy claw.

"The Bith Jedi Ulaha Kore was wounded resisting capture, and I certainly recognize the Solo name."

"Solo?" Wedge Antilles gasped. Along with Garm Bel Iblis, he was standing behind Fey'lya's seat for some reason Viqi did not yet understand. "You have a Solo?"

The chamber fell so quiet that the next question, from General

Bel Iblis, would have carried to the top gallery even without being picked up by Fey'lya's microphone. "Which one? Anakin or the twins?"

The smug look vanished from Nom Anor's face. "Twins?" He quickly forced a sneer, but, to Viqi, the expression looked more sick than snide. "We have the three young ones."

The two generals glanced at each other with fallen faces, and Fey'lya's ears drooped, but only Viqi seemed to perceive Nom Anor's subtle shift of attitude. She did not know what significance twins had to the Yuuzhan Vong, but it seemed clear enough to her that there was one—and that, with a little help from her, Nom Anor would look like a fool to Tsavong Lah for not realizing it.

Viqi leaned forward and glared at the Yuuzhan Vong as though challenging his claim. "Jacen and Jaina are twins, Mr. Ambassador." She leaned back, then added with a disdainful smirk, "It's common knowledge. They're twins, just like their mother and Luke Skywalker."

Nom Anor's good eye narrowed, and he glared at her in open anger. "It does not matter what they are." He forced himself to look back to Fey'lya. "What I came here to say, what the warmaster wishes me to say, is that he is not unreasonable. He will spare the Talfaglion hostages as long as the New Republic continues to turn over its Jedi."

Fey'lya rose from his seat. "Never!"

Nom Anor ignored him and turned to the gallery. "A like number every . . ."

His microphone suddenly went dead, preventing his last three words from reaching the senate gallery.

Viqi keyed her own microphone. "A like number every ten standard days. You have the right to know, whether the chief of state wants you to or not."

Her words instantly had an inflammatory effect, causing such a heated exchange that the security droids actually began to chase a handful of senators toward the exits with sting bolts. Fey'lya pressed a button on his console and rose, his voice now reverberating from both the chamber's public-address system and the individual conferencing consoles.

"What the chief of state wants you to know, whether Councilor Shesh wishes it or not, is how the Yuuzhan Vong conduct their diplomacy."

Mif Kumas, the senate's sergeant at arms, appeared at the edge of the chamber floor, his big Calibop wings fluttering madly as he struggled to keep pace with the three big defense droids used to deal with serious matters in the senate. Fey'lya glanced in Viqi's direction just long enough to bare his fangs, and she suddenly knew the chief of state remained alive not because of Tsavong Lah's tardiness in ordering the kill, but because the assassins had failed. Blood running cold, she calmly stood and turned to leave the high councilors' dais.

Fey'lya touched his control board, and his voice sounded from her conferencing console. "Going somewhere, Councilor?"

Viqi lifted her chin and met his violet eyes as steadily as she was able. "I have a personal need."

He smiled wickedly. "Stay. This won't take long, and I'm sure you will find it most . . . enlightening."

Faced with prospect of being publicly stunned into submission by Kumas's protection droids or maintaining at least a plausible pretense of her innocence, she returned to her seat and tried to pretend she did not feel the thoughtful gazes of the two generals boring into her.

"I will trust you to make this fast."

"Of course. A quick kill is safest." Fey'lya touched a key, once again feeding his microphone into the public-address system, then turned back to Nom Anor. "Recently, a squad of Yuuzhan Vong infiltrators made an attempt on my life."

A half-doubtful murmur filled the chamber, and Viqi's stomach grew so qualmish she feared her "personal need" would soon become legitimate.

Fey'lya raised his hands. "There are certainly some who will view this as a cynical ploy to garner political advantage, but I assure you that is not the case." He glared down at Nom Anor, who had finally noticed the droids and Calibop approaching behind him. "My only desire is to make certain the appeasers in this body understand who they are dealing with. To that end, I have brought two men to substantiate this attack, a pair of generals whose honesty is beyond reproach and who—as many of you know—bear me no particular good faith."

He motioned the generals forward, and Wedge Antilles leaned to the microphone. "It was a well-planned attack."

General Bel Iblis was next. "Unfortunately, we were engaged in classified work and the details must remain secret, but it happened as Chief Fey'lya says. There can be no doubt."

The doubtful murmur quickly assumed a tone of outrage, and Viqi's stomach growled so loudly that her microphone picked up the sound. Fey'lya turned to her expectantly.

"Senator Shesh?" he asked. "Do you have anything to say?"

Viqi glared vibroblades at him. She checked the protection droids and found them hovering beside Nom Anor less than five meters away; only the certain knowledge that they would stun her before she could shoot kept her from palming her stealth blaster.

"What should I say, Borsk? I'm sorry?"

Fey'lya smiled triumphantly. "An apology is hardly necessary, Senator Shesh. You were only trying to save Kuat." He glanced in Nom Anor's direction. "As long as you see your mistake now."

"My mistake?" Viqi gasped, beginning to comprehend that her secret remained secret.

Perhaps her contact had been killed in the attack, or perhaps Yuuzhan Vong infiltrators were trained to withstand even modern interrogation techniques. It hardly mattered. Fey'lya thought he had defeated her challenge—her *political* challenge. Now he wanted to draw her back into the fold and consolidate his support, and he still had no idea what game they were really playing. No idea at all.

Viqi smiled and inclined her head. "I do see my mistake." She turned to glare at Nom Anor. "You just can't trust the Yuuzhan Vong."

"Oh my," C-3PO said to no one in particular. "Did you notice the interest Nom Anor showed when he discovered that Jaina and Jacen were twins?"

Neither Luke nor anyone else answered the droid, for their attention remained riveted on the holopad, where Borsk Fey'lya was gleefully informing Nom Anor of his arrest. It troubled Luke that the Yuuzhan Vong did not bother protesting his innocence. He merely glared at the Bothan as though they both knew the truth.

"Of course, it's impossible to know the significance of twins to the Yuuzhan Vong," C-3PO babbled on. "But in approximately ninety-eight point seven percent of the cultures in our own galaxy, they represent the dualistic nature of the universe: good and evil, light and dark, male and female. When the twins are in harmony, there is balance to the universe . . ."

In the hologram, Mif Kumas fluttered forward with a pair of stun cuffs, his three protection droids arrayed in a triangle around the Yuuzhan Vong. To Luke's great surprise, the Yuuzhan Vong extended his arms and brought his wrists together—then grabbed his own little finger and tore it off. A string of black vapor sprayed out of the base, billowing up around Nom Anor and Mif Kumas in cloud of inky miasma.

The event seemed to lie outside the parameters of the protection droids' programming, for they did not open fire until the Yuuzhan Vong thrust the stump of his finger into the Calibop's startled face. Luke saw the first bolts strike Nom Anor's shimmering robe and blink out without causing him harm, then both figures vanished inside the expanding cloud of darkness.

Paying no attention at all to what was happening in the hologram, C-3PO continued, "But whatever the significance of twins to our enemies, I fear it will only make Jacen and Jaina's captors all the more vigilant. Nom Anor's reaction suggests—"

"See-Threepio!" Leia barked, returning to the room with Ben still quiet in her arms.

"Yes, Mistress Leia?"

"Silence yourself before I decide you need a memory wipe."

"A memory wipe?" C-3PO echoed. "Why in the world would I need a memory wipe?"

R2-D2 tweedled a suggestion.

"Well, I didn't mean to alarm Mistress Leia," C-3PO objected. "I only thought—"

Han reached behind the droid's head and tripped the primary circuit breaker.

"Thank you," Luke said, though he knew Han had silenced the droid for Leia and himself.

The scene in the hologram was confused, dark, and rapidly growing more so. Nom Anor's cloud quickly filled the holocam's view, and the protector droids stopped firing as they lost contact with their target. The operator pulled back to a wider view of the chamber, but the black fumes continued to expand, and even that view was obscured within a few seconds. The audio was filled with panicked screams and the sound of coughing and the thunder of running feet.

There was a moment of static as the chamber's ventilation and fire suppression systems activated, then the image began to clear rapidly. As the stairs and galleries grew visible again, they saw prone bodies lying everywhere—on the stairs, slumped over conferencing consoles, sprawled on communications ramps.

"Sith spawn!" Corran gasped. "He wiped out the entire senate!"

"Knocked out," Luke corrected. He was still trying to puzzle out Nom Anor's strange reaction to Fey'lya's accusation. Luke knew for himself that the attempt on the chief's life had occurred, since both Han and Leia had been at the proving trials when the assassins struck. Yet the Yuuzhan Vong had reacted as though it were political fiction. "This wasn't about destroying the senate. That kind of outrage would draw the New Republic together, and so far the Yuuzhan Vong have been trying to split it apart."

It grew apparent that Luke was correct as the image zoomed back to the chamber floor. Even there, where the cloud had been thickest, the bodies were beginning to stir, hoarse throats to rasp for air. Kumas's wings began to flutter again, while Fey'lya and the other councilors dragged themselves up and punched at their consoles, barking orders that made sense only to their confused minds.

The three protection droids lay inert on the floor, the last swaddled in the still-shimmering robe Nom Anor had been wearing. Of the Yuuzhan Vong himself, there was no sign.

"Got away clean," Han observed. "Probably had one of those masquer things around his waist."

"Maybe palace security will pick him up." Leia turned to Corran, who, as an ex-member of Corellian Security, had more experience in such matters than anyone else. "What do you think?"

Instead of answering, Corran only looked at her and Han with an expression of infinite sadness. He spread his arms and came around the table, Mirax following close behind.

"Han, Leia . . . I'm so sorry."

"Hold on there, fella." Han backed away, one hand raised to ward off the embrace of the former CorSec officer who, a few decades earlier, might have been hunting him down instead of offering him comfort. "There's something you ought to know."

Corran stopped, looking equal parts hurt and confused.

Luke chuckled. "Corran, there's a reason I'm asking the Jedi to gather." He glanced in Booster's direction, then said, "But this has to stay secret—very secret."

Booster spread his palms and looked around the cabin. "Who am I going to tell?"

Luke explained what Anakin and the strike team were doing, and how Eclipse was trying to put together a group of Jedi to defend the Talfaglion hostages.

"Do you remember what you told Jacen after the fall of Ithor, that if there ever came a time when folks looked forward to the return of the man who killed Ithor—"

"Master, I was a little, uh, *disappointed* then," Corran said. "I didn't mean to sound bitter."

"And you didn't," Luke assured him. "But, Corran, the time has come. The invasion is out of hand, and the Jedi need someone of your experience to help us prepare . . . to teach our young pilots how to fight as a unit and survive."

Corran considered this for a moment, then cast a querying look in Mirax's direction.

"What else are we going to do?" She hooked a thumb at her father. "Hang around with this old grouch?"

Booster scowled and started to retort, then threw up his hands. "I'm sworn to secrecy." He eyed Luke. "I suppose you'll be needing a Star Destroyer for this fleet of yours?"

"Not yet—where could we hide you?" As tempting as the offer was, Luke still wanted the academy students kept out of harm's way. "Admiral Kre'fey has converted that old smugglers' hole at

Reecee into a rear base. He'd welcome an extra Star Destroyer there, and you'll be close enough to Eclipse to come running when things start to look bad."

Booster fixed Luke with a sour glare. "I know what you're doing, young fellow."

Luke smiled. "Good. I was starting to think you were slipping."

Chapter 19

*T*he assault on Arkania began quietly enough. A few sensor alarms chimed in warning, then the silky voice of a female tactical controller reported the coordinates of the invasion fleet. A circle of darkness smaller than a thumbnail appeared at the indicated place and blocked the light of the distant stars. The dark area expanded quickly to the size of a human hand, then a head. The stars reappeared, winking in and out of sight as thousands of yorik coral ships passed in front of them.

A flurry of lightpoints sprayed out from the fleet, then swelled into the blue-white dots of plasma balls. They passed harmlessly through the mine shell—the droid brains were programmed to ignore weapons—then flared out of existence against the planetary shields. A volley of magma missiles followed. A storm of low-power stutter lasers flashed out from Arkania's new Balmorran Arms defense platforms to intercept and destroy the missiles on the far side of the mine shells. When the fire inadvertently struck and detonated one mine, the shell instantly realigned itself for optimum coverage.

Finally, what looked like an entire asteroid belt burst into the blue light of Arkania's sun. Dozens of large clearing ships went straight for the mines and opened their pointed noses, spewing

rocky decoys into the shell. The rest of the fleet swirled out to sur-
round the planet, spewing magma missiles and grutchins at the
orbital defense platforms.

The TacCon's silky voice came over the blastboat's comm
channel. "Guard ships take cover behind your platforms. Turbolasers will commence fire in three seconds."

The battered blastboat slid into the sensor shadow of the Wild
Knights' assigned platform, and Danni's readouts went to zero. She
slammed her palm against the console.

"How can I correlate anything from here?"

"You will have your chance, Danni Quee." Their platform
opened up with its variable-pulse turbolasers, filling the darkness
outside with sheets of colored light. Saba, sitting in her command
chair near the front, half turned so she could fix a reptilian eye on
Danni. "Use the wait to calm yourself. It is dangerous to enter a
fight angry."

"I'm not angry."

"You feel angry to me," Wonetun rumbled from the pilot's
seat. "And that'll get someone killed. Calm down or close up."

"You were angry when Mara came to tell us about Anakin's
plan," Saba said. "Perhapz you wished to go along?"

"You're smarter than that," Danni retorted, "or this bunch of
grutchin traps wouldn't have lasted this long. The last place I want
to be is another Yuuzhan Vong holding cell."

"No anger there," Wonetun observed sarcastically.

"She is upset with Master Ssskywalker." Izal sat in the topside
turret, his long tongue flicking the pale salt crust clinging to his
upper lip. "She thinks he should have asked her."

Danni glared up at the Arcona. "Stay out of my mind."

"It is in your face, not your mind."

Danni was not certain she believed him—Izal could be a little
sly when he was holding back on the salt—but there was no
denying the irritation she felt at the suggestion.

"He shouldn't have let Anakin talk him into it," Danni said. "Those kids have no idea what they're getting into."

"The voxyn must be exterminated," Saba said. "Master Skywalker has surely considered the riskz."

"Master Skywalker has not seen a breaking," Danni shot back. "He has no idea."

"The strike team will commandeer the ship before the breaking," Saba said.

"Sure they will," Danni said.

Saba's scaly tail slapped the floor. "What would you have us do? Go after them?"

The sudden apprehension in the Force reminded Danni of what she was saying. Saba's face was so stoic and fearsome-looking that it was easy to forget she had emotions, too, and it had completely slipped Danni's mind that Saba's apprentices and son were with the strike team. Knowing the Barabel did not really understand the concept of an apology and would probably have found it disingenuous if she did, Danni did not even try. She simply gave a small nod.

"If we could find them, Saba, that's exactly what I'd do," Danni said. "I'd go after them."

Saba studied her with a black eye for a moment, then the TacCon's voice came over the comm channel. "Guard ships forward. Remember your areas, and stay close to your platforms."

"Let us do our own jobz first." Saba gestured at Danni's instrument panel. "Knowing *how* the yammosks communicate does us no good until we understand their language. Did you not say that?"

Without awaiting a reply, the Barabel turned away and ordered the squadron forward. Though Danni's anger was gone, the Force was now filled with grimness and apprehension—and not only Saba's. Though the exchange in the blastboat had not been transmitted over the comm channels, the rest of the Wild Knights could sense their leader's anxiety. Danni instantly felt ashamed of her anger and regretted her thoughtless words even more than before.

In a squadron that relied on empathy to bind it together, runaway emotions could get someone killed.

Danni focused her attention on her instruments and promised herself that she would coax every bit of data possible out of the battle. It was the only apology Saba Sebatyne would understand.

They emerged from behind the platform shields not into the maelstrom of whirling fighter craft that Danni expected, but into a meshwork of streaking missiles and flashing laser bolts. Having penetrated the mine shell, the Yuuzhan Vong capital ships were laying off, firing salvos of plasma balls and magma missiles at the orbiting defense platforms. One platform, an older KDY system designed for the turbolaser exchanges of the Rebellion era, was jetting a long plume of boram coolant into space. Otherwise, the enemy barrages were proving remarkably inefficient.

On the other hand, the motley assemblage defending Arkania— the planet's military, volunteer squadrons like Saba's, and a small New Republic task force rushed in to attempt a delaying action— were doing remarkably well. The slow but powerful KDY platforms were breaking up concentrations of enemy ships, preventing the invaders from mounting any sort of planetward thrust. The smaller but newer Balmorran Arms platforms used their long-range stutter lasers to destroy incoming missile volleys and pepper the big Yuuzhan Vong capital ships with showers of random-intensity attacks. Whenever a low-power laser struck yorik coral, a sensor detected the strike and automatically fired a pair of devastating blasts from the platform's charge-storing turbolasers. The system was as deadly as it was efficient, and there were already scores of lumpy derelicts spinning off into space.

What Danni did not see was a swarm of coralskippers rushing to disable the platforms. She checked her instruments and found all readouts hovering down near the bottom.

"What do they wait for?" Wonetun grumbled. "I see the skips on my sensor screen—clouds of them."

"Perhaps they fear the battle platforms," Saba said.

"No," Danni said, suddenly feeling relieved. "They never intended to come in. This is a feint."

"A feint?" Saba turned to look at Danni. "You cannot know that."

"Can't I?" Danni gestured at her instrument panel, where all of the data bars continued to hover near the bottom. "If the attack had truly stalled, don't you think the yammosk would be going wild?"

Saba left her chair and peered over Danni's shoulder for a long time, then finally said, "This makes no sense. They would conquer at half the strength."

"But not without cost," Danni said. "Perhaps their resources are not as limitless as we think."

Saba considered this for a moment, then turned to Wonetun. "Calculate a course for Eclipse."

"What about the Yuuzhan Vong?" Wonetun asked. "They're not going to let us—"

"The Yuuzhan Vong are going to withdraw," Saba said. "They are saving their fleet for something else—something we must warn Master Skywalker about."

Chapter 20

The door valve drew open, and Nom Anor stepped into the sweltering dazzle of the Glory Room. The warmaster, tethered into his cognition throne thirty meters away, could hardly be seen for all the blaze bugs warming the chamber with their crimson abdomens. Some of the creatures moved slowly through the air, and a few winked out or blinked on, but most hovered in place, each representing the known location of a capital starship or significant concentration of smaller craft. The scene was confusing to the eye alone, but a careful listener could identify a blaze bug's affiliation by the sound of its wings—low thrum for Yuuzhan Vong vessels, sharp drone for the New Republic, steady buzz for Imperial Remnant, and shrill whine for other infidels.

With the hum of the invading core enveloped on all sides by the high-pitched whirring of infidel forces, the situation sounded precarious at best. Had not a sour odor filled Nom Anor's nostrils as he moved through the enemy blaze bugs near the entrance of the room, he might have worried. As it was, the reek of disorganization and poor battle preparedness assured a swift Yuuzhan Vong victory, and the executor's success in dividing the New Republic

Senate was undoubtedly responsible for the strongest part of that smell. Certainly, that was why the warmaster had left orders for him to report the instant of his return—or so Nom Anor hoped. The alternative was too horrible to contemplate.

He passed through the infidel areas into the Yuuzhan Vong invasion column, where the sour reek of confusion was replaced by the clyriz-like odor of organization and purpose. Instead of swirling about in confusion when he passed through, as had the blaze bugs in the New Republic section of the room, the bugs here simply fluttered aside, then returned to their places once he was gone.

As Nom Anor drew near the center of the chamber, the warmaster's cognition throne grew more distinct. A little smaller than an infidel landspeeder, the chair lumbered about on six squat legs, flashing a constant series of instructions to the blaze bugs via the soft glowtips at the ends of its hundred antennae.

The warmaster himself sat atop the throne in a neural cusp, his head swaddled in wormlike sensory feeds, his hands thrust into control sacks on the armrests alongside his body. Though Nom Anor had never himself mounted a cognition throne, he knew a skilled rider could join the creature so completely that he experienced the totality of the strategic situation at once. Each blaze bug's coded wingbeats identified not only the class and name of the vessel represented, but also the ship's condition and estimated combat effectiveness. The subtle undertones of odor suggested the morale of the captain and crew—estimates based on a complicated formula of known experience, effectiveness in previous battles, and the general tactical situation. Though Nom would never have said so aloud, he suspected the estimates tended to rate Yuuzhan Vong ships unduly high and infidel ships outrageously low.

The usual crowd of apprentices, subalterns, and readers parted to let Nom Anor pass, but only the apprentices and subalterns crossed their arms over their breasts. An amalgam of diviners and military analysts, the readers were responsible for gathering information on enemy capabilities and translating their knowledge into the blaze bug swarm. Each was also a priest of one of the many different gods to whom the Yuuzhan Vong paid homage, and as such technically subordinate to the *Sunulok*'s priestess, Vaecta, rather than the warmaster—a fact they took every opportunity to emphasize. Nom Anor knew the arrangement to be a constant fang in Tsavong Lah's heel, but, at least to those who believed in such things, the precaution was necessary to avoid placing any of the other gods in symbolic servitude to Yun-Yammka the Slayer.

Trying not to read anything into the lack of envy in the eyes of those around him, Nom Anor stopped before the cognition throne and pounded his own chest in salute. "I come straight from the docking chamber, my master."

Tsavong Lah peered down from the throne, little more than eyes and mouth visible through his cocoon of sensory feeds. "As ordered—good."

Nom Anor's mouth went dry. No words of welcome, no hint of praise. "I am sorry that it took me this long to rejoin the fleet. My journey was delayed by the difficulties of leaving Coruscant."

"Not an easy thing to do with all of Planetary Defense hunting you, I am sure," Vergere's thin voice said. She pushed through the crowd and peered up from between two readers. "You are to be congratulated on your escape. It was most ingenious."

"Yes, planning is everything." Nom Anor had difficulty keeping the rage out of his voice, for he was convinced that Vergere lay behind the attempt on Fey'lya's life. He had considered the matter from every angle, and she had more to gain from it than anyone. "I'm only sorry it was necessary to disappoint you."

"Why would I be disappointed in your escape?" Vergere spread her arms. "Your value to our cause is well known to all."

As accustomed as Nom Anor was to the gamesmanship of

politics, the subtle mockery of this half-pagan creature was too much. Not only had she interfered with his mission and nearly gotten him imprisoned, now she was ridiculing him before his master and peers.

"There is no need to play the shy bunish, Vergere." Nom Anor had to struggle to keep his voice icy, and even then his fury was tangible enough to draw a quiet murmur. "You are to be applauded on your ingenuity. I had not thought a mere pet capable of so much cunning—or daring."

Had Vergere been a Yuuzhan Vong, Nom Anor's words would have been enough to draw a blood challenge. As it was, the little creature only pricked her antennae. "Do you accuse me of what happened in the senate?"

"A bold attempt to remove a rival," Nom Anor confirmed. "Whether or not the assassination succeeds, I am blamed by the infidels and the warmaster both." He shifted his attention to Tsavong Lah. "The fact of my return stands as proof both of my worth to the Great Doctrine and of my faith in the warmaster's ability to see beyond such primitive ruses."

Vergere's beakish mouth opened as though she might hiss, then she caught herself and seemed to calm. "Do not blame me for your failures on Coruscant. It only makes you look more the—"

"Enough."

Though the warmaster spoke quietly, the mere sound of his voice was enough to silence Vergere—and save her life. Had she uttered the fateful *fool,* Nom Anor would have been not only within his rights, but *expected* to kill her on the spot.

"The assassination of Borsk Fey'lya—or the *attempt*—holds little interest for me." The shadow of a smile came to Tsavong Lah's lips. He manipulated something in an arm sack, and the throne's legs folded, lowering the warmaster to a more comfortable speaking level. "Before you arrived, Nom Anor, we were discussing

General Bel Iblis's pathetic scheme to undermine the morale of our warriors with this nonsense about *Jeedai* twins. How did he think of such an idea?"

Nom Anor knew what Tsavong Lah wanted to hear, but he was not foolish enough to lie in the warmaster's presence—not with Vergere waiting to pounce on his every word. "I have no knowledge of how Bel Iblis prepares his plans."

"Then guess," Tsavong Lah said. "I command it."

Nom Anor's throat grew scratchy. The blaze bugs, temporarily released from their station by the idleness of the throne, began to descend on the group. The touch of their hot abdomens stung more than the stab of their proboscises, but such was the price of service. No one did more than shoo the ravenous creatures away from their eyes, and the readers did not do that much.

"My master, humans are not like Yuuzhan Vong. Twins are not an infrequent occurrence," Nom Anor said. In all of Yuuzhan Vong history, there had been only a few twin births—and these only when the gods wished it so. In each instance, one had murdered the other in childhood, then matured to lead the empire through a time of grave crisis. Lord Shimrra himself had murdered his twin brother before growing up to have the dream that foretold the finding of this new galaxy. "Their birth suggests no special favor of the gods."

"Then you are saying the Solo children *are* twins?" The reader who asked this was Kol Yabu of the Undying Flame, a "half-and-half" whose burn-melded body had been carefully shaped to appear male from one profile and female from the other. As an apostle of the Undying Flame, Kol Yabu worshiped the twins Yun-Txiin and Yun-Q'aah, brother and sister gods of love and hate and all things opposite. "You admit that Jacen and Jaina Solo *are* twin *Jeedai* brother and sister?"

Nom Anor tried to wet his throat, but found his swallow as dry as bone dust. "*I admit nothing, Reader.*" He looked toward Tsavong Lah and decided it was probably well that the warmaster's face remained hidden behind a glowing mask of blaze bugs. "Our spy, Viqi Shesh, claims the two Solos are twins, and that their mother and uncle are also twins. Perhaps she is the one we should ask about Bel Iblis's plan."

Tsavong Lah avoided the half-and-half's gaze by glaring at Nom Anor. "Viqi is either a traitor to her own people, or an infidel double agent. I have no faith in her."

"In this matter, we can trust only the opinion of a Yuuzhan Vong," Vergere agreed. Unlike the others, she was not limned in scintillating blaze bug light—perhaps because she kept ruffling her feathers to keep the hungry creatures at bay. "And Nom Anor was on Coruscant. Surely he took time to investigate a matter of such importance before fleeing?"

Nom would have liked to claim there had been no time, but he knew better than to think he could defeat Vergere's trap so easily. Deciding his only hope lay in the unexpected, he took a deep breath, then looked the warmaster in the eye and told the truth.

"There were many records to support Shesh's claim, my master, and I doubt they were planted. Even in obscure sources, I found nothing to contradict her." When the blaze bugs began to leave the warmaster's angry face and take wing, Nom Anor decided his only hope of redemption lay in a risky strategy. "Clearly, fortune was smiling on us when the one named Jacen escaped you at Duro."

The cognition throne trembled and hopped forward—no doubt in response to the clenched fists inside its arm sacks.

"Tell me how." The warmaster's voice was low and harsh, for he did not enjoy being reminded of how Jacen had used the Jedi sorcery a year earlier to rob him of a foot and prevent the sacrifice of Leia Organa Solo.

Nom Anor took a deep breath, then turned to Kol Yabu. "How would Yun-Txiin and Yun-Q'aah view the sacrifice of only one twin?"

The half-and-half considered this for a moment, then said, "The Twins do not demand sacrifices, but the Balance is all."

"That is not what the executor asked," Tsavong Lah said, glowering at the priest. "Answer clearly, or I will ask for a reader who does."

Kol Yabu's eyesacks paled; he—or she, Nom Anor had never checked to see which—answered to Vaecta, but such a request from the warmaster would not be ignored. "*Offended* is not the word, Warmaster. The Great Dance would grow unstable."

Tsavong Lah considered this and nodded. "I thought as much."

"If I may make a suggestion," Nom Anor said, determined to exploit his gains. "Perhaps Lord Shimrra would look favorably on a sacrifice of twin Jedi? You could have them fight each other, as Lord Shimrra fought his brother, just as the gods have ordained that twins must do since the beginning of Yuuzhan Vong history."

Tsavong Lah sat back in the cognition throne, considering. "It would make a great gift to Yun-Yuuzhan, would it not?"

There was no reader to answer, for only Lord Shimrra himself communed with Yun-Yuuzhan, the Cosmic Lord.

"They will never fight each other," Vergere said, always eager to undermine Nom Anor. "They are as close as a pilot and his coralskipper, these two."

Nom Anor was spared the necessity of countering her argument by the warmaster himself.

"We will have to break them first, that is all," Tsavong Lah said. "And Nom Anor should arrange to netcast the combat for the New Republic, I think."

"As you wish, Great Warmaster." Nom Anor allowed himself a quick smirk in Vergere's direction, then said, "Nothing could dishearten the Jedi more, I am sure."

Chapter 21

Anasal Bith voice keened in anguish somewhere in the middle of the *Exquisite Death*'s frigid hold, and Jaina knew Ulaha was in the jaws of the voxyn again. Like the rest of the strike team, Jaina sat facing a wall of red yorik coral, bent uncomfortably forward with her elbows between her knees, her ankles and wrists fastened to the floor by gummy masses of blorash jelly. She was barely clothed and filthy and in too much pain to care, though she did wish it were not so cold. She was shivering, and shivering made everything hurt more.

Ulaha screamed again, and Alema Rar, sitting next to Jaina in much the same condition, mumbled something through swollen lips. Jaina, who was having trouble collecting her thoughts after the voxyn screeched in her face, recalled something about teamwork and opened her emotions to her companions. Immediately, she felt Jacen weaving them into a single entity, calling upon their mutual confidence and fellowship to lend strength to their suffering comrade.

Though everyone except Ganner—who was being held somewhere else in the mistaken belief that he was the group's leader—had faced the breaking at least once, Duman Yaght kept returning to Ulaha, allowing the Bith just enough time to drop into a Jedi healing trance before awakening her to begin again. Poor Ulaha had been to the center of the hold so many times that the others were attempting to prolong their own sessions to buy time for the Bith to recover. Jaina recalled dimly that she had managed only one answer before an angry Duman Yaght pushed her at the creature's face, drawing the compressed-wave screech that had blasted her into unconsciousness.

When Ulaha's cries grew quiet, Duman Yaght said, "Growing accustomed to the drool, are we, Bighead?" His favorite torture was to place Ulaha's wound beneath the voxyn's acid-slavering jaws. "We shall have to try something new."

Ulaha screamed. Jaina struggled to look over her shoulder, but could turn only far enough to see Anakin, Jacen, and several others straining to do the same. For her, that was the worst part of the breaking, the listening to friends scream without knowing what was happening to them. She felt Jacen drawing upon her concern to reinforce the Bith. Ulaha's scream grew a little less visceral, and Duman Yaght sensed the change. He always sensed the change.

"You don't have to tell me where to find the *Jeedai* base," the Yuuzhan Vong said. "Just admit there is one."

Ulaha's scream returned to its anguished pitch, and this time Jacen seemed unable to relieve the Bith's distress. Jaina looked to her other side, where Eryl Besa sat stiff-bodied and wide-eyed, the victim of a neural tail shock—a voxyn attack form they had not known about until Duman Yaght suggested that Eryl experience it. After a moment, Jaina finally caught the other woman's eye and raised her brow.

Eryl frowned in puzzlement, then seemed to understand and shook her head. The daughter of a fanatic space racer, Eryl had been conceived and born on a long cross-galaxy run, then spent most of her childhood speeding up and down the mapped arms of the galaxy. Somewhere along the way, she had developed the ability to tell by the texture of the Force where she was in the galaxy at any given moment. It was her job to alert Anakin once they were safely behind Yuuzhan Vong lines, where they would be far less likely to run into space mines and curious picket ships. Unfortunately, it was taking longer to cross the war zone than anyone expected—perhaps, Jaina suspected, because Duman Yaght hoped to make a name for himself by returning to his masters with the location of the Jedi base.

"What harm is there in admitting it?" Duman Yaght asked. "The Yuuzhan Vong already know of its existence. Just admit what we know already, and you can rest. You can go into your healing sleep."

"There . . . is . . . no base . . ."

"No, don't lie." Duman Yaght's voice remained as eerily calm as always. "Give me your hand. I want to tell you about the neuropoison."

An involuntary whistle of terror escaped Ulaha's nasal cavities, but she said nothing. Jaina imagined the commander holding the Bith's hand over the sensory bristles along the voxyn's back, for Cilghal had detected a powerful neurotoxin coating the spines. There would be an antidote in the equipment pod, but it was as untested as the rest of the inoculations and antivenins she and Tekli had administered before the strike team's departure.

"Your skin is so thin, and the tiniest puncture will inject the poison," Duman Yaght said. "Our shapers claim the effect is not the same on all species. Some fall into convulsions and sink into an endless sleep of pain. Others weaken over many hours, slowly growing so feeble they can no longer breathe or swallow. Some drown in their own saliva."

In the silence that followed, Ulaha's pain and fear grew heavy in the Force. Jaina opened herself to both sensations, hoping to ease her comrade's burden by taking some upon herself, but she was too frightened to be of much help. Bith had only one lung, and the coufee attack aboard the *Lady Luck* had pierced Ulaha's. If she had to fight a neurotoxin, as well . . . Jaina *wanted* her to admit the existence of Eclipse. She couldn't help it; she just did not want to see Ulaha die.

No sooner had she given thought to this emotion than she felt a flood of similar feelings from the others. Jaina knew that persuading Ulaha to admit the planet's existence was only the first step of the breaking, but what harm was there, really? The strike team would be seizing the ship soon, and at least Ulaha would still be alive. She felt a flash of alarm from Alema and a certain bewilderment from the Barabels, but there was no doubting the general feeling of the group. They agreed.

"Bighead, you must think carefully before you answer," Duman Yaght said. "This may be your last chance. Is there a *Jeedai* base?"

Tell him! Jaina wanted to scream.

"You know . . . the answer," Ulaha gasped.

"I am sorry, Bighead. That is not good enough."

Say it!

"Yes!" Ulaha cried.

The group let out an emotional sigh of relief, but now Alema seemed worried and the Barabels sad.

"Yes what?" Duman demanded.

"Yes, there is a Jedi base," Jaina said, yelling into the wall. "She admitted it! Now let her rest."

"Jaina, be quiet!" Alema hissed. "He's trying to break—"

The admonishment was interrupted by a hollow crack, and Jaina looked over to see a Yuuzhan Vong warrior holding the butt of an amphistaff over the Twi'lek's unconscious form. There was a surge of anger from the other Jedi, but Jaina felt only guilt. It had been her outburst that prompted Alema to speak without permission.

Duman Yaght said something in his own language, and the guard tossed a small button-shaped beetle on the floor beside each of Jaina's wrists and ankles. The blorash jelly released its adhesive hold on her flesh and slid away to encase the struggling insects. The guard jerked Jaina to her feet and spun her toward the center of the room, where the commander stood holding Ulaha's hand over the voxyn's sensory bristles. The Bith's normally pale skin had gone translucent with blood loss, and she was so weak that a Yuuzhan Vong warrior had to hold her up. The rest of the strike team sat along the edge of the small hold, partially clothed, filthy, and facing the walls. Only Ganner, whose presence they sometimes sensed forward and sometimes not at all, was absent.

Duman Yaght studied Jaina, then asked, "You think I do not keep my word?"

Jaina fixed her eye on Ulaha's hand. "That remains to be seen."

The commander seemed confused by her challenging tone, then recovered and smirked. "Very well. You are the one in control here."

He said something to the guard holding Ulaha, who returned the injured Jedi to her place next to Tekli, laying the Bith on her back instead of the uncomfortable sitting position in which everyone else was bound.

"The Bith may rest and heal." Duman Yaght smiled at Jaina. "And you will determine how long."

Jaina began to feel sick and frightened, but forced herself to raise her head and step forward without being summoned. Warm feelings of encouragement and confidence flooded into her as the others reached out to prepare her for the breaking. She felt fairly confident that Duman Yaght would not let the voxyn kill her—he had already bragged to her about the place he had been promised at the Great Sacrifice—so she saw every reason to think that with her companions supporting her, she could buy Ulaha enough time to enter a healing trance and stabilize her wounded lung.

But Jaina's confidence was not enough to keep her from trembling as she approached. Only the strength flowing to her through the Force had prevented her from wailing like an infant the first time Duman Yaght tried to break her, and this time would be worse—much worse. The commander could not allow her to challenge him and succeed, and there were so many ways he could hurt her without killing her, so many things to remove or disfigure or break.

A fresh surge of confidence buoyed Jaina up as Jacen relayed Anakin's resolve to keep her healthy, Zekk's admiration of her bravery, Ulaha's weary gratitude, Tekli's calm assurance that all of their injuries could be repaired. She stopped before Duman Yaght and looked up into his face.

"I hope you don't expect me to thank you."

He soured her stomach by clasping the back of her neck. "No need."

He guided her to the voxyn's head. Though the creature's malicious hunger rippled through the Force with a carnal urgency, the thing seemed very much the master of its instincts, quivering with excitement, yet keeping its yellow eyes fixed on its master to await his command. Duman Yaght paused a meter from its jaws, turning Jaina to watch the beads of sour-smelling drool as they dripped from the voxyn's fangs and landed, smoking, on the floor. Jaina swallowed; her back was covered with thumb-sized circles where the drops had fallen the time before. She started to kneel.

Duman Yaght's hand tightened, holding her up. "That is not what I was thinking." He guided her past the voxyn to the wall where her brothers sat affixed to the floor. "Choose."

"What?" Jaina felt the shock of his demand not only in the hollowness of her own stomach, but in the stunned outrage coming to her through the Force. "Choose what?"

"You are the one in control, Jaina Solo. Who will be next?" He kicked first Anakin in the kidneys, then Jacen. "Your brother, or your twin?"

"They're both my brothers." In Jaina's shock, it registered only vaguely that Duman Yaght now realized her relationship to Jacen. "And I choose neither. I choose me."

Duman Yaght shook his head. "That is not your choice. You must choose Anakin or Jacen." Again, he kicked them, drawing involuntary groans from both. "Choose one, or I will be forced to return Ulaha to the breaking. The warmaster knows of her wound, so no one will think anything of it should she happen to die. You are the master now, Jaina Solo."

Jaina felt a surge of anger and would have whirled on Duman Yaght to attack, had a flash of alarm from her brothers not brought her up short. Each wanted to be the one chosen—she would have felt that much from her brothers even without the group's emotional bond—and her tie to Jacen went farther yet. She could sense that for him it was more than a matter of being noble, that he had good reason to believe himself the best choice. Jaina suspected those reasons included the fact that Anakin would need a clear head when the time came to escape—it had to be soon, she hoped—but she could not be certain; even the bond between the twins was not strong enough to share complete thoughts.

"Your choice?" Duman Yaght demanded.

"You can't ask that," Jaina said. She told herself that as facilitator of the battle meld, Jacen was just as important as Anakin, but the truth was that she could not bring herself to harm either one. Though Anakin was a war hero and leader to everyone else, he would always be a little brother to her—someone to look after, protect, keep out of trouble. And Jacen had always been her best friend, the person who understood her when she did not understand herself, the presence that enveloped her like a second skin. How could she send either of them? She looked away from Duman Yaght. "I can't choose."

"No?" His hand tightened on the back of her neck, and he started to pull her away. "A pity for the Bith, then."

Anakin craned his head around. "Jaina, you *can* choose." The weight of the Force was behind his words, not as much to compel her as to make clear that this was an order. "You can choose me."

Jaina's connection to the others diminished as Jacen withdrew into himself. He looked toward their younger brother.

"Anakin—"

"Be quiet, Jacen." Anakin continued to stare at Jaina. "Choose."

Duman Yaght looked at her expectantly. "The Bith will probably die anyway, you know."

Jaina closed her eyes. "Anakin," she said. "Take Anakin."

Duman Yaght nodded to the guard standing behind her brothers, then said something to another standing beside one of the gelatinous membranes that covered the hold doorways. The warrior tickled the membrane until it drew aside, then disappeared into the next room with a thin smile of anticipation.

Instead of returning Jaina to her place on the wall, Duman Yaght forced her to stand beside him as Anakin was secured to the floor facedown. The commander summoned his pet forward and began to give orders, and for the next quarter hour Jaina was forced to watch.

Bolstered by the support of the strike team, Anakin never cried out. Eventually even Duman Yaght clucked his tongue in admiration.

"He takes pain well, your brother," the commander said. "Perhaps we try something new, yes?"

He barked a command, and the voxyn held a foot over Anakin's back. The sharp claws were coated in green slime—the medium, Jaina knew, for the retroviruses that flourished in the thing's toe pads.

"Is that fear in your eyes, Jaina Solo?" Duman asked. "Then there is no need to tell you about the fevers. You know what will become of your brother if he is scratched."

"You wouldn't disappoint your priests." As Jaina spoke, she reached out to the others, sharing with them the uncertainty her brave words concealed. The vaccine Cilghal had given them was untested; it might destroy all the diseases or only some, and she was not happy about experimenting with her brother's life. "Not when they have promised you a place at our sacrifices."

"True, but think of my place if I could tell them in which region the *Jeedai* base is located," Duman Yaght said. "I would be only a few tiers behind the warmaster, close enough so that you could see the gratitude in my eyes."

An overwhelming sense of defiance came to Jaina—Anakin's feelings on the matter, no doubt, as relayed by Jacen.

"You'll just have to watch from the back," Jaina retorted.

Duman Yaght's hand tightened on her neck. "You believe I won't do this?"

He whistled sharply, and the voxyn raked its claw down Anakin's back. Jaina felt a shock through the Force, but somehow her brother still did not scream.

"You overestimate your brother's value," Duman Yaght said. "The priests will be happy as long as I return with you and Jacen. You two are the twins."

He said the word *twins* as though it were some sort of state secret. There was something there Jaina did not understand, but it hardly mattered. One way or the other, she and Jacen were going to disappoint both Duman Yaght and the priests.

The guard who had been sent out earlier reappeared at the hold door. Duman Yaght had a pair of guards lay a lump of blorash jelly over the voxyn's two rear feet, trapping the creature in place. They moved Anakin well beyond the voxyn's reach and secured him to the floor by a single foot.

This was something new, and Jaina did not like the look of it. "What are you preparing, a stare-down?"

Duman Yaght cracked a smile. "In a manner of speaking, yes."

He nodded to the door guard, who stood aside and stretched the membrane back to admit what looked like a small tree. About the size of a grown Wookiee, the plant had a small but thick crown of foliage. In the center of its trunk was a single knothole with a glassy black orb, which it turned in the commander's direction. Duman Yaght pointed at the center of the hold, and the tree clumped forward on three gnarled root burls.

As the thing approached, the voxyn's forked tongue flickered out to test the air. The sensory bristles rose on its back, then it strained to curl its long body around and look behind it.

The tree was about seven meters away when the voxyn went wild, hissing madly and gouging furrows into the floor as it tried to tear itself free. The creature seemed to have lost all its intelligence, acting more like a mindless beast than the shrewd predator the Jedi had learned to fear.

The tree continued to advance, and two meters later Jaina lost all contact with her companions. She reached out with the Force and felt nothing. Then, as the tree drew nearer and the rest of the strike team struggled to see what was cutting them off from the Force, Jaina glimpsed a lizardlike shape clinging to the back of the tree—no doubt trying to hide itself from the voracious predator clambering to get it.

"An ysalamiri," Jaina said loudly. She was a little puzzled, for ysalamiri usually created a much larger bubble of Force absence. "What are you going to do with that?"

"An interesting question." Duman Yaght nodded to the guard who had brought the walking tree into the room. "Show her."

The guard stepped forward and took the ysalamiri from its perch. The creature's hook-shaped claws tore small chunks of bark out of the trunk, drawing a pained leaf-rustle from the tree. With a crooked ridge of vertebrae running down its gaunt back and red sores flecking its smooth hide, the ysalamiri itself looked half dead. The voxyn was mad to get at it, lunging and flicking its tongue at the wary guard as he laid the thing on Anakin's shoulders.

The ysalamiri slid down behind Anakin's back and held on. The voxyn lunged at its restraints, threatening to pull its rear legs out of socket.

"The shapers cannot understand why, but ysalamiri drive voxyn mad," Duman Yaght said. "The voxyn lose their natural cunning. In experiments similar to this, I have seen them tear off their own legs to get the ysalamiri."

"Your point?"

"You know my point," Duman Yaght said. "Sooner or later, the voxyn will stop trying to eat its problem and kill it."

Jaina could not take her eyes off her brother, now so coated in blood he looked almost clothed. In the equipment pod, there was a way to make the ysalamiri leave the hold, of course, but Anakin and Ganner were the only ones who could activate the war droids and get at it. If they both died, the droids would automatically activate to search for strike team survivors—hardly the way Jaina wanted to deal with the problem of the ysalamiri.

"In what region will we find the *Jeedai* base?" Duman Yaght asked. "Take all the time you wish to answer. I am in no hurry."

Jaina tore her gaze from Anakin. Now she understood. In dragging Ulaha before the voxyn all those times, Duman Yaght had not been trying to break the Bith. He had been trying to break the rest of the strike team—and Jaina had shown the first crack. Her body did not seem large enough to hold the disappointment she felt in herself. Lando had warned them, and she clearly had not listened.

Without looking at her tormentor, she asked, "You'll release Anakin if I answer?"

"If that is what you wish," Duman Yaght answered. "You are the one controlling things."

"The Core," Jaina answered. Technically, it was true, though the only way to reach it was via a short hyperlane shaving the edge of the Deep Core. "That should come as no surprise."

Duman Yaght nodded. "It confirms what the readers have surmised." He nodded, and Anakin's guard tore the ysalamiri free, then tossed it to the voxyn. "Never deny a killer her reward."

"I'll keep that in mind," Jaina said. As the voxyn gulped down its treat, her contact with the Force returned, and she felt a surge of support from her companions. "What about my brother?"

"Of course. Just tell me who is next."

Jaina's heart fell. She had expected something like this and knew there was only one response. "Me."

"Not possible."

"It's my only answer."

"Then Anakin will stay. Perhaps he will die."

"You said you would release him," Jaina said. "I thought Yuuzhan Vong were honorable."

The blue beneath the commander's eyes grew darker, but he turned to Anakin's guard and nodded. "Return him to his place and bring the Bith."

Jaina sensed a torrent of conflicting emotions from the rest of the strike team. Some seemed frightened for Ulaha, others supportive of her defiance, but Jacen brought one feeling to the fore— Anakin's calmness and determination. He had a plan; Jaina had no idea what, but just knowing that much gave her the strength to remain silent.

Three meters from the wall, Anakin pulled out of his guard's grasp and, yelling for Ulaha to wake, sprang to her side. He dropped to his knees and whispered frantically into her ear. Ulaha's lidless eyes continued to stare vacantly at the ceiling, but a groggy hint of disappointment in the Force suggested she was more alert than she appeared. Anakin managed another half a dozen words before a guard's amphistaff slammed him in the head. He sank into a place of quiet darkness, and even the strike team's apprehension could not summon him back.

The guard secured him in place with blorash jelly, then released Ulaha and, still holding his amphistaff in one hand, dragged the Bith to the center of the hold. The voxyn tried to face them, but found its rear feet still secured and settled for watching out of one eye. The creature seemed in control of itself again, but its hunger burned through the Force as hot as a blaster bolt.

Too weak to stand on her own, Ulaha was trembling visibly and seemed unwilling to lift her gaze from the floor. Lando had said they would need to do things that sat poorly with their consciences, but Jaina could not believe he had meant standing by while the Yuuzhan Vong killed someone on their team.

"The choice is yours, Jaina." Duman Yaght twisted his scarified face into the semblance of a smirk. "A name or a life."

Jaina reached out to Eryl Besa through the Force, praying for some sign that they had crossed the war zone, that they could finally call the war droids to blast them out of this mess. No such reassurance came.

Jaina lowered her head. There was only one way to correct her mistake, only one way to defeat the breaking, but she could not bring herself to let Ulaha die—to actually speak the words that would kill her.

Jaina did not look up. "This is the last name."

"If you wish it so."

Duman Yaght's mocking tone provoked a sense of deep humiliation. Jaina had been broken. Everyone knew.

Ulaha's feeble voice came to her, and with it a sense of shame not unlike her own. "You mustn't, Jaina . . . Don't let them use me—"

She was silenced by a sharp smack.

"The name, Jaina," Duman Yaght demanded. "Who is next?"

Jaina finally raised her gaze and saw Ulaha struggling to recover her feet. The guard was practically dangling the Bith by her arm, holding her hand over the sensory bristles along the voxyn's spine.

Ulaha turned toward Jacen, gasped, "Give me strength."

"Quiet!" The warrior jerked Ulaha to her feet.

The Force surged with encouragement, support, and something else—something electric and raw, like the zap of a stun bolt.

Suddenly, Ulaha gathered her legs beneath her. The strange energy continued to flow through the Force, and she grew stronger by the moment, pushing her hand down . . . down onto the sensory bristles. It was all the guard could do to keep the Bith from impaling her own palm.

Jaina felt sick. Could this have been Anakin's plan? The anger spilling out of Jacen made clear what he thought, but Jaina could not believe Anakin would order anyone to take her own life—not when he still felt Chewbacca's death so acutely.

Ulaha proved too weak to push her hand down all the way. She appeared to give up—then snatched her captor's coufee from its sheath and flicked the blade across the Yuuzhan Vong's throat. A cascade of blood poured out. With impossible speed for one so wounded, Ulaha jerked him around and caught the voxyn's striking tail on his back.

The barb snapped against the warrior's vonduun crab armor. Duman Yaght roared a command that sent half a dozen warriors dashing in. The voxyn opened its mouth to screech, and Jaina thought it was over for Ulaha. Then Jacen let the battle meld drop, and she felt him reaching out, attuning himself to the voxyn's emotions, infusing it with the idea that Ulaha's attack was only a diversion, that the real danger lay with the Yuuzhan Vong rushing in from the flank. It was a desperate gamble, one that could ruin the mission if Duman Yaght came to understand how the Jedi were playing him. Jaina expected nothing else from a Solo.

The voxyn swung its head around and burped a bubble of green mucilage over the closest guard. The Yuuzhan Vong stumbled half a dozen steps more, groaning, screaming, dissolving. Ulaha used the distraction to slip forward and drive the coufee down between the voxyn's eyes.

The creature shuddered to the floor and began to convulse, and even that ceased when the Bith twisted the blade. Purple blood oozed around the wound, turning to brown fume as it contacted the air. Ulaha staggered back with a hand clasped over her face. She made a second step, then collapsed.

The surviving guards stopped outside the brown cloud. Duman Yaght barked something harsh, and one warrior tossed a ball of blorash onto the coufee knife, sealing the wound. Another covered his mouth and nose and dashed in to recover Ulaha.

She allowed the guard to drag her clear of the toxin cloud, then gathered her legs beneath her and rose. Wide Yuuzhan Vong eyes and gaping Yuuzhan Vong mouths betrayed their surprise at seeing such a mangled body rise, and even Duman Yaght gasped.

A familiar sissing sounded from the far side of the hold, where all three Barabels were sniggering hysterically, their heads twisted around backward and their reptilian eyes glazed with exhaustion.

Jaina allowed herself a smirk, then returned her gaze to Duman Yaght. "Perhaps you have another voxyn to amuse us?"

The Yuuzhan Vong glared down and, much to her surprise, smiled. "That would be foolish, don't you think? I see why the warmaster is so determined to destroy you *Jeedai*." He motioned a pair of guards over, then thrust her into their arms. "Know that we are done playing, Jaina Solo. If you try anything now, the consequences will be fatal."

"Perhaps." Jaina smiled back at him. "But not for us."

The comment drew feelings of alarm from many on the strike team, but Jaina knew by the sudden darkness under Duman Yaght's eyes that she had said exactly the right thing. He turned away, already calling for the star reader to plot a faster course to the rendezvous.

Chapter 22

It would have been simpler to take a tray down to the mess hall and order breakfast from one of Eclipse's military food processors, but Mara was grilling dustcrepes and nausage—a Tatooine favorite—over the single thermpad assigned to the Skywalker living quarters. Hardly a chef under the best of circumstances, she had somehow browned the dustcrepes and puffed the nausage, but she refused to admit defeat. Fetching breakfast would have meant opening the door to the rest of the base, and after a rare full night in her husband's company—a night through which Ben had slept blissfully—Mara wanted Luke to herself for just a few minutes more.

R2-D2 whistled from the other side of the work counter, then ran an urgent message across the sitting room vidscreen.

"There's no reason to alert Emergency Control," she said. "This isn't a fire."

R2-D2 tweedled an objection.

"This isn't cooking, it's . . . heating," Mara growled. "Any suggestion otherwise will earn you a memory wipe. Clear?"

R2-D2 trilled scornfully, then fell silent.

Mara looked down to see the nausage in her makeshift skillet collapsing into black crumbs. Luke picked that moment to emerge from the refresher, pulling a fresh tunic over his wet hair.

"Smells good." He popped a morsel of blackened nausage into his mouth, somehow avoiding a sour face and nodding in approval. "Just like we used to make back home."

"Really?" Mara asked doubtfully. "And I always thought the reason you left Tatooine was to join the Rebellion and save the galaxy."

Luke maintained a deadpan expression. "No, it was the food—definitely the food."

He took a rubbery dustcrepe and began to chew, rolling his eyes as though he were enjoying a bowl of green thakitillo. Disarmed as always by Luke's humble good nature, Mara laughed and leaned across the counter to kiss him.

To everyone else on Eclipse, he might be the enigmatic Jedi Master and last best hope for an imperiled galaxy, but to her he was the gentle husband who always knew what to say, the unassuming moisture farmer who had seen value in her when she could not find it herself. Even knowing of all the things she had done in Palpatine's service, all the lies told and the lives taken, he had accepted her first as a peer, then a friend, and finally—after it had dawned on Mara that the Force was steering them toward a very different relationship than the one envisioned by Emperor Palpatine—a lover and a spouse.

She pulled away from her husband's lips and smiled. "For last night."

Luke glanced across the room to where Ben was sleeping in his crib, watched over by an updated version of the same TDL nanny droid that had tended Anakin and the twins when they were young, and did not need to say what he was thinking. Mara took his hand and started toward the sleeping chamber.

They had almost reached the door when R2-D2 whistled for their attention.

Mara did not even turn around. "Not now, Artoo."

R2-D2 whistled again, then sent a live feed of the hangar to the sitting room vidscreen. Mara glimpsed the *Shadow* and *Falcon* sitting with a dozen other large vessels on the far side of the cavernous bay, where several support technicians were jockeying blastboats to make room for an arriving ship. The central area was packed with seventy new XJ3 X-wings that Admiral Kre'fey had quietly rotated out of his fleet onto Eclipse, while Saba Sebatyne's motley assortment of starfighters and Kyp Durron's battle-scarred X-wings sat untended and inaccessible on the close side of the hangar.

The picture zoomed in on the area between the new X-wings and the older starfighters. Corran Horn stood surrounded by pilots from Kyp's Dozen, the Wild Knights, and the Shockers. This last squadron was Eclipse's own, made up equally of untested Jedi and space-blooded non-Jedi veterans. The three leaders, Kyp Durron, Saba Sebatyne, and the non-Jedi Rigard Matl, were all talking at once while an impatient-looking Corran Horn stood looking into the ceiling holocam.

Luke sighed, then asked Mara, "Do you mind?"

"I'll mind more if we don't win this war," she said. "Corran might seem rigid and moralistic, but he's not the sort who calls for help unless he needs it. Artoo, give us some sound."

Kyp Durron's impatient voice came over the speaker. ". . . don't see what we're waiting for. Maybe Danni will figure out how to jam the yammosks and maybe she won't, but in the meantime the Yuuzhan Vong have Anakin and the others." Like most pilots who had not promised to remain at Eclipse, Kyp had not yet been informed that the strike team's capture was a ruse. "While we train, they move deeper into Yuuzhan Vong territory."

"We'll go after them when Master Skywalker says we go after them," Corran replied. "Until then, we sit tight and wait for orders."

"Orders?" Kyp scoffed. "This isn't the military, *Corran.* Jedi don't wait for orders while the enemy carries their friends off for sacrifice."

"Perhaps not, but they don't rush into battle ill prepared," Rigard said. A former TIE pilot with a battle-scarred face nearly as gruesome as a Yuuzhan Vong's, Rigard hated war with a passion, yet had somehow found himself fighting on one side or the other—and sometimes both—in every major galactic conflict since the Rebellion. "We're waiting for more to fall in place than Danni's research on gravitic modulation. We don't want to lock in our cards until everything's ready."

"It is locking in the cardz that worries this one." Saba Sebatyne addressed this to the holocam, making clear that she was speaking directly to Luke. "She is thinking that when someone stickz an arm out too far, she is liable to lose a hand."

"Blasters!" Luke hissed, echoing a curse Mara had not heard since Jaina and Jacen were at the Jedi academy. "Kyp again."

"Better get down there," Mara said, reaching across the work counter for her comlink. "I'll let Corran know we're coming."

Mara and Luke dressed and, leaving instructions with the nanny droid to comm them when Ben woke, left for the hangar bay. They had to bundle themselves in thermal cloaks, for the base's cooling system was working *too* well now; the corridors were in constant danger of icing over.

As they twined their way through the passages, Mara sensed the disharmony welling up inside Luke. Though their bond was not quite deep enough for her to read his thoughts all the time, she knew he was once again struggling with the difficulties of leadership and family. In a time when the Jedi needed him most, he was worried that Mara's recovery—as mysterious as the disease itself—would not hold. In a time when he needed to be at her side learning to be a good father, he was struggling to hold the fractious Jedi together and find the wisest course along which to guide them.

They rounded a corner and started down the passage toward the big emergency air lock outside the hangar bay, and Mara took his hand.

"Skywalker, sometimes I think I should just kick you in the head."

Not looking all that surprised, Luke glanced over at her. "Really?"

Mara waved a hand at the hangar ahead. "Everything you're doing with the Jedi, it *is* for us." She palmed the air lock's control pad, and its hatch irised open. "Ben is strong in the Force. I know you've felt it, too."

Luke nodded. "I have."

"So the Jedi must win this war," Mara said. "If we don't, where will Ben be safe?"

Luke stopped, and Mara felt the disharmony in him melting away. He motioned her into the air lock. "I hadn't thought of it quite like that."

"Of course not. You're too selfless." She opened the door to the hangar. "But I'm not. Now, are you going to set Kyp and Saba straight—or am I?"

She felt Luke's smile in the back of her head.

"I'd better do it myself. It wouldn't be fair to let you loose on them."

"Fair?" Mara echoed. "What makes you think I care about fair?"

They stepped out of the air lock and walked down a clear path to the gathering of pilots. Danni Quee had also joined the group, no doubt summoned the instant Saba learned Luke was coming. Convinced the strike team could never withstand the breaking, she had been pressing Luke to send a backup mission almost since the *Wild*

Knights' return from Arkania. Luke had yet to rule out the possibility, in part because he feared Saba would take her squadron and attempt the mission herself—but also because he worried Danni was right.

Corran stepped aside, yielding his place at the head of the gathering to Luke.

Luke allowed a note of irritation to creep into his voice and focused only on Corran. "Corran, what's happening here? Why aren't you analyzing the morning exercise?"

Corran's eyes betrayed surprise at Luke's stern tone, but he stiffened his bearing. "Master Skywalker, our exercise came to an early end when the *Lady Luck* entered the system. It should be arriving shortly."

Luke heard Han and Leia approaching and, with a dart of his eyes, sent Mara to intercept them. The sense of purpose he felt from her confirmed that she understood what she needed to do.

As Mara departed, Luke continued to look at Corran. "I don't understand." His voice remained even but firm. "If Lando was in trouble, what are you doing here?"

Saba Sebatyne stepped forward. "It is not Jedi Horn's fault, Master Skywalker. This one left."

Luke raised his brow and waited.

"This one wanted to hear how it went."

"How *what* went?" Kyp demanded, completely ignorant of the part Lando had played in Anakin's "capture." "Somebody had better tell me what's going on around here before I take the Dozen and leave."

Luke stepped toward Kyp. "How can we tell you anything, when you are always so ready to leave us?"

Kyp frowned, then glanced over his shoulder at his pilots. "Are you saying you can't trust us?"

"It isn't a matter of trust," Luke replied.

He let the statement hang and continued to study Kyp as Han

and Leia came up behind him. Neither spoke, and they both fixed silent gazes on Kyp.

Finally, Kyp looked from Luke to Saba. "Saba knows what this is all about," he complained. "And *she* isn't promising to stay."

"Saba has a right to know. Her son is with Anakin," Luke said. "So are her apprentices."

Kyp considered this for a moment, then turned to Saba. "We don't have to take this, you know. We can go after them ourselves."

Han shook his head. "No, kid, you can't." He pointed at the blast doors. "You can take the Dozen and leave if you like, but you can't go after Anakin and the twins—not if friendship means anything to you."

A look of stunned confusion came over Kyp. "Those are *your* kids, Han. You should want us to go after them!"

"I want them back alive," Han said. "And that's not going to happen if you go after them."

"Depending on what Lando Calrissian has to report," Saba corrected. "If he has learned through his villip that the breaking worked—"

"There won't be a backup mission," Luke said. He saw Han stiffen and felt Leia's dismay through the Force, but Mara had prepared them well enough that they betrayed no other sign of concern. "The strike team must succeed or fail on its own. Even if we could reach them, we'll be too busy with other things."

"Strike team?" Kyp looked to Han for enlightenment. "What other things?"

"Sorry, Kyp. You'll have to ask Luke." Ever the gambler, Han sweetened the pot. "There's too much at risk for me to talk out of turn."

Kyp looked back to Luke. "Have you figured out what that feint at Arkania was about? Are we finally going to take the war to the Yuuzhan Vong?"

Luke fought to keep a deadpan face. "I don't know that 'we'

are going to do anything." As he spoke, the *Lady Luck* appeared outside the hangar door and hovered on the other side of the magnetic containment field while the technicians moved the last vessel, Tendra Risant Calrissian's *Gentleman Caller,* out of the way. "If you want to be part of this, I need your promise."

Kyp looked wary. "What kind of promise?"

"An oath of allegiance. What kind do you think?" Han asked, his tone almost angry. "You promise to obey Luke and do what he says as long as he'll have you. If you won't do that, pack your bags and get out now." Han paused, and his tone grew a little more gentle. "It's time you started acting like a Jedi Knight."

Kyp's eyes flared at the admonition. Luke thought for a moment Han had overplayed his hand, but, as usual, the Corellian knew how far to press a bet. Kyp's gaze slowly softened, and something fatherly in Han seemed to get through to him.

He turned to his pilots. "What do you think? Do we throw in with the Jedi and pretend like we're in a real space navy?"

"You know what we want," an insectoid Verpine pilot buzzed—one whose name Luke was ashamed to realize he did not know. "As long as we fight Yuuzhan Vong."

Kyp looked to the rest of his squadron. When they voiced similar sentiments, he turned and nodded to Han. "Okay, we promise."

"Not me, kid." Han quietly pointed to Luke. "He's the boss around here."

Kyp's face reddened, but he swallowed his pride and turned to Luke. "You have our oath, Master Skywalker. We'll stay as long as you'll have us."

"And follow orders?" This from Corran Horn.

Kyp made a sour face. "If we have to."

"You do." Luke saw the *Lady Luck* drifting into the docking bay and turned to Saba Sebatyne. "How about the Wild Knights?"

"Of course, if the Jedi truly intend to carry the war to the invaders," Saba said. "So you have determined the warmaster's purpose in feinting at Arkania?"

"We're still working on that," Luke said. "But we *are* going to carry the war to the Yuuzhan Vong. I would never have risked your son and apprentices if we weren't."

Chapter 23

A groggy Wookiee groan reverberated through the frigid hold of the *Exquisite Death*. Cautiously, Anakin craned his neck around. Lowbacca and many others remained hidden behind a small grove of ysalamiri-laden trees the Yuuzhan Vong had marched into the hold, but he could see Jaina and Eryl opposite him and Jovan and the Barabels on the wall adjacent. Still secured to the floor with their hands between their knees, they were all fidgeting, trying to relieve the strain on their back and legs. The Barabels seemed especially uncomfortable, with their thick tails stretched straight behind them and secured at the tip with blorash jelly.

Anakin glanced over at Zekk and his brother and raised his brow. Zekk nodded eagerly, but Jacen closed his eyes and looked away. Unable to imagine what was troubling his moody brother—and not sure he cared—Anakin lowered his chin toward his left armpit.

"Activate escape," he whispered.

There was a hot tingle as the subcutaneous implant relayed the message, then a heavy foot scuffed the floor behind him. Anakin ducked and caught the expected strike on his much-bruised shoulder.

"Quiet, *Jeedai*," the guard said. "Another word, and I fill your mouth with blorash jelly."

Uncertain how long the war droids would need—or even whether they were still attached to the ship—Anakin fixed his gaze on the floor. The guard hovered another thirty seconds, then shuffled off.

Many minutes later, a series of distant thuds sounded forward in the ship. From the next hold back came a much louder *whumpf*, then the muffled roar of explosive decompression and the clatter and shriek of equipment and creatures tumbling into the void. In the back of the Jedi's hold, the door membranes bowed dangerously outward, but held long enough to turn opaque and stiffen into durasteel-like panels.

The subaltern barked something in Yuuzhan Vong. When no response came from his shoulder villip, he sent two guards forward to investigate, assigned eight more to watch the Jedi prisoners, and took the last two to the rear of the hold. Anakin knew that by now, 2-1S would be standing guard as 2-4S sealed the breach, using emergency patching foam to mate the open equipment pod to the *Death*'s exterior hull. He watched the guards carefully, alert for any hint of an order coming through their shoulder villips.

The subaltern pressed his face close to the door as though to breathe on it, but then a cannon bolt came blasting through the opaque membrane and sprayed black gore everywhere. Anakin's ears popped as the hold pressures equalized, and the subaltern's two escorts were reduced to so much smoking flesh by a series of strobelike weapon flashes.

The rest of the Yuuzhan Vong reached for thud bugs and amphistaffs. Some turned to assault the strike team and fell to a flurry of screaming green bolts as 2-1S crashed into the hold. A coat of icy rime was forming on his space-cold armor, and his photoreceptors were fogging over; Anakin feared the droid would be forced to stand idle while his surface temperature stabilized. Instead,

2-1S activated a thermal defogger and cut down two more enemies as they dived for cover. He raised his other arm and began knocking ysalamiri from their trees with an optional electroray discharger.

Anakin's guard yelled something about *Jeedai* and spun to attack Anakin and was cut in half by a torrent of rapid-fire blaster bolts. The stream swept down the wall, chopping through an ysalamiri tree to dismember a Yuuzhan Vong whirling on Jacen. As 2-1S did all this, he was advancing into the hold, taking thud bugs in the chest and scorching two warriors near Jaina with electrorays. It could not have escaped anyone's notice that the droid was protecting the three Solos—a programming adjustment Lando had neglected to mention—but the others had no cause to complain.

YVH 2-4S entered the hold on the heels of 2-1S, one arm firing a blaster cannon, the other minirockets. He shot through the elbows of a Yuuzhan Vong attempting to behead Jovan Drark, then chased another away from Tekli with a self-guiding minirocket.

Only Tesar had to defend himself, ripping his tail free of the blorash jelly and, leaving the tip behind, sweeping his attacker off his feet. The Yuuzhan Vong landed hard, but leveled his amphistaff at Tesar's midsection—only to have his arms pinned to the floor by Bela's tail, also tipless. Krasov finished the fight by smashing her tail—tipless, as well—across his windpipe.

"Surprise!" Tesar rasped.

This launched the three Barabels into a bewildering fit of laughter. Tesar used the raw end of his tipless tail to flip open the dead Yuuzhan Vong's waist pouch and began flicking beetles at the blorash jelly binding nearby Jedi to the floor.

Anakin looked across the hold to 2-1S. "Secure the doors," he ordered.

A beetle landed beside Anakin's ankle, then several more between him and Jacen, and soon they were free. He assigned one group to retrieve weapons and equipment from the pod, another to dispose of the ysalamiri, and the rest of the Jedi to evaluate the group's medical condition and tend to Ulaha. Only then did he join 2-1S at the forward door, where the droid was peering through the translucent membrane down a long access corridor.

"Report."

"Sir, we are fifteen seconds ahead of schedule. Two-Four-S was able to penetrate the hull with ten coma-gas canisters; effectiveness assessment currently unavailable. Three voxyn were detected in the stern hold and attacked with class-C thermal detonators; postblast sensor sweep detected no sign of surviving life-forms."

"And the vessel itself?" Anakin asked. Tekli appeared beside him, her pudgy Chadra-Fan snout twitching incessantly as she reached up to spray a pain-numbing antiseptic over his raw back. He nodded his thanks, but kept his attention fixed on 2-1S. "Were you able to do any internal mapping?"

"Sir, we are aboard a corvette-analog picket boat, length one hundred twenty-two meters, estimated crew ninety-eight," 2-1S said. "Ultrasonic soundings suggest a two-level design with back-to-back decks sharing a common floor, four main access corridors, three aft holds, forward-facing bridge in the bow, and a substantial network of nondiagrammed ducts."

Anakin groaned inwardly; the ducts would make it easy for the enemy to move around undetected. The Barabels came up behind him loaded with weapons, equipment, and bulky jumpsuits.

"One-One-A fished these out of the flushlock," Tesar said, passing Anakin's lightsaber to him.

As Anakin took it, the lambent crystal inside opened him to the presence of the Yuuzhan Vong, an indistinct fury somewhere forward in the ship.

Bela pointed to a gob of frozen gunk on the handle. "Want that meat?"

"Uh, not really."

Anakin knocked the garbage off the handle and clipped the weapon to the equipment harness Tesar was holding out to him. The Barabels exchanged expressionless reptilian glances, then Krasov retrieved the gunk and divided it into three even pieces. Anakin rolled his eyes and selected a blaster pistol and half a dozen stun grenades from the small arsenal Tesar was carrying, then called the rest of the group over while Tahiri, who had insisted on taking the duty over from Tekli, plastered his back with bacta bandages.

Bela passed jumpsuits to those who were not yet dressed, and within moments everyone on the strike team was garbed in a simple brown uniform that made the Jedi Knights seem both efficient and intimidating. The jumpsuits were also light armor, for they were lined with the same alternating layers of molytex and quantum fiber that made the YVH droids' laminanium armor so impenetrable. In a pinch, they could even serve as vac suits; they had been designed to work with the emergency suits worn back on Eclipse, but attached independently to the appendage pieces and could be made airtight in their own right.

Anakin divided the strike team into two squads—assault and support—and outlined his plan. After allowing everyone a few moments to meditate and rejuvenate their anguished bodies through the Force, they opened their emotions to each other.

As Jacen weaved the battle meld, Anakin sensed a certain reservation in his brother, some misgiving that sent unsettling ripples through the entire strike team. He immediately regretted not sending Jacen back with Lando, but swallowed his irritation and focused on the task at hand. The team would sense his resentment through their emotional bond, and such distractions were the last thing they needed now.

Anakin fitted a breath mask over his nose and mouth, then affixed the attachable hood to his jumpsuit to protect his head.

When the others did the same, he was so awed by the effect that he instantly felt better.

"Astral!" he exclaimed. "Let's go do this."

YVH 2-1S opened his elbow and fired a pair of flash grenades down the corridor, then stepped through the tattered door membrane. Thud bugs began to plink at his laminanium armor. He silenced the source with a flurry of blaster bolts, and the Jedi followed him forward. The interior of the ship looked oddly cavernlike and murky, with hazy circles of bioluminescent lichen clinging to the walls and clouds of coma gas swirling through the air and door valves sagging open every two meters.

Anakin advanced with lightsaber in hand and blaster holstered. Behind him came Tesar Sebatyne, a big B-100 power blaster cradled in both arms, then Alema Rar and the rest of the assault squad. Jacen was in the middle with Tenel Ka, followed by an indignant Tahiri—she wanted to be in front with Anakin—and Bela and Krasov Hara. Last came 2-4S, who was tasked with covering Lowbacca while the Wookiee used a laser drill to insert flechette mines into the system ducts. Jaina remained behind with Ulaha and the support squad, covering the other corridors with powerful blaster minicannons.

As Anakin and the others moved toward the bridge, it grew apparent that the coma gas had done its job well. Unconscious Yuuzhan Vong lay sprawled across sagging door valves, curled up in sleeping nests, slumped over duty stations in shielding nodules and weapon turrets. Several had fallen to the floor in front of gnulliths—the Yuuzhan Vong equivalent of breath masks—and one crew member had even managed to lay the thing on his face before falling prey to the neural effects of the coma gas.

The strike team was attacked only once, when Anakin sensed a sudden flare of enemy anxiety behind a half-open door valve. By the time he turned to warn the others, a gnullith-masked warrior was flinging a pair of thud bugs into Bela's shoulder. The projectiles smashed harmlessly against her jumpsuit's armored lining, and she barely flinched before jerking her attacker from his hiding place and skewering him on her sister's waiting lightsaber.

As they drew near the bow, the assault team lost contact with the Force—no doubt because ysalamiri were near. Anakin lost his sense of the Yuuzhan Vong, as well—a hint that the lambent crystal was somehow connected to the Force. It was good to know, he supposed, but he really didn't care as long as it worked when the Force returned.

Ten meters ahead, the corridor ended in a vertical bulkhead, where an unconscious Yuuzhan Vong warrior hung as though pinned to the wall. The strange sight confused no one; like all good starship designers, the enemy made the most of shipboard space, utilizing their dovin basals to orient gravity in the most convenient direction. The bulkhead looked like a wall from the assault squad's current perspective, but it would become a floor as soon as they crossed the open area and placed a foot on it.

A gentle *whumpf* shook the corridor behind them, and 2-1S said, "Two-Four-S reports mine detonation in the main elimination duct. Ultrasonic soundings suggest the triggering agent was a voxyn, injured but not crippled."

"Voxyn?" Anakin demanded from behind his breath mask. "I thought Two-Four-S disintegrated them!"

"There was a point zero eight chance of a single survival," 2-1S pointed out. "Two-Four-S calculates the odds of a double survival—"

"Don't tell me," Anakin said, raising a hand. "I really don't want to know."

He used his comlink to warn Jaina about the voxyn and sent 2-4S back to watch ducts for her, then asked 2-1S for a see-through sensor sweep.

"Eleven conscious warriors waiting on the deck below, in a cabin adjacent to the bulkhead ahead," the droid reported. "Tactical analysis suggests the likelihood of an ambush."

"You don't say," Anakin said. "What about Ganner?"

"Implant triangulation fixes Ganner Rhysode at five meters starboard and moving forward. Passive acoustics suggest the company of several guards. Vital readings satisfactory, heart rate and respiration indicate deep sleep."

"Coma-gassed, but moving," Anakin surmised. "They must be cutting their way from one cabin to another, or Jaina's squad would see them."

"And they have ysalamiri." Alema Rar laid a hand on Anakin's arm and spoke so quietly that he had to lean his ear toward her breath mask. "The Yuuzhan Vong believe we are soft. They will try to use him against us."

"Against us?" Anakin found himself staring almost hypnotically into Alema's pale Twi'lek eyes. "As bait?"

When she nodded, Anakin disengaged himself and ignited his lightsaber. Being careful not to penetrate all the way through, he plunged the blade into the floor and began to cut a circle. He had no real plan yet except to avoid the ambush, but walking into a trap was not going to save Ganner, either. The yorik coral was easier to cut than durasteel, but it popped and cracked loudly as it melted, and Anakin worried that the enemy would not be as surprised as he hoped.

Jacen stepped to Anakin's side. "What are you doing?" The disappointment was evident in his face, and Anakin knew others could see it, too. "We should be going after Ganner."

"No, we must destroy the ambush party first," Alema said. "This is better."

"Better how?" Jacen asked. "Anakin can't keep sacrificing others to make his plans work. That way lies the dark side."

"Sacrificing others?" Anakin did not look away from his work. "What are you talking about?"

"Ulaha, and now Ganner," Jacen said. "You told Ulaha to attack the voxyn, and now you're abandoning Ganner."

The accusations hit Anakin almost physically. His lightsaber slipped and cut a deep furrow across the floor, and he found himself glaring at his brother, sick with anger and hurt.

"How can you think that?" he demanded. "Ulaha disobeyed orders. I wanted her to tell Duman Yaght the name of the base. I did *not* say to attack!"

Jacen's cheeks flushed, then his jaw dropped, and he stood speechless for a long time. Finally, he stammered, "Anakin, I-I'm sorry. When Ulaha attacked, I thought . . . I just assumed—"

"I know what you assumed," Anakin said. Though his brother's regret was evident on his crimson face, no apology could erase the doubt he had expressed about Anakin's character—nor the fact that he had been so quick to believe the worst, just as their father had when Chewbacca died. Anakin plunged his lightsaber back into the floor and continued to cut. "Get away from me. You're holding things up."

Jacen started to reply, but Tenel Ka caught him by the arm and pulled him away. "This cannot be resolved now, Jacen. You must wait until later."

With Alema's help, Anakin cut the circle to within a few millimeters of the other side, then activated his comlink to warn Jaina about what they were doing. She and 2-4S were busy keeping the wounded voxyn trapped in the systems ducts, but she paused long enough to warn Zekk and Raynar not to fire when figures started appearing in their corridor.

Bela and Krasov kicked the circle out, then lay on their bellies and vanished, one after the other, into the floor. The muffled zing of their repeating blasters immediately came back through the hole. Alema went next, diving headfirst, then Anakin, lightsaber in one hand, concussion grenade in the other. On the other side, he slowed and landed feetfirst on what felt like the ceiling.

The whine of blasterfire and drone-splat of striking thud bugs drove Anakin against the wall. Mind struggling to reorient, he thumbed the arming switch of his grenade. A trio of would-be ambushers lay at the end of the corridor, vonduun crab armor stitched with holes from the Barabel sisters' repeating blasters.

The thud bugs came from the open door of the ambushers' cabin, and also from the bulkhead itself, where a pair of bridge guards wearing gnulliths were attacking through a jagged melt hole. He saw no sign of Ganner, but had not expected to.

Anakin nodded across the corridor to Alema. She armed her own grenade, then they tossed the weapons into the ambush cabin. There were two bright flashes and a gut-deep jolt, and a tongue of flame shot into the corridor reeking of scorched flesh.

Waving the others to follow, Anakin charged forward behind the fiery curtain. A line of thud bugs crackled along the wall, then one took him in the chest and slammed him down on his back. Bela and Krasov pounded past, pouring blasterfire into the bulkhead, and Alema came next, pausing to pull him to his feet. It hurt to breathe and he might have a cracked rib, but his jumpsuit's armored liner had spared him any blood or deep pain. He activated his comlink.

"Two-One-S, secure the bulkhead."

The droid appeared at the end of corridor and dropped onto the bulkhead, now standing perpendicular to Anakin. The bridge guards swarmed him with thud bugs and magma pebbles, burning thumb-sized pits into his armor. He counterattacked with sensor-targeted blaster bolts and electrorays, and the enemy fire withered.

A sporadic stream of thud bugs began to assail 2-1S from the deck where they had first located Ganner. The droid ignored this nuisance and dropped to his knees beside the melt holes, then fired into the bridge itself. Anakin sent Alema and the Barabel sisters to support the droid, then returned to the hole in the floor and dropped back through to the other side.

Tesar and Lowbacca were in the forward cabin, already outlining a new doorway with elastic detonite. As Anakin approached, the pair pressed themselves flat against the wall and ignited the charge with the tip of Lowie's lightsaber. There was a sharp crack and the clatter of spraying shrapnel, then smoke filled the air and the new door remained closed. Tesar stepped away from the wall and sprang into the yorik coral feetfirst.

The slab flew into the adjacent cabin, slammed into something large, and drew a startled Yuuzhan Vong curse. Tesar silenced the voice with the staccato roar of his power blaster, then Lowbacca charged in behind him. Anakin ignited his own lightsaber and . . . heard the all-too-familiar burp of a voxyn expelling acid.

Anakin's thoughts leapt to Lowbacca—he could not bear the thought of telling Chewbacca's family that another member had died with him—then the brown mucus came shooting out of the makeshift door and splashed against the far wall. From inside came a Wookiee growl and the shrill sizzle of a lightsaber straining to cut, then a ghostly squeal of pain that quickly modulated into the opening burst of a screech attack.

Tesar's power blaster roared again.

The screech choked to an end. Anakin stepped through the doorway and found himself looking into a large wardroom, where a blaster-scorched voxyn was scurrying toward a lopsided hole in the rear wall. The thing was missing at least a tail and two rear legs, but remained quick enough to dodge a blaster bolt.

Scattered across the floor were nearly a dozen coma-gassed Yuuzhan Vong, but two more stood behind the claw-scarred remnants of a ysalamiri tree, their faces half hidden behind gnulliths, amphistaffs held ready. Tesar disposed of the sickly looking ysalamiri with a quick shot from his power blaster, and the Yuuzhan Vong warriors rushed to do battle.

Tesar brought his power blaster around and burned a hole through the chest armor of the first one, hurling him back against the wall. Anakin intercepted the second, freeing Lowbacca to make one last stab at the vanishing voxyn.

The Yuuzhan Vong tried to pin Anakin against the wall,

changing his amphistaff into whip form and flicking the fanged head at the Jedi's eyes. It was a tired tactic, almost disrespectful. Anakin feigned a stumble and dropped into a crouch, catching the attack on his lightsaber's fiery blade.

The serpent recoiled. Anakin posted his free hand, whipped his feet around and trapped the Yuuzhan Vong's knees, scissored his legs. The warrior yelled and hit the floor like a bag of rocks. The amphistaff struck again. Anakin blocked, flicked the thing away, brought his own blade down across the enemy's throat.

As the head rolled away, he spun toward the rear wall and was relieved to find Lowbacca holding yet another voxyn leg. The Wookiee's disappointed growls left no doubt that the creature had escaped, but Anakin was happy enough to see him standing. He gathered his own feet beneath him and saw, as he had feared, no sign of Ganner in the room.

Anakin noticed a chill along his spine and realized that his sense of the Yuuzhan Vong had returned, then he felt Jacen's touch brush his mind. There was also another sensation, the familiar hunger of the voxyn, wounded and angry, lurking somewhere in the ducts. They would hunt it down later, after the vessel was secure. Waving his lightsaber out the door to avoid being blasted by a minicannon, Anakin motioned Tesar and Lowbacca after him and stepped into the corridor.

Jaina's voice came over the comlink. "What's that I feel? It can't be a voxyn. Two-Four-S and I killed it. I'm looking at its body right now."

"Just keep an eye on those ducts," Anakin said, resisting the urge to comm 2-1S about the odds of all three escaping the thermal detonator. "There's another one."

He turned toward the bulkhead and found 2-1S kneeling over the shredded door valve, firing an intimidating but relatively harmless stream of nonlethal bolts into the bridge. There was no return fire, but the droid's armor was pocked and smoking from head to foot, with several fist-deep craters where the Yuuzhan Vong had managed to concentrate their attacks. Anakin dropped down beside the droid and the rest of the assault squad. There was a definite Yuuzhan Vong presence on the bridge, but the feeling was too murky for him to tell how many or what condition.

YVH 2-1S turned toward him. "Bulkhead secure, but the enemy is holding one captive—Jedi Rhysode—on the bridge." His photoreceptors were shattered and smeared with thud bug juice. "Currently two minutes eleven seconds ahead of schedule."

"You expected something else?" Anakin had intended to sound cocky like his father, but the effect was ruined when a pang from his bruised ribs made him squeak out the last two words. He glanced onto the bridge, then said, "You don't look so good, Two-One-S. We'll finish without you."

"Affirmative," the droid answered. "Sensor systems unstable."

Rather than risk a security trap by entering through the bridge's battered entrance valve, Anakin dropped to his belly beside the melt holes and peered through. On the other side lay more than a dozen Yuuzhan Vong, most deep in a coma-gas sleep. Some had gnulliths fastened over their faces, no doubt placed there by well-meaning comrades who had not realized that an antidote agent would be required to awaken their comrades. A handful of warriors lay in the awkward positions of their death throes, their wounds still smoking from the heat of the fatal blaster strike.

The cognition hood used to steer the vessel dangled a few centimeters above the comatose pilot's blank face, while the neural interface gloves employed in regulating the ship's systems lay draped over several different control consoles, usually with the hands of a dozing Yuuzhan Vong crew member still wearing them. Anakin was disappointed to find the command chair empty and no one lying within three meters of it; Duman Yaght had escaped the coma gas.

"It doesn't look like there's much happening," Anakin said,

speaking to Lowbacca, Tesar, and the rest of the assault squad. "But be careful. We don't want to get careless and blast Ganner by mistake."

"You're sure?" Tahiri asked, drawing a laugh from the others.

Anakin allowed himself a chuckle, but said, "At least for now."

He ignited his lightsaber and dived through the melt hole headfirst, then felt an attack coming and brought his blade around to block. The thud bug sizzled out of existence with a sharp hiss, and Anakin spun in the direction of the assault, stepping forward to protect those who would be following him.

"Very impressive, *Jeedai*."

Anakin looked toward the voice and found Duman Yaght wearing a gnullith and standing behind an instrument console, Ganner Rhysode's limp form held in front with a coufee to the throat.

"There you are." Anakin peered around the bridge. "All alone, it seems."

"Lay down your weapons," the commander said cautiously, "and your leader will live to meet our warmaster."

Anakin thumbed off his lightsaber—then, as Lowbacca and Tesar stepped onto the bridge, drew his blaster pistol.

"You really don't know Ganner, do you?" Anakin asked. "What makes you think he's that important?"

"You came after him, did you not?" Duman Yaght retreated a few steps, bringing Ganner around to shield him from all three Jedi. "We have studied you *Jeedai*. When it comes to the death of your fellows, you are soft."

"Not that soft." Anakin leveled his blaster pistol at the commander's head, and Tesar did the same with his power blaster. "But I'll offer you a deal. If you surrender, we'll put you off in the shuttle with the rest of your crew."

Duman Yaght's eyes hardened. "And dishonor Domain Yaght?" He ran the coufee lightly along Ganner's throat, drawing a two-centimeter-long trickle of blood. "Yuuzhan Vong do not surrender."

"Really?"

Anakin reached out with the Force and used it to push the coufee away from Ganner's neck. Eyes growing wide, Duman Yaght struggled for a moment to bring the blade back to his captive's throat, then snarled something in his own language and let it fly from his grasp.

When the other hand twitched and started to rise, his head vanished in a convergence of blasterfire.

"By this one's broken tail!" Tesar slung his power blaster over his shoulder and stepped forward to pluck Ganner out of the mess. "They *don't* surrender."

Chapter 24

om Anor could not believe even Vergere
would dare suggest that the warmaster waste his time playing an
infidel game—much less survive the affront. Yet there she sat across
from Tsavong Lah, studying a shaper's version of a dejarik board
complete with animate monsters and a mat of living terrain. The
warmaster was down to a pair of monnoks and a single miniature
mantellion savrip, while his feathery pet still boasted a kintan strider
and three k'lor'slugs. Though Nom Anor had never really enjoyed
the game, he had frequently been forced to play holographic versions during his time in the galaxy—often enough to recognize a
master when he saw one. And Vergere was, undoubtedly, a master.

"If New Republic strategists were the only ones who practiced
this game, it would not be worth the learning," Vergere was saying.
"But there are suggestions that dejarik was once a favorite study of
Jedi Knights."

That explained how she had enticed the warmaster into such a
blasphemy, Nom Anor realized. Tsavong Lah would do anything
that might help him defeat the Jedi.

"The strategies are more subtle than they appear, Nom Anor,"
Tsavong Lah said, not looking away from the game mat—and

surprising Nom Anor, who had thought the warmaster too absorbed to notice the scrutiny. "And a warrior must know the mind of his enemy."

"The game is popular throughout the galaxy," Nom Anor replied. "I have played a few times myself."

"Indeed?" Tsavong Lah tore his gaze from the board. "Then perhaps you have some insight as to the route Jacen and his sister will be taking home?"

"Home?" Nom Anor was confused. The *Exquisite Death* was more than a day overdue, but such delays were not unusual for picket ships, which operated just inside enemy territory and had to be very careful choosing their routes. "I did not know they had escaped."

"You didn't?" Tsavong Lah looked back to the dejarik game, then nudged his savrip forward between two of Vergere's k'lor'-slugs. "Interesting. By now, I would have thought that obvious to any dejarik player."

An angry heat filled Nom Anor's eyesacks. "The supreme commander's last report claimed that this Duman Yaght has things well in hand. Has there been a communication I'm unaware of?"

"Not yet." Tsavong Lah smiled as Vergere sent her strider up to upend his savrip, then he slipped his little monnok through the vacated space to slay her strider from behind. Taking advantage of the surprise-kill second move, the warmaster threatened a k'lor'-slug, then smiled across the table at Vergere. "But the *Jeedai* mind is growing clearer to me. They will keep a low profile, then strike when their captor has grown complacent."

Vergere returned the smirk with one of her own. "They will strike, but not where we think." Instead of moving a second k'lor'-slug to defend the first, she sent it slinking two squares toward Tsavong Lah's side of the mat. "The dejarik vids call that the kintan strider death gambit. It defeats with promises."

She now had her three k'lor'slugs arranged in a right angle, with each of his monnoks trapped between two of her monsters. No matter which he attacked first, both of the others would be in a position to counterstrike from behind, take a surprise move, and trap his remaining monster in an inescapable vise. The warmaster took all this in with a glance, his eyesacks growing dangerously dark as he realized how cleanly Vergere had defeated him.

"I see what you mean." He cleared the game mat with a swipe of his hand, then stood and looked through an exterior viewing lens at the swarm of black-faceted vessels hanging in the starlight beside the *Sunulok*. "So, they have tricked us. To what purpose?"

"The Jedi do not think so differently from you." Vergere scanned through the holographic images of the tiny monsters and selected one, then projected it on the game mat. "They will strike hardest at what they fear most."

Tsavong Lah turned away from the viewing lens and, finding the rancor alone on the mat, nodded.

"I suppose it would be wise to assume the worst." He turned to Nom Anor. "You will take the *Ksstarr* and start for *Baanu Rass* at once."

Nom Anor nodded, needing no explanation. Currently orbiting the planet Myrkr, *Baanu Rass* was the largest of the worldships to enter the galaxy so far. With a dying brain that could no longer control its spin—the shapers there now used dovin basals to give it gravity—*Baanu Rass* was also three-quarters abandoned, a perfect home for the voxyn cloning program that was proving so effective against the Jedi.

"And the *Jeedai*?"

"Do what is necessary, but the Solo twins have been promised to Lord Shimrra. Those you must bring back alive."

"As you command."

The feeling that filled Nom Anor's heart was closer to triumph than joy. While the warmaster had proven surprisingly tolerant of events on Coruscant, neither had he chastened Vergere for interfering with his mission. Nom Anor crossed his fists over his breast and backed toward the door, already planning how he would convert this assignment into a sector prefecture.

"Warmaster, I believe this to be a mistake." Vergere spoke quietly, so that Nom Anor would be forced to admit that he was eavesdropping if he wished to challenge her words. "Given that your reputation with Lord Shimrra is at stake, would it not be wiser to send someone with a more *certain* touch?"

Nom Anor held his tongue—just barely—and continued to back toward the door, ears straining for the warmaster's reply.

"If you are referring to events on Coruscant, I know what happened," Tsavong Lah said. "Nom Anor is not to blame. He did well to return to us at all."

More to Nom Anor's astonishment than his anger, Vergere continued to press. "We must also consider the debacle with Elan and the Peace Brigade, and his failures against Mara Jade Skywalker. Nom Anor has faced Jedi many times and done poorly."

The door valve opened behind Nom Anor, but he remained where he was, not so certain of his position that he could bring himself to depart.

Tsavong Lah turned to face him. "You understand what is at risk, Nom Anor? Vergere's words are rooted in rivalry, but there is substance to what she says. If you are not confident of success, say so now and let us find a better solution together."

"There is no cause for concern, Warmaster." Nom Anor understood perfectly well what was at risk: his prefecture and perhaps his life. "Now that I know you see through Vergere's intrigues, I have no doubts at all."

Tsavong Lah's face darkened. "And you did before?"

"My master, I did not mean to say I doubted *you*, only my own understanding of your methods."

Tsavong Lah motioned him back into the chamber. "And what, exactly, did you not understand?" The warmaster's tone was sharp. "And do not insult me again by lying."

Nom Anor took a deep breath and returned to the dejarik mat. "My master, the sentients of this galaxy also play another game called sabacc, where the chip-cards change identities before their eyes." He cast a pointed glance at his rival. "Vergere was the infidels' prisoner for many weeks, and she has yet to provide a satisfactory explanation of her escape."

"The readers were satisfied," Vergere replied. "As were all of Yun-Harla's priests."

"They have not met Han Solo." Nom Anor kept his eyes fixed on Tsavong Lah. "He is not the type to let an enemy escape."

"He did not *let* me do anything," Vergere replied. "There is more to me than you know."

"And they were in the middle of a battle caused by the ineptitude of *your* hirelings," Tsavong Lah added. "More importantly, Vergere learned more during her captivity than how to play dejarik. Her insights have saved thousands of vessels, and we have destroyed three New Republic fleets when she guessed correctly about their intentions."

"A small price for your favor." The retort was out of Nom Anor's mouth almost before he realized it was in his mind. "I certainly don't mean that Vergere is a traitor—"

"Of course not," Tsavong Lah said. "Only that I lack the judgment to tell if she were."

Nom Anor closed his eyes. "I would never disparage—"

"You just did," Tsavong Lah said. "But that is not what concerns me."

The warmaster fell silent and remained so until Nom Anor dared to open his eyes.

"What concerns me is that you are foolish enough to think I do not see through you." Tsavong Lah studied Nom Anor for a long time, then said, "This assignment is more important than any other I have given you. I think it would be wise for you to take an advisor along."

Having disparaged the warmaster's judgment once that day, Nom Anor knew better than to do so again. "If the warmaster thinks it wise."

"The warmaster does." Tsavong Lah turned to Vergere and, in a voice as stern as he had been using with Nom Anor, said, "You will accompany Nom Anor."

Vergere's feathers bristled. "As his advisor?" she gasped. "One does not advise k'lor'slugs. This will never work."

"It had better." Tsavong Lah gave them both a hard smile. "I have had enough of this jealousy between you two. From this moment on, you succeed—or fail—together."

Chapter 25

hat was I to think when Ulaha attacked?" Jacen asked. Despite his frustration, he kept his voice low to avoid disturbing Ulaha or any of the others lying in healing trances in the Yuuzhan Vong nestbunks. "It looked as though Anakin had ordered her to—and I'm not the only one who thought so."

"Fact," Tenel Ka agreed. She sat hunched into a nestbunk beside him, her shoulder touching his in a manner that was a little more than comfortable. Their lightsabers lay close at hand; with the voxyn still at large in the ship's duct system, they were taking no chances. "But you are his brother. What seems a mistake in others is judgmental from you. And your objections to Lando's advice do not help matters."

"Gamblers and spies can afford to dispense with morality," Jacen replied. "Jedi cannot. It's too easy for our power to lead us down a dark path, and we're not the only ones who suffer when that happens."

"This is so," Tenel Ka said. "But, Jacen, do you remember my first lightsaber?"

"How could I forget?" Jacen asked, wondering where this was

going. Tenel Ka had made the mistake of building her first lightsaber in a hurry, and a flawed crystal had caused it to fail during a sparring match with Jacen. His blade had sliced off her left arm—his first painful lesson in the burden of wielding great power. "For a long time I felt responsible for that accident—I still do, at least partly—but I don't see what that has to do with Anakin and me."

"The accident was no one's fault but mine." Tenel Ka tapped her chest with her one hand to emphasize the point. "What I believed to be confidence in my fighting abilities was arrogance, and that is why I built a faulty lightsaber."

"Arrogance," Jacen repeated. Try as he might, he could not quite see how his mistake resembled Tenel Ka's. "And?"

"Do you believe you are the only Jedi among us who understands the danger of the dark side?"

"Of course not. Most of us have had trouble with the Shadow Academy, and Zekk even turned . . ." Jacen let the sentence trail off, finally comprehending Tenel Ka's point. Anakin knew the danger of the dark side as well as any of them. To believe him capable of ordering Ulaha's mad attack was to doubt more than his judgment; it was to doubt his very character. Jacen shook his head in guilty regret. "That was a mistake. A bad one."

"Fact." Tenel Ka bumped him with her shoulder. "But there is no need to sulk. I will always be fond of you."

Jacen's stomach grew hollow. "You think he's that angry?"

Tenel Ka rolled her eyes, then took a canister of bacta lotion and slipped off the nestbunk to check on their insensate fellows. "It was a joke, Jacen."

"Ah." Jacen grabbed his lightsaber and followed close behind. "Aha. You have a lot to learn about jokes."

She glanced at him over her shoulder. "Actually, I thought it quite good." She came to Ulaha, who was breathing fitfully even in her healing trance, and lifted the Bith's blanket. "Trust him to forgive, Jacen, and things will return to normal."

She rubbed a fresh coat of lotion over Ulaha's wounds. It wasn't nearly as effective as immersion in a tank, but it was better than almost anything else they could do for her.

On the deck below, a Yuuzhan Vong targeting brain lay open on a wardroom table, its nutrient bath filling the chamber with the stink of rotten seaweed. Nestled in a nutlike shell no larger than a human fist, the organ was a tangle of axons and dendrons webbing together a gelatinous muddle of neuron clusters. Though Jaina found the structure of the biotic computer hopelessly bewildering, Lowbacca was engrossed in dissecting the thing, using a small set of steristeel tools to snip here and move there, grunting in satisfaction as the fibers reattached themselves in new locations. Finally, he fused a short thread of axon between two lengths of dendron, then chortled in delight as an eyestalk hanging from the front of the casing rose and focused on Jaina.

Lowbacca growled a request, which Em Teedee, recently retrieved from the equipment pod, translated as, "Master Lowbacca asks if you would be kind enough to circumnavigate the table."

Though Jaina understood Wookiee well enough to know Lowbacca had phrased the request somewhat less eloquently, she did as asked. The eye followed her progress, using a control stem on the back of the shell to spin the brain around as she circled.

"Lowie, get some help," Jaina laughed. "That's just Sith."

Lowbacca growled a chuckle, then steadied the shell with a big hand and slipped a pair of needle-nosed fiber snips inside. Turning away from the targeting brain, Jaina found Zekk waiting with a photon trap from their equipment pod's sensor system.

"There weren't any extra detector films in the droid kit," he said. "Maybe we can take a sheet from this and trim one down."

"It's worth a try."

Jaina led the way across the wardroom to where 2-1S stood, silently regrowing his laminanium armor and running internal diagnostics. Since awakening from their healing trances, Jaina, Zekk, and Lowbacca had been working nonstop to help the war droid repair himself, but 2-1S still looked like he had grabbed the wrong end of a turbolaser. They had replaced his recessed photoreceptors with extras from the repair kit Lando had included in the equipment pod, but several thud bugs had penetrated deep inside the skull casing, smashing circuit boards and detection mediums beyond all hope of repair. Fortunately, having spent much of his life as an equipment forager in Coruscant's dangerous undercity, Zekk had a Force-enhanced talent for finding things. So far, he had scavenged substitutes for the infrared and ultrasonic sensors, and now possibly the gamma analyzers, as well.

Jaina took the thin sheet of detector film from the photon trap and held it up for 2-1S. "What about this for your gamma system?"

YVH 2-1S ran his photoreceptors over the sheet, then crackled, "Affirmative." His voice was a static-filled ghost of Lando's, but that was the least of their worries. "Double the thickness."

"Another success for Zekk," Jaina said. She turned and found herself looking directly into his green two-tone eyes, a sentiment much deeper than friendship evident in the way he held her gaze. Jaina waited a moment for him to look away, and, when he did not, passed the detector film back to him. "Hold this while I get the cutter."

Though hardly blind to the disappointment that clouded Zekk's face, Jaina was careful to maintain a neutral expression as she reached for the lasicutter. Her reaction was not because she lacked feelings for Zekk—in fact, a few years ago she had found it difficult to keep her thoughts off him—but over time her feelings had changed from infatuation to something closer to what she felt for her brothers. It was love, certainly, but nothing physical—nothing like the spark that had passed through her on the *Tafanda Bay,* when Jag Fel had ignored Borsk Fey'lya's entire cabinet to introduce himself to her.

That had made her stomach flutter . . . but she was being silly. She had no idea where Jag Fel was—probably not even in the known galaxy—and even less whether they were ever likely to meet again. If she insisted on waiting for a jolt like *that* again, she would be Mara's age before she ever . . .

"Jaina?" Zekk fluttered the detector film in her face. "Are you going to cut or not?"

"Of course, but we need measurements." Jaina turned away to hide her blush. "Where did I put that hydrospanner?"

Only a few meters away, crawling on his belly through the black muck in the *Exquisite Death*'s central elimination duct, Tesar Sebatyne heard the hiss of a large creature drawing deep breath. He immediately raised his makeshift durasteel shield and used the Force to push it down the low conduit. There was a muffled burp and a loud sizzling as the acid struck, then a dull clang as the shield slammed into the voxyn.

Sissing with laughter, Tesar used the Force to shove voxyn and shield down the duct. When the creature snarled and tried to push its snout through the holes its acid had eaten in the durasteel, the Barabel brought up his blaster pistol and loosed a single bolt. The creature's nose exploded in a spray of black blood, filling the conduit with toxic fumes. Tesar sissed into his breath mask and fired again.

The voxyn roared and, knocking the makeshift shield from its snout, vanished up the duct. Tesar pictured the beast and reached out to his hatchmates with an impression of movement in his mind, and of the creature growing larger.

A moment later, Bela replied with an image of the creature's body glow. Like most Barabels, she could see into the infrared spectrum and often tracked her prey by the heat of its body. She sent a sensation of impending danger, and Tesar knew he had to get clear. He retreated two meters and squeezed himself into a side feed.

He counted three slow reptilian heartbeats before a series of *whumpf-thumpf*s reverberated through the yorik coral. The duct lit with the flashing brilliance of his hatchmates' minicannons, arranged at right angles to each other at the next intersection, and he had to close his eyes. The voxyn's shrill screech sliced through the dank air like a lightsaber, then dropped in tone and began to undulate.

Had they missed? Tesar wondered. How could they?

The irritation his hatchmates shot his way convinced him they had not. His earplugs detected a sudden redshift in the voxyn's squeal and closed tight, sealing his ears against the disorienting impact of a compression wave. He experienced a deep, hard vibration in the pit of his stomach, but shared in the exhilaration of his hatchmates as they continued to pour bolts at their prey. By his cold blood, how he loved hunting with his hatchmates!

Finally, the minicannons fell silent and his earplugs opened again. He flicked his tongue into the breath mask and smelled filter-scrubbed ozone and scorched yorik coral—and an antiseptic, coppery odor he recognized as detoxified voxyn blood.

He sent a question-sense the sisters' way, and received back only an impression of uncertainty. Though Tesar could not exactly *feel* his hatchmates' actions through the Force, he had lived with them side by side all his life and intuitively knew they would be activating a glow stick to supplement their infrared vision. An image of smoking scales came to his mind, then of a voxyn's blaster-scorched leg.

Then Anakin's voice came over the comlink. "Tesar! What's going on back there?"

The sound of clicking claws sounded from around the corner, and Tesar thought, *Uh-oh*. He worked a hand under his chest up toward the comlink clipped to his collar, at the same time worming his way backward down the duct. It was slow going, for the side feed was little larger than Tesar himself, and he was crawling against the lay of his scales. Even through his thick jumpsuit, the rough walls kept catching the tips and bringing his progress to a painful halt.

The voxyn's head appeared at the corner, a red heat silhouette barely two meters in front of him.

"Tesar?" Anakin demanded. "What's going on back there?"

Tesar fired at the voxyn and saw his bolt ricochet off. He should have scales like that! The creature pulled its head out of sight, but pink heat-wisps of breath continued to curl past the corner.

Tesar finally reached his comlink. "You told us to watch the voxyn."

"And?"

"And to call for help if . . ." The pink wisps vanished ahead, and Tesar heard a sharp intake of air. "Uh, keep talking."

He ripped his comlink off and tossed it down the duct. Anakin's distant voice continued to demand an explanation, but Tesar squirmed away as fast as he could. A mangled snout pushed around the corner and buried the squawking instrument beneath a weak stream of acid. Tesar stopped moving and, using the Force to project his voice down the duct, screamed as loud as he could.

He sensed approval from Krasov and, through her, perceived Anakin's panic. He had to be on the comlink, screaming for Tesar to answer.

Bela found this funny; Tesar could feel her sissing. He knew without looking that she would be creeping down the main duct behind the voxyn, lightsaber in hand. Krasov was following along behind, a big T-21 repeating blaster pointed over her sister's shoulder. The voxyn hauled itself around the corner, its claws digging into the yorik coral walls and pulling it forward. Tesar could not see its wounds in infrared, but the creature was definitely moving slowly and in great weariness. It paused at the small pit its acid had burned into the floor, then, not finding the expected body, raised its head and peered down the duct.

Tesar resumed his retreat, firing blaster bolts into the creature's head. Many ricocheted off, but many burned through the armored scales and failed to kill it. Wasting no time with another of its screeches, the voxyn pursued him down the duct, stubby legs pulling it forward faster than the Barabel could retreat. For the first time, Tesar's scales rippled with fear; the beast learned from its mistakes.

Big trouble, he thought.

He sensed the alarm in his hatchmates and heard them begin to splash and rattle in the main duct as they tried to draw the voxyn's attention. Too clever for such antics, the creature pulled to within a meter of Tesar and let out a burp, but either its acid was depleted or the efflux tube had been burned shut; nothing came out. Tesar fired point-blank and smelled scorched flesh.

The voxyn lurched ahead, its mouth closing around the barrel of the Merr-Sonn blaster. Tesar squeezed the trigger—then snarled in pain as the safety circuits sensed a clog in the emitter nozzle and shut down the actuating module. Releasing the weapon into the voxyn's mouth, he squirmed away, pressing his back against the duct roof in what he felt fairly certain would be a futile attempt to free his lightsaber.

Bela's white blade hissed to life somewhere behind the voxyn, but the creature filled the duct so completely that only a few stray rays of light showed past. The beast lunged; Tesar barely saved his breath mask by jerking away, then lashed out and felt his finger talons sink into the thing's wounded snout.

The voxyn continued to drag itself forward, its jaws snapping at the hand clawing on its muzzle. Tesar shoved its head against the wall.

Tesar exuded triumph to his hatchmates. A heavy foot came forward to catch his elbow, its disease-tipped claws dimpling his jumpsuit's molytex lining and nearly pushing through. To his sense of triumph, he added urgency.

The drone of Bela's blade grew louder—then vanished beneath the sharp crack of exploding detonite. An unexpected weight settled on Tesar's back, and suddenly the duct was filled with the soft green light of the bioluminescent wall lichen that illuminated the interior of the *Exquisite Death*. Tesar glimpsed the tangled mass of broken fang and scorched flesh that was the voxyn's mutilated snout, then felt himself rising through the top of the duct as someone levitated him into the cabin above.

The blaster-scarred voxyn scrambled past beneath him, whole chunks of body missing, the stumps of four rear legs dragging uselessly behind.

"You bantha head! It escaped!" Tesar looked over and found himself staring into the blue eyes of Ganner Rhysode, one of the largest and—to judge by his own attitude, at least—most handsome of the human Jedi. "Now it will be twice as hard to kill!"

"Hunting season's over, my scaly friend." Ganner lowered Tesar to the passage floor, then called into the hole. "Come out of there, girls. Anakin wants us on the bridge."

In the adjacent sleeping cabin, Raynar Thul awoke from his healing trance to find himself watching Eryl's bare back as she sat up and stretched on the opposite side of a narrow walkway. Her skin was freckled and milky, with only the faintest hint of the acid scars and claw slashes he had come to know so well during the first voxyn watch. With the others deep in healing trances or busy learning to fly the ship, he and Eryl had spent a great deal of time talking and rubbing bacta lotion into each other's wounds. He had a dim memory of a long lingering kiss just before they finally sank into their own bunks, but it seemed so hazy now it might have been only a dream.

Eryl lowered her arms and, glancing over her shoulder, caught him looking. Instead of covering up, she smiled and asked, "How do I look?"

Raynar's teeth clacked as he snapped his jaw shut, then he managed to stammer, "Fine." Maybe the kiss hadn't been a dream after all. "J-just great, in fact."

Eryl frowned and craned her neck to look down her back, then laughed and, still not covering up, said, "I was talking about my scars, young man. Are they healed?"

"Oh yes." Raynar wanted to drop back onto his bunk and sink into a healing trance. "That's what I meant."

Eryl looked doubtful. "Sure." She reached for her jumpsuit. "But it's okay. After all that bacta rubbing, I don't think anyone on the strike team has any secrets."

"No, I don't think so," Raynar said.

Still, as he reached for his own jumpsuit, Raynar *did* try to hide his disappointment. Eryl might be only a year or two older, but being called a young man had disabused him of any wrong impressions about their relationship.

Tekli appeared from a few bunks down, her brown fur tousled and gray eyes sparkling as she buckled her equipment harness.

"Sleep well?" she asked.

"Yes, very," Raynar answered. "And you?"

"Good." She gave them a tight smile, then lifted her brow as the ship gave a subtle shudder. "We must be coming out of hyperspace."

Both Raynar and Tekli looked to Eryl, who closed her green eyes and reached out with the Force. When she opened them a moment later, she looked just a little younger and more innocent than before.

"I'll have to see some stars to be certain, but it feels right," she said. "We've reached Myrkr."

Chapter 26

As the *Exquisite Death* sped insystem, shedding velocity and swinging into Myrkr's gravity well, the planet swelled from a greenish pinpoint to an emerald disk the size of a thumbnail. Though Anakin did not recall the world having a moon, the pearly fleck hanging beside it was too bright to be a background star and too steady to be an optical illusion. He turned to the sensor station, where Lowbacca sat with his emergency vac suit pulled over his jumpsuit, his head buried in a cognition hood, and his huge hands squeezed into a pair of control gloves.

"Lowie, anything?" Anakin asked.

The Wookiee groaned a reply, which Em Teedee, hovering alongside, translated as, "Master Lowbacca continues to apply his best efforts and assures you he will inform you the moment he succeeds."

Anakin knew well enough what Lowbacca had really said, but he did not remark on the gentle editing or unnecessary translation. Not everyone knew the language, and Em Teedee insisted it was his duty to make certain the whole strike team understood Lowbacca as well as he did them.

Lowbacca growled something short, and Em Teedee added,

"He also wishes me to suggest that frequent requests for information only interrupt his concentration."

"I know," Anakin said. "Sorry."

Though the strike team had quickly mastered most of the *Exquisite Death*'s systems—having studied all available data on Yuuzhan Vong vessels and even experimented with a captured assault boat—the sensors remained a problem. In contrast to the externally oriented observation technologies of the New Republic, the Yuuzhan Vong gathered information by analyzing the infinitesimal distortions that the gravity of distant objects caused in the ship's internal space-time. Given that the galaxy's finest scientists were still struggling to comprehend the basic science of Yuuzhan Vong sensors, it was no wonder Lowbacca was having difficulties operating them—even with Tahiri at his side translating and providing insight into how Yuuzhan Vong thought.

When Anakin looked back to Myrkr, the planet had grown to a cloud-mottled circle the size of Ulaha's head. The gray fleck beside it was now a tiny disk.

"Definitely a moon," Anakin said. At this distance, he could not expect to feel anything through the lambent crystal. But he knew what he was seeing. "A Yuuzhan Vong moon."

Lowbacca let out a victorious growl, and Em Teedee reported, "Master Lowbacca feels it is, indeed, a Yuuzhan Vong worldship." Lowbacca grunted and yowled a few more times, and the translation droid added, "There are several corvette analogs in orbit around it, though the diameter is quite large for a worldship—approximately one hundred and twenty kilometers."

That was as large as the first Death Star. Anakin whistled softly to himself, then reached out toward the distant fleck with the Force. Not one to rule out the possibility of coincidence, he was nevertheless suspicious enough of it to inspect it carefully. He felt an all-too-familiar stirring, the feral agitation of a voxyn—but also something else, another presence full of terror and pain . . . and surprise.

A clear, sharp presence, not hazy. Jedi, not Yuuzhan Vong.

Anakin did not realize he had gasped until a hand took his arm and Alema asked what was wrong. Not answering, he continued to focus on the worldship. The presence touched him back, still full of pain and fear, but now also pity—not for itself, he thought, but for him. He filled his heart with comforting emotions, trying to project an aura of confidence and hope, though he knew the vagaries of the Force might not be capable of conveying the message he wanted. The presence at the other end maintained contact for only a moment longer before abruptly withdrawing, closing itself off to Anakin without any hint of whether it had comprehended what he was trying to communicate.

Tahiri clasped his arm. "Anakin?"

"There are Jedi there," he said. "With the voxyn."

"Well, that puts Plan A right out the lock," Ganner said. Plan A called for them to sneak as close as possible to the cloning facility and destroy it with a baradium-packed missile, then use the resulting confusion to confirm the queen's destruction and escape. "We'll have to try something else."

"That is very brave, of course," Alema said. Standing beside the commander's chair opposite Tahiri, she laid a hand on Anakin's arm and turned to him with a look of entreaty. "But if we forgo our best plan, we stand to lose more Jedi than we would save."

Jacen emerged from the back of the bridge, his eyes rolling at the Twi'lek's pouty tone. "Alema, I think Anakin knows what's at stake here."

"I can handle this, Jacen," Anakin said, doing his best to keep the irritation out of his voice. "And there is no need to remind me about the dark side. I understand the consequences of killing our own."

"Anakin, I only meant—"

"Shouldn't you be at your battle station?" Anakin asked, deliberately cutting Jacen off. He cast a meaningful look at both Alema and Tahiri. "Shouldn't everyone?"

Jacen's face reddened, and Tahiri's eyes narrowed, but all three retreated to their assigned places and left Anakin to his thoughts. This was one of those times Lando had warned them about, when any choice he made felt like the wrong one—but Lando did not have the Force to guide him, and Anakin still had a few minutes before he had to decide anything. If he waited, maybe things would work out for the better; they almost always did.

Jaina swung the *Exquisite Death* into an approach pattern, and the edge of Myrkr's enormous green disk began to slide across the port side of the bridge. From space, at least, there was no visible sign of Yuuzhan Vong planet-shaping; it remained the same steam-shrouded forest world depicted in holovids.

The worldship was rapidly filling the viewing dome, swelling from a little smaller than a Kuati banquet plate to the size of a high command conference table. A thin halo of twinkling stars hinted at the escape of radiant heat, while blotchy circles of gray and brown began to define the planetoid's pocked surface.

Expecting the hailing villip in front of him to activate at any moment, Anakin waved Tahiri close, then used the holoshroud unit on his equipment harness to cloak himself in the prerecorded image of a Yuuzhan Vong warrior. Whether the tattoos and scarrings were appropriate for the commander of a corvette-analog vessel was anybody's guess; there seemed to be the right amount, but New Republic Intelligence was still struggling to learn the significance—if any—of individual patterns.

Lowbacca moaned a warning from the sensor console, informing Anakin that a trio of Yuuzhan Vong corvettes had just appeared from the far side of Myrkr and were lining up for approach behind the *Exquisite Death*. Anakin ordered Jaina to continue as before. Though her face was hidden beneath the pilot's hood she wore to interface with the vessel, he could feel her apprehension. Not knowing the proper procedure for entering a Yuuzhan Vong base, they had opted to try an open approach, trusting that procedural mistakes would prove less alarming than a furtive advance.

Jaina rolled them to starboard and angled into line behind a string of dark specks drifting across the face of the worldship, now so large that it completely filled the dome. Anakin had Ulaha activate a holocam and begin feeding mapping information to her datapad. The long journey between galaxies had left the massive spacecraft dilapidated and spent. A few black, jagged scars denoted breaches in the outer shell, but most of the planetoid seemed a mottled patchwork of gray dust and jagged yorik coral. A sparse network of surface utility lanes curved along the surface, occasionally converging in starburst intersections or vanishing down the dark mouth of an interior access portal.

The worldship still did not hail them, and the back of Anakin's neck began to prickle with danger sense. No New Republic base would allow any ship to approach so closely without making contact. Jaina maintained her spacing behind the other ships, following them around the curve of the planetoid. A complex of cone-shaped grashal peaks appeared on the horizon, protruding up through the outer shell, a little to the starboard of the long line of vessels they were following. Even with the naked eye, Anakin could see that the buildings emerged from the surface close to the city-sized square of a huge black pit.

"Maxmag that, Ulaha," he said. "What's it like?"

Ulaha turned her holocam on the complex and increased the magnification. "It appears to be some kind of spaceport," she wheezed. Though the Bith was much improved after her healing trance, she remained weak and colorless. "There is a large pit surrounded by many entrances, with what look to be loading facilities."

"Abandoned?"

"Empty," Ulaha corrected. "No vessels in sight, but the landing pads are stacked with cargo pods . . . and cages."

Anakin reached out to the facility with the Force. He no longer felt the pained presence he had noticed before, but the hungry stirring of voxyn was still powerful. The tingle in the back of his neck became a nettling, and, noting that their current approach would keep them well away from the complex, he suddenly understood why the worldship had not yet hailed them.

"They're trying to lead us into a trap. Jaina, turn toward that complex now!" Anakin activated the comlink. "Ganner, you and Tesar ready that missile. Stand by for targeting coordinates. Everybody, secure your vac suits. We're in for a rough ride."

As Jaina swung the ship around, Lowbacca rumbled an alarm. "Oh, dear," Em Teedee chirped at Anakin's collar. "Master Lowbacca says there's a cruiser—"

"I *heard* him," Anakin said.

A distant ovoid of yorik coral floated over the horizon, moving to position itself between the *Exquisite Death* and what Anakin now felt certain was the loading area for the cloning complex. Lowbacca warned that the corvettes coming from Myrkr were accelerating and spreading out, and the half-dozen vessels they had been following were turning toward the cruiser. When Em Teedee attempted to repeat this information in Basic, Anakin switched him off.

One of the small villips next to the ship's hailing villip suddenly pushed through its eversion orifice, taking the shape of a lumpy Yuuzhan Vong head ringed around the brow by goiterlike growths. "*Gadma dar,* Ganner Rhysode."

Anakin turned to Tahiri for a translation, but the villip began to speak in Basic before she could supply it.

"Stroke the hailing villip, *Jeedai,* so that we can speak."

Before obeying, Anakin said, "Jaina, continue on course.

Lowie, get a targeting lock on that cruiser and feed the coordinates to Ganner and Tesar."

The Yuuzhan Vong grew impatient. "It should be the leathery disk next to this one, *Jeedai*."

Anakin stroked the appropriate villip. Instead of everting, its central orifice opened and extended toward him a short tentacle with a black eye at the end. The Yuuzhan Vong—or rather, his villip—raised his brow and started to demand something in his own language, then caught himself and smiled.

"Very good, Ganner Rhysode. I see we are not the only ones who use masquers."

Seeing no reason to disabuse an enemy of his mistake, Anakin left the holoshroud on. "I'm sure this is more than a social call, shipmaster."

"Commander," the officer corrected. "It is my obligation to recover the vessel you have stolen."

"Stolen?" Anakin asked. "We're just borrowing it. You can have it back when we finish."

The commander's villip went blank for a moment, then frowned. "I fear it is needed now. Surrender to the matalok ahead, and you will be the only one who suffers for the . . . misuse . . . of the *Exquisite Death*."

Anakin glanced through the bridge dome and saw an ovoid as long his arm. The distance between the vessels had to be no more than a dozen kilometers, and still the cruiser had not opened fire. Perhaps the commander had dreams himself of presenting Tsavong Lah with seventeen Jedi—or perhaps he did not think his cruiser had much to fear from a ship as small as the *Exquisite Death*.

Lowbacca growled a report saying there were half a dozen coralskippers and as many corvette analogs moving into position over the cloning facility.

"It would be futile to make my matalok attack, *Jeedai*," the commander warned. "My trap was well laid, and the warmaster has said that if we must open fire, the Talfaglion hostages are forfeit."

"Has he?" Anakin opened his emotions to the others so they would be ready for what he intended. "I see we have no choice."

Hoping Luke had everything ready on his side of the galaxy, Anakin snatched his lightsaber from his belt and, thumbing the ignition switch, slashed the hailing villip apart.

"Full ahead, Jaina." He activated his comlink. "Ganner, target cruiser. Set fuse to proximity, fire when ready."

"Missile loose."

The report came almost before the order was finished, but it took Anakin until the missile flashed past to realize Ganner had *known* what Anakin intended. The strike team had established its battle meld automatically, perhaps even unconsciously, as soon as the likelihood of combat became apparent.

The missile's unexpected appearance confused the Yuuzhan Vong for only a few seconds. A flurry of plasma balls boiled out to intercept the missile, causing the droid brain to activate its counter-measure program. The missile diverted some of its power to shields and continued toward its target in an evasive corkscrew. Anakin did not need to tell his sister to circle around the target. Baradium was the same substance that made thermal detonators such fearsome weapons, and the missile was carrying enough of the explosive to equip an entire assault division.

The Yuuzhan Vong gunners tried in vain for another few seconds to hit the spiraling target, then gave up and turned the ship's defense over to the shielding crews. A black dot appeared half a kilometer from the ship and sucked the missile toward its doom.

As soon as the droid brain detected the existence of a shielding singularity, it used its guidance laser to measure the distance to target, calculated that 98 percent of the mass fell within its blast radius, and triggered a thousand kilograms of baradium. The cruiser vanished in a blinding sphere of white fire that resembled, for a few seconds, a one-kilometer sun.

The *Exquisite Death* shook beneath the shock wave, then Ganner's voice came over the comlink. "What now? Plan D?"

"Sort of." Anakin looked toward the cloning compound and saw a dozen yorik coral flecks swarming over the buildings. They were not coming out to attack, so it seemed apparent they were conserving their energies and would not open fire until the *Exquisite Death* reached point-blank range. Given the likelihood of a miss hitting the corvette analogs streaking in behind the *Death*, it seemed a wise strategy. "Here's what I want."

Anakin had barely described his plan before Ulaha held out her datapad.

"What's that?"

"I must be the one to stay with the ship," she said.

Anakin felt his sister's alarm as acutely as his own. "No offense, Ulaha," Jaina said, "but you're hardly up to something like this."

"Perhaps not, but I am a pilot—and the *Exquisite Death* is hardly a starfighter." Ulaha pressed the datapad into Anakin's hand. "As stated, your plan has a twenty-one percent success probability, with a casualty projection in excess of ninety percent. Without me to burden you on the ground, your success probability rises to almost fifty percent."

"That high?" Anakin did not even want to hear the casualty projections. "Okay, but just drop Two-One-S's shuttle and go. Do you need anything?"

Ulaha thought for a moment, then said, "If there is time, I would like a length of metal tubing from the droid kit. Leave it in the corridor."

"Count on it." Anakin wanted to hug her or shake her hand or *something*, but that all seemed so final, so irrevocable. Instead, he sent Jaina after the rest of the team, already gathering in the first hold, then paused at the door valve and looked back. "No heroics, Ulaha. That's an order. Just drop Two-One-S and go."

The Bith nodded at him. "It's okay, Anakin. This is the right thing." She turned away and reached for the cognition hood. "Now hurry; every minute of delay reduces the mission's success probability by zero point two percent."

Feeling a little lonely and hollow inside, Anakin rushed down the corridor into the first hold, where the Jedi were already packing themselves and their equipment into five Yuuzhan Vong cargo pods. He left the tubing in the corridor for Ulaha, then sealed the hold door and turned to join the others.

Zekk was packing Tesar in with Ganner, Jovan, and Tenel Ka. "You are sure we have enough thermal detonatorz?" Tesar rasped. "We are going to need many detonatorz for the voxyn."

"I packed all four cases." Zekk pushed the pod shut.

"Only four?" Tesar demanded.

Zekk shook his head, then sealed the seam with a glob of blo-rash jelly and motioned Anakin into a pod with Raynar, Eryl, and Tahiri. "We're the last. I thought it best to separate families and equipment."

There was no need to explain the precaution. Anakin nodded, then pulled up his vac suit hood and crouched beside Tahiri, opposite Eryl and Raynar. Zekk squeezed in beside Anakin, then lit a glow stick and sealed the seam from the inside. The *Exquisite Death* continued forward unopposed for what seemed an eternity, and, through the battle meld, Anakin felt Ulaha's anxiety slowly giving way to bewilderment.

"They are coming out to meet us, but they do not fire," Ulaha commed. "Now they are spreading out, and arrest tentacles are extending from the noses of some ships."

"They're still trying to take us alive!" Anakin gasped. "Why risk so much?"

"They are alienz," one of the Barabel sisters commed. "There is no sense trying to understand them."

The *Exquisite Death* swung sharply to port, then lurched back onto course, dipped sharply, and began to jink like a fighter.

"You must start the drop," Ulaha commed. The ship began to shudder. "They are shooting tentacles at us."

"Projected drop zone two kilometers from spaceport at bearing one-twenty-two," 2-1S reported from the shuttle. "Surprise likelihood high."

Anakin gave the go order, and Ulaha put the *Exquisite Death* into a coral-crackling climb. At the end of the long line of cargo pods, 2-4S used his blaster cannon to open a makeshift bomb bay, and the hold decompressed with a tremendous roaring. Anakin's pod began to slide across the floor toward the breach.

"Decoy away," 2-4S commed.

Anakin's pod, number five, slid toward the hole faster.

"Pod one away." There was a moment of silence, then 2-4S reported, "Enemy arrest tentacle has captured decoy pod."

Anakin held his breath. He had intended the decoy to detonate on the ground, but as long as it convinced the Yuuzhan Vong they were dropping bombs instead of a strike team . . .

A burst of static crackled across the comlinks, then 2-1S's barely audible voice said, "Decoy detonation. Heavy damage to enemy vessel."

The Barabels sissed over the comm channel.

"Pod two away," 2-4S reported. "Pod three . . ."

Anakin did not hear the next report, for a tremendous growling reverberated through their pod as it scraped over the edge of the hole and fell free. His stomach grew queasy with weightlessness and all five of them began to float.

"Two-Four-S away," 2-4S reported.

Tahiri grabbed Anakin's arm, and Eryl began an audible countdown. Anakin opened himself to the Force as completely as possible, alert to any emotion that might suggest the others had been grabbed by an arresting tentacle, or targeted by a defensive blast of plasma. He sensed only apprehensions similar to his own—except from the Barabels, who were radiating the emotional equivalent of a big "yipeee!"

Finally, Eryl said, "Fifteen seconds—mark!"

According to calculations, at least, they were now only a thousand meters above the surface of the worldship. Anakin caught their vessel with the invisible hand of the Force, cushioning their descent just enough so that the deceleration kept them pinned to the floor. The war droids had calculated that a deceleration of approximately one and a half standard gravities would not be overly noticeable, yet the resulting landing would be 99 percent survivable.

Anakin remained silent through the descent, wishing that he could see the surface, or feel the nonexistent atmosphere buffeting them, or anything. After a few more seconds, he decided that they had to be almost down and began to slow their descent still further—and then the bone-jarring shock of impact slammed everyone to the floor. They went weightless as the capsule bounced, then came down on their side and rolled more times than Anakin could count before coming to a rest in a jumbled tangle.

Anakin used the Force to move the others off him, then ignited his lightsaber and hacked through the blorash jelly seam. He had barely opened a fist-sized hole before Zekk and the others activated the delay on four grenades and used the Force to push them up through the crack. Two seconds later, a roiling fireball erupted fifty meters overhead.

Hoping the explosion would look realistic enough from a distance, Anakin finished opening the pod and stepped out into a dusty basin of brown, dead yorik coral. Perhaps three meters deep, the bowl was easily three hundred long and a hundred wide, probably not an impact crater, but the scar of some ancient mishap.

In the far corner, almost directly opposite Anakin, sat the broken husk of a distant cargo pod, a group of minuscule figures scurrying around its base. One of the Jedi felt him watching and waved in greeting, then all four turned and started in his direction. A moment later, the pod vanished in the brilliant flare of a thermal detonator.

Anakin's attention was drawn skyward by a flash of movement. He looked up in time to see a small, unidentifiable shape arc into the near corner of the field, then erupt in a tremendous fireball. Thinking they were under fire from a Yuuzhan Vong warship, he almost dived for the ground—but stopped when he saw the black, star-spangled camouflage armor of a Tendrando Arms YVH S-series war droid emerge from the dust cloud and come toward him at an impossibly fast run.

Anakin assigned Raynar and Eryl to unload their pod and sent Zekk to the basin rim to reconnoiter, then took a moment to concentrate on the others. He sensed a couple of fuzzy heads and a few aches and pains, but the team appeared to be 99 percent intact—just as the droids had promised.

Anakin retrieved the electrobinoculars and turned them overhead. Without the blue glow of streaking ion drives to draw attention to the ships, it took a moment to locate the space battle, which had already drifted far across the sky toward Myrkr. YVH 2-1S was just parting ways with Ulaha, his lumpy black shuttle corkscrewing wildly back toward the worldship as the Bith veered off into deep space in the *Exquisite Death*.

To Anakin's disappointment, the Yuuzhan Vong had swallowed the bait only partially. The coralskippers and four corvettes were surrounding 2-1S's shuttle, arrest tentacles lashing out to capture the careening rock—but the rest of the Yuuzhan Vong were pursuing the *Death*.

A pair of heavy steps came up beside Anakin, then Ganner said over the vac suit comm net, "We're good to go, Anakin. We have the bearings to the spaceport, and Two-Four-S's sensors show no sign they realize we're here."

Anakin lowered the electrobinoculars and turned away. He would have liked to stay and see whether they escaped—they deserved that much—but he knew neither 2-1S nor Ulaha would want that. Every minute of delay reduced the mission's success probability by 0.2 percent.

The strike team had traveled only five hundred meters when 2-4S's metallic voice came over the comm channel. "Two-One-S reports zero survivability rating. Now optimizing—"

An orange fireball blossomed in the sky, drowning the droid's last two words in a tempest of electronic interference. Anakin raised the electrobinoculars in time to see a trio of enemy corvettes burst into white sprays of yorik coral. The fourth vessel, a mere splinter at this distance, spiraled away out of control.

"Loss ratio optimized," 2-4S reported.

Anakin nodded and said, "Maximum efficiency."

They all knew from the training sessions with 1-1A that it was the highest tribute that could be made to one of Lando's droids, and several Jedi repeated the compliment. They continued toward the spaceport, using the Force to smooth the dust behind them and keep it from billowing into the airless sky.

A few minutes later, 2-4S detected two coralskippers approaching. The strike team had to conceal itself beneath the dust and wait as the pair swept over in a slow, curving search pattern. Once the pilots reached the drop zone, they would find four huge baradium craters and nothing to suggest the *Exquisite Death* had dropped anything but four poorly targeted bombs, and they would return to base laughing at their enemy's incompetence. Until then, the Jedi would have to wait and be patient.

Though no one said as much, all of their thoughts were on

Ulaha alone in the *Exquisite Death,* with five corvette analogs and a host of skips on her tail. Though the Bith was growing more distant in the battle meld, Anakin could feel her consumed with the tasks at hand, weary and in pain, but without fear—at peace, even. Daring to hope Ulaha's tranquility meant she was escaping, Anakin raised the electrobinoculars as soon as the search craft were gone and combed the darkness above for the *Exquisite Death,* but it was an impossible task. Even if he were looking in the right direction, by now the Bith and her pursuers would be too distant for electrobinoculars to detect.

The strike team resumed its march. Ulaha's presence continued to fade, then finally vanished altogether. Anakin could tell by the surge of anxiety in the battle meld that the same fear had leapt into the minds of all the Jedi.

Tahiri asked, "Is she—"

"No," Jacen interrupted. "We would have felt that."

"Maybe she jumped to hyperspace," Anakin said. "Two-Four-S?"

"Negative," the droid reported. "*Exquisite Death* still within sensor range."

Then the music started, a reedy, haunting melody that came to Anakin inside his mind. Though there was a mournful hint to it, the strain was more tranquil than sad, and perhaps the most beautiful thing he had ever heard. He turned and found the others staring skyward, some with heads cocked listening, others with a tear or two running down inside their face masks.

"*Exquisite Death* and pursuers decelerating," 2-4S reported. "Analysis suggests tentacle arrest."

No one seemed to hear the report. "I wish . . ." Jaina fell silent as the song drifted into a flighty passage and began to gather energy. "I wish I could record this."

"Yes," Jacen said. "I'm sure Tionne would like it for her archives . . . it's a sad loss for the Jedi."

Anakin could not tell from his brother's flat tone whether Jacen was criticizing or just saying aloud what they all felt. There was no question of Ulaha surrendering the *Death*. Even were she to survive the boarding party's initial assault, she could not endure another breaking.

The music repeated its opening refrain, but more powerfully now and without any hint of sadness, then rose to a robust crescendo . . .

In the sudden silence, Tahiri gasped.

Chapter 27

In the dim planetglow shining down from Myrkr's emerald face, the flattened senalak shafts looked more like ice spikes than any security system Anakin had ever seen. The rigid stalks were only knee-high and no thicker than a finger, but as Jovan Drark's invisible Force wave pushed a safe furrow through the field, their blunt blue caps released a meter-long strand of thorns. The barbed cord would flail around in the vacuum for a couple of seconds, presumably entwining and capturing—if not killing—whatever had disturbed it.

Had Alema not warned them about the trap, the strike team would have entered the security field completely unprepared. Given the trap they had already flown into aboard the *Exquisite Death,* Anakin was beginning to wonder if they were really prepared for this. Ulaha had given them less than a 50 percent chance of success, and as far as he could tell, things were not getting any better. He was beginning to wonder if coming after the voxyn queen had been such a good idea after all.

"Anakin, this has to be done—and you're not making it any easier with that big negatude." Tahiri was crawling along behind Anakin, her blond hair spilling out behind her faceplate.

"So they were expecting us. You dealt with it, and now they aren't."

"Sorry. Thought I had that stuff closed off."

"You did." Tahiri rolled her eyes. "This is *me*, Anakin."

The last of the senalaks fell to Jovan's Force wave, and they found themselves at the edge of the spaceport. Basically a huge pit thirty meters deep and a kilometer across, it was surrounded by a cavernous colonnade sealed behind a transparent membrane and accessed by a ring of air-locked valveways. Twenty biotic berthing bays lay spaced evenly across the floor, all covered by retractable carapaces and sized to accommodate corvette-analog vessels.

On the near side of the spaceport, the latest rescue transport to return from the space battle was just berthing, the two halves of the bay carapace rising up to press themselves against the lumpy hull. Though Anakin and the others had not been able to see the battle as they stole across the worldship's pocked surface, the steady stream of rescue vessels returning from space told them that their comrades had put up a good fight. They also knew the outcome; 2-1S had burst-commed a final situation report to 2-4S, and they had all felt Ulaha's death—one of the reasons, no doubt, for Anakin's "negatude."

Perhaps five kilometers beyond the landing pit rose the hive-shaped grashal peaks they had seen from space. Anakin did not need to stretch out with the Force to know that was where the voxyn were kept. He could feel their hunger clearly, coming straight from that direction. The Jedi prisoner was another matter. He could not sense him—or her, or them—at all, even when he exerted himself.

"Ysalamiri?" Alema asked. She crawled up beside him on the side opposite Tahiri, stopping so that the shoulder of her vac suit touched his. "If they've got a Jedi, they'd need ysalamiri."

Anakin was not really surprised to have the Twi'lek anticipating him. During the trip from the drop zone, the strike team had found itself acting in such harmony that, at times, it seemed they were sharing thoughts.

"I don't think he's dead," Tahiri said. "I realize we don't know who he is or anything, but I still think we'd know."

Anakin did not think so, but there was only one way to find out. He turned to call for the ysalamiri mating pheromones Cilghal had supplied—then grimaced when Jacen was waiting to press the capsule into his glove.

"This is getting weird," he said. "Tesar could have said something."

A grin showed in Jacen's eyes. "Try it from my end." He grew more serious, an aura of distress rising around him. "Anakin, before we start, there's something—"

"Not now, Jacen." Anakin looked away. The last thing he wanted to do was hurt Jacen's feelings, but he had seen at Centerpoint Station what happened when he listened to his brother. "I need to do this my own way."

"I know. I only want to—"

"Please."

Anakin flicked the capsule toward the far side of the landing pit, where a service crew was busy moving provisions out of an open air lock. In Myrkr's greenish planetglow, he quickly lost sight of the tiny capsule, but felt it stop when it entered the lock and came to the inner valve. A few minutes later, the crew finished its task and entered the air lock together. Anakin started to tell the others to be ready, then thought better of it. They were.

The outer valve was just closing when 2-4S reported, "Incoming vessel, enemy, frigate analog."

The report meant the ship's arrival was imminent—as marvelous as YVH war droids were, their sensor package lacked the power for deep-space detection. The news sent a prickle of danger sense down Anakin's spine, but he refused to be rushed. Until he knew where the Jedi was being kept, entering the spaceport would only place the captive—and themselves—at risk.

Finally, a swarm of distant squiggles scurried out of an archway about a third of the way around the colonnade. More than a dozen Yuuzhan Vong followed, stooped over and half stumbling as they attempted to retrieve the escapees. One of the warriors grabbed a squirming form, then jerked his hand back and stomped the creature. Ysalamiri had sharp teeth.

It did not take long before all eyes—at least all eyes visible through transparent membrane—were fixed on the disturbance. Anakin backed away from the edge and stood. When he turned to order the holoshrouds activated, he found himself facing a long line of what looked like Yuuzhan Vong.

"I suppose you know the plan, too?"

"Straight to the ysalamiri house," Bela—or was it Krasov—answered.

"Then back—"

"To steal the rescue shuttle," Ganner finished. "We've got it, Jedi. Two-Four-S and I will cover the descent."

"Well, then."

Anakin activated his own holoshroud and stepped over the edge, dropping alongside the wall and using the Force to cushion his landing. When he did not feel any surge of Yuuzhan Vong alarm through the lambent crystal, he turned to find himself standing before a rancor-sized air lock, a warren of murky tunnels and murkier doorways barely visible through its translucent door valves. He could feel a handful of Yuuzhan Vong somewhere back in the darkness, but his sense of them was too fuzzy to tell whether they were alarmed by his sudden appearance—or even aware of it.

Alema, Tesar, and the others began to arrive beside him. Knowing the Twi'lek to be the most experienced at infiltrating enemy lines, he assigned her to lead the way through the air lock, while he kept an eye on the rest of the spaceport. The landing pit appeared even larger from the floor than from above. In the murky green light, the excitement at the opposite end was visible only as a mass of shadows scurrying around behind the window membrane, and even figures in nearby warrens were difficult to see unless they were silhouetted against a patch of bioluminescent wall lichen. Only the rescue vessel, sitting pinched in its biotic berthing bay, was distinct and easy to see.

By the time Anakin had completed his survey, Ganner and 2-4S were on the floor behind him. They followed the others through the air lock and let their faceplates and breath masks hang over their collars, leaving their throat mikes and earpieces in place so they could communicate quietly. Anakin took the lead and began to hurry along the colonnade at the fastest pace he could without drawing too much attention; the power packs in their holoshrouds would last only two minutes before growing unreliable and needing to be changed.

As they went by the rescue ship, they also passed a rampway leading down to a bustling work level under the landing pit. An unarmored Yuuzhan Vong started up the slope, gesturing at them and calling in his own language. A wave of alarm shot through the strike team, but it was quickly quelled when Jacen used the battle meld to direct everyone's attention to Alema's unruffled composure. The Yuuzhan Vong reached the door and said something more insistent.

Tahiri's voice sounded in everyone's earpieces, giving the proper response. Ganner, who had the most Yuuzhan Vong–like voice, stepped out of line and faced the scarhead.

"*Pol dwag, kane a bar.*"

"*Kanabar?*" the Yuuzhan Vong asked.

There was a moment's pause while Tahiri gave the reply, then Ganner said, "*Dwi, kane a bar!*"

"*Yadag dakl, ignot!*"

The Yuuzhan Vong raised both arms in a rude gesture, then disappeared back down the ramp.

"What was that about?" Anakin whispered.

"Ganner called him the dung of a meat maggot," Tahiri said. "I told him to say *kanabar,* not *kane a bar.*"

"*Kane a bar* was better," Tesar rasped. "How do you say slime under my scales?"

This drew a chorus of sissing from the Hara sisters—and an order from Anakin to save the jokes. 2-4S reported that the incoming enemy vessel was indeed a frigate analog and had gone into orbit around the worldship. The prickles returned to Anakin's neck and did not subside. With a frigate in orbit around the worldship, they would have to be careful about the timing of their escape.

They reached the dark archway leading into the ysalamiri warren. Anakin knew instantly they were in the right place, for the air stank of unwashed bodies, old blood, and even fouler things. The battle meld vanished three steps into the tunnel, and he saw that the passage ahead was lined with walking trees similar to those they had seen aboard the *Death*. Most had broken claws protruding from the trunks, but a handful of the trees still had ysalamiri clinging to them. A pair of Yuuzhan Vong warriors stood behind a yorik coral lobby counter, adroitly plaiting a living cord into a braided whip and somehow ignoring the anguished screams rolling up the corridor.

As Anakin approached, both warriors stopped work and crossed their arms over their chest.

"*Remaga corlat, migan yam?*" the taller one asked.

Anakin walked straight to the gateway.

"Remaga corlat?" the tallest guard asked again, now pulling his amphistaff off his waist and stepping to block Anakin's way.

Anakin's answer was sharp, if not quite angry. *"Kane a bar."*

The Yuuzhan Vong's saggy eyes looked more confused than angry, but he lowered his amphistaff toward Anakin's chest. *"Yaga?"*

Anakin pointed his lightsaber and thumbed the activation switch. The crimson blade shot through the guard's throat and came out through his neck, narrowly missing the warrior behind him. This second Yuuzhan Vong hurled himself backward and opened his mouth to shout the alarm, but was interrupted by the *snap-hiss* of Alema's silver lightsaber slicing through his head.

Anakin switched off his holoshroud and made assignments, sending Jacen, Ganner, and 2-4S to watch the entrance and Jaina, Raynar, and Eryl to dispose of the remaining ysalamiri. Everyone else, he led down the corridor toward the torture sounds. When he reached the doorway and peered around the corner, he found himself staring at a Yuuzhan Vong's vonduun-crab-armored chest.

The warrior gave a startled cry and started to bring his amphistaff around, but Anakin was already slashing his lightsaber across the Yuuzhan Vong's throat. He thrust-kicked the collapsing body back into the chamber, then heard the telltale drone of thud bugs coming his way and dived to the floor. He rolled over his shoulder, trying to scan the chamber as he moved. There was an ysalamiri tree in one corner and two figures spread-eagle against the rear wall, and two more figures moving on his right. He came up with his lightsaber in a high guard—then dropped flat as Tesar's minicannon bolts began *whumpf*ing past his head.

The ysalamiri tree erupted into splinters, and Anakin's contact with the Force returned as the ysalamiri itself was vaporized. He heard the drone of a thud bug coming his way and allowed his Jedi senses to guide his lightsaber around to deflect it, then spun toward the source and found a Yuuzhan Vong charging him with amphistaff in hand. Before Anakin could parry, a bolt from Tesar's minicannon hurled the warrior across the room, and Alema rushed in to thrust her silver lightsaber through the shattered armor.

Only one Yuuzhan Vong remained, smaller than most and thinner, with a spectral female face and a variety of hooked and ser-rated talons protruding from her eight fingers, wrists, and even elbows. A shaper. Anakin stood and started toward her, but a web of shimmering energy lines crackled into existence around her body before he had taken two steps. He thought it was a personal shield of some kind—until her eyes widened and she spat something angry.

Anakin focused his thoughts on the web and felt the famil-iar energies of the Force, but colder and tainted with darkness. He glanced toward the back wall, where the two prisoners still hung spread-eagle, each bleeding from a profusion of wounds. One, a powerfully built woman with dark hair and darker eyes, was glaring at the shaper, quietly mouthing words Anakin did not understand.

The Yuuzhan Vong tried to pluck a strand of the Force energy from her body and succeeded only in severing three fingers. The dark woman smiled, and the web slowly began to shrink, slowly cutting into the shaper's flesh.

Anakin was overcome by a deep sense of wrongness, of hatred and anger . . . and evil. This woman was acting not out of wartime necessity, but out of bloodlust and vengeance. He started toward her. "No! This is wrong."

She ignored him, and the Yuuzhan Vong screamed in anguish. Blood began to patter on the floor, and something larger, as well. Anakin glanced back to see small cubes of flesh dropping off the body of the female shaper.

"Stop!"

Anakin raised the butt of his lightsaber and stepped forward to enforce his command, but the Yuuzhan Vong's scream ended abruptly in a wettish plopping sound. When he glanced back, he found her body heaped on the floor in diced sections. The smell was as horrible as the sight, and he had to fight not to vomit.

That was when Jacen's voice came over his earpiece. "That frigate's sending down a shuttle, Little Brother."

"O-okay," Anakin gasped. "Keep me . . . posted."

There was a pause, then Jacen asked, "Is something wrong?"

"We're fine," Anakin said. "Just a surprise. I'll tell you later."

An acknowledging click came over the comlink, then Anakin turned to find Alema at the back wall, already freeing the dark woman from the blorash jelly holding her in place.

". . . a fascinating technique," the Twi'lek was cooing. "Do you think I could learn it?"

"No, you couldn't," Anakin said. "That attack was cruel. Unnecessarily so."

Alema spun on him, her pale Twi'lek eyes as cold and hard as a Hothan lake. "You may lecture me about cruel when a voxyn has burned the flesh from *your* sister's face." She turned back to the dark woman, who was now free of the wall. "Perhaps I want to be cruel."

The woman gave her an encouraging smile. "There is nothing wrong with vengeance. It is a noble emotion—a powerful one."

"Spoken like a true Nightsister," Zekk said, stepping into the chamber. He glanced from the dark woman to the young man, who was still hanging on the wall behind her. "Hello, Welk."

Welk, a blond-haired human a year or two older than Anakin, narrowed his eyes at Zekk. "Hello, traitor."

"You two know each other?" Anakin asked.

Zekk nodded. "From the Shadow Academy. Welk here was Tamith Kai's best student—after Vilas died, of course."

"After you killed him," Welk corrected, glaring at Zekk. "And Zekk was the Darkest Knight—our leader, until he betrayed the Second Imperium at Yavin Four."

Anakin frowned at this. Though he had been too young to participate in the defense of the Jedi academy when Tamith Kai's Dark Jedi attacked, many of the Jedi Knights on his strike team—including both of his siblings, Lowbacca, Tenel Ka, and Raynar—had fought valiantly in the battle. They would not be happy to learn that they had just risked their lives to save one of the attackers.

Tesar, who had never even *been* to Yavin 4, was the first to object. "We risked our lives to save *Dark* Jedi?" The Barabel trained his minicannon on the pair. "Blaster boltz!"

"Check that, Tesar." Anakin pushed the minicannon down, then turned to the dark woman. "Are there any Jedi—"

"*We* are Jedi," she replied. Though she was oozing blood from a hundred different wounds, the pain seemed to trouble the woman no more than it would a Yuuzhan Vong. "But in answer to your question: not alive. We were the ones you sensed when you entered the system."

"All the same, there's no harm in looking around." Anakin nodded to Tesar and his hatchmates. "Be careful."

"Do as you wish, young Solo." The woman smiled. "But there is no need to doubt us. We will be happy to help destroy the voxyn."

"How do you know—"

"You are certainly not here to rescue *us*." Leaving Welk pinned on the wall behind her, she started for the door. "My name, by the way, is Lomi Plo. Perhaps I should start by telling you what we know of this place."

Anakin raised his brow. "You aren't holding that to bargain? What makes you think we won't leave you?"

Lomi regarded him coldly. "And who would be the dark one then, Anakin?"

Anakin was still trying to figure out how she knew his identity when his earpiece activated again.

"We've got trouble, Little Brother." This time it was Ganner on the other end. "That shuttle? You won't believe who's on it."

"*I* don't," Jacen added. "It looks like Nom Anor!"

Chapter 28

alfaglio lay dead center in Han's cockpit display, a point of fire just three light-years distant. That meant the light in his eye had been created three standard years ago, before the Jedi had become an endangered species and the Yuuzhan Vong had pulled a moon down on Chewbacca. Though seldom one to live in the past, Han would have given his life to ride that orange ray back to its birth, to add one more being to the thousands he had saved on Sernpidal that day. He no longer blamed himself or anyone else for the Wookiee's death, and he was even past wishing he had never tried to rescue anyone in the first place. He only wanted his friend back. He only wanted a galaxy safer for his children than it had been for him, a galaxy where a man and wife could go to sleep at night reasonably sure the world would still be there at dawn.

Some things were too much to ask.

Leia, who had been curled up in the *Falcon*'s Wookiee-sized copilot seat, opened her eyes and sat up straight. There was no grogginess or confusion to her actions; she had not slept—not really—since Anakin's strike team had departed for Myrkr. Neither had Han, for that matter. She slipped her crash webbing over her shoulders and began to cinch it down.

Han activated a self-test routine to warm the *Falcon*'s circuits. "What's happening? You sense something from Luke?"

"Not from Luke." Leia closed her eyes, reaching for her children in a way Han could never share. "Anakin and the twins. They're in the middle of it now, something dangerous." She paused, then added, "I think our turn will come soon."

Han started to activate the intercom, then recalled who would be manning his guns and looked over his shoulder. As expected, the Noghri were standing quietly in the back of the cockpit.

"Take the turrets—and tell See-Threepio to lock himself down," he said. "We're helping Lando and the Wild Knights with the yammosk hunt, so when Corran sends us in, it'll be hot."

The two Noghri dipped their heads and retreated down the corridor. Han watched them go, a little unnerved by the shadow that came to their black eyes whenever combat was at hand, but still grateful for their presence. Over the last fifteen years, the Noghri had saved Leia's life uncounted times and rarely left her unprotected—which was more than he could say for himself. He still found it hard to understand what had come over him after Chewbacca died, why mourning his friend's loss had meant withdrawing from Leia and the kids.

"Remind me to thank those guys," he said.

"You have," Leia said. "At least a dozen times."

Han gave her a crooked smile. "Yeah, but they never say 'you're welcome.' "

For the first time in days, Leia laughed, then Corran Horn's voice came over the comm speaker.

"Time to wake up, people. Outlying sensors show a Yuuzhan Vong assault fleet moving into the Talfaglio system."

Leia stretched over and armed the depressurization safety on Han's combat suit. "I'm scared, Han."

"Me, too." Han reached across and lowered her flash visor. "But what can you do? They're adults now. They get to pick their own fights."

Eclipse had managed to put pilots in fifty of its new XJ3 X-wings, and over half of them were Jedi. Another two dozen Jedi were operating blastboats and other support craft. Given that Luke was risking half the galaxy's Jedi and most of its Masters on a single operation, he should probably have been nervous. He was not. The Force was with them in a way he had never before experienced, a presence so tangible he could almost see it shimmering against the velvet starlight.

Not too calm, Skywalker.

Mara's voice was so clear in Luke's mind that it took him an instant to realize she had not spoken over a comm channel. He glanced at her X-wing, floating close enough that their S-foils almost touched. He wanted to tell her there was nothing to worry about, that Ben would be losing no parents today, but such a thought would have implied a vision of the outcome he had deliberately avoided seeking. If the Force wanted to show him the future, fine; if not, it was better to trust it and take what came. Whatever that was, making this attack was the right thing. He could feel it.

So can I, Mara added.

Luke raised a brow. Through their bond, each could usually sense what the other was feeling, and it was not even uncommon for them to receive short, semiarticulated thoughts. But this was something new; Luke's contemplations had barely risen to the level of consciousness when Mara sensed them. Perhaps the presence of so many powerful Jedi was gathering the Force, drawing it together in the same way a cloud of gas became a star.

"More like a lens gathering light," Mara said. "The effect of so many Jedi concentrating on a common purpose."

"This is really something." Luke added a long thought question to test the limits of their mental link; when his only reply was an impression of curiosity, he asked aloud, "I wonder if the old Jedi Councils focused the Force like this?"

"It certainly would have helped them see clearly—but it might have had its drawbacks."

Luke sensed an uncommon moment of embarrassment in his wife as Mara's mind flashed from the cognitive union they were experiencing to a more physical kind, and he found himself sharing in her hope that nobody else was picking up the connection.

If they were, they had the good sense not to say so.

Smiling both inwardly and outwardly, Luke glanced at his tactical display and saw the enemy assault fleet lumbering into the Talfaglio system. The deliberate approach, he suspected, had less to do with a fear of space mines or ambushes than allowing the hostages plenty of time to contemplate their doom. There were four cruiser analogs, a warship analog, a skip carrier, and twenty frigates. The carrier would have at least two hundred coralskippers, and the five largest vessels would have their own squadrons, as well.

Ouch, Mara thought.

Luke was not worried. The Jedi were there to break the blockade and buy the refugee convoy time to escape, not destroy the fleet. There was one aspect of the mission that would need rethinking, however. He asked R2-D2 for an open channel.

"This is Farmboy." His call sign had been picked by Mara. "Operation Safe Passage is still a go, but there are too many hostiles for the Yammosk Action. Repeat, Yammosk Action is—"

"Hold a moment, Farmboy," Corran said. As the Jedi battle controller, he was aboard the Wild Knights' freighter, *Jolly Man,* using a new subspace eavesdropping suite to monitor the Talfaglion sensors. "We have company exiting hyperspace."

"Company?" Luke's heart did not sink; there was nothing in the Force to suggest an ambush. "Who?"

"An old Rogue," the familiar voice of Wedge Antilles said.

"And an old Rebel."

Though this voice was also familiar, Luke did not recognize it until R2-D2 ran a scan analysis and identified it as that of General Garm Bel Iblis. Luke switched his tactical display to local space and saw a pair of unfamiliar Star Destroyers—the transponder identified them as the *Mon Mothma* and the *Elegos A'Kla*—moving into position behind his fleet. Accompanied by a cruiser and two frigates each, both ships were bleeding squadrons of XJ3 X-wings and Series 4 E-wings into space.

"Gentlemen, welcome!" Luke commed. "But if you don't mind my asking—"

"We just happened by on a shakedown cruise," Bel Iblis said, cutting him off.

"So close to Talfaglio?" This from Mara, whose years in Palpatine's service had given her a deep distrust of unanticipated gifts. "I don't think so."

"An old employer of yours recommended the route," Wedge said. He was referring to the infamous Talon Karrde, onetime smuggling king/information broker and sometime intelligence agent. No one ever knew exactly what Talon Karrde was up to. "He seemed to think we would have a chance to test some new weapons."

"That you might." Luke did not bother to ask how Karrde had learned the timing and location of their operation; Karrde always protected his sources. "Control will fill you in on the plan."

"Karrde already has," Bel Iblis said. "We thought we'd let you punch through ahead, then take cross-fire positions to either side of the escape corridor. We'd assume lead, but we're not sure how well this new stuff is going to work."

"And this is a Jedi operation," Luke finished, reading between the lines. Someone wanted to improve their image on the newsvids. "Thanks."

"We'd be willing to detach a squadron to support the Wild Knights on their mission—say Rogue?" Wedge offered. "We want to keep them off the 'Net anyway."

Though Luke's bond with his sister, Leia, was not as strong as the one with Mara, it was more than potent enough for him to sense her suspicion. The whole thing was beginning to stink of Borsk Fey'lya's influence, which automatically raised the question of what the chief wanted in return—and of who else he might have told about their plans. A simple battle was beginning to look very complicated, but Wedge's offer was too generous to refuse.

"Hisser, what do you think?" Luke asked. "Still want to try for that yammosk?"

"By all meanz," Saba replied. "It would be an honor to hunt with Colonel Darklighter."

"You two work out the details," Luke said. "Everyone else, double-check your jump coordinates, and blast anything that looks like a rock. On your mark, Control."

"Broadcasting escape route coordinates to Talfaglio now," Corran said. "Dozen squadron, jump on my mark. Three, two, mark."

Kyp's Dozen shot forward in a flash of blue efflux, then vanished into hyperspace. Luke switched his tactical screen back to Talfaglio local and watched as, a minute later, the squadron appeared insystem and streaked toward the yellow shell of Yuuzhan Vong blips trapping the refugee fleet in orbit.

At the far edge of the system, the enemy assault fleet began spreading into attack formation and accelerated, no doubt preparing to make a hyperspace microjump toward the planet. The Talfaglion gravity well would prevent them from jumping directly into battle, but Luke knew Corran would need to time their own fleet's arrival carefully.

As the Dozen drew near the blockade, Kyp pulled his squadron in tight and angled for the light cruiser. Half a dozen corvette analogs left their blockade posts to defend the larger ship, and long tongues of plasma began to arc out from the cruiser itself. The Dozen merged into a single blip and continued forward, jinking and juking as one, the pilots weaving in front of each other to keep a fresh pair of shields always facing the enemy.

Kyp's squadron began to pour blue lines of laserfire into the light cruiser. More enemy corvettes accelerated toward the Dozen, abandoning their blockade stations. So far, so good; the Yuuzhan Vong seemed to think this was another rogue operation, a desperate attempt to save the doomed refugees.

A pair of proton torpedoes flashed away from the Dozen and vanished, swallowed by the cruiser's shielding system. There followed another exchange of laser bolts and plasma balls, then an unexpected spray of static as a Jedi shadow bomb exploded. Basically a variation on the tactic Kyp used to slip his proton torpedoes past enemy shielding crews, shadow bombs were proton torpedoes drained of propellant and packed with baradium instead. They were armed with standard proximity fuses and guided to their targets using the Force. The weapons were far more powerful than a standard torpedo, difficult to detect in the heat of battle, and just one of the new tricks in the Jedi arsenal.

Kyp's squadron finished off the cruiser with a pair of standard proton torpedoes, then raced through the debris and swung around as though preparing the escape route. A steady flow of refugee vessels began to leave orbit and stream toward the flight corridor. It did not take long for the blockade to collapse inward as Yuuzhan Vong picket ships rushed to respond.

"Control, time to swing the hammer," Luke commed.

"Concur, Farmboy." Corran actually sounded as though he were cringing when he spoke the call sign. "New Republic task force, Shockers, and Sabers jump to preassigned coordinates on my mark."

The Saber squadron was Luke's personal squadron. It consisted of himself, Mara, seven non-Jedi veterans, and half a dozen newly trained Jedi pilots. Their assignment was to fly cover while the more experienced Shockers drove off the assault fleet.

"Three, two, mark."

Luke jammed his accelerator forward and watched the stars stretch into lines.

"Be careful, kid," Han commed. "We just finished raising three Jedi. We don't need you sticking us with another one."

"Han! That's—"

Talfaglio's orange point vanished into the colorless blur of hyperspace, and Leia's rebuke was lost to the jump blackout. Luke was aware of Mara beside him, calmly running through last-minute systems checks to keep her circuits warm and her attention focused on the coming battle. There had been no need to discuss the wisdom of flying into combat together. They were a team in a way that even Han and Leia could never understand, and they had seen many times before that each was far more likely to survive with the other present.

The blur of hyperspace dissolved into starlines, and Talfaglio appeared outside Luke's canopy, a small orangish crescent hanging alongside the brilliant disk of the system's crimson sun. Though the flotilla had jumped as close as they dared to the gravity well, the battle remained a tiny web of laser bolts and plasma trails hanging in the darkness between them and the planet. The enemy assault fleet was not yet visible to the naked eye, but Luke found it quickly enough on his tactical display. It had already made its microjump and was now on the other side of the blockade, directly opposite the Jedi flotilla, vectoring toward the escape corridor.

Rigard Matl led his Shockers toward the blockade at near-light, a favorite assault tactic that had earned the squadron its name. The Sabers shed just enough velocity to assume their cover position. The tactical display showed the New Republic Star Destroyers decelerating alongside the escape corridor in staggered positions, each retaining an escort of a single frigate and two squadrons of short-range starfighters. The rest of their flotilla streaked toward Talfaglio behind the Sabers.

In Luke's canopy, the battle swelled quickly from a tiny web into a moon-sized snarl of plasma trails and laser flashes. The blockade ships were still constricting around Kyp's Dozen, pouring fire in on the squadron from every direction. The Dozen bounced back and forth inside the sphere, sharing shields and reserving their laserfire for grutchins and magma missiles. There were only nine X-wings visible, but when Luke stretched out with the Force, he felt all three missing pilots scattered throughout the battle area, alone and frightened and no doubt in EV suits. He had R2-D2 send a message to the recovery team and tried not think about what would happen if they were struck by a stray plasma ball or efflux tail.

The nearest blockade ships peeled off to meet the Shockers, who launched a flurry of proton torpedoes and continued forward. The weapons reached their targets almost the instant they were launched. A pair of corvettes broke apart when their shielding crews missed incoming torpedoes; eight more began to vent bodies and atmosphere when the proximity fuses detonated close to their hulls. Then the Shockers were through, streaking past Kyp's Dozen toward the opposite side of the collapsing blockade.

Luke led his squadron into the hole behind the Shockers. They did not waste energy expanding their inertial compensators—the corvettes' dovin basals were more than strong enough to rip their shields. When a pair of corvettes rushed to block their way, Luke dropped a shadow bomb—they were flying too fast to lock their S-foils into firing position—and used the Force to hurl it into the second vessel. There was no need to assign the first to Mara; he *knew* she would take it with the same tactic. An instant later, simultaneous proton detonations broke the spines of both ships.

Wow! Mara sent.

A corvette's dovin basal caught Luke's shields. Warning alarms filled the cockpit. Mara slid her fighter over his to protect him for the instant it took R2-D2 to activate the backup charge. The third member of their shielding trio, the young Tam Azur-Jamin, blasted the attacker with his own shadow bomb.

"Thanks, Quiet," Luke commed.

Tam clicked his transmitter—a garrulous reply for the reticent Jedi—and then they were crossing the kill zone where Kyp had been "trapped." Dozens of refugee ships were already lumbering up from Talfaglio, in their haste to escape willing to brave even the heart of the fighting. Still moving at a substantial percentage of lightspeed, the Sabers flashed past a trio of Dozen X-wings.

Kyp Durron's excited voice came over the tactical net. "Right behind you, Farmboy!"

"Neg that, Headhunter," Luke ordered. If Kyp realized he had three pilots EV, there was no trace of it in his tone. "You're already down three. Stay here and cover refugees."

"Cover? But we're the most experienced—"

"Headhunter," Luke said in a stern voice. "You have your orders."

There was a moment of silence, then, "Copy."

Kyp's resentment lingered in the Force like the aftersmell of a bad blaster burn. Luke was troubled by the continued lack of compassion. If Kyp was ever going to—

Skywalker! Mara's thought was a shout inside Luke's head. *The battle?*

Sorry.

Something inside Luke suggested dropping three shadow

bombs. He did. He had given himself over to the Force completely, and the battle seemed to drop into slow motion. A trio of black-faceted corvettes drifted in from different angles, filling space with magma missiles and grutchins. Luke continued to fly straight and sensed a question rising in the back of Mara's mind—then felt it change to approval when he reached out with the Force and nudged the nearest magma missile into a grutchin.

Luke perceived a sudden need for forward protection and ordered R2-D2 to shift all shielding power to the front. A tiny red speck blossomed from the nose nodule of the closest corvette and, at the squadron's closing speed, flowered almost instantly into a plasma ball. Finding his view blocked, Luke closed his eyes and reached out to the rest of his squadron, using their perceptions to guide his shadow bombs home. He saw the blinding flash of his detonating weapons through their eyes, then felt his X-wing buck as the enemy plasma ball erupted against his forward shields.

There came a surge of trepidation from the Mara-place in the center of his heart—followed almost instantly by a sharp sense of reproach.

Next time jink!

R2-D2 whistled a warning and shut down the overloaded shield generator to begin an emergency cool-off. Luke eased between Mara and Tam, more for his wife's peace of mind than his own. The way he was feeling today, he could have continued without shields. They passed through a field of drifting corvette hulks—Luke was not the only one in his squadron to claim a picket ship—and were through the blockade, following the Shockers past Talfaglio.

The enemy assault fleet moved its frigates forward to form a defensive screen, but continued to withhold its coralskippers, determined to reach the escape corridor before stopping to do battle. With eight New Republic starfighter squadrons, two cruisers, and a pair of frigates close behind him, Luke carried the battle to the enemy and called for long-range fire support.

The New Republic cruisers and frigates laced the darkness with turbolaser flashes. The enemy answered with plasma balls and magma missiles. The Jedi squadrons continued forward, relying on flying ability, danger sense, and shield weaving to twine their way through the fiery mesh. A pair of Shockers turned back when they were damaged by near-hits. One of Luke's pilots lost an S-foil to a grutchin and went EV. The Shockers punched through the frigate screen.

Rigard Matl's X-wing vanished in a ball of fire.

The Shockers' formation disintegrated into a confused swarm of ion trails as the dazed pilots contemplated the loss of their veteran leader. Luke extended himself into the heart of the fireball and experienced a moment of unbearable prickling—then a strange sense of calm familiarity. He focused on the calmness just long enough to confirm that it was what he thought: Rigard had survived the hit and gone EV.

Before Luke could pass on the good news, Rigard's static-laden voice crackled over the emergency channel.

"Tighten up, Shockers!" He sounded pained but confident. "You're embarrassing . . ."

His voice trailed off into sizzle as the assault passed beyond the limited range of his suit's comm unit, but the chastened Shockers formed themselves into three shield trios and continued forward. The Force was truly with them today; so far, the Jedi had lost no one.

The heart of the Yuuzhan Vong assault fleet lay before them now, half a dozen yorik coral pebbles gleaming in the light of Talfaglio's crimson sun. The skip carrier and one of the cruisers were slipping behind the warship analog, while the other three cruisers moved out front and began to deploy skip squadrons. Luke had R2-D2 send the coordinates of the shy cruiser to the Star

Destroyers for a subspace relay back to Saba, then opened a channel to both the Sabers and Shockers.

"Forget the skips. Expand your inertial compensators to full and comet right past them. What we want is the carrier." Of all the ships in the assault fleet, the skip carrier was the most dangerous to the refugee convoy—and to their friends from the New Republic. "We'll make it look like we're going after the cruiser on the left, then launch everything we have the moment we have a clear angle to the real target."

By the time both squadrons acknowledged, the cruisers had swelled to arm-length lozenges of scabrous black yorik coral. Plasma balls streaked past or blossomed against the shields of the leapfrogging X-wings, and the tiny nuggets of the first distant skips glinted in the flashing battle light.

"Split by trios," Luke ordered. "Do what you can to save your shields."

The first handful of coralskippers streaked into range, spitting plasma and grabbing at shields. One pair vanished when they crossed their own cruiser's firing lane, then the X-wings were past the initial wave, still traveling at near-light and moving too fast for the skips to turn and follow. The Shockers angled toward the cruiser on the left. The Yuuzhan Vong captain put his ship into a tight turn, trying desperately to bring his flank around to present the maximum number of shielding dovin basals and weapons nodules.

R2-D2 informed Luke they had reached maximum proton-torpedo range to the skip carrier, but the warship analog was keeping its bulk between them and the target. The cruiser's flank weapons began to open up, filling the darkness with clouds of white energy and spiraling streaks of fire.

"All trios, break formation!" Luke ordered.

He jinked right, checked his tactical display, found the warship still shielding the skip carrier—and the skip carrier slipping past toward the escape corridor.

Luke ground his teeth in frustration, then sensed the bud of an idea forming in Mara's mind. "Go ahead, Mother."

"All pilots, target cruiser," she commanded. "Fire all proton torpedoes and break for safety." *Luke, with me.* "Repeat, target cruiser and fire all proton torpedoes."

In the instant of hesitation that followed Mara's command, a grutchin caught a Shocker X-wing and began to devour the wing. The veteran pilot popped the canopy and went EV, and the starfighter exploded.

"Now!" Mara growled.

Blue tails of ion efflux crisscrossed in front of the cruiser as dozens of torpedoes streaked toward their target. A line of shielding singularities appeared along the flank and began to devour the proton torpedoes, but it was instantly clear the vessel's defenses would be overwhelmed.

A long tail of what appeared to be white flame appeared behind one of Mara's engines, then her X-wing spiraled out of the battle plane. Luke followed, experiencing the barest instant of worry until he felt her drawing on the Force and realized what she was doing.

Nice trick. This came not from Luke, but from Tam, still maintaining the shield trio. "Learn that from Izal?"

Yes, Mara replied. She was a little shaken, Luke sensed, by the idea that Tam was also sharing in their thoughts. "How long have you been eavesdropping?"

Tam responded with a mental shrug. "Wasn't trying." A young navigator-turned-fighter-pilot, the Duros' father—the Jedi Daye Azur-Jamin—had vanished on Nal Hutta a year earlier, and since then, Tam had been having trouble shutting other people's thoughts out of his mind. "You two have just been sort of . . ." *SHOUTING.*

The exchange took only as long as it required the squadrons' fusillade of proton torpedoes to hit the cruiser and detonate. A brilliant light flared above and behind the trio, and Luke's tactical display danced with static as R2-D2 struggled with the electromagnetic pulse.

The Force glow trailing from Mara's engines flashed into a firelike ball that engulfed all three X-wings. "Okay, boys, shut down your sublights."

Luke was already flipping the switch—and drawing an alarmed whistle from R2-D2. "It's okay, Artoo." He flipped the toggle. "This is part of Mara's plan."

R2-D2 tweedled sharply. Luke checked the readout.

"Of course you didn't hear the plan," he explained. "It didn't come over a comm channel."

R2-D2 trilled in doubt.

"Trust me, Artoo, there *is* a plan."

"Time for a little lifting," Mara commed. "Follow along."

Luke felt Mara gathering the Force in, then saw her unpowered X-wing rise slowly out of the light ball. He lifted his own craft after hers and glanced back to see Tam doing the same. Mara let the glowing sphere spiral off. When they still did not draw any Yuuzhan Vong fire, she dispelled it in a final flash of brilliant light.

Luke looked up and saw they were less than a thousand meters beneath the skip carrier's spindly armed form. A full squadron of skips still hung from each of its fifteen arms, and the big warship analog was out in front, paying no attention at all to their dark ships.

Luke started to congratulate Mara on her strategy, but she cut him off. "What'd you expect, Skywalker? Subterfuge is my specialty."

R2-D2 trilled urgently and displayed a warning about non-optical sensors.

"I know they can still detect us," Luke answered. "But they're going to be confused for a second—and a second's all we need."

Mara dropped her shadow bombs, then used the Force to send them sailing up toward the heart of the monstrous ship. Tam's were close behind. Luke was still launching his when the first explosion erupted from the carrier's central disk.

Danni rose into her crash webbing. Fighting to keep breakfast where it belonged, she wondered if the blastboat's overhaul had been a good thing. With every seam rewelded by the maintenance droids on Eclipse and the frame inspected by certified space techs, Wonetun thought he could fly it like the squadron's new X-wings—and he still insisted on keeping the inertial compensator dialed down to 92 percent. The Brubb swung into a vectored-thrust turn so tight the blood pooled in Danni's fingertips. She had to squeeze her eyes shut to keep them in their sockets. A bad thing, she decided. Something popped in the systems bilge beneath her feet. Definitely a bad thing.

A distant flash shone through the forward viewport. Danni looked and saw the white spheres of three proton detonations winking back into nothingness. The Wild Knights had emerged from hyperspace far above Talfaglio's orbital plane and rolled into an inverted nosedrop, so she had the sensation of diving "down" toward the battle. Another proton explosion lit the darkness, vaping the central disk of the big skip carrier. The vessel's arms spun off into space. Burning coralskippers tumbled in every direction.

"Ah—Master Skywalker, he is enjoying his hunt." Saba activated a targeting reticle and slid it across the transparisteel viewport to a Yuuzhan Vong cruiser trailing behind the debris. "There is the shy vessel, Danni. See if it has what we want."

Danni linked her sensors to the reticle. A dozen gravity arrows leapt to life and began dancing to the enemy code.

"Affirmative," she said. "That ship has a yammosk."

"Not for long." Saba sissed uproariously, then transmitted the coordinates to the Rogues and the rest of the Wild Knights. "There is our target. Be careful of her big hatchmate."

The enemy warship was just ahead of the yammosk cruiser,

hurling an unending salvo of plasma balls and magma missiles at the New Republic flotilla blocking its route to the escape corridor. Fortunately, the *Mon Mothma* and *Elegos A'Kla* had made short work of the Yuuzhan Vong blockade and were dashing forward to support the other New Republic forces.

A flurry of bouncing data bars drew Danni's eye back to her holodisplay. "They've seen us."

Fifteen seed-shaped lumps of yorik coral dropped off the enemy cruiser and angled up to meet them, and its weapons nodules began to spew plasma fire and magma missiles in their direction. Danni felt like they were flying into a star.

Wonetun put the blastboat into a wild corkscrew and followed the rest of the squadron into battle, and Izal Waz opened up with the big quad lasers. Danni grabbed the arms of her seat, trying to keep Wonetun's wild gyrations from slamming her against her crash webbing. The gravity arrows in her holodisplay went wild.

"Ready concussion missiles and decoyz."

"Ready." The reply came from both Han Solo's *Millennium Falcon* and Lando Calrissian's *Lady Luck,* flying behind the blast-boat above and below.

"X-wingz, ready all torpedoes," Saba said. "Target cruiser only; ignore skipz."

"Wild Knights ready," Drif Lij commed.

The communication was more for the Rogues' sake than Saba's. With the Force as thick as it was today, the Wild Knights could feel the readiness of their fellow pilots. The Rogues had to rely on more conventional means.

"Rogues ready," Gavin Darklighter confirmed.

Luke Skywalker's voice came over the tactical net. "The Shockers and Sabers are regrouping below the cruiser. We're out of torpedoes, but we'll run interference when that warship starts shedding skips."

"Our thankz, Farmboy."

All of Danni's data bars dropped to near-zero. "The yammosk has gone quiet." She looked forward and saw the cruiser starting to bank around, trying to bring its flank to bear on the ships jumping it from above. How it could have more weapons there than the ones firing at them from its top, Danni could not imagine. "Something's happening."

"Yes. The warship is decelerating and dropping skips," Wonetun added.

"We have convinced them to stay and fight," Saba said. She opened a channel to the tactical net. "Hisser here—"

"That's not it," Danni interrupted. She closed her eyes, using a Jedi concentration technique to help her see the data, comprehend how it fit together. They were too close to Talfaglio for a microjump, and with two Star Destroyers moving up to support the New Republic, the yammosk had to realize that any hope of punching through to the escape corridor was gone. She patched herself into the tactical net. "They're getting ready to microjump—away from the battle."

Saba turned one reptilian eye toward Danni. "Yuuzhan Vong do not run."

Corran Horn's concerned voice came over the tactical net. "All units, break off," he ordered. The *Jolly Man* was far above the system's orbital plane, using its long-range sensors to monitor and coordinate the battle. "They're trying to string you out—"

"Give us a minute, Control," Wedge Antilles said. "There's something we'd like to try. Hisser, please have your squadron launch its missiles."

Saba did not need to be told twice. She gave the order. The brilliant circles of twenty propellant tails flashed past, then multiplied into many times that number as the decoys deployed.

The cruiser completed its turn and began to accelerate, and all of Danni's data bars shot to maximum, and the gravity arrows swung their bases toward the New Republic flotilla. The equipment popped and sizzled, then vented a plume of acrid smoke and went dead. Danni slapped the power cutoff—though she knew by the smell of scorched circuits it was too late to save her processing boards—and turned to answer the question she sensed coming from Saba.

"Gravity surge—something overloaded it."

"So it seemz."

Saba curled her pebbly lips and sissed, then looked forward. With Wonetun spiraling from one direction to another, the enemy cruiser was bouncing back and forth in the viewport. It had stopped firing and seemed to be pivoting around its bow. The first wave of missiles flashed past, their ion tails bending sharply as their guidance systems struggled to adjust course.

Danni thought it was some strange Yuuzhan Vong evasive tactic, until the second wave angled in unopposed and detonated into the hull.

"Disarm the missiles!" Danni yelled. She glanced at Saba's tactical display and saw the warship also spinning out of control. "Disarm them now. We're going to vape our yammosk!"

"You must be right about this," Saba warned, already transmitting the deactivation code, "or this one will eat your arm."

Somehow, Danni did not think the Barabel was exaggerating. "I am."

The cruiser broke into three pieces and began to vent bodies. The next wave of missiles curved in and struck the hull and did not explode, and Danni dared to breathe again. She opened a channel to the *Mon Mothma*. "General Antilles, does one of your ships happen to be an Interdictor?"

"That information would be classified," the reply came. "But it would be safe to assume that we were *just* waiting for them to microjump."

As General Antilles replied, the New Republic flotilla began to rain turbolaser blasts down on the helpless warship, softening it up before attempting to board. Luke and Mara and the rest of the Eclipse X-wings swung away from the conflagration and headed back to help escort the refugee convoy safely out of the system.

With their own target as helpless as the warship, Wonetun flew a straighter course, and Han and Leia and Lando and Tendra came alongside in the *Falcon* and the *Luck*.

Saba turned her chair to face Danni. "Now we know why your equipment exploded?"

Danni nodded. Interdiction technology was nothing new; the Imperials had used it during the Rebellion to project artificial gravity wells in the midst of Rebel fleets to prevent them from fleeing. What was new was that the new Star Destroyers lacked the telltale projector domes of most Interdictor ships. By surprising the Yuuzhan Vong and timing their attack to coincide with the microjumps, they had put both enemy vessels out of control.

Danni opened a channel to the *Lady Luck*. "Gambler, can you send your droids into the cruiser now? I'd like to know if there's anything left of our yammosk."

After Lando acknowledged, Saba said to Danni, "The yammosk will be there, you may be sure, Danni Quee—flash frozen and ready to pack." She slapped her knee and, sissing for some reason only a Barabel would understand, turned to watch as Wonetun fell in behind the *Luck* and the *Falcon*. "The Force is with us today."

Chapter 29

*T*savong Lah was not a rare sight in the *Sunu-lok*'s High Chew—as the ship's officers affectionately called their mess—so he knew the ripple of stunned silence sweeping across the tables behind him had less to do with his presence than that of the person approaching. He did not turn to see who it was; that would have implied curiosity, and he was not curious. The warmaster continued to study the basin of yanskacs before him, his eye fixed on a juicy fellow with an eight-centimeter fence of dorsal spines. The thing seemed to realize it was being watched and kept its tail poised, but it made no move to bury itself beneath the others as wise old yanskacs often did. This one seemed worthy, a true creature of Yun-Yammka.

The voices close behind Tsavong Lah murmured into quiet, and a pair of a feet scuffed the floor. He raised an arm, signaling whoever it was to wait, then darted a hand into the basin and grabbed the yanskac beneath its tail barb. Instead of struggling to escape, the creature reared back, driving its dorsal fence into the warmaster's fingers. Two spines struck bone and another lodged in a knuckle, pumping poison directly into the joint. A cord of white heat shot up Tsavong Lah's arm into his shoulder. The pain was exquisite.

With the spines still embedded in his fingers, the warmaster stepped to the dressing table and braved the yanskac's clacking chelipeds to eviscerate it alive, then tossed it onto the brazier, still thrashing, to cook in its scales. The entrails he flung to the floor for the kaastoag cleaning scavengers, who began to fight over them stinger and tentacle. Such were the gifts the gods gave to their strong: battle, pain, life, death. Tsavong Lah cleaned his coufee in a vat of venogel and drew the edge across his own palm to sanctify the blade, then turned to see who had come.

"Yes?" To his surprise, he found himself facing not a messenger, but a striking young communications attendant with black honor bars burned across her cheeks. "You may speak, Seef."

Seef raised a fist to the opposite shoulder in salute. "News from Talfaglio, Warmaster."

Instead of continuing, she cast a nervous glance around at the other officers in the High Chew.

"I take it the *Jeedai* have shown themselves." The crack of rupturing cheliped told Tsavong Lah that his yanskac had finished cooking. He snatched his meal out of the flames with his bare hands—no officer in the High Chew would dream of using the bone tongs provided for the purpose—then peeled the tail down, pulling the scaly skin off with it. "How many refugees did they save?"

"All of them, my leader, or nearly so." Seef's gaze dropped. "The blockade was defeated, as was our fleet."

"Defeated?" Tsavong Lah grasped the yanskac by its dorsal spines and took a bite. The flesh was firm and tangy, designed by the shapers to be savory as well as nutritious. "You're certain?"

Seef drew her coufee and offered the hilt. "It shames me to bear this news, but the sentinels' view was clear. They attacked with a fleet many times larger than our spies claim they have, and they employed weapons our shapers are still struggling to analyze." She lowered her gaze, not wishing to offend the great warmaster by looking upon him as she delivered the last line of particularly disgracing news. "Their Star Destroyers were even able to capture one of our capital vessels, the *Lowca*."

"Intact?"

"More than not, I fear," Seef answered.

"Interesting. I want to go see this for myself."

"Memory chilabs are on their way from the sentinels now, Warmaster."

"And that won't be necessary." Tsavong Lah pushed the coufee aside. "We have been awaiting this."

"We have?" Seef looked more puzzled than relieved.

"The *Jeedai* have finally let their emotions lead them astray." Though he had been working toward this moment since the fall of Duro, he felt strangely disappointed in his enemies. He had thought them better foes than this, not so easily manipulated. "Seef, you will ask the readers to discover if the gods favor two bold attacks, one to take Borleias, the other to take Reecee."

"Reecee?" This from a master tactician standing in line behind him. "You will bypass the Bilbringi Shipyards?"

"For now." Tsavong Lah placed a hand on Seef's back and pushed her gently toward the exit, then tore the chelipeds off his yanskac. Splaying them open, he raised his arm high enough for everyone in the High Chew to see. "The time has come to prepare our pincers, my warriors."

He brought the claws together. "We are ready for Battle Plan Coruscant."

Chapter 30

Gaunt and thin-lipped, with a much-broken nose and a black-pithed plaeryin bol glaring out of a restructured ocular orbit, Nom Anor was the most recognizable Yuuzhan Vong in the galaxy—at least to a Jedi Knight. The feathery creature hopping along beside him was another matter. Standing a little over waist-high on reverse-jointed knees, it had willowy ears, corkscrew antennae, and delicate whiskers fringing a broad simian mouth. Jacen had never seen a creature quite like this one, and yet he had the uncanny feeling he should know it.

Halfway to its destination—the ramp where Ganner had inadvertently insulted the Yuuzhan Vong at the rescue ship—the thing stopped and turned its head in his direction. Though it was gazing through two layers of window membrane and across a hundred meters of landing pit, it looked straight at him. It let its gaze linger long enough to send a cold shiver down his spine, then smiled slyly and fluttered forward to rejoin Nom Anor.

Beside Jacen, Ganner whispered, "It couldn't have seen us!" Despite his assertion, he retreated deeper into the shadows. "It glanced over by chance."

"It *felt* us," Jacen said, lowering the electrobinoculars. "More than that, it felt our apprehension."

He did not add that the creature had done so through the Force. The shock radiating from Ganner suggested he had already reached the same conclusion.

"What's wrong with you two?" Jaina asked, joining them in the archway. "You feel like you've been hearing the Emperor's voice! Don't tell me you're afraid of a few Yuuzhan Vong."

"There are more than a few." Jacen passed the electrobinoculars to his sister. Her emotions felt oddly disconnected, as they often did when combat was imminent, but he could not criticize her performance. When the thud bugs started flying, she was always the steadiest, most levelheaded Jedi on the strike team. Ignoring the company of Yuuzhan Vong warriors forming up outside Nom Anor's shuttle, he pointed at the bird thing. "But it's Nom Anor's pet that bothers me. I think it touched me with the Force."

Jaina studied the little creature. "You're sure?"

"Not *sure*," Jacen clarified. "But convinced."

"Me, too," Ganner agreed. "That smile . . ."

"Hmm." Jaina frowned in thought. "Does Feathers there remind you of anybody?"

"I keep thinking it should," Jacen said. "But I've never seen anything like it."

"Sorry, I forget that New Republic Intelligence isn't sharing with Uncle Luke these days," Jaina said. "We've seen some interesting holograms in Rogue Squadron. That's Vergere."

"Vergere?" Jacen gasped.

Vergere had been involved in one of the Yuuzhan Vong's first efforts to assassinate the Jedi, but she had also been the one who had given their father the healing tears that had first put Mara's illness into remission. To this day, there remained disagreement over whether Vergere was a friend or foe of the Jedi, a mere pet of the assassin or an agent in her own right.

"It's either Vergere, or another creature like her," Jaina said. "And if she touched you through the Force, we can assume she was more than the assassin's pet 'familiar.' "

Ganner nodded. "She was there to point us out to the killer."

"I'm not so sure," Jacen said. "If she was part of the plot, why did she save Mara's life? Why hasn't she sounded the alarm about us yet?"

"Maybe we were wrong," Ganner suggested. "Maybe she didn't feel us."

"I felt *her*," Jacen insisted.

Their discussion was interrupted by the arrival of Anakin and the rest of the strike team. The two Dark Jedi, Lomi and Welk, were with them, now clothed in their own dark armor and swaddled in Tekli's bacta bandages. Jacen was ashamed to find himself wishing the group had known the pair's identity before his brother decided to rescue them; he felt certain they would still have made the attempt, but *after* killing the voxyn queen.

Ganner passed the electrobinoculars to Anakin at about the same time that Nom Anor and Vergere reached their destination. The unarmored Yuuzhan Vong who had challenged the strike team earlier appeared on the ramp and began to speak with Nom Anor. When Vergere intruded with a harsh comment, he stiffened and brought his fist to his shoulder in salute, then began to include her in the conversation.

Anakin turned the electrobinoculars toward the troops in front of Nom Anor's shuttle. "How many—"

"Too many to fight," Jacen answered.

Anakin ignored him and looked to Ganner. More disappointed by the slight than irritated by it, Jacen swallowed his pride and remained silent. After all, his brother had asked for information, not recommendations.

Ganner said, "I counted a hundred and four warriors—probably three platoons and an overseeing officer."

Anakin's expression did not change, but Jacen felt a rare surge of anxiety in his brother. Their first plan had already failed, and now their second was coming apart. He did his best to mute Anakin's apprehension and prevent it from affecting the others through the battle meld.

Lomi stepped to Anakin's side. "We can escape into the training course. There's an exit into the laboratory complex."

Jacen saw Welk's face pale—and felt his terror through the Force.

"What's the training course?" Jacen asked.

"It's where the Yuuzhan Vong teach voxyn to hunt us," Lomi explained. She narrowed her eyes, clearly resentful at being questioned. "It will be dangerous—but less so than the spaceport."

"And we know the terrain better than the trainers do," Welk said. Despite his fear, he was eager to support his master—perhaps because she frightened him more than the voxyn did. "The voxyn won't be a problem, not for so many of us."

"Unless Skywalker's students do not live up to their reputations?" Lomi taunted Anakin with a sneer. "The choice is yours, young Solo."

"We deserve our reputations," Anakin said.

The unarmored Yuuzhan Vong with Nom Anor pointed down the colonnade toward the detention warren where the group was hiding.

"I don't think he's telling them how to find the refresher," Ganner said. "Things are getting dangerous."

"Not dangerous, just interesting," Anakin replied. He backed out of the archway, then waved Lomi deeper into the detention warren. "Lead on."

Zekk started after him. "Anakin, what are you doing?"

Jacen did his best to dampen the alarm and indignation pouring into the battle meld, but Zekk's feelings were too powerful.

They cascaded through the group, evoking enmity and resentment from Raynar and Eryl, and something more deadly from the Barabels.

Anakin glanced back at the landing pit, where Nom Anor and Vergere were waving to their troops. "We'll never make it around the spaceport. We need to follow Lomi through the training area."

"She's a Nightsister!" Zekk continued. "You can't trust her—you can't even bring her."

"Zekk, we don't have any choice," Jacen said. He was glad to have an opportunity to support his brother—maybe that would convince Anakin to forgive him for his mistake aboard the *Exquisite Death*. "Abandoning them would be the same as killing them."

"Worse," Lomi said, leading the way past the detention cells. "I doubt you have any spare lightsabers, but perhaps a blaster—"

"I said we need you, not trust you," Anakin said.

Lomi smiled guilefully. "As you wish."

She turned down a corridor lined so thickly with ysalamiri trees that Jacen felt as though he were traveling through the jungle floor back on Yavin 4. The battle meld broke briefly as they entered a deep region where the ysalamiri had not smelled the pheromone capsule, then the corridor entered a throat of yorik coral so narrow that even Tekli had to turn sideways. Had the walls not been covered with a slippery blanket of mildew, Lowbacca would not have been able to squeeze through at all.

On the other side, the passage opened into a sparse forest of bitter-smelling trees with drooping crowns and knife-shaped leaves. Through the spindly foliage, Jacen saw that they had entered a canyonlike passage perhaps a hundred meters wide and half that in depth, with a "sky" of brightly glowing lichen clinging to the ceiling above the treetops.

Lomi paused there. "Keep your weapons at hand. The trainers

were working a pack when you arrived, and they pulled us out in a hurry. The voxyn could be anywhere by now."

Jacen looked back through the narrow throat of yorik coral. "Why not the detention warren?"

"The fungus," Lomi explained. "It prevents them from clinging to the walls, and the passage is too narrow for them to pass through otherwise."

They paused long enough for Lowbacca and Ganner to plant a pair of detonite trip-mines in the corridor, then continued down the trail. Jacen reestablished the battle meld and was struck by the discord in the group. With events turning against them and everyone nervous about a voxyn ambush, emotions were running raw.

Lomi guided the strike team down the trail, then turned down an intersecting passage at a convergence Jacen had not even seen. The trees grew instantly darker and denser, their branches draped with long beards of quivering moss. They had traveled no more than fifty paces through this area when a muted crack sounded behind them, followed by the muffled roar of falling stone.

"Mine detonation confirmed," 2-4S reported. "Casualty count unavailable."

"Tell us something we don't know," Tahiri said.

Lomi led the way around several more corners, Tahiri's comments growing more frequent as the forest grew steadily thicker and darker. A pair of coralskippers flew over, then wheeled around just beneath the ceiling and dived toward the treetops.

"Presence detected," 2-4S warned.

Lomi rushed the team down a swampy side rift with scaly trunked trees rising out of green water.

"Two-Four-S, secure the intersection," Anakin ordered.

"Affirmative," the droid responded.

They were barely a hundred splashes into the swamp when the

whumpf-whumpf of the droid's blaster cannon reverberated down the canyon.

"Lead ship destroyed," 2-4S reported over their comlinks.

The fire continued another second before it was joined by the roaring sizzle of a plasma volcano. Through the treetops, Jacen glimpsed the dark disk of a coralskipper swinging toward the canyon mouth, a fan of dark mist pouring from its belly.

"Breath masks!" he shouted.

Most members of the strike team were already pulling the masks over their faces, but the two Dark Jedi could only glance helplessly at the others. Lomi turned to Anakin with an outstretched hand.

"I need a mask."

"Hold your breath," Zekk said nastily.

"And who will guide us if she falls?" Alema demanded.

The Twi'lek tossed her breath mask across the swamp, using the Force to propel it into Lomi's hands, then the roar of 2-4S's propulsion rockets sounded from the intersection. Jacen glanced back to see the droid rising out of the swamp on a column of yellow flame, all weapon systems pouring fire into the nose of the coralskipper. The enemy pilot countered with a pair of plasma balls to the chest. YVH 2-4S vanished inside a ball of white flame, but still managed to steer himself into the oncoming coralskipper and trigger his self-destruct charges.

Coralskipper and droid vanished together in a brilliant flash. Jacen's vision spotted, then the shock wave sent him stumbling backward through the water. He was caught by Tenel Ka's strong hand. After steadying him, she said something he could not hear over the ringing in his ears, but the sentiment of which he recognized through the battle meld: His breath mask would do him no good dangling from his hand.

Jacen pulled the straps over his head, more than a little

distressed by 2-4S's annihilation. Not only had the droid been a valuable and respected comrade, but with both him and 2-1S destroyed, the entire strike team felt far more exposed, as though their protector had vanished and left them to fend for themselves.

When the spots cleared from his eyes, Jacen saw a cloud of oily smoke drifting down the canyon toward them. Beneath it hung the same dark mist that the coralskipper had been releasing when 2-4S destroyed it. He turned to warn the others and found Anakin already motioning the team forward—then he felt the familiar agitation of a voxyn somewhere ahead.

"Sith blood!" Tahiri put her lightsaber in one hand and her blaster in the other. "When does something go right?"

A forest of lightsabers snapped to life, and Anakin ordered, "Keep going—let's stay ahead of that mist until it disperses."

The Barabels inserted their earplugs, then dropped to their bellies and glided out across the water, their thick tails propelling them quietly forward. The rest of the strike team put in their own earplugs and waded after the hatchmates, some with blaster weapons in hand, others with lightsabers, some with both.

They advanced no more than twenty meters before a loud purling rippled through the trees ahead, and Jacen felt an outpouring of surprise from Bela. He pointed toward her side of the gorge and started to shout the alarm, but the rest of the team was already splashing in her direction.

The Barabel shot from the water like a rocket, plastering her body against a nearby tree trunk and scrambling for the top. Behind her came a voxyn's flattish snout, its beady lips drawing open to spray acid. A flurry of blaster bolts converged on the creature's head. Many hit scales and bounced harmlessly away, but several more burned through or buried themselves into the soft tissue around its eyes and ear slits. Ganner and Alema leapt forward and hacked off the smoking head with their lightsabers, leaving the neck stump to slide back beneath the surface.

"Found it!" Bela called, dropping back into the swamp.

The three Barabels broke into a fit of sissing inside their breath masks, then the mist curtain caught up to them and tiny droplets of black vapor began to melt into the water.

"Alema, Welk—into the water!" Jacen yelled.

Alema was already underwater by the time he finished, but, not being part of the battle meld, Welk was slower. He looked around in confusion for a moment, then finally grasped what was happening and threw himself beneath the surface—only to bob to the surface a few seconds later, limp and floating facedown.

Lomi used the Force to summon him to her, then held him above the water while Tekli examined him.

"His breathing is fine," the Chadra-Fan said. "I think it's only . . ."

She let the sentence trail off as she—and everyone else in the battle meld—experienced a sudden surge of panic from Alema.

"You think what?" Lomi asked, unaware of what the others were feeling. "Will he recover, or am I—"

She was interrupted by the crackle of liquid turning instantly to vapor as Alema's lightsaber ignited underwater. The Twi'lek shot out of the swamp in a cloud of steam, using the Force to somersault backward over Ganner.

"Another voxyn!" Alema yelled, pointing. "It caught me by . . . the . . ."

Her eyes closed before she finished, and she splashed into the water on her back. Ganner and Bela ignited their own lightsabers and began to back away, stabbing at the water as they moved. Jacen concentrated on muting the team's negative feelings and keeping the battle meld efficient, and Anakin used the Force to lift Alema out of harm's way and float her over to Tahiri.

"Take her." Anakin pointed back toward the murky forest where the coralskippers had found them. "Take Lomi and Tekli, wait for us on dry land."

"Me?" Tahiri let the Twi'lek sink half into the water before reaching out with the Force to keep her afloat. "Why do I have—"

"Because Anakin asked you to," Jacen said. He stretched a hand toward where Alema had fallen and summoned the Twi'lek's lightsaber from beneath the water, then slapped it into the girl's hand. "Now is no time for jealousy, Tahiri."

"I'm not jealous," Tahiri snapped. "I just don't like being sent off like some child."

With that, she motioned to Lomi and Tekli, then took Alema and retreated up the canyon. Jacen activated his own lightsaber and started forward to join the others searching for the voxyn, but saw the Barabels spreading across the channel with a handful of concussion grenades and realized they had a better idea.

"Everybody back," Anakin ordered, approving the plan even before the Barabels suggested it. "Watch those trees—we don't want them falling on someone."

The Barabels began to throw their grenades in simultaneous trios, working inward from the farthest distance they guessed the voxyn could have traveled. With each column of water the explosions sent shooting into the air, Jacen felt a sharp concussion against his legs. On the second throw, three voxyn floated to the surface with glazed eyes and bleeding ears. Ganner and Lowbacca used their lightsabers to finish the stunned creatures.

"That's four." Anakin deactivated his lightsaber. "The whole pack."

"Perhaps, but it would be wise to be sure," Tenel Ka said, glancing in Jacen's direction. "Do you feel any more?"

Jacen reached out to see if he could locate any other creatures. It took a moment, but he finally located a large group of presences several hundred meters up the canyon.

"There are more," he reported. "A half a dozen, at least. They seem kind of stunned and wary."

"Good," Tenel Ka said. "Then that will give us plenty of time to go the other way."

Anakin nodded, and the strike team turned to go. Twenty meters from the intersection, they found Tahiri and the others rushing back toward them.

"No! Go that way!" Tahiri pointed up the canyon toward the voxyn. "Nom Anor and his bird are coming this way with about a hundred Yuuzhan Vong!"

"What next?" Raynar complained. He slapped a hand to his forehead and ran it over his blond hair. "Can anything else go wrong?"

Zekk glanced at Lomi, then turned away shaking his head as if to say this was what came of consorting with Dark Jedi. Jacen realized that he needed to speak with Zekk at the first opportunity about his impact on the battle meld, but Anakin seemed oblivious to the strike team's growing sense of fatalism.

Not seeming to hear Raynar, Anakin clapped a hand on Tahiri's shoulder and flashed a brash Solo smile. "This is no problem," he said.

Lowbacca growled a question, which Em Teedee translated almost accurately as, "Master Lowbacca wishes to inquire if you have lost your mind."

"That was a long time ago," Jaina answered, not quite laughing. "And if he's thinking what I'm thinking, it's just crazy enough to work."

Hoping to share with the others the positive emotional spark from which Jaina's words sprang, Jacen reached out to his sister—and found only the same battle numbness as before. Trying not to let his concern show, he asked, "What *are* you thinking?"

"Ambush," Jaina said.

Anakin nodded and pointed to four trees. "That will be our killing zone. We'll close the Yuuzhan Vong off from behind and fire from adjacent sides, with high in the back covering low on the side."

The battle meld remained tight enough so that was all he needed to say. The firing teams rushed to their assigned places, the humans spreading out in the water along the canyon wall, while Lowbacca took Jovan Drark and the Barabels high into the trees and spread out across the channel. Tekli used the Force to lift Alema and Welk into the trees well outside the ambush area. Jacen placed himself at the corner of the angle, where he would be as close as possible to everyone in the battle meld.

Lomi waded up to Anakin, who was standing in the water just five meters from Jacen. "Very impressive, young Solo," she said. "Where would you like me?"

"Out of the way. You have no weapon."

Lomi gave him a sarcastic smile. "A Jedi is never without a weapon, Anakin. Would you rather I use a blaster or the dark side?"

Anakin sighed, then used his comlink to have Lowbacca pass down Alema's G-9 power blaster and grenade belt.

"Anakin, you can't!" Zekk protested. He was so loud that Anakin could hear him even without using the comlink.

"Not your choice, Bounty Hunter," Anakin said. "This might get ugly, and she has a right to defend herself."

"Tell him that Welk and I will promise not to use the dark side—as long as we remain armed," Lomi said, sneering. "That should calm him."

Anakin relayed the message.

"I suppose you'll be bringing them into the battle meld next," Zekk said sarcastically.

A warning click came over the comm channel, and the human Jedi lay down beneath the surface of the swamp, relying on their breath masks' backup oxygen canister for air. It was not long before they began to feel the tension of those watching the enemy's approach from the trees, though this sensation was all but overwhelmed by the qualms Zekk and several others felt at seeing an armed Dark Jedi in their midst. Though Jacen was not entirely happy about matter himself, it seemed a better alternative than having her call on the dark side. He did his best to subordinate Zekk's resentment and keep everyone's emotions focused on the task at hand, but the discord was hurting their combat effectiveness. He could feel it.

Finally, the faint sloshing of wading Yuuzhan Vong came to his ears underwater, and an eruption of glee from the Barabels let everyone know it was time to attack. Jacen rose quietly out of the swamp and saw a mass of enemy warriors moving through the trees with far too much confidence—convinced, apparently, that even Jedi would not attack at an odds disadvantage in excess of five to one.

Obviously, they had not done their research on the Solo family. Jacen armed the fragmentation grenade in his hand and threw it into the midst of the still-oblivious Yuuzhan Vong, then raised his T-21 repeating blaster and opened fire.

The Yuuzhan Vong reacted like the well-trained warriors they were. Even with the swamp exploding into shrapnel and blaster bolts all around them, they did not panic or fall into helpless confusion. Their officers immediately began to shout orders— and were promptly picked off by Jovan Drark's deadly sharpshooter blaster rifle—the "longblaster." Jacen caught a glimpse of Nom Anor yelling into a shoulder villip near the back of the company and swung his G-9 power blaster in the executor's direction, but could not bring himself to fire—at least not instantly. It was one thing to attack an impersonal foe in the necessity of battle, quite another to murder a much-despised enemy. Jacen had learned on Duro, when he had been forced to act to prevent Tsavong

Lah from killing his mother, that a Jedi was free—no, *obligated*—to protect others from evil. But targeting a specific person out of anger still felt like murder—and using a battle as an excuse to commit such a sinister act still seemed like the way to the dark side.

Before he could work the matter out, Vergere stepped out from behind a tree, inadvertently placing herself between Jacen and his target. Jacen raised his weapon, training his aim on Nom Anor's head. Vergere glanced at him with her slanted eyes and briefly locked gazes, then grabbed the executor and pulled him to safety behind a tree. Jacen squeezed his trigger and watched the bolt flash harmlessly across the swamp, then swung his weapon back toward the battle.

With their officers dead and vonduun crab armor shattering all around them, the Yuuzhan Vong warriors were seeking cover underwater. Someone called "concussion" over the comlink, and Jacen stopped firing to pull a grenade from his equipment belt—then realized that he had no idea who had spoken. Clearly, the battle meld was suffering.

"Two-second delay," Anakin commed. "Arm."

In the time it took Jacen to thumb the arming switch, the Yuuzhan Vong began to regroup, at least two dozen rising out of the water behind the cover of tree trunks or fallen logs.

"Throw."

Jacen tossed his grenade into the center of the killing zone with everyone else's, then raised his rapid blaster and began firing again. The swamp surface bucked upward, and several Yuuzhan Vong floated up bleeding from eyes and ears, staring vacantly at the sky.

Steady streams of thud and razor bugs began to drone out from behind the trees where the survivors were hiding, and Jacen heard several Jedi groan as they took hits in their armor-lined jumpsuits.

Somewhere down the line, a lightsaber snapped to life, and Ganner waded forward, slapping bugs from the sky.

"Ganner!" Anakin commed. "What are you doing?"

"Can't let them pin us down," Ganner replied.

Lomi started forward, as well, her body weaving and pivoting as she dodged thud bugs, her power blaster filling the air with brilliant flashes as she shot incoming razor bugs out of the sky. If nothing else, her advance impressed the Yuuzhan Vong, who began to concentrate their fire on her.

"Wait!" Jacen commed. He had no doubt that they could advance en masse and wipe out the patrol—but he did not think they could do it without taking losses. "I can flush them." He sensed a query forming in Anakin's mind, then explained, "The voxyn, I think I can use them."

"Think?" Anakin asked.

"Can," Jacen assured him.

Anakin hesitated a moment, then said, "Let's try it."

Ganner and Lomi retreated to cover, and Jacen reached out to the voxyn he had sensed earlier, calling on the Force to soothe them out of their shock, to lull them into thinking there was nothing to fear ahead.

The voxyn responded almost too well. The entire strike team experienced a hungry stirring in the Force as the beasts reached out to locate them, then Jacen felt the creatures start down the canyon toward the ambush. The two sides began to trade fire more sporadically, the Yuuzhan Vong content to sit in cover in the mistaken belief that help would arrive soon, the Jedi content to let them. Jacen thought about comming Jovan to tell him to keep an eye out for Nom Anor and Vergere, then decided against it. He was treading as close as he cared to the dark side.

Less than a minute later, a Yuuzhan Vong snarled in surprise, then gurgled horribly as a voxyn dragged him underwater. Several other Yuuzhan Vong cried out as the creatures brushed past, but only two let out screams suggesting they had been attacked. The voxyn, Jacen realized, were more interested in the Force wielders down the way.

"Out of the water, now!" he commed.

As his fellow Jedi used the Force to boost themselves into the trees, Jacen thumbed a fragmentation grenade active and tossed it into the swamp. While not as powerful as concussion grenade, it would generate enough of a shock wave to serve his purpose. He waited until the grenade exploded, then reached out to the voxyn, encouraging them to blame anything in the water for the attack.

Several more Yuuzhan Vong cried out. A few even stumbled from cover to be picked off by Jovan and the Barabels, but more than a dozen remained in hiding and continued to fling thud bugs into the trees. Climbing into a tree himself, Jacen dropped the battle meld—it was not working that well anyway—and focused only on the voxyn. He threw another fragmentation grenade and urged the creatures to attack anything in the water.

The Yuuzhan Vong attacks dwindled as they turned to battle the attacking voxyn. A handful tried to scramble into the trees as the Jedi had done, but without the Force to boost them, they could not climb fast enough to escape their pursuers. Lowbacca and the Barabels took advantage of the distraction to leap through the tree-tops and attack from above. Soon they were shooting at nothing but voxyn, and a few concussion grenades brought the last of creatures to the surface.

Jacen dropped back into the swamp feeling not exactly guilty about luring the creatures to their doom, but hardly noble either. Maybe Zekk was right; maybe Lomi's mere presence was enough to taint the entire strike team. Jacen was still trying to work this out when Anakin waded over with Tahiri, both of them grinning ear to ear.

Tahiri clasped Jacen's arm and pulled herself up to kiss his cheek. "That was astral!"

"Well done." Anakin slapped Jacen's on the back, and there was more warmth in the gesture than had passed between the two brothers since Centerpoint Station. "You saved a lot of Jedi today."

Jacen would have felt good about that, had the day been over.

Chapter 31

Even with Han sprawled on the couch next to Leia, Ben gurgling in Mara's lap, and the Wild Knights comparing notes with Rogue Squadron in the back of the room, the informal sitting chamber of the Solos' Coruscant residence seemed all too empty. The five Solos had not been in this room together for more than a year, and Leia could not recall ever gathering here with-out the shadow of some faraway crisis hanging over someone's head.

Most of the responsibility rested squarely on Leia's own shoulders. She had devoted her life to the New Republic, and, on its behalf, she had involved Han and Chewbacca and Lando and everyone else she knew in one dangerous mission after another. Even her children had spent most of their lives dwelling apart, first because they needed protection from the Empire's kidnappers, and later because the New Republic needed them to become Jedi Knights. Now they were hundreds of light-years behind enemy lines, fighting a foe as ruthless and cruel as Palpatine himself, facing dangers she could not even guess at, but that she felt constantly through the Force. After fighting a lifetime to make the galaxy a safer place, she wondered if anyone would blame her for questioning her choices; given the danger her children were facing on the galaxy's behalf now, she wondered if anyone would dare.

Leia felt Han reaching out to her even before he touched her shoulder. "You're sure you don't want to be there with Luke?" Han glanced around the packed room conspiratorially. "There's a hovercar hanging around the back platform, and I know your brother isn't all that comfortable addressing the senate himself."

"Send the hovercar away, Han." Leia put just enough sharpness in her voice to let him know she was serious. "I'm through with the senate."

Han rolled his eyes. "Where have I heard that before?"

"It's true, Han." Leia allowed her apprehension for their children to show. "I'm thinking of other things now."

Han studied her for a moment, then nodded. "Okay." He glanced across the room to Lando and Wedge and gave a slight shake of his head, then pulled Leia tight to his side. "All this waiting—it's bad enough without feeling everything through the Force."

Leia squeezed his leg. "We're not accustomed to being the ones left behind."

Izal Waz wandered into the room and stopped behind the couches. "Hey—look at this!" He used a voice command to change the holovid from the senate feed to a news channel. In the foreground, he was shown debarking the Wild Knights' blastboat while a breathless Arcona newswoman explained that a member of their own species had participated in the daring Jedi rescue of the Talfaglion hostages. "I'm a hero!"

Almost since their departure from the system, the HoloNet had been filled with news of the Yuuzhan Vong's total defeat at

Talfaglio. A Kuati network had even managed to obtain a hologram from a Star Destroyer holocam showing an enemy corvette
exploding for no visible reason in front of a Jedi X-wing—the newscaster had identified the wing markings incorrectly as those of
Kyp's Dozen. Fortunately, the shadow bomb responsible could
not be detected even with enhancement, but Luke had prevailed
on the New Republic high command to censor all images of
Jedi combat techniques lest another, better recording betray the
secret.

Saba grabbed Izal by the arm and pulled him away, saying,
"Yes, we are all famous now—so don't embarrasz us!"

Mara stood her son up on her knees and cooed in a high, chirrupy,
and very un-Mara-like voice. "Someone found the salt, didn't he?"

Ben chortled in response, his delight rippling through the
Force just the way Anakin's used to when Leia visited him in hiding
on Anoth—and so powerfully it moved her to tears. She turned
away and tried to hide her face by leaning against Han's shoulder,
but Mara was not one to miss such an obvious sign. She reached
over and placed a hand on Leia's forearm.

"Leia, it's because of you we're here at all," she said. "Remember that. I know Anakin and the twins will."

"Thank you." Leia wiped her eyes and smiled, taking strength
from her sister-in-law's plain words. "That helps . . . a lot."

"Yeah, me too." Han studied Mara, his expression somewhere
between gratitude and envy. "Thanks."

Lando called out that the session was starting. Someone switched
the holovid back to the senate feed, where Luke, dressed simply in a
plain Jedi robe, was riding an escalator to the speaking rostrum on the
chamber floor.

Luke stepped off the escalator beside the speaker's rostrum,
wishing he felt more certain that today he would heal the rift

between the Jedi and the New Republic. The senate chamber was awash in good feelings toward him and the Jedi, but there was also anger for taking matters into their own hands, apprehension about Yuuzhan Vong retaliation, and something more sinister—something dark and dangerous that he sensed would soon reveal itself to him. He lowered the cowl of his robe and, facing the long console on the high councilors' dais, bowed to the Advisory Council.

"Chief Fey'lya, Councilors, you asked to speak with me?"

Somewhere high in the galleries, a Wookiee roared in ovation, and the chamber erupted in cheers and applause. Luke stood calmly, neither acknowledging the outpouring nor discouraging it as he studied the members of the Advisory Council. Most kept their faces carefully neutral, though Fyor Rodan of Commenor sneered in disapproval—no doubt blaming the Jedi for not saving his own planet—and Borsk Fey'lya bared his fangs in a smile that felt surprisingly sincere.

Allowing the applause to continue, the chief of state left his console and descended to stand before Luke. He raised a furry palm and brought the chamber to order with impressive speed, then surprised Luke by clasping his hand warmly.

"Princess Leia was unable to attend?" Fey'lya asked. "The invitation was to you both."

"Leia is occupied elsewhere," Luke said.

Fey'lya nodded sagely. "Anakin and the twins, of course." He lowered his brow in a well-rehearsed expression of concern, then turned slightly toward the hovering sound droid. "Let me assure you, the New Republic is doing everything possible to determine what has become of them—and to find the person responsible."

That much was certainly true. The Wraiths had been snooping along the war zone for several days now, coming so close to identifying the true delivery ship that Luke had been forced to ask Wedge to rein them in. Reportedly, Garik "Face" Loran was furious.

"I am sure the families of all the missing Jedi appreciate your desire to help," Luke said. "But we must not forget that the Yuuzhan Vong threaten more than Jedi."

"The Jedi certainly have not forgotten." Fey'lya pumped Luke's hand enthusiastically. "On behalf of the New Republic, let me congratulate you on the Jedi victory at Talfaglio—and thank you for the lives of our citizens."

"We were glad to be of service," Luke said. "The Jedi have consolidated their forces and hope to be of more service to the New Republic in the future, but it is important to note we did not do this alone."

"We are aware of the support provided to you by the *Mon Mothma* and *Elegos A'Kla*," Viqi Shesh said, speaking from her seat on the dais. Though it was hardly necessary, she leaned closer to the sound pickup in her console and looked down at Luke. "Thanks to the HoloNet coverage, so is the whole galaxy—including, no doubt, the Yuuzhan Vong."

Luke went cold between the shoulders, and he knew he had found the dangerous presence he had been sensing—or rather, it had found him.

"A New Republic task force happened to be in the area, yes," he answered. "It's my understanding they suffered no casualties."

"The galaxy is a vast place, Master Skywalker," Shesh said coolly. "Perhaps you can explain how they 'happened' to be in the area?"

Fey'lya raised a hand to stop Luke from answering, then whirled on Shesh, his lips drawn up to show the tips of his fangs. "We have all read the reports, Councilor. The vessels were on a shakedown cruise. I fail to see the point of your request."

Shesh continued to glare at Luke. "That is precisely the point of my request, Chief Fey'lya. Wedge Antilles and Garm Bel Iblis are two of our best generals—too experienced to take a 'shakedown cruise' into Yuuzhan Vong territory."

"The last I checked, Senator, the Corellian sector was still in the New Republic," Fey'lya said, drawing a chorus of pointed laughter. "As for the generals' experience, I am sure we both agree that they know better than you or I how to shake down a Star Destroyer."

"Undoubtedly—when they are in possession of their wits," Shesh retorted.

The chamber filled with murmurs of outrage and speculation, and Luke saw where Shesh was taking her line of questioning.

"If you are suggesting that the generals were in any way influenced—"

"That is exactly what I am suggesting, Master Skywalker." Leaving her own seat, Shesh stepped over to Fey'lya's console, using his master controls to override the rostrum's microphone with her own. "The Jedi are famous throughout the galaxy for their mind tricks, but you have gone too far when you subvert the legitimate orders of a New Republic task force!"

"Hear, hear!" Fyor Rodan said, rising. "The New Republic cannot tolerate this Jedi abuse."

A surprising number of senators, most from Inner Rim worlds that still hoped to placate the Yuuzhan Vong, rose on cue. The Wookiees and Bothans roared in opposition, and Luke turned slowly, calling upon his Jedi control to keep a calm face. Leia had warned him to be surprised by nothing that happened in the New Republic Senate. Still, he failed to see how intelligent beings could be persuaded that the utter destruction of an enemy fleet and the rescue of a planetful of hostages was a bad thing.

But it was not about the fleet or the hostages, of course. It was about alliances and power, about who had it and who was losing it, who might have it tomorrow and who would share it. No wonder Leia had refused to step foot in the chamber again. No wonder the New Republic was losing the war.

Fey'lya left to reclaim control of his console and found himself delayed when Fyor Rodan blocked his way on the flimsy pretext of discussing some important rule of procedure, and Shesh continued to control the public-address system.

"Master Skywalker, perhaps you fail to realize the damage your selfish antics have caused the New Republic," she said. "In using new weapons aboard the *Mon Mothma* and *Elegos A'Kla* prematurely, you have alerted the Yuuzhan Vong to the existence of two very powerful technologies we are in the process of deploying—two technologies that we had hoped might turn the tide of the war."

This drew a fresh outburst from Shesh's supporters, and the counterprotest began to sound halfhearted. Still finding his way blocked by Fyor Rodan, Fey'lya raised a hand to summon a security droid.

Shesh rushed to press her point home. "Master Skywalker, I am afraid this council must demand that the Jedi disarm and cease their irresponsible activities."

"No." Luke spoke softly but firmly, using the Force to project the word into every niche in the vast chamber. "The Jedi will not disarm."

As he had hoped, the shock of hearing his calm voice quieted the chamber, and he continued, "We have in no way influenced any New Republic officer to disobey orders."

"You expect us to believe you?" Shesh cast a meaningful eye over the suddenly tranquil gallery. "When you are so obviously using your mind tricks on us now?"

Luke allowed himself a wry smile. "No trick," he said. "Only one calm voice."

This drew a chuckle from many in the gallery, and, with the arrival of the security droid, Fyor Rodan feigned surprise and stepped aside.

"All the same, I insist," Shesh said quickly. "If the Jedi will not disarm, the senate must prohibit the New Republic military from having any contact with them whatsoever." The chamber broke into an uproar, but Shesh elevated the speaker volume and spoke over the tumult. "There will be no more 'spare' X-wings rotated into your hangars, Master Skywalker, nor will there be any more intelligence-sharing sessions. If you continue to abuse us—"

"You are exceeding your authority, Senator Shesh," Fey'lya interrupted. The Bothan shouldered her aside and reclaimed control of his console. "Return to your seat, or I will have you removed from the chamber."

Shesh gave him an acid smile and obeyed, but the damage had already been done. She had turned the Jedi's moment of triumph into yet another senate-dividing issue—and Luke had to wonder why. As the supervising senator of SELCORE, the Kuati had certainly proven herself corrupt, and Leia's accusations of misconduct had done nothing to endear the Jedi to her, but this seemed to go beyond even that level of depravity. This was more than opportunistic vengeance; this was treachery with a plan. Had Luke not been able to feel the woman's darkness through the Force, he would have stepped onto the dais and started trying to remove an ooglith masquer; as it was, he vowed to watch this woman until he knew the source of the darkness and danger in her.

Fey'lya repeatedly called for order, then finally gave up and sank into his chair to wait for the tumult to yell itself out. Luke merely crossed his wrists and did likewise, knowing he would only play into Shesh's hands by using another Jedi technique to calm the gathering. He saw no real hope of accomplishing what he had come to do, but he could not leave without appearing arrogant—and arrogance would only be another weapon for Viqi Shesh to use against the Jedi.

The tumult finally began to subside, but Fey'lya was staring so raptly at his vidconsole that he failed to notice. Fearing the Yuuzhan Vong were hurling some new disaster at the New Republic—

and knowing them well enough to realize they would pick just such a moment—Luke reached out to get some sense of what was consuming the Bothan's attention. Like any seasoned politician, Fey'lya held his emotions tightly, but what Luke sensed there seemed more surprise than dismay or panic.

Always quick to seize the initiative, Viqi Shesh rose. "I am very concerned about the Jedi problem—so concerned, in fact, that I propose a resolution."

When Fey'lya remained transfixed by his vidconsole, Luke sent out a gentle Force nudge. The Bothan jerked and turned toward Shesh, but did not interrupt.

She continued, "May it be resolved: that the Jedi are henceforth named dangerous persons to the war effort—"

That was as far she made it before the chamber erupted again. She tried to continue over the din, then turned to Fey'lya, eyes flashing as though he had killed her sound feed.

"Chief Fey'lya, I have every right to make my motion."

Fey'lya smiled. "By all means—but perhaps you would allow me to make a statement first."

He flipped something on his console, and a row of holograms appeared on the chamber floor near the speaker's rostrum. Luke had to step away before he could identify the figures as General Wedge Antilles, General Garm Bel Iblis, Admiral Traest Kre'fey, General Carlist Rieekan, and several other senior commanders. The chamber gradually quieted.

"A surprising number of high officers have contacted me in the past few minutes," Fey'lya said. "After hearing what they have to say, I am directing—not authorizing, but *directing*—the New Republic military to cooperate and coordinate with the Jedi."

The chamber grew even quieter—save for Shesh, who began to stammer, "Y-you can't do that!"

"I can and I have." Fey'lya locked his console out, then stepped down to Shesh's. "If you feel I am exceeding my authority, you may, of course, call for a vote of no confidence at any time. Do you wish to do so now, Senator Shesh?"

Shesh looked into the stunned gallery, trying to gauge whether the Bothan's autocratic mandate might have cost him enough support to lose such a vote. When even her own supporters could not tear their eyes from the holograms of the angry-looking commanders, she saw that she was the one who had overplayed her hand. She lowered her gaze and shook her head.

"No, and I withdraw my resolution."

"Good. We'll talk about your new committee assignments after we finish here." Fey'lya left the high councilors' dais and returned to Luke. "Now, where were we—"

"First, I'd like to ask something." Luke put his hand over the rostrum's microphone, then used the Force to send the sound droid whisking high into the galleries. "What did the generals say to you?"

"Nothing, actually. The communication was from NRMOC; the Yuuzhan Vong are moving on Borleias." Fey'lya turned toward the commanders, his fangs bared in what Luke felt certain the Bothan intended to resemble a smile. "These are file holos."

In the Solo apartment, the cheers were still ringing off the sitting room walls, and Gavin Darklighter was already planning joint missions with Saba Sebatyne and Kyp Durron. New Republic pilots were pouring bubblezap all around—and putting C-3PO into a dither by spilling far too much on the sanibuffed floor. Lando and Tendra were on their comlinks lauding the virtues of YVH war droids to suddenly receptive New Republic procurement officers. If anyone noticed that Wedge Antilles, one of the senior command officers supposedly in contact with Borsk Fey'lya, was actually sitting on the couch with Han and Leia, they did not think the matter worth mentioning.

Feeling far less gleeful than her guests, Leia turned to Han. "Am I the only one who noticed?"

Han gave her a crooked smile. "I noticed." He glanced past her to Wedge, who was continuing to stare at his image on the holovid, his expression somewhere between anger and approval. "Borsk bluffed."

"In politics, it's called misconduct," Leia said. "He had no authority to issue that directive alone."

"Maybe not, but he did the right thing. I seem to recall your telling him to do that."

"He didn't do it because he likes Jedi," Leia retorted. "Borsk wouldn't take the risk. He could have lost his post—he still can, if Viqi finds out what he did and stirs up enough outrage."

"Isn't going to happen," Wedge said, finally stirring himself out of his shock. "Borsk is the one who sent us to help you at Talfaglio. None of the commanders you saw on the chamber floor is going to contradict him—at least not to Viqi Shesh."

A half-dozen comlinks chimed simultaneously, among them Wedge's. He shut off the audible alarm, then he and several other New Republic officers stood and started for a quiet room.

"You'll have to excuse us," he said. "It sounds like General Bedamyr has lost his pet mynocks again."

Han and Leia laughed dutifully. When he was gone, they looked at each other and shrugged.

"I guess we'll find out soon enough," Han said.

Leia's thoughts had already returned to Fey'lya. "First, he wins the commanders over by sending a task force to Talfaglio, then he gives the credit to us." She looked back to the holovid, where Fey'lya was making a great show of presenting Luke with an encryption card that would allow him to navigate the planetary mine shell. "He's solidifying his power base, Han. He needs the Jedi supporters on his side."

"And the Jedi need him," Han said. "We're in this together."

"I know." Leia was mortified to find her own purposes aligned with those of Borsk Fey'lya. "That may frighten me more than the Yuuzhan Vong."

Chapter 32

Fixing his mind on the driving rhythm of Vaecta's chanting voice, Tsavong Lah thought of Yun-Yuuzhan's sacrifices, of the eyes he had surrendered to light the stars and the tentacles he had given to make the galaxies. As the gods had done in their time, now the Yuuzhan Vong must do in theirs. Today's victory would establish the left pincer of his final attack, so it was his left hand that he laid on the cutting block. He understood the place of faith as his predecessors had not; that was why he would succeed where they had died or floundered.

That was why Tsavong Lah had requested the return of the priest Harrar, his own spiritual guide and the only person he would trust to advise him on the offerings necessary to ensure victory to the Yuuzhan Vong. He would have liked to have Harrar lead the ritual himself, but it would not do to insult Vaecta. Today, Harrar would stand at his side as a witness and a friend, not a priest.

As Vaecta blessed the radank claw the shapers would attach in place of his sacrificed hand, Tsavong Lah gazed out at the steamy blue-green disk of Borleias, now swaddled in a flashing meshwork of energy bolts and plasma streaks. By all accounts a world completely lacking in resources useful to the enemy, it was nevertheless an ideal staging area for a strike against Coruscant itself and therefore fortified both heavily and cleverly. The infidels had arranged their orbital defenses in three layers, with the heavy platforms on the exterior, the smaller fast-targeting platforms on the interior, and a dense shell of space mines between.

A plasma ball the size of a small moon finally overloaded the shields of a heavy platform and reduced the unliving abomination to a melting mass of metal, but the island-ship that had made the attack paid dearly for success. A cone of meters-thick turbolaser bolts converged on the vessel, overwhelming its singularity projectors and blasting four huge breaches into the hull. The ship began to bear away, the life inside gushing into open space, a swarm of infidel missiles streaking out from the heavy platforms to complete the kill.

Seef, his communications attendant, stepped into his view bearing the already everted villip of Maal Lah, a shrewd officer from the warmaster's own domain and the supreme commander charged with securing today's victory. Though Tsavong Lah could see the alarm in his subordinate's face, he waited in humbleness until Vaecta finished her blessing, then gestured at the villip.

"Is it permitted?"

Vaecta nodded. "The gods are never offended by one who answers to his duty."

The priestess immediately began to make the obeisances that would be required to Yun-Yuuzhan and the other gods before dedicating the warmaster's sacrifice to the Slayer, and Tsavong Lah turned to the villip.

"Your commanders grow too bold," he said.

"They are eager to win your praise," the villip replied. The image was that of a square-jawed warrior with so many battle swirls that he been forced to start laying red tattoos over blue. "I have warned them that they will not do so by risking their vessels here."

"But you favor bolder tactics yourself," Tsavong surmised.

"I understand the need to conserve ships, Warmaster. Coruscant is well defended."

Tsavong Lah was surprised. After the loss of the great ship, he had expected the supreme commander to argue for an insertion assault to lay dovin basal gravity traps in the inner ring of defense platforms. Costly as the tactic was, it would quickly clear their way to the planet by pulling the minefield down onto the inner ring of orbital platforms. Provided enough of the assault force survived to actually execute the plan, it would also telegraph the tactic he intended to use to clear the far more formidable defenses around Coruscant.

"You are to be commended on your patience, Maal Lah." The warmaster looked out at the battle, where Borleias's dark moon was just swinging around the horizon, tiny flecks of crimson fire erupting in a jagged line down its murky face. "How are matters on the moon?"

"The infidels are putting up a stiff resistance, but they cannot hold much longer," Maal Lah assured him. "The dovin basal will be on the surface within the hour."

They had sent three assault divisions to install a giant dovin basal on Borleias's dark moon. Instead of crashing the satellite into its planet as the Praetorite Vong had done on Sernpidal, however, the dovin basal would be used to sweep the planetary defenses out of position. Given the moon's thirty-two-hour orbit, the stratagem would take more than a day to execute fully, but it would also conserve ships and avoid alerting the infidels to his plan for Coruscant.

Vaecta took Tsavong Lah's coufee from its sheath and began to cut a ritual offering from the thigh of the shaper who would attach the radank claw to his wrist. Realizing he had only a few moments before he would be fully consumed by the ceremony, the warmaster returned his attention to Maal Lah's villip.

"You have matters well in hand, my servant." Tsavong Lah could not help being secretly disappointed. As the warmaster, it was his privilege to decide *what* was to be done and how, but once the battle started, the actual doing fell to his subordinates. "But I doubt that is what you wished to report."

"I would never disturb you only to report that I am performing as you expect, Great Warmaster," Maal Lah said. "The yammosk informs me that her little ones are feeling gravity pulses from the outsystem side of the planet."

In his astonishment, Tsavong Lah forgot himself and nearly removed his hand from the cutting block. The yammosk was Maal Lah's war coordinator, with whom the supreme commander shared thoughts, and her "little ones" were the dovin basals linked to the sensor systems of each vessel. "Gravity pulses, my servant?"

"The modulation is clumsy and erratic, Warmaster, but it is definitely a code of some sort. Certain elements even bear a resemblance to our own. Mass mapping identifies the source as an armored space yacht similar to the *Jade Shadow,* a vessel present at the battle of Duro and later confirmed to be *Jeedai* property."

"Jeedai!" According to Tsavong Lah's spy, the *Jeedai* were still on Coruscant, refueling and rearming their fleet. His readers had assured him they would not reach Borleias until nearly a day after the projected end of the battle. "When did it enter the system?"

"That is unknown," Maal Lah said. "But it is unlikely the vessel was here when we arrived."

"Based on what knowledge?"

"Had the *Jeedai* been here when we arrived, they would already have been in contact with Borleias and established a more secure mode of communication. They have several methods we cannot yet detect, so it would hardly be necessary to draw attention to their presence now by hailing the planet so openly."

"And you have surmised their purpose in taking such a risk?" Tsavong Lah asked.

The villip looked uncomfortable. "Great Warmaster, my judgment in these matters is a blaze bug before the nova of your wisdom, but what if your spy on Coruscant is riding both ends of the rajat?"

Tsavong Lah fell quiet, considering the likelihood of this. It *was* possible that he had underestimated this Viqi Shesh, that she was playing *him* for the fool—or even that the New Republic deception sect knew of her contact with him and was feeding her false information as a means of passing it along. Nor could he place any faith in the HoloNet vidcasts the readers had used to confirm her story; the enemy deception sect could have planted those as easily as his own agents could infiltrate a planetary shielding crew.

As Tsavong Lah puzzled his way through the significance of the supreme commander's report, Vaecta cut a strip of flesh from her own thigh and, letting her black blood run free, twined it with the one she had taken from the shaper. She laid the result on a ceremonial gatag-shell platter and blessed it in the name of Yun-Yammka, then held it out to the warmaster.

"One moment." Tsavong Lah lifted his hand from the cutting block.

Harrar's eyes bulged in disbelief. "You ask the gods to wait?"

"They will understand." Tsavong Lah turned back to Maal Lah and asked, "This is the first pulse-message we have intercepted from the enemy, is it not?"

Maal Lah nodded. "To my knowledge, yes."

"Then why should we believe it is Borleias they are trying to contact?" He switched his gaze to Seef. "Find out what happened to the yammosk at Talfaglio, and issue orders to all supreme commanders that their war coordinators must be destroyed if threatened with capture."

Seef nodded, her eyes now bulging as far as Harrar's. "It will be done."

Maal Lah said, "I will assign a task group to capture the *Jeedai* vessel—"

"It would be better to ignore the vessel than to inform the

Jeedai of their success," Harrar suggested. He motioned to the cutting block. "If you please, Warmaster. The gods are waiting."

"Only a moment longer." Tsavong Lah relayed Harrar's suggestion to the supreme commander in the form of an order, then added, "And I no longer wish to let the moon do our work for us. Order an insertion assault to lay the gravity traps."

"But what of Coruscant?" Maal Lah's expression grew as surprised as Harrar's and Seef's. "If you are right about the yammosks, there is no need to betray ourselves now."

"Perhaps not, but sometimes the blaze bug is right and the nova is wrong." Tsavong returned his hand to the cutting block, then glanced out at the defensive shell protecting Borleias and slid forward until his elbow lay beneath the shaper's saw. "Our need will be great today—give him the arm."

Chapter 33

Jaina crested the latest in a long series of chalk dunes and found an Imperial walker looming over the next one, its white cockpit and armored passenger hump silhouetted against the darkness deeper in the passage. She hissed a warning to those behind her, then dropped into a defensive crouch and snapped her lightsaber from her harness. An obsolete All Terrain Armored Transport was the last thing she expected to see inside a Yuuzhan Vong worldship, but a hundred Rogue Squadron actions had taught her never to be surprised by anything. When a glow stick came to life in the AT-AT's cockpit viewport, she yielded to her battle-honed instincts and hurled herself down the slope in a series of evasive zigzag somersaults.

As Jaina rolled, she felt herself sinking into that odd state of emotional numbness that seemed to accompany any fight these days. Other pilots sometimes spoke of feeling detached or outside themselves in combat—usually about two missions before they made some stupid mistake and let a scarhead send them nova—but this was closer to resignation, to a weary acceptance of the horror and heartache that was battle. She would have liked to attribute such feelings to her trust in the Force, but she knew better. Her reaction was emotional armor, a way to avoid the anguish that came with watching a friend or wingmate die horribly—and to deny the fear that her turn was coming.

Jaina reached the bottom in a billowing cloud of chalk dust and rolled to a stop. She sprang into a low battle crouch and brought her lightsaber around in a middle guard—then heard a familiar hissing sound.

"Stickz, you should grow a tail," Tesar Sebatyne said. "Maybe you would not be so clumsy."

This drew of series of chortles from Krasov and Bela.

"Very funny," Jaina retorted. Even without the battle meld, which Jacen was leaving down in an attempt to dampen the growing discord in the group, she was cognizant of the rest of the strike team's silent amusement. "You could have said something."

"And I could pluck the scales from over my heart," Bela rasped. "But I do not."

There was more sissing.

Jaina stepped out of the chalk cloud to find the Barabels waiting with Anakin and the other team members, their vac suits now folded into their self-storing protection packs and clipped to the back of their equipment harnesses. Caked hood to heels in dust and looking more like Jedi ghosts than Jedi Knights, they were sitting against the passage wall, keeping a sharp watch for the coralskippers that always seemed to come around spraying some enervating breath agent whenever they stopped. Two pairs of footprints—one set huge and obviously Wookiee—led over the next dune toward the AT-AT.

Jaina stretched out through Force and felt Lowbacca inside the walker with Jovan Drark. "Where did that thing come from?"

"The trainers are very thorough," Lomi explained. "They keep an entire city of slaves to operate captured equipment so they can habituate their voxyn to 'lifeless abhorrences.' There is nothing they will not do to rid the galaxy of Jedi."

"There's even a starliner berthed in a grotto hangar," Welk offered.

Notions of crashing a million-ton spacecraft into the cloning facility began to fill Jaina's mind. "Is it—"

"The energy converters have been removed," Lomi said. "Even the walkers and landspeeders run on low-capacity battery banks instead of fuel slugs. They cannot range much farther from the slave city than this."

"Of course," Jaina sighed.

Given a few resources and a little time, she and Lowbacca might well have found a way to restore the machinery—but with the infiltration already thirty hours old, the last thing the strike team could do was give the Yuuzhan Vong *more* time to react. A pale green tint began to come over the chalky passage, and Jaina looked up to see Myrkr pushing its emerald disk across a jagged patch of window membrane that had been used to mend a twenty-meter breach in the outer shell of the worldship. She suddenly felt rejuvenated, a little less jittery and worried. There was something about the arrival of a bright body in the sky that always made her feel as though she had just risen from a long night in a warm bunk.

Jovan Drark's Rodian voice buzzed over the comlink. "The Force has favored us today. The batteries still have a charge, but the power feeds have been isolated by mineral secretions."

A shiver of danger sense raced down Jaina's spine. "Secretions?" she commed.

"It appears to be an insect nest," Jovan reported. "Lowbacca is cleaning it off now."

Jacen's voice came over the comm channel. "What kind of insects?" Though her twin brother was always interested in new creatures, Jaina sensed through their bond that he was asking out of more than curiosity. "If they look like worms with legs—"

"It's no shockapede hive," Jovan commed. "These are little flitnats, completely harmless."

"Nothing the Yuuzhan Vong create is harmless," Alema Rar said to Anakin. "This is a trap."

"Everything's a trap with you," Tahiri objected. As she spoke, the walker's cockpit illumination activated, creating a band of pale light above the next dune. "Why can't the Force just be with us for once? We could all use the ride."

Anakin wisely looked to Lomi. "What do you know about those things?"

"That they are an unnecessary risk." She pointed down the way to where the passage ended in a sheer face of yorik coral. "We have almost reached our destination. The main cloning lab is only a kilometer beyond that wall."

"About time," Zekk said, joining the rest of the group. "I was beginning to think you were stalling."

Lomi smiled sourly. "You will understand if I prefer alive over fast, Zekk. Our fates will be the same in this."

"She's kept us out of trouble so far," Anakin added, scowling at Zekk's provocative tone. In contrast to nearly everyone else on the strike team, Anakin seemed completely untroubled by the time it had taken to negotiate the training course. "Let's make the safe play and avoid the walker. We'll be done and on our way home in two hours anyway . . . four at the most."

"Careful, Anakin," Jaina said. "You're beginning to sound like Dad."

Despite the jovial smile she flashed, Jaina was distressed by her younger brother's overconfidence. Having lost only Ulaha and the two droids despite all their setbacks, Anakin seemed to think that the strike team was untouchable, that even an entire worldship full of Yuuzhan Vong could not stop a single platoon of well-trained Jedi. That might even be true, but Jaina had learned in Rogue Squadron that being best guaranteed nothing, that plans went awry for everyone—and always at the worst possible moment.

Anakin nodded to the Barabels, who never seemed to tire of

walking point, and the strike team started up the dune in a billowing dust cloud. Jaina stayed at her brother's side, debating the
wisdom of pointing out how much trouble they were in. Before
leaving Eclipse, Ulaha and the tacticians had estimated that the mission's likelihood of success would drop 2 percent with every hour
of duration, which meant that the strike team's chances had to be
approaching zero by now. Add to that the fact that the Yuuzhan
Vong had anticipated their assault far enough in advance to set an
ambush and send Nom Anor to recapture them, and the odds had
clearly fallen to minuscule.

Even the Wraiths would have given up at this point and called
for extraction—but that was not an option for the strike team. They
had known from the outset that any flotilla sent to support the
operation would be destroyed either crossing the war zone or once
it was detected near Myrkr. Seeing this as his chance to save the
galaxy, Anakin had insisted on coming anyway, arguing that if the
group needed to be rescued, the Jedi were already doomed—and
with them, the New Republic itself. As much as it frightened her,
Jaina thought he was probably right.

As they neared the top of the dune, Anakin asked, "Jaina?"

She looked over and was struck by how tall her brother had
grown, by how handsome he had become—even with several days
of beard growing through the chalk on his face. "Yeah?"

"What are you doing out of line?" He glanced over his shoulder,
then spoke so quietly he had to use the Force to carry his words to
her ears. "Is there something you want to say?"

Jaina smiled. "There is." She reached over and squeezed his
forearm. "You're doing a good job, Anakin. If we're going to get
this done, it's because of your confidence and determination."

"Thanks, Jaina." Anakin probably meant his lopsided grin to
be cocky, but to his sister it seemed more surprised—perhaps even
relieved. "I know."

"Sure you do." Jaina laughed. She punched him in the shoulder hard enough to make him stumble, then added, "Just remember to keep your guard up."

They crested the dune and found themselves looking into the AT-AT's transparisteel viewport. Jaina thought at first that the interior lighting had been dimmed, but then she noticed Lowbacca's jumpsuit-covered rump protruding up behind the instrument console and realized the murk had less to do with illumination than swarming flitnats. So thick were the insects that the main access tunnel was not even visible, only a slight darkening where it led out of the cockpit back into the passenger compartment.

Anakin was instantly on his comlink. "Streak, what are you doing in there? I said—"

Lowbacca growled a terse reply, his shaggy hand reaching up to slap a filter housing on the console.

"Master Lowbacca reports that he is simply trying to retrieve some needed equipment," Em Teedee translated for those who did not understand Shyriiwook. "And please forgive his brusqueness. The flitnats are starting to bite."

"Bite?" Jaina echoed. She eyed the distance up to the cockpit and began to gather the Force in preparation for a long jump. "What about you, Jovan?"

When no answer came, Anakin commed, "Jovan?"

Lowbacca's furry head appeared from behind the instrument console and turned toward the rear of the cockpit. He barked a query through the access tunnel, then rose to his feet, a second filter housing dangling from his hand.

"Jedi Drark fails to answer," Em Teedee reported. "Master Lowbacca can see him—"

"Dangling from a belly hatch," Tesar interrupted. "Krasov will bring him down."

Lowbacca grunted an acknowledgment and, scratching furiously beneath the collar of his jumpsuit, turned back to the instrument console.

"Lowbacca?" Jaina called. "What are you doing? Get out of there!"

The Wookiee growled a garbled explanation about needing face masks, then dropped heavily to his knees and returned to his work. A long arm rose into view and clumsily piled a handful of hoses with the filter housings, then slipped down behind the console and did not reappear.

"Oh my," Em Teedee reported. "Master Lowbacca seems to be suffering a processor crash."

Using the Force to lift her the extra five meters in height, Jaina somersaulted off the chalk dune and landed lightly atop the cockpit roof, then nearly plummeted backward when Anakin and Zekk landed beside her. Anakin thumbed his lightsaber active and plunged it into the seam of the cockpit escape hatch. Jaina ignited her own blade and began to work in the opposite direction, while Zekk dropped to his belly and dangled over the front to peer in through the viewport.

"I can't believe it!" he said. "He's still trying to get the face masks."

"Perhaps he is getting tired of carrying unconscious Jedi," Lomi said, alighting next to the others. She pointed to two places on opposite sides of the hatch. "Cut there and there."

Jaina and Anakin did as she instructed, their lightsabers whining sharply as they burned through the hatch's locking bolt and reinforced hinges.

As they continued to work, Ganner's voice came over the comlink. "Jovan's alive, but dizzy and sick. Tekli thinks she can save him."

"Save him?" Anakin gasped.

"You should see, Anakin," Tahiri commed. "I didn't know Rodians swelled up like that."

Anakin paled and said nothing, focusing all his effort on getting to Lowbacca.

"Orders?" Ganner requested.

"We must retreat and try another way," Lomi suggested.

Anakin shook his head firmly. "Never."

A muffled thud sounded from inside the cockpit, then Zekk said, "Hutt slime! He's out."

Jaina's lightsaber burned through the hatch bolt with a final acrid sizzle. She snapped the blade off and hung the handle on her equipment harness.

"Anakin, maybe you should listen to her," she said nervously. "If this is a trap, they'll be coming for us."

"So what if they are?" Anakin's knuckles whitened as he continued to cut. "We're Jedi, aren't we?"

"The value of sacrifices has a limit even to Yuuzhan Vong," Lomi warned. "They *will* kill us before allowing us to reach the cloning lab. We must go around."

"I thought that was why we came this way," Zekk said over his shoulder.

"They anticipated us," Lomi said simply. "But there are other ways."

"And when they anticipate those?" Anakin demanded, cutting through the last centimeter of reinforced hinge.

"Then we try another way, and another," Jaina said. She knew their situation would only grow worse as time passed, but she also knew it would be fatal to let the odds pressure Anakin into a rash act. "Sooner or later, we may have to fight—but on *our* terms, not theirs."

The soft hiss of a breaking seal sounded from the hatch as it finally came free and settled deeper into its seating ring. Anakin deactivated his lightsaber and, still not responding to Jaina or Lomi, stepped away.

"Anakin, there's a dust cloud coming up the canyon toward us, and I don't think it's a New Republic landspeeder," Ganner said. "How about those orders?"

"In a second!" Anakin snapped. He let out a calming breath, then knelt beside the hatch and looked to Jaina. "Ready?"

"Ready." Even without the battle meld—perhaps even without the Force—she was close enough to her younger brother to sense what he wanted from her. "Watch yourselves."

Jaina levitated the heavy escape hatch out of its seat and moved it aside. A few flitnats drifted out of the opening, their wings emitting a barely audible buzz as they circled Anakin and began to land on his face. Paying no attention, he peered into the cockpit and used the Force to pull Lowbacca up into the hatchway. Even beneath his thick fur, the flitnats were visible on his face, teeming over his eyelids and swarming inside his black nostrils. His cheeks and lips were swollen to twice their normal size, and his breath came in strangled coughs.

The Wookiee's huge shoulders proved too broad to fit through the hatchway, and Anakin had to lower him back into the cockpit. The instant the opening was clear, clouds of flitnats began to pour out, lighting on Anakin's face and drawing a hissed curse as they started to bite. He leaned into the AT-AT and grabbed Lowbacca's arms, then pulled them through the hatchway first. Along with Zekk, Jaina dropped to her brother's side and grabbed an arm so Anakin could concentrate on squeezing the unconscious Wookiee through the narrow space. Her hands and face exploded in stinging pain as the flitnats swarmed. Lomi stepped behind the others and made a feeble attempt to call up a Force wind, which failed to blow the insects away.

As Lowbacca's torso came through the hatchway, masses of blood-bloated flitnats began to drop from his sleeves. The skin on his hands had been chewed bald and was already erupting into purple lumps the size of Jaina's fingertips.

Anakin's only reply was to pull Lowbacca the rest of the way through. A billowing cloud of flitnats poured out behind the Wookiee, prompting Jaina to turn for the hatch. The flitnat bites were already making her sick, and itching so madly she had to take a second to concentrate before she could levitate the heavy piece of steel. When she turned back around, it was to find Lomi summoning an armful of filter housings and breath masks through the hatchway.

"Mustn't forget these." Lomi gathered the equipment into her arms and started toward the front of the cockpit, where Anakin was already lowering Lowbacca to the dune below. "The Wookiee *did* risk his life for them."

Jaina slipped the hatch into place, then felt Zekk's hand on her arm. She was surprised to find herself stumbling as he pulled her off the front of the cockpit after the others. Though the drop was brief, it was long enough to draw a distracting rise from her queasy stomach. They landed hard between Anakin and Lomi, where Jaina fell to her knees and remained, at once choking on chalk dust, itching madly, and trying to keep her gorge down.

Across her back, Lomi asked, "What do you think now, young Solo? Still determined to fight?"

Anakin thought for a moment, then said, "Blaster bolts!" He pulled Jaina to her feet and sent her stumbling down the back side of the dune, then activated his comlink. "Ganner, let's go. Retreat."

Chapter 34

Ben cradled in one arm, Mara circled the *Shadow*'s hull, looking not for signs of abuse or carelessness—though she knew that was what Danni and Cilghal believed—but for signs of micropits and gas scouring. Such wear was an inevitable result of any journey through the mass-rich space around Eclipse, and she took as much pride in her vessel's sleek appearance as Han did in the *Falcon*'s "character." She found only a handful of items that needed attention, a sign of what must have been an oppressively slow final approach.

Mara stopped at the rear cargo lift, where Danni and Cilghal were unloading the equipment they had taken to Borleias. "You took good care of her. Thanks."

"Thank you for trusting us with her." Danni put something that looked like a giant teething ring with a black eyeball in the center onto the repulsor pallet. "We tried to fit everything in a blastboat, but—"

"It's fine, Danni," Mara said. She and everyone else had still been awaiting Luke's return from the senate when Danni and Cilghal contacted her to ask if they could take the *Shadow* to Borleias. "I'm sure I cringed when I realized you were already under way, but it was in a good cause."

"I only wish we had been more successful," Cilghal said. She placed a blastboat gravity generator on the pallet next to the teething ring thing. "I was sure I understood the structure of the yammosk's gravital resonator. Perhaps the freezing altered something."

Mara felt a rush of joy from Ben and did not need to turn to know that Luke was leading Corran, Leia, and most of Eclipse's leaders across the hangar toward them. "Get ready, ladies," she warned quietly. "They spent the whole trip from Coruscant arguing about how Borleias's defenses could be defeated so quickly."

"That is an easy question to answer," Cilghal said. "The Yuuzhan Vong care less for their own lives than ours. They throw away ships—"

The blaring roar of an assault alarm drowned out the Mon Calamari's final words. Radiating fear and discomfort into the Force, Ben added his own voice to the din, and the hangar erupted into action as ship crews rushed to prepare ships for launch.

The alarm fell silent and was replaced by the watch officer's voice. "Attention all crews: this is no drill. We have incoming yorik coral vessels."

Danni and Cilghal looked at each other guiltily. Mara experienced a flash of anger at them for leading the Yuuzhan Vong here and endangering her child—then realized that was not possible. She had inspected the *Shadow* carefully enough to know there were no tracking barnacles attached to the hull, and it would have been impossible for even the Yuuzhan Vong to track a ship through so many hyperspace jumps without a homing device of some sort.

"No way they followed you here, but that won't make any difference when the bolts start flashing. We'd better take our combat posts." Mara pushed her son into Cilghal's arms, then, as Danni ran off toward the Wild Knights' blastboat, kissed him on the head. "Go to the emergency shelter with Cilghal, Ben."

Ben gurgled uncertainly, then fluttered his arms and legs as Mara rushed off toward her X-wing. Though hardly one to panic in a crisis, she deliberately kept her thoughts focused on the task at hand and felt Luke doing the same. Uncertainty bred fear, and as strong as Ben was in the Force, she did not want him to sense any dark-side emotions in his parents.

By the time she reached her starfighter, the mechs were already lowering her astromech droid—she called him Dancer for no particular reason—into his socket. She grabbed her flight suit off the side of the cockpit and pulled it on, listening intently as the watch officer updated the alarm over her comlink.

"Sentry stations report a light-cruiser-analog task force inbound, in pursuit of a *Mark II*-class Imperial Star Destroyer, possibly the *Errant Venture*."

Corran Horn was instantly on the channel, demanding answers the watch officer could not provide. The Destroyer was not transmitting a transponder signal—not at all unusual for Booster Terrik—nor had it hailed the base. Mara's bewilderment mirrored what she sensed in Luke. The *Errant Venture* was supposed to be hiding the Jedi academy students in the New Republic rear base at Reecee, not hazarding trips to Eclipse, and a light-cruiser task force was hardly the type of fleet the Yuuzhan Vong would send to assault the base of the hated *Jeedai*. Something odd was happening here—something that felt faintly connected to the *Shadow*'s presence at Borleias, and yet something that did not really follow from it.

Mara stopped at the top of her cockpit ladder and glanced over at Luke, whom she sensed looking in her direction. She knew instantly what was troubling him. Corran Horn was still on the comlink, yelling at the duty officer to break base protocol and hail the Destroyer.

Mara nodded, and Luke activated his own comlink.

"Negative on hailing the Destroyer, Watch."

"*Negative?*" Corran's voice was close to a shriek. "My kids are on that Destroyer—I feel them!"

"Then we can assume it is the *Venture*," Mara said. She empathized with his feelings; were Ben being chased by a Yuuzhan Vong flotilla, she did not doubt that she would be just as concerned—and a whole lot more dangerous. "We can also assume Booster has a good reason for staying quiet."

"The Star Destroyer is taking heavy fire," Watch reported. "It's possible that all sensor dishes have been destroyed."

Stang! Mara thought. *Very helpful, Watch.*

Corran's X-wing fired its repulsors and lifted off the hangar floor.

"Commander Horn!" Luke barked. "Where do you think you're going?"

"Where do you think?" This from Mirax. The steady click of heels striking duracrete suggested she was in a corridor somewhere, walking fast. "To chase those rocks off the *Venture*'s tail!"

Corran's X-wing started toward the containment field at the mouth of the hangar. A handful of starfighters followed him. "Watch, request shield deactivation for combat departure."

"Too early," Mara commed. She powered up her systems and had Dancer start running diagnostics to warm the circuits. "We're not ready to form up, and we can take them by surprise if we wait."

"Easy to say when Ben is safe inside and you're still worried about hiding Eclipse's location," Mirax countered. "Not so easy when the *Venture* might go up any minute, taking Valin and Jysella with it."

"Watch, acknowledge departure." Corran's voice had an alarming edge to it. "Deactivate this shield—"

"Corran, Mirax, you're not the only ones with children at risk," Han said. Given the risk that his children were facing at the moment, his words made even Mara feel a little guilty for thinking only of Ben's safety; Corran, they shamed into silence. "And neither of you is thinking very clearly right now. If Booster was in trouble, you can bet he'd be rattling this rock with concussion missiles."

"Contacts have entered visual range," Watch reported. "Identity confirmed as *Errant Venture*."

They were coming fast. Mara activated her tactical display and saw the Star Destroyer streaking toward Eclipse's star, its forward turbolaser batteries blasting a clear path through the enormous asteroid disk that passed for a planetary system even at the edge of the Deep Core. There were eight light cruisers and twice that number of frigate and corvette analogs on his tail, and they were all traveling far too fast to intend decelerating anywhere near Eclipse.

"Corran, what's happening?" Mirax commed. "Why aren't you launching?"

"Han's right, Mirax. Booster has something up his sleeve." There was a moment's pause, then Corran added, "I apologize, Master Skywalker."

Mara was not sure whether the relief she felt was her own or Luke's—or both.

"I'm sure you'd do the same for me, Corran," Luke said. There was no hint of irritation in either his voice or his emotions. "We'll launch after they pass. Can I count on you to keep a clear head?"

"It might be better if Han took Battle Control," Corran admitted. "I seem to have, uh, seated myself in the wrong vessel."

Han did not argue. Like Mara and Luke and most others old enough to have fought in the Rebellion, he had engaged in enough heroics to last five lifetimes; now, he was content to go where he was needed and let the combat come to him.

"The *Venture* has been hulled," Watch reported.

Somehow, Mirax managed to limit her outcry to a strangled gasp. Mara would have filled the channel with curses that would have made even Rigard Matl blush.

"Venting debris now."

Mara looked to her tactical display and saw a cloud of flotsam drifting in Eclipse's general direction as the *Venture* flashed past. The Star Destroyer swayed wildly from side to side, as though struggling to retain control after the hit, then suddenly cleared a new path with a volley from its port turbolasers. Turning as sharply as a Star Destroyer could, it angled for a dense mass of asteroids just in-sun from Eclipse.

"He's setting us up," Han said. "Launch by—"

"Wait!" Mara said, still watching the debris cloud descend toward Eclipse. "Watch, scan that flotsam for life-forms. Booster wasn't hit—he threw that stuff at us."

Before Watch could comply, Corran said, "Mara, thank you. I can feel Jysella and Valin reaching out to me."

"Affirmative," Watch said. "Those are escape pods."

"Leia, can you send Han up to Control and oversee the pod recovery in the *Falcon*?" Luke asked. "And you and Mirax can help her, Corran."

Corran was already setting his X-wing down next to the *Falcon*. "I'd like nothing better. Thank you."

"Everyone else, launch—carefully—by squadrons," Luke ordered. "Watch, lower the shield. Sabers . . . three, two, mark."

Mara activated her repulsorlift and followed Luke's X-wing out of the hangar, sweeping around an escape pod and waving at a pair of wide-eyed young Jedi students watching her through their viewport. By the time the other three squadrons had formed up behind them, the Star Destroyer and its pursuers were already out of visual range and, as they eased into the asteroid cluster, growing difficult to find even on the tactical display.

Mara thought their approach might remain undetected—until a handful of frigates poked their noses out of the asteroid cluster and began to drop their skips.

"They must want Booster pretty desperately," Mara observed.

"Or they don't know who we are," Luke answered. The asteroid cluster came into visual range now, the flash of the Star Destroyer's sixty turbolaser batteries lighting up the interior like a tiny red dwarf star. "All X-wings, lock S-foils into firing position. Don't be stingy with those shadow bombs."

"Farmboy, you'd better hold back a minute," Han commed.

"Hold back?"

"Affirmative, hold—"

Han's voice dissolved into static as the asteroid cluster began to explode mountainous rock by mountainous rock, sixty of them in staccato succession, each one spraying millions of tons of super-heated stone in every direction at several thousand meters a second. On her tactical display, Mara saw a boulder split one of the frigates down the spine and glimpsed a cruiser analog tumbling out of the cluster in three separate sections, then Luke was yelling "Break, break!" and ducking them behind the shelter of a city-sized asteroid.

When Han's voice returned, he was explaining, ". . . old smuggler's trick. Shunt all engine power to the particle shields, then heat an asteroid behind them and wait for it to explode." He paused a moment, then added, "Works really well with a Star Destroyer."

"You could have warned us earlier, Control," Mara observed.

"Hey—do I look like a Jedi mind reader?"

The rubble wave reached them then, tumbling past in light-ninglike streaks of gray, occasionally shattering a nearby asteroid with the flash of a detonating proton torpedo. Their own mountainous shield took several hits that jolted the whole rock noticeably and pelted their particle shields with sprays of loosened pebbles, and finally the storm was past, slowly dissipating as the debris spray dispersed and gave up so much momentum to collisions that the individual shards no longer had the energy to explode on impact.

When they poked their noses out from behind their shield, Mara was astonished to find the *Venture* on her tactical display where there had been only the asteroid cluster before. There were a few blank spots on the array where clouds of dust or frozen vapor confused the sensors, but most alarming were the squadrons of A-wing and Y-wing starfighters spilling from the Star Destroyer's launching bays. The tactical display marked them all as New Republic craft, but . . . the Star Destroyer reduced the number of cruiser analogs to five with a devastating turbolaser volley, and the A-wings reduced it to four with a high-speed concussion missile–proton torpedo combination pass.

"Farmboy, the *Errant Venture* doesn't have a fighter squadron," Mara commed. "Let alone six."

"Try ten, Jedi," an unfamiliar voice said over the tactical net. "And we're just hitching a ride on the *Venture*. We're Reecee fleet—all that remains of it."

A piece fell into place in Mara's mind, and she saw the tenuous connection she had sensed earlier between the *Shadow*'s presence at Borleias and the *Venture*'s unexpected arrival at Eclipse.

"A surprise attack?" she asked. "At the same time as Borleias?"

"On its heels," the voice corrected. "And they meant to keep it that way. The first thing they did was, well, jam our communications. All we've got are our fighter comms—and only when we're outside the Star Destroyer."

"Jam how?" Luke asked.

"Some sort of dovin basal, we think," the pilot answered. "The first Reecee knew of the attack was when they swarmed the base shields. We thought they were some sort of mynock at first, but when we tried to transmit, they pulled the signal in like a black hole."

"*No one* was able to send a message?" Mara asked.

"No one. The *Venture* caught a dose when she came to get us," he said. "We were trying to clean them off when this task force jumped us at the edge of the Deep Core."

"So the New Republic doesn't know that Reecee has fallen," Luke said.

"Or that the Bilbringi Shipyards have been cut off," Han added. "But they will soon. I'll have a message sent now."

The Star Destroyer's form grew visible ahead, its nose coming up before the Sabers as it wheeled around to bring its turbolasers to bear on a cruiser trying to attack from above. Mara could just see something that looked like tiny, heart-shaped freckles dotting the white hull—no doubt the signal-devouring dovin basals that the pilot had described. Another cruiser analog was following behind the *Venture,* pouring plasma balls and magma missiles into its vulnerable exhaust ports.

"Sabers and Shockers, take that cruiser on the tail," Han ordered. "Knights and Dozen, remove the one trying to cut him off."

"You hear that, Reecee?" Luke asked. A flurry of comm clicks acknowledged. "Good, see if you can clear us a path. We're coming in hard."

The Reecee squadrons first engaged the coralskippers in the Jedi's way, then tried to draw them off by turning to flee. The skips started to fall for the ploy—then abruptly reversed course and began to gather in front of the intended targets.

"They have a yammosk!" Danni actually sounded happy about it. "In that port cruiser. If we can—"

"Check," a Reecee voice replied. "Thanks for the tip, Jedi."

Two squadrons of A-wings wheeled on the cruiser instantly, discharging concussion missiles as they dropped. Taking a cue from the fighters, the *Errant Venture* concentrated a whole bank of turbolasers on the vessel, and the hull began to vomit yorik coral immediately.

"Wait!" Danni commed. "I meant capture it! We need it alive!"

The vessel went dead in space and began to drift, bodies and atmosphere streaming from its hull breaches. The coralskippers continued to cluster in the Jedi's path, their volcano cannons now belching plasma.

"Master Skywalker, it's still communicating with the skip," Danni commed. "If we can board it quick enough—"

"Let's finish this run first, Danni," Luke replied. "Sabers and Knights, ease off. Shockers and Dozen, you'll have to clear the way."

Rigard simply took his squadron and shot ahead toward

their target. Kyp, however, did not seem to have fully grasped his assignment.

"Let's go, Dozen," he commed, peeling off. "We have first shot!"

The Shockers rocketed into the enemy coralskippers a kilometer ahead of the Sabers and commenced fire, clearing a path to the cruiser as much by forcing the skips to dodge as by blasting them out of the way. Mara saw one Shocker go EV and slam into a chunk of asteroid when a volcano cannon sheered his S-foils, then watched another vanish in a ball of flame as his starfighter smashed headlong into a magma missile.

She and Tam began to weave shields with Luke, each sensing the other's intentions through the Force, juking and jinking in perfect unison. Mara kept up a constant barrage of laserfire, using the Force more to avoid hitting her own ships than to target the enemy's. Two skips deteriorated into rubble as she rocketed past behind Luke.

The darkness ahead suddenly grew bright as the Shockers launched their proton torpedoes, then it grew brighter still as the decoy flares deployed. The cruiser retaliated with a barrage of grutchins and magma missiles. Rigard's squadron was already diving down and away, leaving the weapons to come streaking toward the Sabers.

"Launch!" Luke ordered.

Mara's shadow bombs were already gone, following Luke's toward the cruiser. Without really thinking about it, she nosed her X-wing over behind his, one eye on her target as she used the Force to guide the weapon home. Tam's laser cannon flashed, blasting a grutchin away from her cockpit before it could attach, and then the brilliant flash of the first proton detonation caused her canopy's blast tinting to darken. More explosions followed in quick succession, and by the time Luke swung the Sabers around, the ship was coming apart.

The inert cruiser lay ahead, surrounded by a cloud of floating bodies and equipment. The rifts in its hull hung dark and ominous, some large enough for an X-wing to enter. Mara checked her tactical display and saw that Luke *could* be thinking what she feared. The *Venture,* now turned on its side next to the Sabers, was already hammering the last cruiser, and the Reecee squadrons were herding the surviving skips into an ever-tightening sphere, picking them off now by the twos and threes.

"Skywalker," Mara commed. "A dead yammosk is one thing—"

"They need a live one—and when is it going to be easier?" Luke eased his X-wing toward the largest breach. "Danni's already shown how valuable it is just to know *when* there's a yammosk present—imagine what we'll be able to do when we can intercept its messages."

"How are you going to carry it back?" Mara asked. "Under your seat?"

"Han, send us the *Jolly Man*."

"Wait a minute," Danni said. "Something's wrong. The yammosk has gone completely silent, and now the skips look confused."

"That's enough, Luke," Mara said. Close to home or not, this felt too easy to be safe. "The Force was with us at Talfaglio. Today, it's not."

Luke was already swinging his X-wing around as the flash of an exploding magma magazine tore the vessel apart, bouncing yorik coral off his particle shields and licking his exhaust ports with hundred-meter flames.

Chapter 35

hough the skyway balcony was always the grandest entrance to any society apartment, Viqi Shesh had long believed that the interior approach revealed more about the occupants' station in life. The Solo apartment sat in a sanibuffed cul-de-sac as wide as a speeder avenue, with a floor of milky larmalstone—a costly nonfabricant available only from the Roche asteroid field—and rare red ladalums blooming in rounded wall niches between pillars of white marde. A barrel-vaulted ceiling of custom-made glow panels infused the area with cloudy light, and a smiling Serv-O-Droid greeter—no doubt with the full tattletale security package—stood patiently outside the crystasteel door.

The Solos had certainly come down in the world since Leia's days as chief of state. Upon learning that they had quietly traded their prestigious Orowood hideaway for something in the more affordable Eastport administrative district, Viqi had at first been inclined to doubt her informer. One did not expect to find two of the Rebellion's most acclaimed heroes and power brokers living among the bureaucrats—much less at an address nearly three hundred meters down from the top of a not-very-tall tower—but the ladalums convinced her. Unique to Alderaan, the shrubs yielded red blossoms only if their line remained pure to their planet of origin. Given the vicissitudes of disease and cross-pollination, they were, like so many things Alderaanian these days, gradually dying out.

That was what happened to those who lost power, Viqi supposed. They withered slowly away, until one day they were just gone. Like Mon Mothma, like Admiral Ackbar, like Leia Organa Solo—like Viqi herself, after being undone in the senate by Luke Skywalker and his Jedi tricks.

Not wishing to draw attention to herself by staring too long at the Solos' apartment, Viqi looked casually away and continued past, just another Eastport bureaucrat heading home on personal business in the middle of the day. Dressed in a fashionable high-collared overcloak and swank slouch hat, she certainly looked the part—well enough to have fooled the young Jedi trailing her when she and an assistant exchanged clothes in the refresher station of a crowded transit hub. She followed the corridor around the corner to a lift bank and stepped into a tube, removing her hat and overcloak as she rose to the rooftop.

Now garbed in the conservative business tabard of a money watcher, she stepped out onto the sky-shuttle landing pad, deposited the clothing in a disintegrator chute, and crossed to another lift bank. After giving the proper visitor authorization for an apartment on the same level, she descended to the Solos' floor and started back toward the apartment, trying to think of how she could insert the sensislug without being observed. Entering the cul-de-sac, even on the pretext of examining the beautiful ladalums, was out of the question. The greeter droid would be very polite and solicitous, but it would also be scanning her image and voiceprint for a data match.

Viqi approached the entry head-on this time, strolling along and peering over the top of a sheaf of flimsiplast documents she had brought as a prop. There was simply no way to enter the cul-de-sac without being seen by the greeter droid, which meant she would have to find some other way to insert the sensislug. Her contact had assured her that the creatures were capable of finding their own way inside once they had been targeted, but the Yuuzhan Vong understood even less about cleaning droids than she did about sensislugs. Having already lost half a dozen of the insects trying to slip just one into the NRMOC committee room, she felt reasonably certain that the instant the sensislug came within twenty meters of a ladalum, some little pest hunter would zip out to destroy it.

Viqi was starting to consider other options—food deliveries or using a third party—when she heard the solution marching up the corridor behind her.

". . . is hardly the time to go sight-seeing, dear," Han Solo was saying.

"It's exactly the time," Leia countered. "They had a reason for trying to keep the capture of Reecee quiet, and that reason will be all the more pressing now that we know about it."

Still pretending to be absorbed in her documents, Viqi quietly slipped one hand into her pocket and palmed what felt like a thumb-sized leech in her fingers. In place of a head, it had a huge compound eye. She turned the eye toward the Solos' crystasteel door and squeezed the creature until she felt its body grow warm with understanding. Han and Leia veered toward the center of the corridor as they came up behind her. Some creature in their party gurgled softly as they passed, and two pairs of metallic feet clanked on the floor behind them.

"Besides, we *know* the reason," Han argued. "Bilbringi."

"That's the obvious reason," Leia countered. "When have you ever known the Yuuzhan Vong to be obvious?"

The Solos swept past Viqi without a second glance, both dressed in rumpled flight suits. Han cradled an infant in one arm. Viqi was hardly an authority on babies—when the time came to bear one, she intended to have a staff and a telbun to care for the thing—but she did know the Solos' offspring to be adults now—or nearly so. This had to be the Skywalker heir.

The couple's famous golden droid came clumping after them, a four-armed TDL nanny droid traveling smoothly at its side. Viqi turned a little more toward the wall. The two humans would not see through her disguise, she knew, because this was the last place they expected to find her. The droids were a different matter. Droids scanned and analyzed and did not let their expectations lead them astray, and she felt fairly certain that the protocol droid, at least, would have her face committed to its memory banks.

The droid seemed more concerned with the discussion between its owners than who she might be. When Han did not answer his wife's objection, it said, "Forgive me for intruding, but I am quite certain that when Master Luke and Mistress Mara said Ben would be safer on Coruscant, they anticipated that we would be staying longer than fifty-seven minutes."

Leia shot a look over her shoulder that would have melted lesser droids. "You let me worry about that, Threepio."

"Yes, Princess."

Viqi guessed from the presence of the Skywalker baby that they had to be coming from the secret Jedi base. Tsavong Lah was still trying to discover its location—that was one of the reasons he had assigned her this task—and, given what Skywalker had done to her in the senate, she was eager to see the warmaster pleased. She waited a moment longer to make certain there was no one else in the Solos' party. Then, as they approached the intersection in front of the apartment, she flicked the sensislug at the protocol droid's back.

The worm hit in absolute silence and slithered down toward the waist coupling, but the droid suddenly paused at the corner and swiveled its head around to look behind it. Viqi hid her face behind her documents and turned the corner—then ran into something barely as high as her chest and cried out in surprise, flinging her flimsiplast props in all directions.

A wispy voice below her rasped, "I beg your forgiveness."

She looked down to see a little bug-eyed alien with gray skin and a mouthful of sharp teeth, gathering her documents in his long-taloned fingers.

The Noghri passed the documents back to her. "I apologize."

Viqi allowed the alien to place the props in her hand, then sensed the Solos watching her. She had taken care to disguise her appearance by coloring her hair drab ash and making liberal use of an NRI disguise kit, but at the moment, she could not help wishing that she had accepted her contact's offer to give her an ooglith masquer. Unable to resist looking, she glanced over at the Solos and found them both staring.

Han's expression grew concerned. "You okay? Would you like to come inside for a minute?"

Viqi's heart jumped into her throat. She mumbled something indecipherable, then scurried off shaking her head.

Chapter 36

Anakin could feel nothing through the battle meld except doubt and resentment, so he was as surprised as anyone when the *crack-crackle* of a thermal detonator reverberated through the street behind him. Raising his lightsaber to high guard and thumbing the activation switch, he pivoted around to discover a ball of blue-white light contracting between Raynar and Eryl, obliterating everything in a five-meter radius and opening a deep crater in the street. Subsurface service ducts began to spew water and sewer gas, filling the hole with steam and flame.

Over the course of several dozen attempts to reach the cloning facility, the Jedi had crossed replications of nearly every environment where voxyn might be sent to hunt them—replications of agritracts, robofactories, swamp farms, even an automated cloud mine. Now they were pushing through the slave city itself. With tiers of windows and balconies built directly into the walls, the metropolis reminded Anakin of the pictures his mother had shown him of Crevasse City on lost Alderaan. In addition to a dozen different species of slave residents, the artificial city contained turbolifts, slidewalks, even droid-operated hovercars.

Anakin stepped past Tahiri and Tekli and peered over Raynar's shoulder into the flaming crater. Nothing remained of whatever had prompted the attack.

"Voxyn?" he asked. Since their retreat from the walker, the voxyn attacks had been coming with increasing frequency.

Raynar shrugged. "I didn't see."

"It came out of the street hatch," Eryl explained from the other side. Her green eyes flickered briefly in Raynar's direction, then she added, "There was no time to do anything but toss a detonator down its throat. Sorry for the waste."

Anakin thumbed his lightsaber off. "I don't know that I'd call it a waste." The team was down to a dozen thermal detonators—now eleven—and perhaps twice that many grenades, but at least they had not lost anyone since Ulaha. "Raynar is probably worth the price of a detonator."

"Probably?" Raynar objected. "If there's any question, the House of Thul will gladly reimburse the Jedi for all detonators used on my behalf."

"You're sure?" Eryl asked doubtfully.

She circled around the burning crater, then pinched Raynar on the cheek and laughed. Behind her came Zekk and Jaina—like Anakin and Lomi, now completely recovered from their encounter with the flitnats. Even Lowbacca and Jovan had nothing worse to show than a bad rash, thanks to Tekli's quick realization that the insects had been engineered to promote a debilitating allergic reaction.

Anakin's earplugs sealed themselves against the disorienting blast of a voxyn screech attack. Such assaults came so regularly now that they were no longer startling. Anakin simply pushed his breath mask into place and started forward to where a mob of slaves was staggering away from a convergence of blasterfire.

A lightsaber flashed, sending the tip of a severed voxyn tail tumbling over the crowd, then the creature itself rose into view as Tenel Ka used the Force to lift it out of a street hatch. Ganner and the Barabels set on it instantly, hacking it apart with their molten blades before Anakin could reach them. Killing voxyn was becoming almost routine; the strike team rarely traveled more than a few kilometers without being attacked by at least one of the things.

Anakin reached out with the Force to search for more. There seemed to be no others lurking beneath the street, but he did perceive someone in anguish lying inside the growing cloud of toxins released by the creature's noxious blood. Slipping past the fighting, he found a mucus-coated slave curled into a fetal ball, so badly acid-burned that only his raw nerve cones identified him as a Gotal.

Anakin called Tekli forward. She should have felt the need on her own, but the battle meld was so full of discord that it served as little more than confirmation that everyone was still alive and conscious. As the Chadra-Fan knelt beside the dying Gotal, Lomi and Welk came up, now wearing the breath masks Lowbacca had risked so much to retrieve. They watched Tekli's ministrations not with the disdain or detachment Anakin had expected, but with visible outrage. He knew better than to think they were empathizing with the slave's suffering; they were simply using the anger it engendered to feed their dark-side power.

"I don't like coming through here." Anakin eyed the growing number of slave residents stumbling away from the toxic fumes. "We're endangering them with our presence."

"They are already in danger," Lomi said. "And you are the one who wishes to try the voxyn warren. This is the only way to reach it."

"You know you're going to get us killed?" Welk asked. "Even Yuuzhan Vong don't go down there."

"Which is why *we* must," Anakin said. Whether Nom Anor intended to or not, he was wearing the strike team down, steadily depleting its munitions and draining its vigor. "We need to break through soon, or we never will."

"If this doesn't work, we may have to accept never," Lomi said. "There comes a time when we must think of our own lives."

"Yeah, like after we've vaped the queen." Tahiri stepped to Anakin's side. "There is no try, only do."

Lomi flashed Tahiri a condescending smirk. "Very impressive, child. You have memorized Skywalker's maxims." She looked back to Anakin. "Seriously, if this does not work, you must signal your extraction team. I won't throw away my life."

"There's more at risk here than your life—or ours," Anakin said.

Lomi rolled her eyes. "I know—the Jedi themselves."

"The Jedi are the galaxy's best hope of survival," Anakin replied. "Otherwise, the Yuuzhan Vong wouldn't be working so hard to destroy us."

Lomi ran her eyes down Anakin's figure, her expression almost seductive. "You are so very earnest, Anakin. It is really quite adorable." Her smile turned icy. "But I did not see Skywalker sending his Jedi Knights to save the Nightsisters when the Yuuzhan Vong captured Dathomir. I will show you to the voxyn cave, but if we cannot fight through, you must call your extraction team."

Anakin hesitated a moment, wondering how earnest she would think him after he lied to her—and then he realized there was no need. He returned her smile with one just as icy.

"Extraction team?" he asked. "What extraction team would that be?"

Lomi's eyes narrowed, and she reached out to test Anakin with the Force. "Do you think you can . . ." When she encountered no resistance, her jaw fell, and she let the probe drop. "You are on a suicide mission?"

"It's no suicide mission," Tahiri said. "We've walked rockier trails than this, lots of times."

Lomi ignored her and continued to stare at Anakin.

"The warmaster anticipated our plans," he explained. "We lost our ship coming in."

"And your backup plan?" Lomi asked. "Surely, you have a backup plan?"

Anakin nodded. "Kill the queen and destroy the lab, then hope we can steal a ship in the confusion."

"I see." The anger in Lomi's eyes grew more intent. "There is no try . . ."

"Only do," Welk finished, his voice mocking. "If that doesn't blast my bones!"

The acid-burned Gotal finally died, and the strike team started up the street again. As soon as they left the toxin cloud, the mob closed in, begging the Jedi to free them, thrusting children out for rescue, volunteering to fight. There were thousands of slaves—Ranats, Ossan, Togorians, even some species Anakin could not name, all cognizant of their fate, all desperate to escape their coming doom, the very people who needed the Jedi—the weak, the downtrodden, the defenseless. Anakin's heart grew heavier each time he was forced to say he could not help, that his mission here was too vital, that he had no way to get them off the worldship. Soon, it grew too painful to explain that much. He simply apologized in a quiet and calm voice, using Jedi persuasion techniques to comfort those in despair and to redirect the wrath of those who were angry.

Lomi started down a cramped alley-canyon that would not have felt out of place in Coruscant's underlevels. Barely three meters wide, the lane descended at a steep angle beneath a network of balconies and catwalks, then vanished into the dank-smelling murk ahead. The windows and doors that pocked the walls to both sides were sealed behind curtains of living membrane. An odd double pathway worn into the dusty ground was spaced about right for the wide-set legs of a voxyn. Noting that the slave residents showed no desire to follow them into the alley, Anakin stopped three steps in.

"Stay sharp, everyone. We need to make this work." He turned to his brother. "If you can do something to keep the voxyn quiet, now is the time."

Jacen paled. "I'll do my best, Anakin." He started forward. "But these aren't normal animals. I can't just reach—"

Anakin did not hear the rest, for the general haze of Yuuzhan Vong presence suddenly grew strong and almost distinct. He turned to scan the crowd and found a group of humans shoving toward Jacen. All five were large men with swarthy faces and blank expressions, men so similar they could have been clones. Four reached for their belts. The fifth tossed a thumb-sized capsule at Jacen's feet, and a thin coat of greenish gel spread across the street.

"Blorash jelly!" Anakin burned a blaster hole through the jelly thrower's throat, then used the Force to pluck his brother off the ground. "Watch the crowd!"

A dozen lightsabers came to life and formed a dancing cage of light around the rear half of the strike team. Anakin put Jacen down in the alley mouth. Someone took a heavy blow, and a tide of darkness swirled through the battle meld as they struggled to stay conscious.

"Jaina!" Jacen yelled.

The mob roared and scattered, trampling each other in their panic. The impostors flung more blorash jelly, capturing slaves and Jedi alike, turning the street into a tangle of confusion. Lowbacca roared, his bronze lightsaber flashing down, cleaving something Anakin could not see. Tenel Ka yelled for support. Alema cursed in Ryl, her silver blade burning through a soft body. Eryl cried out as green gel spread over her foot. She hacked the stuff apart, and the second piece bound her other foot to the ground. She reached into her equipment pouch for a more potent defense.

A razor bug flew out of the crowd, caught her below the nose, and slashed her face in two. Her eyes rolled back, and the lightsaber slipped from her hand, and she fell and began to convulse.

Shock burned through the battle meld like an ion blast. Doubt and resentment gave way to anger, blame, guilt—none of it helpful. The emotions only added to the chaos, blurring Anakin's awareness.

He felt just one thing clearly, the black gauze threatening to engulf his sister.

Anakin stepped out of the alley and heard an amphistaff hiss. He caught the snakish head on his lightsaber, then spun around, driving a back kick into his attacker's midsection and bringing his molten blade around in a neck-high sweep. The impostor collapsed, head tumbling from his shoulders.

Tahiri somersaulted under Anakin's lightsaber and sprang to her feet behind her blade, driving the tip up through the torso of a Duros male. Seeing no amphistaff, Anakin thought she had made a terrible mistake, then sensed Yuuzhan Vong pain and saw a gablith masquer peeling off the Duros' face.

Anakin jerked her behind him. "Careful!"

"You're one to talk!" she snapped.

Tahiri pulled a handful of arsensalts from her equipment pouch and sprinkled them on a blorash jelly sliding toward their feet. The stuff drew back, then began to divide itself into oblivion. Anakin circled past and first sensed, then saw more impostors, three human and two Duros, shouldering their way out of the crowd.

He pushed Tahiri at Ganner and the Barabels and ordered them to secure the alley entrance, then sprang into the air and called on the Force to carry himself over the charging Yuuzhan Vong. As he somersaulted past their heads, he dragged his lightsaber across one impostor's skull and split it down the center. He landed behind the group and thrust-kicked another onto Tesar's waiting blade.

The Barabel ducked a whistling amphistaff, then trapped the arm that had swung it and pulled the elbow into his sharp-toothed mouth. With the odds in the alley now firmly in the strike team's favor, Anakin turned to find Raynar pulling Eryl's limp body into his arms, his face streaked with tears and seemingly unaware of the blorash jelly binding his knee to the ground. Anakin sprinkled some salts on the blob.

Raynar looked up, eyes wide. "I can't feel her, Anakin. She's not in the Force."

Anakin shared his shock. Before, Nom Anor had seemed intent on recapturing the strike team alive. So why were Yuuzhan Vong hurling razor bugs now? Because, suddenly, the strike team had a good chance of reaching the cloning labs, that was why. He pulled Eryl into Raynar's arms, then pushed them both toward the alley.

"I'll send Tekli."

Anakin rushed forward into a mad riot of shrieking slaves. Some lay dead and many were bleeding, but the battle had already drifted out into the street, and most were screaming only because they were trapped. He hurled a few sprinkles of arsensalts as he passed, then met Tenel Ka coming in the opposite direction, levitating Jovan Drark. Tekli was kneeling astride the Rodian, her hands buried to the wrists inside his open chest.

Anakin touched him through the Force and immediately felt sick and hollow inside. Jovan had only the faintest glimmer of life, and even that was fading.

"Jaina's in trouble," Tenel Ka said. "They're trying to—"

Anakin was already racing forward, leaping the bodies of groaning slaves and fallen Yuuzhan Vong, flinging arsensalts at the few remaining patches of blorash jelly. He should have anticipated this, should have realized Nom Anor would use the slave city to ambush them. Now Eryl was dead, Jovan dying, Jaina about to be taken—and the strike team had yet to reach the cloning labs.

He found Jaina pinned against a building, a blob of blorash jelly binding her along one side, blood pouring from a head wound. Despite it all, she was holding two Yuuzhan Vong impostors at bay with a one-handed lightsaber defense. Lowbacca and Zekk were fighting toward her through a half-dozen still-masqued warriors. Alema Rar crouched behind a crashed hovercar, using Jovan Drark's longblaster to delay a company of reinforcements.

Anakin gathered the Force to him and charged, somersaulting into the air as he had a few moments before.

Zekk's opponents broke off, stepping back to hurl their amphistaffs like spears. Anakin batted one aside—then felt a hot pain in his abdomen when the second pierced his jumpsuit's armored lining.

As he finished his tumble, the shaft swung away, the head pivoting inside his abdomen. He heard himself scream, then he was coming down, landing on his feet and hammering the butt into the ground. Cold anguish filled his belly. His knees tried to buckle, but he would not let them—could not let them.

"Anakin!"

Guided by her screaming voice, Anakin flung a handful of arsensalts in Jaina's direction, used the Force to carry them to the jelly.

Then he grabbed the amphistaff and jerked it from his body.

The agony was crushing.

Anakin shunted it aside, used his Jedi training to prevent his suffering from crippling him. He was injured, but not mortally so. One of Jaina's attackers spun to attack, changing his amphistaff to whip form in midswing.

Anakin batted the fanged head aside, leapt forward, feigned a slash. The impostor tried to step inside—*had* to try. Anakin slipped a foot behind his foe's heel and swept the leg. The Yuuzhan Vong went down, rolled, then opened his own throat on Anakin's downturned lightsaber.

Now free of her blorash jelly, Jaina was driving her foe back with a wild web of lightsaber slashes. Calling on the Force for strength, Anakin stepped over and slashed his blade across the Yuuzhan Vong's knees. Jaina opened the warrior's chestplate before he hit the ground, then turned and grabbed Anakin by the elbow.

"By the Sith, Anakin! Why'd you do something like that?"

"Like what?" he asked.

Jaina glared; they both knew his rescue had been rash.

"We lost two . . . and I wasn't going to . . ." The words caught in Anakin's throat, and he had to try again. "You were in trouble."

"And now *you* are." Jaina tried to wipe the blood from her eyes and failed, then started toward the alley. "Anakin, this was really . . . Are you ever going to learn?"

As they turned, Anakin found himself looking at a wall of Jedi, with Lowbacca and Zekk flanked by Jacen, Ganner, and everyone else he had ordered to stay in the alley. The last of the Yuuzhan Vong impostors lay on the ground behind them, their masquers and vonduun crab armor hacked into smoking pieces. Zekk went instantly to Jaina's side. Tahiri beat Lowbacca and Jacen to Anakin's. She tried to pull his hand away from the wound, but he wouldn't allow it. He lifted his chin toward Alema, who was still crouched behind the hovercar burning holes in Yuuzhan Vong chests.

"Call her off," he said. "Let's go before someone else gets killed."

Paying no attention, Tahiri continued to tug at his arm. "Anakin, how bad is it? Let me—"

"Tahiri, stop." Anakin pushed her arm down. "It's just a little cut."

ou call this a shortcut?"

"Trust me." Han looked away from the starless swirl of black nebula gas outside and smiled at his wife. "If the Vong who jumped Booster were protecting something, we'll find it at the end of this run. This is the only way they could have reached the Core region without tripping a picket mine."

"And we aren't going to trip a picket mine *why?*" Leia asked.

"Because there aren't any," Han said. "The New Republic doesn't know about this lane. Nobody does."

"Nobody?"

"Well, Lando knows." Han returned his gaze to the long-range sensors and began to scan for dangerous mass centers. "And Chewbacca, he knew—so did Roa. And, of course, Talon Karrde always knows."

"So, basically you're saying that every smuggler or gambler who ever had a reason to slip into Reecee undetected knows this shortcut?"

"Yeah," Han said. "Like I said, nobody."

They had already made five jumps in as many hours, and now

they were flying the *Falcon* into the inky heart of the Black Bantha. Listed erroneously on most charts as a Gamma Class navigation hazard—which usually meant an unlocated black hole—the Bantha was actually a protostar, a small cloud of relatively cool gas slowly contracting to become a star. In a few million years or so, it would contract enough to start fusing hydrogen, but for now its core emitted nothing more dangerous than a vague aura of infrared heat. A good pilot could fly straight through it at near lightspeed, so long as he stayed clear of its dust ring and avoided the uncharted gamma-ray pulsar on the other side.

An alert chimed once, twice, a half-dozen times, then became a steady bell. A field of dark shapes appeared on the display, ahead of the *Falcon* and a little below, each with a set of numerical readouts below it.

"Han," Leia asked. "What are those?"

"Asteroid cluster," Han said. "It's supposed to be farther out, but it must be drifting toward center."

"Really?" Leia sounded doubtful. "Standard rock-iron asteroids?"

"That's right." Han glanced at the readouts and immediately saw her point. The contacts were too uniform to be asteroids—and not nearly dense enough. He put the *Falcon* into a hard turn, then shut down the ion drives to avoid illuminating their position. "I said we'd find them here."

"At the end of the run."

"It looks like this *is* the end of the run."

Dark shapes continued to appear on the display as they drifted across the protostar. Leia activated a data record and began to run an analysis. Han activated the rest of the passive sensors and kept a wary eye on the dark shapes as they slowed and began to deploy pickets. So far, they did not seem to realize they were being watched, which did not really surprise him—the *Falcon*'s sensors were the equal of any reconnaissance ship, and the New Republic's one small advantage in this war seemed to lie in surveillance. Still, it would be not be long before the picket ships drew near enough to sense their presence.

"Okay, Leia, I think we'd better go."

"Not yet. This is too big," Leia said.

"That's kind of the point."

"No, Han—I mean really big. Isn't the New Republic getting ready to jump to Reecee?"

"In about—" Han glanced at the instrument panel chronometer. "—three hours. Unofficially, of course."

"I don't think they're going to find anything. There must be a thousand vessels already."

Han started to ask Leia what she wanted him to do about it, but realized he already knew. The crooked hyperspace lane behind them zigzagged all the way through the Colonies to the edge of the Core region. From there the Yuuzhan Vong would have a clear path to both Eclipse and Coruscant—and Han did not think even Tsavong Lah was sending a thousand vessels to attack the Jedi base.

"I don't want to do this." They had been in the right place at the right time too often in their lives already. It wasn't fun anymore. "I really don't want to do this."

"I'll ready a message," Leia said.

"Send it to Adarakh and Meewalh," Han said. "We may get only one try, and they're in a better position to make sure the news reaches Wedge and Garm."

"Already thought of that."

"And tell them to find Lando," Han added. "The fleet's gonna need a guide."

"Thought of that, too," Leia said.

"And tell Luke—"

"Han!"

"Hey, coming out here wasn't my idea," Han said. "I'm just trying to help."

Leia gave him a glare that suggested he get on with it.

Han risked a subspace imaging scan and located the real field of asteroids where he had expected, just inside the dust ring down on the protostar's plane of spin. He plotted a short-burn course that would carry them away from the Yuuzhan Vong at an oblique angle and bring them in behind the asteroid cluster. Once they were safely established there, they would be able to monitor the entire gas cloud with long-range sensors and feed the data to the New Republic fleet as it arrived—providing, of course, it *did* arrive. There was always a chance that Fey'lya or some other bureaucrat would panic and decide to keep the fleet at home.

"We'll have to risk an ion glow," Han said. "I don't think anyone will see it in this cloud, but if they do—"

"I've already plotted an emergency hop," Leia said. "It won't be long, but it should buy us some time to come up with something better. The data dump is ready to go."

"Hold on tight," Han said. "We'll be slam-pivoting straight to vector."

"Wonderful. Something to look forward to."

Leia grabbed the arms of the big copilot's chair and nodded grimly. Han clenched his jaw, then activated the ion drive and hit the attitude thrusters. Though the acceleration compensator was dialed to maximum, the *Falcon* slued around so sharply that the crash webbing crackled from the strain. His hands nearly came off the yoke and he had the sensation of tumbling sideways, then his stomach rebelled and he had to clench his jaw to keep from embarrassing himself.

The acceleration compensator caught up as they began to travel in a straight line again, and Leia opened a subspace channel to Coruscant. It took only a few seconds for the signal to find a route through the relay maze to their Eastport apartment, but Han used the time to check the sensor displays and spied a pair of skips peeling off to investigate. The Yuuzhan Vong would have dispatched an entire flotilla if they had seen an ion glow, so it seemed likely the pair were only chasing the wake the *Falcon* was punching through the nebula. Hoping to muddle enemy readings and give his ship the tumbling signature of a rogue asteroid, Han began to cycle power to the particle shields in a top-bottom pattern and deployed the emergency gas scoop—the ship's reactor could fuse raw hydrogen if necessary.

Meewalh's voice finally came over the subspace, a little scratchy due to signal loss inside the absorption nebula. "Lady Vader, we were not expecting to hear from you. All is well?"

"For now." Leia began the data dump. "See that this information reaches—"

Leia gasped and let the sentence break off, one hand rising to her chest, her expression growing pained and distant.

"Lady Vader?"

"Leia?" Han reached over to touch her arm, but she signaled him to wait.

"Here, Meewalh." She closed her eyes and seemed to collect herself, then continued, "I need you to see that the data package I sent reaches Wedge Antilles and Garm Bel Iblis in Fleet Command—at once; do what you must to succeed. Send copies to Luke and to Lando Calrissian, along with my suggestion that they offer their services to Admiral Sovv. This could mean the war for us."

"Lady Vader, it will be done."

Meewalh's tone was so flat she might as well have been promising to tell a neighbor the Solos would not make it home for drinks after all. But if she had to fight her way into Fleet Command, Han pitied the poor sentry or bureaucrat foolish enough to deny her access. Fortunately, the Noghri were as creative as they were stealthy, so she would probably just surprise the generals in the refresher or something and avoid unnecessary bloodshed.

Minuscule as friction was even inside a gas nebula, the drag created by the hydrogen scoop was enough to require an extra two seconds of ion glow. Han watched nervously as the *Falcon*'s vector converged with that of the investigating skips, trying to guess when the light of his ion drives would give them away, but the coralskippers continued as before until the burn finally came to an end. When he saw that they were slowing to swing in behind him—a standard safe approach for any unknown contact—and that their vector would not cross the *Falcon*'s until after it reached the asteroid cluster, he exhaled in relief. They still did not know what they were looking at.

Han found Leia staring out the viewport, her face the color of pearls, her expression distant and guarded. Recalling her unexplained gasp earlier—and her diplomat's habit of not showing her emotions until she had won control of them—he started to ask what was troubling her.

She cut him off before he spoke. "Later, Han." There was an alarming catch in her throat, but also that unyielding edge that he had learned was about as flexible as durasteel. "Pay attention to your flying."

A variation alarm sounded as they passed a straggler from the asteroid cluster large enough to exert its own gravitational pull. Han touched the alarm silent and plotted their new trajectory without making the suggested correction. Any such change would instantly alert the approaching skips of the *Falcon*'s true nature and ruin all hope of the New Republic catching the fleet unprepared.

The new trajectory pointed the *Falcon* out toward the dust ring, where Han would be forced to retract the gas scoop to avoid clogging the intake filters. He was still struggling with how to accomplish that without altering their flight signature when the variation alarm sounded again and another asteroid pulled them back toward the cluster.

Han plotted the new trajectory and saw they would hit—and soon. This was a big one, large enough so that its own gravity would shape it into a rough sphere, and it was bending their vector ever more sharply. Han saw only inky swirls of nebula gas beyond the transparisteel, but the asteroid was out there, off to their left, yet drifting toward the center of the viewport and looming larger every moment.

And it was just what they needed.

Han turned to the navigation computer and began to input blast radii and acceleration rates. The answer came back higher than he liked, and he had to concentrate to keep from cursing aloud.

"Leia, you know that trick Kyp is always doing with Jedi shadow bombs?"

"Define *know*," she said.

"About a kilometer a second," Han said. "I can get some initial acceleration by pressurizing the missile tube—"

"The *missile* tube, Han?"

"—then blowing the hatch," he finished. "But we'll be right behind it when the warhead detonates, and even Han Solo isn't that fast."

Leia's face paled. "You're not going to—"

"We don't have much time here," Han said, arming the missile. "Can you do it?"

Leia closed her eyes. "Which one?"

"Port tube."

Han instructed the computer to open the rear of the tube, then deactivated the missile's ion engine and overrode the launch safeties. By time he had completed all this, a deeper darkness had begun to emerge from the swirling nebula fog, a certain stillness that left no doubt about its solid nature.

Han depressed the launch trigger and heard a soft pop as the hatch cover swung open. Sucked from its tube by the sudden decompression, the missile drifted out from between the *Falcon*'s cargo mandibles and seemed to hang there.

"Now would be a good time," Han urged.

"I'm trying!"

The missile moved forward, picking up speed—but gradually.

"Well, it was a good idea," Han said, prepping the ion drives for a blast start. Leia was no Jedi—she had never had time for the rigorous training—but she could control the Force, and he had seen her move things heavier than the missile. Maybe the nebula interfered with the Force or something. "Nice try, but—"

The missile shot away, then vanished into the darkness.

"—that'll work," Han finished.

He moved his hand to the repulsorlift drives and waited. In the sensor display, the coralskippers omitted the detour caused by the first asteroid and cut straight for the one ahead. They would have a clear view of the impact—though hopefully not so clear they would see the matte-black *Falcon* silhouetted against the flash.

As soon as the first pinpoint of light caused the cockpit blast-tinting to darken, Han activated the repulsorlift drives and swung away, decelerating and turning almost as sharply as his earlier slam-pivot. The coralskippers would be in scanning range by now, but repulsorlifts were not nearly as conspicuous as ion drives, and he was betting the energy burst from the concussion missile would wash out whatever the skips were using for sensors.

They were around the horizon before the impact flash had begun to fade. Flying in the total darkness by sensors and instruments alone, Han slipped the *Falcon* into a deep stress rift, orienting it nose-up and using the landing gear to wedge it against the walls so the efflux nacelles would not be damaged.

"Now what?" Leia asked.

"We wait until they're done searching."

"You think they'll search?" Leia asked. "That concussion missile had to leave a pretty convincing crater."

"Yeah, but that's a big fleet," Han said. "They'll search—then they'll search some more."

Han shut down any of the *Falcon*'s systems that might leak so much as a photon of energy, then he and Leia lay back and stared into the darkness. He had purposely selected a rift facing the interior of the Bantha, so even the stars were too shrouded in nebula gas to count. It reminded Han of being frozen in carbonite—except that he had not been conscious of time in carbonite.

"How long do you think we'll have to wait?" Leia asked.

"Longer than we like." Han had a bad feeling about her gasp earlier and wanted to ask about it, but knew better than to press. "We'll know."

"How?"

"We'll get tired of waiting."

They were silent some more, then Leia just said it. "Anakin's been hurt."

Han's heart collapsed like a black hole. "Hurt?"

He began to depress actuator buttons and toggle circuit switches. Even with so many systems shut down and cool, the *Falcon*'s start-up sequence was remarkably short. They would be launched and on their way in less than three minutes.

"Han?" There was frailty in Leia's voice. "Where are we going?"

"Huh?" Han primed the ion drives and began a twenty-second countdown. "Where do you think we're going?"

"I have no idea," Leia said. "Because I *know* you'd never have let Anakin go through with that hypercrazed surrender plan if there was some other way to reach Myrkr."

The count reached fifteen, and Han's finger automatically swung over to the actuator and hovered there waiting for twenty.

Then he finally grasped why Leia had waited for the *Falcon* to cool down before telling him, and stopped counting.

"There's not another way." He deactivated the primers and began to shut down the rest of the systems, then found the strength to ask, "Is it bad?"

Leia's only response was a nod.

Han wanted to do *something*—protect Anakin or help Leia with what she must be feeling through the Force—but how could he defend a son from a thousand light-years away? Or assume Leia's burden, when he could not even sense the Force, much less feel Anakin's wound through it?

"At least he's not alone." Han reached over to her and noticed that his hand was trembling. He laid it on her arm anyway. "Jaina's there."

"And Jacen."

"Yeah, and Jacen." Given Jacen's recent moral dilemma over using the Force, Han was not accustomed to thinking of his oldest son in the role of a Jedi warrior, but on Duro it had been Jacen who faced Tsavong Lah and saved Leia's life. "The twins will look after him."

"That's right." Leia nodded absently, her thoughts already back on Myrkr a thousand light-years away. "He has the twins."

The last glow faded from the cockpit displays, and they sat in the dark, alone with their thoughts and still close enough to hear each other breathe.

After a time, Han could stand it no longer. "I wish I hadn't said those things when Chewbacca died," he said. "I really wish I hadn't blamed Anakin."

A warm hand found his. "That's over, Han. Really."

They waited in silence, pondering the same unanswerable questions—how serious? how did it happen? was he safe now?—for what seemed an eternity. Once, Han saw a glimmer of purple cross over the rift, but it was so faint and fleeting that he thought it more likely to be a trick of his light-starved eyes than the glow of a Yuuzhan Vong cockpit. For the most part, they just sat and waited, not even able to confirm that the New Republic *would* be sending an attack fleet, since the *Falcon*'s subspace transceiver antenna was shielded by several kilometers of iron asteroid.

With the sensor dish pointed into the heart of the Bantha, the one thing they could do to occupy themselves was periodically risk a passive scan to update their data. Eventually, it grew obvious that the Yuuzhan Vong were drawing vessels not just from the flotilla that had grabbed Reecee, but from active duty stations all over the galaxy. Most of the arriving vessels went straight to the heart of the fleet and lined up to nurse food and munitions at the big ship tenders. Han was relieved to see that the Yuuzhan Vong were only marginally faster at the process than his own fleet had been when he was a general. At the rate the enemy was reprovisioning, even the cumbersome New Republic Fleet Command would have time to make a decision; he only hoped they would bring enough ships.

The first hint of action came when a sensor sweep showed two skips—almost certainly the pair that had followed them to the asteroid—streaking toward the heart of the Bantha. Shuddering at how many times they had discussed leaving their hiding place, Han activated all passive scanning systems and plotted the results on the main data display. The screen looked as though someone had blasted a nest of killer stingnats, with frigate- and corvette-analog yorik coral vessels boiling out toward the protostar's opposite rim and more than a hundred cruiser and destroyer analogs moving to the heart of the formation, forming a sphere of protection around the enormous ship tenders.

"It certainly doesn't look like a jump configuration," Leia commented.

"No, that's their 'taken-by-surprise' configuration," Han said.

"Store this for analysis—it's not a formation the New Republic has seen before."

Han cold-started the repulsorlift drives and lifted the *Falcon* out of the rift. They had barely cleared the rim before the voice of a communications officer came over the tactical comm unit.

"—hailing the *Millennium Falcon*." The energy-absorbing effects of the nebula gas rendered the young woman's voice thready and full of static. "Repeat, this is the New Republic scout vessel *Gabrielle* hailing the *Millennium Falcon*. Please respond on S-thread six zero niner."

"The coordinates don't match the bearing to the battle," Leia said. She tapped the data display, indicating a position a quarter of the way around the circle from where the corvettes and frigates were headed—and on the Reecee side of the Bantha. "Could the Yuuzhan Vong be pulling a Friendly Hutt?"

"If some traitor told them we were out here, why not?" A Friendly Hutt was an old Imperial tactic in which they tried to trick their quarry into giving away its position. "But we have to take the chance. This is no time to be a coward—not with the war hanging in the balance."

Han did not add "and not when our children are risking their own lives," but Leia heard him just the same. As he started to bring the rest of the *Falcon*'s systems on-line, she activated the subspace transceiver and entered the coordinates provided.

"This is the *Millennium Falcon*—"

"Thank the Force!" Wedge Antilles exclaimed. "We've been trying to raise you for an hour. I thought something unfortunate had happened."

Han and Leia glanced at each other, but said nothing about Anakin. "We had a couple of skips sitting on us." Leia's fingers flew across the computer input. "Here's the data we promised."

As she spoke, the first bursts of battle static appeared on the sensor display. The assault fleet itself was too distant to be detected through the nebula gas even with active sensors, but Han could tell by the fire that there were only a few hundred vessels attacking. Still, scores of Yuuzhan Vong frigates and corvettes vanished into stars of dispersing energy before they could organize themselves into a picket wall. The *Falcon* was too distant from the battle to detect anything as small as a starfighter, but Han knew they were present by the sparks of explosion static that appeared all too frequently between the Yuuzhan Vong vessels.

By now, the New Republic fleet had its own surveillance craft watching the battle, but Han and Leia held their position and continued to relay data to the oddly placed command post. In a conflict this size, information was more valuable than ships, and both combatants placed a premium on destroying, blinding, or misleading enemy reconnaissance vessels. That made the *Falcon,* as an undetected observation asset, more important to the attack than any three Star Destroyers.

Slowly—painfully—the Yuuzhan Vong frigates and corvettes overcame their initial disorganization and started to hold the starfighters at bay. With this threat brought under control, the big capital ships left their places in the heart of the formation and went forward to support their smaller companions. As they drew into range of the New Republic's own capital ships, bright bars of energy began to flash back and forth across the data display, at times lighting it up so brightly Han could not see anything else. Eventually, the battle began to drift in the wrong direction, and Han knew their long wait had been for nothing.

He activated the subspace microphone. "Wedge, are you getting this?"

"We are, Han—but you're the only asset still showing the situation in the heart of the protostar. Please stay on station."

"What for?" Han grumbled. "Sovv didn't bring enough ships. Tell him to break off and save what he can."

"Negative, Han." Wedge did not sound nearly upset enough. "We can't do that."

A Yuuzhan Vong destroyer analog pressed the attack too hard and erupted into a two-second flare of light, and frigates and corvettes continued to vanish at a steady rate. But the battle continued to drift in toward New Republic lines. Soon, a discernible gap appeared between the capital ships participating in the attack and those that had remained behind to protect the huge ship tenders. In a gesture of what had to be the ultimate disdain for the New Republic commanders, a quarter of the big ships redocked with the supply vessels and continued to reprovision.

"Now, that is just too arrogant," Wedge commented. "Admiral Sovv needs to teach them a lesson."

"I hope he scolds better than he counts," Han muttered.

"Han . . ." Leia cautioned.

Han ignored her and continued bitterly, "Our message said there were a thousand ships—and more arriving every minute!"

"But I had only nine hundred ready for action," a pinched Sullustan voice said. "And your message also said to hurry."

Leia closed her eyes and let her chin fall. "Admiral Sovv, please excuse my husband's impatience."

"No apology is necessary," Admiral Sovv said. "We'll be out of contact for eight minutes, but I'm sending you our order of battle. Can you have a tactical update ready when we make contact again?"

Instead of answering, Leia turned to Han with an expectant expression.

"Uh, sure thing," Han said. When Leia scowled, he added, "Admiral."

"Good." This from Wedge. "And we have a request from Eclipse. They'll be looking for the yammosk and would appreciate any guidance you can give them."

"Tell them we'll try to narrow the possibilities down to no more than a hundred ships." Han rolled his eyes as Wedge and the admiral signed off, then turned to Leia. "I guess Luke must have found his boarding harpoons."

"Or had someone make them," Leia said. "I only hope they work on yorik coral."

Used legally and illegally across the galaxy by security forces, pirates, and anyone else who wanted to storm a ship, boarding harpoons were a recent development. Basically giant hypodermics filled with coma gas, they melted through a target's hull with a megaheated tip, then lodged themselves in the hole, extended a flexiglass membrane to seal the vacuum breach, and injected the gas. Depending on a ship's size and recirculation system, everyone aboard could be rendered unconscious in anywhere from a minute to a quarter hour. For the sake of the Jedi who would be using them, Han hoped it would be closer to a minute.

They spent the next few minutes scanning the heart of the protostar, identifying high-priority targets, calculating ranges and hit probabilities, estimating how quickly the capital ships on the front line would be able to disengage and return to the heart of the protostar. In less than five minutes, they had a situation report that clearly suggested it would be wise to attack cautiously and conservatively, despite the advantage of surprise. It was not exactly the decisive blow Han had hoped for, but there was no arguing with facts.

Then Leia frowned, said something didn't "feel" right, and began to work the computer again. Han scanned and rescanned the entire Bantha and stared at the data display without blinking. Everything felt right to him. He even managed to narrow the likely yammosk ships down to three destroyer analogs and half a dozen big cruisers.

Leia was still working the computer, muttering softly to herself and taking notes in a datapad, when New Republic contacts began to blizzard onto the sensor display, jumping almost directly into battle because of the protostar's dispersed mass shadow. By the time Admiral Sovv's flagship emerged from hyperspace, the lead vessels were already bleeding starfighters and pouring turbolaser fire into the Yuuzhan Vong capital ships.

The communications officer quickly established a comlink, and Leia sent the tactical update on an encrypted data channel. While they waited for Wedge and Admiral Sovv to digest the new information, Han was surprised to see the Yuuzhan Vong capital ships remaining close to the ship tenders instead of rushing out to engage the incoming fleet and buy time for their comrades to return from the forward battle.

He opened a voice channel. "Wedge, maybe you should have your forward elements hang back. Those rocks are hiding something."

"Yes, they are," Leia said, finally looking up from her datapad. "But don't hang back. Those ships haven't provisioned yet. That's what they're hiding."

Admiral Sovv was on the channel at once. "Are you sure?"

"I am, Admiral. Our computer issued an identifier to each contact, and I just ran a full history of each one. None of them has docked with the tenders."

"I see," Sovv said. "Your recommendation would be?"

Before answering, Leia looked to Han. If her analysis was right, the tactics that followed from their report would be too conservative, perhaps even give the enemy a chance to disengage and escape. But if she was wrong . . . she was not. Han could feel it.

He nodded.

Leia smiled at him, then she said, "Go for sabacc, Admiral. Our recommendation is bet the fleet."

"I see." Sovv was barely able to choke out that much; Sullustans were seldom happy gamblers. "An unusual way to put it, but . . . thank you for your suggestion."

Han winced, then checked to make sure they weren't transmitting. "That's what's wrong with putting Sullustans in command. They're more interested in building careers than winning battles."

"Not this one, I think."

Leia pointed at the display, where the largest part of the New Republic fleet—including all of the Star Destroyers and most of the cruisers—were peeling away from the ship tenders and fanning out toward the far edge of the Bantha. Their turbolasers were already flashing, pouring bolts into the rear of the Yuuzhan Vong battle line. Several cruiser analogs and two destroyer-sized vessels began to break up instantly. Others quickly followed when they turned to meet this new threat and were assaulted from behind by a now-lethal decoy force. The two walls of New Republic ships began to come together, smashing the disorganized Yuuzhan Vong between them.

In the core of the protostar, a swirling cloud of smaller vessels swarmed the tenders and their escorts. The Yuuzhan Vong held their attack until the enemy was almost upon them, then loosed a wave of fire so intense that Han and Leia could actually see the glow, lighting the heart of the Bantha like the star it would one day be. The sensor display required nearly a minute to clear, and when it did, a full quarter of the New Republic contacts had simply vanished.

Leia closed her eyes. "Han, did I—"

"They're Yuuzhan Vong, Leia," he said. "You know they're going to fight back—with rocks, if need be."

They watched in apprehension as the tender escorts continued to lace the heart of the Bantha with plasma balls and magma missiles, sometimes taking whole frigates out in single volleys. Finally, though, the fire began to dwindle, and the destroyer analogs started to take hits. Whole squadrons of New Republic starfighters darted past the lumbering vessels to pelt the defenseless ship tenders with proton torpedoes and concussion missiles. It took only a few minutes of this bombardment before the core of the protostar lit up again even more brightly as one supply vessel after another disintegrated in the heat of its own detonating cargo.

A few minutes later, Luke's voice came over the comm unit. "Han, can you come down here? We've got some cargo we need you to drop off at Eclipse."

"Live cargo?" Leia asked. Danni Quee had been trying to capture a live yammosk since before Booster had told them about the fall of Reecee.

"That's affirmative," Luke reported.

"Sabacc!" Han said. "Pure sabacc!"

Chapter 38

Anakin's anguished body was screaming for a stop, a trance, any kind of escape. But that was not possible, not with Nom Anor and his company coming up the passage. The Yuuzhan Vong were hanging behind now, just far enough so even the Barabels had lost their sound, but Anakin could still feel the enemy through the lambent, a cold aura of anger and malice pressing the strike team onward, always pushing, always threatening.

The Yuuzhan Vong had been back there since the slave city, harrying the Jedi whenever their pace lagged, assailing them with bug attacks and provoking them into firing their weapons. Though the assaults had escalated, Nom Anor had not changed tactics. He was still beleaguering the strike team, still wearing it down, still trying to take a few prizes alive.

And Anakin had given the one-eyed spy no reason to try anything else. He had avoided the trap at the AT-AT, only to wander into the ambush in the slave city like some dustkicker straight off a moisture farm. Distressed by the plight of the inhabitants, he had allowed Nom Anor's impostors to sneak up on the strike team. Now Eryl and Jovan were dead. Anakin should have remembered Nom Anor's predilection for subterfuge and foreseen the attack, should have at least kept the crowd away from his Jedi. He should have been more careful. He—

Jaina thumped him behind the ear. "Stop that."

"What?" Anakin rubbed his ear, then his concentration slipped and pain roared through him in waves of fire. "And thanks for caring."

"You can feel sorry for yourself," Jaina said. A thin line stretched diagonally across her forehead where Tekli had sealed the gash over her eye with synthflesh. "You were reckless, Anakin, and you paid the price—and that's not the point. You need to stop blaming yourself."

The distant rustle of Yuuzhan Vong feet came up the passage. Anakin tried not to let it weaken his concentration and asked, "Who should I blame?"

"The war," Jaina said. "Do you think Uncle Luke sent us here to train? This is important. If people die, people die."

"That's a little cold."

"I'll cry at home." Jaina hazarded a glance over her shoulder, then said, "Maybe you made a mistake, maybe you didn't. But start focusing on the mission, or more people *will* die."

Jaina held his eye for a moment, then the distant rustle of feet grew louder, and they concentrated on running. The strike team passed one of the waist-high tunnels that descended into the warrens of the "feral" voxyn. According to Lomi and Welk, the ferals were creatures the trainers simply lost. Eventually, the beasts found their way to the slave city—the only consistent source of prey in the training maze—and laired in these caves. With an irregular shape, acid-pocked walls, and an overpowering stench of decay, the tunnel certainly seemed like something the creatures might have excavated. Everyone except the Barabels donned their breath masks.

Anakin wore his for perhaps a thousand steps before he pulled it off and discovered that, while the air was fresher, his breath came no easier. He began to feel feverish and realized that his pain was creeping up on him, eating through his Force defenses. Something serious was wrong.

Clearing his mind as he ran, Anakin opened himself completely to the Force. Though hardly a talented healer, he knew his own body well enough to follow the ripples of disturbance down into his wound, to feel that something had come loose inside. He reached under his equipment harness and touched a wet bandage. When he withdrew his hand, his palm was crimson.

"Anakin!" This came from Tahiri, who was, as always, running alongside him. "What's that?"

"Nothing."

Anakin concentrated on the tear inside, tried to use the Force to draw the edges together—and was too weak to concentrate. He stumbled and would have fallen, had not Tahiri reached out with the Force and levitated him.

"Need help!" she cried.

The strike team slowed, Jaina and several others crowding around even as Anakin protested he was all right.

"Neg that!" Tahiri ordered. "You're not all right—not even close."

The sound of the Yuuzhan Vong feet swelled to tramping. Tekli emerged from somewhere under and between Ganner and Raynar, who were sharing the burden of carrying Eryl's body.

"Keep him levitated!" Jaina ordered. She plucked Tekli off the ground and set the Chadra-Fan astride Anakin's legs, then grabbed his wrist and started up the passage. "Everyone, move!"

Anakin tried to insist that he needed no help, but managed only a gurgle. One of the Barabels dropped a flechette mine to delay the Yuuzhan Vong, and the strike team broke into a hard run. Tekli began to undo bandages, her weight barely noticeable on his Force-supported legs. The Chadra-Fan tossed the blood-soaked bacta gauze aside and placed her hand over the wound. The Force flowed into Anakin, yet his strength continued to fade.

"We must stop," Tekli said.

"No." Anakin's voice was barely a whisper. "Can't let . . ."

Tekli ignored him. "He has internal bleeding. I need to see what's happening."

"How much time?" Jaina asked.

"That depends on what I find," Tekli said. "Fifteen minutes, maybe twice that."

The tramping of Yuuzhan Vong feet grew steadier, and the Force stirred with the familiar hunger of voxyn on the hunt. These were not the free-roaming beasts that had been harassing the Jedi so far, but well-trained creatures kept on leashes by experienced handlers. The strike team had killed three already; if the pack was typical, there would be only one more.

Everyone hoped it was a typical pack.

Alema stared back down the passage toward the approaching threat, then turned to Jaina. "I can buy us fifteen minutes." Her voice sounded strangely distant. "I need half a dozen concussion grenades."

Dimly, Anakin heard Ganner say, "Do it," and saw him flip something to the Twi'lek. She danced over to the Barabels, then all four sprinted up the passage ahead of the strike team.

Anakin slipped closer to delirium and began to lose his sense of the others in the Force. He could always feel Tahiri at his side, telling him he was going to be fine. He believed her, but could not muster the strength to say so and squeezed her hand instead.

Time passed—it couldn't have been much—and the hum of a lightsaber filled the passage. They passed close to Tesar, and Anakin glimpsed Alema sitting on his shoulders, pushing her silver blade into the ceiling. Behind her, Bela was on her sister's shoulders, using Jovan Drark's longblaster to tamp a wad of cloth into a similar hole.

Alema took a grenade from Tesar and reached up to push it into the hole she had made, then Tahiri pulled Anakin around a corner and he lost sight of what was happening. He heard—clearly—one of the Barabels rasp "six seconds" and knew Tekli was stabilizing him, perhaps even bringing him back.

Anakin lifted his head and saw Alema and the Barabels come racing around the corner behind the rest of the team, then heard an all-too-familiar drone coming up the passage. A pair of thud bugs splatted into Alema's back; they failed to penetrate her jumpsuit, but sent her sprawling. Tesar caught her on the run, pulling her into his grasp and continuing up the passage without breaking stride.

An instant later, a shock wave jolted Anakin, and his earplugs sealed themselves against the roar of falling yorik coral. Dust billowed off the passage walls, and as the cloud overtook the team, Tekli pushed Anakin's breath mask over his face.

The Jedi continued another thirty paces and stopped. Tekli had Anakin lowered to the floor and gave Jaina a tube of stinksalts to rouse Alema, then pushed her small hands into Anakin's wound and up under his rib cage. He tried not to scream and failed. She continued to work, issuing half-whispered instructions to Tahiri. Anakin looked down once and found Tekli's small arms immersed to the elbow. Darkness closed around the edges of his vision, and he did not look again.

The sound of blasterfire began to drift up the passage from the cave-in. Anakin tried to raise his head, only to have his brother push it back down.

"Don't worry," Jacen said. "Everyone's well covered."

"Alema . . . hurt?" Anakin gasped.

"Angry." Jacen waved in the direction of the battle line. "Already blasting Yuuzhan Vong—and enjoying it."

"Good reason!" Anakin retorted. "After—"

"Easy!" Jacen raised his hands in surrender. "I'm not being judgmental."

Anakin winced as a sharp needle pierced something inside. Then he forced up a doubtful brow.

"Really, I'm not," Jacen said.

The intensity of the blasterfire at the cave-in increased, then Lowbacca roared the announcement of a voxyn kill.

Jacen glanced toward the joyful sound uneasily, then said, "Am I worried about what's happening to us? Sure. This war is bringing out all that's selfish and wicked in the New Republic, corrupting the galaxy star by star. I see it pulling one Jedi after another to the dark side, making us fight to win instead of protect. But I can't push others down my path. Everyone needs to choose for themselves. Centerpoint taught me that much."

"Fooled me."

"Fooled myself," Jacen said. "I thought I was the only one who knows the difference between right and wrong. I realized that wasn't true—actually, Tenel Ka pointed it out—after what I said on the *Exquisite Death*. I've been trying to apologize to you since."

"Really?" Anakin grimaced as one of Tekli's tiny hands brushed an organ that did not like being brushed. "Didn't know."

Jacen flashed a lopsided Solo grin. "I figured."

The zipping sound of blasters gave way to the *snap-hiss* of lightsabers, and Anakin raised his head. Atop the rubble pile, a solid line of colored blades was dancing against the darkness beyond.

"Got to go!" He pushed himself to his elbows. "Not getting anyone else killed."

"Except yourself, if you don't let me finish!" Tekli snapped. She nodded to Tahiri, who promptly pushed Anakin back down. "We can leave in a few seconds."

Anakin dared to look and found the Chadra-Fan coating the interior of his wound with salve. He was alarmed to discover he no longer felt her working.

"You numbed me?" he asked.

"To help with the pain." Tekli took a pad of bacta gauze from Tahiri and packed it into the wound. "But I can only do so much. You need a healing trance."

Anakin nodded. "When we're done."

Tekli looked up, her flattish nose twitching. "Sooner. Much sooner."

"Sooner?" Tahiri echoed. She glanced back toward the fight on the rubble pile. "But healing trances take hours—even days!"

Tekli ignored her and continued to speak to Anakin. "Your spleen was punctured." She looked back to her work, joining the edges of the wound with thread instead of synthflesh in case she needed to reopen it. "I closed the hole, but it will continue to seep until you enter a trance and heal it yourself."

"How's he going to do that?" Tahiri demanded. "We can't stop, not with the Yuuzhan Vong so close!"

There was an uneasy silence as the situation grew clear. Jacen tightened his lips to keep them from trembling and reached out to Anakin through the Force, trying to reassure him. Tahiri grabbed Tekli by the arm and pulled her to her feet.

"Do something! Use the Force!"

The Chadra-Fan laid a comforting hand over the one holding her arm. "I have."

"We must start with what's possible," Jacen said, pulling Tahiri away. "Maybe we'll find a way to buy enough time."

"Not by staying here," Anakin said. He felt more guilty than frightened; it was his wound placing the mission—and his companions' lives—at risk. He rolled to his elbows and sat upright, grimacing when Tekli's bacta numb proved weaker than he had expected. He activated his comlink, then said, "Prepare to break off. Buy some space."

Parrying with her one arm, Tenel Ka used the Force to pluck a fragmentation grenade from her harness and activate the thumb switch, then sent it hurling past her opponent. Two seconds later, it exploded with a brilliant flash, and the battle din quieted to a rumble.

"Lowbacca, Alema, Ganner, Lomi, Raynar—you first," Anakin commanded.

The five Jedi leapt backward off the rubble pile, flipping through the air and landing safely out of the reach of their foes. Anakin assigned Alema, Lomi, and Ganner to cover the others, then motioned Lowbacca and Raynar up the passage to gather their dead, Eryl and Jovan.

"Where?" Raynar demanded. "Eryl's body isn't here! Neither is Jovan's!"

"What?" Anakin glanced back to find Raynar and Lowbacca standing over a pair of bloodstains. "They're gone?"

Lowbacca rumbled indeed they were, then squatted to inspect some marks on the floor. He rumbled something more.

"Master Lowbacca wishes to inquire whether the feral voxyn might have taken them?" To this fairly accurate translation, Em Teedee added his own opinion. "I must say, it hardly seems possible—not from beneath our very noses."

Anakin turned to Jacen, who had already closed his eyes and reached out to the ferals through the Force.

"There are four—no, five—moving up the passage ahead of us. They seem, uh, excited."

"Excited?" Alema asked, turning her attention forward. "How?"

The cacophony atop the rubble pile grew suddenly louder, and Anakin looked up to see Yuuzhan Vong silhouettes clambering into the gaps between his friends.

"Later, Alema," Anakin said. "Keep covering." He activated his comlink. "Break off, everyone!"

As the rest of the Jedi battle line stepped off the rubble pile, Anakin grabbed his brother's arm and pulled himself to his feet—and instantly collapsed. It was as if a lance had pierced his heart, and he screamed so loud his voice echoed back to him a dozen-fold. Then Jacen and Tahiri had him under the arms, dragging him half a dozen steps down the passage before they levitated him into the air.

Bugs swarmed down from the top of the rubble pile, drawing angry curses as they splattered against the strike team's armored jumpsuits. Someone thumbed a remote, triggering the mines planted on opposite sides atop the rubble pile, and the bug storm fell silent. Anakin glanced back to see the area clouded in blast shrapnel, the fragments burying themselves two millimeters deep in bare flesh, vonduun crab armor, or even yorik coral before detonating again. The Yuuzhan Vong literally vanished in a fog of detonite fume and blood spray.

The anguish in Anakin's chest subsided, and was quickly replaced by a different kind, coming to him through the battle meld—a heavier, sadder pain that could be described only as sorrow. He swung his feet around, breaking Tahiri's Force grip, and began to run alongside the others. A large Barabel body was floating between her hatchmates, being pulled along by her arms. The amphistaff that had felled her still wagged between her shoulder blades.

"Bela!" Anakin half turned toward Jacen. "Is she . . ."

There was no need to finish the question. He could feel that she was dead, knew that the amphistaff buried in her back was the source of the pain that had driven him down earlier. He had let another Jedi die—worse, had not even noticed until she was gone. Yet again, he had failed his strike team.

Nom Anor's muted voice shouted an order somewhere on the other side of the rubble heap, and a muffled clatter rolled up the passage as warriors began to clamber over the bodies of their fallen comrades.

Jacen took Anakin's arm. "Let Tahiri lift—"

"No." Anakin jerked free. "Not again. It was my wound. I forced us to stop."

Lowbacca triggered a second set of mines, and again the rubble pile quieted. By now, the strike team was around the corner, out of sight of their pursuers and opening a substantial lead. Anakin drew heavily on the Force and made himself keep pace. He was weakening—and he knew by his friends' anxious glances how obvious it was—but he would not let Tahiri tire herself for him. Not anyone. No more Jedi were going to die because of him. Not even Dark Jedi.

It was not even a minute before Anakin felt the Yuuzhan Vong gaining ground again. There was no ambush, no trap that would delay them. Nom Anor just kept coming, forcing the Jedi onward, soaking up munitions with his warriors' bodies and drawing down power packs with their lives. And the Jedi could do nothing to slow him, could only keep running.

A sour stench began to fill the passage. Everyone but Tesar and Krasov donned their breath masks. They rounded the corner and saw Eryl's red hair disappearing into a low jagged tunnel on the right. Raynar raced forward and dropped to his knees, screaming for the voxyn to release her, reaching inside its acid-melted lair.

Anakin stretched out with the Force and plucked him back into the main passage.

"Hey!" Raynar yelled, flailing.

A low burping sound erupted from the lair, and a spray of sticky acid shot out into the passage. Raynar stopped struggling.

"Uh, thanks." He glanced over. "Anakin, you can put me down. I'm not going in there."

"Are you certain?" Alema went over to the tunnel and—cautiously—stooped in front of it, peering inside. "This is exactly where we need to go."

"You've gone space happy," Welk said.

"Twi'leks do not go space happy," Alema replied mildly.

The distant sound of Yuuzhan Vong feet began to rustle up the passage.

Alema held her palm over the tunnel entrance, then pulled it away and looked up the main passage. "Has anyone else noticed that we have been circling around something?"

Anakin shook his head with the others. "We'll have to trust your instincts on that," he said. As a Twi'lek, Alema's sense of direction was undoubtedly more accurate than that of anyone else; her species inhabited a vast warren of underground cities on the inhospitable planet Ryloth. "What are you thinking?"

"This hole is breathing." Eyes twinkling, she took Anakin's hand and held it in the steady breeze that carried the foul stench from the voxyn tunnel. "It goes somewhere big, and it bisects whatever we're circling around. It could be a shortcut."

"Not one we can use," Jacen said. "The voxyn are protecting something down there. I'm trying to make them think they need to stay with it."

The sound of tramping began to roll up the passage. They all glanced back toward their unseen pursuers.

Ganner said, "Then you make the voxyn leave instead." He turned to Anakin. "We've got to do something."

Even before Anakin turned to ask if what Ganner suggested was possible, Jacen gave an almost imperceptible shake of his head.

Anakin looked to Lomi. "What's down there?"

The Dark Jedi shrugged. "Voxyn, I am sure—but the snake-head may be right. It could be a shortcut. There are more tunnels like this one near the gate."

"Gate?" Anakin was already imagining the difficulty of fighting through a company of gate guards with Nom Anor rushing them from behind. "A guarded gate?"

Lomi nodded. "You can be certain."

Anakin began to feel sick. There was no way, no escape.

The tramping grew louder.

"Anakin?" Ganner asked.

"There's no choice," Jaina said, inserting herself between the two. "We need time for your healing trance."

"We are unlikely to buy much time in a cavern full of voxyn," Tenel Ka observed. "Quite the opposite, I am sure."

Anakin glance guiltily in Bela's direction. He knew what he wanted to do, but he had been wrong so many times on this mission, and every time, someone fell. Now he had to choose again. No matter what he decided, more Jedi would die. Maybe they all would.

"Young Solo?" Lomi inquired. "We are waiting."

Anakin turned to Jacen. "What do—"

"Thanks for asking," Jacen interrupted, not quite hiding his surprise. He took a thermal detonator from his equipment harness and dropped to his hands and knees in front of the foul-smelling tunnel. "But you know what we need to do. I think we *all* do."

Chapter 39

The smell was more sweet than rank, at least to Tsavong Lah, whose limb was the one rotting. The radank leg with which the shapers had replaced his arm was overbonding to his elbow, the aggressive linking cells attacking and killing his own tissue well above the amputation point. Scales and spines were already emerging as high up as his swollen biceps, and above that his arm swarmed with the diptera maggots seeded by the shapers to eat away his dying flesh.

If the alteration stopped at his shoulder, he would be accorded the respect of one who had sacrificed much and risked more in his devotion to the gods. If it continued onto his torso proper, or he lost the arm itself, he would be excused from his duties and shunned by his caste as a Shamed One, disfigured by the gods as a sign of their displeasure. Tsavong Lah suspected that where the alteration stopped would depend on how long he allowed the loss of his Reecee fleet to delay the capture of Coruscant—and that, in turn, depended on how long it required Nom Anor and Vergere to capture the Solo twins. With half his assault force now gone, and the possibility—no, likelihood—that the *Jeedai* had captured a live yammosk, he did not dare attack until he had secured the blessing of the gods.

His mind made up, the warmaster grasped a villip resting beside him and began to tickle it awake. Though he was sitting naked in the purifying steams of his private cleansing cell, Tsavong Lah did not bother to cover himself. The villip in his servant's possession would show only a head.

After an irritating wait of nearly a minute, the villip everted into the likeness of a huffing Nom Anor. Giving the executor no opportunity to apologize for making him wait, Tsavong Lah scowled.

"I trust you are chasing the *Jeedai,* Nom Anor, and not fleeing them."

"Never," the executor assured him. "Even as we speak, I am leading the *Ksstarr*'s Two Scourge in pursuit."

"Will you catch them?"

"Yes," Nom Anor said. "We are taking casualties, but Three Scourge is waiting in ambush at the end of this transit. There is no escape this time."

The casualties did not interest Tsavong Lah. He had already heard how many vessels the *Jeedai* had destroyed above Myrkr and how they had slain the *Ksstarr*'s first company—One Scourge—to a warrior, and he would have considered twice the losses insignificant.

"You will not harm the twin Solos." It had to be the fourth or fifth time Tsavong Lah had given the order, but, now more than ever, he wanted Nom Anor to understand. "Your warriors understand the fate awaiting the one who kills either of them?"

"As do I, Warmaster," Nom Anor said. "The twins are forbidden targets. I have also commanded Yal Phaath to have his own troops stand off—though he bristles at my authority. It would be wise of you to underscore the order."

"As you suggest," Tsavong Lah agreed, ignoring for the

moment his servant's audacity in telling him what to do. "I need those sacrifices, Nom Anor. Our situation is deteriorating while I wait for you."

"You will not need to wait much longer, Warmaster," Nom Anor promised. "My plan is an excellent one."

"That would be healthy for you," Tsavong Lah warned. "I expect to hear from you soon."

He pressed his thumb into the villip's cheek, causing it to break contact and invert. The warmaster set this one aside and picked up Viqi Shesh's, considering whether the time had come to expend this particular asset. Since her removal from the New Republic's military oversight committee, she had been working doubly hard to prove her usefulness to the Yuuzhan Vong—less out of greed or power lust, Tsavong Lah thought, than a simple thirst for vengeance. Such weapons tended to be very explosive—which could be good or bad, depending on when they were detonated.

The steam-cell door spiraled open behind him, admitting a cool draft that wafted pleasantly across his naked back. Without turning around, he snapped, "Did I not say I was cleansing? How dare you disturb me."

"My life in payment, Warmaster." The voice belonged to Seef, his female communications assistant. "But the choice was not mine. Lord Shimrra's villip has everted."

Not bothering to cover himself, Tsavong Lah stood and turned, already reaching for the coufee Seef held ready for him. Except in circumstances involving breeding, it was forbidden for a subordinate to look upon his naked body and live—but when he saw her eyes flickering away from the suppurating flesh above his graft, he left the weapon in her hand. If he killed her now, the gods might well believe that he was simply trying to keep the condition of his arm a secret.

Tsavong Lah studied the communications officer a moment, pushed the coufee away, and narrowed his eyes in a way that left no doubt about his intentions. "You will prepare yourself."

"Yes, Warmaster." Her face betraying no hint of whether she considered this a better fate than death, Seef returned the coufee to its sheath and inclined her head. "I will await you in your chamber."

After she stepped aside, Tsavong Lah left his steam cell and draped a cloak over his shoulder hooks, taking care to keep the sleeve well above his elbow so that the condition of his graft would be visible to all. He found Lord Shimrra's villip set out on the table, its features cloaked in obscurity beneath the cowl-like protrusion of an epidermal mane. The warmaster touched his breast in salute and placed his palm and new talon on the table in front of the villip, then pressed his forehead to the back of his hands.

"Supreme One," he said. "Forgive the delay. I was cleansing."

"The gods value the pure." Shimrra's voice was a wispy rumble. "But also the triumphant. What of this fleet you lost?"

"The gods have reason to be displeased. The loss was total—six clusters."

"An expensive feint, my servant."

Tsavong's throat went dry. "Supreme One, it was no—"

"I am sure your plan warrants the sacrifice," Shimrra said, cutting him off. "That is not why we are speaking."

"Indeed?" Tsavong did not try to correct Shimrra; if the supreme overlord declared the fleet's loss a feint, then it was so. The warmaster's mind leapt immediately to the problem of shattering Coruscant's formidable defenses with only a single-pronged attack—perhaps a variation of the mine-sweeping moon he had intended to use at Borleias, or something involving refugee ships. Refugee ships would be good—the furor over the hostages at Talfaglio had proven how vulnerable to such techniques the New Republic really was. As the rough outline of an idea began to take shape in the warmaster's mind, he said, "I assure you my plan is an excellent one, Supreme One, but I am honored to speak with you regarding any matter."

Before continuing, Shimrra hesitated just long enough to express his displeasure without speaking it, then said, "The success of your new grafting is in doubt?"

"It is so," Tsavong Lah answered. He did not ask, even of himself, how Lord Shimrra knew of his troubles with the radank leg. "I fear my arm may have offended the gods."

"It is not your arm, my servant. I saw nothing of that."

Tsavong Lah remained quiet, desperately trying to work out in his own mind whether Shimrra's vision was the reason they were speaking or merely the excuse.

"It is the twins, my servant," Shimrra said. "The gods will give us Coruscant, and you will give them these twins."

"It will be so, Supreme One," Tsavong Lah said. "Even now, my servants are running them to ground."

"You are certain?" Shimrra asked. "The gods will not be disappointed again."

"My servants assure me their plan is an excellent one." It did not escape Tsavong Lah's notice that Nom Anor's words had been much the same as his own to Lord Shimrra. "There is no escape."

"Let it be so." Shimrra was silent for a moment, then said, "See and be seen, my servant."

Tsavong raised his head, but said nothing. He had been invited to look, not speak.

"Know this, Tsavong Lah," Shimrra said. "In allowing your villip tender to live, you have kept for yourself one who should belong to the gods."

Tsavong Lah went cold inside. "Supreme One, this is so, but it was not my intention—"

"It pleases the gods to let you keep her. Do not insult them by explaining what they know." Shimrra's villip began to invert. "Use her well, my servant. All things are forgiven in victory."

Chapter 40

Tattooed sparsely beneath his sagging eyes and bearing no mutilations except a hole beneath his lip that looked like a second mouth, the Yuuzhan Vong was clearly a raw recruit, probably assigned to point duty for the sole purpose of drawing fire. Praying that the shadows in the tunnel were deep enough to hide her, Jaina used the Force to press her back more tightly to the ceiling. She held her breath as the warrior crawled another meter into the cave. Holding an activated lambent at arm's length, he used his amphistaff to prod the floor beneath Jaina. She could see the weapon's snakish shape and knew her own silhouette had to be just as visible, but the Yuuzhan Vong did not look up. He merely gagged on the stench of the place and retreated. When he reached the entrance, he rose and yelled *"fas!"* and continued up the main passage.

Jaina remained where she was, watching vonduun-crab-armored legs march past, desperately hoping the next thing to peer inside would not be a voxyn. Though they had already killed four of the beasts—Lowbacca had blasted the last one at the cave-in—the possibility that Nom Anor had brought more than the standard number was the one weak point in strike team's plan. The Yuuzhan Vong could be expected to miss the Jedi's detour, but a voxyn could not. A voxyn would *feel* the change of direction.

A second Yuuzhan Vong, this time with the fringed earlobes and heavily branded face of a veteran, thrust his lambent crystal into the jagged tunnel. Like most of the Jedi on the strike team, Jaina had toyed with the idea of capturing one of the crystals, but it was certainly not worth the risk. Anakin's bond to his was unique, no doubt because of his role in growing it, and even he doubted that he could re-create the feat. Certainly, no one in the Eclipse Program had even been able to figure how the things reproduced. This time, the warrior searched the ceiling as well as the floor, but he rose and continued up the main passage without crawling inside.

Finally allowing herself a full breath, Jaina removed the flechette mine from her equipment harness. She set the signal feature to their comlink frequency and attached it to the ceiling in front of her. She did not activate it. Once she set the detonation selector to "motion," she would have only three seconds to leave sensor range, and she could not risk moving until all the Yuuzhan Vong had gone by.

The company seemed to take forever to pass. Without their pet voxyn to warn when Jedi were near, they moved warily, keeping a five-meter interval and looking for booby traps. Despite everything, the strike team remained alive, mobile, and—with a little help from the Force—capable of destroying the queen. Were Anakin in one piece, Jaina would have considered that a victory in itself.

She alternated between being scared for her brother and furious with him. She could not really blame Anakin for coming to her rescue—she would have done the same for him or Jacen—but she did. It had been a reckless and typically Anakin thing to do, spectacular, rash, effective—foolish. Tekli had made clear what would happen if they didn't find time to let him heal, and Anakin had made it just as clear that they were to place the mission above his life. Jaina was determined to do both, but if she had to make a choice . . . well, she had only two brothers, and she did not intend to leave either one behind.

Jaina felt Jacen reaching out to her through their twin bond and knew that, somewhere deeper in the tunnel, the others had encountered the first of the feral voxyn. She opened herself to the battle meld and was relieved to discover that Anakin's wound had drawn the group back together, though Zekk remained resentful about the Dark Jedi, and the others were distracted by concern for Anakin. Worried that any battle sounds from behind her would reverberate into the main passage, she summoned to mind the stillness of a Massassi temple and used the Force to expand this silence outside herself, creating—she hoped—a sphere of quiet between her companions and the Yuuzhan Vong.

Another set of vonduun-crab-armored legs passed the mouth of the tunnel. A pair of thin, reverse-articulated legs arrived next. They paused, folded down on themselves, and lowered a feathered torso into view. Jaina had to calm herself for fear that her pounding heartbeats would break the sphere of silence. A simian face with slanted eyes and delicate whiskers appeared atop the featherball and peered into the tunnel.

Vergere, or some being like her.

An alien presence touched Jaina's mind, startling her so badly she lost her concentration and dropped a hand's breadth before she regained composure and lifted herself back to the ceiling. She leveled her blaster pistol at Vergere's face.

A wry smile crossed the odd being's lips, and Jaina knew Vergere had touched her on purpose. But how—through the Force? It didn't seem possible. If Vergere was a Force-wielder, then the voxyn would hunt her, as well. Wouldn't they?

A thicket of vonduun-crab-armored legs gathered outside the tunnel. The silence barrier prevented Jaina from hearing whether the Yuuzhan Vong were speaking, but she did not doubt that Vergere knew of her proximity—even if she had not actually seen her. The alien presence was still touching her, taunting her, almost daring her to attack.

Jaina activated the flechette mine, then pushed herself back out of sensor range. Vergere's smile changed to a smirk, and the alien touch faded from Jaina's mind so quickly she began to wonder if she had felt it at all.

Vergere spoke to someone behind her. Jaina thumbed off her blaster safety lock, but her target turned and hopped up the passage before she could fire. The Yuuzhan Vong followed, and then even the memory of the alien touch dwindled away.

Jaina lowered her blaster and, shaking so hard she had to use both hands, reengaged the weapon's safety lock. She did not understand why she was so frightened. The creature had not even known she was there.

The other end of the voxyn tunnel opened into a grand corridor, six or seven meters high and wide enough to be a hovercar lane, but still dank and foul-smelling. Even in the small area lit by Jacen's glow stick, it curved away noticeably but gently, vanishing into darkness at both ends. The wall opposite the strike team's hiding place was breached by a pair of archways, set about twenty meters apart and each large enough for a rancor. Between these arches stood Wookiee-sized alcoves containing sculptures of the Yuuzhan Vong's bulbous-headed, many-tentacled god of war, Yun-Yammka. Above every alcove hung another alcove, empty and upside down, with the top pointing at the floor.

Once, Lomi had explained, the giant worldship had spun on an axis, generating artificial gravity through centrifugal force just as smaller versions did. Sometime during the journey between galaxies, the central brain had lost its ability to control the spin, breaking off the vessel's spiral arms and destabilizing the whole system. The shapers had switched to dovin basal–induced gravity, forcing the entire worldship to reorient its concept of up and down. There were a few places, such as this, where signs of the transition remained.

Through the archways whispered the ceaseless rustling of scales and—occasionally—the belch of an angry voxyn. Jacen could feel more than a dozen of the creatures lurking in the darkness just beyond the light of his glow stick, as patient as spice spiders and far more deadly.

"Looks like the outside of an arena," Anakin whispered. He was lying on the tunnel floor next to Jacen. "A really big one."

"Or a temple," Lomi said. She and Ganner were squatting on their haunches above the brothers' feet, with Tesar and Krasov stooped behind them, and everyone else waiting deeper in the cramped tunnel. "If Jacen can use his power to keep the grand corridor clear, perhaps we can sneak—"

"We can't," Anakin interrupted. "One way or another, we have to fight. How many, Jacen?"

"Too many."

Jacen could not perceive individual creatures well enough to make an accurate count, but he could sense them hiding in the cavity of darkness beyond the archways, scattered along the slopes of a bowl-shaped depression that felt easily a kilometer across. He recognized in most of the creatures the same determination to defend their territory that he had sensed in many species, but there was something fanatic about it, the suggestion of a familiar kind of selfless devotion.

"Nests!" The outline of a plan began to form in Jacen's mind. "They're defending their nests."

"Nests?" Lomi demanded. "What do clones need with—"

Anakin silenced her with a raised hand. "Let him concentrate."

"Not too long," Ganner said from somewhere in back. "Sooner or later, even Nom Anor will notice we've slipped away."

Jacen focused on the voxyn across the way and sensed not

protectiveness, nor even hunger, but something closer to longing. One by one, he reached out to the other creatures beneath the arches and, perceiving a similar craving, knew he had guessed right. He backed deeper into the tunnel and faced Tesar and Krasov.

"I have an idea—"

"Do it," Tesar rasped. "Bela will be honored."

"Do what?" Welk demanded, looking from one Jedi to another. "How come nobody around here ever finishes a sentence?"

"No time," Ganner said. "Let's go. The Yuuzhan Vong have got to have noticed we're gone."

Jacen ignored him and asked Krasov, "You understand—"

"She gave her life to the Jedi," Krasov said. She and Tesar squeezed aside, then levitated their hatchmate forward in between them. "Her body is nothing."

They rubbed their muzzles briefly against hers, then removed Bela's equipment harness and vac suit pack. Tesar set the timer of a class-A thermal detonator to four minutes, then secured it deep within her reptilian throat. Krasov affixed her sister's lightsaber in hand with synthflesh, and they exchanged places with Lomi and Ganner and floated Bela's body into the grand corridor.

Choking back tears—and wondering if he could have done the same thing had it been Anakin's body—Jacen watched in horror as more than a dozen feral voxyn rushed into the light of his glow stick. The creatures filled the corridor with sonic screeches, and his earplugs activated. Tesar used the Force to ignite Bela's lightsaber and slice the muzzle off the first voxyn to reach her body. The second bit the arm off at the shoulder. The third bowled the corpse over and straddled it.

The other voxyn hurled themselves into this one, snarling and snapping at its legs. Several together caught hold and dragged the beast down the corridor, where the battle erupted into a vicious acid-belching melee that reduced the combatants to smoking heaps of scales. The rest continued in a more restrained manner, each trying to straddle Bela's body, the others fighting to unseat the current possessor, slowly dragging her down the corridor toward one of the archways.

The battle moved into the darkness, and the strike team was left to listen as the snarling and hissing grew more distant and muffled. Finally, the crackle of a thermal detonator shattered the quiet, and a brilliant glare flashed through an archway far down the corridor. Jacen reached out to the voxyn with soothing thoughts, trying to reassure them the light would not come again. The surviving creatures—and it felt like there were plenty—greeted his efforts with sonic squeals and clattering claws, but gradually settled down and returned to their nests.

Jacen checked to make sure no voxyn lurked in ambush, then led the way out into the grand corridor. The stench was so bad that even his breath mask could not filter it out. He reached out to summon Jaina and felt her already approaching, apprehensive and baffled, but not panicked.

Anakin joined the Barabels and began to speak with them quietly. Though Jacen knew Tesar and Krasov would be more unsettled by an apology than gratified by it, he kept his distance. Anakin needed his talk with the Barabels; maybe they would do for him what Jacen could not.

Jaina arrived and, at Ganner's insistence, the team set off up the corridor. Anakin reluctantly allowed Tesar and Krasov to assume their usual position in front, though only because they appeared insulted by the suggestion that it was someone else's turn at point. Every thirty meters, another archway led into the rustling darkness. Though Jacen never perceived more voxyn lurking in these openings, the Barabels took no chances. They always leapt onto the wall and, extending their claws to hold themselves in place, peered through the opening to be certain.

Jacen stepped to his sister's side. "Everything okay back there? You seem uneasy."

"Fact," Tenel Ka said, joining them. "You have more furrows between your eyebrows than a Hutt's purser."

"Thanks," Jaina said. "I saw Vergere."

Jacen waited, then finally asked, "And?"

Jaina's eyes went vacant. "And nothing . . . she left." She pointed her chin ahead. "How's Little Brother doing?"

Jacen looked forward to where Anakin was keeping pace with Lowbacca's long stride. Their brother was so powerful in the Force that it was difficult to tell how much pain he was burying, or how much strength he was burning, but Jacen could feel the fatigue nipping at the edges of Anakin's carefully maintained facade of vigor.

"Hard to know," he said. "I'm scared."

Jaina fell quiet, then surprised Jacen by grasping his arm. "Don't be. We're not going to let anything happen to him."

Tenel Ka took Jacen's other arm. "Fact."

Anakin followed Tesar and Krasov up the grand corridor. Every time they leapt onto a wall to peer around the haunch of an archway, he cringed. His efforts to explain how sorry he was about Bela's death had only bewildered them, prompting the pair to apologize to *him* for the strike team's other casualties. He had ended up feeling more guilty than before, and the Barabels had seemed vaguely affronted by the idea they might need comforting. Reminding the hatchmates to be careful was out of the question, but the Force in the immense chamber beyond the arches was full of brutish agitation, and he kept expecting a mass of brown bile to blast one or both of them.

Instead, he felt a sudden surge of primal longing. Anakin ignited his lightsaber and, along with everyone else, shouted. A pair of open jaws darted into view. Krasov hissed and pulled back—not quickly enough. A tooth snagged her breath mask and tore it free.

Anakin jumped forward, slashed the voxyn under the jaw, reversed strokes and cut off the muzzle. The creature reared, then Tesar and Krasov swung down in front of him and severed its swiping claws.

What remained of the voxyn's jaws began to open. Krasov dragged her white blade across its throat, then staggered back, her face covered in gummy acid. Tesar used the Force to hold the reeling voxyn upright as Anakin drove his lightsaber into its chest and spun away, pulling his purple blade through its body. The voxyn went limp and hung suspended in the air.

Krasov's face was masked by rising fumes, but the sizzle of melting keratin left no doubt about what was happening to her. "Tesar!" she gasped. "My eyes . . ."

"Here, Krasov."

Leaving the voxyn to fall, Tesar pulled her out of the archway.

A loud clatter sounded from the darkness beyond. Anakin pulled a thermal detonator off his harness and threw it well down into the room. There was a familiar sizzle and a bright flash, but no shock wave or heat blast. Precision was what made thermal detonators so useful. Everything within the blast radius was utterly disintegrated; everything beyond remained completely untouched.

When Anakin sensed no more voxyn charging the door, he turned to call Tekli and found her already guiding Krasov to a seat against the wall. The Chadra-Fan began to scrape off the sticky bile with the blade of a multitool. Too many scales came with it.

Anakin looked away, said nothing. Every decision cost someone something. Their mission began to seem distant and impossible.

"Trouble coming!"

Anakin barely heard Jacen's words. He did not want to make any more decisions, cause any more casualties.

"Anakin?"

He felt Jacen probing, checking to see if the battle had caused his wound to open. It had not. The pain remained bearable, and the Force gave Anakin strength.

A muffled rustling came down the corridor from both directions.

"Sith blood!" Jaina cursed. "He's cracking."

Someone fired a blaster. Someone else fired in the other direction. The Force became permeated with primal longing, and voxyn poured into the grand corridor to both sides of the strike team. The blasterfire grew deafening. Anakin drew his own weapon. It would be easier this way; no decisions to make. All he had to do was aim and fire.

Anakin started forward, and Lowbacca clamped hold of his shoulder and pointed toward the arch at their backs and groaned a question.

Anakin shook his head. "Tahiri can keep watch. I'm fighting with everyone else."

"Better if you watch," Tesar rasped. He pushed Anakin toward the arch. "For Krasov."

"I'm not hurt." Anakin followed the Barabel toward the battle line. "I can still fight."

"Anakin! Will you stay?" Jaina pointed her blaster into the arch. "Get yourself together."

Though spoken softly, the words struck Anakin like a fist. His own sister did not want him fighting at her side. Had he bungled things that badly?

Jaina joined the others on the firing lines. Anakin squatted behind the dead voxyn and stared into the rustling darkness, alert to any change in sound or in the Force that meant more creatures coming. Though hardly as sensitive to the beasts as Jacen, he could tell that most of the creatures on the other side of the archway were bloodthirsty but defensive—and almost stationary.

"You don't have to let them push you around," Tahiri said, dropping to her knees and almost yelling to make herself heard over the battle roar. "You're still team leader."

"Some leader," Anakin said.

Tahiri waited almost a full second before demanding, "What's that mean?"

"I keep getting people killed."

"People are getting killed. Who says it's your fault?"

"I do." Anakin glanced toward the battle. "They do."

"Neg that! They just want you to get us out of here." A concussion grenade shook the corridor and was answered by a dozen sonic screeches. "So do I. Think of something—fast."

Tahiri kissed him and turned toward the battle, her blaster drawn. So far, the bolt storm was holding the voxyn at bay, but that would change. It would change soon. Several Jedi were already drawing down their last power packs, and eventually the voxyn would mount an attack through Anakin's archway—unless the strike team left first.

Tesar rasped a curse, hurled his minicannon at a voxyn, and summoned Krasov's weapon to hand. His target sprang at his head, claws lashing. Raynar Thul caught the creature on a hissing lightsaber, opened a three-meter slash down its belly, then leapt away—into the path of its lashing tail.

The barb penetrated. Raynar winced and retreated into the Jedi ranks, severing the tail a meter from his jumpsuit and leaving the stump to hang. Anakin spun to call Tekli and found her scurrying forward, antidote in hand.

They had to move, they had to move *soon*.

Anakin turned his glow stick to maximum and tossed it through the archway, catching it with the Force and holding it high in the air. The voxyn belched acid at it, but settled down as they grew accustomed to the radiance. Anakin glimpsed many dozen creatures—probably not a hundred—spread over the tiers of a vast stadium. Most were squatting over the corpses of slaves they had dragged in from the city, glaring and ruffling their neck scales at each other.

No way to levitate across that. Jedi could not fly, after all, and the distance had to be more than a kilometer. Maybe if they used their Force acrobatics . . .

Jacen came to Anakin's side and, sensing the drift of his thoughts through the battle meld, peered into the arena. "We don't want to startle them. They won't leave their, uh, nests unless they feel threatened. I might be able to keep them from attacking at all."

"Good," Anakin said. "It'd be nice if something went right."

He turned to find Ganner pointing toward an acid-melted voxyn tunnel just up the corridor and yelling that they had to make a run for it. Afraid he wouldn't be heard over the battle roar, Anakin activated his comlink.

"Right idea, Ganner, wrong direction." He pointed through the archway. "This way."

"The arena?" This from Jaina. "You can't heal—"

"I'll heal when this is done," Anakin interrupted. What he wouldn't do was hole up in some voxyn tunnel and get everyone trapped. "This way."

Tesar Sebatyne was the first to nod. "As you order." He laid a barrage of covering fire. "Fall back!"

Lowbacca did the same for those facing the opposite direction, and Jacen led the way into the arena, dropping the battle meld so he could concentrate on soothing voxyn. The closest creatures ruffled their scales and scratched furrows into their tiers. They also remained in their nests and did not attack.

Anakin let out a breath and turned to Krasov. Though her face was covered by Bela's breath mask, plenty of bones and teeth showed around the rim. Anakin caught Tekli's eye and raised his brow.

"Not thiz time, Little Brother." Krasov's voice was barely a croak. "Allow this one to cover your . . . departure."

"No," Anakin said. "We'll toss a detonator back—"

"Too late." Krasov opened her hand to reveal a thermal detonator, fuse set to ignite three seconds after her thumb left the trigger. "This iz better."

Alema Rar slipped past, pulling a stuporous Raynar Thul along. His condition was due to the antidote, not the poison. Anakin sent Tekli after the pair and laid covering fire for Lowbacca.

"Krasov, secure that trigger," Anakin ordered. Half a dozen voxyn came boiling down the corridor. He dropped the leader with a bolt to the eye. "Krasov?"

"Krasov iz gone." Tesar tossed a concussion grenade into the rest of the pack and, as the blast rocked the corridor, kneeled to press his cheek to Krasov's. He held it there until the residual acid began to make his own scales smoke, then rose and pointed to her thumb, now barely holding the trigger. "This one thinkz we should hurry."

Chapter 41

Anakin ducked through the arch into the arena, Tesar close on his heels. The rest of the strike team was already three tiers below, lighting their way with glow sticks and nervously snaking past a nesting voxyn. The two Jedi started after them, circling around a forty-meter crater that Anakin had made moments earlier with a thermal detonator.

A tumult of snarling and bellowing rumbled through the arch behind them, prompting Anakin and Tesar to launch themselves headlong down the tiers. The thermal detonator Krasov had been clutching when she died would go off three seconds after the ravaging voxyn knocked it from her lifeless hand. Something tore inside Anakin's wound and sent a half-numbed pain shooting up through his belly. He ignored it and completed his somersault, then landed dead-legged two tiers below and tumbled over the edge.

Two things happened next. First, the voxyn that he had disturbed took offense and opened its mouth to spew acid. Second, the thermal detonator went off above him, flashing a fan of white brilliance across the arena and disintegrating a forty-meter length of wall, and bringing untold tons of yorik coral crashing down into the arena.

Anakin was a lot more worried about the angry voxyn. Fumbling for his lightsaber, he rolled away and leapt to his feet—only to find the beast scratching at its own throat, mysteriously choking on its tongue and dribbling brown acid out the side of its mouth. A dark shiver raced down his spine, and he turned to find Welk standing behind him, one hand curled into a strangling claw, his face contorted into an angry mask of concentration.

"Jacen needs everybody down!" Tenel Ka's hushed voice came over the comlink. "Stay low and silent!"

Anakin obeyed quickly, Welk less so, and Anakin watched in silence as the Dark Jedi used the Force to strangle the life out of the creature. Certainly, neither Anakin nor anyone else on the strike team would have used the Force to kill directly—calling upon its power to extinguish the very life that sustained it was a certain path to the dark side—but Anakin would have been hard-pressed to call it immoral. Had the situation been reversed, he would not have hesitated to use a blaster or lightsaber to save Welk.

As the rumble of falling yorik coral faded away, the voxyn continued to snarl and scratch at the yorik coral beneath their feet. Anakin felt Jacen reaching out with the Force, soothing the beasts with reassuring thoughts, working to persuade them that this was the last of the disturbances. Given the commotion of the last hour, the task was difficult, but the voxyn were so eager to remain on their nests that they calmed.

"It is okay to move slowly," Tenel Ka advised. "But do nothing threatening. Under no circumstances must anyone attack."

As Anakin rose, a wave of dizziness made him brace himself against the wall, but no one noticed. All eyes were focused on Zekk, who was marching over to Welk with fury in his eyes.

"You used the dark side!" he hissed.

"Better to let the beast kill young Solo?" Lomi asked, placing herself between the two.

"You broke your promise," Zekk said.

"He saved my life." Anakin stepped to Zekk's side, then glanced pointedly around. There were no live voxyn closer than twenty meters, but all of the beasts within the range of their glow sticks were ruffling their neck scales and staring at the strike team. "And if we can feel your outrage, so can the voxyn."

The heat went out of Zekk's expression. "Sorry, Anakin." He glared at Welk and Lomi, then said, "Don't use the Force again—not around me."

With that, he spun on his heel and started down the tier after Jacen and Jaina. Anakin watched him go, suddenly too weary to concern himself over Zekk's rigid view of the dark side. His legs shook from the mere effort of standing. He took a moment to concentrate, using the Force to muster his strength, then waved Welk and Lomi forward and fell in behind.

"By the way, thanks for saving my life," he said to Welk.

"Then you do not feel tainted by the dark side?" Lomi asked.

"I'm not afraid of it, if that's what you mean," Anakin replied. "But Zekk's right, you did break your promise."

"Don't worry," Welk said, not looking back. "I won't do it again."

They descended the tiers in a zigzagging course as Jacen gave the widest possible berth to the nesting voxyn. Even through the breath masks, the stench grew ever more unbearable, and they saw bodies in all states of decomposition, the hopeful mothers still standing guard over the food they expected to nourish their sterile eggs. In a few cases, the voxyn herself had starved to death and collapsed on top of her nest's bare bones. The sight struck Anakin as morbidly sad, though it did not really surprise him. He knew from his studies—and from Jacen's endless discourses during long space voyages—that many creatures faced death to bring forth the next generation. This willingness—and the fact that in some species it was even necessary—was tangible evidence of the eternal nature of the Force, Jacen said.

About halfway down, they came to a ten-meter drop, which proved to be another tier of arches similar to the ones out of which they had come. Rather than risk drawing any more nestless voxyn through these portals, they began to circle the arena—or whatever it was—clambering up and down tiers in order to avoid voxyn nests. The effort quickly began to tell on Anakin, even when he used the Force to assist himself. It was not long before his knees were trembling and his belly burning.

Tahiri, of course, noticed right away. "Anakin, you're shaking."

Anakin nodded. "The smell is getting to me."

"The smell makes no one else shake," Tesar noted, coming up behind Anakin. "This one will carry you."

Before Anakin could object, the Barabel scooped him up in his arms. Tahiri insisted on reporting Anakin's condition to Tekli, whose examination came to an abrupt end when an angry voxyn stuck its head over the tier above and belched acid in their direction. Fearful of agitating the rest of the beasts, the strike team resumed its march, with Anakin cradled in Tesar's scaly arms.

As they continued around the arena, Anakin saw that the tiers below were better appointed than those through which he and his companions were traveling. The walls were decorated with statues of Yun-Yammka, many showing the god tearing off his own limbs or draining his blood. A few showed Yuuzhan Vong warriors being devoured by the god or emerging whole again from among its tentacles. When he began to glimpse long spikes and sharp hooks protruding from the walls surrounding the arena floor, Anakin thought this was probably a stadium where the Yuuzhan Vong had once entertained themselves by pitting slave gladiators against each other.

Then Anakin noticed the series of ramps extending from the

lower tier onto the arena floor and realized he had it wrong. The Yuuzhan Vong had been the ones who fought here—or at least those lucky enough to sit in the privileged lower tier. Viewed in that light, the statues of Yun-Yammka took on a religious tone, and he began to imagine the arena as an enormous church. He could almost see the place filled with Yuuzhan Vong faithful as the worldship hurtled through the darkness between galaxies, the most prominent citizens and celebrated leaders down on the arena floor, honoring their gods with their blood, by their deaths assuring the Yuuzhan Vong of a new home in the distant galaxy of the New Republic.

"Put me down," Anakin said. Warriors like those would not be defeated by someone who had to be borne into battle in another's arms. "I won't be carried, not in here—not until this is done."

Tesar returned Anakin to his unsteady feet.

Lowbacca groaned, then moaned a question.

"Then how do you expect—"

"Tesar can help me," Anakin said, interrupting Em Teedee's translation. He turned to the Barabel. "When Ulaha was being tortured, you gave her strength."

"It will not be as much," Tesar warned. "There were three then."

"I'll take what I can," Anakin said. "I just want to finish this on my feet."

The Barabel showed his needlelike teeth. "Then this one would be honored."

Anakin felt Tesar make contact through the Force, then experienced a peculiar reptilian chill as the Barabel brought them together emotionally. The world turned strangely crimson, and Anakin felt his weakness pouring into Tesar, and Tesar's strength flowing into him. With it came a strange sense of loneliness, not quite sorrow as humans knew it, but two aching absences that would never be filled.

Without realizing that he had closed them, Anakin opened his eyes. "I—it isn't quite what I expected."

"No?" Tesar rasped. "You wanted scales?"

Astonished to discover he actually understood the joke, Anakin chuckled and started after the others. His connection to Tesar felt similar to the battle meld, save that now it was the Barabel's *strength* that was being shared.

A few minutes later, Alema announced that they had circled around the arena to a point opposite their entry arch, and the team began to ascend the stairs. Anakin was able to climb under his own power, but Raynar was still suffering from the effects of the poison antidote and had to be lifted from one tier to the next with the Force. They were only one tier from the exit when Raynar, waiting for Alema to climb up after him, pointed ten meters down the tier.

"Look!" His tongue was so thick that Anakin did not understand him at first. "Eryl!"

Raynar turned and started to stagger in the direction he was pointing, drawing a warning neck rustle from a nearby voxyn. Alema pulled herself up in one swift motion and rushed after the disoriented Jedi, while Anakin and several others reached out with the Force and jerked him back.

The voxyn belched acid and missed, then lunged forward and slashed Raynar twice. The first attack tore through his armored jumpsuit, the second opened four deep gashes. Leaving the wounded Jedi to his companions, Anakin jerked his lightsaber off his harness and activated the blade.

"Anakin, no!" Jacen warned. "Let it go back to its nest."

Anakin deactivated the blade, but kept the weapon at high guard. Tesar floated Raynar's babbling figure over to Ganner and Alema, who quickly disappeared behind the edge with him. The voxyn continued to glare down, its beady eyes fixed on the lightsaber in Anakin's hands.

"Need help, young Solo?" Lomi asked. "I can kill it, but there is that promise—"

"Keep your promise," Anakin said. He slowly lowered his light-saber and backed away. "You really don't want to see Zekk angry."

"Do not be so sure," Lomi said. "I hear he is very powerful when he is angry."

The voxyn retreated to its nest. Anakin dared to breathe again, then he and the others scrambled up the last tier to the exit. Alema and Zekk were already on the other side with Tekli and Raynar, but Jacen and the rest were waiting just inside the arch.

Anakin stepped through and peered at Raynar over the Chadra-Fan's small shoulder. Four deep gashes ran diagonally across his chest, but the bleeding was not severe and no bone was showing.

"How is he?"

"Well enough for now," Tekli said, filling the wounds with cleansing foam. "But much will depend on how Cilghal's anti-disease agents work."

Anakin continued to stare at Raynar. Another casualty, this one a close friend of Jacen and Jaina—but they had made it across the voxyn warrens. He felt both sorrowful and relieved, but not guilty. He had chosen as well as he could.

Though Raynar was probably too incoherent to notice, Anakin kneeled down and patted his shoulder. "Can he be moved?"

"Have someone levitate him," Tekli said. "I'll ride."

Zekk had the patient in the air before Anakin could give the order. Alema was beside him, holding Tekli's medpac, her face distressed. Anakin gave her arm a reassuring squeeze, then gently took the medpac from her and passed it to Tahiri.

"We need you to navigate," he said to Alema. "Lomi's never been outside the training course, and everyone else is lost down here."

Alema thought for a moment, then guided them down the passage in what seemed the opposite direction they had been traveling. This corridor resembled the one they had followed into the arena, save that it lacked acid-scarred caves connected to a parallel tunnel. Eventually, the team passed an intersection that had been blocked with a yorik coral plug, presumably to discourage voxyn from escaping onto the rest of the worldship. Alema passed by the first, then the next, and finally stopped at a third.

"It feels like we're very near the surface here." A shudder ran down her lekku as she spoke. "I'm guessing we are far from the gate they were herding us toward. Maybe we can finally take them by surprise."

Jaina checked her comlink. "Maybe we can. They still haven't tripped the flechette mine."

Anakin gestured at the barricade. "Who wants the honors?"

Lowbacca and Tesar ignited their lightsabers simultaneously and set to work. The yorik coral was much harder than that aboard the *Exquisite Death,* and it required nearly twenty minutes to cut through the meter-deep plug. Anakin spent much of the time in meditation, doing what he could for his injury, but Tekli did not want to open it again. Even if a stitch had popped, there would be nothing solid to reattach it to.

Finally, Ganner levitated the last block out of the intersection. Ahead of them, a large access tunnel ascended toward the surface at a shallow angle. About fifty meters distant, it ended in a transparent wall of membrane and an air-locked valveway that opened into one of the deep-walled service routes they had seen from space. This travelway, however, was obviously no longer in use. It was crammed with captured equipment—landspeeders, utility lifts, hovertaxis, even a SoroSuub cloud car—all of it no doubt being stored out of sight until it was needed in the training course.

And there, sitting cockeyed in the middle of the tangle with hatches sealed tight and one landing gear only half extended, was a battered light freighter.

"Well," Anakin said. "It looks like the Force is finally with us."

Chapter 42

It was a forty-second turbolift drop to the Solos' floor in their Eastport residential tower, and forty seconds had never seemed so long. Leia pulled her lightsaber from the thigh pocket of her grease-stained flight suit, and Han checked the power level of his famous BlasTech DL-44. Given the tower's unobtrusive but watchful security department, Leia felt certain there would be a pair of guard droids and a sentient supervisor waiting with a retina scanner when they stepped out of the lift. As long as Han didn't start a firefight, that would probably even be a good thing. It was always smart to have a little support in situations like these.

"Can't this thing drop any faster?" Han grumbled.

"They don't put acceleration compensators in turbolifts," Leia reminded. "Be patient, Han. We'll be more useful without our knees in our chests."

Han was silent for a moment, then asked, "Did Adarakh say they were on the way, or already in the building?"

"On our floor," Leia said. "He said they were already on our floor."

*   *   *

With its rare red ladalums and milky larmalstone floor, the Solo atrium appeared as deserted and placid as the first time Viqi Shesh had visited it. Instead of ambling casually by as she had before, she walked straight toward the cul-de-sac, the looming figures of an entire Yuuzhan Vong infiltration cell following close on her heels.

Dressed in the blue jumpsuits of the Municipal Health Bureau and wearing conspicuously similar ooglith masquers, Viqi's companions looked more like a squad of sextuplet assassins than a vermin control team—though it hardly mattered. Droids were not capable of making the leap of thought necessary to interpret the odd similarity as a threat, and there would be no sentients awake inside to notice. Ten minutes ago, she had walked past and innocuously blown an ultrasonic whistle, causing her sensislug surveillance bug to self-destruct and release an invisible cloud of sleep-inducing spores. By now, everyone in the Solo apartment, including Ben Skywalker, would be slumbering peacefully.

Viqi had almost entered the atrium when a sudden rustle broke out behind her, and she turned to find the infiltrators opening their collars to reach for the gnulliths concealed beneath their jumpsuits.

"Not yet, gentlemen." In an attempt to keep the security system from identifying the stress pattern in her voice, Viqi spoke in a bare whisper. "We don't want to alarm anyone."

"But the spores—"

"Grow ineffective after five minutes, or so I was given to believe." Viqi was not at all happy about having her judgment questioned by a male inferior. "It has been *ten* minutes."

"They settle to the ground after five minutes," the leader corrected. His name was Inko or Eagko or something similarly odd. "If they are stirred into the air again—"

"We'll mask when we are inside, Inkle." Viqi pushed the leader's hand back beneath his jumpsuit, then tipped her chin toward the Serv-O-Droid GL-7 standing patiently outside the crystasteel door.

"If the greeter droid sees a vermin control team approaching in gnul-liths, he'll have tower security down here before we cross the atrium. We must disable him before revealing ourselves."

The leader considered this for a moment, then nodded to his warriors and removed his hand without the gnullith. "Ingo Dar," he said. "I am called Ingo Dar."

"Of course you are." Viqi rolled her eyes and turned back to the atrium. "Follow me, Ingo—and do only what I command."

Though Viqi was about to expose herself as one of the most notorious traitors in the short history of the New Republic, she had not bothered to mask either her appearance or her voice. A thorough analysis of the security data would penetrate such a disguise anyway, and she knew from her spy in the security department that any attempt to avoid all the tower's hidden holocams and microphones would be hopeless. Besides, there was a part of her—a big part of her—that wanted Luke Skywalker to know who had taken his son. No one could cross Viqi Shesh and hope to escape the consequences—not even the Master of the Jedi.

There would also be consequences for Viqi, of course. She would become a hunted woman and a reviled traitor, and her whole planet would be stigmatized by her betrayal—but not for long, she was certain. Since losing her seat on NRMOC, she had actually expanded her value to the warmaster, recruiting a network of spies who believed she was merely working to regain her lost prestige. She had provided him with not only the secret of the Jedi shadow bombs, but also the technical readouts of the gravity projectors aboard the *Mon Mothma* and the *Elegos A'Kla* and the disposition of the New Republic hyperspace mines now being laid between Borleias and Coruscant. Tsavong Lah knew that in commanding her to distract the Jedi in this manner, he was forfeiting his most valuable intelligence asset—and Viqi could think of only one reason for him to do that.

Tsavong Lah was coming to Coruscant, and soon.

As Viqi approached the door, the GL-7 swiveled its smiling face in her direction and made a show of scanning her features—though she knew that it had already done that from twenty meters away, when she stepped onto the hidden pressure pad at the entrance to the atrium. She smiled warmly and slipped a hand into her stylish hip pouch, reaching for the powerful two-shot hold-out blaster she had hidden inside a scan-proof cosmetics case.

"Senator Shesh, how kind of you to call!" The GL-7 radiated electronic enthusiasm. "See-Threepio informs me that the household is napping at the moment, but he expects them to awaken shortly. If you and your friends care to wait, he is prepared to offer refreshments."

"Refreshments?" It was hardly the type of greeting Viqi expected, but perhaps the droid's programming had not been updated since her "retirement" as the chair of SELCORE. Certainly, Leia Solo would have been eager to offer a warm reception to the senator in control of the refugee effort's purse strings. Leaving the hold-out blaster in her hip pouch, Viqi said, "Yes, refreshments would be nice."

"See-Threepio is waiting for you inside." The crystasteel door slid open. "Please enjoy your visit."

Only her experience as a politician kept Viqi's jaw from dropping. "Thank you. I am sure we will."

Hoping that the infiltrators behind her were not doing something foolish like reaching under their jumpsuits for the amphistaffs twined around their waists, Viqi crossed the threshold and stepped into the foyer, a domed atrium similar to the one from which they had just come, though much smaller and even less grandiose. To the left, a large double door opened onto the apartment's skyway balcony, where, two meters below, a hoversled from a popular airbed vendor was waiting to provide a fast escape.

The Solos' golden protocol droid appeared from deeper inside the apartment. "I am See-Threepio, human-cyborg relations."

"The whole galaxy knows who you are, See-Threepio," Viqi remarked dryly.

"How kind of you to say so, Senator Shesh." C-3PO gestured at a set of pouf couches arrayed around a potted ladalum, then said, "We have been expecting you. Please be seated, and I will take drink orders for your and your friends shortly."

The droid's tone was so pleasantly matter-of-fact that the significance of what he had said did not strike Viqi until he had turned away and vanished around the corner. The infiltrators instantly began to rustle beneath their jumpsuits for their gnulliths, but Viqi pulled her hold-out blaster from its hiding place and started after the droid.

"See-Threepio! You were *expecting* us?"

"Why, yes, Senator Shesh." The droid reappeared instantly, his metallic hands grasping a delicate, Vors-glass orb spattered on the inside with some sort of organic material. "I was given to understand that this belongs to you."

Still struggling to make sense of the situation, Viqi leveled her hold-out blaster at the droid's head. "Stay there."

C-3PO stopped. "Oh my." The glass sphere slipped from between his hands. "Is that really necessary?"

Viqi had time enough to draw one breath before the orb shattered on the tile floor, then a small gray-skinned alien slipped past the droid with a T-21 repeating blaster in his hands. He was, she saw, wearing a breath mask.

Viqi fired once in his direction and heard the first infiltrator thump to the floor. The alien fired past her twice, and two more warriors crashed down. When a fourth fell, Viqi realized the situation was hopeless and turned to flee. Even if any of the Yuuzhan Vong remained conscious long enough to don their gnulliths, they would never fight past the Noghri.

As she approached the skyway balcony, the double doors slid open automatically, and a second Noghri dropped onto the floor. Viqi took two more steps and loosed the hold-out blaster's last bolt. The shot missed, of course, but it did force the alien to waste an instant pivoting away.

That instant was all Viqi needed. She raced across the balcony and hurdled the safety rail blind.

With any luck at all, the hoversled would still be there, two meters down.

The crook of Luke's arm felt strangely empty without Ben there to keep it occupied. At the oddest times, he found himself holding his hand in front of his belly and his elbow slightly out from his body, rocking from one foot to another and humming softly to himself. Sometimes, such as now, it even seemed to him that his ribs were warm where his son would be pressed against him, or that the air was sweet with the smell of the milk on Ben's breath.

Sensing a sudden silence in the air, Luke looked up to find the three women in the room—Mara, Danni, Cilghal—studying him with knowing smirks. He felt himself blush and knew there was no use denying that his thoughts had been elsewhere.

"Well, nothing else seems to work." He shrugged and smiled sheepishly, then looked through the transparisteel viewport at the writhing mass of tentacles in the nutrient tank. "I thought we might as well try music."

"Sure you did, Luke," Mara said. "I'm sure that every yammosk war coordinator will be mesmerized by 'Dance, Dance, Little Ewok.' "

"Why not?" Cilghal asked. "It works as well as anything we have tried. We know they communicate through gravitic modulation, but there must be something in the wave pattern we are missing. Whatever we try, it fails to answer."

"Fails, or refuses?" Luke asked, studying the creature more closely. "We keep talking about yammosks like they're animals, but I'm not sure. What if it doesn't *want* to answer? If they're smart enough to run a battle—"

"Then they're smart enough to avoid helping us," Danni said. She shook her head wearily. "For every step forward . . ."

Luke's comlink buzzed, then Mara's.

Mara got to hers first. "Mara here."

"Everything's fine, but Leia thinks you should know we just had a little excitement here." Han's voice was tinny and scratchy, a result of the relay from Eclipse's comm center being split between two comlinks. Luke turned his off, and the voice sounded more like Han. "There's nothing to worry about."

Luke and Mara looked at each other, then Mara demanded, "What do you mean there's nothing to worry about? If there was nothing to worry about, would you be comming us to say there was nothing to worry about?"

"Viqi Shesh paid us a visit," Leia said. "She had a squad of infiltrators with her."

"They were after Ben?" Luke asked.

"That's how it looks," Han said. "Adarakh and Meewalh took them in the foyer. The Yuuzhan Vong are either dead or on their way to an NRI interrogation facility."

"And Viqi?" Mara asked.

"She jumped off the balcony," Leia said.

"She didn't fall far," Han added. "She had a delivery sled one floor below. NRI is tracing it now."

"But it won't take long to find her," Leia hastened to add. "Within the hour, every voice scanner on Coruscant will be trying to match her print."

Luke and Mara looked at each other again, then Mara shrugged.

"So who said I was worried?" Mara asked. "If anyone in the galaxy knows how to deal with kidnappers, it has to be Han and Leia Solo."

This drew a laugh from both Han and Leia, who had almost lost count of the number of times their children had been abducted.

"But you two stay put," Mara ordered. "No more sneaking off on secret reconnaissance missions when you're supposed to be watching my son."

" 'Firm that," Han said. "I could use some time on the couch."

After they clicked off, Luke could still sense a lingering uneasiness in Mara. He waited until they had stepped into the frigid corridor—Eclipse's heating system was again performing below specifications—then spun Mara around and zipped her thermasuit to her throat.

"It isn't easy being here," he said. "Not with the Yuuzhan Vong after Ben on Coruscant."

Mara managed a smile. "And with everything so quiet right now . . ."

"You could probably take a few days. Ben might like to see his mother, too."

"And his mother would like to see him," Mara said. She fell silent, considering, then shook her head. "But she also wants to protect him, and the only way to do that is to keep the Yuuzhan Vong away from Coruscant. With all those refugee convoys disappearing from Ralltiir and Rhinnal, this is more than just quiet."

Luke nodded. "I feel it, too." He took her hand and started toward the hangar caves, where Corran Horn wanted to show him a supplemental targeting system being installed on the XJ3s. "This is the dark before the nova."

Chapter 43

Good news—Master Lowbacca wishes to report that the *Tachyon Flier* will be ready for launch before you attack the queen."

Horrified that Em Teedee's sharp voice would carry down the dusty slopes to the grashal's protective thorn hedge, Anakin and several others fumbled for their hanging earpieces. They were studying the cloning lab from more than a hundred meters distant, but the air in this part of the worldship was so still that even soft sounds carried.

"He's reinserting the reactor cores now," Em Teedee said. "We're going home, Master Anakin. You're going to survive after all!"

"Affirmative." Anakin's voice was barely a whisper. Earlier, Jacen had felt a single voxyn presence inside the huge grashal, so it seemed likely they had at last reached the queen. Now all they had to do was kill her before the Yuuzhan Vong realized they were here. "Maintain comm silence."

"Comm silence?" Em Teedee's voice was quieter now. "Does that mean you're in—"

The question came to an abrupt end as the droid was switched off, then Lowbacca acknowledged with a comm click. Anakin responded with a double click and continued his reconnaissance. The cone-shaped grashal stood in the heart of what had once been a vaulted dome, but which had become an immense basin when the shapers reoriented the worldship's gravity. As the strike team had seen from the other side of the spaceport, the peak of the huge structure protruded through the outer shell of the worldship and—judging by the number of patching membranes—provided some much-needed support for the makeshift ceiling.

Whether Nom Anor understood that this was where his prey had gone was impossible to say, but Anakin felt an urgency in the Force. The strike team had escaped through the voxyn lair over an hour ago, so the executor certainly realized by now that his quarry had disappeared. Provided he knew a shorter route, he might even be waiting inside. Someone should have been able to help with this question, but Anakin could not think who. Alema? Tahiri? Both had experience with Yuuzhan Vong bases, but their knowledge of this complex was no more specific than anyone else's. He shook his head. There was someone else, but for the life of him he could not remember who . . .

Inside the *Tachyon Flier*, a battered but serviceable Corellian Engineering Corporation YV-888 light freighter, Lowbacca tightened the last shielding bolt to its proper torque, then initiated a self-test. The instrument panel broke into a flurry of dancing lights as the reactor brain checked its circuits. Finally, bright green steam began to rise behind the shielding door's observation panel. When none of it appeared to be seeping through the seal, he authorized a pressure check, slipped the hydrospanner into his equipment belt, and started forward to check on his patient. Tekli had assured him that the dose of tranqarest would keep even a Jedi quiet until long after the others returned, but Lowbacca wanted to be sure. He had already been forced to secure Raynar in crash webbing after the feverish Jedi Knight thrashed his wrist against the bunk's safety rail.

As Lowbacca passed the air lock, he heard someone banging on the outer hatch. He went to the security panel and activated the external monitor. The vidcam was so dust-caked he could see only the vague shape of a small vac-suited human, hammering at the durasteel with the butt of a minicannon. He activated his comlink and started to ask what was wrong, then recalled Anakin's request for comm silence and stepped into the equalization chamber. He sealed his vac suit, then shorted two wires dangling from the control box.

As the outer seal broke, he experienced a sudden ripple of danger sense and snapped his lightsaber off his belt. The hatch opened, and Lomi Plo's voice came over his personal channel.

"There's no need for that." She tossed the minicannon at his waist, forcing him to lower his arms to catch it. "Come along—the scarheads have your friends cornered."

She turned and started down the boarding ramp, unslinging her own T-21 repeating blaster as she ran. Pausing only to clip his lightsaber on his harness, Lowbacca rushed after her.

The Wookiee was already at the bottom of the ramp when he sensed another human behind him, lurking somewhere beneath the *Tachyon Flier*. Instinctively bringing the minicannon up, Lowbacca spun around to find Welk stepping out from behind a landing strut, a blaster pistol aimed at his chest. Needing no further evidence of the pair's treachery, Lowbacca squeezed the minicannon's trigger.

The power pack did not even contain enough energy to activate the depletion alarm. Struck by the depth of the betrayal, Lowbacca lowered the minicannon and switched to Welk's personal channel, then growled a one-word question.

"Because your friends are going to get themselves and everyone with them killed, that's why," Welk answered.

He fired, catching Lowbacca full in the chest with a blue stun bolt. The Wookiee choked out a pained growl and dropped to a knee, drawing on the Force to keep himself conscious. He hurled the minicannon at Welk and reached for his lightsaber, then rolled over his shoulder and came up on a knee, molten bronze blade slashing toward the Dark Jedi's waist.

Stun bolts began to pour in from behind.

"Play nice, Wookiee," Lomi said. "We could have set our weapons to kill."

Anakin had almost finished explaining his plan when a blue glow shone down through the transparent ceiling patches. He lifted his gaze and saw the *Tachyon Flier* shooting into the green sky, its efflux nacelles glowing brilliantly as the ion drives flared to life.

"Lowie?" he gasped.

Jaina and the others were instantly on their comlinks, trying to raise Lowbacca and find out why he was leaving. They received only static in return.

"Strange," Tesar Sebatyne rasped. "This one has always heard that nothing is more loyal than a Wookiee."

"That's right," Jacen said. "And Lowbacca is more loyal than most. Something's wrong."

"Fact," Tenel Ka said.

The strike team stared at each other blankly while Anakin tried to raise Lowbacca again. When that did not work, Jaina switched channels and sent an activation signal to Em Teedee.

"—danger?" the droid asked, finishing the question that had been in his circuits when Lowbacca shut him down. "Oh dear, when did we launch?"

"Em Teedee, what's Lowie doing?" Jacen asked. "Why's he leaving?"

"Leaving? Why, Master Lowbacca is doing nothing of the sort. He's right here with . . ." The droid let the sentence drift off, then screeched, "Help! They're stealing me!"

"*Who?*" Anakin asked.

"Who?" Em Teedee echoed. "Lomi and—"

The explanation ended in a crackle of static.

"Welk," Zekk finished, his voice hard and angry. "Lomi and Welk."

As soon as he heard the names, Anakin recalled the Dark Master who had guided them through the training course—and whose last sentence to him had been something along the lines of "We were never here." He had seen her hand rise and felt the Force behind her words, but Lomi was as subtle as she was powerful. He could not even remember if there had been time to resist.

Ganner might not have been the first to realize what the ship's theft meant for Anakin, but, as usual, he was the only one bold enough to say it. "Anakin, I'm sorry. Once we found out they were Dark Jedi, we should never have—"

"Yes, we should have," Anakin said. He was surprised to discover how calm he felt, how focused he was on the duty at hand. "Without them, we wouldn't have made it this far—and I would have died in the arena anyway."

"Not *anyway,*" Tahiri insisted. "We'll find another way off this rock."

"First things first," Anakin said softly. Though Tekli was still working on him, reaching into his wound with the Force to repair his torn organs, he could feel his strength fading and his pain rising. "Let's concentrate on the mission."

The blue dot of the *Tachyon Flier*'s ion drives blinked completely out of sight, then a flight of coralskippers streaked across a patching membrane and shot into space. A moment after that, the dark shape of Nom Anor's frigate floated over the horizon, also pursuing the YV-888.

"I hope the scarheads catch them," Alema Rar said, her voice full of bitterness. "I hope they dump 'em in a voxyn pen."

"I do not." Tenel Ka displayed her comlink, which was already pulsing static as the first plasma balls battered the *Flier*'s shields. "Our friend Raynar is still aboard."

The sinking feeling in Anakin's chest was all too familiar. He activated Lowbacca's comlink remotely and found it completely silent.

"But not Lowie," he said. "And if he had been killed, I'm pretty sure we would have felt him die."

When no one said anything, he looked up from his comlink and found everyone else studying him. There were tears welling in Jacen's and Jaina's eyes, and Tahiri was wiping her cheeks with the cuff of her sleeve.

"We'd better do this now," Anakin said, not wanting to lose focus. He disengaged from Tekli, then took Raynar's G-9 power blaster off his shoulder and raised the long-range sight. "Jaina, keep a channel open to Raynar. Maybe we'll hear what becomes of him."

And maybe they wouldn't, Anakin knew. In war, people sometimes just disappeared. No one ever found out what had happened to them, leaving friends and family with lifetimes of longing and uncertainty.

When no one moved to ready themselves, Anakin said, "*Now* might be nice."

Spurred into action, the strike team readied their weapons and opened their emotions. Despite the lingering outrage—and some feelings of blame—over the Dark Jedi's betrayal, the battle meld felt the tightest it had been since the detention warrens. Anakin knelt a few meters from the passage mouth and took aim at one of the dark shapes visible through the thorn hedge. When he felt the others also find their targets—two to each guard—he fired.

Eight streaks of color fanned down the dusty slope and tore through the hedge into the four dark shapes beyond. None of the bolts missed. No Jedi would bungle such an important attack, not with the Force to guide his aim. But only two shots burned through. Six ricocheted off the guards' vonduun crab armor, blasting dust columns into the air or burning pits into the grashal wall.

The surviving guards dropped and crawled for cover. Half the strike team was already rushing down the slope, firing as they ran, their T-21 repeating blasters keeping the Yuuzhan Vong pinned and clearing the hedge for the more powerful weapons behind.

Anakin and Jaina fired again. Prone to deflection and straying at that distance, their power blasters could only flush the guards. One warrior fell to Alema's longblaster. The other was staggered by Tesar's minicannon, then finished by the T-21s as they reached effective range. Now the second wave was up and running. Despite the strength Tesar was sharing, Anakin could not keep pace. Tahiri, Jaina, and Tesar dropped back to stay with him.

"Go! I'll catch up."

"When Jawas swim!" Tahiri shot back.

"Anakin, you're in no condition," Jaina said. "Go back to the equipment pit and locate Lowie. Maybe if you find a safe place to hole up and go into a healing trance—"

"Too late for that," Anakin said. "I'm seeing this through."

"Even if it means putting others at risk?" Jaina demanded. "If you're slow, you're a danger to us all. At least *try* a trance."

Things had gone too far for a trance, Anakin knew. He was thirsty enough to drink sweat, and his abdomen was hard with trapped blood, and the effort of finding a place safe enough to enter a trance would probably kill him anyway. But the thought that he might be endangering others did give him pause. It was one thing to face the inevitable, quite another to take others along. He sought guidance from the Force, opening himself to its tide, trying to sense where it was carrying him.

The sound of the ruffling voxyn scales rose to mind. He felt again the awe he had experienced in the arena, when he realized it had been Yuuzhan Vong patricians who fought there. The Force had spoken to him then.

"I'm going," he said.

Jaina clenched her jaw, then looked away. "I thought so."

The first wave reached the hedge and ducked through the burn holes. Stalks began to strike like snakes. Half a dozen lightsabers snapped to life and hacked the brambles away, then the Jedi stumbled out the other side ripping thorn tangles from around their throats and legs. The hedge struck again as the second wave crossed. The first wave left them to their own devices and continued on toward the grashal. Speed was crucial. During their reconnaissance, Anakin had sensed a company of Yuuzhan Vong lurking a few hundred meters beyond the cloning lab, presumably where the strike team had been expected to leave the voxyn warrens.

By the time Anakin and his three companions penetrated the hedge, the first wave had already cut through the grashal wall. Tenel Ka, Zekk, and Alema pressed themselves against the block and rode along as Ganner used the Force to shove the monolith inside.

A burring cloud of bugs came boiling out. The Jedi huddled down in their armored jumpsuits, their blades tracing crackling color fans as they batted insects from the air. A grenade explosion rocked the grashal, then another and another, and the bug storm withered to a trickle.

"Clear!" Zekk yelled.

Ganner and Jacen ducked inside. Jaina hefted her power blaster to follow, but then everyone's comlinks popped and hissed static. There came a ripple in the Force, maybe strong enough to be Raynar's death. Anakin looked to the ceiling, saw nothing through the patching membranes but Myrkr's green glow. He would never know.

"They'll pay." Jaina tore her eyes from the ceiling. "They *will* pay."

"Then so will we," Anakin said. Jaina's eyes were sunken with fatigue and her mouth was drooping with sorrow, and she looked more frail and troubled than Anakin had ever seen her. "We're here to destroy the queen, not take revenge."

"Right." Jaina stepped through the opening. "Revenge comes later."

Anakin left Tahiri and Tekli at the breach with Alema's long-blaster and followed his sister into the grashal. It was like stepping into a Yavin 4 nightstorm, a dark fog hanging overhead, glow lichen up there somewhere casting sallow halos, blaster bolts and lightsabers flashing like colored lightning—and the humid air muffling the scream and roar of combat, making all that death seem more distant than it was.

Anakin spun out from behind the door block and batted a razor bug from the air, found himself staring through a jungle of pulsing white vines, their corkscrew stalks rising out of planting bins filled with briny-smelling mud. The Yuuzhan Vong were ahead everywhere, their presence too dispersed and indistinct to tell him much. A pair of thud bugs sent him diving for cover. He exchanged his lightsaber for the power blaster and came up firing.

The first shots left him so light-dazzled he glimpsed only a dark shape on the opposite side of the bin, diving for cover. He spun around the end of the box, heard the *snap-hiss* of an igniting lightsaber, then Tesar Sebatyne's familiar hissing. The Yuuzhan Vong had thrown his last bug.

Anakin reached out with the Force and found the rest of the

strike team taking heavy swarm, pinned down in the darkness. Easy enough to fix. He reached for his incendiary grenades, but felt Tesar already lifting three objects into the dark fog overhead.

A smug Yuuzhan Vong presence drew Anakin's attention to the next planting bin. Rolling from his hiding place, he saw a dark figure leaping across the aisle ahead, amphistaff poised to strike. He lifted his power blaster . . . and pitched forward as a razor bug sliced across his neck from behind, vibro-sharp mandibles gliding off his jumpsuit's armored lining. The insect banked and came back, pincers stretching for his face. Anakin pivoted and took a cheek slash, fired at his original target.

The bolt caught the Yuuzhan Vong in a shoulder seam and spun him around. An arm flew off trailing the smell of scorched flesh, but the warrior did not even scream. He just pirouetted and, now swinging one-armed, brought his amphistaff down.

Anakin's razor bug came around again, this time slashing for the throat, and he had to turn away. Behind him, Tesar's lightsaber snapped to life and sputtered harshly. Anakin blocked with the body of the power blaster, then took a pair of thud bugs in the flank and slammed to the floor. He heard the dull thump of an amphistaff hitting a thick reptilian skull, and the flow of strength trailed off as the Barabel plummeted into insensibility.

Anakin did not consciously fire his power blaster. He was too busy reaching up into the darkness, searching for falling grenades. How many seconds left? The power blaster just flashed, and Tesar's attacker crashed to the floor.

Anakin found what he was looking for and pushed. A ripple of danger sense made him roll away as the razor bug crashed to the floor where his head had been. He hammered the thing dead, then heard the telltale crackle of the grenade detonations. Hoping he would still be there when the sound fell silent, he closed his eyes and reached out to find his attacker through the lambent crystal.

Not easy—too many Yuuzhan Vong in too many places—but he felt something off to his left. He spun and fired.

The depletion alarm sounded, just loud enough to be heard over the crackling flames above. The Yuuzhan Vong presence was closer now, eager. Flinging the useless blaster aside, he plucked his lightsaber from his belt and thumbed it to life, brought it into a cross-body guard—caught an amphistaff descending toward his head. Eyes still squeezed shut against the brilliant glare above, he swung his legs around and scissored his attacker's knees. The contest ended in a quick lightsaber thrust.

The flames crackled out. Anakin opened his eyes and saw yellow glow lichen shining bright, the last wisps of vapor cloud evaporating into the hot air. He lay there for a long time, taking stock of his condition, trying to fight off his anguish. It took five full breaths to establish that the pain was caused only by his old wound, ten heartbeats more to bring it under control.

Gradually, Anakin grew aware of the battle meld again, of the strike team's mounting elation. Pushing his agony aside, calling on the Force, he lifted himself to his feet. The Jedi were advancing on the left side of the grashal, driving back the last handful of shapers and guards, slashing nutrient vines and cloning pods as they went. Through the pulsing tangle of stalks, he could not see what they were hunting—but he could feel it, over by the grashal wall, trapped a little below floor level, unsettled, wild, ferocious. Afraid.

Behind Anakin, the longblaster boomed. He felt panic from Tahiri and turned to find her rushing into the grashal. A ball of fire followed her through the breach and exploded into the monolith standing there, and Tahiri went flying.

Anakin rushed to help, but she was up before he took two steps. "Magma spitters! We're cut off."

Anakin did not bother to look. "Tekli?"

Tahiri pointed behind him, where the Chadra-Fan was sprinkling stinksalts on Tesar's forked tongue. The Barabel was smiling, but not waking.

"Take him . . . and go." Every word filled Anakin's belly with fire. He pointed toward the others. "You may need to cut a way out."

" *You*?" Tahiri said. "I'm not going—"

"Do it!" Anakin snapped. When Tahiri's face fell, he spoke more gently. "You need . . . to help Tekli. I'll be along."

"Yes, Tahiri," Tekli said. She cast a knowing glance at Anakin, then kneeled astride the Barabel and began to slap him. "Tesar is not responding. I cannot move him and work on him both."

Tahiri looked doubtful, but could hardly refuse to help. Blinking back a tear, she stretched up to kiss Anakin on the lips—then caught herself and shook her head. "No—for that, you have to come back."

Anakin gave her his best lopsided smile. "Soon, then."

"Soon," Tahiri repeated. "May the Force be with you."

This second part, she added so quietly that Anakin did not think she meant him to hear it. All too aware of the growing weakness in his legs, he went to the makeshift doorway and peered around the edge. An artillery squad had set up beyond the thorn hedge, their four magma spitters trained on the opening. No one was attempting to move closer, which meant the main force would be attacking from the other side. Anakin turned toward the primary entrance and focused on what he felt through the lambent crystal. It did not surprise him at all to sense a heavy Yuuzhan Vong presence streaming in from the ambush site.

He set off at a painfully slow run. Twice, he dropped to a knee when his legs buckled—once while trading blows with a glassy-eyed Yuuzhan Vong who had no more business in hand-to-hand combat than he did. He won that fight by slashing open a planting bin, then levitating himself while the nutrient mud spilled out and swept his foe off balance. The next combat he nearly did not survive at all, catching an amphistaff butt in his wound and popping the external stitches. His life was saved only when he used the Force to bounce his blaster off the warrior's tattooed brow.

As he retrieved his weapon and rose, Anakin vomited blood. Even before he was finished, he was using the Force to lift himself to his feet, willing himself to run. He had to beat the enemy assault force to the door. At last, he cleared the planting bins and spied the door membrane twenty meters to his left, as wide as an X-wing was long and twice as high. The far corner of the membrane rose slightly. Anakin ducked back into the planting beds, free hand already pulling a thermal detonator from his harness.

When Anakin saw the figure who stepped through, he nearly dropped the detonator. The newcomer's back was turned, but he wore a tattered jumpsuit and stood a head taller than most humans. He set off for the voxyn pen at a sprint.

"Lowie?" Anakin called, using the Force to make his weak voice carry.

He reached out, but felt only the same hazy Yuuzhan Vong presence as before. The newcomer turned, revealing the profile of a sandy-haired human, and raised an old E-11 blaster rifle.

Anakin was already behind a planting bin, activating his comlink. "Impostor!" he warned. "Trying for pens."

The blasterfire crescendoed to a deafening roar, as did the Jedi frustration. The firing angles were impossible. A grenade detonated somewhere, and Jaina yelled for a charge.

The door membrane began to roll upward, revealing forty pairs of Yuuzhan Vong feet waiting to rush inside. Anakin opened himself to the Force completely, drawing it into himself through the power of his emotions—not through his anger or fear like a Dark Jedi, but through his love for his family and his fellow Jedi Knights, through his faith in the Jedi purpose and the promise of the future. The Force poured in from all sides, filling him with a swirling maelstrom of power and purpose, saturating him and devouring him. There was nothing to be frightened of, no reason to grieve. He could feel it flowing into him and himself flowing into it. Anakin *was* the Force, and the Force was Anakin.

Anakin rose. His body emitted a faint aura of light—the glow of his cells burning out—and the air crackled around him. His injuries no longer pained him. He was acutely aware of everything in the grashal—the musty smell of the droning thud bugs, the sultry heat rising from the planting bins, the huffing breath of his fellow Jedi, even the Yuuzhan Vong. Their presence was as distinct to him as that of his own companions, almost as though the Force had somehow expanded to include them.

Firing as he ran, Anakin raced along the rising door. Every bolt blasted a Yuuzhan Vong foot. Muffled roars reverberated through the membrane. Ahead of him, half a dozen warriors dropped and rolled into the grashal. He blasted these before they could rise, then reached the other end and stroked the tickle pad. The door lowered again.

"Hutt breath!" Jaina cursed over the comlink. "She's escaping."

Anakin could feel it, too. The voxyn was moving down and away. He activated his own comlink. "The impostor must have opened an escape tunnel." It no longer hurt to speak, but his aura had gone from faint to bright. His cells were burning like fire. "Jacen, you're in charge. Take everyone and go after her."

Jaina's surprise at not having her own name called carried through the Force like a shout across water, but she stifled any resentment she felt and said, "Can't get there, Little Brother."

"The path will clear."

Anakin slashed the membrane tickle pad and circled toward the empty voxyn pen. He could feel Yuuzhan Vong ahead, crouching behind the last row of planting bins, secure in the knowledge that help was coming. That changed a moment later, when Anakin began to pour blasterfire into their flank. His angle was poor for head shots and his bolts too weak to penetrate vonduun crab armor, but by the time the Yuuzhan Vong realized that, they were being overrun by Jedi.

A plasma ball roared through the grashal door and set fire to a twenty-meter swath of cloning vines. Anakin charged back toward the melted membrane, miniature forks of lightning dancing off his arms and legs, the Force swirling through him like fire, burning more ferociously every moment. He was completely filled with the strength of the light side now; his injured body could hold no more. The energy was burning its way out of him, consuming a vessel too weakened to contain it.

Yuuzhan Vong—their feet fully intact—poured in five abreast. He dropped the first rank from fifteen meters out, his blaster pistol singing out twice between each step, every bolt burning through a face or a throat. The volcano cannon roared again, and a sphere of white fire blossomed in front of him, seemingly from nowhere. Anakin dived and rolled into the wall, hit boots-first, sprang into a back flip, returned to his feet ten meters from the explosion.

"Anakin!" Jaina's cry resembled a scream.

Go! He commanded her through the Force. *She's getting away!*

The blaster sang out in Anakin's hand, dropping Yuuzhan Vong as fast as it could fire. More warriors poured in. A razor bug buried itself in his shoulder, his jumpsuit half disintegrated by the Force energy escaping his body and no longer much protection. He allowed the impact to spin him around, fired again and once more, heard the depletion alarm. The Yuuzhan Vong hurled handfuls of thud bugs and rushed, already pulling amphistaffs off their waists.

Anakin threw the blaster pistol at the first and dropped him and leapt the second, thumbing his lightsaber to life in the air. He landed in front of the entrance and began a whirling dance of slash and parry, blocking once and striking twice, every attack a killing blow. His aura was burning so brightly that he cast shadows behind his foes. He batted the blade left to right, overpowering two blocks to open two throats, then sent another warrior tumbling with a hook kick to the head.

And still they came, piercing Anakin in three places, one amphistaff sinking its fangs into his flesh. The Force scalded the poison from his system before he felt it, and the new wounds troubled him less than the old one—but there were a dozen more warriors behind them, and he could not hold forever. He killed another, then another, took a crippling slash to his thigh, and gave ground. The Yuuzhan Vong rushed, trying to slip past to the right.

The longblaster roared from the pen area, blowing a head-sized hole through one Yuuzhan Vong and a fist-sized hole through the one behind him. Anakin launched himself into a back flip and landed five meters away. His aura flickered wildly as his cells began to burn and burst. He hazarded a glance over his shoulder and saw Jaina peering over the pit wall, tears streaming down her cheeks, the longblaster propped against her shoulder. Jacen was beside her, likewise weeping, trying to pull her away.

Go! Anakin said through the Force. *I can't hold.*

The Yuuzhan Vong charged again, and Jaina fired. Another warrior fell, and the rest came. Anakin flipped another five meters back—then felt someone, a Yuuzhan Vong, creeping along the far wall of the grashal. He retreated until he could see the figure: the Jedi impostor, perhaps thirty meters distant, dragging a heavy cargo pod toward the strike team's makeshift opening.

The warriors arrived again, and Anakin had to defend himself. Purple blade ticking back and forth, blocking and parrying and slipping strike after strike, he faded two steps and saw an opening. He brought his feet up and planted his heels in the center Yuuzhan Vong's chest. His lightsaber flashed twice, cleaving the skulls of the adjacent warriors, then he kicked off, launching himself into a series of Force-assisted cartwheels.

Anakin continued far enough to see where the impostor had come from, a work area near the queen's pen. Dozens of tendrils lay stretched along a workbench, each ending in a small cloning pod, some open, some closed. It looked like a tissue transfer station.

That was what the impostor had, a cargo pod full of voxyn tissue, enough to clone a million. Anakin's aura flashed and dimmed, flashed again and dimmed more, his cells rupturing in chain reactions, the cycles coming faster and faster as less of him remained to contain the energy. He felt himself not exactly departing, but melting back into the Force. He pulled his last thermal detonator off his harness and thumbed the timer three clicks.

Go now.

"Anakin, I can't!" Jaina commed.

Anakin raised the detonator so his brother and sister could see. *Thirty seconds.* He released the trigger. *Take her, Jacen. Kiss Tahiri for me.*

With the charging warriors almost on him again, Anakin threw the detonator across the grashal. He wasn't conscious of using the Force to guide it, but he must have, because it hit the impostor in the head.

Anakin was too busy parrying to see what happened for the next few seconds, but when he finally managed to spring away from his attackers—he was no longer strong enough to flip or cartwheel—the impostor was gathering himself up, rubbing his head and searching for what had struck him. Even from thirty meters, his broken nose and misshapen eye orbit identified him clearly as Nom Anor.

When the executor's gaze fell on the silver sphere, his real eye grew as large as his plaeryin bol. He reached down.

Anakin used the Force to nudge the sphere away, then caught an amphistaff in the ribs and went down hard, letting his lightsaber fall from his hand. His aura was only a faint glow, flickering between dim and nonexistent. The maelstrom inside was dying away now, flowing back into the Force.

Nom Anor rushed for the detonator again. Anakin waited, waited until the executor was almost on it, then reached out with the Force one last time, rolling the sphere toward the cargo pod.

He did not hear the angry curse that followed, nor did he see Nom Anor fleeing at a dead run.

By then, Anakin was gone.

Chapter 44

No way they're coming for Eclipse, not with the armada that left Borleias," Kenth Hamner was saying. Now serving as the official liaison between the Jedi and the New Republic, he had arrived an hour before to report some alarming Yuuzhan Vong fleet movements. "Even if they *could* bring that many ships in here, it would take a standard year to stage through the hyperspace gauntlet."

The Jedi's best tacticians were gathered in the Eclipse war room, studying the three displays Luke had put up. One hologram showed the array of hyperspace routes spraying outward from the planet Borleias. Another showed the tortuous route into Eclipse, along with the planet itself hidden behind its screen of asteroid belts and gas giant neighbors. The third hologram showed the entire Coruscant system, and it was to this map that everyone's eye kept drifting—specifically, to an obscure cluster of comets on the capital planet's side of the system.

Mara pointed into the swirling mass of comet tails. "And there are uncharted asteroids orbiting with the OboRins?"

"We're keeping an eye on them," Kenth said. "We can take them out anytime."

No one suggested that the asteroids might be anything but reconnaissance vessels. Corran Horn, who was one of the Jedi studying the display, had confirmed not long before that space rock was a favorite camouflage for Yuuzhan Vong scout ships.

"This is it, then," Luke said.

He adjusted the holoprojector, annulling the displays of the Borleias hyperspace routes and the Eclipse system—then, when his connection to Anakin suddenly began to strengthen, failed to enlarge the Coruscant map. He flashed on an image of Yuuzhan Vong charging past a tangle of burning vines, of a purple blade ticking back and forth, of a golden light burning in a dark place. Luke could feel that his nephew was calm and focused, in harmony with the Force and himself—but weak and growing weaker.

"Master Skywalker?" Corran asked. "What is it?"

Luke turned away and did not answer. He knew that Saba Sebatyne had felt the Hara sisters die, and others were gone, too— he could not feel *who*, only that there was a growing Jedi absence in the Force. Now the strike team was losing Anakin, as well—and Luke had sent him, had sent them *all*.

"Luke?" Mara was standing behind him, taking his hand.

Luke let her, but reached out for Jacen and Jaina, found them filled with sorrow and horror, fear and rage, but alive, at least, and strong.

Then Anakin was gone.

Luke felt like the Yuuzhan Vong had reached inside and torn his nephew out of his own body. There was a black void in his heart, a tempest so fierce and cold he began to shake uncontrollably.

"Luke, stop!" Mara's fingers dug into his arm and jerked him around to face her. "You've got to shut it down. Ben will feel you. Think of what this will do to him!"

"Ben . . ."

Luke covered Mara's hand with his and drew in on himself, dampening his presence in the Force—and losing his connection to the twins. Unable to contain the anger rising up inside him, and unwilling to inflict it on his son, he turned and brought his hand down on the holoprojector.

"Master Skywalker!" Kenth gasped.

"It's Anakin," Mara said.

"Anakin? Oh . . ." The room broke into groans and startled outcries, then Corran managed to ask, "Master Skywalker . . . what can we do?"

What indeed, Luke wondered. He looked to Mara, struggling to regain his composure and focus his thoughts. The question was not what they *could* do, but what they *had* to do.

"Anakin . . ." Luke choked on the words, tried again. "Anakin died for a reason."

Corran and the others waited in silence, and looked to him expectantly.

"What we need to do is prep our battle wings," Mara said, taking charge. She turned to Kenth. "And get in touch with Admiral Sovv. We're going to need a place to berth when we get to Coruscant."

With circles under his eyes almost as dark as his glassy black Sullustan pupils themselves, General Yeel's vidimage suggested that of a chubby-cheeked Yuuzhan Vong child—a *spoiled* chubby-cheeked Yuuzhan Vong child. Han banged the heel of his palm on the comm desk—out of vidcam pickup—and pasted a forbearing smile on his face.

"I'm not saying installation security is lax, General Yeel," Han said. He was with Lando in the study of his Eastport apartment, trying to do the New Republic a favor and finding it impossible as usual. "But Viqi Shesh was on NRMOC. She could have slipped an infiltrator onto a shielding crew anytime in the last two years. Why take a chance?"

"Do you have evidence of that, Solo?" Not *General* Solo, or

Retired General, or even Han, but just *Solo.* "If you have evidence, I will institute a review at once."

"I don't have evidence. That's the point." Han ran a hand over his brow. "Look, what could it hurt to assign a couple of YVHs to every generator station? This is a great deal."

"Yes, *free* is a great deal," Yeel replied. "What's wrong with them?"

Lando slipped into the vidcam's view. "Nothing is wrong with them, General, I assure you. I'm a loyal citizen of the New Republic doing everything he can to help."

Yeel looked doubtful. "Wasn't it a YVH droid that failed to protect Chief of State Fey'lya when infiltrators attacked *him?*"

"That was a glitch in the demonstration program," Lando said patiently. "The droids I'm donating to the New Republic will be combat ready—*fully* combat ready."

"That is what frightens me, Calrissian." Yeel blinked twice, then placed his arms on his table and leaned toward his vidcam. "Chief of State Fey'lya asked me to take your call, and I have. But I am *not* going to put new technology into my generating stations without a full compatibility evaluation—and Planetary Shielding will not be conducting any evaluations until we know where the fleet at Borleias has gone. I'm sorry, Calrissian—"

An anguished wail echoed down the corridor, so shrill and frenzied that Han did not recognize the voice as human—much less Leia's—until he was already out of his chair and snatching his blaster holster off the table.

"Leia!"

If anything, the wailing grew louder and less human. Han raced down the corridor to Leia's private study, where he found Adarakh and Meewalh flanking the desk and looking uncharacteristically confused and helpless. The furred image of the Bothan general of the Orbital Defense Command was staring out of the vidscreen, looking confused and inanely repeating "Princess Leia? Princess

Leia?" Leia herself was lying on the floor, curled into a fetal ball and screaming something incomprehensible.

When Han saw no obvious threat in the room, he knelt at Leia's side and grabbed her arm. "Leia?"

She did not seem to realize he was there. Her eyes were rimmed in red and her tears were pooling on the floor, and the only thing Han could get out of her was a long "—aaaaaaa—"

The Bothan general continued to repeat "Princess Leia? Princess Leia?"

Lando came into the room and, ignoring the comm unit, put a hand on Han's shoulder. "What is it?"

Han shook his head and looked to the Noghri.

"Lady Vader was speaking with General Ba'tra," Meewalh explained. "She was explaining how Lady Risant Calrissian is already on her way with a thousand Hunter Ones, then she suddenly stopped speaking—"

Leia grasped Han's arm and began to sputter, "Aa . . . aaa . . ."

And Han knew. Anakin was gone.

And Leia had felt him die.

"Princess Leia?" Ba'tra droned. "Princess, are you—"

Finding the DL-44 still in his hand, Han used it to blast the comm unit silent. It felt so good that he turned the weapon on the holopad and blasted that, too—and then the security system vid bank and anything else that crackled and made sparks when a supercharged particle beam burned a hole through it.

"Han!" Lando cried. "Han? What are you doing?"

"He's dead." Han shot a datapad off Leia's desk, then sent Lando diving by swinging the blaster around to target a holographic wall panel. "They killed our boy."

Han pulled the trigger and watched the pinnacles of Terrarium City erupt into a spark storm, then Adarakh was on him, trapping his blaster arm in a control lock and wrenching the weapon away.

Han collapsed to his haunches and began to sob, now too weary to be angry, too certain of the look in Leia's eyes to doubt the truth.

Leia did not seem to notice any of this. Still wailing in anguish, she gathered herself up and ran from the room. Han watched her go, realized somewhere in the back of his mind that Ben was crying. Lando squatted at his side. Blaster arm still locked in Adarakh's grasp, Han looked over at his old friend.

"Anakin is gone."

"Han, I'm sorry." Lando squatted at Han's side, then caught Adarakh's eye and nodded toward the door. "First Chewie, and now this. I can't imagine."

"I can't either. Those terrible things I said to him . . . ," Han said. In the back of the apartment, Ben was crying more ferociously than ever, and Leia was sobbing even more loudly. "I drove him to it. He had to prove—"

"No." Lando leaned in close and locked gazes. "Listen to me, old buddy. Anakin died because he was a Jedi Knight doing what Jedi Knights do—not because of what happened to Chewbacca, not because he was trying to prove anything to you."

"How would you know?" Han snapped. He was lashing out not because Lando had said anything wrong, but because the anger was returning and he need to be angry with someone. "He wasn't your son."

"No, he wasn't." A pained—perhaps even guilty—look came to Lando's eyes. "But I was the one who turned him over to the Yuuzhan Vong. He didn't blame himself for what happened to Chewbacca . . . and he knew how much you loved him. Everyone could see that."

The gentleness in Lando's voice robbed Han of his anger, and substituted despair instead. He knew that his friend was only trying to comfort him, to keep him from falling apart like he had after Chewbacca's death—but the words rang hollow. Han knew how he had behaved after Chewie died, how he had taken out his anger on Anakin and let the rest of his family drift apart while he wallowed in his grief. He had nearly lost them, and now it was happening again—and this time, Leia was not going to be there to pull them all together again. This time, Leia would need someone else to be strong.

C-3PO clunked into the room, his electronic voice shrill with alarm. "Someone, please help! Mistress Leia has switched Nana off, and now she's going to crush him!"

Keeping one hand on Han's shoulder, Lando rose. "Crush who, See-Threepio?"

C-3PO threw his golden arms into the air. "Ben! She won't let him go."

"I'll see what I can do." Lando pushed C-3PO at Han and started for the door. "Watch him."

"No, Lando—I'll go." Han grabbed C-3PO's arm and pulled himself to his feet. "It'll need to be me."

Lando lifted his brow. "Are you up to this?"

Han nodded. "I'll have to be."

He led the way to the nursery in the back of the apartment. Leia was standing in front of a transparisteel viewing pane, clutching Ben to her shoulder and staring out at the passing hover traffic, patting him on the back and swaying gently from foot to foot. If she realized that he was crying at all, she did not seem to recognize that it was because of her own keening.

Han went to her side and shooed the Noghri away, then slipped a hand between Leia and the baby.

"Let go, Leia." He gently began to pry Ben free. "You need to let me take him."

Her gaze drifted toward his face, but her eyes seemed to look through him without seeing anything. "Han?"

"That's right." Han caught Lando's eye and passed him Ben, then wrapped Leia in his arms and held her—just held her. "I'm here, Princess. I'll always be here."

Chapter 45

hey came like snow, at first a few contacts dropping out of hyperspace, then a steady shower cascading down toward the OboRin Comet Cluster, then finally a data blizzard that swept Luke's tactical display white with vector lines and bogey symbols.

"Outlying sensors confirm hostile contacts." Even over the battle net, the signals coordinator—SigCor—sounded jittery. "Stand by for a message from Admiral Sovv."

The admiral's nasal voice came over the battle net, addressing what amounted to half of the New Republic Space Navy in a less-than-inspiring Sullustan monotone. Luke's attention began to wander almost immediately. Still reeling from Anakin's death, he could not help second-guessing himself, reexamining his decision to let his nephew embark on such a dangerous mission. Had he overestimated the strike team's abilities—or underestimated those of the Yuuzhan Vong?

Mara's voice came over a private channel. "Luke, stop beating yourself up. You can't carry a load like that into battle."

"I know, Mara." There were times when Luke truly wished his emotions were not an open book to his wife—this was one of them. "But it's not so easy. I keep thinking I let them go on a suicide mission."

"You didn't," Mara said. "Does Leia blame you?"

"Leia is in no condition to blame anyone," Luke said. He could feel his sister's anguish beneath his own—a numb, almost physical pain not so different from what he had experienced when he lost his hand to Darth Vader. She was in shock, struggling to accept that a part of herself was gone forever. "But you heard how Han was."

"He was worried about Leia."

"That's what he said," Luke replied.

This time, Mara did not argue. Luke could sense how frightened she was about leaving Ben with Han and Leia while they were both so grief-stricken, but he knew better than to suggest again that she go to Coruscant. She had already told him she would go *after* the battle, and even Luke Skywalker—especially Luke Skywalker—knew better than to press Mara once she had made up her mind.

A moment later, Mara said, "Luke, it would have been wrong to deny your nephew his chance to save the Jedi, and Han and Leia know it, too. Think back to that meeting in the crater room. They're the ones who told you to let him go."

Knowing Mara would sense his nod even if she could not see it, Luke remained quiet and began to concentrate on his breathing, employing a Jedi relaxation technique to focus his thoughts. The truth was, he had a bad feeling about the coming battle that had nothing to do with Anakin. With what they had planned, Eclipse was going to lose pilots—maybe a lot of them.

Admiral Sovv captured Luke's attention again by thanking him and the Jedi "intelligence apparatus" for alerting the Defense Force to the time and place of the enemy's arrival. This drew a chuckle from Mara and the rest of the Jedi Knights; the "apparatus" had been a growing sense among the more powerful Masters that there was trouble coming from the OboRin Comet Cluster. Given that the Force was blind to the Yuuzhan Vong, the Jedi had been mystified by the feelings and reluctant to act on them—until they learned from Talon Karrde that a huge Yuuzhan Vong assault fleet had departed Borleias about the same time the sensations began. Admiral Sovv, who had been looking for political cover to concentrate his defenses around Coruscant, had seized on the feelings as a "reliable report from Jedi intelligence" and used them as an excuse to recall several outlying fleets. Wedge had told Luke privately that the admiral did not really expect the Yuuzhan Vong to show, but had set up today's ambush for the sake of maintaining appearances.

When contacts finally stopped dropping out of hyperspace on the tactical display, Sovv said, "The moment is upon us, my friends. Please switch to your assigned battle channel now, and may the Force be with you."

Luke opened the channel assigned to Eclipse. "You all know what we're attempting and why. Stay in formation, and follow your squadron leader's orders. The battle will turn on us—"

"And the war on the battle," several voices replied.

"We know, Master Skywalker," Saba Sebatyne said. "You have said this seven times already."

This drew a nervous laugh from both Eclipse wings.

Luke would have liked to do his part to ease the tension with a witty comeback, but found that part of his mind still too fogged by grief. "Sorry. Just wanted to be sure. Control?"

"Stand by for target identification," Corran said. "Hisser, go ahead and stick your nose out. Everyone else hold positions."

Saba's blastboat slipped out of formation and eased alongside the comet—a wide-swinging stray—behind which the Eclipse squadrons were hiding. Luke switched his tactical feed from fleet to Jedi. The display image rotated ninety degrees, so that the main body of the comet cluster now hung along one side and the contacts were streaking horizontally across the screen. The counter at the bottom of the display read in the tens of thousands and still rising.

A small square appeared in the center of Luke's tactical display, outlining a set of five blips near the heart of the invading fleet. Danni Quee's voice came over the comm channel.

"Yammosk located. We'll pinpoint which vessel when the fighting heats up."

"Everyone fast and furious?" Corran asked.

Luke checked his command display to confirm that the status readout for each craft in his squadron read full DSW—drives, shields, and weapons. When he found everything at full capability, he opened his emotions to Tam—the third member of his and Mara's shielding trio—and chinned his microphone.

"Sabers are good."

When the other three squadrons also verified, Corran cleared them for launch. Both wings—seventy-two X-wings and eight supercharged blastboats—dropped out from behind their comet and accelerated to near-light, closing so rapidly that they were past the perimeter pickets before the Yuuzhan Vong could loose a magma missile. Luke took the lead, plotting an interception vector that would carry them into the heart of the main fleet without making their target obvious.

"Well done," Corran commed.

The tactical display shifted scales, now showing Luke's two wings of blue symbols surrounded by a sea of yellow Yuuzhan Vong symbols, each displaying the ship's mass, analog class, and—when the *Jolly Man*'s computers could match the attributes to a profile in the data bank—occasionally even a name. Intent on pushing through the comet cluster and carrying through on its surprise attack, the enemy fleet maintained its loose formation so that each vessel would have maneuvering room. When Luke looked outside the cockpit, he could see the ships only as black areas blotting out the distant starlight; this far from Coruscant's sun, there was little light to illuminate their dark hulls.

A frigate identified as the *Reaver* loosed the first Yuuzhan Vong salvo, but only one plasma ball was leading the fast-moving attack wings far enough to strike home. It hit one of the Shockers' X-wings and, overwhelming the shields, reduced the starfighter to a flash of photons and atoms.

"Hold your fire," Luke ordered. He began to jink and swerve, deliberately keeping both combat wings between two vessels at all times so enemy gunners would risk hitting their own ships if they fired and missed. "If we stop to fight, we're lost."

As they streaked deeper into the fleet, the Yuuzhan Vong kept up a steady but ineffectual dribble of fire, all the while maneuvering to clear a firing lane. It was a futile exercise against the nimble X-wings and their blastboat escorts. With the surveillance crews on the *Jolly Man* watching their backs, Luke always knew when a lane was opening and slid into a new attack vector. The Shockers lost one of their blastboats to a magma missile, but the crew retaliated by mass-firing their torpedoes and bombs before going EV. Almost half the volley penetrated the cruiser's shielding singularities, and a long line of breaches began to vent bodies and atmosphere from the port side.

A skip carrier decelerated and turned to cut them off. As soon as coralskippers began to drop off the vessel and form up, Danni's targeting square shrank and isolated an unnamed heavy cruiser in the heart of the five-ship group she had designated earlier.

"Yammosk confirmed."

Luke studied the tactical display, then touched a finger to a destroyer analog well off their current vector. The name beneath the destroyer was *Sunulok*.

"Designate secondary, Artoo." A circle appeared around the

vessel, and Luke opened a comm channel to Corran. "Control, are we clear for a diversionary launch on that one? We'll bump over and slide away on the other side."

"You're good to go, Farmboy." Corran divided the target into attack sectors by squadron, then commed Luke, "By the way, SigCor says they're reading ion tails at the front of the fleet."

"Ion tails?"

Yuuzhan Vong did not use ion drives.

"Maybe they're bringing the Peace Brigade along," Mara said. "That would explain how we felt them coming."

Luke stretched his awareness of the Force forward. He found nothing for a moment, then felt a whole wall of life at the forward edge of the fleet. "Too many for a crime cartel. I feel two or three million beings there."

"Must be one of their slave armies," Tam said.

Luke was not so sure. The presence lacked the muted, staticlike sense caused by the head growths the Yuuzhan Vong used to control their slaves, but he had no time to contemplate what else he might be feeling. The skip carrier was dropping the last of its coralskippers, and the first squadrons were already coming out to meet them.

"X-wings slow, blastboats break!" Luke ordered.

The seven surviving blastboats turned hard, swinging in behind the destroyer analog's rearmost escort frigates. Luke waited until their vector had straightened, then gave the command for the X-wings to follow. All four squadrons pivoted on their bellies, reverse-firing two engines and overthrusting the opposite pair, and were instantly flashing past the blastboats toward the two escorts.

Flashes of ruby fire blossomed from the frigates' rocky sterns as they belched magma missiles at their attackers. Luke dropped his nose and dived for two seconds to force the Yuuzhan Vong gunners to fully depress their launchers, then snapped into a climb and accelerated past their sterns while they tried to readjust. He checked his tactical display and saw a dozen squadrons of coralskippers swinging after them from the skip carrier, but their pursuit angle was so poor they would never reach the killing zone behind the X-wings.

When Luke raised his eyes again, it was to find space burning around him. He thought for an instant he had been hit, but felt no surge of concern from Mara or Tam. He gave his hand over to the Force and continued to jink and juke in tandem with his shielding companions, and the firestorm quickly resolved itself into exploding plasma balls and streaking magma missiles. A crackle of static announced the destruction of someone in his squadron, and R2-D2 scolded him with long series of whistles.

"I don't like it either, Artoo," Luke said. "But Admiral Sovv is depending on us."

The maelstrom faded as quickly as it had erupted, and Luke checked his tactical display. He had taken his squadrons exactly where he intended, midway between the two escorts, but this pair had shown no fear of firing in each other's direction. He had lost one of the Sabers' blastboats, while the Dozen and the Shockers had both lost an X-wing. The frigates had paid a steep price for missed attacks, however; both symbols were blinking steadily to show that they were moderately damaged.

"We must be doing something right," Kyp commed. "They really don't want us near that big rock."

Another pair of escorts came into view, their sterns sparkling with missile launches. The *Sunulok*'s tail was now visible between them, a dark disk the size of a thumb tip. Luke went into an evasive dive-and-rise, and missile trails began to streak past above and below. He checked the tactical display and found the dozen squadrons from the skip carrier still on their tail.

"It looks like we'll have to take this ruse all the way," he commed. "We'll separate by squadrons and run hulls past the escorts. Shockers and Dozen left, Sabers and Knights right."

The order was acknowledged by a flurry of comm clicks, then

the four squadrons separated into pairs. Luke led the Sabers and Knights on an undulating course toward the escort on the right. Narrowly escaping a trio of plasma balls launched in a desperation spread, he brought his X-wing in above the frigate's weapon banks and skimmed its flank barely two meters off the hull. To his surprise, both escorts continued to attack the squadrons opposite, pouring so much fire into each other that R2-D2 had to reinforce the particle shields because of all the yorik coral geysering up in their path.

"Danni, you're sure the yammosk is on the cruiser?" Kyp commed. "Because the way they're—"

"I'm sure. The yammosk is going crazy." Danni's transmission ended in a crackle of static, then she came back yelling, "Drif!"

Luke did not need to check his command display to know that Saba had lost one of her Jedi pilots. He felt the Barabel die. The Sabers reached the bow of the frigate, and he immediately angled across the nose, both to confuse the enemy weapon crews and to set the squadron up for their diversionary attack run.

Then the comm speaker crackled with a huge pulse of static, and a nova-bright flash illuminated space behind Luke. He checked his tactical display and saw the adjacent escort coming apart just behind the Shockers, engulfing Kyp's Dozen in flame and debris and hurling X-wings in every direction. Three, four, and finally five symbols winked out as starfighters exploded, then the blastboats went, and two more pilots went EV.

"Headhunter?" Corran commed. "Headhunter, are you there?"

No answer.

"Any Dozener?"

Again, no answer.

"Just fried circuits," Rigard said optimistically. "We had a good spike ourselves."

"Let's hope so," Luke said. He checked his display and saw

that six of the skip squadrons pursuing them were peeling off to go after what remained of the Dozen. "Dozeners, if you can hear this, you're out of action. Run if you can, or shut down and try to hide."

The order was answered by a single scratchy comm click. Luke felt Mara reach out to him, silently urging him to forget the sinking feeling in his stomach and concentrate on the task at hand. Luke turned back to the *Sunulok* and found the destroyer analog's stern swelling up before him, as big as a sandcrawler and growing fast, a half-dozen weapon stations spitting plasma balls the size of banthas.

"Arm one proton torpedo," Luke ordered. "Fire on my mark, then go over the top and be ready to break."

By the time the last comm click had acknowledged his order, Luke had lost his second blastboat to one of the big plasma balls, and the *Sunulok*'s wing of coralskippers was streaming back beneath the destroyer's belly to engage the X-wings.

"Ready, mark!" Luke ordered.

The blue glow of fifty ion drives filled the darkness and resolved itself into a dazzling wall of receding circles. The shielding crews began to work their dovin basals, capturing perhaps a third of the proton torpedoes and forcing the proximity fuses to detonate a safe distance from the *Sunulok*. Luke pulled up, angling for the top of the destroyer analog, and watched with satisfaction as the rest of the torpedoes struck home. The entire stern came apart, hurling a wall of flame and yorik coral pebbles in front of the approaching X-wings.

Relying on their shields for protection, they shot through the rubble and streaked along the spine of the wounded ship. Luke continued for perhaps a half kilometer, then broke off sharply and dived toward the heavy cruiser. R2-D2 tweedled helpfully and displayed a message for Luke.

"Thanks, Artoo." Luke armed the rest of his torpedoes and

shadow bombs. "Twenty seconds to target. Preparing for the main attack run."

"Copy." Corran was quiet for an instant, then said, "Message relayed. Good hunting."

They were halfway to their target when a wall of New Republic turbolaser fire erupted from the main body of the comet cluster and briefly silhouetted the entire Yuuzhan Vong fleet. It looked like nothing more menacing than a vast field of black lozenge-shaped asteroids, but Luke experienced a terrible disturbance in the Force as several thousand beings from their own galaxy were blasted back to their elemental atoms.

Everything went dark again, and an uneasy silence settled over the Eclipse comm channels. Though only half of the pilots and crew in the combat wings were Force-sensitive, the rest had been around Jedi long enough to have some idea of what their battle mates were experiencing.

An instant later, the vanguard of the Yuuzhan Vong fleet responded to the ambush with a lightning storm of crimson flashes and streaking fireballs. The New Republic turbolasers flashed to life again, the Force quavered with another thousand deaths, and the battle exploded into its full horror.

Luke saw a pair of frigates accelerating to cut them off from the cruiser. He touched his tactical display, designating the rearmost one as a secondary target.

"We'll go through this one," he said. "Hisser, will you take the lead?"

"My honor," the Barabel replied.

The Wild Knights drew into a tight formation and moved forward, a golden aura slowly expanding around Saba's blastboat. The frigates dropped their skips and began to pour more fire into the glowing ball of radiance, which only made it grow faster as Izal Waz used the Force to trap the light. Once the sphere was large enough, Luke lined the other two squadrons up behind it, picking off skips as they tried desperately to fight their way into the golden orb and stop the Wild Knights.

As Danni had described happening at Arkania, the frigate eventually grew so nervous about the approaching sphere that it turned a shielding singularity on it. The glowball abruptly lengthened as it was caught and accelerated by the gravity of the tiny black hole.

"Drop the block!" Saba ordered.

By the time she finished giving the command, the glowball had stretched into an ovoid twice as long as it was thick. Izal Waz let the golden sphere fade away, and the Wild Knights' X-wings fanned out, already firing proton torpedoes. The shielding crews scrambled to redirect their singularities—and never saw the two-ton block of black durasteel that it had just accelerated to several hundred thousand kilometers an hour. The frigate did not explode so much as flash out of existence, and the wings from Eclipse suddenly found themselves diving on their target through a cloud of superheated dust.

A full wing of skips came boiling out of the cruiser to intercept them. The ship itself opened up with all batteries, pouring constant streams of fire from its bow and stern in an attempt to force the attacking X-wings to come at it amidships and meet its coralskippers.

"Time to try out Control's new targeting system," Luke said. "Break into your shielding trios and go down the center."

"And don't stop to dogfight—those skips from the carrier are still on your tail," Corran said. He switched to a private channel, then added, "And, Farmboy, you need to get this right the first time. Listen."

There was a scratchy pause as Corran patched in the civilian emergency channel, then a confused babble filled Luke's cockpit. A moment later, he began to recognize individual voices—and wished he hadn't.

"—on us, please! We're civilians from—"

"—is the *Happy Hutt* with five thousand refugees—"

"—*Meteor Racer* out."

"Six hundred transponders just came on, Luke," Corran said. "They confirm what you're hearing."

"Of course they do."

Luke needed no further explanation to know what was happening. He recognized the *Happy Hutt* as one of the refugee ships missing from the evacuation of Ralltiir, and he felt certain that a records search would turn up the *Meteor Racer*'s name, as well.

The yammosk cruiser's wing of skips began to fire at maximum range, no doubt trying to force their attackers to decelerate and be caught from behind. Instead, the X-wings and blastboats continued forward at maximum firing velocity.

Luke clicked off with Corran and had R2-D2 activate his supplementary targeting system. The reticle quickly locked onto the gravitational pulses coming from the dovin basal in his target's nose. With lasers quadded on full power, he squeezed the trigger. One bolt streaked out a millisecond ahead of the others, following the targeting lock straight toward the skip's nose. The rest diverged according to a carefully calculated ratio of distance and velocity until they were caught by the gravity of the skip's shielding system and bent back inward. The first bolt vanished into the singularity; the other three converged three meters behind it, taking the coralskipper directly in the pilot's compartment.

"Almost as good as the Force," Luke said.

He found a pair of skips coming out of the field of detonations that had been the cruiser wing a moment before and set his targeting reticle on the one on the left.

"Already spoken for," Mara said. She and Tam fired simultaneously; a moment later, both skips vanished. "Sorry, Farmboy."

"You're forgiven," Luke said.

With its entire detachment of skips eliminated in the flash of an eye, the cruiser began to concentrate its fire in the approach lane.

Knowing that even one of its big plasma balls would take out an entire shielding trio, Luke ordered his wings to fan out. As quick as the pilots were to obey, one trio of Sabers evaporated into the flame, and the Shockers lost their last blastboat.

But now the cruiser was laid out before them, a kilometer-long lozenge of dark yorik coral striped with bands of knobby weapons banks. With Mara to one side and Tam to the other, Luke juked and jinked for a three count, firing his quadded lasers into roiling clouds of flame while he gave the rest of his pilots time to reach firing position.

Finally, they were ready. "Fire everything you have—we won't be coming back."

Luke fired the two proton torpedoes from his open bank, fired three more from the other bank, then dropped the shadow bombs stored in the XJ3's third set of launchers and used the Force to send them on their way. He saw the first two torpedoes vanish into a shielding singularity, then a plasma ball erupted from a weapon nodule ahead, coming so quickly at this distance that he barely had time to slide out of the way and kiss wings with Mara.

"Close, Farmboy."

Luke eased away, then winced inwardly as she dipped her own X-wing and sent a magma missile ricocheting off her shields.

"You're one to talk," Luke commed.

Then the attacks dwindled away, and finally they could see the flames and debris erupting from the breaches their shadow bombs and torpedoes had torn into the hull. In some places, secondary explosions could be seen rolling down sections of exposed deck, and there were clouds of bodies and matériel billowing out into the vacuum. Luke decelerated as much as he dared with the skips coming behind them and locked down the trigger of his laser cannon, burning round after round into the interior of the cruiser.

"Danni, what's the yammosk status?"

"Quieting, but still alive."

Luke checked the tactical display and found the skips from the carrier still thirty seconds behind them.

"What part of the vessel?" Luke asked.

"Negative, Farmboy," Corran said. "We talked about this—you had your shot, now get out of there."

"Danni, what part?" Luke demanded.

Mara's apprehension level spiked. "Farmboy, one dead hero—"

"There are a lot of dead heroes out there today—too many to leave this undone." Luke checked his tactical display; twenty seconds. "Where? Now!"

"Try lower deck, midships," Danni said. "I can't be sure."

"I'll take one more shot." Luke angled toward the middle of the ship and continued to decelerate. "Everyone else, go."

"Not on your life," Mara said.

She and Tam decelerated along with him. With the rest of the wing flying cover, they began to work their way along the cruiser's hull, pushing through the body clouds and sticking their noses into likely looking holes.

"Farmboy, you have fifteen seconds before those skips are all over you," Corran said. "And there's something else."

He patched the Fleet Command channel through.

"—you to cease fire!" Sovv's nasal voice was shouting. "The New Republic navy does not butcher its own people!"

"*We* are not butchering them," Garm Bel Iblis countered. "The Yuuzhan Vong are. *We* are trying to fire around them."

"And failing miserably, General," Traest Kre'fey countered.

"What about Coruscant?" Garm argued. "What about the Jedi? Do you know how many pilots they lost to give us this chance?"

Corran deactivated the channel. "Luke, the Yuuzhan Vong are already pushing through the comet cluster. Rather than fire through the refugee screen, Traest is falling back and trying to maneuver. Garm will have to join him soon or be cut off, and Wedge is two minutes behind schedule because the battle is moving toward Coruscant."

According to Sovv's original plan, Wedge would be the hammer falling on Garm and Traest's anvil, sweeping in from behind the Yuuzhan Vong to drive them into the ambush.

"Wedge can still surprise them—if the yammosk is dead," Luke said. He could sense that Mara felt betrayed by Sovv's decision not to fire on the refugees, but Luke was not so sure. Would a New Republic willing to attack through a fleet of its own people be worth saving? "This isn't over yet."

"Five seconds, Farmboy."

Luke stuck his X-wing's nose into a breach just below the dormant weapons bank and burned through two more decks, puncturing a sealed bulkhead and sucking a long stream of startled Yuuzhan Vong out into the vacuum.

"You found it!" Danni exclaimed.

He was joined by Mara and Tam. Combined, their fire was enough to blast through the other side of the vessel, and Luke glimpsed a many-tentacled creature flying out the breach amid a cloud of frozen vapor.

"That's—"

Danni's confirmation dissolved into static as a skip's plasma ball dissipated against the blastboat's shields. The attack was answered instantly by a storm of laser cannon fire, but staying to fight was the last thing on Luke's mind. He pulled his X-wing out of the breach and dropped the nose.

"Break off!"

Luke led the way under the cruiser and up on the other side, forcing the oncoming skips to decelerate or risk having the X-wings pop up on their tails. Without the yammosk to coordinate them, the coralskippers reacted in disarray. Some streaked over the cruiser at full speed and some under, while others stopped cautiously on the other side.

Luke sighed in silent relief, then commed, "Let's go find Wedge. We've got to refuel, rearm—"

"And return," Saba said. She sounded more eager than determined. "There are still plenty of Yuuzhan Vong for everyone."

Chapter 46

They had eaten worse things—the sour fungus growing on the walls of Nolaa Tarkona's ryll mines came to mind—so Jacen knew it was not his sister's delicate sensibilities that kept her from choking down the tasteless pulp Alema had commandeered from their terrified Yuuzhan Vong host. Nor was it the urgency of their situation. The strike team was hiding in a one-room lodging cell on the outskirts of a domicile warren deep inside the worldship, trying to stay out of sight until Tesar reported back with news of the queen's location. They had seen no sign of Nom Anor or his troops since the battle in the grashal, when they had escaped by bringing the passage ceiling down behind them and fleeing into the heart of the worldship.

Jacen scooped a bowlful of pulp from a shell-like serving basin and pressed it into Jaina's hands. "I don't feel like eating either, but you need to keep up your strength."

Jaina hurled the gruel against the bioluminescent wall. Their Yuuzhan Vong captive, a lowly worker who was almost attractive in her utter lack of mutilations or tattoos, cringed in the corner as though the bowl had been thrown at her. The lichen began to glow more brightly as it absorbed nutrients, and no one spoke.

Jacen could feel the guilt and anger tearing his sister apart, though her emotions were so intermingled with his own that he could barely distinguish them. They shared a void that would never again be whole, an emptiness that he sensed pulling at Jaina like a vacuum breach. He laid a hand on her knee, hoping his touch might serve as her anchor.

"We can't give up. We still need to destroy the queen."

Jaina looked up, a faint spark of presence finally showing in her vacant eyes. "You left him to the Yuuzhan Vong."

"We had to," Jacen said, accepting the rebuke. As much as he himself was hurting, he would rather Jaina lay the blame boiling up inside her on his shoulders than her own. "They were all over him. You saw that."

Jaina pushed his hand from her leg. "He put you in charge, and you left him behind."

Jacen said nothing. Though he knew his sister's own feelings of guilt were driving her to accuse him, he did not trust himself to keep an even voice.

"Jacen does not deserve your blame." Tenel Ka was sitting on the other side of the small room, her legs crossed beneath her and her posture as erect as ever. "Everyone heard the command, and we all know why he gave it. To disregard such an order would have been to dishonor Anakin's memory and dismiss his sacrifice."

"Stay out of this, Tenel Ka," Jaina said. "You can't possibly know anything about it. You have the emotional depth of a ronto."

The speed with which Tenel Ka unfolded her legs and stepped around the low table proved how mistaken Jaina was. Jacen thought for a moment the Dathomiri would slap his sister, but Tenel Ka only continued to glare until Jaina finally grew uncomfortable and looked away.

When she did, Tenel Ka said, "We are all hurting, Jaina. Your brother, too."

It was difficult to tell from Tenel Ka's tone whether she meant the words to be conciliatory or cutting, but they caused Jaina to stand. Jacen reached for Jaina's hand, but he needn't have worried. Zekk was already stepping between the pair, positioning himself to intercept any blow that might be thrown.

"What's this going to help?" Zekk addressed himself more to Tenel Ka than to Jaina. "Calm down."

Both women opened their hands, but continued to stand and stare, each waiting for the other to apologize. The room remained uncomfortable and silent. The other Jedi stared into their gruel.

They were spared the necessity of a long wait by a low growl over their comlinks. Jacen snatched up his own comlink.

"Tesar?" he asked. As the strike team's stealthiest member and only natural night hunter, the Barabel had been the obvious choice to send slinking through the murky lanes of the domicile warren. "Did you find her?"

He was answered not by the Barabel's voice, but by another low growl. It took him a moment to recognize the sound as a Shyrii-wook word, as Wookiee voices did not carry well over comlinks.

"Lowie?" Jaina gasped, grabbing her own comlink. "Is that you?"

Lowbacca confirmed his identity with a groan, then began a long apology for allowing the *Tachyon Flier* to be stolen.

"Lowie, forget it—they fooled us, too," Jacen said. "Where are you now?"

The answer Lowbacca rumbled was considerably more than a location.

"Why would they do that?" Jacen asked.

Lowbacca grunted a guess.

"Keep watching," Jaina said. "And whatever you do, stay with him. I'll be there as soon as I can."

She snapped her comlink off, and Jacen barely caught her arm before she reached the door.

"What are you doing?"

"Going after Anakin's body—what do you think?" It was

Tahiri who said this, speaking for the first time since they had fled the grashal. "They're not taking him anywhere."

She rose and went to Jaina's side, as did Alema and, a moment later, Zekk. Jacen ignored them all and continued to hold his sister's arm.

"What about Anakin's last words?" he asked. "He told us to destroy the queen."

"Then destroy her." Jaina tore her arm free of his hand and slapped the tickle pad. "But I'm going back."

Not even checking to see if she would be seen, Jaina jerked her lightsaber off her belt and led the others out into the dark.

Chapter 47

ave that Leia was smelling Ben's sweet breath instead of her own nervous sweat and the couch was not sluing around beneath her, war looked much the same on a wall-sized holovid as it did from the cockpit of the *Millennium Falcon*. Plasma balls still rolled over their targets in blossoms of white fire, turbolasers still laced the air with dazzling lances of color, wounded vessels still bled dark clouds of flash-frozen crew. The inset image of a grim-voiced Duros war correspondent described how the massive Yuuzhan Vong fleet was steadily pressing forward behind the screen of refugee ships despite a fierce running assault on its rear by Wedge Antilles's Fleet Group Three. The invaders had already crossed the orbit of Nabatu, the tenth planet of the Coruscant system, and were expected to reach the Ulabos ice bands by the end of the standard day.

The newsvid changed scenes, now showing the starliner *Swift Dreams* as it strayed into a barrage of turbolaser fire. Leia knew she should have felt something, should have been angered or frightened or something by the huge Yuuzhan Vong fleet sweeping down on Coruscant, but she was not. All she cared about was holding Ben in her arms, keeping his warmth pressed to her body.

As the *Swift Dreams* began to vent a cloud of tumbling refugees, a Bith correspondent appeared in the inset and reported that Garm Bel Iblis's Fleet Group Two continued to attack through the refugee screen, ignoring friendly-fire accidents such as the one shown and repeated orders from Admiral Sovv to stop. Several reliable sources claimed that Sovv had actually relieved Bel Iblis of command, an order that the general and his entire force also ignored. There were unsubstantiated reports of whole attack groups leaving Traest Kre'fey's Fleet Group One to join Bel Iblis in his effort to stop the Yuuzhan Vong at any price.

A pair of military analysts came on the newsvid and began to argue about whether Garm Bel Iblis's actions were the only way to delay the enemy until reinforcements arrived, or the first sign of the disintegration of the New Republic military.

"What a mess," Han said.

Leia did not reply. It was the first either of them had spoken since turning on the vidscreen, and she had actually forgotten he was sitting beside her. He had been following her around since it happened, as though he were afraid it might be necessary to snatch Ben out of her arms again. His constant presence was starting to annoy her, though she could not bear even the small emotional turmoil that she would cause by telling him so.

The analysts were replaced by an image of Luke and Mara climbing out of their starfighters. As they joined a long line of exhausted Jedi stumbling across a Star Destroyer's docking bay, a behorned Devaronian reporter appeared in the foreground and described how the Jedi-led attack wing continued their daring penetration missions, destroying more than fifteen capital ships in the heart of the Yuuzhan Vong fleet. While Eclipse's losses were classified for intelligence reasons, casualties in both personnel and equipment were rumored to be high. No one had seen the famous Kyp Durron or any of his Dozen since the battle began.

Han used a voice command to change to the senate feed. Good

old Han, worried about Leia being upset by news of the danger her brother was facing. She would have *liked* to be upset. She would have liked to feel something—anything—other than the hollow ache that consumed her now. Why had Han needed to change the feed? She just wanted him to go away and leave her alone.

The holovid split into two images, one showing the packed chamber, the other a hologram of Admiral Sovv standing before the high councilor's console. The Sullustan was demanding that NRMOC confirm his dismissal of General Bel Iblis and a long list of officers who had deserted to serve under his command. Borsk Fey'lya appeared in an inset, his fur tangled and his eyes sunken with stress.

"You have another way to hold the enemy at bay, Admiral Sovv?" Fey'lya asked.

The Sullustan's hologram continued to stare directly ahead. "Bel Iblis's mutiny is undermining the command integrity of the whole military."

"So the answer would be no," Fey'lya said. "In that case, I suggest that instead of interfering with General Bel Iblis's efforts, you follow his lead. You will not stop the Yuuzhan Vong by nipping at their heels."

This caused enough of a tumult in the senate chamber that Ben opened his eyes and began to cry. The TDL nanny droid was instantly at Leia's side, reaching for the infant with her four synthskin arms. Leia shielded Ben with her body and shooed the droid away. Nobody was taking this child from her.

Apparently speaking to Fey'lya via direct feed and unaware of the uproar in the chamber, Admiral Sovv did not wait for the audio to equalize, and his response was lost in the general tumult.

"I am also aware of how many lives we stand to lose here if you let the enemy drive that refugee fleet into our planetary shields," Fey'lya said. "Admiral Sovv, as the chairman of NRMOC, I am not only instructing you to fire through the hostage screen, I am *ordering* you to. If necessary, you are to fire on those ships directly."

Again, Admiral Sovv did not wait for the audio to equalize, and his reply was lost to the general uproar.

Fey'lya's response was not. "Then you are relieved of command, Admiral Sovv. I am sure General Bel Iblis understands the necessity of my order."

This time, the audio could not be adjusted to filter out the din in the chamber. Hundreds of senators stood and began to shout their disdain of the Bothan; a smaller number rose to applaud his courage and decisiveness. Then, one by one, holograms of Sovv's Sullustan protégés began to appear on the speaking floor beside the admiral. There were the Generals Muun and Yeel, Admiral Rabb, Commander Godt, and a dozen others, all powerful figures in the New Republic military who owed their rise to Admiral Sovv. Fey'lya did not seem all that surprised to see them appearing before him, but his beard fur bristled when General Rieekan, Commodore Brand, and even his fellow Bothan Traest Kre'fey added their holograms to those standing with Admiral Sovv.

"We don't need to watch this," Han declared, still trying to shield her from anything upsetting. "How about one of Garik Loran's old holodramas? Those always used to make you laugh."

Leia shook her head. "This is fine."

The disintegration of the New Republic military ought to keep her mind off the empty hurt inside. She signaled the droid for a collapsipack of formula and settled back to feed Ben. Now, if she could get Han to go away and leave her alone, she just might make it through the day.

Fey'lya rose and tried for a while to quiet the chamber. When this resulted only in a louder outburst of shouts, he gave up and returned to his seat, then disappeared behind his instrument console and began to work the controls. Apparently, he noticed that his face was still on the vidfeed, because he scowled and flipped something, and the inset disappeared.

The Solos' comm unit began to beep for attention. Han frowned and started to rise.

"Han!" Surprised by the alarm in her own voice, Leia caught him by the arm. "Where are you going?"

Han gestured vaguely in the direction of the study. "To answer the comm."

Leia shook her head and pulled Han back to the couch. "Don't leave me."

Han's face melted. "Never. I'm not going anywhere."

The comm unit continued to beep. The vidscreen split into three images, one showing the uproar in the senate galleries, another the holograms of Sovv and his supporters, and the third the top of Borsk Fey'lya's head as he stared at his instrument console.

C-3PO stepped into the door. "Excuse me, Master Han, but the comm unit is requesting attention."

"We know, Goldenrod," Han said. "We lost a son, not our hearing."

C-3PO's photoreceptors dimmed noticeably. "Oh, of course."

He clumped out of the room. The turmoil in the senate chamber finally began to fade, though there was still too much noise for the sound droid to pick up Admiral Sovv's voice when his hologram spoke to Fey'lya again.

The chief of state looked up long enough to signal the commanders to wait, then returned his attention to his instruments and spoke briefly.

A moment later, C-3PO walked into the room with a portable comm screen. He glanced at the vidscreen and tipped his head in robotic bewilderment, then turned to the couch.

"I'm sorry to interrupt, but Chief of State Fey'lya is asking to speak with Mistress Leia."

"Me?" Leia's mind would normally have leapt immediately to speculations as to why Fey'lya would be calling her at such a time, but all she could think of now was that she hadn't slept or bathed or even brushed her hair since it happened. "No. Absolutely not."

C-3PO glanced at the vidscreen again, then said, "He said to tell you it was matter of galactic security."

Leia looked to Han, and she did not even need to say anything. He simply took the comm screen from C-3PO and put it on the couch between them, with the built-in holocam facing him.

"This is Han, Chief Fey'lya. Leia can't talk right now."

On the wall screen, Leia watched Fey'lya's hand run through his head fur. "Yes, I've heard that something might have happened to Anakin. If that's so, I'd like to express not only my own sympathy, but that of the entire New Republic."

"We appreciate that." Han glanced at the wall screen and rolled his eyes, then looked back into the comm unit's holocam. "Now, I'm sure you'll understand if I sign off."

Fey'lya's hand darted out toward his instrument panel. "Wait— there was one other thing, General Solo."

"General?" Han looked over the comm screen at Leia and cocked an eyebrow. "Don't tell me you're reactivating my commission? You can't be that desperate for line officers."

It finally occurred to Leia that her husband was playing with the New Republic's chief of state not for his own amusement, but in an attempt to cheer her up. The effort touched her, even if it failed to come close to drawing a smile.

"Not yet, General Solo." Fey'lya's ears twitched, a rare sign of being flustered. "Actually, I was hoping to prevail on Leia to say a few words of support for my government to some of her old friends in the military."

Han glanced over the comm screen.

Fey'lya seemed to realize Leia was listening in, because he

quickly added, "I'm sure Leia realizes how supportive I have been of the Jedi recently, and the military has several sizable droid orders pending approval with Tendrando Arms."

Leia sighed and stared at the floor. Was this what Anakin had given his life for? The thought was so depressing that she started to sob again.

"Sorry, Chief Fey'lya," Han said, reaching for the comm screen power switch. "This time, you're on your own."

To Cilghal's sensitive nostrils, the foamy fungus eating away the scorched metal of the surviving X-wings smelled almost as foul as the soiled flight suits of the eight exhausted pilots themselves. There was an acidic edge to it, and the metallic mustiness of corrosion—a common-enough smell on oceanic worlds like her own Mon Calamari, but certainly a rarity coming from the rust-proof alloys used in starfighters.

Cilghal used a plastifibe agitator to scrape some of the yellow growth into a sample bag, and the musty smell grew stronger. Though she had already scanned for the typical Yuuzhan Vong attack toxins, she found herself wondering if she should have taken the time to return to her laboratory for her breath mask.

Behind her, Kyp Durron sneezed, then asked, "What do you think?" After several dozen terrifying hours zipped tight in his EV suit because of a vacuum leak in his cracked canopy, he was by far the worst-smelling of the survivors. "A new kind of weapon?"

"Not a very effective one, if it is," Cilghal said. "If this is all it grew in the time you needed to limp back to Eclipse, it will not destroy many fighters before the tech crews steam it off."

She continued to scrape and finally reached bare hull. As her nose had led her to suspect, the metal was pitted with corrosion. The fungus was metabolizing the X-wing itself—but why? The

Yuuzhan Vong would not have gone to the trouble of creating a self-heating, vacuum-hardened fungus unless there was a purpose to it.

Kyp sneezed, and Cilghal turned to face him.

"How long have you been doing that?" she asked. "Were you sneezing in your EV suit?"

Kyp shook his head and wiped his nose on the cuff of his flight suit. "It started when I unzipped."

"Spores." Motioning Kyp to follow along, Cilghal took her sample bag and started toward the hangar hatch. "They wanted it to produce spores."

Cilghal was just about to palm the control pad when the blaring roar of an assault alarm reverberated through the cavern. It continued for fifteen ear-piercing seconds, then was replaced by the watch officer's voice.

"Attention all crews: This is no drill. We have an incoming yorik coral vessel."

"Sith blood! It has to be that frigate again." Kyp had already explained to the watch officer that their return had taken so long because of a frigate that kept turning up behind them. "I could have sworn we had lost him."

Before Cilghal could stop him, Kyp turned and ran off to join the bustle as the ship crews prepared Eclipse's motley assortment of backup starfighters for launch. With the *Errant Venture* in a protective orbit around the base and well crewed by refugees from Reecee, there was no question of a single frigate destroying the Jedi stronghold.

Unfortunately, Cilghal knew, there was no longer any chance of keeping the secret of its location. As a vessel traveled through hyperspace, its hull built up a tachyon charge that was not released until it entered realspace again. If she was right about the fungus growing on the eight X-wings—and apparently she was, given the approaching Yuuzhan Vong frigate—the spores were freeing the tachyons in hyperspace, creating a long thread of faster-than-light particles leading straight to Eclipse.

So absorbed in this theory was Cilghal that when she returned to her laboratory, she immediately set to work stripping a tachyon gun from a spare S-thread spinner. The Mon Calamari was not very good with human mechanical equipment—she preferred to rely on Jaina or Danni for such jobs—so the task absorbed all of her concentration for the next quarter hour, until the base alarm blared again and the dismayed watch officer announced that the frigate had sacrificed itself to slip three skips past Eclipse's outer defenses.

The whole base shook as the two big turbolasers opened up on the small vessels. At first, Cilghal took the erratic ticking she heard to be subsurface vibration from the weapons, but then she noticed a complicated repeating pattern, and it was coming from the gravitic pulse coder standing in front of the captured yammosk's cell.

Cilghal rushed over to the observation window and found the creature's tentacles splayed straight out in the pool, its body membranes pulsing in consonance with the ticking of the pulse coder.

"So you *do* talk!"

Cilghal turned to the pulse coder and found it scratching a complicated series of peak and trough readings onto a flimsiplast drum. They did not yet have enough data to convert the marks into a meaningful message, but it seemed likely that the scratches would translate into identity codes, vectoring instructions, and target priorities. Cilghal activated their own makeshift gravitic wave modulator, adjusted the amplitude to match that being recorded, and began to generate the gravitic equivalent of white noise.

The yammosk stopped pulsing for an instant, then whirled around in its tank and launched itself into the viewport with a resonant thud. Cilghal stumbled back, and the creature held itself against the transparisteel, its tentacles lashing along the edges in search of a seam.

Cilghal turned off her modulator. When the yammosk dropped

back into the water and began to pulse again, she knew they had succeeded.

The watch officer's voice came over the internal comm system again. "Suicide run! Close all airtight hatches, secure environment suits, and prepare for impact in ten, nine . . ."

Cilghal glanced at the pulse coder's flimsiplast drum and suddenly knew what was recorded there. Though she could not have translated the message directly, she felt certain it said something like, "Here I am. Destroy me—destroy me at any cost."

There was no time to disconnect all of the power and data feeds and save the pulse coder. Cilghal ripped the flimsiplast off the scratch drum and flew out of the doomed laboratory, almost forgetting to slap the emergency hatch seal as she left.

Chapter 48

The Sabers dropped out of the *Mon Mothma*'s forward fighter bay and saw Coruscant's thumb-sized disk twinkling at them through a gap in the Yuuzhan Vong fleet, the planet's trillion-light aura a genial reminder of what they were fighting to protect. Ben was down there beneath one of those lights, sleeping soundly in his aunt's apartment and dreaming of his mother's return. That much, Mara could feel through the Force. What she could not feel was when his dream would be answered. Despite the steady flow of New Republic reinforcements—even Admiral Ackbar was rumored to be on his way with a Mon Calamari fleet—the Yuuzhan Vong continued to press their advance. Their route insystem could be traced by the swath of derelict vessels littering space, but they still had half their fleet, and now they were within sight of Coruscant.

It was as close to her child as Mara intended to let them come.

A sheet of blue energy lit space overhead as the *Mon Mothma*'s turbolaser banks opened fire again. A moment later, a Yuuzhan Vong frigate vanished from the tactical display, and the cockpit sensor alarms started to scream as a flight of skips headed their way.

Wedge Antilles's voice came over the comm. "All squadrons,

stand by for close defense. This time, we're going to make them stop and pay attention."

Mara was engulfed by the reassuring warmth of her husband's Force touch. "He's going to be all right," Luke said. "We're not going to let anything happen to him."

Blue eyes widening as the safe band narrowed, the *Bail Organa*'s young comm officer asked, "Shall I ask Planetary Defense to deactivate a mine sector for us, General?"

Garm Bel Iblis twirled his mustache and, ignoring the tactical display on the bridge's wall screen, stared out the viewport at the plasma storm blossoming against the Star Destroyer's forward shields. Between flashes, it was just possible to see a swarm of blocky silhouettes moving forward behind the assault, rapidly swelling into the shapes of New Republic starliners and mass transports. Never one to substitute technology for his own judgment, he knew instinctively that the refugee screen would be on him in less than a minute—just as he knew that Planetary Defense would need to deactivate two sectors of mines—not one—if Fleet Group Two was going to withdraw in order.

"General?" the young woman asked. "I have an open channel to Planetary Defense."

"Very good, Anga." Garm's eyes shot briefly to the tactical display, where he saw that with all the defections from Fleet Group One, his force was actually larger than at the beginning of the battle. "You may tell Planetary Defense to keep all sectors of the mine shell active. We won't be retreating."

Anga's face went as pale as her hair. "Excuse me, General?"

"Give me an open channel to all fleet groups," Garm ordered. "I'll need to say a few words."

Located in a repulsor-equipped satellite hovering on a station in front of the Yuuzhan Vong invasion route, Orbital Defense

Headquarters was as large as a Mon Calamari floating city, and the control hub at its heart was the size of a full shock-ball court. Despite being packed to overflowing with weapons directors and traffic coordinators, the nerve center was also, at the moment Lando followed his escort through the hatch, as still as space.

Noting that every pair of eyes in the place was fixed on the ceiling, Lando lifted his chin and found himself staring through a large transparisteel dome at a vast abyss of spiraling magma trails and blossoming fireballs. Some of the explosions appeared close enough to lick the shields. Lando's instinct was to drop for cover and crawl back to the *Lady Luck* as quickly as his hands and knees would carry him, but it was a matter of pride with him never to be the first to panic. Despite what his eyes were telling him, the station remained stable and, in a room packed with electronics, there was not a single crackle of pulse static.

In a deliberately calm voice, he asked, "Optical ceiling?"

"That's right," his escort, a winsome petty officer who would have made even Tendra frown with jealousy, said. "Sometimes it helps to point the station and *see* what's going on."

"Uh-huh," Lando said.

Now that he was sorting out the scene, he could see the blue circles of several thousand ion drives receding into the firestorm. Garm Bel Iblis had turned on the invaders like a cornered wampa, and Fleet Group Two was accelerating through the refugee screen to meet the enemy head-on. New Republic corvettes and frigates were vanishing by the dozens; cruisers and Star Destroyers were belching fire and falling away one after another.

Lando took his comlink off his belt and opened a channel to Tendra. "Have you finished with the weapons platforms yet?"

"I'm making the last delivery now," she answered. "There's still an open shield section on the far side of the planet, so I thought I'd drop the extras at the Imperial Palace."

"You'd better hold off on that," Lando said. "I think they'll be closing that hole shortly. I'll meet you at our rendezvous."

"When?" Tendra sounded worried.

"Soon," Lando replied. "Very soon."

The petty officer leaned through the hatch and summoned the two YVH war droids Lando was delivering, then led the way across the control hub. By the time they had twined their way through the maze of aisles and checkpoints to the lift tube on the other side, Fleet Group Two had penetrated the refugee screen and was webbing the darkness beyond with turbolaser fire. The hostage ships themselves were accelerating forward, their dark shapes backlit by blue halos of ion glow.

The petty officer pressed her palm to a security pad to authorize access, then led Lando and his droids onto the command deck. Though General Ba'tra was already surrounded by aides and junior command officers—all speaking to him at once—the Bothan motioned the newcomers over immediately. Muzzle curled into a faint snarl, he looked the war droids over and grunted approval.

Gratified to finally find someone who appreciated the craftsmanship of the droids, Lando smiled warmly and extended his hand. "General Ba'tra, how nice to meet—"

"Cache it, Calrissian," Ba'tra snarled. "We're in the middle of a battle."

Lando let his hand drop with his spirits, but kept the smile. "Yes, sir, that's why I'm donating these war droids to your security detail."

"Donating?"

"Free of charge," Lando confirmed.

Ba'tra looked doubtful. "And what do you get in return?"

"Nothing, yet," Lando said. "These are good droids, and I'm just trying to preserve the market long enough for people to realize that."

"Preserve the market?" The Bothan smiled wryly, then plinked a claw off YVH 1-302A's armor. "Quantum?"

"Better," Lando said, deliberately duplicating the general's brusque manner. Echoing the customer's tone was one of his most effective sales techniques. "Laminanium. Developed it ourselves."

"Ah."

Sensing the Bothan's approval, Lando said, "I have twenty more aboard the *Lady Luck,* if you have a use for them."

"They're not spoken for?"

Lando shook his head. "This is my last stop."

A flare of orange light strobed through the control hub's observation dome as a pair of space mines fired their rockets and accelerated toward a Ralltiiri refugee vessel. The converted freighter's shields absorbed the detonation of the first mine, but the second slammed into the bow, igniting a wave of secondary explosions that vaporized the ship stem to stern.

"Answers that question," Ba'tra commented, watching the vessel explode. "Definitely Vong guards aboard."

A flickering sheet of orange filled the control hub as a dozen more mine rockets ignited.

The faces of the general's assistants fell, and a Bith female asked, "Shall I have sector two-twenty-three deactivate, General?"

Before answering, Ba'tra turned to consult a tactical display hanging on the command deck wall. Wedge's Fleet Group Three was sweeping down from behind, but even a quick glance at the situation revealed that Garm's force could not hold the Yuuzhan Vong in place. While the remnants of Fleet Group Two had already carved out a sizable hollow at the front of the column, enemy vessels were sweeping past on all sides, chasing the refugee ships toward the mine shell.

The orange light in the control hub died away suddenly and was not replaced by the flash of detonating mines. Ba'tra's head snapped back long enough to take in the sight of a dozen refugee vessels streaking through the mine shell unimpeded.

The Bothan whirled on the Bith who had suggested deactivating the sector. "I did not authorize that!"

What little color there was faded from the Bith's face. "Neither did I."

Ba'tra snatched his comlink from a pocket and stepped to the transparisteel wall that overlooked the control hub's main floor.

"Activate sector two-twenty-three!"

The Bothan was staring at a lone Mon Calamari seated forty meters away in the heart of the giant floor. She merely folded her hands in her lap and looked out the ceiling. The mine controllers flanking her did likewise.

"I see." Ba'tra snapped his comlink off and turned to Lando. "Are your droids as adept at dealing with traitors as they are infiltrators?"

Lando glanced at the controllers and swallowed, not certain that he wanted to answer truthfully.

"Do you know how quickly the enemy will reach us once they have cleared the mine shell?" Ba'tra asked. "And I should mention that you will not be leaving this station until I have an answer."

"You designate targets and issue an override command," Lando said.

"Which is?"

Lando did not answer, for his thoughts were suddenly full of thrust calculations and pitfalls.

"Calrissian?"

"General, do you have any way to keep your mines from targeting your orbital defense platforms?"

Ba'tra scowled, but looked to an Arcona assistant.

"We could give them the deactivation codes," the aide suggested. "With a tight-beam transmission, they could kill the warhead and let the mine bounce off their shields."

"Good," Lando said. "Then I suggest you deactivate *all* sectors."

"What?"

"Let them through," Lando clarified. "The refugees, the Yuuzhan Vong, everyone."

Ba'tra's eyes narrowed in thought, and Lando could see that the general was already thinking along the same lines. This particular Bothan, at least, deserved his post.

After a moment, Ba'tra asked, "You know what will happen when those ships hit the planetary shields?"

Lando shrugged. "Your mines might stop the first hundred ships—"

"Not even that many," the Bith said.

"So you might as well put your assets to their best use."

Ba'tra glanced up at the stream of hostage vessels pouring through the deactivated sector toward the surface of Coruscant. The first transports were already vanishing behind the rim of the observation dome, long needles of ion efflux trailing them as they accelerated into the planetary shield.

"You know this won't save the hostages?" Ba'tra asked.

"But at least the New Republic won't be the ones killing them," Lando said. "And it just might save Coruscant."

A bowl of golden light rose from the planet as the first refugee ship disintegrated against the shield.

Ba'tra winced, then nodded. "Very well, Calrissian. Do it."

Lando's jaw fell. "Me?"

"Your idea, your assignment," the Bothan said. "I'll have someone fetch you some stars, General. You've just been reactivated."

By the time Fleet Group Three connected with Fleet Group Two, local space was too littered with battle debris to enter at anything approaching combat speed. Through the flotsam cloud, Mara could see half a dozen Star Destroyers and perhaps twenty or thirty smaller vessels using their turbolasers to clear an exit path, but even they were barely crawling. At least half were venting bodies and atmosphere, and a dozen were moving only under the power of a nearby vessel's tractor beam. Clearly, Garm Bel Iblis and his followers were out of the battle.

The Yuuzhan Vong rearguard was pouring around the devastation on all sides, trading fusillades with Fleet Group One as they streamed past into the deactivated mine shell. Traest Kre'fey had apparently chosen not to engage until he joined up with Wedge's group. The few thousand vessels remaining to him were all standing off, content to attack from a distance while the invaders poured into orbit and swarmed Coruscant's defense platforms. Though they were badly outnumbered, Mara found it difficult to believe the admiral would be so cowardly. Despite his Bothan heritage, he had always struck her as an honorable soldier and loyal citizen.

The scene at the edges of Coruscant's atmosphere made Mara's heart race for Ben's safety. A thousand-kilometer circle of shield glowed gold beneath the constant bombardment of hostage ships. Every new impact launched a kilometers-high pillar of fire and sent shock circles rippling across the surface. Occasionally, a refugee vessel broke away at the last second as the crew finally overpowered their captors. Every attempt ended badly, with the craft crashing into the shield anyway, or being blasted out of space by a waiting frigate, or disintegrating under the stress of trying to escape. For the most part, the Yuuzhan Vong suicide squads were forcing the pilots to hit the same area, and the largest detonations were already causing forks of disruption static to dance across the shield.

Danni Quee's voice came over the channel. "We've got another yammosk."

Mara dropped her gaze to the tactical display, where a targeting box had appeared around a heavy cruiser already deep inside the mine shell. A dozen weary sighs sounded from the comm speaker.

This would be Eclipse's fourth yammosk kill. They had taken out the second one with Saba's glowball tactic, but the third kill had cost so many pilots that Luke had reorganized Eclipse's forces into a single wing of two fifteen-pilot squadrons. When Danni had detected no more gravitic pulses, they had all dared hope they had killed the last one, but it now seemed apparent the invaders had been holding it in reserve.

Luke opened a channel to the *Mon Mothma.* "We'll need that support, Command." During their last rearming break, Wedge had offered the support of both Rogue Squadron and the Wraiths—who were being tapped for combat duty despite their status as an intelligence unit—for the next yammosk attack. "This is a tough one."

"Negative, Farmboy," Wedge responded. "You are not authorized for attack."

Mara felt Luke bristle and knew how tired he was. Luke *never* let himself get so angry she could feel it.

"This is not time to be looking out for old buddies, Command. You can see how desperate things are. If we don't take out that—"

"I said *no,*" Wedge interrupted. "I can't order you to hold back, but trust me. There are some things I can't say over a combat channel."

Mara felt Luke perform the Jedi equivalent of counting ten. They still had no reason to believe the Yuuzhan Vong could eavesdrop on their communications—much less break military codes—but the same could not be said for the refugee ships. If any of those pilots happened to be smugglers in the Han Solo or Talon Karrde mold, they would have the finest comm-scanning equipment in the galaxy.

"Copy," Luke said. "Let us know when we have authorization."

"Count on it."

"Wedge?" Mara was as surprised as anyone to hear herself saying Wedge's name over the comm—and even she wasn't sure why she had done it until she asked, "Can you patch me through to Coruscant civil communications?"

There was a slight pause, then Wedge said, "Sure, we can do that. Who do you want to talk to?"

"My brother-in-law," she said.

The curiosity she felt from Luke lasted only as long as it took the next refugee ship to strike Coruscant's shields. This time, the disruption static shrank back on itself and burned through the shields. Two more vessels crashed beside the hole, enlarging it by a factor of ten, then a third pilot guided his lumbering starliner through the breach to safety. The comm channels crackled with an odd sort of half cheer as Fleet Group Three gave voice to the jubilation of finally seeing a refugee ship survive. The accolades ceased when a pair of Yuuzhan Vong frigates darted through the hole after it.

Han Solo's voice came over the comm speaker. "Mara? What happened?" The channel was full of static. "Is Luke—"

"He's fine," Mara interrupted. "Listen to me. The shields are going. Can you get Ben offplanet?"

"Threepio is already packing," Han said. "We'll be in the air as soon as we can reach the *Falcon*."

"Thank you." There was an awkward pause during which Mara found herself caught between saying again how sorry she was and apologizing for thinking Anakin's mission had been a good idea, then she asked, "How's Leia?"

"Hanging on," Han answered. Mara flashed on an image of Leia clutching Ben to her breast, then Han said, "We'll see ya."

He switched off, leaving Mara and Luke alone with the war. She felt Luke reaching out to her through the Force, trying to fill her with a sense of reassurance she could tell he did not quite feel himself.

I'm fine, Luke, she thought.

But Mara could feel Luke's irritation mounting, as well. Even

Master Earnest was growing impatient with this strange game of follow-and-wait. More than a dozen Yuuzhan Vong vessels slipped through the overload breach into Coruscant's atmosphere before planetary shielding finally brought a replacement generator on-line.

Fleet Group Three was almost at the mine shell when Wedge gave the order to cease pursuit. Though there had not been an enemy vessel close enough for X-wings to fire at in twenty minutes, Luke ordered the Sabers and Wild Knights to take up static combat stations two hundred kilometers ahead of the Star Destroyer. Puzzled by Wedge's hesitation, both squadrons settled in to watch the deadly light storm being hurled back and forth by the big capital ships.

The puzzle was solved less than a minute later, when the entire mine shell sprouted rocket candles. The capital ships ceased firing. An astonished silence fell over the comm channels as the mines locked onto enemy vessels and curved after them. The Yuuzhan Vong maneuvered wildly, but they were trapped against Coruscant with nowhere to go. No sooner would they escape one mine than they ran afoul of another. Some vessels skimmed the planetary shields and were instantly torn into rubble. A few collided with each other, and still others grew so distracted they fell prey to missiles and turbolaser fire from the orbital defense platforms.

Eventually, the Yuuzhan Vong realized they were better off to stop and weather the storm, relying on their weapons and shielding singularities to destroy the approaching mines. Many failed and were blasted into rubble. A thousand more suffered hull breaches and began to vent internal systems. Almost all took at least one hit, but an astonishing number showed little sign of damage. They returned to their missions, attacking the orbital defense platforms and herding refugee ships to destruction.

Then, almost as one, the crippled Yuuzhan Vong vessels dropped out of orbit, hurling themselves into the planetary shields. Disruption static shot across the atmosphere. Whole grids shimmered and winked out. Planet-bound generator stations exploded with flashes brilliant enough to be seen from space. Skips began to drop off the surviving Yuuzhan Vong vessels and dive toward the surface.

On Mara's tactical display, the cruiser carrying the fourth yam-mosk was blinking slowly to show damage. But it was still intact, drifting toward the sunny side of the planet.

"Okay, Farmboy," Wedge commed. "*Now* you are authorized to attack."

Chapter 49

Even before Jaina peered into the sunken compound, she feared they might be too late. An oily column of pyre smoke was rising out of the pit, gathering beneath in a blackened valve that periodically cracked open to puff the fumes out into the vacuum. The air reeked of charred flesh and scorched bone, but also of slower kinds of decomposition that made clear why the place lay so far from anything else. Whatever the Yuuzhan Vong did with their dead, it did not involve preserving them.

Despite the guidance of her comlink's signal finder, Jaina did not see Lowbacca until a powdery arm rose out of the ash and waved them onto the observation balcony outside the tunnel mouth. She dropped to her belly and, trying not to think about the fact that she was crawling through the incinerated remains of untold thousands of Yuuzhan Vong, advanced to the edge of the pit.

What lay below struck her as more of a processing center than a mortuary. About a tenth the size of the spaceport, the five-sided facility lay at the hub of a dozen large travelways, most of them emerging from the worldship's murky interior. Many of the subterranean passages had been permanently sealed with yorik coral plugs. The rest were choked with Yuuzhan Vong mourners, their numbers no doubt swollen by the strike team's efficiency—a thought in which Jaina found herself taking some solace. The Yuuzhan Vong had finally shattered the emotional armor that had been accumulating around her since Anni Capstan, her first regular Rogue Squadron wingmate, perished over Ithor. They had made the war *hurt* again, and now she wanted to hurt them back.

As in the spaceport, long colonnades at the bottom of the five outer walls opened into a network of utility warrens whose purpose Jaina could only guess at and cared little about. The five grottoes that stood in the facility's five corners were more interesting. The effigy of a major Yuuzhan Vong god sat in each recess, gazing out at a deep pit directly in front of his—or her—eyes. Beside each pit stood a priest and several assistants, chanting prayers to the gods and inviting the mourners, one group at a time, to step forward and throw a piece of their loved one into the pit. Which piece seemed to depend on the particular effigy. Into one pit, they lowered the skins; into another, they tossed the major bones of the body; into Yun-Yammka's pit—the only god Jaina recognized—they poured the blood.

The actual preparation of the corpse was performed at one of any number of stations of varying opulence scattered around the interior of the compound. Selection of a preparer seemed to involve a fair amount of barter, as Jaina could see mourners arguing— sometimes violently—with the aproned body-dressers who performed the work. After the work was done, the first stop was always a blazing pyre in the center of the compound, where the skull and hands were thrown.

Jaina grew cold inside. "If they did that to Anakin—"

Lowbacca groaned softly and pointed over the rim. Being careful not to push any ash over the edge, Jaina eased herself forward and saw, twenty meters below, a handful of Yuuzhan Vong warriors playing some game that involved kicking a snarling spike-creature into the opponent's bare chest hard enough to make it stick. Standing off to one side, weaving Anakin's lightsaber through a surprisingly smooth practice routine, was Vergere.

"So where's Anakin?" Tahiri hissed.

Lowbacca gestured at the warren beside the warriors, then to a nearby air lock, explaining in a soft rumble that the lock opened into a small docking pit where Vergere and her companions had a shuttle waiting. Jaina and the others donned their vac suits, then camouflaged themselves with a coat of ash and spent the next hour watching the gruesome rites below. Had they not seen a pair of Yuuzhan Vong emerge from the warren with the husk-encased body of a comrade and depart in one of the small yorik coral transports the Yuuzhan Vong sometimes used inside the world-ship, the wait would have been interminable. As it was, it merely gave Jaina a chance to watch the ghastly spectacle and hope the warriors who had killed Anakin were among those being offered to their gods.

At last, a Yuuzhan Vong subaltern emerged from the warren and summoned two of the crew inside. The others quickly began to dress, pulling thin tunics over their heads and coaxing their living armor open so they could don it again. Jaina cautiously lifted her power blaster out of the ash, clearing the emitter nozzle and tar-geting sensors with a quick breath and rub of her tunic.

"Blast them when Anakin's out where we can see him," Jaina said over the comlink. She missed the intimacy of the battle meld, but it was probably a good thing that Jacen was not here to link them all together; as angry as she was feeling, she did not want to open her emotions to the others. "We'll jump down and get him, then commandeer the shuttle, go find Jacen, and finish this thing."

"Check," Zekk said, acknowledging the order.

By the time the others had checked off, as well, the subaltern was walking into view. Behind him came the two crew members, an Anakin-sized husk suspended between.

"May I have the officer?" Alema asked, setting the longblaster's sight on the subaltern.

"Take him," Jaina said.

The others named their targets, as well, Tahiri taking the front husk-carrier and Zekk the back. Lowbacca set his sights on the pilot, and Jaina aimed her power blaster at Vergere.

"I've got Featherbag," she said. "Fire at—"

Four blaster bolts lanced down into the mortuary pit, but Zekk's hand crashed down across Jaina's barrel and her shot went wide, burning into the ground next to Vergere's feet. The creature was already jumping to one side, Anakin's lightsaber coming around smoothly, as though she actually knew how to use it—a notion that was dispelled when she let it slip from her hand and clatter bladeless to the ground.

Jaina whirled on Zekk. "What'd you do that for? I had her!"

"And we don't know you should have," Zekk retorted almost as hotly. "She's done us no harm, and she's had the chance."

"The company she keeps is harm enough!" Jaina peered back into the pit, but her target had already snatched Anakin's lightsaber up and ducked out of sight—as had the spared husk-carrier, taking with him her brother's body. "Zekk, don't do that again. Don't you dare stand in my way!"

By now, an astonished murmur was rolling across the compound as the crowd below began to realize they were under attack. Jaina shouldered her blaster, then snapped her lightsaber off her belt and hurled herself headlong into the pit. Using the Force to slow her descent, she performed a twisting flip and landed facing into the warren, midway between Tahiri and Lowbacca. Alema was on the other side of Tahiri, her longblaster rising to her shoulder. The warrior whose life Zekk had spared was backing under the wall, using Anakin's body to shield himself from the Twi'lek's weapon and drawing his coufee.

"You two secure the shuttle," Jaina ordered Lowie and Tahiri. "Alema and I will get Anakin."

As they scrambled to obey, the Yuuzhan Vong plunged his coufee into the husk and cut it open near the head. "You want your *Jeedai?*" He thrust the blade through a layer of clear gelatinous slime and placed the tip on Anakin's cheek. "Stay back, or I give him to you in pieces!"

The longblaster roared, missing the Yuuzhan Vong but demolishing the keystone of the arch behind him. He flinched and looked over his shoulder at the tons of rubble crashing down behind him, then turned back toward Jaina and moved his knife toward Anakin's eye.

Rage boiling inside her like magma, Jaina reached out with the Force and shoved Anakin's body hard. The Yuuzhan Vong yelled in surprise and stumbled back into the collapsing arch, his coufee sliding away from the eye. Jaina jerked her brother free of the warrior's grasp and sent him floating in Alema's direction.

"Take Anakin," she said.

As Jaina spoke, she was opening herself to her anger, using the power of its emotion to draw the Force into her as the Dark Masters Brakiss and Tamith Kai had tried to force her to do so long ago, when she and Jacen had been imprisoned at the Shadow Academy with Lowbacca. The power came surging into her in cold waves, feeding on her hatred of the Yuuzhan Vong and pouring it back to her twofold.

In a motion so fast Jaina barely saw it, the warrior sat up and flicked his coufee at her throat. She could have dodged or blocked with her lightsaber, but she did not. Instead, with the fierce energy crackling inside her, she used her free hand to bat the weapon aside, then raised her hand toward her attacker and released the dark power inside. A fork of lightning crackled into existence a few centimeters beyond her glove tips, then blasted a hole through the

Yuuzhan Vong's chest and hurled him onto the rubble pile smoking and motionless.

Jaina felt someone watching and turned to find Vergere staring at her from the shelter of a nearby archway, Anakin's lightsaber dangling from one hand and her narrow eyes angled in what seemed a peculiar expression of dismay. Jaina sneered at the creature, then raised her hand and loosed another bolt of Force lightning.

Anakin's lightsaber snapped to life in Vergere's hand and rose to intercept the attack. Then, eyes going wide, she turned and fled into the warren, the lit blade wagging behind her like a tail.

Alema came to Jaina's side and, somewhat tentatively, took her by the arm. "We'd better go."

Jaina grew aware of a roar building on the other side of the vessel and realized that the outraged priests were exhorting their mourners to attack. "The shuttle?"

"Secure," Alema reported. "Everyone's aboard but us."

"Good." Jaina took Anakin from the Twi'lek, then entered the air lock. As the outer valve opened, she thumbed the fuse of her last thermal detonator to ten seconds and dropped it on the middle of the lock. "The vac breach that leaves ought to burst a few scarhead lungs."

Chapter 50

*L*ike some insectoid model of a Coruscant skyline, the hives had over countless years of habitation climbed entirely out of the bug pit, their serpentine spires now scratching at the vaulted ceiling from atop a thirty-meter mound of carapace detritus and discarded chrysalides. Though the colony was as deserted as much of the worldship, the long-neglected glow lichen still shined just brightly enough to reveal the legs of a dead Yuuzhan Vong protruding from an acid hole in the base of the innermost tower, jerking and jiggling as the body was devoured by a voxyn.

The voxyn, Jacen hoped. With leaden arms and shaking legs, he felt like they had tracked the thing through the entire diameter of the worldship—though it was impossible to know for sure without Alema's sense of subterranean direction.

"The reading is good," Tekli whispered. She used both hands to raise the cell analyzer and show the numbers to Jacen. "Do we want to test a second sample? I see some droppings up there."

"Not necessary," Jacen replied. They were studying the colony from the mouth of a dark passageway, and it would have been impossible to retrieve the droppings without either leaving their cover or using the Force—both of which would have exposed their presence to the voxyn. "Tesar has already said the trail is the queen's. Let's just kill it."

"Too bad we don't have the longblaster," Ganner said softly. "I can guess where she is, and we could burn a hole right through that nest."

"This one thinkz it is better for him to sneak around to her blind side," Tesar hissed. "If she flees, you will be here to attack and pursue."

When Jacen nodded, the Barabel leapt onto the wall and climbed silently to the ceiling, where he seemed to melt into the shadows. A faint tingle crept down the back of Jacen's neck—a tingle that continued to grow as Tesar neared the tunnel mouth. There was something wrong here, something they were not seeing. Tenel Ka touched Jacen's arm, and he knew she felt it, too.

"Tesar!" Jacen hissed. He did not want to reach out with the Force; they had already learned that doing so would alert the queen to their presence. "Wait!"

"Wait?" Ganner asked, disbelieving. "What for?"

"Be quiet," Tekli whispered. Ganner had the danger sense of a mynock; he had nearly walked into Yuuzhan Vong search parties twice. "It feels wrong."

When the Barabel did not immediately return, Jacen began to have visions of losing Saba's last student. Taking care to remain in the shadows, he slipped along the wall, then nearly cried out when a deep thump shook the passage. Tesar hissed in shock and re-tracted his claws, almost taking Jacen's head off as he dropped along the wall. They retreated deeper into the tunnel, their eyes on the dimly shining colony ceiling.

"Something landing?" Ganner asked.

Tesar nodded. "Something big."

"Ah. Aha. They *were* trying to lure us into a trap." Tenel Ka bumped her shoulder into Jacen's. "Perhaps the time has come to withdraw, my friend."

"Perhaps." Jacen did not turn back. There was still something wrong here, something yet to be revealed. "But if it's a trap, why give themselves away?"

Another thump, this one smaller, rumbled down through the yorik coral.

"This one could go look," Tesar suggested.

Jacen passed over the electrobinoculars, and the Barabel bounded up the passage on all fours. This area of the worldship seemed devoted to producing foodstuffs and other necessities, and every kilometer or so, there were large air locks opening onto the surface access routes. Jacen had traveled enough of the worldship to know that the surface network would be a more efficient system for moving freight than the sometimes cramped, always meandering passages inside.

A minute later, Tesar reported, "Frigate analog—perhapz the one that brought Nom Anor. Its shuttle is missing."

Despite the extra weaponry and personnel such a vessel carried, Jacen was no more worried than before. Frigates of this size were known to carry only three assault companies, and by his count, they had already destroyed one and cut up the other two pretty badly. If Nom Anor intended to launch an attack from this ship, it would either be with worldship personnel or the vessel crew—neither of which was likely to be experienced enough to keep them from escaping.

"Any sign of an assault company?" Jacen asked.

"The boarding ramp is down," Tesar replied. "But the ones who used it are already gone."

"Then there couldn't be many." Tekli's voice sounded more hopeful than confident.

"Okay, Tesar," Jacen said. "Keep an eye on things while we decide what to do here."

"We could telekinese a thermal detonator at the voxyn and hope for the best," Ganner suggested. "Or I could carry it up."

"And that would work better than the other times why?" Tenel Ka asked. "We have only two detonators left. We must conserve."

Ganner acknowledged her point with a shrug, and the Jedi fell to contemplating the situation in silence. No one felt any compulsion to flee—at least not until they knew what was happening. They had been dodging Yuuzhan Vong search parties since their escape from the cloning grashal, and the frigate's arrival was the first hint that the enemy had guessed their location.

A few minutes later, Tenel Ka said, "Perhaps the Force brought the frigate to us, after all."

She pointed into the hive colony, where several dozen Yuuzhan Vong silhouettes had emerged from hiding places near the voxyn. The unarmored leader appeared from inside a spire and stomped down the detritus mound, circling toward a passage about seventy meters around the pit from that of the Jedi. He was met just inside the colony by an eight-fingered shaper whose cage of glow bugs revealed the leader's face to be that of Nom Anor.

The two immediately began to speak and gesture harshly. A moment later, Vergere came waddling out of the tunnel, Anakin's equipment belt strapped around her body like a bandolier, lightsaber and utility pouches still hanging in place, his comlink set dangling in the empty blaster holster.

The sight of his brother's captured equipment filled Jacen with sorrow and self-reproach. Jaina's angry accusations had compelled him to rethink nearly everything he had done since his blunder aboard the *Exquisite Death,* and he could not help believing that had he been less worried about making amends and more concerned with tempering his brother's rashness, Anakin might still be alive. Jacen was troubled, as well, by the refuge he had taken in Anakin's calm response to the theft of the *Tachyon Flier.* If Jaina, who remained collected under even the most heated attack, could not bear their brother's death, how could he still be worrying about the mission? How come *his* grief was not driving him mad?

Vergere glanced in the direction of the Jedi. Her hand brushed Anakin's comlink, and suddenly two angry Yuuzhan Vong voices were coming over the comm net.

Jacen barely noticed. His gaze remained fixed on Vergere. As much as it hurt to see her wearing Anakin's gear as a war trophy, he felt no urge to attack her, nor even Nom Anor. Truth be told, though he was determined to destroy the queen, he really did not *want* to kill her either. None of it was going to bring Anakin back.

Tenel Ka squeezed the back of his arm, then quietly reached over and killed his comlink mike. "I do not know what game she is playing at, but it would be better if they could not hear us, as well."

"Thanks," Jacen said.

Though he could not understand the conversation coming over his comlink, he did hear two familiar words—*Jeedai* and *Anakin*. Nom Anor gestured angrily toward the voxyn's hiding place. Vergere spread her hands, then pointed up the passage from which she and the shaper had come. She rattled off something that included the word *Jaina,* which prompted the eight-fingered shaper to turn and gesture into the hives, repeating the word *voxyn* time and again.

Nom Anor snapped at him, then he and Vergere began to yell at Nom Anor, and soon all three were shouting at once.

"Looks like Jaina has been busy," Ganner observed.

"Why am I not surprised?" Tenel Ka asked. "But it is going to be difficult to destroy the queen now. That frigate will complicate matters."

"Not for long," Jacen said. He could feel something in the Jaina-place inside him, something angry and dark coming their way. "Not if I know my sister."

Relying heavily on both lightsaber technology and several borrowed focusing crystals to help control the enormous power it would need to jam yammosk waves, Cilghal's new gravitic amplitude modulator was part gravity generator and part plasteel rectenna. It was also even larger than the one that had been destroyed when the skips from the Yuuzhan Vong tracking vessel had attacked her lab, so when she and Kyp started across the hangar with the unwieldy apparatus in tow, Booster Terrik did not look happy. He came striding down the *Jade Shadow*'s boarding ramp to meet them, shaking his head and wagging his finger.

"Your orders are to evacuate, not relocate," he growled. "The *Venture*'s already packed bilge to bridge with Reecee refugees. We've no room for Jedi sculptures."

"This is no sculpture," Kyp said. "This is a GAM, and it just might win the war for us."

Booster rolled his eyes. "And a Gamorrean *might* be the next chief of state—but it won't happen today."

Kyp's face reddened with temper. "Listen, you old—"

"That's enough, Kyp," Cilghal said, cutting him off. She passed him the hoversled controls, then turned to Booster and raised her hand toward him. "I'm sure that when Captain Terrik sees this instrument in action, he will be happy to find a place for it aboard the *Errant Venture*."

Booster scowled and started to reiterate his denial—then cried out in surprise as his feet rose off the ground and Cilghal floated him out of the way.

"Okay, okay," he growled. "If it means that much to you, I'll take a look at this gizmo in action."

"A wise idea," Cilghal said. She disliked using the Force on a friend in this manner, but Booster was stubborn and time was short. "I am sure that you'll be impressed—so impressed that you'll let us run a power feed off one of your fusion reactors."

Booster's scowl returned to its most stubborn. "Don't push it, Cilghal. We'll talk about that *after* you show me what this thing can do."

* * *

As weary as Jacen was of watching Vergere and the shaper argue with Nom Anor, he could think of no way to reach the voxyn. With a frigate full of Yuuzhan Vong in the area, sneaking up on it was out of the question. So was floating a detonator or incendiary at it; the creature had proved many times that it would flee as soon as it felt them using the Force. That left only waiting, but wait he would—until he was fifty, if that was what it took to destroy the queen. He had promised Anakin.

Vergere and the others were still arguing when a series of frantic clicks came over the comm net. Jacen reached out to Tesar and felt the Barabel still waiting at his station on the surface, concerned but not nearly excited enough to be fighting someone. A single click confirmed that Tesar had felt his touch, then the boom of an exploding missile reverberated through the yorik coral. Vergere turned and bounded away around the detritus mound. Nom Anor and the shaper remained where they were, barking questions at her vanishing back.

"Jaina?" Ganner gasped.

"Who else?" Tenel Ka replied.

Jacen reached out to his sister through the Force, found only the same cold anger that he had felt since Anakin's death, and tried to break through to some vestige of the Jaina he had known all his life. He touched only swirling darkness, stormy and unreasoning and full of hate. Afraid to use the comlink—he could not be sure what channels Vergere had open—Jacen opened his emotions to the others, drawing them into a battle meld and reaching out to Tesar with the same question on their minds: Was this Jaina's doing?

They were answered with a confirming click.

"An excellent plan, catching the frigate off guard," Tenel Ka said. "It will greatly aid our final escape."

Another blast shook the passage, this one closer than the first, then a second eruption even louder. Flakes of glow lichen began to snow from the ceiling. High in the colony interior, the legs of the dead Yuuzhan Vong vanished from sight as the startled voxyn dragged him out the back side of the hive and disappeared, never presenting a shot to the Jedi below. A third explosion shocked the dust off the walls, and loose chunks of ceiling began to bombard the insect city.

Tesar's desperate voice came over the comlink. "Stickz, not there—stop!"

Even as Tesar yelled, a fourth explosion dropped an avalanche of vault ribbing on the colony. An entire borough of the insect city collapsed into rubble around Nom Anor and the shaper, and then the whole bug pit was filled with an impenetrable cloud of dust.

When a sporadic rain of yorik coral continued to fall from the weakened ceiling, Jacen backed deeper into the tunnel and pulled his equipment harness off his back.

"We'd better get into our vac suits," he whispered.

After failing to destroy the frigate on the first two passes, Tesar thought the assault shuttle would turn and flee. That would have been the tactic of a wise hunter striking at such dangerous prey. But Jaina was in a killing frenzy and unable to resist the temptation of a 150-meter Yuuzhan Vong frigate sitting motionless on the surface, its debarking ramp still hanging open like the mouth of a winded dewback. She wheeled around, coming in close for a point-blank shot, and loosed a pair of plasma balls that vanished almost instantly into shielding singularities.

The assault shuttle flashed over its target and pulled up sharply, preparing to wheel around for yet another attack.

The frigate finally answered, launching a flurry of magma missiles and plasma balls from its port-side weapons bank. At such short range, the missiles lacked time to fix on their target and streaked past harmlessly, but two plasma balls exploded into the shuttle's rear quarter, blasting through the firewall and sending it spinning into the sky.

Tesar feared for a moment that the shuttle would explode or spin itself into pieces, but then Jaina—at least he assumed she was the pilot—somehow brought it under control and banked away. The craft climbed five hundred meters, then belched flame and began a long, wobbling descent toward the horizon.

Tesar snapped his tongue against his faceplate in anger, then thought for a moment and finally decided to risk a message over Jacen's personal comm channel. Even if the Yuuzhan Vong were eavesdropping, this was not something he wanted to try relaying through clicks and Force sensations.

"No!" Jacen gasped.

He had felt something wrong even before Tesar commed, but had not known what. Forgetting about Anakin's captured comlink, he opened a general channel and would have started calling for a report, had Tenel Ka not ripped the mike off his throat.

"You will not help anyone by getting us killed," she said. "Jaina will bring them down softly. You know that."

"No, I don't. Not anymore." Jacen took a deep breath, using a meditative calming technique to bring himself back under control. "But you're right about the rest."

Jacen reached out to his sister and spent the next minute or so struggling to stay in contact with the dark emotions that now filled her. She did not seem frightened, only angry and focused on the effort at hand. Then, as he sensed her efforts growing even more intense, her anger abruptly deepened to a level that Jacen could not bear, and he lost her.

"She's gone," he gasped.

"Dead?" Ganner asked.

"I don't know." Jacen looked up. "I didn't feel that. I just don't feel her at all."

Tenel Ka enfolded him in her one arm and pulled him close. "Jacen, I am so sorry."

Out in the bug pit, the dust had settled enough to see the Yuuzhan Vong clearing rubble. Although pieces of ceiling continued to fall at increasing frequency, it soon grew apparent that the collapse had so far caused few casualties. Nom Anor was already standing at the edge of a fallen hive, glaring down with a sour expression as a pair of assistants pulled the shaper from beneath the debris.

Once the shaper regained his feet and a little of his dignity, he brushed himself off and began to speak sharply to Nom Anor. Jacen thought for a moment they would continue their argument, but after a while Nom Anor only nodded and pointed up the tunnel leading to the surface and their frigate. The shaper nodded back, then took the warriors and started across the colony in pursuit of the voxyn queen. The executor shook his head wearily and started up the tunnel toward the frigate.

He had barely departed before a squeaky voice came over their comlinks. "It is safe to come out now, young Jedi. You have nothing to fear from me."

Jacen motioned the others to ready their weapons, then activated his comlink microphone. "Who is this?"

"There is no time to explain that now." As she spoke, Vergere came around the colony on the side opposite the one she had departed, then pointed in the direction the voxyn queen had fled. "Your quarry is escaping."

Chapter 51

The Solo entourage was halfway across the last pedestrian bridge outside the Eastport Docking Facility when a deafening crackle roared out of the sky and shook the surrounding skyscrapers. Reflexes conditioned to instant reaction by far too many brushes with death, Han dropped to his haunches and looked for the source of the trouble. He found it in the form of a million orange fireballs reflecting off the transparisteel panes of a million tower viewports, silhouetting the dazed figure of his wife with Ben cradled in her arms.

Like almost everyone else on the bridge, Leia was still standing upright, craning her neck to see what was making all the noise. Han grasped her elbow and pulled her down beside him.

"Get down, sweetheart."

The smell of ozone and ash wafted down on a hot wind. A corvette-sized fireball roared overhead and impacted half a kilometer up the durasteel canyon, vaporizing forty floors of a residential tower and blasting the walls out of three adjacent buildings. The shock wave cleared the hoverlane of traffic, then hit the bridge and turned the air as hot as a Tatooine drought. Adarakh and Meewalh dropped the luggage and used their own bodies to cover Han and Leia, C-3PO skidded three steps across the walkway before both he and the potted ladalum he was carrying were caught by the YVH war droid Lando had given them, and Ben's TDL nanny was swept off the bridge along with a hundred screaming pedestrians.

"How dreadful!" C-3PO peered over the safety rail. "She'll be smashed beyond components!"

"And so will we if we don't get off this bridge," Han said, rising.

Still holding Leia's arm, he started to push forward through the crowd. With the battle for Coruscant now being fought in an orbit so low the weapon discharges looked like a colossal skydazzle show, the planet was being bombarded with a steady rain of flaming spacecraft. The kilometer-long walk from the apartment had been one long smoke-stroll, and twice they had been forced to detour around impact craters where the bridge came to an abrupt end a hundred meters above the stump of a truncated building.

The closer they came to the docking facility, the slower the crowd seemed to move. Han finally saw why as they drew to within a few meters of the building. A pair of burly Defense Force soldiers in full biosuits and headgear flanked the half-closed access gate, carefully scanning identichips and waving pedestrians through one at a time. It seemed a ludicrous endeavor given the circumstances.

One of the guards turned his dark-visored gaze on Han and held out his scanner. "Identichip."

"You don't know?" Han asked, presenting the group's chips. Not being in disguise, he and Leia had been the subject of countless whispers and pointed fingers along the way; at times, only the menacing presence of Lando's YVH war droid had kept frightened citizens from besieging them with questions they could not answer and bringing their progress to a halt. "Where'd they recruit you guys, Pzob?"

"Procedure . . ." The soldier looked at the datareader on the back of his scanner. "Solo. I read only four chips. There are five of you."

"Give me a break," Han said. He felt the YVH war droid easing up behind him and quietly signaled him to stay back. "The baby's only four months old."

The soldier continued to stare out from behind his visor.

"It takes *six* months to get the chip," Han bluffed. If this guy didn't recognize him and Leia, chances were he wouldn't know Coruscant documentation law either. "Until then, the kid travels on a parent's chip."

"Of course." The soldier lowered his scanner, then pointed down an exterior walkway to a large balcony packed with droids. "You may enter, but your mechanicals must remain. There is no room to evacuate them."

"Remain?" C-3PO echoed. "But my place is with—"

Han waved the protocol droid silent. "They won't be taking a public berth. We have our own vessel."

"Which you should use to evacuate living beings," the second guard said, stepping over. "Not these lifeless—"

"Please remain calm," the YVH war droid said, pushing an arm between Han and Leia. "This is a military emergency."

Han started to turn. "What—"

A pair of blaster bolts streaked past his face, burning holes through the chests of both soldiers. Leia shrieked and Ben wailed, and an astonished murmur rustled through the crowd. C-3PO, still holding the pot with Leia's blast-stripped ladalum, began to distance himself from the larger droid.

"Really, One-dash-Five-Oh-Seven, that was uncalled for! Your primary programming must be garbled."

The war droid squealed something in machine language that made C-3PO take a step back, then turned to Han. "I apologize for the identification delay. The biosuits were obscuring the criteria."

"Criteria?" Han broke the seal on one of the helmets and found an ooglith masquer already peeling away from the face of its host. "And I thought you just didn't want to be left behind."

* * *

Bureaucrats, businessbeings, and bankers, the people pouring through Gate 3700 of the Eastport Docking Facility were not the ordinary sort of refugee. They swirled into the terminal area escorted by droids, sentient assistants, and hoversleds loaded with art treasures and portable gem vaults. Most were protected by hastily armed servants, bodyguards of various intimidating species, and even Ulban Arms S-EP1 security droids. But only one family had Noghri luggage porters, a protocol droid carrying a heat-blasted ladalum, and a fully operational YVH 1 war droid providing crowd control. As ever, the Solos were the most conspicuous of the conspicuous.

Pores still raging against the ooglith masquer she had been wearing since the failed kidnapping at their apartment, Viqi Shesh turned to the child standing with her at the observation deck safety rail. With a mop of unruly brown hair and big blue eyes as round as Old Republic valor medals, he could have been a twin to the twelve-year-old Anakin Solo portrayed in newsvid archives. He ought to have been; it had cost Viqi a small fortune in cosmisurgeon and bacta tank fees to make him look that way.

"You see them, Dab? The ones with the big war droid?"

"How could I miss them?" the boy answered. "Everybody in the galaxy knows the Solos. You didn't say they were the ones."

"I didn't say a lot of things," Viqi said. Thanks to a thumb-sized Yuuzhan Vong leech-creature lodged in her throat, Viqi's once-silky voice was now almost reedy and quavery. "But if you and your family want passage off Coruscant with me, I won't need to."

The boy looked away. "I understand."

His mother and two sisters were already aboard Viqi's yacht, which was berthed under a false name on the other side of the *Falcon,* just beyond a public starferry named the *Byrt.* She studied the boy, wondering if she had perhaps misjudged the urchin's character when she spotted him in the underlevels rifling the pockets of a salted Arcona. If the child turned out to have a sense of honor—or even the shadow of a conscience—she was as doomed as Coruscant itself. After the HoloNet had reported her failure at the Solos' apartment, Tsavong Lah's villip had everted just long enough to say as much.

"I hope you *do* understand, Dab," Viqi said. "I will not suffer failure lightly . . . I will not suffer it at all."

Leave it to the Eastport docking master to squeeze a ronto into a rabac hole. By keeping the dome irised open and landing the *Byrt* nacelles-down inside a magnolock hull-hoist, the remarkable Shev Watsn had squeezed a two-hundred-meter starferry into a berthing bay designed for yachts and light transports.

Leia could have slapped him with a lightsaber.

Ten thousand terrified people stood waiting to board a vessel that would hold five thousand at best, most standing in front of Docking Bay 3733 where the *Falcon* was kept under an assumed name. As much as Leia wanted to board their ship and get off Coruscant with Ben, she knew they would be mobbed by desperate refugees the instant they tried to push through the throng. For now, the best thing to do was wait at the edge until the *Byrt* began to board, then work their way over to their berth as the crowd pressed forward.

Leia hoped they would have enough time. Through the narrow crescent of sky visible above the *Byrt*'s nose, she could see a steady stream of government yachts rising out of Imperial City—the New Republic's dedicated senators and loyal government officials abandoning their posts. So far, the Yuuzhan Vong were still too busy with the New Republic military to harass fleeing civilians, but that would change soon. She had even heard of senators asking admirals from their own sectors to escort them home, and in far too many cases those requests were being honored. She found it difficult to believe this was the same New Republic she had helped found— and for which Anakin had given his life.

"General?" The voice that asked this was reedy and quavering. "General, is that you?"

Leia turned with Han, the Noghri, and the droids to see a luggage-burdened woman with a large nose and tired eyes pushing through the crowd toward them. Trailing along at her side was a sandy-haired boy of about twelve, also struggling beneath a mound of baggage.

"General!" As the woman said this, she suddenly found her path blocked by Adarakh and Meewalh. "It *is* you!"

"I haven't been a general for a long time." Han spoke quietly and tried not to be too obvious as he glanced around to see who might be eavesdropping. "Do we know each other?"

"You don't remember?"

The woman used a bag to sweep her son forward, and Leia was struck by just how much he looked like Anakin at that age. It was more than just the upturned nose and the ice-blue eyes; his whole face was shaped the same, and he even had the same round little chin. Her heart went out to this boy and his mother.

Han studied the woman and her son, then said, "No, I *don't* remember."

The woman did not seem offended. "Well, of course, I'm sure it was more important to me than to you. After all, you were the general, and Ran was only a flight officer in Rogue Squadron."

"Ran?" Han asked. "Ran Kether?"

"Yes," the woman said. "I was only his girlfriend then, but I met you twice on Chandrila—"

"Okay," Han said, warming instantly. He motioned the Noghri aside. "I'm sorry I don't remember you. How is Ran?"

The woman's expression fell. "You didn't hear?"

Han shook his head. "I've been, uh, out of touch."

"He was flying refugee transports for SELCORE. We lost him at Kalarba." The woman glanced at Leia for the first time. "I understand your daughter was injured there, too."

"She recovered quickly." Balancing Ben on a hip, Leia reached out to squeeze the woman's hand. It was the first time since Anakin's death that she had felt sorry for someone other than herself, and in a self-centered sort of way it was almost a relief. "I'm so sorry about Ran. There's too much of that these days."

"Thank you, Princess."

"Leia, please." Leia touched the shoulder of the boy who looked so much like Anakin. "I'm sorry about your father, young man."

The boy nodded and looked uncomfortable. "Thanks."

"This is Tarc, I'm Welda." The woman smiled at the child in Leia's arms. "The gossip vids haven't said anything about you being pregnant, so I assume this beautiful boy is Ben Skywalker?"

"Actually, we're trying to keep that quiet," Leia said. She cast a meaningful look around the crowd. "You understand."

"I'm sorry." Welda's tone was abashed, but she did not blush. "How foolish of me."

A loud clunk sounded from five meters up the *Byrt,* and a cloud of vapor shot into the air as the boarding hatch broke its seal and opened. Although the boarding ramp had not yet been lowered, the crowd immediately began to compress forward.

"It looks like they've worked out the artificial gravity alignment problems." Welda looked at the still-growing crowd, which now had to be closer to twelve thousand than ten. "I hope there'll be room for us all."

Han looked behind the woman's head and raised his brow at Leia. She nodded. They would be taking as many refugees with them as the *Falcon* could carry anyway, and she had no intention of leaving this pair behind.

Han smiled crookedly and leaned close to Welda's ear. "Actually, that won't be a problem."

The boarding ramp came down. The crowd started to ascend rapidly, each group being detained at the hatch long enough for an epidermal scan to ensure they were not Yuuzhan Vong infiltrators.

The Noghri took advantage of the movement to start easing the group toward the *Falcon*'s berth. There were a few angry glares and muttered comments about pushy Solos, but the presence of a war droid and the fact that the group was not cutting forward limited the objections to the nonphysical kind. Leia was careful to keep Tarc and Welda close at hand, and the group reached the entrance to Docking Bay 3733 intact. Now came the tricky part—getting inside without being trampled by desperate refugees. Han quietly stationed YVH 1-507A in front of the durasteel door and reached for the security pad.

"If you're trying to slice the security, save yourself the bother," a gravelly voice said. Leia turned to find a horn-headed Gotal in a gaudy scintathread tunic speaking to them from within the crowd. "Whoever owns that junk heap couldn't afford the berthing fees. The umbilicals are all disconnected."

"What?" Han cupped his hands to the viewing panel and peered inside. "You've got to be kidding! There's containment fluid all over the floor."

Even after sitting idle for several days, the *Falcon* could be cold-started in only a few minutes—but not without a fully charged fusion containment unit. Too devastated to ask the helpful Gotal what he had been doing looking at the *Falcon*—she had no doubt he had considered trying to slice the security panel himself—Leia turned to apologize to Welda.

The woman was no longer beside her.

Something metallic hit the floor a couple of meters away, and Leia glimpsed Tarc pushing through the crowd. She switched Ben to the other hip so her weapon hand would be free, then YVH

1-507A clanged past toward the sound, his powerful arms batting people aside as gently as possible.

"Remain calm and please seek shelter," he intoned. "There is an active thermal detonator in the area."

Of course, the crowd did anything but stay calm. Determined to board the *Byrt* at any cost, someone kicked the detonator and sent it skittering across the floor, and the mob began to push toward the boarding ramp even more urgently.

"Do not kick the detonator," YVH 1-507A ordered. "Remain calm and step away."

Someone booted it back at the original kicker, and the droid skidded over a family of Aqualish trying to change direction. Incredibly, the crowd continued to shove forward, between the Solos and to both sides of them. Determined to avoid becoming separated from Han, Leia snapped her lightsaber from beneath her jacket and turned back toward the berth. She found Welda blocking the way, raising a small hold-out blaster and pointing it at Leia's chest.

The weapon remained there for about half a second before Adarakh, still holding the luggage he had been carrying, sank his teeth into the woman's arm. There was a sickening crunch, and Welda's hand fell open and let the blaster fall. The Noghri used a bag to knock her feet out from beneath her, and then he was on her, tearing at her head with both hands. Even this did not stop the desperate mob from pressing forward around the fight.

Far too accustomed to assassins and kidnappers to waste time wondering who had sent them or why, Leia positioned her body between Ben and Welda and started to push her way around the fight. Han was two steps away from her, holding his blaster in one hand and using the other to punch the admittance code into the security panel.

"See-Threepio, where's Meewalh?" Leia asked.

"She went after Tarc, mistress." Still holding her blast-scorched ladalum, the droid was following Leia around the fight. "I do hope the boy set a long fuse on that thermal detonator! One-dash-Five-Oh-Seven is so terribly clumsy."

The soft drone of a vibroblade sounded behind Leia. Surprised that Adarakh had not finished the fight already, she turned to find a powershiv rising in Welda's good hand. The Noghri blocked easily, then countered with a slash that caught the woman beside the ear and lifted her entire face off. The woman's scream was nowhere near as ghastly as it should have been. Her face squirmed in Adarakh's hand like a thing alive, and neither Leia nor the Noghri understood for an instant what they were looking at.

That was all the time Welda needed to drive the powershiv into Adarakh's ribs. The Noghri's eyes grew wide with shock and his mouth fell open, then Leia felt the life leave his body. All of the disappointment and sadness she had been feeling since Anakin's death turned instantly to anger. She thumbed her lightsaber active and, still holding Ben, stepped forward to attack.

Welda hurled Adarakh's body into Leia's knees, knocking her legs from beneath her and rolling away. Leia was barely quick enough to catch herself with the Force and avoid landing on Ben. A pair of blaster bolts zinged overhead from Han's direction, forcing her attacker back and eliciting an even louder uproar from the panicked crowd. Leia gathered her feet beneath her in a fighting crouch and found the assassin mirroring her position from two meters away, a wide-eyed Ho'Din family squeezing past behind her.

Even with every pore still oozing blood where the ooglith masquer had been forcibly ripped away, the slender face across from her was unmistakable.

"Viqi Shesh," Leia said. Ben finally had enough and began to cry, but Leia was too outraged to pay attention. "I would've thought you'd be down in the grotto levels waiting for your masters with the rest of the granite slugs."

"Leia—always the proper word for every occasion."

Shesh flicked her wrist, hurling the powershiv at Ben. Leia blocked easily with her lightsaber, then cursed inwardly as Han chased the traitor off by zinging another pair of blaster bolts over her head.

"You're a better shot than that, Han!" Leia snarled, although she knew he had only been trying to avoid hitting innocent bystanders. She thrust Ben at C-3PO. "Put that tree down and hold him."

"Me?" The droid dropped the pot and cupped his metallic hands under the child. "But, Mistress Leia, you had my child-care module wiped after that time—"

"Wait on the *Falcon*," Leia ordered.

"Of course, Princess, but I must remind you . . ."

The droid's objection was lost to the general din as Leia pursued Shesh into the crowd. She heard Han call her name, but did not turn back for him either. The traitor would not escape, not after betraying the New Republic, selling out SELCORE, and no doubt arranging the deaths of a great many Jedi. Perhaps she had even had a hand in Anakin's.

The whine of a pair of repulsor-enhanced legs echoed through the docking facility girders and YVH 1-507A bounded over the crowd toward Gate 3700.

"Make a hole! Thermal detonator coming through!" The droid crashed down on a hoversled loaded with priceless sculptures and immediately bounded into the air again. "Remain calm and—"

The command ended in a deafening crackle as the detonator ignited, taking with it five hundred cubic meters of docking facility, sentient biomass, and durasteel substructure. As the sizzling sphere contracted on itself, a long metallic groan reverberated through the docking facility, then a large section of floor suddenly began to sink toward the now-nonexistent Gate 3700.

The crowd roared and somehow began to run at the *Byrt,* half pushing, half carrying those in front up the boarding ramp. Leia found herself being carried backward by the crowd and had to use the Force to stay in place. Her quarry was nowhere to be seen, but she did spy a blood-smeared Rodian rushing in her direction. She pushed through the crowd and planted herself in his path, raising her inactive lightsaber to stop him.

He buzzed an objection at her in Huttese.

"Everyone is trying to board that ship." As she spoke, Leia gestured at him with an open palm. "And I'm sure you'll make it that much sooner, if you just take the time now to tell me where the woman who smeared this on you went."

The Rodian repeated her suggestion, then pointed to Docking Bay 3732—the next one after the *Falcon*'s. Leia let him go and fought her way fifty meters up the corridor, her fury growing with every step. The damage Viqi Shesh had done to the New Republic was immeasurable, the pain she had caused the Solos unforgivable. Leia owed it to Anakin—and to all of the millions of others who had given their life defending an ideal—to repay her in kind.

Leia reached the bay to find it already secured. Not bothering to try the control button, she ignited her lightsaber and jammed the blade into the seam, slicing through the durasteel locking bolt as though it were so much tin. The security alarm that began to blare both inside the berth and outside did little to add to the general commotion in the docking facility. Following close behind to shield herself from attack, she used the Force to push the durasteel door open—and was surprised to find blaster bolts already ricocheting around the launch bay's dreary interior.

In the center of the bay sat a sleek KDY staryacht, the pilot peering through the cockpit viewing panel as he powered up the repulsor drives. Viqi Shesh was about a third of the way around the circle, holding her mangled arm and dodging for the boarding ramp while Han fired at her through a hole that someone had recently cut through the durasteel wall separating Docking Bay

3732 from Bay 3733. He was being fired on, in turn, by a pair of crew members trying to cover their employer from the well of the boarding ramp.

Leia started across the bay after her quarry, only to hear the ominous whir of the yacht's roof-mounted weapons turret revolving in her direction. She barely had time to hurl herself to the floor before the weapon depressed and fired, burning a fifty-centimeter hole into the durasteel beside her head.

Leia rolled and came up with her blade ignited.

"Leia, are you crazy?" Han yelled, forgetting himself and rising up in front of the hole. "You're not that good with that thing!"

The crew members poured a flurry of blaster bolts through the hole, forcing Han to dive for the floor and giving Shesh a clear path to the boarding ramp. The turret laser fired again, but Leia was already dodging across the floor—if a bit awkwardly, at least fast enough to keep from getting hit. She stumbled and nearly fell, then heard a blaster rifle off to one side. She turned toward the sound and found Viqi Shesh rushing under the yacht toward its boarding ramp.

Trying to ignore the blaster bolts pinging off the durasteel all around her, Leia locked her lightsaber on and hurled the weapon at the traitor, using the Force to keep it spinning toward its target. The turret laser fired again, as did the crew members at the top of the boarding ramp. Leia gave her body over to her instincts and continued to focus her mind on the attack, trusting to the Force to move her arms and legs in the correct manner.

Shesh hurled herself down on the boarding ramp. Instead of cutting her in half, the blade slipped along her back, burning away her clothing and a thick layer of skin and bone. She screamed and collapsed, then reached up with her arms and began to pull herself toward the interior of the ship. The ramp rose, and the last thing Leia saw of the traitor was a pair of male hands pulling her aboard.

Leia did not even realize she was also being dragged out of

harm's way until she heard Meewalh say, "Lady Vader, you must get down!"

Leia allowed the Noghri to pull her to the floor just as another cannon bolt tore through the wall above her. When the yacht's repulsor engines whirred to life and a second bolt did not follow, she reluctantly raised her head, her heart already bursting with the news she would have to give Meewalh.

But instead of the Noghri, she found herself staring at Anakin's twelve-year-old face.

"Do whatever you want to me," Tarc said. He was sitting with his back to the wall and his hands bound by a pair of Meewalh's plasteel restraining cuffs. "At least my mom and sisters are safe."

"Safe?" Leia could only shake her head. "Is that what you think?"

"It's what I know." The boy tipped his head back and looked up at the ceiling, where Shesh's yacht was being forced to wait until the docking master cleared it for departure by opening the dome. "They're on the *Wicked Pleasure* right now."

Leia was already reaching for her comlink when Han came running up.

"Forget it," he said, displaying his own comlink. "I tried. Shev's not holding vessels for anyone."

Leia nodded. It hardly mattered what Shev said; with its big laser cannon, the yacht could blast out of the bay anyway.

Han held out her deactivated lightsaber. "Feel any better?"

"Not really," Leia admitted. She stood and took the lightsaber, hanging it inside her jacket again. "How about you?"

"Worse," Han said. He pointed at Tarc. "What are we going to do about him?"

The last thing Leia wanted to do was take this particular child along on the *Falcon,* but she was certainly not going to abandon a twelve-year-old boy on Coruscant. She grabbed him by the wrist restraints and pulled him to his feet.

"Yeah, that's what I thought." Han frowned, then looked expectantly toward the door. "What'd you do with See-Threepio and Ben?"

"They're supposed to be with the *Falcon*."

Han's face fell. "Not likely. When you ran off, I secured the door to keep the mob out."

A low rumble shook the berth as the dome irised open, and they looked up to see the *Byrt* rising on a pillar of ion efflux. The *Wicked Pleasure* slipped out of the bay and followed it skyward, then C-3PO's voice came over the comlink.

"Master Han? Mistress Leia?"

Leia and Han activated their comlinks together. "Where are you?"

"This isn't my doing!" the droid said. "The berth was locked, and I was helpless to defend us."

"See-Threepio!" Leia said. "Are you telling me you're aboard the *Byrt*?"

"I'm afraid so, Mistress Leia," he said. "And they're threatening to put a restraining bolt on me!"

Chapter 52

*T*he skips were stacked like the stones in an ancient Massassi wall, each craft hovering above the gap between the two below, every gap covered by interlocking fire from an inner ring of corvettes. Behind the corvettes waited frigates, and somewhere behind the frigates was the cruiser bearing the yammosk. Luke and his shield mates launched another volley of shadow bombs and watched the weapons veer into shielding singularities. The three Jedi continued on vector long enough to taunt the Yuuzhan Vong pilots with a fusillade of cannonfire, then broke off amid a storm of hot plasma and angry grutchins. Though all three were careful to present inviting attack angles as they turned, none of the enemy coralskippers abandoned station to pursue. The warmaster had finally learned how to protect his yammosk, and woe to the warrior who broke formation.

Luke opened a channel to Orbital Defense Headquarters, to whom they had been passed off as the battle drifted closer in to Coruscant. "Zero on the chasers, Gambler. That yammosk is in the battle for good."

"Copy, Farmboy. No reason to be disappointed," Lando replied. "You've forced them to take half a fleet out of the fight."

"That's something." Luke had no idea how Lando had come to be General Ba'tra's special operations commander, but he was glad to have someone of such composure serving as their battle coordinator. Judging by the static and booming on the channel, the ODH itself was under heavy attack. "Let's try a wave attack. Maybe we can just punch through."

"Negative," Lando said. "Stand by for a planetside comm patch."

Luke felt Mara grow instantly apprehensive. Han and Leia should have been off Coruscant an hour ago, but it could not be anyone else.

Han came on the channel. "Can you break free up there?"

"You know we can," Mara answered.

"You need to catch the starferry *Byrt*." As Han spoke, the tactical display shifted scales. A targeting square appeared a quarter of the way around the planet, on a 200-meter transport rising into space. "C-3PO is aboard with your package."

"It's my fault." Leia's voice was as brittle as a glitterstim web. "Viqi Shesh ambushed us in the docking bay, and I was so furious—"

"Leia, don't worry," Mara said. There was only resolve in her voice, no blame or worry. "We'll get him back."

"Okay." Han sounded relieved. "We're stuck planetside until we find some containment fluid. The senator did a job on our feed lines and umbilicals."

Now Mara was worried, Luke sensed. Charging an empty containment unit could take hours. Coruscant didn't have hours. Given the number of coralskippers and airskiffs already dropping out of orbit, it might not have *one* hour.

Luke was about to send Saba Sebatyne down in her blastboat when Lando came on the channel. "Old buddy, the scarheads will blast this bucket of bolts out from under me any minute. I could drop down in the *Luck* and give you a lift."

"And leave the bird behind? Never!" Han commed. "You guys take care of things up there."

"Will do," Luke said. "And may the Force be with you."

"Yeah, kid—you, too," Han said. "Solo out."

Luke's thoughts turned to his son. Mara had already plotted an atmosphere-skimming vector that would intercept the *Byrt* and a thousand other vessels streaming up from the Eastport/Imperial City area. But they would have to hurry. The tactical display showed a Yuuzhan Vong frigate group moving to intercept the fleeing starships.

"Gambler—"

"Go," Lando commed. "A couple of Jedi won't make a difference here."

Luke peeled off after Mara, who was already diving away. Noticing that Tam was following, he commed, "Quiet, stay with the wing. Hisser, you're in charge. Make it look good until things fall apart, then comet for the rendezvous."

"You do not want help, Master Farmboy?"

"I want it." Luke pushed the stick forward and followed Mara under the flaming belly of a kilometer-long KDY New Republic battle cruiser. "But every minute you hold that task force here saves ten thousand New Republic lives."

"Copy," Saba said. "Count on us to save a million."

The comm speaker gave a sharp crackle, then Luke came up on the other side of the cruiser to find a rolling fireball where the tactical display showed Mara's X-wing.

Jinking around the explosion, he commed, "Mara?"

No answer, but she reached out through the Force, urging him not to worry. *Get Ben.*

R2-D2 tweedled a warning. Luke swung left and narrowly avoided a barrage from the enemy vessel—also a cruiser—that had set the KDY aflame. He designated it a high-priority watch for R2-D2 and automatically fell into a random jink-and-juke evasive pattern.

He found Mara silhouetted against the lights of Coruscant's night side, her number three engine trailing yellow flame, her astromech droid domeless, her S-foils stuck half open—no good for firing or speed.

Has she been anyone else, or their task any but retrieving Ben, Luke would have ordered her to a safe base. With Mara, that was out of the question until their son was safe. He pulled his X-wing alongside hers and pointed at her shield generator.

Mara shook her head. No shields.

Finally frightened, Luke reached out with the Force, consciously reinforcing their bond. Mara reached back and slid into place beneath his X-wing—before he could gesture her over.

They skimmed through the upper atmosphere, giving wide berth to a small battle raging around a skyhook residential platform tethered in low orbit, then began to take incidental fire dodging through an airskiff insertion zone. As they drew nearer the *Byrt,* R2-D2 kept changing the tactical display's scale to show more detail. It soon grew apparent that the Yuuzhan Vong frigate group was moving to intercept the same starferry they were.

They left the atmosphere again and found themselves surrounded by a dozen small battles as Yuuzhan Vong assault groups struggled through the interlocking fire zones of Coruscant's orbital defense platforms. The invaders were succeeding, but slowly and only by weight of superior numbers. In view of the naked eye alone, there were a dozen enemy cruisers venting their entrails into space and hundreds of smaller craft drifting about in aimless, decaying orbits.

Luke started to detour around the combat cluster—and drew an admonishing whistle from R2-D2. A pair of time estimates appeared on the main display, showing that the frigate would beat them to the *Byrt* as it was. Luke adjusted the threat alarms to their most sensitive and set the X-wing on a straight vector.

Something bumped his starfighter's belly. Luke's first thought

was of Mara, that maybe she'd been hit again; then he felt her apprehension and knew she was there. His X-wing jumped again. He
looked over and saw her flying down to one side. She pulled back on
her stick and banged her S-foils into his undercarriage, hard.

When she bounced away, they were closed. A new time esti-
mate appeared on Luke's display. They would intercept the *Byrt*
within a few seconds of the Yuuzhan Vong.

"Artoo, is Mara seeing this?"

The droid chirped impatiently, then an explanation appeared
on the primary display. R2-D2 was using his transceiver to feed
data directly onto her vid displays.

"You could have told me," Luke said. "Ask how many shadow
bombs she has available."

Mara held up three fingers.

Luke nodded, then flashed three fingers twice and closed his
S-foils. "Give us a two-second count."

The count appeared, and two seconds later they were flying
through the combat area at two-thirds an X-wing's top speed—the
best Mara could manage on three engines without drifting into
overload ranges. Luke lost his own shields when an enemy corvette
used half a dozen dovin basals to rip them in swift succession,
drawing down the grab-safety and overloading the generator as it
tried to bring up new protection too quickly. But then they were
above the defense platforms and out of those battles, streaking after
the *Byrt*.

Luke opened a channel to the liner. "Starferry *Byrt*, please alter
vector toward incoming X-wings. We'll eliminate your pursuit."

There was a short pause, then a deep voice came over the
channel. "You gone vac-brain? There are only two of you!" A
second New Republic vessel, a sleek KDY staryacht flying with its
transponder off, appeared on the tactical display behind the *Byrt*.
"We'll take our chances. No particular reason they'd be after us."

"There is," Luke said. On the display, the frigate group—a

frigate analog and two corvettes—was gaining on the starferry. "This is Luke Skywalker. You have my son aboard."

"What?" the captain cried. "This is no time for jokes."

"No joke," Luke said. "Alter your vector *now*."

Though he doubted it would carry over comm waves, Luke put the weight of the Force behind his words.

The *Byrt*'s vector started to bend.

Mara's relief washed up from below. Luke checked the tactical display and found the KDY staryacht continuing along its original vector—one less factor to worry about. The *Byrt* came into visible range, a finger-length needle of ion efflux illuminating the yorik coral noses of the three pursuing vessels.

Luke touched the symbol of the rearmost corvette. "Artoo, designate that one for Mara . . . and tell her to be careful."

R2-D2 bleeped an acknowledgment. The Jedi split, streaking toward their targets in wild corkscrews. The frigate group dropped skips and began to spray plasma. Lacking shields, Luke and Mara poured on speed and gave their stick hands over to the Force. The enemy vessels swelled into stony monoliths, scabrous and black and half hidden behind whirling curtains of flame. Mara broke toward her corvette, barrel-rolled past half a dozen skips, and launched her shadow bombs.

Luke swung after her. The skips took the bait and rushed to intercept him. He broke back toward the frigate and dodged past a magma missile, slashed a grutchin apart on his closed S-foils, and made an oblique run down the vessel's flank.

A shielding crew snared his first shadow bomb twenty meters from target. The other two blossomed against the hull. One breached at midships, the other behind the bow. The frigate fell silent and began to vent flotsam. Luke dodged over the top and began a tight turn toward the last corvette.

Her first target already reduced to rubble, Mara was also swinging toward the corvette. Luke could feel her resolve as clearly as his own, but with her shadow bombs gone and her S-foils stuck closed, that was all she had.

"Artoo, tell her to dock with the *Byrt*."

The droid whistled negatively. They were too far apart to project data directly onto her screens.

"Great."

Luke finished his turn, found skips swarming over the corvette to cut him off. The *Byrt*'s two laser cannons began to spray red bolts at the vessel's nose. The corvette held its fire and extruded capture tentacles.

Luke deployed his S-foils and began to trade fire with the skips. With Corran's new targeting system, he quickly destroyed the first pair and forced the rest to spread out. A notice alarm beeped on the tactical display. The unidentified staryacht had changed vector, was coming in behind Mara.

"What now?" Luke grumbled. "Get this onto Mara's display."

R2-D2 whistled doubtfully.

"Try." Luke juked past a plasma ball and poured cannon bolts into the skip that had launched it. "And open a channel to that yacht."

A half-dozen skips swung toward Mara. He started after them, then heard her voice in his mind.

No!

The image of the corvette flashed in Luke's mind, and he knew that Mara wanted him to concentrate on saving Ben.

Behind you, Luke returned. He sent a flurry of bolts streaming at the skips, then rolled back toward the corvette. "How about that channel, Artoo?"

An explanation appeared on the primary display.

"They won't?"

The reason for the staryacht's silence grew clear when it fired on Mara from behind. Luke twisted around and saw bolts streaming into her starfighter, then the bright flash of a hit. A piece of wing spun off flaming.

Go! Mara urged. The panic in her thought was for Ben, not herself.

A single word more, *eject,* came to Luke's mind. Mara wheeled toward the planet, using the Force to hold her X-wing level so it would not go into a tumble when she hit the atmosphere. Luke reached out to envelop her with his love, then looked to his tactical display and found her craft already marked for tracking. There was now a transponder identification below the staryacht: the *Wicked Pleasure,* registered to Senator Viqi Shesh. Luke took a breath and let it out, let his fury go with it. *Then* he marked the vessel as a target of opportunity.

A plasma ball skipped across his nose cone, and the tactical display went dead beneath his fingers. R2-D2 shrieked with static, then fell into an electronic babble as melted comm components and burning sensor packages spilled into space.

Luke soared in among the skips, dodging and rolling and pivoting, targeting by the Force alone and still scoring hits. He blasted one skip into pebbles and suddenly found a clear hole to the corvette. He closed his S-foils and accelerated. The skips whirled after him, pouring fire from behind. The X-wing bucked. Alarm screeches filled the cockpit. The engines lost power, and he decelerated.

Luke launched his shadow bombs anyway. The first veered into a skip's shielding singularity and detonated barely a hundred meters away. The other two vanished against the corvette's black silhouette. He kept pushing until their proximity fuses detected the pull of a dovin basal and blasted a pair of deep hollows in the vessel's hull.

Close, but no breach.

R2-D2 wailed for Luke's attention. He glanced back and

found two engines, possibly all four, burning. He slapped the emergency shutdown, wheeled toward Coruscant, and reached out with the Force, pulling himself toward Mara and her plummeting X-wing.

I couldn't get to him, he told her. *I just couldn't make it.*

Jaina woke to the sound of laughter, with a bright light shining in her eye and a stink in her nose like a Gamorrean refresher station. The laugh was just the sort of mad cackle one would expect in a Kala'uun ryll den, but she knew better than to think her throbbing head and aching shoulder were the by-products of a spice dream. This nightmare was real. Nom Anor's frigate had shot down her stolen shuttle, Jacen and the rest were stranded on an enemy world-ship, Anakin was dead.

The longblaster roared, and another mad cackle sounded somewhere forward of Jaina.

"Did you see that one?" Alema Rar chortled. "I cut him in two."

"Good," Jaina rasped. The effort filled her head with pain, but she welcomed it, drew strength from it. "Kill some more."

"Be quiet, Jaina," Zekk said, his voice condemning. The light shifted to her other eye. "You don't know what you're talking about."

"And you do?" Jaina slapped the glow stick aside, and the foul-smelling stinksalts, as well. "You don't even *have* a brother."

"But I do know the dark side," he said. "It isn't the answer."

"Who said I was turning to the dark side?" Jaina asked.

"You used the Force to kill."

Zekk did not say more.

Jaina looked away from Zekk's dark eyes. "He had it coming." Her numbness had been replaced with raw fury, and she was glad. "You saw what he did to Anakin."

"Anakin is beyond insults," Zekk said evenly. "And what about Vergere? You attacked her, too."

"I was angry."

Gritting her teeth against the pain, Jaina sat up and looked around. The inside of the shuttle was a listing mass of clutter, with a long crack running the length of the hull and a fluid-smeared tangle of cognition hoods and burst villips strewn across the flight deck. Jaina flashed on a garbled memory of struggling with those controls to keep the nose up, of skimming a crater rim and coming down like the rock the shuttle was, of skipping across the basin floor and rolling sideways and decelerating sharply as the nose caught . . . then there was nothing, only a vague feeling of pitching forward and the sound of screaming voices and a sudden darkness.

Across from Jaina, Tahiri lay on a litter next to Anakin, one obviously broken arm resting across the husk in which his body was encased. Barely half lucid, she was still talking to him, describing how they had tracked him down in the Yuuzhan Vong mortuary.

In the back of the vessel, Lowbacca let out low groan as he moved something heavy into place. He rumbled softly to himself in the half-slurred voice of a Wookiee with a concussion, then let what sounded like a rock plop into a pool of viscous liquid. A sodden bang followed, and an instant after that, the distant crackle of an erupting plasma ball.

"A little short," Alema called from the forward door. "Raise it one degree, and you'll burn them crisp."

"I take it we're under attack," Jaina said to Zekk.

"Not exactly under attack, but they're coming," Zekk confirmed. "Nom Anor is trying to capture us alive."

A sneer came to Jaina's lips. "Let him try." She swung her legs off her makeshift litter and reached for her power blaster. "I'm going to enjoy this."

*   *   *

In all his decades of kicking around the galaxy, Han had never heard anything quite as eerie as the ululation of an anguished Noghri female. It reminded him of the sound of crumpling durasteel, or of the comm shriek a star gives off just before going nova. Even shielded from the noise by the flight deck door and half the length of the *Falcon,* it sent a shiver down his spine—and drew tears from his eyes. After eighteen years with the Noghri, he still could not say he understood them—but he knew how much he owed them, and it always hurt when one fell defending his family.

Han wiped his eyes, then looked away from the rain of burning ships outside the *Falcon*'s cockpit long enough to check the temperature in the fusion power unit. "We have about ninety seconds before we become just another fireball crashing down on a tower. Think we still have enough pull to recharge at Imperial City? Or should we try Calocour Heights?" He waited one second, five, then ten. "Leia?"

When there was still no answer, he glanced over at her. She was sitting stiffly upright in the oversized copilot's seat, her hands folded in her lap and her blank gaze fixed on her feet. For the first time, Han noticed that Chewbacca's old seat was so large that it left her toes dangling ten centimeters above the floor.

Han shook her arm. "Leia, wake up. I need you here."

Leia looked up, but stared out the cockpit at the distant smoke plume of a crashing Star Destroyer. "Why would you need me, Han? I'll only let you down."

"Let me down?" Han echoed. "That's crazy. You've never let me down."

Finally, Leia looked at him. "Yes, Han, I have. I went after Viqi Shesh—"

"So did I."

"But you didn't lose Ben and get Adarakh killed."

"Really?" Han sneaked a glance at the temperature of the

fusion unit, then glanced around the cockpit theatrically. "Funny, I don't see them here."

"Han." Leia sighed the word, then looked out over Coruscant's smoking, broken-toothed skyline. "You know what I mean."

"I suppose I do," Han said. "I just didn't think you'd go away like I did. I thought you were stronger than that."

Leia faced him and, for the first time, really seemed to be looking. "How can you say that?" Though her voice remained even, her very calmness betrayed the depth of her anger. "This must hurt you, too—or do you care only for Wookiees?"

"I care." Han managed to hold his anger in check by reminding himself that her bitterness was a good sign; any emotional reaction was. "And that's why I'm not giving up this time—not ever again. Anakin and Chewbacca may be gone, and Adarakh and maybe even Ben and Luke and Mara—but we still have each other."

"That's about all." Leia looked back out the window.

"And we have hope," Han insisted. "As long as we have each other, there's still hope for us, for Jacen and Jaina—wherever they are—even for the New Republic."

"The New Republic?" Leia's voice rose so sharply it rivaled Meewalh's ululation. "Are you blind? There is no New Republic! It died before the Yuuzhan Vong came!"

"It didn't!" Han yelled back, no longer able to contain his anger. "Because if it did, then Anakin died for nothing!"

He glanced down at the temperature of the fusion unit again and saw that they were about thirty seconds from becoming a crater. Han said nothing; if his wife had really given up, he did not care to keep fighting himself.

Leia's mouth opened as though she were going to yell back, then she saw where he was looking, and all of the emotion left her face. Han felt her watching him watch the gauge. He said nothing. The gauge ticked up another bar.

"You're bluffing," Leia said.

"I'm betting," Han said. Jaina and Jacen were still alive, and she would not let her grief make her give up on them.

Leia watched the temperature rise another bar, then said, "Imperial City."

Han let out his breath. "Calocour's closer."

"Han!"

Han swung the *Falcon* around and began a silent countdown.

"Go to the chief of state's landing pad," Leia said. "We need to see Borsk."

"You think Borsk is still on Coruscant?" Han gasped.

"Where else? He certainly won't be going to Bothawui." Leia pulled a datapad out of the stowage slot on her seat and, with the ease of a practiced statesperson, began to make speech notes. "There's something I need to do for him."

Chapter 53

With the Orbital Defense Headquarters burning like a second sun as it plummeted across Coruscant's opalescent sky, the tapered spires and delicate towers of the Imperial Palace were bathed in scintillating orange light. As they descended toward the chief of state's private landing pad, Leia felt like they were dropping into a forest ablaze. Han brought them down less than a meter behind the tailfins of Fey'lya's garish Kothlis Systems Luxuflier and shut down the fusion unit even before the *Falcon* settled onto its struts. Leaving Anakin's look-alike—his true name was Dab Hantaq—aboard under Meewalh's care, they lowered the boarding ramp and found themselves looking down the barrel of a tripod-mounted G-40 portable cannon.

"Something wrong with the *Falcon*'s transponder, Garv?" Leia asked, not all that surprised by the cautious reception. "We tried to comm, but couldn't get through."

"Just being careful, Princess." A thin man in the uniform of a New Republic general stepped into view. "Sorry about the comm problem. The Yuuzhan Vong are starting to take out the satellite web, so Chief of State Fey'lya has ordered a blackout on all nonmilitary communications."

"That's sure to help the evacuation," Han said.

Garv—General Tomas to everyone except his superiors and former superiors—responded with an enigmatic half nod. Leia had personally named Garv the commander of palace security, and in all the time she had known him, that was as close to a comment on a superior as she had ever seen from him.

"Garv, we ran into a little sabotage problem with Viqi Shesh," Leia explained. "Would it be too much to have someone recharge our containment fluid? And I'd like to speak with Chief of State Fey'lya."

"We can arrange both." Garv sent a furry-cheeked Bothan aide off to fetch the maintenance crew, then turned back to Leia looking uncharacteristically doubtful. "Forgive me if I'm intruding, but I've heard rumors about Anakin. I can't tell you how sorry I am."

"Thank you," Leia said. Knowing she would need to accustom herself to people offering condolences, she laid a hand on Garv's arm. "That means a great deal to us."

Han nodded. "We're going to miss him."

"As will the New Republic," Garv said.

"And speaking of the New Republic," Leia said, glad for an excuse to change the subject, "I noticed the data towers are still intact. Shouldn't someone be destroying those records?"

"Someone *should* be," Garv said. "But Fey'lya refuses to give the order."

"He thinks he can hold the planet?" Han asked, disbelieving. "The idiot! If the scarheads capture those survey abstracts, there won't be a safe place in the galaxy to put a base."

Garv's expression turned sour. "I *have* mentioned as much."

"I'm sure the chief of state will give the order when the time comes," Leia said. With shafts of turbolaser fire starting to strike at hostile vessels from rooftops all across Coruscant, she felt certain the time had come already—but Garv Tomas was too good an officer to exceed his authority even under these circumstances.

"Still, it wouldn't be improper to arm the charges now, would it, General?"

Garv smiled. "Not improper at all."

He keyed the order into a datapad and dispatched an officer to see it carried through, then led the way through the hangar to the chief of state's towertop office suite. After a brief dispute with an agenda droid, which Garv won by virtue of a security override command, the general admitted them to the restricted chambers and withdrew to continue his duties. They found Fey'lya bereft of his usual gaggle of advisers and sycophants, standing alone in the heart of his opulent office, studying a holographic display of Coruscant's crumbling defenses.

The situation was hopeless. What remained of the New Republic fleets were surrounded or cut off from the planet, sometimes both. Half of the defense platforms were falling out of orbit, the rest blinking with critical damage indicators. The atmospheric security force was fighting fiercely in their V-wings and Howlrunners, but the superiority of their air-dedicated craft could not overcome the enemy's sheer numbers. Yuuzhan Vong drop ships were already forming up to make their runs, and Leia knew this battle would soon be moving to the rooftops.

It took Fey'lya a minute to notice he had guests. "Come to gloat, Princess?"

Leia forced a warm tone. "Not at all, Chief." Hoping Han's face would not betray the opinion of Fey'lya he had expressed earlier, she extended her hands and crossed to the Bothan. "I came to apologize."

Fey'lya's ears flattened. "Apologize?"

"For not helping with the military," she explained. "I'm afraid I was too consumed with grief."

Fey'lya's attitude changed instantly, and he took her hands between his paws. "Not at all. I am the one who should apologize— to call upon you at such a time!"

"It must have been important, or you wouldn't have in-truded." Confident that Fey'lya was already considering how he might use her to bolster his evaporated support, Leia shifted her gaze to the display and let the comment hang. "Our position cer-tainly looks tenuous. Can we hold?"

"We must," Fey'lya answered. "If Coruscant falls, so does my government."

"Yeah, wouldn't that be a shame?" Han said.

Resisting the urge to stomp on his foot, Leia smiled and pre-tended not to notice the sarcasm. "What my husband means to say, Chief Fey'lya, is that you have our support." She pulled Han to her side. "Isn't that right, dear?"

"Of course, dear." Han sounded sincere—or close enough to draw an accepting nod from Fey'lya. "Chief Fey'lya can count on us."

Leia put on an earnest look. "If you thought a few words from me would do any good . . ."

Fey'lya's smile looked more relieved than appreciative. "What could it hurt? If the military knows you're with me, they'll stand firm behind my government. That's been the problem, you see—all these senators running for home and grabbing a piece of any fleet they can."

"I know," Leia said. "I've seen the newsvids. Is the comm center still over by the window?"

"That was such an easy place for Baldavian lip-readers to watch." Fey'lya took her arm and guided her toward what had been, when she occupied the office, a coat closet.

"One body of open water on the whole planet, and you drop our X-wings in it?" Mara said, wrapping an airsplint around her broken ankle. "The *only* one? What were you thinking, Skywalker?"

"Mara, I really didn't have a choice," Luke said. The heat of his engine fires had fused the fibers on the back of his flight suit, and he would need a close cut before his singed hair looked human again. "It was put them here or crash them into a tower."

Mara and Luke were staring across the firelit waters of the Western Sea, a vast artificial lake and multispecies recreation area spread across thousands—maybe tens of thousands—of rooftops. A dozen whirlpools marked where crashes less controlled than their own had punctured the durasteel bed and freed the contents to rain down on Coruscant's underlevels. All in all, it had not been a bad place to push the X-wings after they ejected, but the bottom was so strewn with discarded droids and junked airspeeders that locating their cherished R2 unit was proving difficult even for Luke.

She pulled the airsplint's inflation tab and did not allow herself to wince as it compressed her broken bones, then took an injector out of the ejection medpac and gave herself a shot of bacta numb. Mara would normally have avoided any kind of painkiller, but they would be moving fast over the next few hours, and she did not want her injury slowing her down. The Yuuzhan Vong were starting to bring their big vessels down to suppress the rooftop turbolasers, and she could sense that the *Byrt* had not escaped into hyperspace with Ben. They had to find a way back into orbit, and fast.

Luke finally stretched a hand over the water. A distant speck broke the surface and swelled into the shape of a scorched X-wing. A pair of Yuuzhan Vong airskiffs promptly dropped out of the sun to attack, in turn drawing fire from a nearby turbolaser battery. For a few short seconds, the sky above the lake erupted into a gridwork of streaking plasma balls and flashing energy bolts, then one skiff burst into rubble and the other pulled up, vanishing into the sun with a stream of laser shafts chasing its tail.

Mara waved their thanks up to the battery crew, which was so well camouflaged on a nearby rooftop that she had difficulty finding it until she used the Force. Luke brought the X-wing to shore and lifted a wildly chirping R2-D2 from the astromech socket. Other than heat scarring, the droid looked sound, and the fuss he was making confirmed that his hermetic seals remained intact after both fire and submersion.

Something big exploded high above, momentarily outshining the sun and spraying long tongues of white flame across the sky. Mara and Luke watched until the brilliance dimmed enough to reveal individual pieces of debris fluttering planetward, but there was no way to know whether the vessel had been New Republic or Yuuzhan Vong. Suddenly overcome by the desperation of their situation, she looped her arm through Luke's elbow and allowed him to take the weight off her broken ankle.

"Luke, how are we going to do this?" They had seen from the air that the hoverlanes were either jammed with traffic or blocked by debris, and they both knew that even if they did reach a space-port, any spacecraft worthy of the name would be long gone. "We'll be lucky to get ourselves offplanet, much less rescue Ben."

Luke took her in his arm. "Trust in the Force, Mara."

"Is that the best you can do?" Mara asked bitterly. "Did trusting the Force save Anakin?"

"Perhaps Anakin was meant to save us," Luke said gently. He knelt in front of R2-D2 and used his sleeve cuff to dry the droid's auditory sensors. "We're not in this alone, Mara. If Artoo can get through on a military channel, maybe someone else can help."

"Maybe." Mara looked away and tried to keep the dark emotions from rising inside her. She did not want to blame Han and Leia for their son's peril, but it had been "help" that had endangered Ben in the first place. "Will you hurry, Skywalker?"

"Got it," Luke said. "Artoo—"

The droid whistled in excitement.

"You're sure?" Luke began to dry R2-D2's speaker grille. "You found Leia?"

"This is not the end," Leia said. "Two years ago, the Yuuzhan Vong entered our galaxy. They came not as friends and equals, though we would gladly have welcomed them as such, but as thieves and conquerors. They saw a galaxy at peace and mistook the strength of our convictions for frailty of arms, the wisdom of compromise for the timidity of cowards. They attacked without provocation or mercy, slaying billions of our citizens, enslaving entire worlds, and sacrificing millions of beings to appease the bloodlust of their imaginary gods. They believed we would be easily defeated, because they believed we would yield without a fight.

"They were wrong. We have fought at Dubrillion, Ithor, the Black Bantha, Borleias, and Corellia—we have fought them every leg of the way from the Outer Rim into the Core. We have lost untold numbers of loved ones, my own son Anakin and my husband's dear friend Chewbacca among them, and now we are battling in the skies over Coruscant itself. We are still fighting.

"Soon, the enemy will be on our rooftops, in our homes, roaming the dark underlayers of our city. To those able to evacuate and to those trapped behind, I say the same thing I would tell my twins—were I able to reach them behind enemy lines: Keep fighting.

"This is not the end. Twice already, Jedi-led forces have decimated Yuuzhan Vong fleets, and we enter each battle with new weapons and better tactics. We have prevailed against ruthless enemies before, against Palpatine, against Thrawn, against the Ssi-ruuk. This is a war we know how to win. Keep fighting until you can fight no longer, then exhaust the enemy chasing you, and turn and fight some more. Keep fighting. I promise you, we will prevail."

The *Lady Luck*'s flight deck fell as silent as a Noghri with a vibroblade. Lando pretended to adjust the shield power until he knew his eyes would remain dry, then heard an odd half growl from the copilot's seat. He looked over to find General Ba'tra drying his cheek fur.

"That woman could talk a Hutt onto a diet." The Bothan spent the next few seconds looking out the forward viewport, where the *Byrt*'s finger-sized profile was rapidly swelling to arm-sized. A smaller lozenge, black and scabrous, was tentacled to its belly, and Viqi Shesh's sleek KDY staryacht hovered nearby. Finally, Ba'tra grunted, "General Calrissian, none of those vessels looks like the *Errant Venture*."

"They're not," Lando said, offering no other explanation. As far as he was concerned, his reactivation had ended with the fall of the Orbital Defense Headquarters. Now, Ba'tra and his soldiers were just evacuees hitching a ride. He opened a ship-to-ship channel to his wife. "Has—"

"Where are you?" Tendra demanded. "I've been worried sick."

"Everything's fine. I was, uh, delayed at the ODH." As Lando spoke, he was sending her coordinates on a separate data band. "When Booster arrives, ask him to swing by this location. I'm doing a favor for some mutual friends, and it would be good to have a Star Destroyer standing by."

"What *kind* of favor?"

"It's important." Though the channel was encrypted, Lando hesitated to say more for fear of Peace Brigade slicers. "Just tell Booster. I'll see you soon."

"You'd better."

"Bet on it."

Not wishing to alarm Tendra, Lando signed off without telling her he loved her. Ba'tra studied him out of the corner of his eye.

"Didn't figure you for a hero, Calrissian."

"Me? Not at all." Lando flashed his salesman's smile. "But I couldn't pass on a chance to demonstrate my droids to a captive audience."

Ba'tra snorted, then half smiled and glanced at the primary display. Even this high in orbit, space was crowded with vehicles. For the most part, the Yuuzhan Vong were too busy with Coruscant's still-formidable defenses to molest civilian ships, but a dozen skips patrolled the area around the *Byrt*, chasing off any vessel that came near.

Ba'tra tapped a claw on the display. "Wouldn't hurt to bring some escort. We could call the Jedi wing off that yammosk."

"And draw attention to ourselves?" Lando cocked his brow mischievously, then activated the *Luck*'s intercom. "Tighten your crash webbing back there. One-One-A, is your company ready to go?"

"Affirmative, General."

"I'm not a general. The reactivation was temporary."

"A general is always a general, General."

Lando rolled his eyes and opened a panel on the arm of his pilot's seat. He pressed a safety-locked button, and a valve in the starboard engine pod began spraying nonsealed Tibanna gas into the ion drives. The *Luck* sprouted a kilometer-long tail of what looked like white flame, but was actually a harmless fulgurous discharge caused by the ionization of Tibanna gas. Lando put the yacht into a corkscrew spin and set an oblique course for the *Byrt*, maintaining enough angle to clear the starferry by a safe margin. The skips scattered, but held their fire. A hit might change the "damaged" yacht's course and send it careening into the vessels they were guarding.

"Compliments, General." Ba'tra squeezed his eyes shut against the nauseating star spin outside. "Haven't seen a Bothan runaway gambit this tight in years."

Lando continued on a vector that would miss by half a kilometer. The skips wheeled around behind him, but stayed well back from the Tibanna tail. The *Byrt* swelled to the size of a building, and Lando nosed down toward it and decelerated hard, and then there was nothing but durasteel hull in the forward viewport, and the two ships kissed particle shields hard enough to push the starferry into the Yuuzhan Vong tether ship. Lando swung his stern around and tractored the *Luck* alongside the *Byrt*.

The first two coralskippers arrived, belching plasma balls into the *Luck*'s energy shields. Lando shut down the sublight fuel feed and closed the efflux nacelles. Tibanna gas billowed out through the cooling vents, becoming trapped under the shields and engulfing the *Luck* in fused-photon "flames."

The next two skips pulled up without firing, and Lando lowered the shields on the *Byrt*'s side of the yacht. "One-One-A, go!"

When General Calrissian's attack authorization came, YVH 1-1A was already magnoclamped to the *Byrt*, affixing a bead of elastic detonite to the hull. Still troubled by his failure at the Coruscant proving trial, he had dedicated a processing band to weapon-circuitry tests. All systems checked full power and ammunition—but so they had on Coruscant. YVH 1-1A's self-preservation routines kept accessing the memory of his blaster bolts dancing off the armored Yuuzhan Vong, kept reporting an undetected flaw in his power-selection module. His logic center knew the assertion to be groundless, but if it was only a ghost loop, why did it persist even after he degaussed his circuits?

In 1.2 seconds after General Calrissian issued the "go" order, two subordinate units secured the *Lady Luck*'s cofferdam around him. YVH 1-1A withdrew to the air lock and activated the detonite. A door-sized section of hull popped free and clanged off 1-1A's chest armor as the pressures equalized.

Scanning ahead with both optical and acoustic sensors, 1-1A rushed through the breach into a small power-relay control station. Three crew members lay on the floor, holding their ears, groaning from the pressure shift. YVH 1-1A ignored them and crossed the cabin, then stopped when his see-through sensors detected a squad of Yuuzhan Vong in the main corridor outside.

Ambush? 1-24A asked.

Affirmative.

YVH 1-1A projected red dots onto the wall to show the location of each individual. He was about to outline an attack strategy when 1-24A clunked through the hatch and started firing. The results left no doubt that *his* weapon systems were functional.

Corridor secure, 1-24A reported.

Maximum efficiency, 1-1A complimented.

Circuits chilling at his own hesitation, 1-1A assigned firing teams to sever the enemy tether, to secure the *Byrt*'s drive units, and to begin a Yuuzhan Vong search-and-destroy sweep. The most important task he reserved for himself. Leaving two squads to secure the breach until General Calrissian arrived with the biotics, 1-1A set his auditory sensors to their most sensitive and stepped through the hatch.

Though only 4.5 seconds had passed, the corridor walls were pocked with spent thud bugs, the floor strewn with Yuuzhan Vong bodies. Droid squads were advancing in both directions, their blaster arms filling the passage with flashes of color. As his processing unit began to interpret auditory data, 1-1A realized he had underestimated the difficulty of his own mission. Within current sensor range alone, he detected fifty-two vocalizing infants. Loudly vocalizing infants.

Starting with the nearest, 1-1A stepped over a still-smoking Yuuzhan Vong corpse and followed the wailing through a short maze of corridors to the first-class berthings. An enemy search party was pulling refugees out of their sleeping cabins, shoving them to the floor. The leader was dangling a crying infant by one leg, shaking it at a sobbing human female, and demanding, "Tell me! Is this the *Jeedai* baby?"

YVH 1-1A raised his blaster arm, and the whir of his servomotors caused the Yuuzhan Vong to whirl around. Some pushed their captives back into the cabins, others dragged them out to use as shields. YVH 1-1A sprang forward, firing. There was no question of faulty selection modules or dampened power outputs. He dropped five foes in five shots. When the leader attempted to dash the baby against the wall, he even felt confident enough to shoot the warrior's hand off at the wrist.

The astonished mother caught the child in her arms, then turned to 1-1A babbling incomprehensible words of gratitude.

"Remain calm," 1-1A replied. "Seek shelter immediately."

Viqi Shesh looked like something resurrected by a Krath death witch. Her cheeks were hollow, her pupils dilated, her skin as gray as a Noghri's, and her gait suggested the influence of some powerful painkiller. But she held her head high and seemed most determined to impress the Yuuzhan Vong following her down the corridor. Fearful that the glow of his photoreceptors would betray his presence, C-3PO stepped to one side of the evacuation bay hatch and continued to peer through the viewport at an oblique angle.

"And then the nasty Senator Shesh came looking for Ben Skywalker," he said quietly. In a futile attempt to calm the distressed infant, he was using his agile TranLang III vocabulator to replicate Mara's breathy voice. The imitation was flawless, but there was nothing he could do about the coldness of his metallic flesh—or about what the child sensed through the Force. "So brave Ben grew very quiet."

Ben whimpered loudly.

Out in the corridor, Viqi Shesh cocked her head to one side.

"I *told* Mistress Leia I was the wrong droid for this," C-3PO whined in Mara's voice. He opened the emergency medpac he had taken from the escape pod and removed the safetranq. "Please be quiet, Master Ben. I am quite certain your mother wouldn't want me administering sedatives."

Viqi Shesh spoke to her escorts, and they began to open hatches and search escape bays. C-3PO had primed their own pod for launch, but he was not eager to take another escape pod ride. Besides, they would only find themselves back on Coruscant.

The searchers were three hatches away when a hulking YVH war droid appeared behind them.

"Thank the maker!" C-3PO said.

He thought it was a 1-1 series, but that hardly mattered. The whole YVH line was top quality, and the mere fact that there was one aboard was a positive sign. C-3PO sent a burst transmission identifying himself and his charge and requesting aid. He received a terse reply informing him that rescuing him and Ben *was* the mission. Then the droid loosed a flurry of minicannon fire, taking out four of Shesh's escorts in half as many seconds.

Ben erupted into a fit of wailing. Given the roar in the corridor, C-3PO thought that three centimeters of durasteel wall might prevent the baby from being heard. He was disabused of that notion when he peered through the viewport and found Viqi Shesh crouching behind a bulkhead opposite him, staring through the viewport directly at him.

"Ben! Now look what you've done!"

It was just the sort of tactical problem suited to a deceptive Bothan mind: one narrow doorway defended by a dozen well-armed foes in possession of an undetermined number of hostages. Ba'tra would normally have sent a team through an air duct, or tried to lure the enemy out by feigning withdrawal. This time, he turned to a YVH war droid and pointed at the door.

"One-Thirty-two, secure the bridge."

"Yes, General."

YVH 1-32A waded forward into a bug swarm so thick Ba'tra lost sight of him. The droid countered with a lightning storm of blasterfire. Three seconds later, he stood in the doorway, both blaster arms smoking, laminanium armor pitted to the circuit casing.

"Bridge secure, General."

"Well done." Ba'tra raised his comlink and spoke to a subordinate waiting in Lando's yacht. "You may send the *Lady Luck* on her way, Captain—and give it some speed. I'm sure General Calrissian would appreciate the vessel still being intact when he activates his recall unit."

The general clicked off without awaiting an acknowledgment, then followed a dozen soldiers onto the bridge. Though there were no signs that the *Byrt*'s crew had put up a fight, two had been tortured to death, the rest bloodied to various degrees. Ba'tra looked around until he found a Rodian with a captain's epaulet hanging off one shoulder.

"This ship is being commandeered." Ba'tra handed him a piece of flimsiplast with a set of coordinates. "Take us here."

"You're not commandeering us, General, you're rescuing us." The Rodian studied the flimsiplast, then looked out the viewport as the uncrewed *Lady Luck* streaked past with an entire squadron of coralskippers in pursuit. The funnels atop his head twisted outward in confusion, then he said, "But I don't understand. This is barely beyond the battle. We won't be safe there."

Ba'tra smiled. "We will when the *Venture* arrives."

Lando was halfway down the service ladder when a shock wave slammed the *Byrt* so hard there was no need to finish the descent. He lost his grip and simply found himself squatting on the starferry's lowest deck, listening to the roar of a pitched battle around the corner.

"Thermal detonator ignition, General," 1-1A reported, already standing on the deck. "Tether ship destroyed."

"Thanks for the warning."

Lando stood, then heard a familiar drone and dropped back to his haunches as a stray razor bug streaked around the corner. The thing dived at his throat, but 1-1A zinged a low-power bolt past his ear and zapped it out of the air. Lando managed a weak smile, trying not to show his fright, but knowing the war droid had already detected his increased heartrate and the slight rise in skin temperature. He drew his blaster and peered around the corner.

Viqi Shesh and two dozen Yuuzhan Vong were withdrawing into Escape Bay 14, leaving the floor behind them strewn with tiny black seedpods. Though Lando had never seen this particular weapon, he felt sure the husks contained some unpleasant surprise.

"Analysis?" he asked.

"Unknown caltrop device," 1-1A replied. "High potential for biotoxin attack."

"Thanks for nothing."

The *Byrt* lurched slightly as the sublight drives kicked in, and Lando knew they were on their way to the *Venture*. He removed his breath mask from his combat belt.

"You're sure it's the right baby this time?" Lando asked. "We're not going after some Squib trapped in a locker?"

"The sound signature was identical," 1-1A said defensively. "And the confidence level here is high. YVH One-Twenty-five received a burst transmission from a 3PO protocol droid claiming to have the correct child."

"That's them." Lando covered his face with the breath mask. "Send in a droid, One-One-A."

Lando had barely finished before 1-25A rushed forward, deftly dancing through husks. He made it two steps, then the pods began to roll toward him. Another two steps, and his foot came down on one. Nothing happened.

Then he moved his foot, and a heart-shaped kernel shot into the air behind him. The droid went motionless, then drained into the nugget.

"Singularity mines." Lando pulled his breath mask down. "Nasty."

"Analysis predicts obstacle impassable," 1-1A reported. "All techniques for bypassing or clearing minefields will fail."

Lando shook his head in disappointment. "Remind me to speak with the brain department about your ingenuity routines." He took out his comlink and opened a channel to the bridge. "Calrissian here. Request two-second suspension of artificial gravity and inertial compensation."

"Copy."

Lando grabbed a bulkhead and had the droids magnoclamp themselves to the floor. A moment later, his stomach fluttered, and the singularity mines floated into the air. They drifted toward the stern and filled the corridor with eerie grating sounds as they brushed the walls and ripped two-meter holes in the durasteel. When gravity was restored, the remaining husks dropped to the floor and destroyed a five-meter section of service corridor.

Lando released the bulkhead and sprinted toward Escape Bay 14. He had intended to lead the charge himself, but the droids were already there, pouring blasterfire through the hatchway.

"Careful!" Lando ordered. "Watch the baby—and Threepio!"

He peered around the corner. The last Yuuzhan Vong were squeezing into the crowded escape pod, flinging thud bugs at the bay hatch. Viqi Shesh was nowhere to be seen, and the muffled wailing of a terrified infant could just be heard from inside the pod.

"Go!" Lando screamed. "Don't let it launch!"

YVH 1-1A was already charging. The bug swarm trailed off, then C-3PO's golden form tumbled out.

"Don't shoot!" C-3PO screamed. He picked himself up and raised his hands. "I'm one of you!"

The war droids continued to pour fire past C-3PO as they rushed across the launch bay. The pod hatch started to close. YVH 1-1A sprang forward, reached for the gap, arrived a millisecond too late to prevent it from sealing.

C-3PO palmed the automatic launch button.

"See-Threepio!"

Lando rushed for the control panel and hit the cancel pad.

There was a soft clunk . . . then the rockets pounded the blast shielding with efflux.

"What a relief!" C-3PO started across the bay. "I thought they would take me along."

Lando followed close behind. "See-Threepio, who was that crying in the escape pod?"

"Oh, that was me, General Calrissian," C-3PO answered in an infant's voice. He stopped next to an emergency breath-mask locker and withdrew a medpac pouch containing a soundly sleeping infant. "Ben won't be crying for several more hours, I am quite certain."

Chapter 54

With both valves of the distant air lock drawn open, a bright crescent of blue sun could be seen blazing out from behind Myrkr's rising disk, illuminating the million pillars of the serpent hall in gloomy streaks of sapphire. The shaper and his escorts were little more than stick silhouettes filing toward the exit in a single line. The voxyn queen was not visible at all, though Jacen knew she was there, in the gap two figures from the front.

"This is not right," Tesar rasped quietly. "That air lock can't be open."

"It is better to seek an explanation than to deny what we all see clearly," Tenel Ka replied. "There is an atmosphere outside that lock."

"Yes, but what else?" Vergere asked. "That is the question, is it not?"

"How about you answer it for us?" Ganner replied.

When Vergere spread her arms and gave a feathery shrug, Jacen looked back to the line of Yuuzhan Vong. He filled his mind with thoughts of fear and suspicion and reached out to the queen for the eighth time since leaving the hive colony.

The voxyn reacted even more quickly than she had the last time, whirling on the warriors behind her. She must already have struck the first Yuuzhan Vong with her poison tail barb, for she ignored him and belched acid at the second in line, then leapt past both to slash at the next one. All three warriors went down, and she was attacking a fourth before the shaper and two of his remaining assistants got hold of her leashes and restrained her.

Jacen withdrew his presence. The queen slowly calmed to the point where the shaper felt confident in approaching her, stroking her muzzle and no doubt speaking to her in soothing tones. It would not be long before that act of bravery turned into a deadly mistake, but Jacen did not want the beast to kill the handler yet. As wary as the warriors were already, the death of the shaper would cause them to send for reinforcements.

The shaper finally backed away and signaled his assistants to release the tethers. They had learned the hard way that the queen would not move with someone holding the other end of a leash— the result of another uneasy feeling planted by Jacen. When the voxyn showed its willingness to resume travel by not killing anyone, the Yuuzhan Vong turned and—leaving their dead and wounded where they lay—vanished through the open air lock.

"Only four left," Vergere said, rising from the group's hiding place. "Well done, Jacen Solo."

Jacen did not thank the strange little creature. He disliked killing, and he disliked even more tricking an animal into doing it for him. But he had his promise to Anakin to keep and his sister to track down—he still could not feel Jaina through the Force—and encouraging the voxyn to follow its nature was his only hope of doing either. He nodded to Tesar, who rose and set off. The Barabel kept them concealed in a fungus-lined rift, for the area was strewn with Yuuzhan Vong workers scavenging the exhausted serpent yards for a usable amphistaff or tsaisi baton.

As they traveled, Ganner remained a step behind Vergere, his repeating blaster pointed at her feathery back. Though she had been of considerable use in tracking the Yuuzhan Vong, the Jedi still did not trust her. Not only had she declined to identify her species—claiming they would not recognize it anyway—she had also refused to explain her presence during Elan's attempt on the Jedi, or her reason for providing the tears that had saved Mara's life. While unsure that she was an enemy, Jacen hardly considered her a friend, either. Needless to say, he now had Anakin's lightsaber clipped to a spare hook on his equipment harness, and Ganner had pointedly confirmed that he would blast her into a feathercloud at the first sign of treachery. Vergere had indulged them with a shudder, undoubtedly insincere.

The fissure and fungus both dwindled away as the group neared the air lock. To avoid drawing attention, the Jedi activated their holoshrouds and, keeping Vergere screened from view, marched through the air lock disguised as Yuuzhan Vong.

They found themselves standing on the inside rim of what looked like an enormous impact crater, save that the slope was surprisingly featureless and the crest unnaturally even. There was no covering overhead, but the atmosphere was as thick and warm as inside the worldship. In the bottom of the basin lay what resembled a giant honeycomb, save that each cell was a meter across and held a single dovin basal.

Jacen could not sense the emotions of the dovin basals—creatures with no connection to the Force remained as unreadable to him as the Yuuzhan Vong themselves—but he could see by their labored pulsing and flaking hides that the things were in distress. There were even large tracts where the cells contained nothing but shriveled husks. Whether this stemmed from old age, exhaustion, or disease he did not know, but it did suggest another reason the Yuuzhan Vong were deserting the dilapidated worldship.

The shaper and his escorts were already on the floor of the basin, moving along the edge of the basal-comb toward Nom Anor's frigate, which lay about a fifth of the way around the circle. The executor himself and perhaps fifty Yuuzhan Vong were half a kilometer out on the structure itself, crawling along the narrow walls between the cells and being careful to avoid the dovin basals themselves. From the group's different dress—many of them wore armor only over their torsos—it was apparent the executor had stripped the ship's crew to supplement his company.

Nom Anor and his followers were making their way toward the center of the basal-comb, where a huge sweep of cells contained either shriveled husks or nothing at all. In the heart of this dead area rested Jaina's stolen shuttle, cracked and overturned, but still in one piece. The sporadic stream of blaster bolts and magma missiles arcing out of the wreckage suggested that at least a few Jedi had survived the crash.

Vergere hunched beside Jacen, her gaze running from the queen over to Nom Anor's frigate, where four warriors stood watch at the base of the boarding ramp. "Interesting . . . Will you destroy the voxyn, Jacen Solo, or save your sister?"

Jacen ignored the question and continued to study the situation. The longblaster roared and split open a warrior in front of Nom Anor. The executor shuddered, but lowered his head and continued forward.

"I don't understand," Tekli said. "The shuttle is helpless. The frigate should be attacking."

"Yes," Tenel Ka agreed. "Why crawl so far under fire?"

"Why, indeed?" Vergere said. "Perhaps there is something aboard they want alive?"

"Jaina," Jacen said.

Vergere spread her hands. "And you. Tsavong Lah promised Yun-Yammka a pair of Jedi twins for the fall of Coruscant. Matters will go badly for Nom Anor if she is already dead." She stopped there and studied Jacen a moment, then said, "But you could save him the trouble of looking, could you not? I understand that Jedi twins have a special . . . sense of each other."

Jacen studied her from the corner of his eye. "I wouldn't place too much trust in cantina tales, were I you."

"No?" Vergere smirked. "Are you just cautious, I wonder, or do you have a suspicious nature?"

"Both are the same around you, this one thinkz," Tesar said. He checked the power level of his minicannon, then braced it on the crest of the slope and trained it on the voxyn. "Jacen, this one has two shots, maybe three. We must destroy the queen."

Jacen nodded. "And save—" He almost said *Jaina,* then caught himself. "—our friends on the shuttle."

"You cannot do both," Vergere warned. "The Yuuzhan Vong have a saying: 'The fleet that fights two battles loses twice.' "

"Do we look like Yuuzhan Vong?" Ganner demanded, pointing at his eyes. "We're Jedi."

"So you are," Vergere said mildly. "But the Yuuzhan Vong have their strengths, as well. Do not dismiss those strengths because the Force is blind to them."

"I don't," Jacen said. "But we *are* going to win two battles— and here's how."

He explained his plan to the others, then watched as a plasma ball arced over Nom Anor and crashed twenty paces away. The strike vaporized a ten-meter circle of basal-comb, but as the super-heated gas spread over the adjacent cells, it condensed into noth-ingness and vanished in a sheet of flashing color.

"What about her?" Ganner motioned at Vergere with his blaster.

"Once you're on the frigate, she's free to stay or leave with us as she likes," Jacen said. "Until then, if she makes a false move—"

"Blast her," Vergere finished. She gave a flip of her four-fingered hands, then turned to Tesar. "On the bridge of the *Ksstarr* you will find a pilot, a copilot, and a communications subaltern. The master keeper will also be aboard somewhere. They are not permitted to leave while the vessel is in action."

"This one shall keep the information in mind," Tesar said. "And also where it came from."

Tesar passed his minicannon to Ganner, then removed his jumpsuit and slipped over the rim of the basin on all fours. His rough scales camouflaged him against the yorik coral's dark background, and he moved with such slow reptilian grace that it immediately grew difficult to pick him out.

Jacen filled his mind with an image of his cramped cell in the Shadow Academy and allowed himself to feel again the terror of the kidnapping, his fear and confusion when he realized he no longer controlled his own destiny. Never far from the surface even this many years after the event—and perhaps made more accessible by his anguish over Anakin's loss—the emotions returned easily. When a cold sweat began to bead on his forehead, he reached out to the voxyn, infusing her with his own feelings, urging her to flee.

The voxyn screeched and sent two escorts reeling despite the protective membranes in their ears, then turned to run and found a third warrior blocking her way. She snatched him up and bit him cleanly in two. The shaper raced after her, calling out commands, trying to calm her. Jacen urged the beast not to trust her "tormentor." She whirled and spat acid, but the shaper was quick enough to dodge and let one of his escorts be hit instead.

Jacen unclipped his lightsaber. "I'll need to concentrate on the voxyn, so we have to do this without the battle meld. May the Force be with you, my friends."

Taking her own lightsaber in hand, Tenel Ka stepped over to kiss him—and was cut off by Vergere.

"And with you, Jacen Solo." The little creature shooed him down the slope. "Now go, before your quarry escapes."

Jacen looked over her to Tenel Ka and rolled his eyes, then flashed the Dathomiri a lopsided grin and pushed up his breath mask. Using the Force to descend the basin's inner rim in two bounds, he landed undetected behind the last stunned escort. Thinking he could knock the lurching warrior unconscious rather than kill him, he reached out to pull off the Yuuzhan Vong's helmet—and saw his mistake when the fellow spun on him.

Jacen thumbed his activation switch. The weapon sprang to life in front of the approaching arm and severed it at the elbow, but losing a limb would never stop a Yuuzhan Vong. Jacen turned his weapon ninety degrees and drew the blade across his foe's neck. The warrior collapsed in a heap.

"Jacen?" The voice on the comlink belonged not to Jaina, but to Zekk. "That you?"

"Who else?" Jacen continued forward, tried not to be disappointed that he wasn't talking to Jaina. "What's your condition?"

"A few injuries, but everybody's stable," Zekk reported. "We have Lowbacca—and Anakin's body."

"And Jaina?" Jacen asked, concerned by what Zekk left unsaid.

Zekk paused, no doubt surprised Jacen would need to ask. "She's here, Jacen."

Something in Zekk's tone hinted at the cold darkness Jacen found whenever he reached out to his sister, but he was happy enough for now to hear she was still alive. "Good. Wait there— somebody's coming for you."

Jacen risked a glance at the frigate. Whether or not the ramp guards realized who he was, the sudden appearance of a single Jedi had proved too much of a temptation. Leaving one warrior on-station, the other three were racing after him, amphistaffs in hand. Behind them, Tesar Sebatyne's dark figure was creeping into the shadows beneath the frigate's nose, gathering himself to pounce on the last sentry.

Jacen raced after the shaper and fleeing voxyn. The minicannon roared once, then twice, and two of his pursuers fell. The third dropped under a torrent of T-21 bolts. Jacen did not even look back. By now, Tesar would be boarding the frigate, the others rushing to join him.

The voxyn pulled away fast, the shaper less so. Jacen reached out with the Force, this time to soothe the voxyn. Not a chance. With plasma balls bursting and lasers flashing just a few hundred meters away, the queen continued to run. He tried to call her hunting instincts into play. No good either. Where her clones were trained to stalk Jedi, she was trained only to preserve her own life. Jacen pulled one of two thermal detonators from his belt, thumbed the fuse to the first click, and used the Force to hurl it into her path.

The queen whirled away from the silver ball, found her handler in the way, and slapped him aside. Jacen saw an arm fly in one direction and the rest of the shaper tumble in another, then the voxyn was racing toward him, head rising to belch acid. He activated his lightsaber and charged to meet her.

She disgorged her acid at three paces. Jacen launched into an airborne round-off, and the brown spray shot past below. Then the detonator crackled behind him, and he found himself swinging at empty air. He landed lightly and sprang into a half twist that brought him around facing the same direction as before, and his heart rose into his throat. No voxyn, only the brilliant flash of the detonator shrinking in on itself. Blinded, Jacen brought his lightsaber around in a block-and-slash and reached out to locate his quarry.

She was off to the side, moving away slowly. He blinked the dazzle from his eyes and found her crawling out onto the basal-comb, angling away from the battle, angling away from Jacen, her body so broad she had to straddle the wall between the cells. He left his T-21 slung on his shoulder and started after her. He had only a handful of shots remaining, and the bolts would not penetrate her thick scales anyway.

Tenel Ka's voice crackled over the comlink. "Frigate secured. We have a way home, but also a complication."

Lowbacca rumbled a question.

"*How* does not matter," Tenel Ka replied. "When we found the communications officer, he was in contact with the spaceport."

Jacen groaned inwardly, then asked, "Vergere?"

"She said she had no wish to be atomized, then departed," Tenel Ka said. "She seems to be following you."

"Check. You hurry." Jacen reached the basal-comb and had to slow. The walls between cells were a half meter wide, but so steeply crowned that running over them was like running on a board's edge. "Shuttle first."

"Us?" Zekk complained. "You *do* know the Yuuzhan Vong are chasing you?"

Jacen had no time to look. He was gaining on the queen. "Shuttle first," he repeated. "I have to finish here."

The voxyn stopped at the next cell convergence, where the walls met to form a sort of island, then whirled. Jacen leapt across the dovin basal and landed at her rear flank, tottering and activating his lightsaber. The voxyn screeched, but could not bring her head around far enough to assault Jacen. He danced forward and brought his blade down behind her forward leg.

Internal organs began to slip from the gap, leaking blood into the air and filling it with toxic fumes. Jacen slashed sideways, taking the second leg off at the joint, then thrust deep and brought the blade up. The voxyn pulled away, retreating onto the adjacent wall so she could turn on him. He leapt across to stay behind her—then heard a razor bug droning in his direction.

Jacen dropped into a squat and brought his weapon up to block, and the bug crackled out of existence. The voxyn continued to retreat until she could face him again. Jacen launched himself into a back flip and came down on the cramped convergence behind him, dared to glance away from the queen.

The stolen frigate was already sweeping across the basin toward the crashed shuttle, the forward ramp hanging open for quick boarding. Nom Anor and his warriors were within a hundred meters now, some staring up at the stolen frigate with gaping jaws, others still crawling toward Jacen, but all too distant to have thrown the razor bug.

A shiver of danger sense drew Jacen's attention in the opposite direction. He turned and saw a large Yuuzhan Vong flying at him across the cell.

"No, *Jeedai!*" The figure extended a single arm.

Jacen swept his lightsaber up and cut the fellow through at the waist and did not even recognize him as the shaper until an eight-fingered hand caught hold of his breath mask and nearly jerked him over. He lowered his head, and the breath mask came off. The Yuuzhan Vong's torso tumbled into the cell beside him, angry eyes glaring up, and barely touched the dovin basal before the creature reacted with its only defense. A tiny gravitic singularity sprang into existence, then the shaper's corpse collapsed in on itself and disappeared in a flash of dancing color.

The acrid smell of toxic blood reminded Jacen of the peril he faced without a breath mask. He looked up to find the queen staring at him from two meters away, eyes expressionless and black, the Force heavy with her grim resolve. The creature knew why he was here. She was not angry, not hateful—only determined to save herself. Jacen did not want to kill her—he had never wanted to kill any animal. Perhaps she sensed that in him.

Jacen's head started to spin. He had to finish this. Flicking his lightsaber to hold the creature's attention, he dropped his free hand toward his last thermal detonator. The queen came bounding. He pulled the detonator off his harness. She stretched forward to snap at his head, then surprised him with a claw to the shoulder.

The talons bit deep, launched him off his perch. The detonator flew, inactivated, from his hand, and the dovin basal appeared beneath him, rising fast. He whipped his legs over his head, flinging himself to the opposite side of the cell. Landing dizzy and off balance, Jacen continued in the same direction, this time flipping higher to buy more time.

He came down on his heels, vision closing, nostrils burning. He fell backward onto a convergence. His shoulder was throbbing already, but at least it still supported the weight of an arm.

A trio of coralskippers streaked past overhead, their noses pouring plasma balls toward the center of the basin. Coughing, fighting to stay conscious, Jacen sat up and saw the stolen frigate lumbering skyward beneath the bombardment. It launched a magma missile, which vanished into a shielding singularity the instant it neared a skip. With a large-enough crew, the frigate would overwhelm the smaller craft easily. With a handful of Jedi, it would be torn apart piecemeal.

Jacen activated his comlink, but was interrupted by a familiar burping sound. He rolled over his good shoulder and came unsteadily to his feet. A fan of brown mucus landed where he had been lying, then the voxyn began to advance. The acrid stench of her blood staggered him, made his lungs burn and his head spin, and nearly sent him tumbling down onto a dovin basal.

The queen reached the convergence and stopped. They were separated now by a sizzling pool of her acid. Jacen brought his lightsaber to middle guard, tip angled forward, his wounded arm hanging limp. Behind the voxyn, the hundred-meter bulk of a yorik coral corvette swept in and cut him off from the rest of the strike team. They were battling now, his friends and a whole flotilla of arriving Yuuzhan Vong.

A wave of nausea dropped Jacen to a knee. Eager to press the advantage, the voxyn gathered herself to spring.

A thermal detonator splashed into the pool of acid. The fuse had not been activated, but that was all Jacen saw before the silver casing sank into the sludge.

"Could that be important?" Vergere called. She was coming toward him, thin arms extended for balance. "I saw you drop it."

Jacen's jaw fell. "How did you—"

"No time."

Vergere pointed. The voxyn was scrambling along the edge of the convergence, fleeing the silver sphere. The detonator could never ignite without a properly set fuse, but what did the queen know about detonators? All spheres of shiny silver were spheres to be feared.

Jacen sprang feet-first, caught the queen dead center, heels driving high into her ribs, forcing her over the edge. She dug her claws deep into the yorik coral and saved herself. Jacen landed beside her, hard, and the breath left his burning lungs. The darkness began to rise inside him.

No, *tried* to rise. He stabbed his lightsaber into the yorik coral and began to cut it from beneath the queen's claws. Still intent on escaping the detonator, she released her front leg and reached for the adjacent wall, then her support began to crumble, and her front quarters slipped into the cell. She brought her tail around, the poisonous barb driving for Jacen's neck. He ducked behind his wounded shoulder, took the tip in an open gash, felt venom pulsing into his torn flesh. Hot. Stinging.

Too weak to kick, Jacen pushed with the Force. Another leg came free. The queen, also weakened by injury, slipped deeper. A foot grazed the dovin basal, then she was plummeting over the edge, collapsing in on herself, shrinking out of sight.

Jacen did not see the final flash of color. The barb tore free of his shoulder, and he was overwhelmed by dizziness, collapsing backward onto the convergence. Something began to sizzle, and his hand began to burn, then someone lifted his arm and propped him up.

There came a terrible thunder overhead, a firestorm so bright it lit the darkness behind Jacen's closed eyelids. He heard a voice calling—a voice he had known all his life, yet one that now seemed as alien as that of any Yuuzhan Vong.

"Jacen?" A pause, cold and demanding. "Jacen, answer me!"

A delicate hand brushed back Jacen's hair, took the comlink from his head. "You can do nothing for Jacen now," a second voice said—also familiar. "Save yourselves."

"Vergere?" the first voice demanded. "Is that you? I want to talk to my brother—"

The demand was clicked silent. Jacen opened his eyes and saw a delicate, four-fingered hand flinging his headset into the air. In the sky far above raged a battle, a Yuuzhan Vong frigate trying to blast through a screen of Yuuzhan Vong corvettes.

Jacen was confused, but only for a moment. The frigate was Nom Anor's, stolen by his friends, now trying to reach him. He struggled upright and saw a one-eyed Yuuzhan Vong leading several dozen warriors through a rain of plasma balls and magma missiles. Toward him. He tried to roll, found himself restrained by a four-fingered hand.

"No." Despite the apparent frailty of the hand, its strength was irresistible—at least in Jacen's condition. It took his lightsaber from his grasp, then unclipped Anakin's from his equipment harness and took that one as well. "You have won your battles. Now you pay."

Jacen recalled the tortures he and the others had endured aboard the *Exquisite Death*. His stomach grew queasy. His hands trembled. He opened himself to the Force and smiled at his body's fear. The Jedi were safe. Compared to that, his pain meant nothing.

"It will, Jacen," Vergere said, surprising him. He did not recall speaking his thoughts aloud. "That I promise you—it will."

A warm drop struck his face, then another and another. Jacen craned his neck and found Vergere wiping tears from her cheeks. Her face was turned so Nom Anor and the others could not see.

"Vergere, were you—"

"Yes, Jacen." She pressed a finger to his lips. "I was crying for you."

Chapter 55

The drop fleets hit like an Nkllonian meteor storm, slanting across the sky in fiery armadas a hundred kilometers across, crackling and hissing like S-thread static and trailing anvil-shaped towers of night-black smoke. Standing in the open cannon turret atop Fey'lya's office, Leia allowed herself two seconds to be awed by the spectacle of it all and let the thunder reverberate through her body. There was something primal and beautiful in the power of the drop, something that stirred in her a passion of purpose that, until Anakin's death, she had thought lost with her youth.

Han came to her side and handed her a comlinked artillery helmet. "The end of the world," he said. "Who'd've thought we'd live to see it?"

"There'll be other worlds, Han." She put the helmet on and buckled the chin strap. "There was after Alderaan."

The smile Han gave her was as crooked as usual, but now more wistful than cocky. "Then let's hope this one lasts until they finish charging our containment fluid."

Shafts of color rose from distant rooftops to stab at the descending drop fleets, and vessels almost invisible to the naked eye showed damage in the form of white starbursts and flickering disks of orange. The turbolaser fire was answered by a torrent of plasma balls. Towers melted into liquid pillars of durasteel slag. In some cases, building shields endured the first strike, only to fall to the second, or the third. Dark swarms of coralskippers and airskiffs boiled down ahead of the drop fleets, taking advantage of the steady barrage to locate and attack the turbolasers. These attack craft were met by a far smaller number of New Republic atmospheric fighters, and a steady drizzle of smaller craft began to rain down on Coruscant.

General Rieekan's voice came over the helmet comlink. "Light artillery, take your stations. Hold fire."

Han slipped into the gunner's seat on one side of the laser cannon, and Leia took the spotter's station on the other. She would actually have the more difficult of the two jobs, finding and prioritizing threats on the weapon's display. All Han would have to do was shoot them down. Leia activated the sensor feed and began to plot trajectories, assigning precedence based on which drop ships would be approaching nearest to their position.

Over the next ten seconds, the number of turbolasers firing decreased steadily, but they punched so many holes in the drop fleets that Leia had to update her targeting priorities twice. By the time the ships themselves began swelling from fingertip-sized circles of friction flame into glossy black wedge-wings, the turbolasers had opened holes the size of lakes in the great armadas.

"Open fire," Rieekan commanded.

Han squeezed the trigger, and the air filled with the deafening screech of discharging actuators. Their attack took the first drop ship by surprise, burning away a wing and sending the wedge-shaped vessel tumbling in two different directions. Subsequent targets proved more difficult. Han had to pulse the trigger and stitch bolts across the hull to defeat the shielding crews, but it was easier to fire from a stationary turret than to defend aboard a wildly gyrating craft, and he and Leia sent two more drop ships crashing into the towers. They paid no attention to the skips and airskiffs diving on their position from all sides. Those were the responsibility of even lighter blaster cannons firing from adjacent towers, and their expert crews never let an attacker get close.

Finally, Leia could find no more targets on the tacscreen. She looked up into a dark miasma of smoke, fed by flaming ruins and fuming wrecks all across Coruscant. For a moment, all was quiet, then Rieekan's voice came over the comlink again.

"Look sharp out there. They're sending in the hunter-killers."

Leia studied the tactical display and saw a line of blastboat analogs—she and Han called them blast boulders—streaking toward their position. Large enough to take a hit or two from a light blaster cannon, yet nimble enough to dodge the slower laser cannons, these craft posed a more serious threat than anything that had come before. Leia began to designate priorities and feed Han targets.

Borsk Fey'lya chose that moment to appear on the access lift, flanked by a pair of tall Orbital Defense soldiers with sandy hair and square chins. Their other features were also so similar they had to be brothers. In Leia's time, relatives would never have been permitted to serve in the same unit, but those rules had changed under Fey'lya. Bothans had a different view of family.

"Leia, you have a comm message in my office," Fey'lya said. His brisk tone suggested he had lifted himself out of the torpor into which he had sunk when her speech failed to bring the deserting senators and their pilfered flotillas back to Coruscant. "You can take it at my desk."

"We're kind of busy right now," Han growled, pouring fire into the first blast boulder. "You might have noticed?"

"It's Luke Skywalker," Fey'lya said. "He seems to be trapped."

Han stopped firing. "On the planet?"

"Over at the Western Sea, if I heard him correctly," Fey'lya said. "The channel was scratchy."

Han looked over the cannon at Leia, and she knew he was thinking the same thing. If Luke was on Coruscant, there was no telling where Ben was.

"These guards will take your station," Fey'lya said, motioning to the brothers.

Leia slipped out of her seat and moved toward the lift. Instead of stepping out of her way as most soldiers would for a former chief of state, this pair stared down at her blank-faced. She knew instantly something was wrong, and confirmed it when she reached out with the Force and felt nothing from them.

"Forgive me, soldier."

Turning to hide her lightsaber from view, Leia stepped aside to let the infiltrator by, then caught her husband's eye as he did the same thing. Han furrowed his brow. She glanced pointedly at his blaster and snapped the lightsaber off her belt. An alarmed light came to his eye, and he reached for his blaster pistol.

His Yuuzhan Vong spun on him, knocking him into the back wall. Han slumped to the floor and, never taking his weapon from its swing-free holster, blasted the infiltrator.

Leia was already pressing her lightsaber against her own foe's ribs. "Surren—"

He whirled, elbow driving at her head. She ducked, thumbed the activation switch, then stepped away as the impostor collapsed at her feet.

Fey'lya stared at the corpses, jaw snapping as the ooglith masquers peeled away from their faces. "In my own office!"

"Perhaps the time has come to destroy the data towers, Chief," Leia suggested mildly.

Fey'lya's eyes flashed, but any reply was cut off by a blaring attack alarm. One glance at the display told Leia the infiltrators had succeeded at least in part; with three blast boulders lining up for approach, they had no chance of saving their weapon.

"Go!"

She pushed Han and Fey'lya onto the service lift, then followed. They commed a report to General Tomas's aide, then emerged ten meters below in the chief of state's office. An instant later, a series of explosions shook the blast-hardened ceiling, and the cannon turret was gone. Leia saw Garv Tomas coming through the far door, but she removed her artillery helmet and went straight to Fey'lya's comm center.

"Luke . . . Luke, this is your sister . . . Luke?"

There might have been an answer; it was difficult to tell over the battle roar in the background. She stretched out and sensed her brother's presence somewhere beyond the horizon. Though she was not sensitive enough to guess his condition or situation, Leia could feel that he was alive.

"Luke, if you hear me, we'll be there as soon as the *Falcon*'s containment fluid is recharged."

"Actually, it's recharged now."

Leia glanced over her shoulder to find Garv Tomas glowering at Fey'lya.

"I asked Chief Fey'lya to relay that news some time ago."

Fey'lya shrugged. "They were needed in the cannon turret."

"Check that, Luke." Leia was not even angry. Being upset at the Bothan's selfishness would have been like being angry at a Wookiee's shedding—and they *had* been needed in the turret. "The *Falcon* is ready now. We'll be coming soon, Luke."

Again, there was no answer—only a small surge in her sense of her brother. Though Leia hoped it meant Luke had heard her, there was no way to be sure. It could have meant he was trying to find her, thinking about her, going to miss her—anything. Leia stood and turned to find Han already describing the infiltrators to Garv. The general was shaking his head angrily.

"The door guards have epidermal scanners and orders to use them, but disordered troops are pouring in by the tens of thousands, and no one wants to turn away a fellow soldier." Garv ran his fingers through his hair. "For all I know, they're *all* infiltrators."

"It was bound to happen, Garv." Leia turned to Fey'lya. "The time has come to destroy the data towers, Chief. To delay longer is to give the enemy his most precious advantage."

Fey'lya's eyes flashed angrily, almost madly, and Leia thought he would refuse. He spun away and went to stare at the carnage outside.

"You're deserting me, aren't you?" he asked. "Just like the senators."

Han rolled his eyes, then hefted his blaster like a club and cocked his brow at the others.

Leia pushed his hand down, then went to stand behind Fey'lya. "*Not* like the senators. It's time."

Fey'lya stared over the smoking city for another moment and finally let his chin sink. "I suppose it is." He took a moment to gather his strength, then turned to Garv. "General Tomas, give the order to destroy the data towers—if you haven't already."

"Very good, Chief Fey'lya." The fact that Garv did not reach for his comlink suggested the order had indeed been issued. "I'll have *First Citizen* prepared for departure."

Fey'lya nodded wearily. "Evacuate as many as you can—and be sure you are aboard. That's an order, General."

"Yes, sir, as long as my duties here are completed."

"They are," Fey'lya said. "Don't make me dismiss you."

Garv reluctantly inclined his head. "Very well, then."

"Good." Fey'lya turned back to the transparisteel. "And tell Captain Durm not to wait. I won't be joining you."

"What?" Han asked. "If you think you can make some kind of deal—"

"Han, that's not what the chief is thinking." Leia held a finger to her lips, then said, "Chief Fey'lya, you can't accomplish anything here."

"And what could I accomplish anywhere else? Who would follow me after *this*?" He waved a hand outside. "History will blame me for what happened today. Don't try to tell me otherwise."

Leia did not. Even if she had wanted to lie, Fey'lya was too smart. "There are other ways of serving."

Fey'lya snorted. "Perhaps for you, Princess." He turned his back and walked to his desk. "But not for me. Not for Borsk Fey'lya."

"Snap to, people!" The captain had to yell to make himself heard inside the turbolaser's cavernous turret; the battery intercom had gone with the rest of the communications. "Here comes the second wave."

Luke hardly needed the officer's warning. He had only to crane his neck to look through a ten-meter hole in the ceiling and see a sheet of orange friction flames crackling down from above. If anything, this assault looked larger and faster than the first, and the first had reduced Coruscant's turbolaser capacity by two-thirds.

"They're coming through this time," Mara said, not quite reading Luke's thoughts. She was sitting on a bench in the observation bay, her bacta-casted ankle propped on a spare blast helmet. "That first wave was just to soften us up."

Luke took her hand. "Han and Leia will get here," he said. "I told Borsk where we were."

"But did he tell *them*?"

Luke knew better than to offer hollow reassurance. The fear they had been sensing in Ben all morning had become a strange disconnectedness, and Mara—always more of a realist than an optimist—assumed the worst. Never one who liked counting on others, she blamed herself for leaving the baby with Han and Leia after Anakin's death—which only made her all the more determined not to count on anyone else for his rescue. Luke chose to place his trust in the Force, though he knew that an unhappy outcome would certainly lead to a profound crisis of belief.

The twin turbolasers began to hurl blue streaks skyward, each discharge shaking the huge turret so hard that Luke's knees felt like they would buckle. This time, far fewer starbursts and orange flares appeared in the heart of the drop fleet. A steady stream of white pinpoints swelled into crackling orbs of white plasma and burst against the battery's hastily repaired shields. Each time, the internal lighting dimmed a little more, and a few more pieces of equipment sparked out.

In the middle of it all, R2-D2 started to tweet and whistle so fiercely that he was audible even two bays away. Luke looked toward the number two targeting bay, where the little droid was filling in for a damaged R7 unit, and saw a scowling fire control officer waving him over.

"I'll be right back," Luke said to Mara.

A plasma ball finally crashed through the shield and burned a second hole through the armored ceiling. In the next instant, two more fiery balls roared into the turret itself and erupted against the back wall, filling the chamber with smoke and screams. One of the big turbolasers fell silent, and the evacuation alarms blared.

"Hold on, Skywalker." Mara stood and limped after him. "You're not going anywhere without me."

Computer operators began to pour out of both targeting bays, but the officer who had waved at Luke stayed long enough to shake a finger at a vid display.

"Your droid frizzed out and said you had to see this." He turned to depart with the others, calling over his shoulder, "He picked it out of a teletargeter data stream—it was in one of the old flash codes."

The display showed a string of times and orbital coordinates, then a four-word message: "*Byrt* bet covered—Calrissian."

"Lando!" Mara exclaimed. "I could kiss him."

Luke tapped the console keys, ordering a flimsiplast printout. "And I could let you."

Instead of continuing down into the teeth of Coruscant's still-plentiful light artillery, the second wave of drop fleets pulled up at two thousand meters and began to disgorge spiraling lines of dark flecks. As they came closer, the flecks resolved into V-shaped wings over tiny dark rectangles, then into Yuuzhan Vong warriors suspended in the grasp of huge, mynocklike creatures. Watching from the privacy of his office balcony, Borsk found himself admiring the way Tsavong Lah built one attack off another, lulling the enemy into believing he was trying one thing while actually doing something else. It was classic cutthroat dejarik strategy, and the war-master was executing it like one of the old Bothan masters.

Borsk hated him for it. The Yuuzhan Vong were robbing him of all he had spent a lifetime seeking, and they were ensuring that he would be forever remembered as the Bothan who lost Corus-cant. For that, Borsk would have liked to teach the kintan strider death gambit to Tsavong Lah; such a coup would certainly have changed how New Republic historians remembered Chief of State Fey'lya.

When the descending warriors began to fling firejellies down on the palace, Borsk took a last gulp from the snifter of Endorian port in his hand, then stood and went to his desk. Not allowing himself to hesitate or tremble, he reached down to his bottom drawer and keyed a code he had never expected to use. He removed a small medkit scanner/transmitter, then depressed the activation switch and held the device next to his heart. When the function light began to beep in time with his pulse, he placed it in the center of the desk and reached down again, this time arming a fuse attached to the proton bomb that filled most of the drawer. The bomb was not

huge, but it was large enough to destroy this wing of the palace—
and all the secrets within it.

By the time he finished, the enemy drop troopers were circling
the palace's burning data towers and fighting their way onto its bitterly defended balconies. Finding no guards outside the chief of
state's office, a squad dropped onto the balcony where he had been
sitting. Borsk waited behind his desk and watched as the warriors
kicked in a door they could have opened with the touch of a
button. The first two raced to his side and thrust amphistaffs
toward his throat, but stopped short of killing him when they saw
his furred paws resting in plain sight. Several more rushed through
the room to secure the doors and equipment, then a heavily tattooed officer came to his desk.

Before the Yuuzhan Vong could ask, Borsk said, "I am Borsk
Fey'lya, chief of state of the New Republic. Harm me at your own
peril."

This drew a derisive snort. "It does not look like I have much
to fear from you or your New Republic, Borsk Fey'lya."

"Then from your own warmaster," Borsk said evenly. "Tsavong Lah will certainly wish to speak with me. You may tell him I
will receive him here."

"You will see the warmaster when and where it pleases him."
The officer glanced at the heart-rate scanner on Borsk's desk.
"What is this abomination?"

"A communications device," Borsk lied. "I can use it to communicate with all New Republic troops on Coruscant."

Quicker to see the obvious than the chief of state had dared
hope, the officer thrust it at Borsk's face. "Tell your troops to lay
down their arms, and they will be spared."

"*After* I have worked out terms with Tsavong Lah."

The officer slapped his amphistaff across Borsk's hand. Something sharp penetrated his furry flesh, then the Bothan felt a fiery

tide of venom rolling up his veins and noticed the frantic blinking of his heart-rate scanner. Quickly regaining his composure, he reached over with his free hand and pinched the pressure point inside his armpit, then looked up at the officer and shrugged.

"Pump me full of all the poison you wish. It makes no difference to me if you offer your gods a spoiled sacrifice."

"You assume much in thinking yourself worthy, Fey'lya."

Despite his words, the officer turned and spoke into the air. One of the villips on his shoulder said something in reply. He nodded curtly and, saying nothing else to his prisoner, stationed his squad at various points around the tower suite. Borsk wished he had thought to bring in the port from the balcony. He felt sure he would die the instant he released the pressure point, but the pain was not bad enough to prevent him from holding the snifter in the poisoned hand—and, judging by his success so far, he could probably have bluffed the officer into letting him finish it.

Outside, Yuuzhan Vong drop troopers continued to swirl around Coruscant's aeries, trading fire with light artillery emplacements and slowly claiming control of the towertop strongholds. As the cannonfire dwindled, the blast boulders started to venture down again, melting stubborn pockets of resistance into naked skeletons of durasteel. Finally, the drop ships descended, landing whole brigades of reptoid slave-soldiers on captured rooftops. The Yuuzhan Vong might claim to be great warriors, but Borsk knew who would be doing the hard fighting down in the underlevels.

Despite the pains shooting up his arm, Borsk called upon his long experience as a diplomat to keep an impassive face. At last, a large blast boulder stopped outside his balcony and disembarked a company of much-tattooed warriors.

An earless individual wearing a cape of colorful scales over armor entered the office and came to Borsk's side. He had fringed lips and a face so mutilated it was difficult to tell the tattoos from the scars, but Borsk knew this was not Tsavong Lah. Like nearly everyone else in the New Republic, the chief had watched the warmaster's broadcast after the fall of Duro, when he had demanded the surrender of the Jedi, and even this grisly face could not compare to Tsavong Lah's.

"You may stand," the newcomer said.

"When I see Tsavong Lah."

The Yuuzhan Vong held his hand out and received an amphistaff from one of his subordinates. He brought the butt of the weapon down on Borsk's poisoned hand. The Bothan bit his tongue to keep from screaming and grew immediately dizzy.

"Tell the warmaster to hurry," Borsk said, fighting to stay upright. "I will be dying soon."

"I am Romm Zqar, commander of the drop," the Yuuzhan Vong said. "You must surrender to me."

Borsk shook his head. "Then there will be no surrender."

Instead of striking again, Zqar pressed the amphistaff's fanged head to the hand holding the pressure point. "Why must you speak with the warmaster personally?"

"Honor." Borsk had been expecting this question and had long ago thought of a suitable answer. "If I am to surrender, I must do it to someone of equal station."

Zqar surprised him by speaking into the air in Yuuzhan Vong. There were a few minutes of silence. Borsk continued to grow dizzy, and the light on his heart-rate scanner began to blink more slowly. Finally, one of the commander's shoulder villips answered. Zqar nodded and uttered a single Yuuzhan Vong word, then ordered the others to evacuate the office.

When his subordinates filed onto the waiting blast boulder, Zqar said, "You are not Tsavong Lah's equal, but he sends his compliments." He flicked the amphistaff, and the head sank its poisoned fangs deep into the hand holding the pressure point. "He believes the kintan strider death gambit to be the only worthy move in your infidel dejarik game."

* * *

The detonation flash would have been visible from orbit even without the magnification of the *Kratak*'s great eye, but through the lens Tsavong Lah saw the white sphere of Borsk Fey'lya's death bomb flash into existence across a full kilometer. It hung there for many seconds, its heat melting the faces of the surrounding towers and shattering every yorik coral vessel within two hundred meters. In addition to Zqar's departing command vessel, the blast destroyed two drop ships and at least twenty airskiffs, and the warriors inside a good portion of the Imperial Palace, as well—in all, perhaps twenty-five thousand Yuuzhan Vong.

"I should have had Zqar let him bleed to death," Tsavong Lah said. "Our losses today are already too heavy."

"I am glad you are not among them, Warmaster." Seef was standing next to him at the edge of the great eye, staring down on the world they were conquering. In her hands, she held the villip of the priest Harrar, whom the warmaster had dispatched to Myrkr to consecrate the capture and return of the Solo twins. "Eminence Harrar was wise to advise you not to go."

Tsavong Lah considered this, then addressed the villip. "Seef praises your wisdom, my friend. She does not think me ready to stand before Yun-Yammka either."

"It is not a matter of your readiness, Warmaster," Harrar's villip said. "It is a matter of what the gods desire. If it was not their wish to take you when the *Sunulok* was destroyed, it would have been a blasphemy to let the infidel leader slay you."

The warmaster looked back to the Imperial Palace and watched the fiery sphere contract into its own vacuum, drawing clouds of smoke and rubble and tumbling bodies after it. The blast had annihilated most of what Viqi Shesh's diagrams identified as the executive and administrative wings of the Imperial Palace. Only the Grand Convocation Chamber and senatorial offices remained more or less intact, and there was no reason to believe they would contain many of the vital records the readers had hoped to capture.

"I am not so certain the gods will be all that pleased with my survival, Eminence Harrar." Tsavong Lah glanced down at the scales and spines protruding from the still-rotting flesh at his shoulder, then said, "It is better to die in the service of a victorious end than suffer the disgrace of a Shamed One."

"Then the corruption is advancing again?" Harrar asked.

"It has not abated," Tsavong Lah corrected. "The gods have given me Coruscant. Now I must give them their *Jeedai* twins."

"You will, Mighty One." It was a mark of their friendship that Harrar addressed him so, for priests rarely afforded warriors such respect. "Vergere's ruse was successful. She reports that Jacen Solo is her prisoner even now."

"And Jaina Solo?"

"When last we spoke, Nom Anor assured me she was within his reach."

Seef exhaled in relief, but the warmaster's stomach grew queasy. Yal Phaath had already contacted him to complain about the destruction of the cloning grashal and the loss of the voxyn primary, so he knew just how short Nom Anor's reach truly was. He folded his hand and radank claw together before his chest and bowed to Harrar's villip.

"Glory to the gods, Eminence. All Coruscant awaits your return."

They brought the *Ksstarr* around again. The targeting mask on Jaina's face showed three yorik coral corvettes coming straight at them. Behind the trio, the worldship was silhouetted against Myrkr, a huge gray disk overlapping an even larger green disk. The basin where she had last seen Jacen was smaller than the last time they had come around, about the size of a fefze's compound eye.

"Zekk!" she yelled into the targeting mask. "We're farther away!"

"Because *they* keep getting closer," Zekk growled back. "We won't save him by getting blasted ourselves. Clear me a lane!"

"Done!"

Cursing Zekk for a Sith-spawned coward, Jaina raised her left thumb. The control glove on her hand activated the mask's targeting reticle, basically a set of increasingly blurry rings. She fixed her gaze on the rightmost blur and—working through trial and error, with no idea what the strange flashes in the viewfinder might mean—ran her right hand through an awkward finger dance that brought each concentric ring into focus. When the center disk showed a clear image of her target, she made a fist with her left hand.

From the other side of the blastule came the loud plop of the plasma gun's automatic loader, then the deafening bang of the actuator charge ionizing the medium. Jaina's mask went dark, and the blazing sphere streaked away.

The viewfinder cleared two seconds later. Her plasma ball was arcing toward her target—and a long line of enemy rounds was streaking back toward her.

"Incoming!" she yelled.

Zekk put the frigate into a tight rising turn, and they swung away from the worldship.

"Zekk!"

Lowbacca cut her off with an urgent bellow.

"A *fleet*?" Jaina cried.

She craned her neck around, and a dozen oblong flecks appeared in her targeting mask, streaking in from the edge of the system. Her heart fell. It wasn't a fleet—not exactly—but if they tried to return to the worldship, they would be trapped.

A flurry of plasma balls blazed past under the *Ksstarr*'s belly, then one slipped past Tesar at the stern shielding station and impacted the hull. The frigate shuddered.

Zekk's voice came through the mask. "Jaina, what do you want to do?"

Jaina could not answer. There was only one thing *to* do. But how could she abandon Jacen? After rebuking him for leaving Anakin, how? The *Ksstarr* shuddered again. A wet pop sounded somewhere aft, a door valve sealing against a vacuum breach.

"Jaina!" Zekk yelled.

"I—"

The words caught in her throat, like she was choking. She closed her fist and sent a plasma ball streaking into space.

"Better for Jacen if we flee," Tenel Ka said. "With only one twin, perhaps they will delay the sacrifice until we can organize a rescue."

What rescue? Jaina thought. They had lost so many Jedi already. Even Luke would risk no more to rescue Jacen. But he would not stop Jaina. Nobody would.

"That's what we do," Ganner said. "Best thing for Jacen."

"Jaina?" Zekk asked. "Your brother."

Just do it, Jaina thought. *Don't make me say it.*

"All right." Zekk turned the ship away. "I think I understand."

"This one thinkz you do," Tesar said. "We all do."

Not possible. Mask filling with tears, Jaina craned her head around, and the worldship came into view, no larger than a fist. She closed her eyes, concentrated on that place in her chest that had always belonged to Jacen. She felt him there, just a flicker for just an instant, and then she lost him, then she could feel nothing except her own anger and hatred and despair.

"We'll be back, Jacen," she said, finding the strength to speak. "You hold on. We'll come for you."

* * *

Generally speaking, it was not good to skim a planetary surface with a ship's artificial gravity fully activated. The conflicting perceptions of up and down played havoc with most species' sense of balance, and Leia could feel the effects in her own queasy stomach and spinning head. She could also hear over the intercom, and smell in the circulation system, the effect it was having on the passengers.

There was nothing to be done about it. With the holds packed full of unrestrained passengers and the *Falcon* dodging and swinging through Coruscant's hoverlanes and a skip squadron nosing their tail, they needed some way to hold everyone on the floor. If that meant Leia had to sanisteam the entire ship later, she would consider it a privilege to be alive to do it.

Han rolled the *Falcon* upside down and bobbed over a bridge, then found two skips coming head-on and had to dive for the dark underlevels. Both laser turrets chuffed as Meewalh and a gunner from the palace poured fire over the stern. One of them hit, and a deafening rumble shook the towers. Their success had no effect on the number of magma balls streaking down all around.

Leia pulled herself back to the center of the oversized copilot's chair, checked the map on her vid display, and cursed. "Missed our turn."

"I knew that."

"Of course, dear."

Han leveled the *Falcon* out and headed back. The upper quad cannons chuffed constantly as Meewalh ripped into the bellies of half a dozen surprised skips, then Han stood the *Falcon* on its side and banked into the narrow side lane, and Leia had to grab the arm of her chair to hold herself up where she could see the map display.

"Left in three, two—"

"Got it."

Han flipped the *Falcon* over on its other side, then they were shooting through the dank catacombs beneath the Great Western Sea. Meewalh and the palace gunner took out another pair of skips. Han splashed the *Falcon* through a swirling waterfall, made three quick turns, and the skips were gone.

"Not bad for an old man." Leia centered herself in her chair. "Maybe Corran can teach you to fly an X-wing when we get out of this."

"If Eclipse has any left," Han said.

They picked their way through the dark maze of mildewed buildings and mossy pillars that supported the lake bed, then poked the *Falcon*'s nose out from under the ferrocrete beach and hovered on their repulsor engines. Directly ahead lay the smoking ruins of a planetary turbolaser battery. The weapons themselves were melted to slag. The massive support structure looked more like a meteor crater than a building.

"This the one?" Han's voice was full of disbelief.

Leia checked the display. "This is it."

Han cursed.

Leia could tell what he was thinking, that he was afraid they were too late, but knowing she had other resources, he waited and said nothing. He was the same Han, certainly, but somehow attuned to her in a way the old Han could never have been. She was beginning to like this—really like it.

Leia closed her eyes and reached for her brother, trying to let her sense of his presence lead her to him, as it had that time on Bespin when Darth Vader took his hand. After a moment, she raised her arm and, without looking, pointed in the direction she felt him.

"There," she said.

"You mean right over there?" Han asked. "Where that drop ship is coming down?"

Leia opened her eyes and saw the small mountain of a Yuuzhan Vong drop ship descending toward the towertop she was pointing at. "Yes," she said. "That would be about right."

*   *   *

Pirouetting on her good foot, Mara raised her bacta cast and hook-kicked a Yuuzhan Vong in the temple. He dropped, and she continued her spin and slashed her lightsaber across the one behind him, then ducked an amphistaff striking from the right and saw Luke leave himself open to run her attacker through. She brought her blaster under her arm and fired twice, once to either side of Luke's head, and burned holes between the eyes of two Yuuzhan Vong rushing to attack him.

Luke smiled and swept the feet from beneath a fresh warrior as he skipped in to attack. For each warrior they killed, a dozen more rushed forward to die. They launched themselves into side-by-side backflips and came down in the middle of the turbolaser crew's firing line and began to bat swarm and lay bolt. The Yuuzhan Vong charge faltered, then dribbled to an end as the crew members opened up with their blaster rifles.

A junior officer—one of two remaining to the battery—stepped to their side. "We're out of here—going under."

"No!" Mara told him. "The *Falcon* can't find us *inside* a building."

"Won't much matter." The officer pointed into the sky, where a thousand-meter drop ship was moving into position over the building. "Like the lady said, 'Fight until you can fight no longer.' Your friends aren't coming. We'll do more damage below."

The drop ship started to rain firejellies, melting hand-sized holes into the durasteel roof. One landed too close and drew an alarmed whistle from R2-D2, and Mara and Luke began to use the Force to redirect those coming in their direction.

"What do you think?" Mara asked Luke. She knew he still felt Leia searching for them. "Maybe we're just drawing them into a world of hurt."

The drop ship's belly hatches opened and began to dangle lines, reptoid slave-soldiers already sliding down. A dozen ropes landed on their building alone.

Luke raised his blaster and opened fire. "We have to stay. Han and Leia won't leave until they know one way or another."

Mara nodded. "Fine. Ben is safe. I'll trust the Force for the rest."

"Hey, where's everybody going?" Han demanded of nobody in particular—least of all Leia. "Wouldn't you think they could stay in one place for five minutes?"

The tower was one of those mirrsteel jobs with a stepped roof, and of course the lightsabers and blaster flashes had been on the wrong side when Leia finally spotted Luke and Mara and the battery crew. It had taken five minutes of wild flying to circle the area and approach from Luke's side of the roof, and now the New Republic crew members were running for the stairwell.

"Tighten your crash webbing," Han said. "And arm the concussion missiles."

"The concussion missiles?" Leia gasped. "Han—"

Han took his eye off the rooftops and glanced over. "Yeah?"

Leia swallowed, then reached for the arming switches. "How many?"

Han smiled crookedly. "How many do you think?"

"All of them." Leia started flipping toggles.

Han brought them in fast and low, streaking under the drop ship barely three meters above roof level. Too slow to react, the big vessel released a volley of firejellies that did more harm to the reptoids on its drop lines than to the well-shielded *Falcon*. Han slammed the decelerators and—hoping he wouldn't ion-scorch Luke or Mara—brought the ship up on its tail.

"Launch!"

Leia hit the launcher. The first pair of missiles flashed away and slammed into the drop ship's belly before the shielding crews could react. The shock wave banged the *Falcon* down on its tail, and she launched the second and third volleys. By the time she hit the fourth wave, the massive vessel was belching fire from its drop hatches and raining shards of yorik coral from its hull.

The New Republic troops reversed course, racing for the *Falcon*. Han could not see Luke and Mara, but felt sure they were already running up behind.

"Get the boarding ramp." Han set the *Falcon* down on its struts. "And make it—"

Leia was already rushing down the outrigger access tunnel. Meewalh and the palace gunner opened up on the reptoids with the quad cannons. Han lowered the retractable repeating blaster for good measure. He kept expecting the drop ship to lay down a suppression barrage, but soon realized the real danger was being crushed beneath the flaming boulders that kept crashing down around the *Falcon*. Maybe there *was* such a thing as overkill.

Han withdrew the retractable blaster. As soon as the status light indicated the ramp was rising, he lifted off and streaked out from under the drop ship, diving into the hoverlanes and shooting under the Great Western Sea, navigating more by sensor and display map than by what he could see. They were about halfway across when Luke entered the cockpit with Mara, Leia, and R2-D2.

"Thanks for the lift." Luke clasped Han's shoulder and slipped into the copilot's seat. "We were beginning to think you wouldn't make it."

"The hoverlanes were murder." Han glanced at the map on Leia's display and started to ask Luke to find a good place to break for orbit—then thought better of it and hitched his thumb toward the back of the cockpit. "Sorry, kid, that seat belongs to Leia."

Luke's face fell. "I'm sorry." He stood and fished a piece of flimsiplast from his pocket. "I just needed to give this to you."

An uneasy silence fell over the cockpit. Luke started to hand the flimsiplast to Han, then caught himself and turned to Leia instead.

Han rolled his eyes. "Look, I didn't mean anything. I just need my copilot in her own seat and you on the belly gun. That's all."

The relief in the cockpit was thick enough to taste, and Han was content to leave it that way. The last thing he wanted was someone apologizing for Anakin's death. That would have cheapened it, implied that Anakin had died for nothing.

"Will you guys get to it?" Han demanded. "Mara, maybe you can see about reloading the missile launchers. We've got a lot of people on this tub who'd like to get out of here."

"Sure."

Mara and Luke stepped aside so Leia could slip into her chair, then Luke handed her the flimsiplast and explained where it had come from. By the time he finished, the *Falcon* was streaking out from beneath the far side of the Western Sea. Han took it down deep in the hoverlanes and began to bob and weave through broken-down bridges. Leaving R2-D2 to plug into the droid socket, Luke and Mara retreated to their combat posts.

Leia looked over. "My seat, huh?"

"You've been doing all right." Han eyed the huge copilot's chair—Chewbacca's old chair—then added, "If we get out of here alive, we'll make it official and get you a seat that fits."

Leia raised her brow. "Now that *would* be something." She studied the flimsiplast, checked the chronometer, then punched in a set of coordinates. "Take us up, flyboy."

Han laid on the power and pulled the yoke, and the *Falcon* streaked out of the tower canyons into the opalescent sky.

They were past the drop ships and assault ships before the Yuuzhan Vong had time to react, but as they left the upper atmosphere, a cruiser analog tagged as the *Kratak* dropped skips and moved to cut them off. Luke and Meewalh sounded off with the quad cannons. R2-D2 chirped and whistled, searching the comm channels for a friendly voice.

Han activated the intercom. "Mara, how are those—"

"Three loaded."

"That'll do." Han tried to sound confident. "Stand—"

R2-D2 trilled wildly, then Danni Quee's familiar voice broke in. "*Falcon,* break to ten degrees. Continue with all due speed— and *don't* fire those concussion missiles."

Han obeyed instinctively—then looked at his tactical display. Nothing but skips ahead.

"Uh, ten degrees doesn't look good."

"It will." This from Lando.

Mara was instantly on the channel. "Calrissian? What are you *doing?* I don't want—"

"Your package is safe with Tendra," Lando replied. "Aboard the *Venture.*"

Han looked over. Leia could only shrug and wave the flimsi- plast Luke had given her.

"Trust me," Danni said.

R2-D2 tweedled, then the Jedi wing appeared on the tactical display streaking in the skips' flank.

"Copy." Han continued toward the converging coralskippers. "What have we got to lose?"

The enemy closed another few seconds and began to fire. Luke and Meewalh answered, and the *Kratak* rushed to join the battle. The first plasma balls blossomed against the forward shields.

Then the Jedi wing reached range and opened fire, and half the skips vanished.

The cruiser suddenly had other concerns and veered away from the battle, and the skips fell into chaos. Four wheeled around to meet this new challenge, all moving in different directions with no hope of concentrating their fire. Another pair collided. The six skips in the lead continued forward, oblivious to the danger behind. The Jedi wing loosed another volley, then nothing lay between the *Falcon* and freedom.

"Think you can put the bird through there, you old pirate?" Lando commed. "Even you ought to be able to handle that."

Han was speechless. A disciplined skip squadron did not dissolve into a mess that would have embarrassed a swoop gang—yet that was what he had seen. He piloted the *Falcon* past the few remaining skips. The *Venture* appeared on the tactical display, and he veered toward it.

Finally, he asked, "Did that really happen back there?"

"I think so," Luke said over the intercom. "A yammosk has just been jammed." He switched to the general comm channel, then added, "Danni, Cilghal, congratulations. Your success came too late for Coruscant, but it gives me hope for the future."

"It gives us *all* hope," Leia said. "Thank you."

The rest of Eclipse's forces added their congratulations, then Luke came on the channel again.

"Let's form up on the *Venture* and proceed to the rendezvous," he said. "And be careful. With Coruscant captured, the responsibility for keeping the New Republic alive will fall to the Jedi."

Han swung the *Falcon* into line with the rest of the convoy, then started to calculate whether they could make even the short jump to the rendezvous site with so many passengers aboard. "Leia, how many troopers did we pick up on the roof?"

When there was no answer, Han looked over to find Leia lost in meditation, her face weary and full of sorrow. His heart rose into his throat, for it was a look he had seen on her face only once before. He reached over and shook her arm.

"What?" he asked. "Not the twins?"

Leia's face remained weary and sad, but also grew fearfully calm. "They're alive, but in trouble. Terrible trouble."

"Artoo, give me a line to the *Venture*," Han ordered. "We'll dump this bunch and go after them, Leia. Just you and me."

Leia placed her hand on his and shook her head. "No, Han.

Even if we knew where to look—and could reach there alive—it doesn't feel like that kind of trouble. They must rescue themselves."

Han scowled. It sounded like Jedi trouble, and that was the worst kind. "And if they don't?"

"They will." Leia closed her eyes and held his hand. "They will."